SHIELD OF
THE EMPEROR
–AN ASTRA MILITARUM OMNIBUS–

More tales of the Astra Militarum from Black Library

HONOURBOUND
A novel by Rachel Harrison

STEEL DAEMON
A novella by Ian St. Martin

CADIA STANDS
A novel by Justin D Hill

CADIAN HONOUR
A novel by Justin D Hill

SHADOWSWORD
A novel by Guy Haley

BANEBLADE
A novel by Guy Haley

THE MACHARIAN CRUSADE
An omnibus edition of the novels *Angels of Fire, Fist of Demetrius* and *Fall of Macharius* by William King

• **GAUNT'S GHOSTS** •
By Dan Abnett

THE FOUNDING
An omnibus edition containing books 1–3:
First and Only, Ghostmaker and *Necropolis*

THE SAINT
An omnibus edition containing books 4–7:
Honour Guard, The Guns of Tanith, Straight Silver and *Sabbat Martyr*

THE LOST
An omnibus edition containing books 8–11:
Traitor General, His Last Command, The Armour of Contempt and
Only in Death

THE VICTORY PART ONE
An omnibus edition containing books 12–13:
Blood Pact and *Salvation's Reach*

BOOK 14: THE WARMASTER
BOOK 15: ANARCH

• **THE ELYSIANS** •
Audio dramas by Chris Dows
PART 1: SCIONS OF ELYSIA
PART 2: RENEGADES OF ELYSIA
PART 3: MARTYRS OF ELYSIA

SHIELD OF THE EMPEROR

–AN ASTRA MILITARUM OMNIBUS–

STEVE PARKER | STEVE LYONS
MITCHEL SCANLON

BLACK LIBRARY

A BLACK LIBRARY PUBLICATION

Fifteen Hours first published in 2005.
Death World first published in 2006.
Rebel Winter first published in 2007.
Knee Deep, Better the Devil and *The Citadel* first published in
Imperial Guard Omnibus: Volume One in 2008.
This edition published in Great Britain in 2019 by
Black Library,
Games Workshop Ltd.,
Willow Road,
Nottingham, NG7 2WS, UK.

10 9 8 7 6 5 4 3 2 1

Produced by Games Workshop in Nottingham.
Cover illustration by Anna Lakisova.

A CIP record for this book is available from the British Library.

ISBN 13: 978-1-78193-987-1

See Black Library on the internet at

blacklibrary.com

Find out more about Games Workshop
and the world of Warhammer 40,000 at

games-workshop.com

Printed and bound by CPI Group (UK) Ltd, Croydon, CR0 4YY

It is the 41st millennium. For more than a hundred centuries the
Emperor has sat immobile on the Golden Throne of Earth. He
is the Master of Mankind by the will of the gods, and master of
a million worlds by the might of His inexhaustible armies. He
is a rotting carcass writhing invisibly with power from the Dark
Age of Technology. He is the Carrion Lord of the Imperium for
whom a thousand souls are sacrificed every day,
so that He may never truly die.

Yet even in His deathless state, the Emperor continues His
eternal vigilance. Mighty battlefleets cross the daemon-infested
miasma of the warp, the only route between distant stars,
their way lit by the Astronomican, the psychic manifestation
of the Emperor's will. Vast armies give battle in His name
on uncounted worlds. Greatest amongst His soldiers are
the Adeptus Astartes, the Space Marines, bioengineered
super-warriors. Their comrades in arms are legion: the
Astra Militarum and countless planetary defence forces, the
ever-vigilant Inquisition and the tech-priests of the Adeptus
Mechanicus to name only a few. But for all their multitudes,
they are barely enough to hold off the ever-present threat from
aliens, heretics, mutants – and worse.

To be a man in such times is to be one amongst untold billions.
It is to live in the cruellest and most bloody regime imaginable.
These are the tales of those times. Forget the power of
technology and science, for so much has been forgotten, never to
be re-learned. Forget the promise of progress and understanding,
for in the grim dark future there is only war. There is no peace
amongst the stars, only an eternity of carnage and slaughter, and
the laughter of thirsting gods.

CONTENTS

FIFTEEN HOURS

Mitchel Scanlon

The sky was dark, and he knew he was dying.

Alone and frightened, unable to stand or even move his legs, he lay on his back in the frozen mud of no-man's-land. Lay there helpless, his body shrouded in darkness, eyes gazing up at the nighttime sky overhead as though trying to read some portent of his future in the cold distant stars. Tonight, the stars kept their own counsel. Tonight, the bleak and foreboding heavens held no comfort.

How long has it been now, he thought. *How many hours?*

Finding no answer to his question, he turned his head to look out at the scenery about him – hoping at last to see some sign of rescue but there was nothing: no movement in the darkness, no cause for hope. Around him, the bleak expanses of no-man's-land lay still and silent. A landscape rendered featureless by the hand of night, painted black with threatening shadows, holding nothing that spoke to his hopes or could even help him to find his bearings. He was lost and alone, abandoned to a world of darkness, with no prospect of help or salvation. For a moment it seemed to him he might as well be the last man left alive in the entire galaxy. Then, the thought of it gave him cause for fear and he quickly put it from his mind.

How long now, he thought again. *How many hours?*

He had felt nothing when the bullet struck him. No pain, no agony, nor even anguish, just a strange and sudden numbness

11

in his legs as he slid toward the ground. At first, not understanding what had happened, he had thought he had tripped. Until, cursing himself for his clumsiness, he had tried to rise only to find his legs curiously unresponsive. It was then, as he felt the spreading warmth of his own blood seeping across his belly, that he had realised his mistake.

In the hours since, unable to see the extent of his wounds in the darkness, he had used his probing fingers to tell him what his eyes could not. He had been hit at the base of the spine, the bullet leaving a fist-sized hole at the front of his stomach as it exited his body. Treating his wounds to the best of his medical knowledge, he had stuffed them with gauze to stem the bleeding and placed dressings over them. Though there were phials of morphia in his Guard-issue med-pack and he had learned the 'Prayer of Relief from Torment' by heart, he had no need for them. There was no pain from his wounds – even when his probing fingers had slid past the knuckle into the ragged hole in his stomach he had felt no physical discomfort. He did not need to be possessed of any great medical knowledge to know that was not a good sign.

How long now, the question came to his mind again, unbidden. *How many hours?*

There were other discomforts, though. The chill of the cold night air biting at the exposed skin of his face and neck, a terrible mind-wearying fatigue that made his thoughts seem dull and leaden: the fear, the loneliness, the isolation. Worst of all, there was the silence. When first he had fallen wounded, the night had thundered with all the cacophony of battle: the high-pitched whine of lasguns, the *crack* of slugthrowers, the roar of explosions, the screams and cries of the wounded and the dying. Sounds that gradually subsided, growing slowly more distant before finally giving way to silence. He would never have thought a man could draw comfort from such sounds. As terrifying as the clamour of battle had been, the quiet that followed was worse. It compounded his isolation, leaving him alone with all his fears. Here, in the darkness, fear had become his constant companion, plaguing his heart without remorse or respite.

How long now? The question would not leave him. *How many hours?*

At times, the compulsion came over him to cry out. To shout for help, to beg for mercy, to scream, to yell, to pray – anything to break that dreadful silence. Every time it came he fought it with all his strength, biting his lip hard to stop the words from spilling out. He knew that to make even the slightest sound would only be to bring death upon him all the sooner. For though his comrades might hear him, so would the enemy. Somewhere, out there on the other side of no-man's-land, the enemy waited in their countless millions. Waited, ever eager to fight, to maim, to kill. No matter how terrifying it was to be trapped alone and wounded in no-man's-land, the thought of being found by the enemy was worse. For what seemed like hours now, he had endured the silence. Knowing that, as desperately as he might hope for rescue, he could do nothing to speed it on its way towards him.

How long now, the thought pounded insistently in his head. *How many hours?*

There was so little left to him now. So little of real substance. All the things that had once meant so much – his family, his home-world, his faith in the Emperor – now seemed dim and distant. Even his memories were insubstantial, as though his past was fading away before his eyes as swiftly as was his future. His inner world, the world of his life which had once seemed so full and bright with promise, had been diminished and reduced by circumstance. He was left with only a few simple choices: to cry out or keep his silence; to bleed to death or take his knife and end it quickly; to stay awake or fall asleep. At the moment, sleep seemed a tempting prospect. He was tired and bone-weary, fatigue pulling at his sluggish mind like an insistent friend, but he would not yield to it. He knew if he fell asleep now he would likely never awaken. Just as he knew that all these so-called choices were simply illusions. In the end, there was only one stark choice left to him now – to live or to die – and he refused to die.

How long now, the question again, relentless. *How many hours?*

But there was no answer. Resigning himself to the thought that his fate was now in the hands of others, he waited in the silence of no-man's-land. Waited, hoping that somewhere out in the night his comrades were already searching for him. Waited, refusing to give in or fall asleep. He waited, caught between life and death. His life a last fitful burning spark lost amid a sea of darkness, his mind wondering how it was he had ever come to be there at all...

CHAPTER ONE

The Last of a Thousand Sunsets – A Letter Edged in
Black – A Ghost in the Cellar – The Lottery and the Tale
of his Fathers

The sun was setting, its slow descent reddening the vast reaches
of the westward sky and bathing the endless wheat fields below it
in shades of gold and amber as they stirred gently in the evening
breeze. In his seventeen years of life to date, Arvin Larn had seen
perhaps a thousand such sunsets, there was something about the
beauty of this one that gave him pause. Enraptured, his chores
for the moment forgotten, for the first time since his childhood
he simply stood and watched the setting of the sun. Stood there,
with the world still and peaceful all about him, gazing toward
the gathering fall of night as he felt a nameless emotion rising
deep within his heart.

There will be other sunsets, he thought to himself. *Other suns,
though none of them will mean as much to me as this one does,
here and now. Nothing could mean as much as this moment does,
standing here among these wheat fields, watching the last sunset
I will ever see at home.*

Home. The mere thought of the word was enough to make him
turn his head and look over his shoulder across the swaying rows
of ripening grain toward the small collection of farm buildings
on the other side of the field behind him. He saw the old barn

with its sloping, wood-shingled roof. He saw the round tower of the grain silo; the ginny-hen coops he had helped build with his father; the small stock pen where they kept the draft horses and a herd of half-a-dozen alpacas.

Most of all, he saw the farmhouse where he had been born and raised. Two-storeyed, with a low wooden porch out front and the shutters on the windows left open to let in the last of the light. Given the unchanging routines of his family's existence, Larn did not need to see inside to know what was happening within. His mother would be in the kitchen cooking the evening meal, his sisters helping her set the table, his father in the cellar work-shop with his tools. Then, just as they did every night, once their chores were done the family would sit down at the table together and eat. Tomorrow night they would do the same again, the pattern of their lives repeating endlessly day after day, varying only with the changing of the seasons.

It was a pattern that had endured here for as long as anyone could remember. A pattern that would continue so long as there was anyone left to farm these lands. Though, come tomorrow night at least, there would be one small difference.

Come tomorrow, he would no longer be here to see it.

Sighing, Larn returned to his work, turning once more to the task of trying to repair the ancient rust-pitted irrigation pump in front of him. Before the sunset had distracted him he had removed the outer access panel to reveal the inner workings of the pump's motor. Now, in the fading light of twilight, he removed the motor's burnt-out starter and replaced it with a new one, mindful to say a prayer to the machine spirit inside it as he tightened and re-checked the connections.

Taking a spouted canister from beside the foot of the pump he dribbled a few drops of unguent from it into the workings. Then, satisfied everything was in order, he reached out for the large lever at the side and worked it slowly up and down a dozen times to prime the pump before pressing the ignition stud to start the motor. Abruptly, the pump shuddered into noisy life, the motor whining as it strained to pull water up from aquifers lying deep below the ground. For a moment, Larn congratulated himself on a job well done. Until, just as the first few muddy drops of water emerged from the mouth of the pump to stain the dry earth of the irrigation trench before it, the motor coughed and died.

Disappointed, Larn pressed the ignition stud again. This time though, the motor stayed sullenly silent. Leaning forward, he carefully inspected the parts of the mechanism once more – checking the connections for corrosion, making sure the moving parts were well-lubricated and free from grit, searching for broken wires or worn components – all the things the mechanician-acolyte in Ferrusville had warned them about the last time the pump was serviced. Frustratingly, Larn could find nothing wrong. As far as he could see, the pump should be working.

Finally, reluctantly forced to concede defeat, Larn lifted the discarded access panel and began to screw it into place once more. He had so badly wanted to be able to fix the pump; with harvest time still three weeks away, it was important the farm's irrigation system should be in good working order. Granted, it had been a good season so far and the wheat was growing well but the life of a farmer was always enslaved to the weather. Without the irrigation system to fall back upon, a couple of dry weeks now could mean the difference between feast and famine for an entire year.

But in the end he knew that was only part of it. Standing there, looking down at the pump after he had screwed the panel back in place, Larn realised his reasons for wanting to see it repaired went far beyond such practical considerations. Like it or not, tomorrow he would be leaving the farm forever and saying farewell to the only land and life he had ever known, never to return. He understood now that he had felt the need to perform some last act of service to those he would be leaving behind. He had wanted to complete some final labour on their behalf. An act of penance almost, to give closure to his grief.

This morning, when his father had asked him to look at the pump and see if he could fix it, it had seemed the perfect opportunity to achieve that aim. Now though, the recalcitrant machine spirits inside the pump and his own lack of knowledge had conspired against him. No matter how hard he tried, the pump was broken beyond his powers to repair it and his last act of penance would go unfulfilled.

Larn collected his tools together and made ready to turn for home, only to pause again as he noticed a change in the sunset. Ahead, the sun had already half disappeared below the horizon, while the sky around it had turned a deeper and more angry red. What gave him pause was not the sun or the sky, but the fields below them. Where once they had been bathed in spectacular shades of gold and amber, now the colour of the fields had become more uniform, changing to a dark and unsettling shade of brownish red, like the colour of blood. At the same time the evening breeze had risen almost imperceptibly, catching the rows of wheat in the fields and causing them to flow and shift before Larn's eyes as though the fields themselves had become some vast and restless sea. *It could almost be a sea of blood*, he said to himself, the very thought of it causing him to shiver a little.

A sea of blood.

And, try as hard as he might, he could read no good omen in that sign.

By the time Larn had put his tools away, the sun had all but set. Leaving the barn behind, he walked towards the farmhouse, the yellow glow of lamplight barely visible ahead of him through the slats of the wooden shutters now closed over the farmhouse windows. Stepping onto the porch Larn lifted the latch to the front door and walked inside, carefully removing his boots at the threshold so as not to track mud from the fields into the hallway. Then, leaving the boots just inside the doorway, he walked down the hall towards the kitchen, unconsciously making the sign of the aquila with his fingers as he passed the open door of the sitting room with its devotional picture of the Emperor hung over the fireplace.

Reaching the kitchen he found it deserted, the smell of wood-smoke and the delicious aromas of all his favourite foods rising from the pans simmering on the stove. Roasted xorncob, boiled derna beans, alpaca stew and taysenberry pie; together, the dishes of the last meal he would ever eat at home. Abruptly it occurred to him, in whatever years of his life might yet come, those self-same aromas would forever now be linked with a feeling of desperate sadness.

Ahead, the kitchen table was already laid out with plates and cutlery ready for the meal. As he stepped past the table toward the sink, he remembered returning from the fields two nights earlier to find his parents sitting in the kitchen waiting for him, the black-edged parchment of the induction notice lying mutely on the table between them. From the first it had been obvious they had both been crying, their eyes red and raw from grief. He had not needed to ask them the reason for their tears. Their expressions, and the Imperial eagle embossed on the surface of the parchment, had said it all.

Now, as he moved past the table Larn spotted the same parchment lying folded in half on top of one of the kitchen cupboards. Diverted from his original intentions, he walked towards it. Then, picking up the parchment and unfolding it, he found himself once more reading the words written there below the official masthead.

Citizens of Jumael IV, the parchment read. *Rejoice! In accordance with Imperial Law and the powers of his Office, your Governor has decreed two new regiments of the Imperial Guard are to be raised from among his people. Furthermore, he has ordered those conscripted to these new regiments are to be assembled with all due haste, so that they may begin their training without delay and take their place among the most Holy and Righteous armies of the Blessed Emperor of All Mankind.*

From there the parchment went on to list the names of those who had been conscripted, outlining the details of the mustering process and emphasising the penalties awaiting anyone who failed to report. Larn did not need to read the rest of it – in the last two days he had read the parchment so many times he knew the words by heart. Yet despite all that, as though unable to stop picking at the scab of a half-healed wound, he continued to read the words written on the parchment before him.

'Arvin?' He heard his mother's voice behind him, breaking his chain of thought. 'You startled me, standing there like that. I didn't hear you come in.'

Turning, Larn saw his mother standing beside him, a jar of kuedin seeds in her hand and her eyes red with recently dried tears.

'I just got here, Ma,' he said, feeling vaguely embarrassed as he put the parchment back where he had found it. 'I finished my chores, and thought I should wash my hands before dinner.'

For a moment his mother stood there quietly staring at him. Facing her in uncomfortable silence, Larn realised how hard it was for her to speak at all now she knew she would be losing him tomorrow. It lent their every word a deeper meaning, making even the most simple of conversations difficult while with every instant there was the threat that a single ill-chosen word might release the painful tide of grief welling up inside her.

'You took your boots off?' she said at last, retreating to the commonplace in search of safety.

'Yes, Ma. I left them just inside the hallway.'

'Good,' she said. 'You'd better clean them tonight, so as to be ready for tomorrow...' At that word his mother paused, her voice on the edge of breaking, her teeth biting her lower lip and her eyelids closed as though warding off a distant sensation of pain. Then, half turning away so he could no longer see her eyes, she spoke again.

'But anyway, you can do that later,' she said. 'For now, you'd better go down to the cellar. Your Pa's already down there and he said he wanted to see you when you got back from the fields.'

Turning further away from him now, she moved over to the stove and lifted the lid off one of the pans to drop a handful of kuedin seeds into it. Ever the dutiful son, Larn turned away. Towards the cellar and his father.

The cellar steps creaked noisily as Larn made his way down them. Despite the noise, at first his father did not seem to notice his approach. Lost in concentration, he sat bent over his workbench at the far end of the cellar, a whetstone in his hand as he sharpened his wool-shears. For a moment, watching his father unawares as he worked, Larn felt almost like a ghost – as though he had passed from his family's world already and they could no longer see or hear him. Then, finding the thought of it gave him a shiver, he spoke at last and broke the silence.

'You wanted to see me, Pa?'

Starting at the sound of his voice, his father laid the shears and the whetstone down before turning to look towards his son and smile.

'You startled me, Arv,' he said. 'Zell's oath, but you can walk quiet when you've a mind to. So, did you manage to fix the pump?'

'Sorry, Pa,' Larn said. 'I tried replacing the starter and every other thing I could think of, but none of it worked.'

'You tried your best, son,' his father said. 'That's all that matters. Besides, the machine spirits in that pump are so old and ornery the damned thing never worked right half the time anyway. I'll have to see if I can get a mechanician to come out from Ferrusville to give it a good look-over next week. In the meantime, the rain's been pretty good so we shouldn't have a problem. But anyway, there was something else I wanted to see you about. Why don't you grab yourself a stool so the two of us men can talk?'

Pulling an extra stool from beneath the workbench, his father gestured for him to sit down. Then, waiting until he saw his son had made himself comfortable, he began once more.

'I don't suppose I ever told you too much about your great-grandfather before, did I?' he said.

'I know he was an off-worlder, Pa,' Larn said, earnestly. 'And I know his name was Augustus, same as my middle name is.'

'True enough,' his father replied. 'It was a tradition on your great-grandfather's world to pass on a family name to the first-born son in every generation. Course, he was long dead by the time you were born. Mind you, he died even before I was born. But he was a good man, and so we did it to honour him all the same. A good man should always be honoured, they say, no matter how long he's been dead.'

For a moment, his face grave and thoughtful, his father fell silent. Then, as though he had made some decision, he raised his face up to look his son clearly in the eye and spoke again.

'As I say, your great-grandfather was dead long before I could have known him, Arvie. But when I was seventeen and just about to come of age my father called me down into this cellar and told me the tale of him – just like I'm about to tell you now. You see, my father had decided that before I became a man it was important I knew where I came from. And I'm glad he did, 'cause what he told me then has stood me in good stead ever since. Just like I'm hoping that what I'm going to tell you now will stand you in good stead likewise. Course, with what's happened in the last few days – and where you're bound for – I've got extra reasons for telling it to you. Reasons that, Emperor love him, my own father never had to face. But that's the way of things: each generation has its own sorrows, and has to make the best of them they can. That's all as may be, though. Guess I should just stop dancing around it and come out and say what it is I have to say.'

Again, as though wrestling inwardly for the right words, his father paused. As he waited for him to begin, Larn found himself suddenly thinking how old his father looked. Gazing at him as though for the first time he became aware of the lines and creases across his father's face, the slightly rounded slump of his shoulders, the spreading fingers of grey in his once black and lustrous hair. Signs of aging he would have sworn had not been there a week previously. It was almost as though his father had aged a decade in the last few days.

'Your great-grandfather was in the Imperial Guard,' his father said at last. 'Just like you're going to be.' Then, seeing his son about to blurt out a string of questions, he held his hand up to gesture silence. 'You can ask whatever you want later, Arvie. For now, it's better if you just let me tell it to you like my father told me. Believe me, once you've heard it you'll know why it is I said I thought you should hear it.'

Hanging on every word in the quiet stillness of the cellar, Larn heard his father tell his tale.

'Your great-grandfather was a Guardsman,' his father said again. 'Course, he didn't start out to be one. No one does. To begin with he was just another farmer's son like you or me, born on a world called Arcadus V. A world not unlike this one, he would later say. A peaceful place, with lots of good land for farming and plenty of room for a man to raise a family. And if things had followed their natural course, that's just what your great-grandfather would have done. He would have found a wife, raised babies, farmed the land, same as generations of his kin on Arcadus V had done before him. And in time he would have died and been buried there, his flesh returning to the fertile earth while his soul went to join his Emperor in paradise. That's what your great-grandfather thought his future held for him when he came of age at seventeen. Then he heard the news he'd been conscripted into the Guard and everything changed.

'Now, seventeen or not, your great-grandfather was no fool. He knew what being conscripted meant. He knew there was a heavy burden that goes with being a Guardsman – a burden worse than the threat of danger or the fear of dying alone and in pain under some cold and distant sun. A burden of *loss*. The kind of loss that comes when a man knows he is leaving his home forever. It's a burden every Guardsman carries. The burden of knowing that no matter how long he lives he will never see his friends, his family, or even his homeworld again. A Guardsman never returns, Arvie. The best he can hope for, if he survives long enough and serves his Emperor well, is to be allowed to retire and settle a new world somewhere, out among the stars. And knowing this – knowing he was leaving his world and his people for good – your great-grandfather's heart was heavy as he said farewell to his family and made ready to report for muster.

'Though it may have felt like his heart was breaking then, your great-grandfather was a good and pious man. Wise beyond his years, he knew mankind is not alone in the darkness. He knew the Emperor is always with us. Same as he knew that nothing happens in all the wide galaxy without the Emperor willing it to be so. And if the Emperor had willed that he must leave his family and his homeworld and never see them again, then your great-grandfather knew it must serve some greater purpose. He understood what the preachers mean when they tell us it isn't the place of Man to know the ways of the Emperor. He knew it was his duty to follow the course laid out for him, no matter that he didn't understand why that course had been set. And so trusting his life to the Emperor's kindness and grace, your great-grandfather left his homeworld to go find his destiny among the stars.

'Now, the years that followed then were hard ones. Although he would never speak of it much afterwards, in his time as a Guardsman your great-grandfather saw more than his fair share of wonders and horrors. He saw worlds where billions of people lived right on top of each other like insects in giant towers, never able to breathe clean air or see the sun. He saw worlds that lay gripped all year long in perpetual winter, and dry desert worlds that never saw a flake of snow nor felt a drop of rain. He saw the blessed warriors of the holy Astartes – god-like giants in human form, he called them – and great walking machines so big this entire farmhouse would fit inside one of their footprints. He saw terrors by the score, in the shape of all manner of twisted *xenos* and things even ten times worse.

Though he faced a thousand and more dangers, though he was at times wounded and seemed close to death, still his faith in the Emperor never faltered. Five years become ten. Ten became fifteen. Fifteen became twenty. And still your great-grandfather followed his orders without thought of complaint, never once asking when he would be released from service. Until at last, nearly thirty years after he'd first been conscripted, he was posted to Jumael IV.

'Course this world didn't mean much to him then. Not at first. By then he'd seen dozens of different planets, and at first sight Jumael didn't seem to have anything much to recommend it more than most. His regiment had just finished a long campaign, and they had been sent to Jumael to rest up and recuperate for a month before being shipped out to war once more. By then your great-grandfather didn't have too many wars left in him. Oh, he tried to put a brave face on it, never complaining. But he was getting old, and the wounds he'd sustained in thirty years of battles were starting to take their toll. Worst of all was his lungs – they'd never healed right after he breathed a mouthful of poison gas on a world called Torpus III, yet still he didn't waver in his duty. He had given his life over to the service of the Emperor, and he was content that it was at the Emperor's will whether he lived or died.

'Then one day, as the time grew closer when they would be leaving Jumael, news came among the regiment of something extraordinary. Emperor's Day was coming, and with it the thirtieth anniversary of the founding of their regiment. As an act of celebration it was decreed that lots would be drawn from among all the men, and whichever man won would be released from service and allowed to remain behind when the regiment left

Jumael. A lottery that, for one man among thousands, might well mean the difference between life and death. As the day of the lottery came upon them there was a sudden outbreak of piety among the men, as each man in the regiment prayed fervently to the Emperor to be the one to be chosen. All except your great-grandfather. For though he prayed to the Emperor every morning and night, it was never his way to ask for anything for himself.'

'And so great-grandfather won the lottery?' Larn asked, breathless with excitement and no longer able to keep his peace. 'He won it, and that's how he came to live on Jumael?'

'No, Arvie,' his father smiled benignly. 'Another man won. A man from the same squad as your great-grandfather, who'd fought by his side through thirty years of campaigning. Though that man could've just taken his ticket and walked away, he didn't. Instead, he looked at your great-grandfather with his worn-out face and half-healed lungs and handed him the ticket. You see, he'd decided your great-grandfather needed to be released from service more than he did. And that's how your great-grandfather came to settle on Jumael IV, through the kindness and self-sacrifice of a comrade. Though in the years to come, your great-grandfather would always say there was more to it than that. He would say sometimes the hand of the Emperor can be seen in the smallest of things, and that it was the Emperor who had decided to work through this man to save his life. In the end it was a miracle of sorts. A quiet miracle, perhaps, but a miracle all the same.'

With that, his father fell silent again. Looking at him Larn could see the first beginnings of tears shining wetly in his eyes. Then, at length, his father spoke once more, his every word heavy with barely suppressed emotion.

'You see now why I thought you should hear the tale, Arvie?' he said. 'Tomorrow, just like your great-grandfather before you, you're going to have to leave your home and your kin behind, never to return. And, knowing full well you may have some hard years ahead of you, before you left I wanted you to hear the tale of your great-grandfather and how he survived. I wanted you to be able to take that tale with you. So that no matter how dark, even hopeless, things might seem to you at times, you'd know the Emperor was always with you. Trust to the Emperor, Arvie. Sometimes it's all that we can do. Trust to the Emperor, and everything will be all right.'

No longer able to keep the tears from flowing, his father turned away so his son could not see his eyes. While his father cried into the shadows Larn sat there with him as long uncomfortable moments passed, struggling to find the right words to soothe his grief. Until finally, deciding it was better to say something than nothing at all, he spoke and broke the silence.

'I'll remember that, Pa' he said, the words coming with faltering slowness from him as he tried to choose the best way of saying it. 'I'll remember every word of it. Like you said, I'll take it with me and I'll think of it whenever things get bad. And I promise you: I'll do what you said. I'll trust to the Emperor, just like you said. I promise it, Pa. And something else. I promise, you don't have to worry about me doing my best when I go to war. No matter what happens, I'll always do my duty.'

'I know you will, Arvie,' his father said at last as he wiped the tears from his eyes. 'You're the best son a man could have. And when you're a Guardsman, I know you'll make your Ma and me proud.'

CHAPTER TWO

Marching Practice – Conversations with Sergeant
Ferres – A Meal Among Comrades

'Hup Two Three four. Hup two three four,' Sergeant Ferres yelled, keeping pace with the men of 3rd Platoon as they marched the dusty length of the parade ground. 'You call that marching? I've seen more order and discipline in a pack of shithouse rats.'

Marching in time with the others, painfully aware of his own visibility, Larn found himself silently praying his feet kept in step. His place midway along the platoon's left outer file put him out in plain view right under the sergeant's eyes. The two months' worth of basic training he had endured so far had left him with few illusions as to what happened to those who failed to live up to the sergeant's exacting standards.

'Keep your feet up,' the sergeant screamed. 'You're not courting in the wheat fields with your cousins now, you inbreeds! You are soldiers of the Imperial Guard, Emperor help us. Put some vim into it.' Then, seeing the platoon was nearly at the far edge of the parade ground, Ferres yelled again, his voice strident and shrill with command. 'Platoon. About face. And march.'

Turning smartly on his heel with the others, as they resumed marching Larn found himself feeling dog-tired and exhausted. So far today, like each of the sixty days before it, Ferres had had them running training exercises since dawn. Marching, weapons drill, kit inspection, hand-to-hand training, basic survival skills: every day was a never-ending series of challenges and tests. Larn felt he had learnt more in the last two months than he had in his entire life. Yet, no matter how much he and the rest of the platoon learned or how well they did, none of it seemed to satisfy their vengeful sergeant.

'Hup two three four. Keep in step, damn you.' the sergeant bellowed. 'I'll keep the whole damned lot of you drilling here for another two hours if that's what it takes to make you keep to time!'

Larn did not doubt Ferres meant his threat. Over the last two months the sergeant had repeatedly shown an inclination to hand out draconian punishments for even the most minor infractions. Having been on the receiving end of such punishments more than once already, Larn had learned to dread the sergeant and his idea of discipline.

'Company halt,' Sergeant Ferres yelled at last, hawkish eyes watching to see if any of the Guardsmen overran their mark. Then, apparently satisfied that every man had stopped the instant they heard his order, he yelled again, loudly elongating every syllable of the command. 'Turn to the left!'

With a sudden clatter of clicking heels the company turned to face their sergeant. Seeing Ferres advance purposefully towards them, Larn did his best to keep his shoulders back and his spine ramrod straight, his eyes staring fixedly ahead as though gazing blindly into the middle distance. He knew enough of Sergeant Ferres's ways by now to know that an inspection would follow immediately they had finished marching. Just as he knew Ferres would not be any kinder to the soldier who failed to pass muster now than he would to anyone whose marching did not meet his standards.

From the corner of his eye Larn saw Sergeant Ferres move to the end of the outer file of Guardsmen to begin his inspection. Moving slowly along the line to inspect each man in turn, the sergeant's dark eyes darted swiftly up and down, scanning for any flaw in equipment, dress or manner. At times like these, no matter where in line he stood, it always felt to Larn as though it took the sergeant forever to reach him. A slow torturous eternity, spent waiting like the head of a nail to be struck by the hammer – all the time knowing that, no matter how well he had worked or what precautions he had taken, the hammer would fall regardless.

Abruptly, still three men away from Larn, the sergeant stopped to turn and face the fair-haired trooper standing in front of him. It was Trooper Leden – his favourite target. Tall and broad-shouldered, with a thick neck and big hands, Leden looked even more the farmboy than the rest of the men in the company. Even now, standing to attention under Ferres's withering glare, Leden's face was open and guileless, his mouth looking as though it could break into a warm and friendly smile at any moment.

'Your lasgun, trooper,' the sergeant said. 'Give it to me.' Then, taking the gun from Leden's outstretched hands, he checked the safety, before inspecting the rest of the gun in turn.

'What is the best way for a Guardsmen to prevent his lasgun from failing him in battle?' Ferres asked, eyes boring into Leden's face as he spoke.

'I... uh... first he should check the power pack is not empty. Then, reciting the Litany of Unjamming, he should...'

'I asked what is the best way to *prevent* a Guardsman's lasgun from failing him, Leden,' the sergeant said, cutting him off. 'Not how he should clear a jam after it malfunctions!'

'Umm...' for a moment Leden seemed stymied, until his eyes lit up with sudden inspiration. 'The Guardsman should clean his lasgun every day, taking care to recite the Litany of Cleanliness as he...'

'And if, because he has *failed* in his duty to keep his lasgun clean, the Guardsman finds his weapon jams in the heat of battle and he cannot fix it?' the sergeant cut him off again. 'What then, Leden? How should the Guardsman proceed?'

'He should fix his bayonet to the mounting lugs on his lasgun's flash suppressor, sergeant, and use it to defend himself,' Leden replied, an edge of pride to his voice now as though he was sure he had finally answered one of his sergeant's questions correctly.

'In the heat of combat? With the enemy right on top of him? What if he doesn't have time to fix his bayonet, Leden?'

'Then, he should use his lasgun as a club, sergeant.'

'A club you say?' the sergeant asked, suddenly placing both his hands at the end of the lasgun's barrel and lifting the butt of the weapon above his head. 'What, he should hold his lasgun above his head as though it were a bat-stick and he was playing shreev-ball?'

'Oh no, sergeant,' Leden replied mildly, apparently unaware that with every word he was digging a deeper hole for himself. 'He should hold his lasgun horizontally with his hands widely spaced as though it were a short-staff and strike the enemy with the butt.'

'Ah, I see,' the sergeant said, bringing the lasgun down and holding it in front of him with his hands in the positions Leden had indicated. 'And to best disable the enemy, what target should the Guardsman aim at – the face, the chest, or the gut?'

'The face,' Leden said, an idiot smile on his face, while every other Guardsman in the company winced inwardly at what they knew was coming.

'I see,' Sergeant Ferres said, bringing the butt of the lasgun up quickly to smash Leden in the bridge of the nose. Screaming, a gout of blood geysering from his nose, Leden collapsed to his knees.

'Get up, Leden,' the sergeant said, tossing the lasgun back to him as Leden shakily rose to his feet once more. 'You aren't seriously injured. Much less disabled. Look on it as a lesson. Perhaps next time you'll remember to clean your lasgun more carefully. The power node on this one is so filthy, chances are it'd burn out after a few shots.'

Turning away from Leden, the sergeant resumed his inspection. Standing three men down the line, Larn felt weighed down by the expectation of impending disaster. *Ferres is really on the warpath today*, he thought. *There's no way he'll let me pass muster. He'll find something I've done wrong. Some little thing. He always does*. Then, his heart rising in his mouth, Larn saw the sergeant pause in his slow procession down the line and turn to face him.

'Your lasgun, trooper!' the sergeant said. Then, as he had done with Leden before him, he checked the safety before inspecting the rest of the gun in turn. Sights, barrel, stock, holding lugs – for long seconds Ferres pored minutely over the lasgun as Larn felt sweat gathering at the back of his collar. Next, pressing the release catch Ferres pulled the power pack free to check the contacts and the cell well were clean. Then, glowering as he snapped the power pack back into place, Ferres raised his eyes to look at Larn once more.

'Name and number!' he barked.

'Trooper First Class Larn, Arvin A, sergeant. Number: eight one five seven six dash three eight nine dash four seven two dash one!'

'I see. Then, tell me, Trooper First Class Larn, Arvin A, why did you join the Guard?'

'To defend the Imperium, sergeant. To serve the Emperor's will. To protect humanity from the alien and the unclean.'

'And how will you do those things, trooper?'

'I will obey orders, sergeant. I will follow the chain of command. I will fight the Emperor's enemies. And I will die for my Emperor, if He so wills it.'

'What are your rights as a member of the Imperial Guard?'

'I have no rights, sergeant. The Guardsman willingly forfeits his rights in return for the glory of fighting for the just cause of our Immortal Emperor.'

'And why does the Guardsman willingly forfeit his rights?'

'He forfeits them to better serve the Emperor, sergeant. The

Guardsman has no need of rights – not when he is guided by the infinite wisdom of the Emperor and, through Him, by the divinely ordained command structure of the Imperial Guard.'

'And if you should meet a man who tells you these things are wrong, Larn? If you should meet a man who claims the Guard's command structure sometimes makes mistakes and needlessly wastes the lives of the men under its command?'

'Then I will kill him, sergeant. That is the only way to treat with traitors and dissenters.'

'Hnn. And if you should hear a man spout heresy, Larn, how will you persuade him of the error of his ways?'

'I will kill him, sergeant. That is the only way to treat with the heretic.'

'And if you should meet the *xenos*?'

'I will kill it, sergeant. That is the only way to treat with the *xenos*.'

'Very good, Larn,' the sergeant said to him, tossing Larn's lasgun back to him before turning to inspect the next man in line. 'You're learning. Perhaps we'll make a Guardsman of you yet.'

'No bruises, no extra laps, not even a demerit,' Jenks said. It was an hour later, and Larn sat with the other men of his fire-team at one of the long tables inside the mess hall as their company waited for the midday meal to be served. 'You passed muster with flying colours this time, Larnie. Looks like Old Ferres is starting to like you.'

'Like me? I don't think he likes *anyone*,' Larn replied. 'Still, I can hardly believe it myself. The way he glowers at you, you always think he's going to put you on report no matter what you do.'

'Ah, the sergeant isn't so bad,' said Hallan, the squad medic, from nearby as he busied himself putting a dressing on Leden's damaged nose. 'I mean, granted he can be tough, but he's pretty fair with it.'

'Dair?' Leden said, outraged. 'Da dastard doke by dose!'

'It could have been worse, Leden,' Hallan said. 'Usually when Ferres thinks a trooper's gun isn't clean enough he kicks him in the balls. At least this way I haven't got to get you to drop your pants to tend your injuries. And besides, next time the sergeant gives you a choice between face, chest, or gut maybe you'll be smart enough to say "toe".'

'Ha, say that and you'll definitely catch one in the balls,' Jenks laughed. 'No, once Ferres has a burr riding him he's going to hurt you one way or another. You ask me, only thing you can do is take your lumps and tough it out. Unless you're like Larnie here, of course. The perfect Guardsman.'

At that, they all smiled. Even though the jibe – such as it was – was directed at him, Larn smiled with them. Even without the light tone in his companion's voice, he would have known Jenks was only joking. *The perfect Guardsman.* Larn might well have just passed muster, but he did not have any pretensions in that regard. Even after two months of basic training, he felt no more a Guardsman now than he had on the day when he had first been drafted.

For a moment, while the others continued their conversation around him, Larn considered how much his life had changed in the space of a few short months. The day after his conversation with his father in the cellar he had taken the landrailer to the town of Willans Ferry, and from there on to the regional capital Durnanville to report for induction. From Durnanville he had been sent two hundred kilometres east, to a remote staging post where for the last two months they had trained him to become a Guardsman.

He found himself looking at his comrades. Hallan was small and dark, Jenks tall and fair, but despite the differences between them he realised they did not look any more like Guardsmen than either him or Leden. Himself included, they all still looked like what they were – farmboys. Like him, they were all the sons of farmers. So for that matter were most of the men in the regiment.

They were all of them farmboys, fresh from the fields and accustomed to lives of peaceful obscurity. The arrival of the induction notices had changed that forever. Now, for better or worse, they found themselves conscripted as Guardsmen. Two thousand green and unproven recruits, sent for basic training at this staging post before they left Jumael IV for good. Two thousand would-be Guardsmen, given over to the tender mercies of men like Sergeant Ferres in the hope they could be made into soldiers by the time they got their first taste of action.

'Anyway, if you ask me, Hallan is right,' Jenks said, his voice breaking into Larn's thoughts. 'I mean, hard as Ferres is, at least you know where you stand with him. Besides, I suppose he's earned the right to be hard. Unlike the rest of us, I hear he was regular PDF back before he got drafted. He's probably the only man in this entire regiment who knows anything about soldiering. And, believe you me, when we make our first drop and the las-fire starts flying we'll be glad they gave us a man like that to lead us.'

'Do you ever think about it, Jenks?' Larn asked. 'Do you ever think about what it will be like the first time we see action?'

In response the others fell silent then, their faces troubled and uneasy. For as long as the silence lasted, Larn worried he had said too much. He worried that something in his voice, some tremor perhaps or even the very fact he had thought to ask the question at all had been enough to cause the others to start to doubt him. Then, finally, Hallan smiled at him; the smile telling him that all of them felt the same nervousness he did at the thought of seeing combat.

'Don't worry, Larnie,' he said, 'Even if you do get hit I'll be on hand to patch you up.'

'Lot of comfort that is,' Jenks said. 'I thought you said the only reason they made you a medic was because you were a veterinary back home.'

'Actually, it was my *father* who was the veterinary – I just used to help him out,' Hallan said. 'So not only do I know how to mend wounds, Jenks, but if we come across a pregnant grox I'll be able to assist with the birthing as well.'

'Just so long as you don't get the two mixed up, Hals,' Jenks said. 'Bad enough if I should get wounded, without having to worry about you trying to put your hand up my backside because you think I'm about to calf.'

They all laughed, the sombre mood of a few moments before gratefully forgotten. Then, seeing something at the other end of the mess hall, Jenks nodded towards it.

'Hey oh,' he said. 'Looks like dinner's here at last.'

Following the direction of Jenks's nod, Larn looked over to see Vorrans – the fifth member of their fire-team – hurrying over towards them with a stack of mess trays balanced in his hands in front of him.

'It's about time,' Hallan said. 'I swear my stomach's so empty I was starting to think my throat'd been cut.' Then, as Vorrans arrived at the table and began to hand out the mess trays: 'Zell's tears, what took you so long, Vors? This food is barely warm!'

'It's not my fault the mess line is so crowded this time of day, Hals Vorrans said. 'Besides, yesterday when it was *your* turn at mess duty I don't remember you getting the food here any faster. And anyway, remember what you said then? Your exact words were "It's not like this slop tastes any better hot". That's what you said.'

'Excuses, excuses,' Hallan replied, before turning his attention fully to the contents of his mess tray. 'Though I was right enough about this slop. Back home we wouldn't have fed this to the grox. Still it fills a hole, I suppose.'

'Fills a hole is right,' Jenks said, pulling a spoon from his mess kit and using it to prod suspiciously at the sticky grey stew in his own mess tray. 'You should keep back some of this and take it into battle with you, Hals. Anybody gets wounded you can use this stuff to glue them back together.'

'I try to pretend to myself it's alpaca stew,' Larn said. 'You know, like they make back home.'

'And does that work, Larnie?' Jenks said. 'Does it make it taste any better?'

'Not so far,' Larn admitted with a shrug.

'What amazes me,' said Vorrans, 'is here we are, surrounded by wheat fields on every side in one of the most productive farming regions on the entire planet. Yet, every day, instead of giving us real food they give us this reconstituted swill. If you ask me, it makes no sense.'

'Well, that's your mistake right there, Vors,' Jenks said. 'Asking questions. Don't you remember the big speech Colonel Stronhim gave us on the first day of induction?'

'Men of the Jumael 14th,' Hallan said, his voice taking on a false gravity as he mocked the stern patrician tones of their regimental commander. 'In the months and years to come you will find yourselves assailed by a thousand questions every time you are dispatched to a new theatre of operations. You will ask yourselves where you are going, how long will it take to get there, what will the conditions be like when you arrive. You must put such things from your mind. The Guard's divinely ordained command structure will tell you what you need to know, when you need to know it. Always remember, there is no place in a Guardsman's mind for questions. Only obedience!'

'That was really good, Hals,' Larn said. 'You captured the old man's voice perfectly.'

'Well, I've been practising,' Hallan said, delighted. 'Though I tell you there are only two questions I want answered: *where* are they sending us for our first posting, and *when* is it going to happen.'

'I wouldn't hold your breath on that count, Hals,' Jenks said. 'I wouldn't expect them to tell us anything of the sort until they're good and ready. And anyway, even if they have decided where and when we're going, you can be sure we'll be the last to know about it.'

CHAPTER THREE

Answers in the Briefing Room – Warp Sickness and the Rhythms of Sleep – On the Care and Handling of Imaginary Ordnance

'We should be there in three weeks, maybe four,' the naval officer said, standing illuminated in the glow of the star chart on the pict-display behind him. 'Though given the vagaries of warp travel and the relativity of time in the empyrean, you should understand that giving anything even resembling a definite answer in this regard is entirely out of the question. Furthermore, there is always the possibility that what may seem like three weeks to us may prove to have been a somewhat longer period once we emerge from the warp. As I say, time is relative in the empyrean.'

The officer droned on, his sentences strewn with terms like 'trans-temporal fluidity', 'real-space eddies', and a dozen other similarly indecipherable phrases. Sitting in the confines of a briefing room already made cramped and stifling by the presence of an entire company of Guardsmen crammed inside it, Larn found himself forced to suppress a sudden yawn. Two months had gone by since the day he had first passed muster on the parade ground, and for the last four weeks of that period Larn's regiment had been billeted on an Imperial troopship en route to what promised to be their first campaign. Four weeks, and today at last their superiors had finally decided to tell them where in hell it was they would be going.

'Seltura VII, gentlemen,' Lieutenant Vinters the company commander said, stepping forward to address his men as the naval part of the briefing ended. 'That's where we are going. And that is where you will get your first chance to serve your immortal Emperor.'

Behind the lieutenant the image on the pict-display abruptly changed, the naval star chart giving way to a static image of a round blue world set against the blackness of space. With it there was a stirring in the room as, almost as one, two hundred Guardsmen leaned forward from their lines of metal chairs for a better view. Then, satisfied he had their attention, Lieutenant Vinters used the remote device in his hand to change the pict-display once more, revealing an aerial view of a forest landscape.

'Seltura VII is heavily forested,' Vinters continued. 'Over eighty per cent of the planet's landmass is covered in temperate rain forest. The climate is mild – not unlike that back on Jumael IV, I'm told – though with something like twice the mean average rainfall per annum. It should be about early summer by the time we arrive to make planetfall, so you can expect the weather to be hot and wet.'

Finding himself yawning once more, Larn hurriedly raised his hand to cover his mouth. Even travelling through the depths of the void, Sergeant Ferres had not let up on them. If anything, Ferres's daily training regime since they had left their homeworld was harder than it had been back on Jumael IV, the only difference being they did their training now in one of the troopship's loading bays while sardonic naval crewmen paused in their own duties to watch them with sneering smiles. Every day, Ferres had had them running training exercises from breakfast to lights out. It was not just the effect of today's exertions that had left Larn feeling so exhausted.

They had been on the troopship nearly a month now, jumping

in and out of the Immaterium for a few days' warp travel here, a few days there. Each time, during every night they spent in the warp, Larn had been troubled by terrible nightmares. In his dreams he saw alien landscapes populated with strange and horrific creatures – dreams that had him waking in a cold sweat in his bunk every night, his heart heavy with a sickening and nameless dread. *Warp sickness*, the ship apothecary had called it when half of the regiment had reported for sick duty after their first night in the warp. *You will get used to it in time*. For Larn, the pills the apothecary had given him to help him sleep had proven of little use. He had not had a decent night's sleep in weeks. While, no matter how many pills he took, every night he spent in the warp seemed just as bad as the first.

'Obviously, for reasons of secrecy, there is a limit to the details I can give you at this stage as to the specific operational aspects of our mission on Seltura VII,' Lieutenant Vinters said. 'What I can tell you is that we have been sent to help suppress a mutiny among elements of the local PDF and restore the legitimate government to power. If Intelligence is to be believed we can expect heavy resistance on the part of rebels. We are the Imperial Guard, gentlemen. We will prevail. Of course, we may take it for granted we are likely to experience some hardships at first – not least in matters of acclimatisation to local conditions.'

Acclimatisation, thought Larn, *that's half my problem. The warp sickness is bad enough but it feels to me like it should have been lights out hours ago*. Larn knew that in order to acclimatise their body clocks to the thirty-hour day/night cycle of their destination world, the light-cycle in the parts of the ship inhabited by his regiment had been altered accordingly. Even after weeks now of living by the new cycle, Larn was still finding it difficult to adjust. He felt time-lagged, in the grip of constant fatigue, as though his body was wondering why it was still awake. As hard as the warp sickness was to endure, Larn found the strange sleep rhythms he was now forced to live by made his sleeplessness infinitely worse.

'But as I say, gentlemen,' Vinters said, 'we are Guardsmen and we will prevail. I know this is to be your first campaign. Be assured, your commanders have faith in you all the same. Now, I think that covers everything. If you have any questions you may refer them to your sergeants.'

With that, the lieutenant pressed the remote device once more, causing the image on the pict-display to fade away to darkness as the assembled Guardsmen rose and filed silently from the room. Though as Larn walked away with the others, he found himself wondering how well Lieutenant Vinters really knew the character of the men under his command.

For, from among all the men in the company, who in their right mind would ever dare refer a question to Sergeant Ferres?

'You call yourselves soldiers?' Sergeant Ferres yelled, his voice echoing stridently off the bulkhead walls of the loading bay. 'I've seen higher lifeforms sticking to my father's arse after his ablutions. Now, attack that blockhouse like you mean it or I'll make the whole lot of you sorry you ever crawled from your inbred mothers' idiot wombs!'

Five hours had passed since the briefing. Five hours which Larn had spent in one of the troopship's loading bays with the rest of his platoon, experiencing the latest training regime to issue from the febrile mind of Sergeant Ferres. All around them rectangular shapes had been painted on the metal floor. Shapes representing the imaginary outlines of bunkers, fixed emplacements, and blockhouses, on which the Guardsmen were expected to hone their skills in close tactical assault. Despite the hours spent already in conflict with invisible enemies, Sergeant Ferres seemed far from happy.

'Keep crouched as you run,' the sergeant yelled, running alongside Larn and his fire-team as they assaulted another non-existent objective. 'There's las-fire and shrapnel whistling all around you. Keep crouched and stay in cover if you don't want to get hit.'

To Larn, the whole thing seemed like madness. Even accounting for his normal fear of the sergeant, as they raced from one imaginary target to another it was all he could do to stop from bursting into laughter. The only thing that stopped him was the expression on Ferres's face. Whatever Larn and the others might think of the folly of spending five hours attacking the outlines of imaginary buildings full of invisible enemies, it was clear that to Sergeant Ferres it was no laughing matter.

'Faster,' Ferres shouted, his voice so shrill it seemed on the verge of breaking. 'I want you to clear that blockhouse room by room. No quarter to the enemy. No survivors. For the Emperor!'

Reaching the outer wall of the 'blockhouse' Jenks took point while the others covered him, kicking in an imaginary door in time for Leden to throw an imaginary grenade into the room to kill the imaginary enemies inside.

'Halt!' the sergeant screamed, spittle spraying from his mouth with the force of the command.

In an instant, Larn and the others froze where they stood. Then, unsure what to do next, they watched as Sergeant Ferres marched past them towards the blockhouse. Stepping carefully into the blockhouse as though he picking his way through a splintered doorway only he could see, Ferres advanced into the centre of the imaginary room before bending forward to wrap his fist around some imaginary object. Straightening his back, he turned and walked towards Leden, his fist held knuckles down in front of him at waist height as though he was still carrying something there.

'What is this, Leden?' the sergeant asked, indicating the invisible object gripped in his fist.

'I... I don't know, sergeant,' Leden replied, jaw sagging open in confusion.

'This is the grenade you just threw into the blockhouse, Leden,' Ferres said. 'Now, can you tell me, what is *wrong* with this grenade?'

'Umm... I don't know, sergeant,' Leden said, shrinking down

into himself as he answered as though melting beneath the hot glare of Sergeant Ferres's eyes.

'What is wrong with this grenade is that its pin is still in place, Leden,' the sergeant said. 'And the reason I know the pin is still in place is because when you threw it, you didn't remove it. Now, tell me, Leden: what use is a thrown grenade that still has its pin in place?'

'I... I... didn't think I had to remove the grenade pin, sergeant,' Leden said, his voice trailing away to nothing as he realised what he was saying. 'It is only an imaginary grenade...'

'Imaginary? Not at all, Leden. I assure you, this grenade is quite solid. Here, let me show you,' the sergeant said, suddenly balling his hand into a fist and punching Leden in the stomach. The air exploding from his mouth, Leden fell to his knees. Then, Ferres turned to face the others.

'There,' he said, holding the imaginary grenade up in the air for them all to see it, 'you see I was right – this grenade is just as solid as my fist. As solid as the door of this blockhouse, the walls of the emplacement, even the plasteel of that bunker. The next man who dares even to suggests to me that these things are not real and solid will get the same as Leden just got, but worse. Now, I want to see you attack that blockhouse again. And, this time, I want to see you doing it like Guardsmen!'

At that, the sergeant screamed the order to attack. Chastened by the example of Leden, Larn and the others hurried to assault the blockhouse once more while Leden painfully pulled himself to his feet and came to join them. So it continued, with assault after assault on imaginary buildings and invisible enemies, as Sergeant Ferres moved from fire-team to fire-team to inspect their labours. Larn felt himself growing more and more tired as his sleeplessness took its toll until at last, after hours more of manoeuvres, the sergeant finally called a halt to training and dismissed them. So tired by then, Larn was sure he knew what it meant to be a dead man walking.

INTERLUDE

A Day in the Life of Erasmos Ng

'Coordinate: two three three point eight six three nine,' the voice blared into Erasmos Ng's ear as he dutifully typed the number 233.8639 into the cogitator before him. 'Coordinate: two four two point seven four six eight. Coordinate: two three eight point five nine six one. Correction: two three eight point five *eight* six one. Further coordinates pending. Wait.'

With that, the voice in his earpiece fell abruptly silent. Granted brief respite from the endless stream of numbers that assailed him every minute of his working life, Erasmos Ng turned his tired eyes to gaze at the cavernous interior of the room around him. As ever, Data Processing Room 312 was a hive of mindless activity as a thousand other bored and dispirited souls just like him went about their labours. Here, numbers were crunched, data entries updated, reports filed, then collated, then cross-indexed – all amid a constant din of clattering type-keys and whirring logic-wheels that put him in mind of nothing so much as the sound of an insect army on the march. Still, he realised it was a spurious analogy. The labours of insects at least served some useful purpose. While he had long ago begun to doubt that what went on in Room 312 served any purpose at all.

'Coordinate: two three five point one five three zero,' the voice in his earpiece crackled into life again. 'Coordinate: two two two point six one seven four. Coordinate: two three six point one zero one five.' And so on, *ad infinitum*.

Resuming his task with a weary sigh, as he typed the new set of coordinates into the cogitator, Ng found himself reflecting sadly on how often the shape of a man's life came to be dictated by the happenstance of birth. If he had been born on another planet he might have been a miner, a farmer, or even a huntsman. As it was he had been born on *this* world – on Libris-VI. A world whose only industry of note resided in a single enormous Administratum complex the size of a city – one of many thousands of such complexes the Administratum maintained across the galaxy. Lacking other prospects, like his parents before him Erasmos Ng had entered Imperial service, becoming just another small cog in the vast bureaucratic machine responsible for the functioning – smooth or otherwise – of the entire Imperium. A selfless and noble calling, or so they told him. Though, as with so much else he had been told in his life, he no longer believed it.

'Coordinate: two one eight point four one zero zero,' the voice – his unseen tormentor – said, his tone smug and mocking even through the static. 'Coordinate: two two one point one seven two nine.'

Now, at the age of forty-five and with thirty years of mind-numbing tedium behind him Ng knew he had risen as far in the Administratum hierarchy as he was likely to go. Specifically, to the heady heights of Assistant Scribe, Grade Secundus Minoris. A records clerk by any other name, condemned to spend every day of his life hunched over the cogitator at his workstation in Room 312. His appointed task: to type into the cogitator the never-ending series of numbers spoken to him by the disembodied voice over his earpiece. A task he performed seven days a week, twelve hours a day, barring two permitted fifteen-minute rest-breaks, a full half-hour for his midday meal, and a single day's unpaid holiday every year on Emperor's Day.

Beaten down by the bleak dreariness of his existence, Erasmos Ng found he had long ago stopped caring what purpose his labours served. Instead, for thirty years now, he had simply performed his allotted task, repetitively typing coordinates into the cogitator again and again and again, no longer caring what – if anything – they meant. A lost soul, adrift in a dark and endless sea of numbers.

'Coordinate: two three three point three three two one,' the voice said, grinding his soul down a little more with every word. 'Coordinate: two two three point seven seven one two.'

Then, just as he finished typing a new set of coordinates into the machine, Erasmos Ng abruptly realised he might have made a mistake. That last coordinate – was it 223.7712 or 223.7721? But long past giving a damn one way or another he simply shrugged, put it from his mind, and went on to the next one. After all, he consoled himself, it hardly really mattered whether or not he had made a mistake. He had long ago realised his labours, like his life, were of no importance.

And, in the end, they were only numbers...

CHAPTER FOUR

Curious Orders and Unwelcome Destinations –
Exhortations to Duty and Unanswered Questions – The
Lander and Intimations of Falling

Magnified by the enhancement devices cunningly hidden in
the transparent surface of the forward viewing portal the planet
looked huge and foreboding, its red-brown bulk reminiscent of
nothing so much as an enormous globule of half-dried blood. As
he stood watching it from his usual vantage on the bridge of the
troopship he commanded, Captain Vidius Strell found himself
briefly pitying the men who would be forced to make planetfall
there. *Poor devils*, he thought. *I have seen a lot of planets, absolute hellholes some of them, but there is something about the look
of that damn place that makes you think landing there wouldn't
be pleasant.*

'Captain?' he heard the voice of his first officer, Gudarsen,
behind him. 'Navigation Liaison reports we are currently fifteen
point three five minutes from reaching orbit. Gravitational conditions normal. All systems running clean and smooth. We are
green for go, Captain. Request permission to relay the order to
launch control to prepare a lander for planetary descent.'

'Permission denied,' Strell said. 'I want you to check the confirmation codes on that last astropathic message again, Number
One. Then, report back to me.'

'Aye, sir. Understood,' Gudarsen replied, before bustling energetically away with what seemed to his captain a commendable eagerness to follow his instructions.

Left to his thoughts once more, while around him the crew of the command bridge went about their duties, Strell again turned his attention to the planet looming ever larger through the viewing portal. As he did, he wondered if the disquiet he felt gazing at the world before him had less to do with anything sinister in the appearance of the planet itself and more to do with his puzzlement at the orders that had brought them to it. His ship, *Inevitable Victory*, had been en route with escorts and another thirty troopships to the Seltura system when they had received orders to break convoy and proceed here alone. It had been only a small detour requiring no more than a four hour jump through the warp, but the precise nature of the mission they had come here to perform was enough to have the *Victory's* captain grinding his teeth in frustration.

A single company, thought Strell. *Why in the name of the Divine would Naval Operations Command divert an entire starship just to drop a single company of Imperial Guardsmen on some backwater, Emperor-forsaken world?*

Aggravated by the thought, Strell cast an ill-humoured eye over the printout of the ship's transport manifest held in his hand until he came to the listing for the offending company. *6th Company, the 14th Jumael Volunteers, Company Commander: Lieutenant Vinters*. There was nothing out of the ordinary in the company's listing on the manifest. Nothing to explain why he and his crew had been diverted from their duties and the protection of the convoy to ferry two hundred men to a planet that, in galactic terms, might as well be in the middle of nowhere.

Perhaps there is more to this than meets the eye, thought Strell again. *Perhaps the manifest listing is only a cover, and they are special troops on a secret mission. Why else would we have been sent here? The only other reason could be if some mistake had been made but the Imperium does not make mistakes. Yes, a secret mission. It is the only explanation that makes any sense...*

Satisfied at last that he had found the answer, Strell turned to see Gudarsen hurrying towards him once more, holding the text of the astropathic message gripped tightly before him.

'All confirmation codes read correct, captain,' Gudarsen said. 'The specifics of our mission are confirmed.'

'Very good. You have my permission to relay instructions to Launch Control to prepare a lander for launch. Oh, and Number One? This is strictly a "drop-and-depart" mission. Tell Liaison to have the navigator plot a new course for Seltura-III. Once the lander has dropped its passengers planetside and returned to the ship, I want us to underway within the hour.'

'Orders received and understood, captain,' said Gudarsen, ending with a standard phrase of acknowledgement as he hurried away to carry out his duties. 'The Emperor protects.'

'The Emperor protects, Number One,' Strell echoed, already turning to redirect his gaze towards the planet once more as he waited for the lander to be launched so he could watch its descent.

Yes, he thought. *A secret mission. That's the only thing it could be. If Operations Command has decided we are to be denied information as to the nature of that mission, so be it. It is like they used to teach us in the scholarium.* Then, he allowed himself a small smile of nostalgia as his mind turned to the half-remembered wisdoms of long ago days. *How did it go now*, he thought. *Ah yes, it was something like: 'Ours is not to reason why.'*

'Ours is but to do and die.'

'It is better to die for the Emperor than live for yourself!' the vox-caster screamed, drowning out the sound of trampling feet and shouted orders as the men of 6th Company ran through the troopship's cramped corridors towards the launch bay. 'The blood of martyrs is the seed of the Imperium! If you want peace, prepare for war!'

The vox-caster blared on through the bowels of the troopship, on and on in a pre-recorded loop of exhortations to duty, as Larn ran stumbling with the others under the weight of the heavy pack on his back. Barely three hours had passed since Sergeant Ferres had at last relented and dismissed them from training to return to their quarters. Three hours since, exhausted, Larn had finally been allowed to go to sleep. Only to be roused blearily from his slumbers two and a quarter hours later by the wail of sirens as Sergeant Ferres had ordered the men of the platoon from their bunks and told them to make ready for a planetary drop.

'Be vigilant and be strong!' the vox-caster shrieked ever louder, harsh echoes rebounding from loudspeakers set in the metal walls and ceiling all around them. 'The Emperor is your shield and protector!'

Now, three quarters of an hour's worth of hurried preparations later, Larn found himself running in full kit as he and the rest of his company were herded like sheep through the troopship's maze of corridors. Here and there they passed naval crewmen who paused from their duties long enough to cheer them on, offering half-heard words of encouragement in place of the sardonic laughter that had greeted their earlier training exercises. With the prospect that their erstwhile passengers might soon be seeing combat, it seemed the normal antipathy between the Navy and the Guard had abruptly given way to mutual respect. With a sudden tremor in the pit of his stomach, Larn realised he was about to go to war.

'You shall know no reward other than the Emperor's satisfaction!' the vox-caster continued. 'You shall know no truth other than that which the servants of your Emperor tell you!'

This is it, Larn thought. *After all the training and briefings, all the preparations, the moment for which it was all in aid of is here at last. I am finally going to war.* As much as that thought filled his mind, he found himself distracted as a second thought pushed itself insistently to the fore. *Three weeks,* he thought. *Three*

*weeks, maybe four. That is what the naval officer said in the brief-
ing only yesterday. He said it would be at least three weeks before
we saw any action.* Confused, Larn wondered what could have
changed in the meantime. If yesterday they were still three weeks
from combat, how was it today they were about to make their
first drop?

'The mind of the Guardsman has no place for questions,' the
vox-caster screamed unnervingly. 'Doubt is a vile cancer whose
symptoms are cowardice and fear, steel yourself against it. There
is room for but three things in the mind of the Guardsman: obedience, duty, and love of the Emperor.'

Abruptly, as though the blaring of the vox-caster was somehow the sound of his own conscience, Larn felt a sudden shame.
He thought of his family far away on Jumael, and how every
night they would be offering a prayer for his safety as they knelt
before the votive picture of the Emperor above the fire man-
tle. He thought about the tale his father had told him, about his
great-grandfather and the lottery. He thought about all the promises he had made his Pa about doing his duty. He realised, for all
his talk and promises then, how close he had coming to failing
them at the very first hurdle. It did not matter that the facts given
him in yesterday's briefing now seemed at odds with today's reality. He was a Guardsman, and all that mattered was that he did
his duty. Putting his questions aside he found himself comforted
by the memory of his father's words in the cellar, his recollection
of his father's voice serving as a kinder and more gentle counterpoint to the vox-caster's wail and bombast.

'Trust to the Emperor,' his father had told him with tears in
his eyes. 'Trust to the Emperor, and everything will be all right.'

Emerging from the cramp and narrowness of the corridor, the
launch bay seemed huge as Larn followed the men in front of him
inside it. Ahead he saw the imposing bulk of a lander, steam rising from the hydraulics of the platform it rested on as tech-adepts

scurried around it like mindful ants giving succour to a fallen giant. He saw adepts manning the massive fuel lines that ran from a recessed spout in the far wall of the launch bay to the lander's engines, while others anointed the surfaces of the lander with unguents, burned incense, performed blessings, or made final adjustments to the lander's systems with the diverse instruments of holy calibration. All the while the lander hummed with power, the thrumming of its restive engines vibrating through the metal floor of the launch bay towards where Larn and the others stood gazing at it uncertainly, like wary travellers unsure whether to risk waking a sleeping tiger.

'Get moving, you inbreeds!' Sergeant Ferres yelled, the volume of the continuing vox-caster broadcasts around them having been diminished enough by the open spaces of the launch bay for them to at last hear their sergeant's commands. 'A man might almost think you bumpkins hadn't seen a lander before.'

In truth, none of them had: their journey from Jumael to the orbiting troopship having been undertaken inside local planetary shuttles of much less startling dimensions. As Larn rushed towards the lander with the others he found himself in awe to be approaching so enormous a vehicle. *It looks like it could hold a couple of thousand men at least*, he thought. *Not to mention tanks and artillery besides.* For the first time he truly appreciated the extraordinary scale of the troopship he had been travelling within for the last twenty-nine days. *Sweet Emperor*, he thought in amazement, *to think they say this ship carries twenty such landers!*

At the front the mouth of the lander lay open, the primary assault ramp stretching towards them like the tongue of some improbable metal beast. Running up the ramp into the cavernous and dimly lit interior of the lander itself, Larn and the others found a grim-faced member of the lander's crew waiting to point them in the direction of a nearby stairwell. Then, following the stairwell to its summit, they came to the vast rows and aisles of seats of the lander's upper troop-deck.

'Find a seat and fasten your restraints,' Ferres barked. 'I want you seated together in fire-team, section, and platoon order. Any man who isn't in his seat and ready for drop in two minutes' time is going to find himself on a charge.'

Hurrying to his seat Larn quickly sat down, carefully fastening the buckles of the seat's impact restraints across his waist, shoulders and chest, before tightening them to fit him. Making sure the safety on his lasgun was set to 'safe', he pushed the gun upright and butt-first into the shallow recess of the weapon holder set at the front of his seat and clipped the barrel lock closed to hold the gun in place. Then, looking about him at the other Guardsmen as they did likewise, Larn found himself briefly confused as he realised just how few men there were inside the lander. Despite the fact that the lander was built to house a minimum of two thousand men, there was at most a single company of men inside it. *It looks like they are only dropping my company,* he thought. *6th Company. But that would make no sense. Why would they only put only two hundred men on board, when this lander can hold ten times that? No. They must be going to load more men on board. No doubt we are just the first aboard and rest of the regiment will be following us soon enough.*

'Ready for launch in T minus two point zero zero minutes,' a harsh metallic voice announced over a hidden vox-caster speaker as, in the distance, Larn heard the slow grinding of the lander's assault ramp closing.

'Sounds like we got into our seats just in time, Larnie,' Jenks said, as Larn realised he had taken the seat next to him. 'Good thing, too. Never mind old Ferres and his threats, I wouldn't want to be wandering around out of my seat when this monster finally gets going.'

With that Jenks turned away to fasten his own seat-restraints. For a moment, still confused, Larn found himself fighting the urge to ask Jenks where he thought the rest of the regiment was. Then, abruptly, he realised it made no difference. It was too late to turn back now. Like it or not, it looked like 6th Company would be making their first planetary drop on their own.

'Ready for launch in T minus one point zero zero minutes,' the voice said again, as Larn felt the vibrations of the lander's engines grow stronger.

'Don't worry, Larnie,' said Jenks by his side as, trying as much to allay his own anxieties as comfort a friend, he turned to give Larn a kindly smile. 'They say it's not the *fall* you need to worry about. It's hitting the *ground* that kills you.'

'Ready for launch in T minus zero point three zero minutes,' the metallic voice continued its countdown as Larn realised, too late, he had forgotten to pray to the Emperor for a safe descent.

'Ready for launch in T minus zero,' the voice said as the lander's engines fired and Larn found himself feeling suddenly weightless. 'All systems ready. Launch!'

And then, quicker than Larn would have thought possible, they were falling.

CHAPTER FIVE

Evasive Manoeuvres – Falling and the Taste of Vomit –
Landfall, Death and Grim Realisations – The Calamity of
Sergeant Ferres – No-Man's Land and the Eagle in the
Distance – Welcome to Broucheroc

'Bearing one eight degrees one five minutes,' the navigation servitor's voice croaked, the parchment-thin tones of its voice barely audible in the lander's crew compartment over the roar of engines. 'Recommend course correction of minus zero three degrees zero eight minutes for optimal atmospheric entry. All other systems reading normal.'

'Check,' said the pilot, automatically pushing his control stick forward to make the adjustment. 'New bearing: one five degrees zero seven minutes. Confirm course correction.'

'Course correction confirmed,' the servitor said, its yellowing sightless eyes rolling back in their sockets as it rechecked its calculations. 'Atmospheric entry in T minus five seconds. Two. One. Atmospheric entry achieved. All systems reading normal.'

'Look at that glow, Dren,' Zil the co-pilot said, his eyes lifting from his instruments for a fraction of a second to look out the view-portal at the nose of the lander as it was surrounded by a nimbus of bright red fire. 'No matter how many planetary drops we do, I never get used to it. It's like riding in a ball of flame. It makes you thank the Emperor for whoever first made heat shields.'

'Heat shields reading normal,' said the servitor, gears whirring inside it as it mistook the comment for a question. 'Exterior temperature within permitted operational thresholds. All systems reading normal.'

'That's because you've only got a dozen drops behind you,' the pilot said. 'Trust me, by the time you've done another dozen you won't even notice it. How's the signal from the landing beacon? I don't want to miss the drop point.'

'Beacon signal reading strong and clear,' Zil replied. 'No air traffic, friendly or hostile. Looks like we've got the sky to ourselves. Wait! Auspex is reading some–'

'Warning! Warning!' the servitor interrupted, the whirring of its mechanisms reaching an abrupt crescendo as it burst into life. 'Registering hostile missile launch from ground-based battery. Recommend evasive manoeuvres. Missile trajectory eight seven degrees zero three minutes, airspeed six hundred knots. Warning! Registering second missile launch. Missile trajectory–'

'Evasive manoeuvres confirmed!' the pilot said, pressing his control stick forward as he pushed the lander into a dive. 'Servitor: belay hostile trajectories and airspeeds until further orders. Zil, deploy chaff!'

'Chaff activated. Instruments reading chaff successfully deployed,' Zil said, his voice growing suddenly hoarse as he looked at one of the screens before him. 'Wait. The chaff, it's not done any good. It's as though... Holy Emperor! None of the hostile missiles have guidance systems!'

'What do you mean?' the pilot asked as he saw Zil's face go pale. 'If that's the case we have nothing to worry about. If they're firing blind there's not one chance in a thousand of them being able to hit us.'

'But that's exactly it,' said Zil, his voice frantic. 'I'm reading a *thousand* hostile missiles as airborne already. And hundreds more are being launched every second. Holy Throne! We're flying into the biggest shitstorm I've ever seen!'

'Emergency evasion procedures!' the pilot said, barking out orders as he pushed the lander forward into an even steeper dive while from outside they could hear the first of the missiles exploding. 'Servitor: override standard flaps and navigation safety protocols – I want full control! Make sure your strapped in tight, Zil – we're going to have to go in hard and heavy! Looks like this is going to be a *close* one...'

Falling.
They were falling.
With nothing to slow or stop them.
Like a comet.
Falling headlong from the stars.

In the lander's troop compartment, slammed back in his seat by the force of acceleration, it felt to Larn as though his stomach was trying to push its way up from his throat. Around him he could hear men screaming, the sound all but drowned out by the dull thud of explosions from outside the lander. He heard cries for pity and muttered oaths, all the while the skin being pulled so tight across his face he was sure it was about to rip free from his bones. Then, sounding much louder than any noise he had ever known before, there came the boom of another explosion and with it the gut-wrenching sound of tearing metal. With those sounds he found himself forced back against his seat with even greater force as the fall began in earnest.

We've been hit, he thought, overcome with sudden panic while the world began to spin crazily around him as the lander turned over and over on its axis out of control. *We've been hit*, the thought crowded his mind and held him at its mercy. *We've been hit! Holy Emperor, we're in freefall!*

He felt himself struck in the face by a warm and semi-solid liquid, the acrid smell and the taste of the droplets dribbling past his lips telling him it was vomit. Half mad with desperation, he found himself wondering incongruously whether it was from his own stomach or someone else's. Then another thought forced its way fearfully into his mind and he no longer cared who the vomit belonged to. A thought more terrible than any he had ever considered in his seventeen years of life to date.

We are falling from the sky, he thought. *We are falling from the sky and we're going to die!*

He felt his gorge rise in a tide of sickly acids, the half-digested remnants of his last meal spewing uncontrollably from his mouth to soak some other unfortunate elsewhere in the lander. Certain he was on the brink of oblivion he tried to replay the events of his life in his mind. He tried to remember his family, the farm, his homeworld. He tried to think of fields of flowing wheat, magnificent sunsets, the sound of his father's voice. Anything to blot out the terrifying reality around him. It was hopeless though and he realised the last moments of his life would be spent with the following sensations: the taste of vomit; the sound of men going screaming to their deaths; the feeling of his own heart beating wildly in his chest. These were the things he would take with him to death: the last sensations he would ever know. Just as he began to wonder at the unfairness of it all the world stopped spinning as, with a bone-jarring impact and a terrible screech like the death-knell of some mortally wounded beast, the lander finally hit the ground.

For a moment there was silence while the interior of the lander was plunged into total darkness. Next, Larn heard the sound of coughing and quiet prayers as the men in the lander drew a collective breath to find, despite some initial misgivings, they were very much alive. Abruptly, darkness gave way to dim shadowy light at the activation of the lander's emergency illumination system. Then, he heard a familiar strident voice begin to bark out orders as Sergeant Ferres sought to re-establish control of his troops.

'Fall in!' the sergeant shouted. 'Fall in and prepare to disembark.

Get off your arses, damn you, and start acting like soldiers. You've got a war to fight, you lazy bastards.'

Releasing his seat-restraints Larn staggered unsteadily to his feet, his hands warily prodding his body as he checked to see whether any of his bones were broken. To his relief, it seemed he had survived the landing little the worse for wear. His shoulders were sore, and he had the painful beginnings of a bruise where the clasp of one of the seat-straps had bitten into his flesh. Other than that, he had escaped from what had seemed like certain death remarkably unscathed. Then, just as he began to congratulate himself on surviving his first drop, Larn turned to retrieve his lasgun and saw that the man sitting in the seat next to him had not been so lucky.

It was Jenks. Head lolling sideways at a sickening angle, eyes staring blankly from a lifeless and slack-jawed face, Jenks sat in his seat dead and unmoving. Staring at his friend's body in numb disbelief, Larn noticed a thin stream of blood trickling from Jenks's mouth to stain his chin. Then, spotting a small bloody-ended piece of pink flesh lying on the floor of the lander beside his feet, Larn realised that with the force of the landing Jenks must have inadvertently bitten off the end of his tongue. As horrified as he was by that discovery, Larn could not at first understand how Jenks had died. Until, looking once more at arrangement of seat-restraints around his friend's body and the way his head lolled sideways like a broken puppet, Larn realised the restraints had been improperly fastened, causing Jenks's neck to snap at the moment of their landing. The realisation brought him no comfort. Jenks was dead. Understanding how his friend had died did nothing to lessen Larn's grief.

'Fall in.' the sergeant shouted again. 'Fall in and get ready to move out.'

Still numb with shock, Larn grabbed his lasgun and stumbled past Jenks's body to join the rest of the company as they lined up in one of the aisles between the upper deck's endless rows of seating. As he did, he became aware for the first time of the sound of distant ricochets clanging off the exterior of the hull. *We are being fired at*, he thought dully, his mind still reeling at the sight of Jenks's corpse. Until, noticing an almost palpable sense of unrest among the other Guardsmen as he took his place in the line and waited for the order to move out, Larn realised he could smell smoke and with it, there came an unwelcome realisation that cut through the fog of his grief and seemed to grip at his heart with clutching icy fingers.

The lander was on fire.

Spurred on by horror at the prospect of being trapped in a burning lander, the Guardsmen began to hurry for the stairwell while behind them Sergeant Ferres shouted profanities in the vain hope of maintaining some form of order. No one was listening. Frenzied, they rushed down the stairs towards the lower deck, treading on the corpses of those already killed in the landing.

Running with the others, Larn caught a brief glimpse of their company commander, Lieutenant Vinters, sitting dead in his seat with his neck broken just like Jenks. He had no time to dwell on the lieutenant's death; caught in the crush of fleeing Guardsmen he could only run with the crowd as they made for the lower deck, to the assault ramp and freedom. As they came within sight of it they found that the assault ramp was still sealed shut, while from all around them the smell of smoke grew ever stronger.

'Open that ramp!' screamed Sergeant Ferres, pushing his way through the crowd of milling Guardsmen to where a small group stood studying the control panel governing the ramp's mechanism. Seeing the group raise their eyes to look at him in confusion, he pushed them aside and stretched out a hand towards a metal lever set in a recess by the edge of the ramp. 'Useless bastards!' he spat in contempt, his hand closing around the lever. 'The master control panel must have been damaged in the landing. You need to pull the emergency release lever – like this.'

Pulling the lever, Sergeant Ferres shrieked in sudden agony

as one of the ramp's explosive release bolts misfired, a bright tongue of yellow fire bursting from the side of ramp to engulf his face. Screaming, a halo of flame dancing around his head, he stumbled blindly against the assault ramp as the other bolts fired and the ramp fell open behind him. Falling into the suddenly vacated space, his body rolled down the ramp and came to a stop partway down it as one of his legs caught on a protrusion at its side. For a moment, seeing the strugglings of their sergeant's body grow still as the life left him, his troops stood gazing at him in shocked silence, hypnotised by the brutal calamity of their leader's death.

'We have to move,' Larn heard someone say behind him as he realised how warm it had grown in the lander. 'The smoke is getting closer. If we don't get out of here now we'll either burn to death or choke.'

As one, the Guardsmen burst forward to rush down the ramp. The light outside seemed blinding in its intensity after the shadowed dimness of the interior of the lander. Barely able to keep his feet as the men behind him pushed to get out, Larn stumbled down the ramp with the rest, his first experiences of the new world before him registering as a disconnected jumble of sights and sensations. He caught snatches of an empty landscape through the press of bodies around him, saw a grey and brooding sky above them, felt a savage chill that bit gnawingly into his flesh. Worst of all was the sight of Sergeant Ferres's burnt and disfigured face. The fire-blackened sockets that had once held his eyes glimpsed briefly at the edge of Larn's vision as he followed the others down the ramp. Then, as the first ranks of Guardsmen reached the foot of the ramp and apparent safety, the frenzied herd instinct of a few moments before abruptly abated.

Released from the crushing pressure of the crowd as the Guardsmen in front moved to take advantage of the open space before them, Larn was relieved to find himself able to breathe properly once more. Then, standing uncertainly with the others as they milled leaderless in the shadow of the lander, he turned to take his first clear view of the planet around him.

This is it, he thought, his breath turning to white vapour in the cold. *This is Seltura-III? It doesn't look much like how they described it in the briefing.*

Around him, as endless as the wheat fields of his homeworld, was a bleak and barren landscape – a flat treeless vista of frozen grey-black mud, punctuated here and there by shell craters and the rusting silhouettes of burned-out vehicles. To the east of him, he saw a distant cityscape of ruined buildings, as grey, foreboding and abandoned as every other aspect of the landscape around it. *It looks like a ghost town,* he thought with a shiver. *A ghost town, hungry for more ghosts.*

'I don't understand it,' he heard a questioning voice say as he realised Leden, Hallan and Vorrans had come to stand beside him. 'Where are the trees?' Leden asked. 'They said Seltura-III was covered in forests. And it's cold. They said it would be summer.'

'Never mind that,' said Hallan, terse at his side. 'We need to get into cover. I heard shots hitting the hull when we landed. There must be hostiles around here some–' He paused, stopping to look up with anxious eyes at the sky as, overhead, they heard the whistle of a shell coming closer.

'Incoming!' someone screamed as the entire company raced frantically to seek shelter at the side of the lander. Seconds later, an explosion lifted up dancing clods of frozen mud thirty metres away from where they were standing.

'I think it was a mortar.' Vorrans said, an edge of panic to his voice as he huddled with the others beside the lander. 'It sounded like a mortar,' he said, jabbering uncontrollably in a breathless rush of fear. 'A mortar, don't you think? A mortar. I think it was a mortar. A mortar...'

'I wish to the Emperor that was *all* it was,' Hallan said. Around them, more shots and explosions rang out. A fusillade that seemed to ominously increase in volume with every instant, as the noise of bullets and shells striking the hull on the other side of the lander grew so loud they had to shout to be heard over the roar. 'Lucky for us whoever's shooting is on the other side of this lander but we can't stay here forever. We need to find better cover, or it's only a matter of time before their artillery finds the range and starts to loop shells over the lander to land right on top of us.'

'Maybe this is all a mistake?' Vorrans said, his face alive with the glimmer of desperate hope. 'That's it, mistaken identity. Maybe it's our own side doing the shooting and they don't know who we are. We could make a white flag and try to signal them.'

'Shut up, Vors. You're talking like an idiot.' Hallan snapped. Then, seeing Vorrans look at him in shock, he softened his tone. 'Believe me, Vors, there's nothing *mistaken* about it. There's a ten-metre tall Imperial eagle painted on each side of the hull of the lander. The people shooting at us know *exactly* who we are. That's why they're trying to *kill* us. Our only way out of this is to try and make for our own lines. Though we'll need to find out where they are first.'

'There!' Leden said, his finger pointing eastward. 'You see it – the eagle in the distance. Sweet Emperor, we're saved.'

Turning to follow the direction of Leden's jabbing finger, Larn saw a flagpole rising from the rubble-strewn outskirts of the city. At its top a worn and ragged flag: an Imperial eagle, fluttering in the breeze.

'You're right, Leden,' Hallan said, the excitement in his voice drawing the attention of the rest of the company as dozens of eyes turned to look toward the flag. 'It's our own lines, all right. If you look closely you can see the outlines of camouflaged bunkers and firing emplacements. That's where we should be headed.'

'But it's got to be seven or eight hundred metres away at least, Hals,' Vorrans protested. 'With nothing between us and that flag but open ground. We'll never make it.'

'We don't have any choice, Vors,' Hallan said. Then, seeing the eyes of every other Guardsman in the company were on him, he turned to them, his voice raised loud enough to be heard among the din of gunfire. 'Listen to me, all of you. I know you're scared. Zell knows, I am too. But if we stay here we are as good as dead. Our only chance is to make for that flag!'

For a moment there was no response as the Guardsmen cast frightened eyes from the now burning lander to the wide expanse of open ground before them. Each man weighing an unwelcome decision: to stay and risk an undetermined death sometime in the future, or to run and risk an immediate death in the present. Then, suddenly, a shell landed on their side of the lander no more than five metres from where they were standing and the decision was made for them.

They ran.

Breathless, terror dogging his every step, Larn ran with them. He ran, as from behind them there came a remorseless tide of gunfire as the unseen enemy tried to shoot them down. He saw men die screaming all around him, red gore spraying from chests and arms and heads as the bullets struck them. He saw men killed by falling shells, bodies torn apart by blast and shrapnel, heads and limbs dismembered in an instant. All the time he kept his eyes glued on the flag – his would-be refuge – in the distance before him. His every breath a silent prayer in the hope of salvation. His every step one closer to making that salvation a reality.

As he ran, he saw friends and comrades die. He saw Hallan fall first, his right eye exploding from its socket to make way for the bullet passing though it, his mouth open in a cry of encouragement to his fellow Guardsmen that would never be finished. Then Vorrans, his torso ruptured and mutilated as a dozen pieces of shrapnel exploded through his chest. Other men fell: some he had known by name, others he had known only by sight. All of them killed as, just as breathless and desperate as he was, they ran for the flag. Until at last, with most of his comrades dead already and the flag still a hundred metres away, Larn realised he would never make it.

'Here! Over here! Quickly, this way! Over here!'

Suddenly, hearing shouting voices nearby Larn turned to see a group of Guardsmen in grey-black camouflage appear as if from nowhere to beckon him towards them. Changing direction to head for them, he saw they had emerged from a firing trench and raced towards it with enemy bullets chewing up the ground around him. Until at last, reaching the trench, he leapt inside to safety.

Trying to catch his breath as he lay at the bottom of the trench, looking about him Larn saw five Guardsmen standing around him in the confines of the trench: all clad in the same uniform of grey-black patterned greatcoats, mufflers and fur-shrouded helmets. At first they ignored him, their eyes turned to scan the killing fields he had just escaped from. Then, one of the Guardsmen turned to look down towards him with a grimace and finally spoke.

'This is Vidmir in trench three, sergeant,' the Guardsmen said, pressing a stud at his collar as Larn realised he was speaking down a comm-link. 'We have one survivor. I think a few more made it to the other trenches. But most of those poor dumb bastards are dead out there in no-man's-land. Over.'

'I can see movement on the ork side,' one of the other Guardsmen said, standing looking over the trench parapet. 'All this killing must have got their blood up. They're getting ready for an attack.' Then, while Larn was still wondering if he had really heard the word 'ork', he saw the man turn away from the parapet to look towards him. 'Assuming that uniform you're wearing is not just for show, new fish, you might want to stand up and get your lasgun ready. There's going to be shooting.'

Pulling himself to his feet, Larn unslung his lasgun, stepping forward as the other Guardsmen moved sideways to make space for him on the trench's firing step. Then, as he checked his lasgun and made ready to put it to his shoulder, he saw something that caused him to wonder if his first combat drop might have gone even more badly wrong than he could have thought. As, from the corner of his eye, he spotted a bullet-riddled wooden sign erected behind and slightly to one side of the trench. A sign whose ironic greeting gave him pause to wonder if he really was where he thought he was at all.

A sign that said:

Welcome to Broucheroc.

CHAPTER SIX

Questions of Interstellar Geography and Other
Revelations – A Bad Day in Hell – The Waaagh! – A
Baptism of Fire – Hand-To-Hand against the Enemy – An
Opinion as to the Best Method of Killing a Gretchin

'They're getting ready to move all right,' the Guardsman said next
to him, spitting a wad of greasy phlegm over the trench parapet.
'They'll hit us hard this time, and in numbers. It's the blood that
does it, you see. Our blood, I mean. *Human* blood. The sight and
smell of it always makes 'em more willing and eager for a fight.
Though, Emperor knows, your average ork is usually pretty *eager*
to begin with.'

His name was Repzik: Larn could see the faded letters of the
name stencilled on the tunic of the man's uniform under his
greatcoat. Standing beside him on the firing step, Larn followed
the direction of his eyes to look into the landscape he now knew
as no-man's-land. No matter how intently he stared across the
bleak fields of frozen mud before them he could see no movement, nor for that matter any other sign of the enemy. Ahead,
no-man's-land seemed as flat, featureless and devoid of life as
it had when he had emerged from the lander to his first view of
it barely ten minutes ago. The only difference now was the addition of the burning shell of the lander itself, and with it the bodies
of his company strewn haphazard and bloody across the frozen
landscape. Abruptly, as he looked out at the remains of men he

had known as friends and comrades, Larn felt the beginnings of tears stinging wetly at the corners of his eyes.

Jenks is dead, he thought. *And Hallan, Vorrans, Lieutenant Vinters, even Sergeant Ferres. I don't see Leden. Perhaps he is still alive somewhere. But nearly every man I came here with from Jumael is lying dead out there in no-man's-land. All of them slaughtered within minutes of landing, without even having fired a shot.*

'It's a pity about your comrades,' Repzik said, his voice almost kindly as Larn clenched his eyes to try and stop the other men in the trench from seeing his tears. 'But they're dead and you ain't. What you need to start thinking about now is how you're going to stop yourself from *joining* them. The orks are coming, new fish. If you want to live you're going to have to keep yourself hard and tight.'

'Orks?' Larn said, trying to concentrate his mind on the practical in an effort to lay his grief aside. 'You said "orks"? I didn't know there were any orks on Seltura VII?'

'Could be that's true,' Repzik said, as beside him one of the other Guardsmen looked to the sky in silent exasperation. 'Fact is, you'd have to ask somebody who's actually *been* there. Here in Broucheroc though we generally have more orks than we know what to do with.'

'Wait,' asked Larn, confused, 'are you telling me this planet isn't Seltura VII?'

'Well, I wasn't specifically commenting on it, new fish,' Repzik said. 'But since you ask, you'd be right enough. This place isn't Seltura VII – wherever in *hell* that is.'

Stunned, for a moment Larn wondered if he had somehow misunderstood the man's meaning. Then, he looked out again at the treeless landscape and was struck by all the troubling inconsistencies between what he had been told to expect on Seltura VII and the stark brutal realities of the world he saw before him. They had made the drop three weeks early. There were no forests. It was winter rather than summer. The war here was against orks, not PDF rebels. A catalogue of facts that, with a dawning horror born of slow realisation, pushed him inexorably toward a sudden and shocking conclusion.

Holy Throne, he thought. *They sent us to the wrong planet!*

'I shouldn't be here,' he said aloud.

'It's funny how everyone tends to think that when they're waiting for an attack to begin,' said Repzik. 'I wouldn't worry about it, new fish. Once the orks get here you'll soon find yourself feeling right at home.'

'No, you don't understand.' Larn said. 'There has been a terrible mistake. My company was supposed to be going to the Seltura system. To a world called Seltura VII, to put down a mutiny among the local PDF. Something must have gone wrong because I'm on the wrong planet.'

'So? What is that to me?' Repzik said, his eyes as he looked at Larn seemed little warmer than the landscape around them. 'You are on the wrong planet. You are in the wrong system. Not to mention probably the wrong war. Get used to it, new fish. If that is the *worst* thing that happens to you today, you will have been lucky.'

'But you don't understand–'

'No. It is *you* who does not understand, new fish. This is Broucheroc. We are surrounded by ten million orks. And right now some of those orks – maybe only a few thousand or so, if we are lucky – are getting ready to attack us. They don't care what planet you think you should be on. They don't care that you think you're in the wrong place, that you're wet behind the ears, or that you're probably not even old enough to shave. All they care about is *killing* you. So if you know what is good for you, new fish, you will put all this crap aside and start worrying about killing them instead.'

Shocked at the man's outburst Larn said nothing, his reply dying on his tongue as he saw Repzik turn away from him to gaze darkly into no-man's-land once more. As though by some sixth sense the other Guardsmen in the trench had already done the same, all of them staring hard into no-man's-land as though watching something happening out there of which Larn was entirely unaware. No matter how hard Larn tried, he could see nothing. Nothing except grey-black mud and desolation.

Frustrated, wary of asking the others what they were looking at for fear of drawing another angry outburst, Larn turned to glance around him. Behind him, hidden from his sight when he had first landed by a gentle sloping of the ground, was a series of firing trenches and foxholes. All of them led down towards sandbag emplacements that covered the entrances to a number of underground dugouts set among the shattered husks of buildings at the outskirts of the city. Now his eyes had become accustomed to the relentless grey of the landscape, Larn could see other firing trenches around and to the side of their trench – their parapets cunningly camouflaged to look no different from the countless chunks of crumbling half-buried plascrete and other detritus that lay scattered across this wasteland. From time to time a Guardsman would suddenly emerge from one of the trenches to run half-crouched, zigzagging from one piece of cover to the next until he reached the safety of either another trench or the entrance to one of the dugouts. Behind them, in the distance, the main body of the city stood brooding across the horizon as though watching their lives and labours with disdain. A city of ruined and battle-scarred buildings set against a grey and uncaring sky.

This is Broucheroc, Larn reminded himself. *That is what they said the city was called.*

'There,' one of the Guardsmen said beside him. 'I see green. The bastards are moving.'

Turning to gaze once more into no-man's-land with the others, for a moment Larn found himself vainly struggling to see anything among the wearying grey of the world about them. Then, suddenly, at ground level, perhaps a kilometre away, he saw a brief glimpse of green flesh as its owner stood upright for a split second before abruptly disappearing once more.

'I see it,' Larn said, the words jumping breathless from him, unbidden. 'Holy Emperor! Is that an ork?'

'Hhh. I only wish orks were as small as that, new fish,' Repzik said, spitting over the parapet into no-man's-land again. 'That's a gretch. A gretchin. Keep looking and you should be able to see some more.'

He was right. Ahead, Larn saw the creature stand upright once more. This time it stood where it was unmoving, its green flesh plainly visible against the contrast of the grey backdrop of the landscape behind it. Then, after a moment, Larn saw another dozen creatures appear beside it, all of them standing still and motionless as though trying to smell something on the wind. Each of them perhaps a metre tall at most, their stunted green bodies appearing curiously hunched and misshapen inside their rough grey garments. Watching them, Larn felt himself recoil in instinctive horror at his first sight of an alien species. Until, before he even knew what he was doing, his finger was on the trigger of lasgun at his shoulder as he sighted in on the *Xenos*.

'Don't bother, new fish,' Repzik said, laying a hand across his barrel. 'Even if you did manage to hit one of the gretch at this range, you would be wasting your ammo. Save it 'til later. Save it for the orks.'

'I don't like it,' one of the other Guardsmen said. 'If the orks are sending their gretch out like that it means they're planning on hitting us with a frontal assault. Another one. What is that now? Something like the *third* one today?'

'Third time is right, Kell,' the Guardsman called Vidmir said, his face grim as he pressed a finger to his ear to listen to something on his comm bead. 'You'll have to remember to remonstrate with the orks about their lack of originality when they get here. From the reports I'm hearing over the tactical net, you should soon be getting the opportunity to do so.'

'What is it?' the other Guardsman – Kell – asked, while the rest of the men in the trench turned to look at Vidmir. 'What have you heard?'

'Sector Command says auspex is reading a lot of movement in the ork lines,' Vidmir replied. 'Sounds like Repzik was right. They're going to be hitting us hard, and in numbers. Though, from the sound of it, I think there's more to this than just a matter of the orks getting excited over killing the new fish's friends. Could be they were already getting ready to launch an offensive. Which would be bad enough, except it sounds like our own side is trying to get us killed as well. Battery Command are refusing to give us artillery support until they are sure this is really a full-blown assault and not just a feint.'

'A feint, my arse,' Kell grunted. 'When have you ever known an ork to do anything by halves?'

'Agreed,' Vidmir said. 'But, irrespective, it looks like we're going to have to repel the orks on our own. Emperor help us.' Then, turning towards Larn, Vidmir gave him the cold flash of a graveyard smile.

'Congratulations, new fish,' he said. 'Looks like not only did you manage to get yourself dropped right into the middle of hell but you picked a bad day in hell besides.'

Repzik, Vidmir, Donn, Ralvs and Kell. These were the names of the five men who shared the trench with him. Larn had learned that much about them at least in the quiet time as they waited for the battle to begin. They were from a planet called Vardan, they told him. They and their regiment, a group of hardened veterans known as the 902nd Vardan Rifles, had come to the city of Broucheroc more than ten years ago and had been here even since. *Ten years!* He could hardly believe it. Nor where those the only things that Larn had learned from the Vardans.

'I don't understand it,' he said, looking out at the group of gretchin on the other side of no-man's-land. 'What are they waiting for?'

Ten minutes had passed since the first alien appeared. Though the numbers of those waiting with it had now increased to perhaps a couple of hundred, still the ranks of gretchin stood exposed and out in the open on the other side of no-man's-land. Occasionally a squabble would break out, two or three of the aliens suddenly breaking away from the main group to fight a bloody battle with tooth and claw while their fellows watched with lazy interest. For the most part the aliens simply stood there unmoving, their feral faces turned to stare unblinkingly towards the human lines. It was an unnerving spectacle. Not for the first time, Larn found himself fighting the urge to take his lasgun and fire at them. To shoot over and over again until every one of the ugly inhuman faces he could see before him had been obliterated.

'It's an old trick, new fish,' Repzik said. 'They're waiting for us to shoot at them and give away our positions.'

'But that's suicide,' Larn said. 'Why would they be willing to sacrifice themselves like that?'

'Hhh. They're gretch, new fish,' Repzik replied. 'Willing doesn't come into it. If their Warboss tells 'em to go stand out in no-man's-land and wait to get killed, it's not like they get much say over it. Of course, even the fact that their boss is smart enough to think of using his gretch that way tells us something. It means the greenskin leading the assault is likely to be one crafty son of a bitch, relatively speaking. And that's likely to be bad news for us, believe me. There's not much worse than a crafty ork. Now quiet down, new fish. There will be plenty of time for questions later, after the attack. Assuming, of course, we survive it.'

At that Repzik fell silent once more, his eyes staring into no-man's-land with the rest of the Vardans. Denied the distraction of further conversation, Larn began to realise just how tense the atmosphere was in the trench. *An attack is coming,* he thought. *Although these men have faced dozens, perhaps even hundreds of such attacks in the past, still the tension is plain on every line of their faces for anyone to see.* Briefly, he tried to find comfort in that thought. He tried to tell himself that if hardened veterans like these felt queasy in the face of the impending assault, there was no shame in the churning of his own stomach but he remained unconvinced. *Am I a coward*, he thought. *I am afraid, but will my nerve hold so I can do my duty? Or will it fail? Will I fight when the attack comes or will I break and run?* But as forcefully as those questions rebounded around inside his head, he could find no answer.

The waiting was the worst of it. Abruptly, as he stood there on the firing step, Larn realised that until now he had been inoculated against fear by the sheer breathless pace of events since the lander had been hit. Now, in the silence of the lull before battle, there was no hiding place from his fears. He felt alone. Far from home. Terrified that he was about to die on a strange world under a cold and distant sun.

'Ready your weapons,' Vidmir said, as more gretchin began to appear on the other side of no-man's-land. 'This is it. Looks like they got tired of waiting.'

'We hold our fire until they're three hundred metres away,' Repzik said to Larn. 'See that flat grey-black rock over there? That's your mark. We wait 'til the first rank of gretch reach that before we fire.' Then, seeing Larn looking in confusion into no-man's-land as he tried to distinguish which of the thousands of grey-black rocks was the mark, Repzik sighed in exasperation. 'Never mind, new fish. You shoot when we do. You follow orders. You do what we tell you to do, when we tell you to do it, and you don't ask any questions. Trust me, that's the only way you going to survive your first fifteen hours.'

Ahead, the group of gretchin out in no-man's-land had swelled to become a horde several thousands strong. They seemed agitated now, jabbering to each other in incomprehensible alien gibberish while the more brave or foolhardy among them pushed their way to the front of the group as though restless for their wait to be at an end. Then, finally, the waiting was over as for the first time Larn heard the sound of massed alien voices screaming a terrifying war cry.

Waaaaaaaghhhh!

As one, firing their guns into the air, the horde of gretchin came charging towards them. As unnerving as the sight of the aliens had seemed to Larn earlier, they were nothing compared to the horrors he now saw emerging into view in their wake. Just behind the onrushing gretchin he saw countless numbers of much larger greenskins rise up to join the charge. Each one of them a grotesquely muscled broad-shouldered monster more than two metres tall, screaming with ferocious savagery as they took up the battle cry of their smaller brethren.

Waaaaaaaaghhh!

Sweet Emperor, Larn thought, half-beside himself with terror. *Those must be the orks. There's so many of them and every one of them is huge!*

'Eight hundred metres,' Vidmir said, sighting in on the enemy with the targeter clipped to the side of his lasgun, his calm voice barely audible above the sound of approaching thunder as the greenskins charged ever closer. 'Keep yourselves cold and sharp. No firing until they reach the kill zone.'

'Don't fire until you see the reds of their eyes,' Kell snickered, as if he had found some grim humour in the situation that eluded Larn.

'Six hundred metres,' Vidmir said, ignoring him.

'Remember to aim high, new fish,' Repzik said. 'Don't worry about the gretchin – they're no threat. It's the orks you want to hit. We open up with single shots at first – continuous volley fire. Oh, and new fish? You might want to release the safety catch on your lasgun. You'll find killing orks is easier that way.'

Fumbling at his lasgun in embarrassment as he realised the Vardan was right, Larn switched the firing control from safe to 'single shot'. Then, remembering his training and the words of *The Imperial Infantryman's Uplifting Primer*, he silently recited the Litany of the Lasgun in his mind.

Bringer of death, speak your name,
For you are my life, and the foe's death.

'Four hundred metres,' Vidmir said. 'Prepare to fire.'

The greenskins were closing. Looking past the scuttling ranks of gretchin, Larn could see the orks more clearly now. Close enough to see sloping brows and baleful eyes, while thousands of jutting jaws and mouths filled with murderous tusks seemed to smile towards him with eager and savage intent. With every passing second the orks were coming closer. As he watched them charging towards the trench, Larn felt himself gripped by an almost overpowering urge to turn and flee. He wanted to hide. To run away as far and fast as he could and never look back. Something deep inside of him – some mysterious reservoir of inner strength he had never known before – stopped him. Despite all his fears, the dryness of his mouth, the trembling of his hands that he hoped the others could not see, despite all that he stood his ground.

'Three hundred and fifty metres!' Vidmir shouted, while Larn could hear the distant popping sound of mortars being fired behind them. 'Three hundred metres! On my mark! Fire!'

In the same instant every Guardsman on the line opened fire, sending a bright fusillade of las-fire burning through the air towards the orks. With it came a sudden flurry of airbursts as dozens of falling mortar and grenade launcher rounds exploded in mid-air in a deadly hail of shrapnel. Then came the blinding flash of lascannon beams; the rat-a-tat crack of autocannons; the flare of frag missiles streaking towards their targets. A withering torrent of fire that tore into the charging orks, decimating them. Through it all, as the Vardans in the trench beside him ceaselessly worked the triggers of their lasguns to send more greenskins screaming to *xenos* hell, Larn fired with them.

He fired without pause, as merciless as the others. Over and over again, his fears abating with every shot, the terrors that had once assailed him replaced by a growing sense of exultation as he saw the greenskins die. For the first time in his life, Larn knew the savage joy of killing. For the first time, seeing orks fall wounded and dying to be trampled under the heedless boot heels of their fellows, he knew the value of hate. Seeing the enemy die, he felt no sorrow for them, no sadness, no remorse for their deaths. They were *xenos*. They were the alien. The unclean. They were monsters, every one of them.

Monsters.

With a sudden insight, he finally understood the wisdoms of the Imperium. He understood the teachings he had received in the scholarium, in the sermons of the preachers, in basic training. He understood why Man made war upon the *xenos*. In the midst of that war, he felt no pity for them.

A good soldier feels nothing but hate.

Then, through the heat and noise of battle, Larn saw something that brought all his fears rushing back to him. Incredibly, despite all the casualties inflicted by the Guardsmen's fire, the greenskins' charge had not wavered. Though the torrent of fire continued from the Vardans' positions, the orks kept on coming. They seemed unstoppable. Abruptly, Larn found himself uncomfortably aware just how much he wanted to avoid having to face an ork in hand-to-hand combat.

'One hundred and twenty metres!' he heard Vidmir yell through the din. 'Change cells and switch to rapid fire!'

'They're getting closer!' Larn said, his hands clumsy with desperation as he struggled to change the cell in his lasgun. 'Shouldn't we fix bayonets – just in case?'

'Hardly, new fish,' Repzik said, his cell already changed and firing with the rest. 'If this battle gets to bayonet range we've as good as lost it. Now, shut up and start shooting!'

Out in no-man's-land the charging orks came ever closer. By now most of the gretchin were dead, winnowed away by blast and shrapnel. Though the ranks of the orks had also been thinned, from where Larn stood there looked to be thousands of them left.

All bearing down across the battered landscape of no-man's-land in a relentless and barbaric tide hell bent on slaughter.

There's no stopping them, Larn thought. *We're going to be overrun!*

He saw orks armed with short bulbous-headed sticks running at the head of the mob, the sticks covered in a lethal profusion of spikes, blades and flanges. At first he took the weapons in their hands to be some form of primitive mace or club. Until he saw the front rank of orks suddenly throw the same 'clubs' to land in the frozen mud before the trenches, each one exploding in a shower of shrapnel. Instinctively, seeing one of the stick-grenades land a few metres from his trench, Larn ducked his head to avoid the deadly fragments whistling through the air above it. An action that drew a terse reprimand for Repzik.

'Damnation, new fish. Keep your fool head up and keep on shooting!' Repzik yelled. 'They're trying to make us keep our heads down so they can get in close.'

Doing as he was told, Larn resumed firing. Only to look on in horror with the rest of the men as, flying through the air so slowly it might almost have been moving in slow motion, another of the stick grenades hit the parapet and bounced inside their trench.

'Stikk bomb!' Vidmir screamed. 'Bail out!'

Rushing to evacuate the trench with the others, Larn scrambled over the trench wall behind him, stumbling over his own two feet as he made it to ground level and turned to run for cover. He tripped, his body already falling towards the ground as the blast of the stikk bomb ripped through the air behind him. He felt a pain in his shoulder and a sudden pressure in his ears.

Then, he hit the ground and everything went black.

He became aware of a ringing in his ears, his face cold against the hard frozen mud beneath him. Through the haze of returning consciousness, he heard men screaming and shouting, the sound of lasguns being fired, the bestial roars and bellows of what could have only been orks. The noises of a battle going on all around him.

Starting abruptly awake, with a surge of fear Larn lifted his head from the mud and looked about him to try and gain his bearings. He was lying face down on the ground, the pain in his shoulder having diminished to nothing more than a distant ache, while on every side around him Guardsmen and orks fought in brutal combat. He saw an ork shot point-blank in the face, its feral inhuman features burned away in the blink of an eye by a lasgun on full burst. He saw a Guardsman in the uniform of the Jumael 14th die screaming as another ork disembowelled him with the blade of a great gore-stained axe. He saw men and orks fighting, their feet slipping and stumbling over the bodies of their fallen comrades beneath them, the details of which side was winning or losing unclear in the fog and haze of combat. He saw blood and he saw slaughter. He saw savagery from human and alien alike. His eyes opened, he saw the reality of war once all the noble pretensions were stripped away.

Then, as the appalling spectacle continued to unfold around him, Larn's heart began to beat wildly in his chest as a dreadful thought suddenly occurred to him.

Where is my lasgun, he thought, looking about him in panic. *Sweet Emperor, I must have lost it when I fell.*

Feeling suddenly naked, Larn began scrabbling frantically among the fallen bodies lying nearby in search of a weapon. No sooner had he started than he all but fell over a gretchin searching among the bodies for reasons of its own. For a second they stood face-to-face, the creature was as astonished to see Larn as he was to see it. Then, noticing a sly smile come over the gretchin's face as it made to lift its gun and point it at him, Larn leapt screaming towards it.

Knocking the gun from the gretchin's hands before it could shoot, Larn made to grab for it himself, only for the gun to skip away from both of them as the force of their impact sent them falling to the ground. Pushing himself on top of the creature, desperately trying to hold it off with one hand as it clawed and bit at him, Larn felt the fingers of his free hand brush a hard object lying on the ground beside him and he grabbed it. As he raised the object and brought it crashing down into the gretchin's face, Larn became dimly aware he was holding his own helmet but he was past caring. In a frenzy born of self-preservation, he raised the helmet and smashed it down into the gretchin's face again and again. Repeatedly smashing the creature in the face until the helmet in his hand was slick with black ichor. Then, finally realising the gretchin had stopped moving long ago, Larn paused to catch his breath. By then, there was no trace left of the smile he had seen from the gretchin when it had tried to kill him. Below him, the gretchin's face had been reduced to a battered shapeless pulp. The creature was dead. It could no longer hurt him.

Hearing the chilling sound of an alien battlecry, Larn looked up from the dead body beneath him to see a group of a dozen orks charging towards him. For a moment he almost turned, whether to run away or scramble after the gretchin's fallen gun to defend himself he did not know. Only to realise that no matter what he did now it would make no difference. The orks were too close. He was as good as dead already.

This is it, he thought, his panic abruptly displaced by an unnerving sense of calm. *I am going to die here. I am a dead man and there is nothing anyone can do to save me.*

'Forward!' he heard a voice yell as a shotgun boomed behind him and the face of the foremost ork disappeared in an explosion of gore. 'Vardans, by my mark! Advance and rapid fire!'

Amazed, Larn saw a battle-scarred sergeant in a grey-black greatcoat stride past him leading a ragtag band of Vardans in a counter-charge against the orks. Moving at a slow walk, firing from the hip with shotguns, lasguns and flamers blazing, they advanced towards the oncoming orks, taking a gruesome toll of the enemy with every step towards them. While before them orks screamed and died, the sergeant led his men forward with bullets and las-beams flying all around him, his pace never faltering, his voice a clear beacon of authority among the confusion of battle. Watching the sergeant lead his men from the front, his every gesture calm and unafraid, Larn found himself wondering if one of the long-dead saints of the Imperium had somehow regained human form and now walked among them. The sergeant seemed immortal. Unkillable. Like a hero from the tales they told in the scholarium.

A legend, leading his men to victory.

'Forward!' the sergeant yelled, the counterattack gaining momentum as every man still alive in the trenches gathered to advance beside him. 'Keep on firing. Forward and advance!'

Following the sergeant's lead the advance continued, the constant fire of the Vardan guns and the slow measured pace of their progress seemed every bit as relentless and unstoppable as had the orks' charge earlier. Until, wilting before the remorseless ferocity of the Vardans' attack, the orks did something which Larn had never thought he would live to see.

They turned and ran.

Watching the surviving orks run back towards their lines, Larn slowly became aware of a brief hush falling across the battlefield as the Vardans' advance halted and they stopped firing. Soon, as it became plain the orks' attack was ended, new sounds broke the silence: the cries of wounded men; the shouts of their comrades calling for a medic; the noise of nervous laughter and disbelieving oaths as other men found they were still very much alive. Hearing those sounds, Larn felt the tension abruptly leave him as the realisation hit him that he had survived. Still kneeling over the body of the dead gretchin, he looked down at the thing's ruined face in with sudden queasiness; afraid he was going to vomit. Then, he saw a shadow fall across him as a nearby Guardsman came to stand beside him.

'You must be a new fish?' a cynical voice asked him. 'One of the new groxlings to the slaughter they sent us in the lander? I think this belongs to you.'

Looking up, Larn found himself staring at an ugly dwarfish Vardan with a shaven head and a mouthful of stained and crooked teeth. The Vardan was holding a lasgun in each hand, one of which Larn recognised sheepishly as his own gun – the same weapon he had lost earlier.

'Here, new fish,' the runt said, giving him a sardonic broken-toothed smile as he tossed the lasgun towards him. 'Next time you need to kill a gretch, you might try using this.'

CHAPTER SEVEN

The Field Station – Lessons in Futility, Parts One &
Two – Friends & Heroes Awaiting Disposal – Welcome
to the 902nd Vardan – Corporal Vladek and the
Distribution of Resources – Meeting Sergeant Chelkar
and an Addition to Davir's Woes

Pausing for a moment to catch his breath while he waited for the stretcher bearers to bring another patient, Surgeon-Major Martus Volpenz was surprised to realise how inured he had become to the sound of men screaming. Around him, the walls of the apothecarium field station reverberated with it constantly. He could hear men shouting, begging, moaning, shrieking, muttering profane oaths and whispering half-remembered prayers. Not for the first time, ever mindful that it was his calling to alleviate the pain of others, the surgeon-major looked about him at the place where he practised his craft and felt despair.

To a man less accustomed to it, the dimly lit interior of the field station's main operating theatre might have been mistaken for a scene from hell. Along one wall of the station, hundreds of severely wounded men lay in litters stacked four men high on a series of metal racks. Against the other wall a dozen exhausted surgeons worked feverishly to clear the most urgent cases from tables that stank with the blood that stained every surface of the floors and walls. For each man they healed, a dozen more men waited amid the suffocating stink of blood and pus and death, desperately wailing and pleading for help in a cacophony of suffering that never reached its end.

'Stomach wound,' his surgical assistant Jaleal said, breaking into his thoughts. 'He's been given morphia,' he added, checking the treatment notification tag on the patient's ankle as the stretcher-bearers lifted the unconscious form of a wounded Guardsman onto the operating table before them. 'Two doses.'

Taking a pair of scissors, Jaleal removed the tag, before cutting away the Guardsman's tunic in blood-encrusted strips to reveal the wound hidden beneath it. Then, taking a wet cloth from a bucket at the foot of the table, he washed the worst of the blood away from the edges of the wound.

'Looks like a through and through,' he said. 'From the size of the wound I'd say an ork gun was the culprit. The blood's dark. Looks like his liver's been punctured.'

'Give him some ether somnolentus,' Volpenz said, taking a scalpel from a tray of instruments nearby as he stepped to the side of table. 'Standard dosage.'

'We have none,' Curlen, his other assistant, said. 'We used what was left on the last patient.'

'What about the other anaesthetics?' Volpenz said. 'The nitrous oxide?'

'Gone as well,' Jaleal said. 'If he wakes up we'll just have to hold him down.'

'At least tell me we have some blood plasma left?' Volpenz said. 'If I have to go digging around this man's insides in search of a wound in his liver he's going to bleed like a stuck pig.'

'Not a drop,' Jaleal said, shrugging in helplessness. 'Remember the sucking chest wound twenty minutes ago? He got the last of it.'

'How much blood is there in the overspill bag, Jaleal?' Volpenz asked.

Ducking his head under the table, Jaleal checked the contents of the transparent bag underneath it designed to catch the blood bleeding out of the patient as it oozed along the disposal gutters set in the table's sides.

'About half a litre,' he said, pulling the bag up from beneath the table. 'Maybe three-quarters.'

'All right,' Volpenz said. 'Replace that bag with a new one and use the contents of the one you've got to autosanginuate him.'

'You want to transfuse him with his own blood?' Jaleal said. 'There's barely enough in here to keep a dog alive, never mind a man.'

'There's no other choice,' Volpenz said, leaning forward with a practiced hand to make the first incision. 'He'll die anyway if this wound isn't seen to. Now, look sharp, gentlemen. We're going to have to do this fast, before he bleeds to death.'

Cutting an incision to open the wound, Volpenz quickly peeled back the skin around it and fixed a clamp in place to keep it open. Then, while beside him Jaleal used his cloth to mop at the blood welling in the wound cavity, Volpenz searched desperately for the source of the bleeding. It was hopeless. There was so much blood in the wound he could hardly see a thing.

'Vital signs are weak,' Curlen said, his fingers at the man's neck to feel his pulse. 'We're losing him.'

'Lift his legs up, Jaleal. It'll send more blood to his heart,' Volpenz said. 'I only need a few more seconds. There! I think I've found it. He's got a tear in the main artery leading to the liver.'

Pushing his hands deep into the wound cavity, Volpenz clamped the bleeding artery shut. Only to find his hopes frustrated as, abruptly, the cavity began to fill with blood once more.

'Damnation! There must be another bleeder! Curlen, how's he doing?'

'I can't find a pulse any more, sir. We could try to manually resuscitate him?'

'No,' Volpenz said, throwing his bloody scalpel down on the instrument tray in frustration. 'It wouldn't do any good. He's bled out. The round probably hit a rib and caused bone fragments to perforate his liver in a dozen places. Clear the table. We can't save this one.'

Grabbing a piece of discarded cloth to clean his hands, Volpenz stepped away from the table, pausing only to glance at the dead Guardsman as Curlen signalled for the stretcher bearers to take him away. *How old was he,* he thought. *He looks to be in his forties, but that means nothing here. Broucheroc has a way of aging a man. He might only be in his early thirties, even late twenties.* Then, as they lifted the dead man's body from the table, Volpenz noticed an old scar in the patient's side. *He's been wounded before,* he thought. *And patched up. I wonder, was it my work or someone else's? Doesn't matter now, I suppose. Whoever saved the poor bastard's life before, there was no saving him this time.*

Sighing, he turned away to gaze once more at the confines of the operating room around him. As he did, he realised how little good could be done there for the dying and suffering men who came to the field station day after day. *It's not the war or even the orks that kills most of them,* he thought. *It's the shortages. We're short of anaesthetics, antibiotics, plasma; even the most basic of medical equipment. Short it seems of everything except pain, death and futility. Here in Broucheroc, these things at least are never in short supply.*

Then, as he made to throw away the cloth he had used to clean his hands, Volpenz noticed something was written on it. Looking at it more closely, he saw there was a name stencilled in the cloth. Repzik. Abruptly, he realised the cloth must have come from the dead Guardsman's tunic – one of the pieces Jaleal had cut away earlier to reveal the man's wound. *Repzik,* Volpenz thought sadly. *So that was what his name was.* Then, just as abruptly, he realised that it made no difference.

Whatever name the man had come here with, he did not need it now.

In the shadow of the dugout emplacements, a little way behind the trenches, the corpses of the men killed in the last hour-and-a-half

had been piled in a line three cadavers deep. Their feet boot-
less, their bodies stripped of their equipment, some with faces
wrapped in concealing cloth, others with dead features left naked
to the biting cold: all of them laid haphazardly atop each other like
so many logs ready for the burning. *Like firewood*, Larn thought
as he stood gazing down on the dead bodies of the men who had
made the journey with him from Jumael IV. Men he had known
and liked. Men who had crossed the unimaginable distances of
the void only to waste their lives on the wrong planet and in the
wrong campaign. His comrades, now reduced to nothing more
than a temporary landmark in the unforgiving and war-torn landscape he saw all about him. For what? To Larn, it seemed the most
pointless of the many horrors he had witnessed already in this
desolate place. A lesson in utter futility.

Hearing the protesting squeal of a rusted axle, Larn turned
to see four bent-backed old women bundled in ragged layers
of civilian dress pushing an empty handcart across the frozen
ground towards him. Noticing the faded insignia of the Depart-
mento Munitorium on the khaki-green armbands they wore on
their sleeves, Larn realised they must be militia auxiliaries lev-
ied from among the local population. Wheeling the cart past
him, they halted beside the line of corpse and wearily began to
lift them into the cart. Until at last, as their labours revealed the
face of a corpse hidden deeper in the pile, Larn saw something
that made him cry out and race towards them.

'Wait!' he yelled.

Startled, cringing away as though afraid he might hurt them,
the women stopped their work. Then, seeing Larn standing by
the pile to peer down at the face of a corpse, one of the women
spoke to him in a voice made dull and lifeless with fatigue.

'You knew him?' she said. 'One of the dead men?'

'Yes,' Larn said. 'I knew him. He was a friend. A comrade.'

It was Leden. His face slack and pale, his body covered in gruesome and horrendous wounds, he lay at the centre of the pile

with dead eyes staring up at the foreboding sky overhead. Having not seen Leden die during their mad flight across no-man's-land, Larn had harboured the hope the simple-minded farmboy might have made it to the Vardan lines and survived just as he had. Now that hope was dashed. Looking down at Leden's face, Larn realised his last living link with his homeworld had been severed. He was truly alone now. More alone than he could have ever thought possible. Alone, on a strange new world that seemed entirely given over to randomness, brutality and madness.

'He was a hero,' the old woman said.

'A hero?'

Unsure of her meaning, Larn looked at her in confusion. For a moment, her eyes dim and uncomprehending with exhaustion, she returned his gaze in silence. Then, barely more animated than the dead bodies before her, she tiredly shrugged and spoke once more.

'They are heroes,' she said in a listless voice, as though reciting a speech she had heard a thousand times herself. 'They all are: all the Guardsmen who die here. They are martyrs. By giving their blood to defend this place they have made the soil of this city into sacred ground. Broucheroc is a holy and impregnable fortress. The orks will never take it. We will break their assault here. Then, we will push them back and reclaim this entire planet.'

'So the commissars tell us,' she added, without conviction.

Returning to their work the women made to lift Leden from the pile. Finding him held fast and stuck to the other bodies by frozen and congealed blood, one of the women took a pry bar from the side of the cart. Sickened to his stomach, Larn watched her slide the bar under Leden's body and put her weight on it, the corpse rising with a crack of splintered ice as her sisters pulled it free and tossed it on the cart. Then, two of them pushing down the handles of the cart while the others stood by the side to stop its contents from falling out, the old women began to wheel away the bodies they had collected.

'What will you do with them?' Larn called out after them, not altogether sure he wanted to know the answer.

'They will be buried,' the women he had spoken to earlier said. 'Like heroes should be. Buried, up on the hill past the old plasteel works on the Grennady Plass. Heroes' Hill, it is called. Or at least that is what they tell us,' she shrugged again. 'We just transport the bodies. Others deal with their disposal.'

With that she turned back to the burden of the cart, pushing it away with the other women in the direction of the outskirts of the city. As he watched them go, Larn belatedly tried to remember one of the prayers he had been taught as a child. A prayer to ease the passage of the departed souls of his comrades into the afterlife as they went to join their Emperor in paradise. His mind was a blank, his heart so sick with grief it felt dull and empty. All his prayers had left him.

'Take off your jacket and pull back your tunic,' he heard a voice say behind him.

Turning, Larn found himself face-to-face with a gaunt Vardan medic wearing a blood-splattered greatcoat and carrying a satchel slung across his shoulder.

'If you want me to treat that shoulder wound I will have to be able to see it,' the medic said, opening his satchel.

Looking at his own left shoulder, much to his surprise Larn noticed a small bloodstained hole in the epaulette of his jacket. Dimly remembering the sudden pain he had felt there when the ork bomb had exploded in the trench behind him, he did as the medic had asked, removing his jacket and pulling down his tunic shirt to allow him access to the wound.

'Hmm. The good news is you'll live,' the medic said, prodding at the wound while Larn shivered in the cold. 'Looks like you were winged by a piece of shrapnel. Took a little bit of flesh with it, but it doesn't look as though the bone is broken.'

Taking a sachet of white powder from inside his bag the medic poured it liberally on the wound and pressed a gauze pad over the hole, applying half-a-dozen pieces of adhesive tape to hold the dressing in place.

'You didn't realise you had a hole in you, I take it?' he said. Then, seeing Larn nod, he continued. 'Probably shock. Get yourself some recaf. Food too, if you can find it. It'll help you get yourself together. Though I warn you, you probably won't thank me for that advice in an hour's time. Once you get your feeling back, chances are you'll find that wound aches like a bitch. You have morphia?'

'Four phials,' said Larn. 'In my med-pack.'

'Good. Let me see it,' the medic said. Then, when he saw Larn hesitate, he held out his hand in command. 'Kit inspection. As company medical officer, it is my job to make sure you are properly equipped.'

Pulling the slim oblong wooden case of the med-pack he had been issued with on Jumael from his belt, Larn handed it over. Breaking the seals on the box lid the medic slid it open and checked the contents.

'Morphia. Vein clamps. Sterilising fluid. Synth-skin canister. Wherever you're from they obviously don't believe in sending their sons under equipped to war. Still, my need is greater than yours. I'm going to have to requisition some of your supplies.'

'But you can't just help yourself to my med-pack,' Larn said in outrage. 'The regulations say–'

'The regulations say a lot of things, new fish,' the medic replied, taking a handful of items from inside the med-pack and dropping them into his satchel. 'Though you can be sure whichever genius wrote them never troubled himself actually finding out if they worked in practice. Anyway, I'm leaving you with half of the gauze, morphia, and clamps. Plus, you get to keep the insect repellent. Given the climate, there's not much call for it hereabouts.'

'But if I should get seriously wounded–'

'Then you'll need a medic. Just scream loudly and I'll come running.'

Tossing the depleted med-pack back to him, the medic closed his satchel before looking at Larn once more.

'Now,' he said, 'seeing as you're standing about here on your own, I take it you've not been assigned to duties yet?'

'No... I... my company was destroyed and...'

'Go see Corporal Vladek,' the medic said. 'He'll sort you out. Tell him Medical Officer Svenk sent you.'

'Corporal Vladek?'

'Over there,' the medic said, pointing to one of the dugout entrances as he turned to walk away. 'Barracks Dugout One. Vladek is our quartermaster – the biggest scavenger, thief, pack rat, and all round scrounger in the sector. You'll know him when you see him. Oh, and a word to the wise, new fish. Don't drink any more than two cups of Vladek's recaf. Or else, next thing you know you could be charging the ork lines on your own in a one-man assault.'

Walking down the rough earthen steps underground into the dugout, Larn was greeted with a warm blast of air thick with the smell of smoke and the odour of stale sweat. Eyes watering at the stench of it, he stepped past a couple of Guardsmen playing dice just inside the doorway and made his way into the barracks. Inside, he saw two lines of rusting metal bunks arranged either side of an iron stove at the centre of the room where a group of Vardans sat talking, eating, or cleaning their weapons. For a moment, Larn considered asking them if any of them had seen Corporal Vladek. Then, seeing a flabby unshaven Vardan in a stained undershirt sitting alone at a table in a corner of the room, Larn remembered the medic's description and knew he had found his man.

Crammed on ramshackle shelves and in alcoves cut directly into the earth of the wall behind the corporal was a treasure trove of scavenged equipment. Larn could see lasgun power packs, frag grenades, boxes of dry rations, shotgun shells, bayonets and knives of all shapes and sizes, spades, picks, hand axes, lanterns, uniforms, helmets, flak jackets, even a large metal claw that could only have come from the arm of a dead ork. Meanwhile, on the table and the floor around him were a number of standard issue Guardsmen's field rucksacks, the contents of which the corporal was currently busy digging through with the grim enthusiasm of a bandit chieftain surveying his latest spoils.

'Corporal Vladek?' Larn asked, approaching the table. 'Medical Officer Svenk said I should come see you.'

'Ah, more cannon fodder,' the corporal said, pushing the rucksacks aside to clear a space as he looked up at Larn with the glint of a smile in his red-rimmed eyes. 'Always good to see some new grist for the mill. Welcome to the 902nd Vardan, new fish. Find yourself a chair. You would like some recaf? I have some brewing.'

Turning to the battered pot of recaf perched precariously on a small hotplate beside him, the corporal produced a pair of enamel cups and filled them to the brim with black steaming liquid. He noticed Larn staring darkly down at one of the rucksacks still left on the table.

'Here we go. Two cups of Vladek's special recaf, nice and hot,' the corporal said. 'Sadly, we have to make do with a ground-up concoction of local roots and tubers rather than the real thing. Even the Emperor himself would be hard pressed to find any real recaf in this hellhole, and we all know he can work miracles. To give it a bit more kick I mix in a tenth of a dose of powdered stimms which, incidentally, works wonders for the flavour. But I see you seem to be interested in one of my latest acquisitions, new fish. Though, from the expression on your face, I have a feeling you're not about to make me an offer.'

'This rucksack,' Larn said, feeling dead inside as he looked at the words *Jumael 14th* stamped on the side. 'It could have belonged to one of my friends.'

'I wouldn't be surprised,' Vladek said, then gestured at the pile of rucksacks lying on the floor beside him. 'If not this one, then perhaps one of these other packs did. So? What of it? It is not as though this equipment is likely to be of help to its previous owners any more. While it *could* mean the difference between life and death for someone still living on the line. It is a simple matter of the fair and logical distribution of resources, new fish. Which, in this case, means that the living get to keep the things the dead no longer have any use for. Besides, if I hadn't had the foresight to liberate these packs from the bodies of the dead, someone else would have. You would have preferred I had let the militia auxiliaries get them so they could make us trade for the contents? This is Broucheroc, new fish. Forget all that nine-tenths rubbish. Here, possession is the *whole* of the law.'

'And if I was killed?' said Larn, angrily. 'Would you loot my body as well?'

'In a heartbeat, new fish. Your lasgun, your bayonet, your pack, your boots, not to mention whatever medical supplies the esteemed Svenk was kind enough to leave you with. Anything that might be of use to us. But you needn't feel so put upon. It is the same for everyone here, myself included. If I am killed tomorrow, I should expect to have my equipment stripped and re-allocated before my body even goes cold.'

'Not much likelihood of that happening,' Larn spat. 'Not with you sitting warm and safe in here in this dugout while outside good men are dying!'

'Good men?' Vladek said, his voice low with menace as the warm facade of moments earlier abruptly faded. 'Don't talk to me about good men dying, new fish. In ten years in this stinking cesspit I've seen men – good and bad – die by their thousands. Some of them were friends of mine. Others weren't. But any one of them was worth more than you and all your idiot recruit friends put together. You think just because I'm sitting here I don't know what it is to fight? I was killing the Emperor's enemies when you were still sucking greedily at your mother's teat. How else do you think I ended up with a leg like this?'

Taking an enormous combat knife from the table before him Vladek smacked it down against his left leg for emphasis, the flat of the blade making a dull metallic noise through his trouser leg as it struck his knee.

'You have an augmetic leg?' Larn said, shocked.

'Augmetic? Phah. The chance would be a fine thing! Along with everything else bionics are in short supply hereabouts. This is a Mark 3 Non-Motive Prosthetic, Left Leg Model. I had to barter the salvaged parts from a knocked-out sentinel for it, never mind what it cost me to get the damned apothecary to fit it. Now, I think it's time you sat down and stopped your mewling, new fish. Before I become so offended at your big mouth and flagrant disregard for my hospitality that I waste this good recaf by throwing it in your stupid snot-nosed face.'

Hearing someone laugh in another part of the dugout, Larn suddenly realised the other Vardans must have heard every word Vladek had said to him. His face burning with shame and embarrassment Larn took a chair and sat opposite the corporal with eyes lowered, unwilling to meet the other man's gaze for fear his cheeks were still flaring scarlet.

'Drink your recaf, new fish,' the corporal said, the storm of his anger passing as abruptly as it had started. 'We will begin again, you and I. Wipe the slate clean. I know it has been a hard day for you after all, and so I am willing to make allowances. It is not every day that a Guardsman finds he has been dropped on the wrong planet.'

'You know about that?' Larn said, stunned. 'Did one of the men I was in the trench with tell you? Repzik said—'

'Repzik is dead, new fish,' Vladek said. 'He died in the last attack. We talked about good men? Well, Repzik was one of the best. I knew him nearly twenty years, all told. From back on Vardan, even before we were drafted into the Guard together. The parts from the sentinel I used to buy this leg? It was Repzik who went into no-man's-land to get them for me. Like I said, a good man. But no, to answer your question, it wasn't Repzik who told me about your misfortune. It was Kell. Though by then I had heard about it from other sources anyway.'

'Other sources? Who?'

'The Navy. About half an hour ago Sector Command forwarded us a message from an orbiting troopship, requesting that we inform the Guard company they'd just dropped that this planet wasn't in fact Seltura VII. Apparently they forgot to tell you this, what with all the excitement of the drop and so forth. *A regrettable oversight caused by a temporary failure in the lines of communication.* Those were their exact words I believe. A snafu, as we call such things in these parts.'

'A snafu?'

'Situation Normal All Fouled Up. An apt and well-used acronym here in Broucheroc. Though you can substitute other words for fouled if you so desire.'

'But if they have realised their mistake, does that mean I am being reassigned?' Larn asked, his heart grown suddenly hopeful.

'No, new fish. Frankly, the fact the troopship chose to relay the news of your company's predicament at all was more by the way of an afterthought. The main purpose of their message was to demand to know what the hell we had done with their lander. I am told their response when they heard the lander had been shot down and would not be returning was unrepeatable. By now, they are likely already underway again and far from this planet.'

'So, I am stuck here,' Larn said glumly.

'You and the rest of us, new fish.' Vladek said, bending forward to delve through a boxful of grey-black coats sitting under the table. 'Now, drink your recaf and we will see about getting you sorted. A new greatcoat in urban camouflage pattern would seem as good a place to start as any. It will help you blend in and make you less of a target, not to mention keeping you warm. This time of year it's cold enough to have a man passing ice cubes every time he voids his bladder. I have one here that should fit you perfectly, give or take. No need to worry too much about the blood on the lapels. I am sure you will find it brushes off easily enough once it has had time to dry.'

Ten minutes later, courtesy of Corporal Vladek's scavenged stores, Larn found himself the new owner of a greatcoat, a pair of woollen gloves, two frag grenades, a fur-covered helmet, a small lump of whetstone, and a comm-bead tuned to the local comm-link frequencies used by the Vardans. Then, as Larn finished the last bitter mouthful of ersatz recaf from his cup, Vladek asked to see his dog-tags and wrote his name and number on a clipboard beside him.

'That is it for now, new fish,' Vladek said. 'You will need to come back here and see me again in fifteen hours' time. Then I can issue you with some of the more valuable and sought-after pieces of equipment: hotshot power packs for your lasgun, extra frag grenades, a laspistol, smoke grenades, and so on.'

'Why fifteen hours?' Larn asked.

'Phah. You will learn soon enough in this place there are some questions it is better not to ask, new fish. That is one of them. Just come see me again in fifteen hours, and try not to think about it in the meantime. Oh, and new fish? I almost forgot. You will need one of these.'

Removing a slim black copy of *The Imperial Infantryman's Uplifting Primer* from a shelf behind him, Vladek offered it to Larn across the table.

'But I already have one, corporal,' Larn said. 'I was issued with my copy of the Primer on my first day of basic training back on Jumael.'

'Congratulations, new fish,' Vladek said. 'Now, you have two copies. You will need them, and it is better not to get caught short. You will find this little book to be a vital tool when it comes to the nitty-gritty of day-to-day living here in Broucheroc. The paper it is printed on is most absorbent.'

Handing him the book along with his dog-tags, Vladek turned to the hotplate to pour another steaming cup of recaf.

'Anyway, that's enough equipment for you to be getting on with, new fish,' Vladek said, turning back towards Larn and nodding at something behind him. 'Next, we should see about getting you fixed up with a fire-team. Fortunately here comes our company commander, right on cue.'

Seeing a figure in a greatcoat approaching through the corner of his eye, Larn stood bolt upright from his chair and saluted smartly. Only to find himself facing the same Vardan sergeant he had seen lead the counterattack against the orks earlier.

'Why is there a new fish saluting me, Vladek?' the sergeant said, stepping past Larn to take a cup of recaf from the corporal's hand. 'He has mistaken me for a general perhaps?'

'An entirely understandable mistake given your commanding presence and natural air of authority, sergeant,' Vladek said, smiling. 'Then again, I had just told him you are our company commander. Perhaps he thinks that makes you a lieutenant.'

'A lieutenant? I am disappointed, Vladek. If I am going to be mistaken for an officer, I thought I would have rated colonel at least.' Then, the merest suggestion of a smile ghosting at his lips, the sergeant turned back to Larn. 'You can put your hand down by the way, trooper. Even if I was a lieutenant, we don't hold much with saluting here. It only gives the orks something extra to aim at. I assume you have a name? Other than new fish I mean?'

'Trooper First Class Larn, Arvin A, reporting for duty, sergeant!' Larn said, his hand falling but his back still ramrod straight as he stood to attention. 'Number: eight one five seven six dash—

'At ease, Larn,' the sergeant told him. 'Save it for the parade ground. As I say, we don't stand much on ceremony here. All right then. I take it you have already given your name and number to Corporal Vladek so he can forward them to General HQ?'

'Yes, sergeant.'

'Good. It may be that HQ will order you reassigned to duties elsewhere in the city. In the meantime standing orders on the disposition of new troops are clear. You were dropped into our sector: that means you belong to us. You are hereby seconded to the 902nd Vardan until further notice, Larn. Welcome to Company Alpha. My name is Chelkar. Until you are assigned elsewhere or HQ gets around to sending us a new lieutenant you will be taking your orders from me. We are clear?'

'Clear, sergeant.'

'How long since you took the eagle?'

'The eagle, sergeant?'

'I mean: how long is it since you were inducted into the Guard?'

'Four months, sergeant.'

'Four months? You are green then? You haven't seen much action?'

'No. Today was my first engagement, sergeant.'

'Hmm. Well, you survived it at least. I suppose that shows us something.' For a moment, his eyes grown suddenly sad and distant, Chelkar fell silent. Certain he was being judged some-how by that silence, Larn felt a rising urge to defend his worth.

'You do not need to worry, sergeant,' he said. 'I will not let any-one down. I am a Guardsman. I will do my duty.'

'I am sure you will, Larn.' Chelkar's expression was grave. 'But remember, part of that duty is for you to keep yourself alive so you can fight again tomorrow. To that end, you will do the fol-lowing things. You will follow orders. You will keep your eyes and ears open. You will watch your comrades' backs, just as they will watch yours. But most of all, there will be no heroics. No fool-hardiness. No unnecessary risks. This is Broucheroc, Larn. There are no heroes here; the orks keep killing them. Do we under-stand each other?'

'Yes, sergeant.'

'All right then,' Chelkar said, before turning to call out to one of the Guardsmen standing beside the stove. 'Davir. Come over here and meet our new recruit.'

In response to Chelkar's call, Larn saw a stocky diminutive Vardan move away from the stove and come walking towards them. With a sinking heart, he recognised him at once as the same ugly dwarfish Guardsman who had given him his lasgun back after the battle.

'Davir, this is Larn.'

'We have met already, sergeant. Hello, new fish.'

'Good,' said the sergeant. 'Larn, I am assigning you to Fire-team Three under Davir's command.'

'With all due respect, sergeant,' Davir said, 'given the new fish's lack of experience, wouldn't it be better to assign him somewhere else until he finds his feet. Fire-team Three is a frontline unit, after all.'

'This whole company is a frontline unit, Davir,' Chelkar said. 'If you can think of anywhere I could send him in this entire sector where the orks wouldn't be shooting at him, I'd be glad to hear of it. Besides, your fire-team is under strength. You need him and I am sure I can rely upon you to look after him and show him the ropes.'

'You are right of course, sergeant,' Davir said, grudgingly. 'Come on then, new fish. Get your kit and follow me. We have orks to kill, you and I.'

Turning, Davir strode away at a surprisingly brisk stride, forcing Larn to hurry his own pace to catch up. Then, as Davir walked through the door at the end of the barracks and headed up the steps out of the dugout, from behind him Larn heard the Vardan muttering venomously to himself under his breath.

'Need him,' he heard Davir whisper to himself. 'Need him, my Vardan arse! Like I need to be nursemaiding a damn new fish. As though having had to spend ten years in the company of that fat halfwit Bulaven wasn't bad enough, now they've gone and saddled me with a war virgin just to add to my woes. Damnation!'

Reaching the head of the steps to emerge into the cold air outside, Davir turned to give Larn a withering glare as he waited for him to catch up.

'Come on, new fish. I haven't got all day. Though I suppose I should thank the heavens for small mercies that you've managed to negotiate the stairs without losing your lasgun again. Not that I mean that as an invitation, mind. You lose that damned thing again, don't expect me to go finding it for you. You want to go around confronting orks with no other weapons than what nature gave you, next time you're on your own. I'll leave you to it. Now, come on. Let's get moving and when we're heading for the trench, keep your damned fool head down. Not that I've got any qualms about seeing the orks blow your head off, you understand. I just don't want to run the risk of the damned greenskins missing and hitting me instead.'

So it went on, with Davir unleashing a constant tirade of insults and complaints as, trailing in his wake, Larn followed him up the low rise towards the firing trenches and the frontline. As they ran half-crouched towards their destination and the tirade continued, Larn abruptly found himself briefly entertaining a notion that until a few minutes before would have never occurred to him.

Suddenly, he found himself feeling strangely nostalgic for the good old days of Sergeant Ferres.

CHAPTER EIGHT

Casualties of War – Thoughts on the Killing of Generals –
Scholarly Answers and Insights – On Vital Supplies
& The Many and Varied Uses of Prophylactics – The
Mathematics of Slaughter & Questions of Life Expectancy
at the Front – The Facts of Life as According to Davir

For once, the printing press was silent. Though Lieutenant Dellas had always considered the constant clattering of the machine to be a source of much-cursed irritation, now it was idle he found the sound of its silence filled him with dread. Sitting at his desk in the claustrophobic confines of his cluttered office, he looked across the fractured glass of the top half of the partition wall separating him from the print room and felt his stomach churn in anxiety as he watched the militia auxiliaries who made up his staff go about their labours. The aged caretakers Cern and Votank were busy maintaining the ancient parts of the press itself: Cern oiling the machine's rollers, while Votank topped up the ink reservoir ready for the next edition. Nearby, head bobbing and his face moving in involuntary tics, the feeble-minded cripple Shulen stumbled past them with a broom flailing spasmodically in his hands as he attempted to sweep the floor. Only the compositor Pheran was without a task. His features pinched in an expression somewhere between expectancy and annoyance, he stood beside the empty expanse of the typesetting board and gazed back towards Dellas through the glass. Then, seeing he had met the lieutenant's eyes, Pheran raised a hand to point at the chronometer hanging above the printing press in a gesture of mute accusation.

1500 hours, Dellas thought, his heart sinking as his eyes followed the direction of Pheran's bony finger to glance at the chronometer. *We only have an hour now before I have to deliver the late edition to Commissar Valk for approval. A single hour! I must find something to write. Anything!*

Despairing, Dellas returned his attention to the dozens of official papers piled in confusion across his desk. Among the jumbled mass of documents before him were copies of situation reports, battlefield dispatches, casualty statistics, terse communiqués, comms transcripts: between them comprising a record of every event of consequence that had happened in the city of Broucheroc in the past twelve hours. Despite what seemed like hours now spent surveying the assembled weight of information before him, Dellas had found nothing there to suit his purpose.

There is no good news to report, he thought bleakly. *Today, the same as every other day, there is only bad news and I cannot print that. The commissar would have me shot on the spot.*

His thoughts drifted back to the day two years previously when he had first heard the news that he was being posted to the imposing edifice of the General Headquarters building in the centre of Broucheroc. At first, sure he was going to be rewarded with a staff assignment, he had rejoiced. Then, when they brought him to the dingy basement print room to tell him it would be his task to produce a twice-daily newsletter and propaganda sheet for the edification of the city's defenders, his heart had thrilled even more. It had seemed the answer to all his prayers: a staff and an office of his own, and more importantly a prestigious assignment that would keep him far from the fighting. He had soon learned however that the lot in life of an official propagandist was rarely a happy one. Even less so when it was his duty to put a brave face to a conflict as prone to sudden reverses and unmitigated disasters as was the war in Broucheroc.

We are losing this war, he thought, so lost in the depths of his own misery now he was barely aware of any wider implication. *We are losing this war. That is the reality and yet I have barely an hour to find some small piece of good news that will allow the newsletter to pretend otherwise. An hour. It just can't be done. I need more time.*

Hearing the sound of his office door opening, Dellas looked up to see Shulen shuffling through the doorway. Mouth working soundlessly, his body twitching with uncontrollable palsies, Shulen tottered towards him with a wastebasket in his hands, the ugly scar left by the ork bullet that had addled his brain clearly visible at his temple.

'What is it, Shulen?' Dellas sighed.

'Cuh cuh cuh... cleaning!' Shulen said, stammering out a spray of spittle as he stooped to start shovelling the papers littering Dellas's desk into the wastebasket.

Aggravated, for a moment Dellas idly wondered if there was a way of making Shulen bear the blame for his problems. *I could tell Commissar Valk it is all Shulen's fault*, he thought. *That we were just putting the finishing touches to the latest edition when Shulen blundered into the typesetting board, knocking it to the floor and destroying all our work. If the commissar decides to shoot the useless oaf in retribution, I for one would not miss him.* Just as quickly he realised for the plan to work the other members of his staff would have to support his story. Pheran and the others would not wear it. They had always protected Shulen, coddling him like some idiot child, and would be sure to oppose any attempt to make him the sacrificial goat. Then, abruptly, Dellas caught a glimpse of the words written on one of the crumpled pieces of paper in Shulen's hand and knew he finally had the answer.

'Stop that!' he snapped at Shulen, reaching out with a metal ruler to rap his knuckles. 'Leave the wastebasket here and go tell

Pheran I will have the copy for tonight's edition ready for him in fifteen minutes.'

'Fuh fuh fuh...'

'Fifteen minutes,' Dellas said, retrieving the paper he had seen in Shulen's hand and smoothing out the creases so he could read it. 'Now, get out of my sight.'

It was a contact report, reporting an ork assault in Sector 1-13 two and a half hours earlier. What interested Dellas more was the attached account of the event that had presaged the assault. A single lander bearing a company's worth of battlefield replacements had crashed in no-man's-land. Reading it, Dellas realised it was exactly what he had been looking for. Granted, the course of events would need a little rewriting. To keep Commissar Valk happy what had been an entirely futile waste of human life would need to become a resounding victory. All the basic substance of what he needed was there already: he would only have to change the details and the events in Sector 1-13 should suit his purposes admirably. *Yes, this is exactly what I need*, Dellas thought, quickly running through a series of potential headlines in his mind. *Enemy Assault Defeated By Landing From Space. A Sector-Wide Breakthrough. Orks Retreating in Disarray.* Then, the hairs rising at the back of his neck, he thought of a new headline and knew he had cracked it.

Orks Defeated in Sector 1-13: Jumael 14th Victorious!

Smiling, Dellas picked up a stylus and began to write a glowing report of the battle, carefully embroidering the account with a variety of the stock words and phrases he had developed over the years in the course of his duties. *Heroic resistance! Brave and resolute defence! A triumph of faith and righteous fury over Xenos savagery!* Occasionally, as he paused to construct some new sentence full of rhetorical zeal and fire, he felt the vague stirrings of his conscience troubling him but he ignored it. It was not his fault he was forced to lie and twist the facts, he told himself. The truth was always the first casualty in warfare. As an information officer, sometimes it was his task to be creative: to do otherwise would be to risk offering aid and comfort to the enemy. Yes, it was a matter of duty.

And, after all, it was important to do everything humanly possible to keep up the morale of the troops.

'A fire,' Davir said as they sat in the firing trench. 'That's what I would like to see. A fire to burn down General Headquarters and torch all the stupid bastards inside it. If another blaze could somehow be ignited at Sector Command as well then, all the better. It wouldn't be that difficult. Give me a grenade launcher and a couple of phosphorus rounds, and I would have both damn places on fire in no time.'

Appalled, Larn listened in disbelieving silence. In the last half an hour since they had reached the trench, Davir's constant stream of complaints had slowly given way to extended musings in which he openly discussed methods of killing the General Staff responsible for the progress of the Broucheroc campaign. Though even more extraordinary to Larn's mind was the fact that the other men in the trench had simply sat there and listened to it, as though it was the most normal thing in the world to talk lightly of mutiny and sedition. As Davir's monologue wore on, Larn found himself with fewer and fewer doubts as to the reasons why the war in this city seemed to be going so badly if these men represented a representative cross-section of the city's defenders.

'Of course, I accept it will be difficult getting close enough to use a grenade launcher,' Davir continued. 'What with the security perimeters around both buildings being so heavily patrolled and defended. But I have already foreseen a solution. It is only a matter of stealing the right credentials, and I can be inside the perimeter and killing the members of the General Staff before you can say poetic justice.'

These men can't be Guardsmen, Larn thought as he looked at the faces of the four men sitting around him in the trench. *Granted, they fought off the ork attack well enough two hours ago. But where is their discipline? Their devotion to the Emperor? It is as though all the traditions and regulations of the Guard mean nothing to them. How can they just sit here and listen to this man spew treason without taking action?*

'You would never get away with it, Davir,' the Vardan sitting opposite Davir said. A tall thin man in his mid-thirties, his name was Scholar. Or at least that was what the others called him. Whether it was his profession or a simple nickname, given his stoop-shouldered build and the owlish cast of his face, the name seemed to fit him.

'I am afraid it is a question of there being major flaws in your *modus operandi*,' Scholar said, fingers playing unconsciously at his chin as though stroking a non-existent beard. 'Even granting that you manage to obtain the necessary credentials, I doubt the perimeter guards would be willing to stand idly by while you shoot grenades at their generals willy-nilly. There are rules in the Guard against the wasting of ammunition, after all. Besides, even if you could somehow elude the guards, you can be sure that the buildings housing General HQ and Sector Command have both been extensively fireproofed. Not to mention equipped with damage controls systems, blast shields, extinguishing devices, and so forth. No, Davir, I think you will have to find some other method of getting your tally.'

Could they be joking somehow, Larn thought. *Is that it? Is this all some kind of joke, intended to do no more than help them pass the time? But they are talking about murdering officers! How could anyone mistake that for a laughing matter?*

'Then I will simply have to seize control of an artillery battery,' Davir said. 'A few high explosive rounds aimed at the GHQ building and I should kill a few generals at least.'

'But you wouldn't want to do that either,' the third one, Bulaven, said earnestly. A hulking figure with a thick neck, brawny arms and a broad bearish build, Bulaven was the fire-team's heavy weapons specialist. He also seemed the only man among the group to harbour anything in the way of concern for the lives of his superiors. 'If you start killing generals, Davir, who would we have left to give us orders?'

'You talk as though that is a bad thing, pigbrain,' Davir spat. 'It is thanks to those arseholes in General HQ and their orders that we are in this mess to begin with! Not that I expect us to suddenly starting magically winning this war when they are all dead, you understand. Killing them couldn't make it any worse. At least doing it would give me some small moments of satisfaction. Orders? *Phah!* As though they ever achieved anything with all their damned orders other than making things ten times worse. You want to know about orders? Ask Repzik. If it hadn't been for some fool ordering Battery Command to withhold artillery support during the last attack, he'd probably still be alive. For that matter, what about our new friend here? You all saw what happened to that lander earlier. Ask the new fish what he thinks of the orders that sent him halfway across the galaxy just to make landfall on the wrong planet.'

Abruptly, the other men in the trench turned to look towards him. Fully aware he must have looked like a rabbit caught in the searchlights of an oncoming vehicle, Larn could only gawp back at them, unsure of what to say.

'Perhaps he is still in shock?' Bulaven said, his tone solicitous. 'Is that it, new fish? Are you in shock?'

'Wetting his pants in fear more like,' Zeebers, the fourth man in the trench, said. Thin and wiry, of average build, Zeebers looked younger than the others: perhaps in his mid-twenties where Davir and the rest were in their early to mid-thirties. Red-haired, with a pitted and pockmarked face, Zeebers looked nastily towards Larn and sneered at him. 'Look at him. If his skin was any greyer you wouldn't be able to see him against the mud. You ask me, he's afraid if he says what he really thinks some commissar will hear him and have him shot.'

'Hhh. Not much to be worried about on that score,' Davir said. 'You hear me, new fish? You can speak freely. Granted, time was we'd always be getting commissars coming to the line to lead attacks and so forth. Thankfully, our friends the orks soon put paid to that. Any commissar who was crazy enough to want to join a frontline combat unit got himself killed off long ago. The commissars left now tend to be those with a sharper instinct for their own survival. Sharp enough to stay away from the front at any rate. So, come on, new fish. You must have an opinion? Let us hear it.'

'Yes, indeed,' said Scholar. 'I for one would be fascinated to know what you think.'

'Come on, new fish,' Zeebers said, his tone harsh and goading. 'What are you waiting for? Gretch got your tongue?'

'Don't rush him,' Bulaven said, more kindly. 'Like I say, I think he's still in shock. I'm sure he'll tell us in time.'

Faces expectant, the Guardsmen fell quiet as they waited for Larn to answer. Uncomfortable, painfully aware of the four pairs of eyes staring at him in silence, for a moment Larn could only sit there with his mouth open, the words dying on his tongue before he could even say them. Then, thinking about all he had seen and heard in the last few hours, in a voice thick with misery he gave them the only answer he had.

'I... I don't understand any of this,' he said at last. 'None of it. Nothing that has happened to me so far today seems to make any sense.'

'What is there to understand, new fish?' Davir had said. 'We are stuck in this damned city. We are surrounded by millions of orks. Every day they try to kill us. We try not to let them succeed. End of story.'

'A concise summary granted, Davir,' Scholar had said next. 'Though you omitted to mention the promethium. And the stalemate. Not to mention some of the wider parameters.'

'Fine, Scholar,' Davir had shrugged. 'I think you're wasting your time, but you tell him all about it then. While you're at it, you might as well tell him how to go about brushing his teeth and wiping his backside. After all, I wouldn't like to see the consequences if the new fish here somehow got those two vital functions mixed up. Whatever you do, do it from the firing step. It is still your turn to stand watch. And remember: just because we have to nursemaid a war virgin doesn't mean the orks have forgotten they want to kill us.'

'You see them?' Scholar said a few minutes later, standing pointing into no-man's-land from the firing step next to Larn while Davir and the others sat playing a card game on the trench floor below them. 'That dark grey ragged line about eight hundred metres away? That's the ork lines.'

Looking through the field glasses Scholar had lent him, Larn followed the direction of the tall man's pointing finger to stare into the wasteland before them. There. He saw it. A sinuous line of ditches that ran the entire length of the sector on the other side of no-man's-land. Watching it, from time to time he saw a gretchin or ork head suddenly come into view. Only for the head to then swiftly disappear as its owner dropped out of sight below the parapets on the ork side once more.

'I don't understand how I didn't see it before,' Larn said. 'Having the field glasses helps. But it seems so clear now. How could I have missed it?'

'It is a question of perception,' Scholar said. 'You have noticed how grey the landscape is? The mud, the rocks, the sky, even the buildings? When a person first arrives here the details of the world about them can easily be lost in the same monotonous tone of grey. But there are subtle differences. Differences you become slowly aware of the longer you spend in this city. You have heard how some jungle-worlders have forty different words for green? In reality of course those forty words correspond to different shades of green. Shades which would all look the same to us. But to them, their perceptions heightened by living their entire lives in a green environment, the difference between each shade is as obvious as the difference between black and white. It is the same here in Broucheroc. Believe me, you'll be amazed how acute you become to the palette of greys once you've been in this city a few months.'

'Of course,' he continued, delighted to finally have an audience willing to hear a lecture, 'normally you wouldn't be able to miss the ork lines if you tried. There'd be an array of makeshift walls, dirt ramparts and bosspoles stretching from one side of the sector to the other. Or piles of burned-out vehicles and corpses used in place of sandbags. The details differ from sector to sector. Up to a month ago we were stationed in Sector 1-11. There, the orks used these large jury-rigged barricades that they would just smash their way through whenever they attacked us. Then they would rebuild them, smashing their way through them again whenever there was a major assault, and so on.

You see, the orks don't follow a centralised command structure as we do. Granted, when their Warbosses are not busy fighting it out amongst each other, they are usually united behind a single Warlord. But when it comes to the disposition of any particular ork sector, the local Warboss is free to do as he wants. And, as it happens, this particular boss seems to have taken a leaf out of our book – ordering his followers to dig camouflaged underground dugouts, foxholes and trenches rather than the usual ostentatious fortress. It could be he is brighter than the usual ork leader. Then again, perhaps he's just aping our tactics without any kind of clear plan in mind. Really, it can be hard to tell with orks. Even after ten years here, I still find it difficult to tell the difference between a stupid ork and a clever one.'

'You have been here ten years as well?' Larn said. 'I could barely believe it when Repzik said he had been here that long.'

'We all have,' Scholar said. 'Me, Davir, Bulaven, Vladek, Chelkar,

Svenk, Kell. All the men in the company have. The ones from Vardan, anyhow. Of course, there are plenty of replacements like you and Zeebers who have been here considerably less time.'

'Zeebers isn't from Vardan?'

'Him? No, as I say, he is a replacement. Joined us about two months ago, give or take.'

'What about the rest of the regiment? Are there many replacements among them as well?'

'The rest? You misunderstand me, new fish,' Scholar said sadly. 'Company Alpha *is* the Vardan 902nd. We're all that's left among the Vardans here. The others are dead.'

'You mean your regiment was wiped out?' Larn said horrified. 'Out of an entire regiment, only two hundred men are still alive?'

'Worse than that, new fish. There were three Vardan regiments when we first set down in Broucheroc. But over time we suffered heavy losses. We lost the Vardan 722nd in our first week here, wiped out when General HQ ordered one of their now famous all-out assaults on the ork lines. The survivors were amalgamated into the Vardan 831st, who in turn eventually became part of the 902nd. Then, over the years, there were more casualties and the number of companies in the 902nd were reduced and amalgamated. Until, now, only Company Alpha is left. At last count I believe our current fighting strength is something in the order of two hundred and forty-four men, perhaps three-quarters of whom are from Vardan. Something like one hundred and eighty or so Vardans then, left from the more than six thousand men who first made planetfall in this city ten years ago. Really it is not so different from your situation with your own former company. It is a matter of attrition, you see. It's the same for ever other Guard regiment in this city. Of course, having been on the frontlines so long, we've had it worse than most. I doubt there's a regiment left in this city that is at any more than thirty per cent of its original strength. This is Broucheroc; here, everything is a matter of attrition. But then, given the name of the place, it is hardly surprising.'

'The name?' Larn asked, still stunned by the thought that the men he saw about him were all that was left from six thousand Guardsmen.

'Yes. A while back we spent a month dug in at an old bombed-out building that turned out to be a storage facility for some of the city's oldest archives. I managed to read some of them before Davir and the rest used them for toilet paper. In the days before it became a city the name of this place was Butcher's Rock, or *Bouchers Roc* in the local planetary dialect. Over time, as the city grew, its name was corrupted to the pronunciation we know now. *Broo-sher-rok*. As for the origin of the name, apparently the first settlement to be founded here served as the centre for the planet's meat trade. Of course it still does, in a manner of speaking.'

'Still does?' Larn said. 'I don't understand what you mean.'

'He means that this whole damned city is one big meat grinder, new fish,' Davir growled from the bottom of the trench. 'And we are the meat.'

'You should tell the new fish about the promethium, Scholar,' Bulaven said from beside him. 'It is better if he knows what we are fighting for.'

'Ah yes. The promethium,' Scholar said, taking the field glasses back from Larn and placing them in a case on his belt. 'That is what the battle here is about, more or less.' Then, nodding towards Davir, he added: 'Of course, I'm sure if you asked Davir he would tell you the war here is only about survival. Which would be right as well. But you cannot understand the broader issues of strategy here without knowing something about the promethium.'

'Strategy, my broad Vardan arse,' Davir said. 'What does strategy mean to us? You think a man cares about strategy when he feels an ork blade go into his belly? You and Bulaven are fooling yourselves, Scholar. What, you think if it wasn't for the promethium the orks would just go away? If that were the case I'd have found some way of giving it to them myself by now, never mind all this fantasising about killing generals. You make things too complicated, Scholar. The orks want to kill us for one simple reason. They are orks. That is all there is to it. Though by all means tell the new fish about your grand theories. I'm sure they'll come in very handy next time the bullets start flying and he finds himself face to face with a horde of screaming greenskins. Though from what I've seen already, you might be doing him more of a favour if you told him to tie a string around his belt and tie the other end to his lasgun so he doesn't lose it again.'

Grimacing in dismissive annoyance Davir returned his attention to the card game, leaving Scholar to go on with his lecture.

'The promethium, new fish,' Scholar said. 'That's why the orks are here and that's what makes the city important to both us and them. Remember I told you this city started off as a centre for the meat trade? Well, that was thousands of years ago. In more recent times Broucheroc became a centre for the planet's promethium industry. Time was when this city was little more than one giant refinery, where crude promethium would be brought from the drilling fields further south to be refined into fuel. Even though the pipelines that brought that crude here were cut long ago, this city is still rich in promethium. Billions of barrels' worth, stored in massive underground tanks underlying most of the city.'

'But what do the orks want with it?' Larn asked him.

'Fuel,' Scholar said. 'Ten years ago, just as we first made landfall here, it looked like the orks were going to conquer this entire planet. Until they started to run out of fuel for their armour. When that happened they laid siege to Broucheroc, hoping to seize the city's fuel reserves. But we managed to hold out, and without fuel the ork assault elsewhere on the planet simply ground to a halt. Ever since then it has been a stalemate, with us trapped inside the city and the orks outside it trying to get in. A stalemate that shows no sign of ending anytime soon.'

'But what about the Imperial forces in other parts of the planet?'

Larn said. 'Or even Imperial forces from off-world? Why haven't they tried to relieve the siege?'

'As for the Imperial forces elsewhere on this planet, it could be they have tried to relieve us, new fish,' Scholar said. 'Certainly, if you asked General HQ they would tell you the city is on the verge of being relieved. However, seeing as they have been saying the same thing for ten years now, no one much believes them anymore. You will find that here in Broucheroc our commanders tell us a lot of things. That we are winning the war. That the orks are leaderless and on the verge of collapse. That the big breakthrough they have been promising us for the last ten years is finally imminent. You will find that after a while hearing the same old things, day after day after day, you simply learn not to listen. For myself, I suspect that our brother Guardsmen in other parts of this Emperor-forsaken world are in no better shape than we are. Not that I can say definitely whether or not this is the case you understand, given that the only part of this planet I've ever seen is Broucheroc. As theories go however, it seems no worse than any other.'

'But, of course, that doesn't fully answer your question,' Scholar said, fully lost now in the flow of his own erudition. 'As to why Imperial forces from off-world don't intervene; I suspect the war here is simply not important enough to justify a full-scale landing. From time to time there are smaller more isolated landings – by a lander say, or a single dropship – but nothing that could be mistaken for anything even resembling a real attempt to break the siege. Sometimes, as in the case of you and your company, these landings turn out to be simple mistakes. Other times, it is as though some distant bureaucrat has finally decided to send us a few more troops or supplies in order to reassure us we have not been forgotten. For the most part, these occasional drops are as pointless and ridiculous as every other aspect of life here in Broucheroc. In the past we have been sent entire pods full of supplies, only to find when we fight our way to them the boxes inside the pods are full of the most useless things imaginable: paperclips, mosquito netting, laxatives, boot laces, and so on.'

'Remember when they sent us an entire drop-pod full of prophylactics?' Davir said from nearby. 'I never could decide whether they wanted us to use them as barrage balloons, or simply thought the orks must have a fear of rubber.'

'A good example of what I was talking about,' Scholar said. 'But anyway, I think that pretty much covers everything for now, new fish. Do you have any questions?'

'Never mind his questions,' Zeebers said, suddenly looking up from his cards to gaze at Larn with a sly and malignant smile. 'You didn't quite cover everything for the new fish, Scholar. There is still one thing you forgot to tell him.'

'Forgot?' Scholar said. 'Really? I don't think there was anything else of importance...'

'Yes there is,' Zeebers said, staring hard at Larn now with cold malice. 'You forgot to tell him why it was Davir said you'd be wasting your time telling the new fish anything. Why all the things you told him already are probably totally useless to him. Why, come tomorrow, there's likely only going to be four men in this trench, not five. Oh yes, I think you forgot to tell him something, Scholar. You forgot to tell him the single most important thing of them all.'

For a moment Zeebers paused, the silence growing tense and ugly as he stared at Larn while the others shifted uneasily in their positions as though suddenly uncomfortable. Then, the corners of his lips rising tightly in a gloating smile of victory, Zeebers smirked at Larn and spoke once more.

'You forgot to tell him about the fifteen hours.'

They were quiet at first. Scholar and Bulaven looked down at the ground in apparent embarrassment, while even Davir avoided Larn's eyes as though feeling the same vague sense of discomfort as the others. Only Zeebers looked his way. Staring back at

him, Larn found himself party to an unwelcome insight. Zeebers hated him. Though why, or for what reason, he could not
even begin to guess.

'What is this fifteen hours?' Larn said at last to break the silence.
'Repzik said something about it just before the last attack. And
Corporal Vladek mentioned it as well. He said he would issue
me with more equipment if I came back to see him again in fifteen hours' time.'

Long moments passed and no one answered. Instead there
was only more silence while Davir, Scholar, and Bulaven looked
uneasily at one another as though mentally drawing lots to
decide which of them would perform an unwelcome duty. Until
at length, still refusing to meet Larn's eyes, Davir finally spoke.

'Tell him, Scholar.'

In response Scholar fidgeted for a moment before, clearing his
throat, he turned to face Larn directly.

'It is a matter of statistics, new fish,' Scholar said with a pained
expression. 'You must understand that in many ways every marshal and general at headquarters is as much a bureaucrat as the
most pedantic scribe in the Administratum. To them war is not
just a thing of blood and death; nor entirely a question of tactics and strategy. To them, it is as much as anything a matter
of calculation. A calculation based on casualty reports, rates of
attrition, the numbers of units in the field, estimates of the enemy's strength, and so on; all the myriad facts and figures that,
together, can be used to establish a mathematics of slaughter.
Every day, from all over Broucheroc, these figures are recorded,
collated and sent to General Headquarters for the bean counters there to work on them. As for this fifteen hours that Zeebers
mentioned, it is one of the products of these daily calculations.'

'You are over complicating things again, Scholar,' Davir said. 'It
does no good to sugar the pill for the new fish. He asked a direct
question; you should answer him accordingly.'

'It is a matter of life expectancy, new fish,' Scholar sighed.

'Fifteen hours is the average length of time a replacement Guardsman survives in Broucheroc after he has been posted to a combat unit at the frontlines.'

'A replacement Guardsman?' Larn said, still unsure whether he fully understood what Scholar had just told him. 'Like me, you mean? Is that what you are telling me? That's how long you expect me to survive here? You think I am going to be dead inside fifteen hours?'

'Less than that, new fish,' Zeebers said, his tone smug and mocking. 'You must have been here at least three hours by now. Leaving you only twelve hours left. Maybe less. Why do you think Vladek told you to return to him in fifteen hours? He didn't want to risk wasting a lot of good equipment on a dead man.'

'Shut up, Zeebers,' Bulaven rumbled. For a moment Zeebers glared back at him until, seeing the angry expression on the big man's face, he dropped his eyes to look down at the mud of the trench floor in sullen silence. 'Tell him that isn't the way it is, Scholar,' Bulaven began again, his expression softening and his voice almost pleading. 'Explain it to him. Tell him we have every faith he will still be alive tomorrow.'

'What, you think we should lie to him?' Davir said to Bulaven. 'Zeebers here may be an evil little shit with a big mouth, but at least he was telling the truth. You think we should treat the new fish like a child? Tell him that everything will be all right? That his kindly old uncles Davir, Scholar and Bulaven will keep him safe from the mean and nasty orks? Even after ten years of your fat-headed stupidity, you never cease to amaze me, Bulaven.'

'It wouldn't be lying, Davir,' Bulaven said sulkily. 'There is nothing wrong with giving a man some hope.'

'Hope, my arse,' Davir spat. 'I keep telling you, fatman: hope is a bitch with bloody claws. You'd think after ten years in this damned hellhole you would have learned that lesson by now at least.'

'All the same, Bulaven is not entirely wrong,' Scholar said, turning towards the others to join the discussion. 'The new fish does indeed have some small cause for hope. True. General HQ may have calculated the life expectancy of a replacement to be fifteen hours. But that is only an average figure. Perhaps the new fish will be more fortunate. He could survive longer. He has already beaten the odds once already by surviving that landing.'

'Phah. Sometimes, Scholar, you can be as bad as Bulaven,' Davir said. 'But where he witters on about hope and optimism, you act like you were still in the scholarium. You would do better to remind yourself we are in the real world here. Your talk of odds and averages is all very well, but this is Broucheroc. It doesn't matter that the new fish survived the landing. Any more than it matters whether or not you and Bulaven try to coddle him. He is as good as a corpse already. A dead man walking. Trust me, the orks will see to that. There's nothing they like better than a new fish, still wet behind the ears and ready for the gutting.'

'All I am saying is that we are perhaps being too literal-minded when it comes to talking about this figure fifteen hours,' Scholar said, all three of them so caught up in the heat of their argument now that they ignored Larn as he stood there listening to them. 'It is not an absolute figure. It is only an average. Why, for all we know, the new fish might end up surviving days, weeks, even years.'

'Years?' Davir said. 'You know you really are a wonder to me, Scholar. I've never seen a man talk so eloquently and at such length from his arse before. You think the new fish is going to manage to survive years in this place? Next you will be telling me you expect Sector Command to make Bulaven a general! You obviously haven't seen the new fish in action–'

'Stop it,' Larn said quietly, no longer willing to be talked about as though he were invisible. 'I've heard enough. Stop calling me *new fish*. My name is Larn.'

For a moment, as though surprised by the interruption, the

other men in the trench simply blinked and turned to look at him in silence.

'What? You don't like us calling you new fish, then?' Davir said after a time, sarcastically. 'We have offended you perhaps? Your feelings are hurt?'

'No,' said Larn, uncertainly. 'I... You don't understand. I just think you should use my name is all. My real name, I mean. Larn. Not new fish.'

'Really?' Davir said, gazing at him with cold eyes while Zeebers glared at him in hostility and Scholar and Bulaven looked at him in sadness. 'Then, it is you who does not understand the facts of life here, new fish. You think I care what your name is? I have enough baggage in my head already; never mind learning something that will likely be written on a grave marker before the day is out. You want me to remember your name? Tell me it again in fifteen hours' time.

'By then, perhaps it just may be worth knowing.'

CHAPTER NINE

A Figure Moving Closer Through No-Man's Land –
Standing Watch with Bulaven – Matters of Gretchin and
Human Marksmanship – A Splash of Colour Amidst the
Wasteland – Lessons on How Best to Act as Bait

He had been moving slowly now for hours.

Crawling on his belly, painted from head to hind claws in grey clay with the long kustom barrel of his blasta wrapped in layers of grey sacking, he crept forward a centimetre at a time through the frozen mud of what the humies called no-man's-land. Slow, like a slaver hunting a squig with a grabba stik, he moved an inch and then waited. He moved an inch and then waited. He moved an inch then and waited. Over and over again, always careful in case his prey was watching.

Suddenly, seeing a glint in the distance ahead of him, he stopped. Sure one of the humies' spotters must have seen him, he tensed, expecting at any moment to feel the pain from a las-beam or hear the sound of a shot, but neither of them came. He remained motionless. Until, as the minutes passed and he became convinced he was none the worse for wear, his journey began again. Moving slowly, inch by inch, across the frozen mud toward his destination.

Finally, perhaps halfway across no-man's-land, he reached the lip of a shallow shell crater. For a moment he looked at it. Then, responding to some inner instinct he could have never named, he crawled inside. Out of sight now, he moved more quickly, crawling up the opposite slope of the crater to look through the sights of his blasta in search of a target. At first, nothing. Then he saw a head in a fur-shrouded helmet peeking out of a hole in the ground some way away and he knew the instinct had been right. He had found his kill.

Breathing through his nose, careful not to make any sudden moves that might spook his prey, he aimed at it through his sights, his finger tightening incrementally on the blasta's trigger. As he did, he felt a warm sensation rush through his head as something like a clear and coherent thought occurred to him.

If he made this shot, the boss would be pleased...

'You shouldn't take it too much to heart what Davir said before, new fish,' Bulaven said. 'He didn't mean anything by it. It is just his way is all.'

Bulaven was standing on watch on the firing step, looking out into no-man's-land with Larn beside him. Meanwhile, in the firing trench below them, the other men were mostly quiet. Wrapped in an extra greatcoat in place of a blanket, his muffler pulled forward to cover most of his face, Davir lay dozing with his back against some spare flamer canisters. Beside him, Scholar sat silently reading from the tattered pages of a battered and obviously well-used book. Only Zeebers was making anything much in the way of noise. Sitting on the trench floor, he could be seen sharpening the blade of his entrenching tool with a whetstone, the low scraping sound of the stone running over the metal added a malicious counterpoint to the occasional hostile glances he periodically made in Larn's direction.

'Yes, that is a good trick, new fish,' Bulaven said, noticing that Larn was looking at Zeebers. 'If you sharpen the blade of your entrenching tool it makes a good weapon if you find yourself in hand-to-hand with an ork. Better than a bayonet, anyway. Of course, you need to be careful you don't sharpen the edges of the spade head too fine. Otherwise, it can split if you actually have to dig the earth with it.'

'Does it happen a lot?' Larn asked him, giving an involuntary shiver as he remembered his earlier encounter with the gretchin. 'Going hand-to-hand with the orks, I mean?'

'Not so much if we can help it,' Bulaven said, tapping the imposing bulk of the heavy flamer by his side. 'For myself, when it comes to killing orks I prefer to use my friend here. Sometimes though, the orks get in close and it can't be helped. Then you just have to kill them with laspistols, knives, spade heads: whatever comes to hand. But you don't need to worry too much about that, new fish. Stay close to me, Scholar and Davir, and you'll be all right.'

'You will forgive me, Bulaven,' Larn said to the big man. 'But it didn't sound too much like that when you were talking before.'

'Ach, I told you: you shouldn't worry about that, new fish,' Bulaven said. 'As I say, Davir didn't mean too much by it. It is simply his manner to sound off from time to time, and you just happened to get in his way. Personally, I think it is because he is shortarse. He likes to talk a lot to make himself seem important. Trust me, you should just put it from your mind as though it never happened.'

'And the fifteen hours?' Larn said quietly. 'What about that?'

In reply Bulaven fell silent for a moment, his broad and kindly features abruptly given over to an almost pensive brooding. Until, at length, he spoke once more.

'Sometimes, it is better not to think too much on such things, new fish,' he sighed. 'Sometimes, it is better just to have faith.'

'Faith?' Larn asked. 'You mean in the Emperor?'

'Yes. No. Perhaps,' Bulaven said, his words growing as slow and thoughtful as his expression. 'I don't know, new fish. I used to believe in so many things back when I first became a Guardsman. I believed in the generals. I believed in the commissars. Most of all, I believed in the Emperor. Now, I certainly don't believe in the first two any more. And as for the Emperor? Sometimes it is hard to see His grace among all this carnage. But a man must have faith in something. And so, yes, I still believe in the Emperor. I believe in Him. And I believe in Sergeant Chelkar. Those are the two articles of my faith, such as they are.'

'But there is something else, new fish,' he continued. 'Something just as important as faith. *Hope*. Davir is wrong about that, you see. A man must have hope, or he might as well not be alive. It is as important as the air we breathe. So, no matter how bad things get, new fish – no matter how bleak they seem – you must remember not to give up hope. Trust me, if you can hold on to your hope, everything will be all right.'

With that, Bulaven fell silent again and Larn found himself remembering his talk with his father in the farmhouse cellar on his last night at home. *Trust to the Emperor*, his father had told him then. And, now, Bulaven had told him to trust to hope. Though in his heart he knew them both to be good pieces of advice, as he looked out at the desolate and foreboding landscape around him they seemed of little comfort.

A single shot rang out, the sound of it unnaturally loud after the silence. Acting on reflex Larn jumped back from the firing step in search of cover, only to fall backwards into the trench to land on top of Davir, causing the stocky runt to awaken in a flurry of profanities.

'Marshal Kerchan's bloody arse!' Davir cursed as he pushed Larn away. 'Can't a man get any sleep around here without some idiot jumping on top of him with two boots first! What, you have mistaken me for your mother, new fish, and you wanted a cuddle? Get the hell off me!'

'There was a shot, Davir,' Bulaven said, still standing on the firing step, head crouched to peer cautiously over the trench parapet. 'From out in no-man's-land. A sniper, I think. That is what the new fish was reacting to.'

'Well, he can react to it all he wants so long as he doesn't keep leaping on me,' Davir said, grabbing his lasgun and stepping up to the firing step beside Bulaven to gaze wolfishly into no-man's-land. 'So. A sniper, eh? Scholar, hand me your field glasses and we will see if we can find him.'

Soon, Scholar and Zeebers had joined Davir and Bulaven on the firing step. Then, handing the field glasses to Davir, Scholar turned to look over his shoulder at Larn standing at the bottom of the trench behind him.

'You should come up and watch this, new fish,' Scholar said. 'It is important you learn how to deal with a sniper.'

Taking his place on the step next to Scholar, Larn watched as the other men stared intently into no-man's-land, scanning for anything out of place. Until, indicating a shell crater perhaps three hundred metres away from their trench, Davir's wolfish smile became a broad grin of delight.

'There,' he said. 'I see him. Keep your heads down – the little gretch bastard is already looking for his next shot. He's not the brightest of sparks, however. He may have painted himself grey to blend in with the mud, but apparently, nobody told him a sniper's not supposed to fire twice from the same position.'

As though in response another shot rang out, raising a clod of earth as the bullet struck the ground three metres to the left of the trench.

'Ha! He's not much a shot either,' Davir said, handing the field glasses to Bulaven beside him. 'Really, I think we should consider sending a letter of complaint to the orks about the quality of the gretchin they choose for sniper duty. This one is so poor a marksman, killing him seems almost a waste of a las-blast.'

'It is another one of the hazards here, new fish,' Scholar said to Larn. 'Every now and again the orks will equip a particularly level-headed gretchin with a long rifle and send him out into no-man's-land to act as a sniper. Of course, gretchin are hardly renowned for their marksmanship, so mostly they are just a nuisance. But we have to take them out, all the same. Which unfortunately means that one of us here will have to act as bait.'

'I vote for the new fish,' Zeebers said, sneering at him. 'He is expendable, after all, and you never known when a gretch might get lucky.'

'Very kind of you to volunteer him,' Davir said, his lasgun at his shoulder as he sighted in on the shell crater. 'Especially since, if memory serves, it is actually your turn to act as sniper bait. Now shut your stinkhole and get out there. And make sure you give the gretch plenty of opportunity to shoot at you. I want a clear view of him so I can be sure of a clean kill.'

Muttering darkly under his breath, Zeebers grabbed his lasgun and put his hands on the top of the trench wall to the side of him. Then, giving Larn a last poisonous glare, he pulled himself up out of the trench and jumped into the open. The moment his feet hit the ground he was off and running; zigzagging with his body half-crouched as he sprinted across open ground to the next nearest firing trench and threw himself inside to safety.

'No,' said Davir, still peering through his sights towards the shell crater. 'He is still in cover. Maybe our friend is smarter than we think. Or perhaps he simply finds Zeebers to be a rather scrawny and uninspiring target. Either way, I haven't got a shot yet.'

'Again, Zeebers!' Scholar yelled, waving toward the next trench.

Discontent clearly visible on every line of his face even from a distance, Zeebers leapt from the trench again and ran zigzag once more toward the next trench in line.

'He's moving,' Bulaven said, gazing through the field glasses towards the crater. 'Looks like he's taken the bait.'

'Quiet.' Davir hissed. 'You are putting me off.' Then, exhaling slowly, he pulled the trigger, producing a single sharp crack as the lasgun fired.

'You got him!' Bulaven said, passing the field glasses to Larn with a smile of exultation. 'Look, new fish. You see that? He got him.'

'Of course I got him,' Davir said. Then, as he clicked the firing control switch on his lasgun to safe, the wolfish smile returned. 'Though it was a remarkably fine shot, even if I do say so myself.'

Gazing through the field glasses Larn looked toward the shell crater, at first unable to distinguish any sign of the gretchin in the grey landscape. Then, he saw it: a small red stain lying across a grey rock at the lip of the crater. Abruptly, adjusting the magnification of the field glasses to take a closer look, Larn realised he had been mistaken. What he thought was a rock was in fact the gretchin's head; the red stain being the contents of the creature's brains as they oozed through the hole in its ruptured skull and dribbled towards the ground. The creature was dead; the only sign of its passing a smear of red against the all-encompassing greyness of the world around it. A bright splash of colour in the midst of a wasteland.

'Did you see how Zeebers did it, new fish?' Bulaven asked him. 'Did you see how he kept crouched and ran zigzag from one trench to the next, so he wouldn't give the gretch too much of a target?'

'Yes, I saw it,' Larn said, sensing some unwelcome portent in the concern evident in the big man's manner. It was almost as though Bulaven was warning him about something. 'But, why do you ask?'

'Why do you think, new fish?' Davir grunted. 'Because, now Zeebers has been kind enough to show you how it is done, next time we have a sniper it is your turn to act as bait.'

CHAPTER TEN

A Daily Dose of Hell – Further Musings on the
Frontline – Friendly Fire – Intimations of an Unwelcome
Burial – Another Consultation with Medical Officer
Svenk – Corporal Grishen and Certain Failures in
Communications – Sergeant Chelkar Finds a Way to
Make his Point

'Battery, make ready!' he heard Sergeant Dumat's voice shouting in his earpiece. 'Gun crews remove camo-covers and make ready to open the breech!'

As though an army of quiescent insects had been provoked into action, in an instant the artillery park became a nest of activity. Everywhere, gun crews rushed to their posts to pull away camouflaged tarpaulins and make ready for firing. Watching as the camo-covers were discarded to reveal the huge and gleaming bores of the dozen Hellbreaker class cannons under his command, Captain Alvard Valerius Meran allowed himself a moment of pleasure as he saw the extra firing drills he had ordered for his men had worked. There was no sign of slackness, ill discipline or confusion in the workings of the gun crews. The entire battery operated with all the smooth efficiency of a single, finely tuned, well-oiled machine.

'Load ordnance.' Sergeant Dumat yelled, the strident tones of the command carried to the ears of every man in the battery through the comm-beads inside the ear-protectors they wore to protect them from the sound of their guns. 'High explosive rounds.'

Standing in the shadow of the burnt-out building that served as his de facto headquarters, Captain Meran watched the four-man loading teams attached to each gun crew as they hurried to disappear into the tarpaulin-covered ammunition stacks beside each gun. A moment later they emerged once more, each loading team gently cradling the shining and deadly weight of a metre long high explosive shell between them. Then, carrying them to their guns, the loaders lifted their shells into the open breeches for the other members of the guns crews to ram them home.

'Load propellant.'

Again, delighting at every well-trained movement and flawless action, Meran watched as the loading teams returned to the stacks to fetch the heavy barrel-sized cylindrical sacks of cordite that served as propellant for the cannons. Grunting under the weight, taking even more care with the volatile cordite than they had with the shells, the loading teams lifted the sacks into the guns' breeches, then retreated to their positions beside the ammunition stacks once more.

'Close breeches. Set firing trajectories as follows. Horizontal traverse: five degrees twenty-six minutes. Repeat: zero five degrees two six minutes. Vertical elevation: seventy-eight degrees thirty-one minutes. Repeat: seven eight degrees three one minutes. Windage: zero point five degrees. Repeat: zero point five degrees.'

And so the sergeant's voice went on, repeating the bearings again as the gun crews worked the wheels and gearings of their guns' aiming systems to adjust the Hellbreakers to the proper trajectories. Until, their preparations at last completed, the gun crews stepped back from their guns and awaited the firing instruction.

Yes, Captain Meran thought. *Just like a machine. Really, that was a most excellent display of gunmanship. It is a shame no one*

from Battery Command was here to see it. If they had been, they
would have been sure to have given me a commendation.

Briefly, he wondered whether he should order an extra ration
of recaf for the gun crews by way of a reward. Just as swiftly he
abandoned the idea. It might set a dangerous precedent to give
the men any additional reward for simply doing their duty. No,
it would be pleasure enough that they could all go to their beds
tonight knowing they had performed their duties with admirable dispatch. Then, noticing his men looking towards him with
expectant faces as they awaited the order to fire, Meran made an
elaborate show of taking his pocket chronometer from its chain
and opening it to check the time. *16:30 hours exactly*, he thought
with a smile, hand going to the comm-stud at the collar of his uniform as he make ready to vox the command to Sergeant Dumat
to give the order to let loose the guns.

Time to give the orks their daily dose of hell.

Perhaps half an hour had passed since they had killed the sniper.
Half an hour. Yet still, having returned to the trench in the wake
of acting as bait, Zeebers sat sullenly in a corner glaring mur-
derously at Davir and the others. Most of all, he glared at Larn;
his eyes full to the brim with hatred and loathing. Not for the
first time, Larn found himself wondering how it was the man
had taken so badly against him for no apparent reason. Though,
given Zeebers's current demeanour, he thought better of asking
him outright why he hated him.

Elsewhere in the trench, the others had resumed the same
positions they had occupied before the sniper's opening shot.
Davir had his back against the spare flamer canisters and was
wrapped dozing in an extra greatcoat once more. Scholar had
returned to his book. Bulaven was still on the firing step, gazing
out into no-man's-land on watch with Larn beside him. Now,
with the passing of the brief excitement caused by the sniper,
the big man had fallen as quiet as the others.

So much has changed, Larn thought, finding the brooding silence of the past half-hour had at least given him time to think. *A few hours ago I was with Jenks and the others, getting ready to make our first planetary drop and wondering what to expect. Even in our worst nightmares none of us could have thought of this. Certainly, Jenks wouldn't have expected to die in his chair without even leaving the lander. Any more than Sergeant Ferres would have expected to be killed by a misfiring explosive bolt. The same goes for Hallan, Vorrans and Leden. It is like I remember that old preacher saying one time. You never know what the shape of your death is going to be until it has got you. And, by then, it is already too late to do anything about it.*

Sobered by the thought, shivering against the cold, Larn looked out into no-man's-land and tried to make some sense of how it was he had come to be there. Try as he might he could see no sense in it. No sense in the mistake that had brought him to this place. No sense in the deaths of his friends and comrades. No sense to the fact that it seemed his life was now under a fifteen-hour sentence of death. He could see no sense in it. No sense at all.

Turning to glance down at the others from his position on the firing step, Larn noticed he could just about see the faded gold leaf lettering of the title on the cracked leather cover of the time-worn and battered book that Scholar was reading. *Under The Eagle*, the book's title read. *Glorious Accounts of Valour from the Annals of the Imperial Guard.* Larn had heard the book mentioned in basic training. It was a compilation of stirring accounts of the brave actions and past successes of just a few of the many millions of different regiments of the Emperor's armies.

Watching Scholar as he read the book, Larn saw the man's face break into an occasional smile from time to time as though in sarcastic amusement at some passage he had seen there. Again, Larn found himself wondering about Scholar's background. Davir had mentioned something about him no longer being in the scholarium. *Could it be that Scholar had once been a student in some place of higher learning?* He certainly had the disposition for it, and he seemed better informed than any of the other men in the trench. *If he really was a scholar, what was he doing serving in a forward firing position on the frontlines?* It was a mystery. As much of a mystery as everything else about the behaviour and motivations of the men around him.

With a sudden sadness born of isolation, Larn realised he understood nothing about the men who shared the trench with him. Nor for that matter did he understand any of the other men he had met so far in Broucheroc. Corporal Vladek, Medical Officer Svenk, Sergeant Chelkar, Vidmir, Davir, Zeebers, poor dead Repzik – none of them seemed remotely like any of the people he had known before he had come to this planet. By turns they were gruff, sardonic, cynical, world-weary, intimidating, not to say largely contemptuous of all the institutions and traditions Larn had been raised to cherish. Even with Bulaven, the most sympathetic and friendly of the Vardans, Larn could sense a certain reserve as though the big man was wary of getting to know him too well. It was more than that. More than any remoteness of manner or lack of empathy. These men seemed entirely unknowable to him: almost as alien in their own way as the orks. It was as though some strange and entirely new species of Man, far removed from Larn's understanding, had been given life by this place.

A new species, he thought with a shiver that owed nothing whatsoever to the coldness of the air. *A new species, forged in hell and nurtured on the fields of slaughter.*

'You seem caught up in your troubles, new fish,' Bulaven said beside him, the sound of his voice after so much silence making Larn jump. 'As though the weight of this entire world was on your shoulders. It cannot be so bad as that, though. A centi-credit for your thoughts?'

For a moment, wondering if it was possible to give words to all the confused welter of thoughts and emotions whirling inside him, Larn was silent. Then, just as he was about to speak in answer to Bulaven's question, they heard the forboding thunder of artillery fire in the distance behind them.

'Hmm. Sounds like they're firing the HeeBees,' Bulaven said, turning to look toward the sound of firing.

'HeeBees?' Larn asked.

'Hellbreakers,' said Bulaven distractedly, 'A local variant on the Earthshaker, just *bigger*. Now please be quiet, new fish. We need to listen.'

From far away Larn began to hear the high-pitched scream of artillery shells in flight. Moving ever closer, the sound of the shells' passage high in the air above them grew louder by the instant. Until, by the time the noise was directly overhead, the character of the shells' screaming abruptly changed, reaching a terrifyingly shrill and strident crescendo as the shells began their final death-dive shriek.

'Incoming!' Bulaven yelled, grabbing Larn by the collar and pulling him down with him as he suddenly leapt towards the bottom of the trench.

His stomach rebounding hard against an ammunition box as he landed on the trench floor, Larn found he was not alone there. Roused by Bulaven's warning shout, Davir and the others had already thrown themselves prostrate at the trench bottom, hugging the ground with all the fervour of lovers reunited after a long separation. Finding himself face down among a heap of bodies with someone else's boot heel jabbing painfully against his ear, Larn tried to rise, only to find it was impossible to even move so long as Bulaven's not-inconsiderable bulk was lying on top of him. Though any questions Larn might have had as to the reasons behind his comrades' strange behaviour were quickly answered as the screaming of shells in the air above them abruptly ended, replaced by the roar of explosions as the shells began to fall to earth all around their trench.

'The stupid sons of bitches!' Davir yelled, his shouting voice barely loud enough to be heard above the din. 'That's the third time this month.'

His body shaking as the ground quaked from multiple detonations, Larn closed his eyes and buried his face in the mud, his lips mumbling a litany of choked and terrified devotions as he prayed for salvation. As he prayed, his mind raced with desperate and outraged questions. *How can this be*, he thought. *Bulaven said they were our guns. Why is our own side shooting at us?* But there was no answer. Only more explosions and flying soil as the bombardment continued.

Then, abruptly, thankfully, the explosions stopped.

'Move! Move! Move! Out of the trench!' Davir shouted. 'Quickly. Before the bastards finish reloading!'

Scrambling to his feet as the others leaped up and over the rear trench wall, Larn followed them. Clearing the wall, he saw they had already sprinted halfway down the rise towards the line of dugouts. Running desperately to catch up, for a moment Larn was aware of nothing more than the rush of blood in his ears and the pounding of his heart. Then, as though with a slow dawning realisation akin to a nightmare, he heard the deathdive scream of falling shells once more and knew he would never reach the dugouts in time.

Abruptly, an explosion ripped through the air to the side of him, knocking him to the ground and showering him with falling earth. Finding himself on his back and covered in soil, Larn felt a sudden fear at the thought he had been buried alive, before he saw the grey sky overhead and realised he was still above ground. Spluttering out a mouthful of earth as he stumbled to his feet again, he spent long dangerous instants staggering aimlessly about in a daze as more explosions wracked the ground beneath him. Then, relieved, he heard the sound of a familiar voice shouting through the haze of his confusion.

'Here, new fish,' he heard the voice yell. 'This way! Over here!'

It was Bulaven. Standing sheltered within the sandbag walls of one of the dugout emplacements, the big man was gesturing frantically to him. Seeing him, Larn half-ran, half-stumbled towards him, all but collapsing into Bulaven's outstretched arms as he finally reached the safety of the emplacement. Then, hurriedly, Bulaven helped Larn down the steps into the dugout while another grim-faced Vardan slammed the door closed behind them.

'...new fish...' Bulaven said, the words mostly drowned out by the ringing in Larn's ears. '...close one... thought... los.. you...'

'...new fish...' Bulaven said again, what few words Larn could understand were dim and muffled, as though the big man's voice was a dying whisper echoing down the length of a long tunnel. '...are... ou... ll... right...'

'...new fish... ' Bulaven's face was painted with concern as Larn felt a sudden weakness and the world about him grew dark and distant.

'...new fish...'

And then, everything went black.

He awoke to darkness and the smell of earth. Opening his eyes, Larn looked up to see a slim rectangle of cold grey sky above him surrounded on all sides by dark walls of soil. As he tried to stand, he found his limbs would not answer him. He could not move; the fact of his paralysis accepted with a curious sense of detachment and calm resignation. Abruptly, he saw four bent and ragged figures appear overheard to peer down at him as though from a dizzying height. Seeing the lines and creases on each ancient wizened face, he recognised them at once. They were the old women he had seen carting corpses away after the battle. Then, looking down at him with tired disinterest, the women began to speak, each one taking up where the other had left off as though performing some ritual they had enacted a thousand times already.

'He was a hero,' the first old women said as Larn slowly began to understand something was terribly wrong here. 'They all are, all the Guardsmen who die here.'

'They are martyrs,' one of her sisters said beside her. 'By giving their blood to defend this place they have made the soil of this city into sacred ground.'

'Broucheroc is a holy and impregnable fortress,' the third one said. 'The orks will never take it. We will break their assault here. Then, we will push them back and reclaim this entire planet.'

'So the commissars tell us,' the fourth one added, without conviction.

Turning away, the rustling noise made by their tattered layers of clothing not unlike the flutterings of the black wings of crows, the women disappeared from his sight again. Lying on his back still looking up at the rectangle of grey sky above him, Larn felt his previous sense of calm replaced by a sudden presentiment of terror. *There is something wrong here*, he thought. *They are talking as though I were dead. Are they blind? Can't they see I am still alive.* He made to speak, to call out and tell them to come back and help him up out of this strange pit he found himself lying in but the words would not come. His mouth and tongue were as paralysed as every other part of his body. Then, Larn heard a scratching sound as though somewhere a shovel had been pushed into a mound of earth, and knew all his horrified premonitions of a moment earlier were about to be made reality.

This is not a pit, he thought, his mind frantic with despair. *It is a grave! And they are about to bury me alive!*

'Grieve not for this departed soul,' he heard a stern and even voice say from above as the first shovelful of earth fell towards him. 'Man born of woman was not made to be eternal. And, insofar as he was given life by the Immortal Emperor, so it is by His will that Man should die.'

Feeling the earth strike his face, Larn tried to struggle to his feet. To scream. To shout. To cry out. It was hopeless. He could not move.

'For though the soul may be immortal, the body was made to pass from this world,' the voice smoothly continued. 'And let the flesh of the remains of Man be given over to the processes of decay, for only the Emperor is undying.'

Helpless, Larn found himself blinded as another shovelful of earth landed on his face. Then, as fragments of soil dribbled into his mouth and nostrils, he felt more earth hit his body, the weight of it growing slowly more intolerable as, one remorseless shovelful at a time, the unseen grave diggers went about their work. Soon, his lungs crushed under the weight of the soil on his chest, his mouth and nose choked from the soil inside them, he could no longer breathe. Mute and blind now, his heart growing feeble, in the throes of his last desperate paroxysms of helpless terror the final thing he heard was the words of the calm and pitiless voice droning endlessly on above him.

'Ashes to ashes,' the voice said, uncaring. 'Dust to dust. A life is over. Let the body of this man be given to the earth.'

'There. You see now I was right,' he heard Davir say. 'I told you all he wasn't dead. Naturally I defer to your medical judgement in such matters, Svenk, but I understand it is exceedingly rare to find a dead man who is still breathing.'

Groggily opening his eyes, Larn was briefly confused to find he was lying on his back on the floor of an unfamiliar dugout with the gaunt figure of Medical Officer Svenk kneeling over him. For a moment he wondered what had happened to the open grave and the weight of earth on top of his chest. *It must have been a nightmare*, he thought. Then, becoming aware of a pungent odour making his eyes water, he realised Svenk had broken open a vial of smelling salts and was wafting them under his nose. Weakly pushing the vial away Larn tried to stand, only for Svenk to place a firm hand on his chest to stop him.

'Not just yet, new fish,' he said, raising a hand to hold three fingers up in front of Larn's face. 'How many fingers do you see?'

'Three,' Larn said, noticing Bulaven kneeling on the other side of him and looking down at his face with an expression of concern.

'We thought we had lost you there for a moment, new fish,' Bulaven said. 'When you collapsed I was sure a near miss from one of the shells must have liquefied your insides. The blast does that sometimes, even if the shrapnel does not hit you. I am glad to see you are still all right though.'

'How many now?' Svenk asked, changing the number of raised fingers and holding them in front of Larn once more.

'Two.'

'Good,' Svenk said. 'You can remember your name?'

'Larn. Arvin Larn.'

'And where do you come from, Larn?'

'From? Outside... there was shelling...'

'True. But I mean where is your homeworld, Larn? Where were you born?'

'Jumael,' Larn replied. 'Jumael IV.'

'Excellent,' Svenk said, his face at last cracking into a smile. 'Let me extend my warmest congratulations to you, new fish. You are hereby pronounced fit for duty and free from concussion. Should you find yourself experiencing any sudden dizziness or nausea over the next twelve hours, please take two glasses of water and call me in the morning. Oh, and as for that headache you are no doubt feeling at the moment? Don't worry, it is a good sign. It means you are still alive.'

'The warmth of your bedside manner is most extraordinary, Svenk,' Davir said, suddenly appearing to stand over the medic's shoulder and gaze down at Larn. 'Remarkable, even. Really, you are a credit to your profession.'

'Thank you, Davir,' Svenk replied, putting the loop of his satchel strap over his shoulder once more as he made to stand. 'I always find such unsolicited testimonials deeply moving. Now, if you will excuse me, I had better go and check the other dugouts for casualties. Given the thoroughness of the bombardment our own side are currently subjecting us to, chances are there are others elsewhere who may be in more need of my talents. Though I warn you, new fish,' he added, looking down with mock seriousness at Larn. 'While getting injured twice in one day is scarcely unheard of hereabouts, it does suggest a certain carelessness about your own well-being. Come to me again today, and I may be forced to start charging you for my services.'

With that Svenk turned on his heel and walked briskly away, headed for the doorway at the far end of the dugout. As he watched the medic open the door and start up the stairs towards the surface, Larn became abruptly aware of the muffled sounds of explosions as shells struck the earth overhead. *We are still being bombarded*, he thought, the fog of his mind slowly clearing as he came more back to himself. *And Medical Officer Svenk is about to go out in the middle of it in search of wounded men in need of treatment. Unbelievable. Whatever the strangeness of his manner, he is either insane or the bravest man I have ever seen.*

'You still do not look too well, new fish' Bulaven said, still kneeling beside Larn and frowning at him with concern. 'Your face is very pale.'

'So?' said Davir. 'For all we know that is his normal colour when he has just had the shit knocked out of him. Anyway, you heard what Svenk said, Bulaven: the new fish is perfectly fine. Now, stopping clucking over him like some idiot mother hen and get him to his feet. If the new fish isn't dying he has no right to be taking up valuable space by lying there like that.'

'Come on then, new fish,' Bulaven said, helping him stand up as Larn looked for the first time at the interior of the dugout around them. 'Careful now. If you feel like your knees are about to go, just put your weight on me.'

Inside, the dugout was smaller than the one he had been in

before; perhaps a third of the size at most of the barracks dug-out where he had first met Sergeant Chelkar and Corporal Vladek. Looking through the crowd of a dozen or so Guardsmen standing near him Larn saw a table in the corner covered in communications equipment. In a chair beside it an unshaven and harried-looking Vardan corporal sat holding a pair of headphones to his ear with one hand, while pressing down the 'send' button of the vox-com before him with the other.

'Yes, I understand that, captain,' the corporal said, talking into the vox-com. 'But regardless of what your situation maps may say, I assure you we are still in possession of sector 1-13.'

'That is Corporal Grishen,' said Bulaven once he had seen Larn watching the man. 'Our comms officer. Right now he is talking to the commander of the artillery battery that is shelling us.'

'What? You mean they *know* they are shooting at us?' Larn asked in disbelief.

'I wouldn't sound so surprised, new fish,' said Davir. 'This is Broucheroc, after all. Here, such snafus are not uncommon. You have heard the expression by now, I take it? Snafu? I tell you: there could be no better term for describing this whole damn war.'

'It is usually a question of parts, I understand,' Scholar said as he came over to join them. 'The cause of these incidents when our own artillery suddenly starts shooting at us, I mean. Old parts wear out; the new ones are incorrectly calibrated, or else they have been recycled and refurbished so many times as to be all but useless. Whatever the cause though, I'm sure once the battery commander has become aware of our situation the shelling will stop.'

'*Phah*. More groundless optimism,' Davir spat. 'Really, Scholar, you are getting as bad as this fat oaf Bulaven here. Grishen has been at the comm-link working his way up that battery's chain of command for the last twenty minutes. So far, the most he has managed to accomplish is for his backside to go numb from sitting in that chair. No, I wouldn't expect this bombardment to end any time soon. For that to happen the moron shooting at us would have to admit he has made a mistake. And why should he do that, after all? If he kills us, some arsehole at General Head-quarters will probably pin a medal on him.'

'Yes, captain, I know you have your orders,' said Corporal Grishen nearby, still talking into the vox-com before pausing to listen to a reply through his headphones. Then, with every man in the dugout now silent as they stood listening to the stop-start rhythms of Grishen's side of the conversation, the corporal began once more.

'Yes, I realise that, captain,' Grishen said. 'And you are right: the Guardsman's first duty is obedience. But, even granting that you have your orders and it is your duty to obey them, if those orders are mistaken...'

A pause.

'No, of course, you are right, sir. The divinely ordained com-mand structure of the Imperial Guard precludes any possibility of your orders being mistaken. If I may rephrase myself, how-ever? What I really meant to say, of course, was that perhaps the problem here lies not in the orders themselves, but in the prac-tical aspects of their execution...'

Another pause.

'Oh no, sir. I wasn't for a moment questioning your competence...'

And another.

'Yes, sir, as you say: your battery runs like a well-oiled machine. But you must concede that, seeing as we are unquestionably under bombardment, a mistake must have occurred somewhere...'

Another pause.

'Yes, of course, sir. You concede nothing. Yes, I understand. No, sir, you are correct. General Headquarters is not known for promoting fools to the rank of captain...'

And so it went on, while from above Larn heard the distant roar of explosions as the bombardment continued. Until, at last, he heard a door open behind him and turned to see Sergeant Chelkar step grim-faced into the dugout. Then, as the group of assembled Vardans huddled in the dugout silently parted to give way before their sergeant, Larn saw Chelkar stride purposefully over to Grishen at the comms system.

'Yes, sir,' Corporal Grishen said, raising his eyes as he saw Chelkar approach him. 'Naturally, you are right. If there is any mistake here it was ours in being present in a sector scheduled for bombardment. But, if you will excuse me for a moment, my company commander has just entered the room. Perhaps it would be better if you and he discussed this matter directly.'

'What is going on, Grishen?' Chelkar said, laying the shotgun he had been carrying down across the table before him. 'Why in hell are those idiots still shelling us?'

'I am on the line to the captain commanding the battery in question now, sergeant,' Grishen said, diplomatically releasing the 'send' button on the vox-com so his listener at the other end could no longer hear them. 'I have tried to explain things to him, but he refuses to accept anything I say. He claims that according to his situation map this entire sector fell to the orks three days ago – meaning he would be quite within his rights to bombard it even if he didn't already have signed orders from Battery Command telling him to do so. And as for ending the bombardment? He says in keeping with his orders the shelling will cease in precisely one hour and twenty-seven minutes' time. Not a moment sooner. He is most definite on that point, sergeant. Frankly, some might even say a little intransigent.'

'I see,' said Chelkar. 'Hand me the vox-com, Grishen. I want to talk to this son of a bitch myself.'

'This is Sergeant Eugin Chelkar,' he said, taking the headphones and pressing the button to activate the vox-com. 'Acting regimental commander of the 902nd Vardan Rifles. Who am I speaking to?'

For a moment, like Grishen before him, Chelkar went quiet

as he listened to the voice on the other end of the line through his headphones. Then, his tone becoming grave and forceful, he spoke once more.

'Captain Meran, the 16th Landran Artillery?' Chelkar said. 'I see. Well, I have a message for you, captain. No, I am well aware you outrank me, but you will listen to what I have to say all the same. I am giving you two minutes, captain. Two minutes. And, if this bombardment hasn't ended by then, I am going to come over to whatever hole you are hiding in and kick you up the arse so hard that you will taste leather every time you swallow. Not that you will have to worry about that for long, you understand. The arse kicking will only be for my own amusement. After that, I fully intend to put a shotgun blast through your skull. Have I made myself clear?'

Again, there was another pause while Chelkar listened to the captain's reply on his headphones.

'No, it is you who does not understand the situation, captain,' Chelkar said after a moment. 'I don't give a damn about your rank or your orders. Nor do I care if you report me to the Commissariat. In fact, please feel free to do so: if nothing else, they can serve as pallbearers at your funeral. What you fail to understand is that, even if you have me arrested, there is an entire regiment of men standing around me who are quite prepared to make good on my threat. And, if you think the Commissariat will be willing to arrest an entire frontline combat unit to save you, I think you overestimate your own value to the war effort of this city. Oh, and by the way, captain, the chronometer is counting down. You now have only one minute and twenty seconds to make a decision. Chelkar out.'

Giving the vox-com and headphones back to Grishen, Chelkar stood waiting beside the table. Listening intently, like every other man in the dugout to the sound of shelling going on above their heads.

'I don't understand,' Larn whispered. 'Surely the sergeant has just written his own death warrant by talking to an officer that way?'

'Maybe,' Bulaven whispered back. 'You don't know Chelkar though, new fish. In seventeen years I have never seen him be afraid of anything. If there is something that needs to be done, he is the man to do it. Whatever the cost. All the same, I wonder if even he has gone too far this time. If the captain should vox a complaint to the Commissariat...'

'Ach, you are both like children frightened of your own shadows,' Davir muttered beside them. 'You especially should know better, Bulaven. When has Chelkar ever failed us? The sergeant knows what he is doing. These artillery monkeys always think frontline troops are crazy to begin with. This arsehole captain won't dare call the Commissariat. Trust me, he is probably already soiling himself in fear and is giving the order to cease fire even as we speak.'

Above, as though in confirmation of Davir's opinions, the guns abruptly fell silent. At first no one spoke, all of them listening to hear whether the shelling would begin again. Until, as the seconds passed into a full minute with no further sound of explosions, it became clear the bombardment was ended.

'There, you see, Grishen?' Chelkar half-smiled. 'It is simply a matter of knowing how best to talk to these people to get your point across.' Then, taking up his shotgun once more and turning away from the corporal, Chelkar noticed every man in the dugout was looking at him with faces caught in expressions of awe and gratitude.

'It was nothing so much,' Chelkar said to them. 'Still, it was probably better that I let our friend the captain think he was going to have an entire regiment after his blood if he didn't stop the shelling. If he'd known the 902nd Vardan was only made up of a single company perhaps he would have felt man enough to take us all on. It is not unusual for these rear echelon heroes to have a bloated sense of their own abilities.'

At that the men smiled, some even laughed in nervous relief. Seeing the mood of reverence had been successfully dispelled, the sergeant's manner became more business-like.

'All right,' he said. 'Now, enough of this hiding underground. Back to your posts. We don't want to leave the firing trenches undefended and make the orks think it is a worthwhile time launching another attack. Go on. Get moving, all of you.'

As the men in the dugout began to hurry out towards their trenches again, Larn's last sight of Chelkar came as he saw the sergeant turn to towards Corporal Grishen once more with further instructions.

'Grishen, I want you to contact General Headquarters,' he heard the sergeant say. 'Inform them Sector 1-13 is most certainly not in ork hands and make it clear we would consider it a great personal favour if they would adjust their situation maps accordingly. Oh, and you had better try voxing Battery Command as well to ask them if in future they could please refrain from ordering people to shoot at us. It probably won't work, of course. But I suppose we should at least pretend we believe the men in charge of this war have some idea of what it is they are doing.'

INTERLUDE

As Above, So Below or Grand Marshal Kerchan
and the Genius of Command

By any standard of measurement, the war was going badly.

Brooding as he sat through yet another interminable briefing His Excellency Grand Marshal Tirnas Kerchan, Hero of the Varentis Campaign and Supreme Commander (All Forces) of the Most Glorious Armies of the Emperor in Broucheroc, considered the facts he had learned so far that day and found there was nothing there to please him. For the best part of two hours now, from his place at the head of the long table inside General HQ's Central Briefing Room One, he had listened as a succession of his commanders read aloud their latest situation reports to the assembled General Staff. Through it all, through all their pasty-faced dissemblings and pathetically transparent attempts to lay the blame for their failures on others, the message at the heart of each man's report was exactly the same.

They were losing the war.

'Grand Marshal?' he heard his adjutant, Colonel Vlin, whisper from his chair by the side of him, breaking his train of thought.

Disturbed from his despairing reverie, the Grand Marshal abruptly realised he had lost track of the briefings. Looking up he saw the eyes of every man at the table were turned to gaze his way, nervously awaiting his reaction to the substance of the last report. For a moment, unable to remember the name of the man standing before him who had presented it, he found himself stymied.

'Yes, good. Very good,' Kerchan harrumphed, then floundered. 'Most cogent and concise. An excellent analysis, General... ah...'

'Dushan,' Vlin said *sotto voce*, raising a sheath of papers in front of his mouth to hide the words as he spoke them.

'Yes, General Dushan,' the Grand Marshal said, inclining his head toward the officer in question and giving him a curt nod by way of encouragement. 'Your grasp of the situation is to be commended.'

Clearly relieved, his face all but beaming at the praise, the ferret-faced Dushan puffed out his chest with pride and bent forward in a low bow in grateful acknowledgement before taking his seat once more.

Look at him, the Grand Marshal thought sourly. *The man is an idiot. Still he is hardly unique in that regard. I am surrounded by idiots. This whole damned city would seem to be staffed from first to last with idiots, cowards and incompetents.*

Briefly, the Grand Marshal idly wondered whether it might not be better to make an example of Dushan. To denounce him, here and now, and order him taken away to stand court martial on charges of incompetence. *That might put the fear of the Emperor into the rest of them for a while,* he thought. *Force them to buck their ideas up for fear they'd be facing more of the same themselves.* As attractive as the idea was, he found himself forced to dismiss it. He had just praised the man, after all. To go back on that praise so quickly might make him seem indecisive. No, like it or not, for the rest of the day at least the idiot Dushan was beyond arrest; almost as inviolable to the Grand Marshal's powers as the body of an Imperial saint. It was a matter of maintaining the proper respect for the chain of command. Once the Grand Marshal had given voice to an opinion on a man there could be no turning back.

And besides, thought Kerchan, *I was the one who gave Dushan his position in the first place. To punish him for his inadequacies now might be perceived as an admission I was wrong to promote*

*him. No matter what, a Grand Marshal can never admit to having
made a mistake. He must be seen to be infallible. To give credence
to any thought otherwise would be to fatally undermine the rightful awe every Guardsman naturally feels for the wisdom of their
superiors. Well, the awe that most of them feel anyway. It is the
nature of war that, occasionally and inevitably, there will always
be dissenters.*

With a distant stab of quiet anger, the Grand Marshal found
himself remembering the officer whose place Dushan had taken
on the General Staff. *What was the man's name,* he thought.
Minar? Minaris? Minovan? He was about to turn to Colonel Vlin
to ask him the name of Dushan's predecessor, when abruptly it
came to him. *Mirovan! That was the man's name.* The remembered name brought with it a clearer picture in his mind of the
individual to whom it belonged and Grand Marshal Kerchan
found his bleak and unhappy mood growing even darker.

Of all the men on his staff, Mirovan had always seemed the
best and brightest. An exemplary field officer with an admirable
record of citations for bravery behind him, Mirovan had made
general in a creditably short space of time. If the man had any
flaw at all, it was in the one single characteristic Kerchan could
never abide in a subordinate.

Insolence.

Mirovan had been so insolent in fact that two weeks ago he had
even had the temerity to question one of the Grand Marshal's
military decisions during a staff meeting. Enraged, Kerchan had
demoted the man on the spot, busting him down to the rank of
common trooper and ordering him to be immediately posted
to a frontline combat unit. Next, in a hasty decision the Grand
Marshal now bitterly regretted, he had promoted the man's less
than able second-in-command, the then-colonel Dushan, and
ordered him to serve on the General Staff in Mirovan's place.
Though he had felt quite sure humbling Mirovan had been the
right thing to do at the time, the Grand Marshal now experienced

a troubling sense of ill-defined unease. *In many ways Mirovan was an admirable man*, he thought sadly. *Certainly, he was a damn sight more competent than most of the toadies and feckless lackeys who bedevil me sitting around this table day after day. I wonder what happened to him?*

'He was a good man in his way,' the Grand Marshal said. 'It would be a pity if such a man were dead.'

All around the table, the others were staring at him. Kerchan realised he must have inadvertently spoken his musings aloud, interrupting the flow of conversation around him as the members of the General Staff discussed the significance or not of Dushan's report. On every side of him, as though not entirely sure how they should react, generals stared towards him with expressions ranging from uncertainty to quiet trepidation. Even the ever-faithful Vlin seemed to be looking at him strangely. Kerchan, however, felt no embarrassment. If nothing else, a lifetime spent commanding soldiers had taught him a simple truth. A man with the absolute authority of life-or-death over others should never feel any need to have to apologise for his own behaviour.

'I was remembering Mirovan,' he said, turning to look toward General Dushan. 'After his demotion he was given over to your command, Dushan. What happened to him?'

'I... I am not sure, your excellency,' Dushan said, almost squirming before the Grand Marshal's gaze. 'I left the matter of assigning him to a new posting to one of my aides. As to where precisely he was sent, I should have to check the battalion rosters...'

Faltering, failing miserably to hide his discomfort, Dushan's voice gradually trailed away to guilty silence. *He probably had the man posted to the worst unit and the most dangerous duties he could find*, Kerchan thought. *Somewhere right in the thick of the action no doubt, where Mirovan would have been lucky to survive a week. After all, with their former general still alive there would always be the danger of dissent and mutiny among the men who had served under him. So, Mirovan is likely dead then.*

Not that I can fault Dushan's decision-making in that regard, of course. Dissent is a cancer. If I had been in his position, I would have done the same myself.

Then, looking at the eyes of the men seated around him, the Grand Marshal realised his mention of Mirovan's name had apparently had an entirely unforeseen consequence. Every man there seemed in the grip of the same queasy discomfort as Dushan, as though the recollection of Mirovan's sudden fall from grace had spooked them. Watching them, the Grand Marshal began to understand he had quite inadvertently achieved his original purpose. *Mentioning Mirovan did the trick*, he thought. *That seems to have put the fear of the Emperor in them, all right.* Not for the first time, Kerchan was left dazzled by the extent of his own genius when it came to motivating the men under his command. *I didn't even realise I was doing it*, he thought. *And yet still, by some happy accident, I seem to have created exactly the effect I wanted. No, not an accident.. Unconsciously or not, the fact I achieved my aim means I must have intended to do so all along. There are no accidents when one is a Grand Marshal.* Then, making the effort to summon his most carefully unreadable sinister half-smile, the Grand Marshal spoke to Dushan once more.

'No matter, Dushan,' he said, noting with satisfaction that the man seemed little reassured by his manner. 'It was simply an idle thought, nothing more. Now, on to other matters. Colonel Vlin? Who is scheduled to give the next briefing?'

'Magos Garan, your excellency,' his adjutant said. 'He wishes to advise us on the monthly production figures from the city's munitions manufactoriums.'

His brief mood of good humour abruptly evaporating, the Grand Marshal watched with a sinking heart as the hooded figure of the archmagos of the Adeptus Mechanicus in Broucheroc rose slowly to his feet. As much machine as man, covered in whirring devices that had kept their owner alive for far past the normal span of life, what could be seen of the magos's aged and withered body from beneath his cloak no longer looked entirely human. Most disquieting of all were the mechadendrites: four thin tentacle-like mechanical arms that would periodically emerge from the folds of the magos's cloak to make minute adjustments to the other machines that covered his flesh.

Though as disturbing as he had always found the creature's appearance, the real root of the Grand Marshal's dislike of Magos Garan lay more in practical considerations than in anything so flighty as matters of aesthetics. Unlike the rest of the men seated around the briefing table, Magos Garan did not serve at the Grand Marshal's whim. As the most senior member of the Adeptus Mechanicus in the city Garan was not here as a subordinate. Without the machine-adepts to keep the city's manufactoriums working, the Grand Marshal would have no munitions for his troops. No new lasguns. No missile launchers. No replacement power packs. No grenades, mortar rounds, artillery shells, or any of the hundreds of other things the Guardsmen of the city needed daily to help them keep the orks at bay. As such, the Grand Marshal found himself forced to deal with Magos Garan as though he was the representative of some foreign power. A man to be negotiated and entreated with, but never commanded. An equal, not an inferior. Not being by inclination a man much given to the subtle intricacies of diplomacy, Kerchan had long found dealing with the haughty magos to be a difficult burden to bear.

'In the last thirty days the productivity of the city's manufactoriums has fallen by a figure of four point three four per cent,' the Magos said in a dry monotone voice, apparently so long past remembering what it was to be human he made no attempt to leaven the bad news as he delivered it. 'The reasons for this fall in productivity are as follows. One, the loss of five manufactoriums in Sector 1-49 when the sector in question was partially overrun by the orks. Two, the destruction of another manufactorium in Sector 1-37 by an ork raiding party who had gained entrance past the city's defensive perimeter by unknown means. Three, damage to a further fifteen manufactoriums in Sectors 1-22 through 1-25 caused by the orks' long-range artillery. Four, further damage to three of the same manufactoriums caused by gretchin suicide bombers. Five, the slowness of repair to these facilities caused by a chronic lack of qualified personnel. Six, the outbreak of an unknown viral pathogen among the lay manufactorium workers of Sector 1-19, causing the loss of 180,757 working man-hours through either sickness or death. Seven, the loss of 162,983 working man-hours caused through civil unrest occasioned by food shortages among the lay manufactorium workers of Sector 1-32, said unrest having since been suppressed at the result of a further 34,234 working man-hours lost through either injury or death...'

His face emotionless, the magos continued, droning out an apparently endless catalogue of doom. As he listened, Grand Marshal Kerchan once more found himself falling into despair. According to his strategic calculations, the battle for Broucheroc should have been won weeks, if not months, ago. More than that, by now they should have broken out of this Emperor-forsaken city and be pushing the enemy back on every front. Yet, impossibly, after ten years of warfare the orks still showed no sign of defeat or collapse. While day after day, hour after hour, Grand Marshal found himself confronted by defeatism at every turn: his every waking moment spent in the company of dozens of mewling incompetents, all of them with their pleas of extenuation and tales of woe.

The Adeptus Mechanicus complained about not having enough workers or raw materials for the manufactoriums. The Medical Corps complained of not having enough surgeons or medicines for the apothecariums. The militia authorities he had placed in command of the civilian infrastructure complained of not having the resources to provide enough food or clean water for the city's population. Worst of all, his own generals complained of not having enough men, or arms, or artillery support, or any other damned thing. Complaint, after complaint, after damn complaint.

All the while, the Grand Marshal knew all these complaints for what they truly were. Excuses. It was hardly any wonder that sometimes he felt such outrage he was tempted to pick out one of his generals at random and put a las-blast through his head just as an example to the others.

A las-blast, he thought, hand straying unconsciously to the finely filigreed surface of the ceremonial laspistol at his side. *Right here and now. That really would put the fear of the Emperor into them!*

'Fifteen, the loss of 38,964 working man-hours through reason of power shortages in Sectors 1-42 through 1-47,' the magos droned relentlessly on, his mechadendrites still attending to the machines of his body as though with a life of their own. 'Sixteen, the loss of a manufactorium to explosion in Sector 1-26, said explosion believed to have been caused by a malfunction in an incorrectly fitted power conduit. Seventeen...'

And on and on and on. Seeking relief from the depressing tedium of the magos's report, hearing the sound of a door opening behind him the Grand Marshal turned his head enough to the side to watch from the corner of his eye as one of Vlin's aides stepped into the briefing room from the anteroom outside. Holding a data-slate the aide advanced to the table to hand it to Colonel Vlin, before saluting and smartly turning on his heel to march away. Pressing the display stud to bring up the report stored on the data-slate, Vlin studied it for a full minute. Then, his face visibly growing pale, he raised his eyes to look uneasily toward the Grand Marshal.

'What is it, Vlin?' Kerchan asked as, from further down the table, the magos's briefing continued inexorably.

'I have just received the latest estimates from the Office of Strategic Analysis, your excellency,' Vlin said, a wavering tone of uncertainty in his voice. 'But there must be some mistake–'

'Let me see it,' the Grand Marshal said, holding his hand out for Vlin to give him the data-slate.

For a moment, as though unsure whether he should surrender it, Vlin hesitated. Then, the habits of obedience engrained by fifteen years in the Grand Marshal's service proving too strong to resist, he reluctantly complied. Curious as to what could have so unnerved his adjutant, Kerchan took the data-slate and skimmed through the report to see for himself. At first glance it seemed no more than Vlin had said: another dry analysis of facts and figures from the number crunchers in the OSA. At least until the Grand Marshal happened to look at the report's conclusions.

'Damnation!' he roared.

Incensed, before he even knew what he was doing the Grand Marshal had thrown the data-slate away in a rage, flinging it across the room to smash against the wall in a crash of breaking plexiglass as its display screen shattered. Stunned by his outburst, mouths gaping open in idiot expressions of surprise, the men around the table sat frozen in shock. Even Magos Garan was not immune, his mechadendrites becoming suddenly motionless, he paused in his report and stood gazing at Kerchan as though unsure how best to react. All of them silently staring at the Grand Marshal with wary expressions whose combined meanings were almost palpably clear.

They think I have turned into a madman, Kerchan thought, the storm of his anger having subsided immediately he had vented his rage against the helpless data-slate. *The old man is losing it. That is what they are all telling themselves.*

'Leave me,' he said quietly, his face a mask, his mind feeling suddenly tired and no longer willing to see the looks in their eyes. 'Leave me,' he directed. 'All of you. Get out of here now.'

Cowed, heads bent so as not to meet his gaze, the members of the General Staff stood, bowed at him, and filed from the room in uneasy silence. All except Vlin. Treading cautiously over to the fallen data-slate while the others went to the door, the adjutant picked it up and made to take it with him.

'Leave it, Vlin,' the Grand Marshal said. 'Put it on the table, and then get out with the rest of them.'

Soon, he was alone. The mammoth expanse of the briefing room seemed desolate and empty about him now it was deserted, Grand Marshal Kerchan began to wonder if he perhaps should have held himself better in check. Generals were by their nature inveterate gossips. Within the hour news of his outburst would be known throughout General Headquarters; by tomorrow it would likely be known across the city. In these trying times even a Grand Marshal must be careful. Whatever the rules and regulations of the Imperial Guard might say to the contrary, as the commanding officer of a besieged city his position was precarious. Idle gossip about the data-slate incident could easily lead to discussions about the state of his mental health; discussions that in turn might undermine his authority, creating fertile soil in which the twin ugly flowers of dissent and mutiny could grow. He was not afraid. Experience had taught him there was always one sure way for a Grand Marshal to maintain order.

It is time for another purge, he thought. *Tonight, I will tell Vlin to contact the Commissariat and have them send over a list of anyone above the rank of major they suspect of disloyalty. A few show trials and shootings should nip any problems in the bud in that regard. And while we're at it, I will tell Vlin to add Dushan to the list. Yes, another purge. That is exactly what is needing here.*

Calm and satisfied now, he turned his attention back to the object that had originally provoked his displeasure. Lifting the data-slate from its position on the table where Vlin had left it, the Grand Marshal looked again at the words and graphs of the report still visible on the shattered surface of its display screen. The findings of the report were bleak. Based on current estimates of ork birth-rates and the rate of attrition of men and materiel inside the city, it concluded Broucheroc could only survive another six months at most.

Six months, the Grand Marshal thought grimly. *I shall have to remember to tell Vlin to add the name of whatever traitor compiled this report to the list as well. Imagine claiming this city has only six months left to live, when any fool knows the siege is on the verge of crumbling and victory is within our grasp.*

Mentally making another note to himself to have the report suppressed, Kerchan tossed the data-slate away and sat in silence for several minutes. Feeling weighed down by the heavy burden of responsibility on his shoulders, his brooding mood of earlier returned. *I am assailed on all sides by troubles,* he thought. *Bad enough after a long and glorious career for a man to find himself shunted to a sideshow war on a planet of no importance. Worse, to then be condemned to a long siege with no prospect of relief from other sources. But it does not matter. The genius that won me my battles in the past has not deserted me. I am still a great leader, and my plan is sound. Soon, I will break this siege and reclaim this planet for the Emperor. And, when I do, the fools among the Lord Generals Militant responsible for sidelining me to this awful place will find themselves embarrassed to see me celebrated and revered for all my victories. I am the Grand Marshal Tirnas Kerchan. I am still in control of my own destiny. I will win this war. And, soon enough, I will be able to add the name 'Hero of Broucheroc' to all my different titles. I will not allow matters here to go any other way.*

Then, noticing a single page sitting alone among the flotsam spread of maps and documents lying across the table, the Grand Marshal saw something there that excited his interest. It was the latest edition of *The Veritas,* the city's twice-daily newsletter and, as so often in the past when he felt weighed down by all his troubles, the Grand Marshal turned to the newsletter in the hope of comfort.

Orks Defeated in Sector 1-13, the headline read. *Jumael 14th Victorious!*

Yes, he thought, reading the story written below it. *It doesn't matter what the others say, here is the proof that I was right all along. The proof of impending victory and the proof my battle plans are sound. We are winning victories. We are defeating the orks. We are winning this war.*

It says so right here in the news.

CHAPTER ELEVEN

Boy and the Taking of Broucheroc's Children – Trench
Repairs Parts 1, 2 & 3 – Questions as to the Whys and
Wherefores of Survival – A Reappraisal of the Tale of
his Fathers

His name was Boy. Granted, his Ma had given him another name
but she had been dead for more than three something years now
and he had been so young he could no longer remember what
it was she had called him. Instead, he had taken the name the
auxies used for him when they tried to catch him to take him
to the machine-men and their big making-places. *'Come here,
boy'* they would say. *'We don't want to hurt you, boy',* their voices
breathless from running, their stupid faces red and panting, trying to chase him as he danced away from them across the rubble.
Some of them, the clever ones he guessed, would even try to
trick him. *'We have food, boy,'* they'd say. *'Come down here and
we will share some with you.'* But they could never fool him. He
was Boy, and he lived wild and swift and free in the ruins of this
city. Try as they might, the auxies and the machine-men would
never get him.

Now, the cloak he had made from rat skins and scavenged
sacking-cloth wrapped tight about him to keep out the cold, Boy
crouched hidden in a hollow in the rubble waiting to see if one
of the children of Cap'n Rat would take his bait. The pickings had
been good this week, with Cap'n Rat sending at least one of his

children along each day for Boy to kill and eat. In return Boy had done right by the Cap'n just liked he'd promised him: forsaking all other gods and praying to Cap'n Rat over each of his kills. As far as agreements went Boy reckoned it had been a pretty good one. Only problem was, despite the fact he had been waiting in the same place for hours now, so far today the Cap'n didn't seem in any great hurry to live up to his end of the bargain.

Then, at last, Boy saw signs of progress. Tempted from his burrow by the promise of easy pickings, a rat emerged from a nearby hole in the rubble and moved quickly across the rocks towards the bait. Until, coming to the small piece of greasy flesh Boy had set out as a lure, the rat paused with whiskers twitching warily as though some inner instinct had alerted it to danger.

Too late to be twitching with your whiskers now, Brother Rat, Boy thought, a feral smile playing across his cracked lips as he aimed his slingshot and loosed the taut string to let fly with a two-inch metal nail. *Shouldn't oughta have been so greedy, coming out in the open in the suntime like that.*

Flying fast and true the nail took the rat square in the back of the neck, stabbing through its spine and into the skull. On his feet and moving before the nail had even hit its target, Boy jumped from cover to race scampering across the rubble to retrieve his prize. Grabbing the dead rat by the tail, he turned and ran back to find refuge again in his hiding place. Then, pulling the nail free and daubing two smears of the rat's blood across his cheeks, he knelt to send a silent prayer of thanksgiving to his unseen benefactor.

Praise'm, Cap'n Rat, he thought as he looked down at the body of his catch and considered its worth. *Praise'm for making so many of your children. Praise'm for making them big and fat. And praise'm for sending them to me so I don't starve.*

It was a good rat, fine and sleek, with the kind of big meaty haunches he knew would make for tasty eatings. Nor did the value of the rat to Boy end there. He could make clothing from its pelt, sewing thread from its sinews, needles and traphooks from its bones, teeth, and claws. No part of the rat's body would go wasted. By virtue of the survival skills he had learned first by watching his mother and then on his own after her death, Boy could find a use for anything.

Abruptly, he found himself thinking of how things used to be when his Ma was still alive. He remembered the cellar where they used to live, her kind and care-worn face, the soft lullabies she would sing to drift him off to sleep. He remembered sitting on her knee as she told him the reasons they must stay in hiding. *'They say we must give up our children,'* she had told them. *'The generals. They say children are a distraction in wartime; that the people of Broucheroc must all serve in the auxiliaries while their children are cared for in the orphanariums. But I don't believe them. I think they want to give the children over to the Adeptus Mechanicus – the machine-men – so they can train them to be workers in the manufactoriums, the big dangerous making-places. But I won't let them do it, my baby boy. I won't let them take you. No matter what happens, you can always know your Ma will keep you safe.'*

His heart growing heavy, Boy remembered other things as well. He remembered the sound of thunder rolling across the ground above their heads one night while they crouched huddled in the cellar. He remembered the cave-in and his mother's body lying crushed among the rubble. He remembered her eyes staring at him, cold and dead from a face covered in a thick layer of dust. He remembered crying for hours, scared and lonely, not understanding how it was she could have left him. Then, his own eyes stinging wetly at the corners, Boy found he didn't want to have anything more to do with remembering for a while.

Sucking a breath of air and rubbing the back of his hand across his face to clear his eyes, Boy decided it was time to head back to his warren and get to eating Brother Rat. Too smart to just head there directly in case anyone was looking, he took the long way, cutting a twisting path through the maze of shattered buildings and mounds of rubble all around him. Then, as he crossed near the summit of one of the mounds, he noticed something that gave him pause. A smell, almost. Something gathering on the wind...

For a moment, feeling a sudden chill at the base of his spine, Boy stood looking out toward the east. Before him the city seemed quiet, its deserted streets appearing every bit as dead and life-less as the ruined burnt-out buildings that surrounded them on every turn. Boy was not fooled. After three something years liv-ing alone among the rubble now he had developed a sixth sense when it came to the city and its ways. A sense that, right here and now, told him he had best be wary.

Oughta be getting myself back underground and staying there a while, he thought as he finally turned to make for home. *There's trouble brewing: the wind says it clear and loud. A bad day is com-ing, and like as not a lots of peoples is gonna die...*

'What was life like where you were born?' Larn asked Bulaven, lifting another shovelful of earth onto the blade of his entrench-ing tool as the big man stood beside him. 'On your homeworld, I mean?'

'On Vardan?' Bulaven said, pausing in his work long enough to wipe the sweat from his chapped brow before it could freeze. 'It was good enough I suppose, new fish. Certainly, there are a lot of worse planets a man could be from.'

They were standing in the trench with shovels in their hands, Davir and Scholar beside them while Zeebers stood on the firing step on watch, trying to repair the damage done to the trench in the course of the shelling. Returning to their trench in the after-math of the bombardment, the fire-team had arrived to find the explosion of a nearby shell had caused part of the trench's rear wall to collapse, half-burying the trench interior in clods of frozen earth. Now, after half an hour of backbreaking labour the trench floor was mostly cleared, the excess earth having been piled out of the way into another corner of the trench.

'Personally, I would say you are doing our homeworld a grave disservice, Bulaven,' Davir said, sitting on the end of his shovel and watching them as they moved the last of the fallen earth. 'Frankly, my own recollections suggest Vardan was every bit as much a stinking hellhole as Broucheroc. Granted, we didn't have all these orks to contend with there. I'm sure I don't remember having to do so much digging back home though.'

'I don't seem to have noticed you doing too much digging here either,' Bulaven said. 'Most of the time in fact you have been standing there and leaving all the work to others.'

'Phah. It is a simply a matter of maintaining a proper division of labour,' Davir said. 'Each man performs the task to which he is best suited. Which, in this case, means that you, Scholar, and the new fish do the donkeywork while I oversee your labours in a supervisory capacity. Besides, someone must watch to make sure the new fish can tell one end of a spade from the other.'

'Not to mention your vital role in keeping us all warm,' Larn said, so annoyed now at the ugly dwarf's constant insults that he found himself responding in kind without even thinking. 'Emperor knows, if it wasn't for all your hot air spewing about this trench we might have frozen to death long ago.'

For a moment, shocked at his response, the others looked at him in silence. Then, abruptly, Scholar and Bulaven broke into surprised laughter. Even Davir's face briefly cracked into a grudging smile. Only Zeebers seemed unmoved, scowling down at Larn from the firing step with the same hostile expressions he always wore.

'Hah! Hot air!' Bulaven said, laughing. 'That's a good one. The new fish may not have been here very long, Davir, but you have to admit he got your number fast enough!'

'Yar, yar, yar. Keep on laughing, pigbrain,' Davir said, his gruff demeanour abruptly restored as he turned to look at Larn in tight-lipped derision. 'So, it seems our little puppy has claws. Very good, new fish. Well done. You made a joke. Ha, ha, you are very funny. But don't let your head get too big now. The orks like nothing better than to see a new fish with a big head. It gives them more of a target to aim at.'

The repairs continued. Having finally cleared the trench of earth, they laid down their shovels. Then, as Larn watched them, Bulaven and Scholar picked up an oblong sheet of metal lying across the trench floor and pressed it against the ragged hole in the trench wall, holding upright it as Davir took a wooden prop and used his shovel to hammer the prop in place to keep the sheet in position.

'There,' Davir said, checking the hole was fully covered and putting his weight against the prop to make sure it was tight. 'That should hold it long enough for us to finish the repairs.'

'What now?' Larn asked. 'We have cleared the floor. How do we repair the hole itself?'

'How?' said Davir. 'Well, first thing, you pick up your shovel again, new fish. You see that pile of earth over there?' he said, pointing towards the clods of frozen earth they had already moved over to the corner of the trench. 'The pile you just moved? Well now, you take your shovel and move it back over here. Then, you use it to fill in the original hole. I know, I know, you needn't say it. With all this endless excitement, who can believe that anyone ever told you that life in the Guard might be boring?'

'I don't understand how this is supposed to work,' Larn said later, his hands blistered through his gloves and his back aching from using the shovel as they refilled the hole in the trench wall with soil. 'Even after we have filled the hole in, won't the wall just collapsed again the moment we take the prop away?'

'We don't take the prop away, new fish,' Bulaven said, shovelling beside him. 'Not at first, anyway. First, we fill in the hole. Next, we wet the soil. Then, we tamp it all down and leave it to freeze for a while. Then, after a couple of hours, we finally remove the prop and the wall will be as good as new. Trust me, new fish, it always works. You wouldn't believe how many times we've had to repair this trench since we first dug it.'

'Wet it?' Larn asked. 'Don't we need a bucket then to fetch more water? We haven't got much left in our canteens.'

'Bucket? Canteens?' Bulaven said, pausing in his labours to look at Larn with raised eyebrows. 'We are repairing a trench wall, new fish. We don't use *drinking* water for that.'

'But then, what do we use?' Larn asked, beginning to feel foolish as he realised the others were smirking at him.

'What do we use, he says,' Davir said, rolling his eyes towards the heavens. 'My broad Vardan backside. I swear, new fish, just when I was starting to think you might not be a total idiot you say something stupid and ruin my good opinion of you. If it helps you to answer your question, here are a couple of hints. One, it is always better to use warm water when repairing trench walls in frozen conditions. Two, every human being carries a ready supply of the stuff in question about their person.'

'Warm?' said Larn, a new understanding slowly dawning on him. 'You mean we...'

'Ah, finally, he understands,' Davir said. 'Yes, that's right, new fish. And guess what? It's your turn first. Now, get up there and start pissing. I only hope to hell you haven't got a nervous bladder. Emperor knows, I have better things to do with my time than standing around here waiting for you to piss.'

'What about your own world then, new fish?' Bulaven asked afterwards, as they sat in the trench waiting for the newly repaired wall to freeze. 'You asked me about Vardan before. What was your own homeworld like?'

Trying to think of an answer, for a moment Larn was quiet. He thought about his parents' farm, the endless golden wheatfields swaying in the breeze. He thought of his family, all of them sitting at their places around the table in the kitchen as they made ready for their evening meal. He thought of that last beautiful sunset, the sky reddening as the fiery orb of the descending sun fell slowly towards the horizon. He thought of the world he had left behind, and of all the things he would never see again.

It all seems so long ago and far away now, he thought. *As though all those things were a million kilometres away from me. The sad thing is they are even farther away than that. Not just a million, but millions of millions of kilometres; however far it was we came in that troopship.*

'I don't know,' he said at last, unable to find the words to say what he really felt. 'It was different anyway. A lot different from this place.'

'Hnn. I think our new fish is starting to feel homesick,' Davir said. 'Not that I blame him, you understand, any place would seem rosy when compared to this damn stinkhole. You find me in a strangely magnanimous mood however, new fish, so let me give you a piece of advice. Whatever wistful longings you may harbour for the world of your birth, forget them. This is Broucheroc. There is no room for sentiment here. Here, a man must keep himself hard and tight if we wants to live to see tomorrow.'

'Is that it then?' Larn asked. 'I remember Scholar told me you were all that had survived from over six thousand men. Is that how you did it? By keeping yourselves hard and tight?'

'Ah, now there you have touched upon an interesting question, new fish' Scholar said. 'How was it we survived when so many of our fellows didn't? You can be sure it is a regular topic of conversation hereabouts. Each man has his own opinions. Some say that to have managed to live so long in Broucheroc at all, we must have been born survivors to begin with. Others say it must have been a combination of fate and good judgement, or perhaps only a matter of poor dumb luck. As I say, everyone has their own opinions. Their own theories. For myself, I am not sure I put much store in any of them. We survived where others died. That is all I can tell you.'

'I always thought the Emperor must have had a hand in it,' Bulaven said, his expression quiet and thoughtful. 'That perhaps He was saving us for some greater purpose. At least, that is what I used to believe. After so many years in Broucheroc, a man begins to wonder.'

'The Emperor?' Davir said, throwing his hands up in a gesture of frustration. 'Really, this time you have excelled yourself, Bulaven. Of all the lumpen-headed stupidities I have heard pouring from your mouth over the last seventeen years since we were inducted into the Guard, that is without a doubt the most idiotic. The Emperor! Phah! You think the Emperor has nothing better to do than watch over your fat backside and make sure it comes to no harm? Wake up, you big pile of horse manure. The Emperor doesn't even know we exist. And, if he does know, he doesn't care.'

'No!' Larn shouted, the sudden loudness of his voice in the trench startling them. 'You are wrong. You don't know what you're talking about!' Then, seeing the others looking at him in bewilderment, Larn began to speak again. More quietly now, the words spilling heartfelt from his mouth.

'I am sorry,' he said. 'I didn't mean to yell. But I heard what you were saying and... You are wrong, Davir. The Emperor does care. He watches over all of us. I know he does. And I can prove it. If the Emperor wasn't good and kind and just, he never would have saved my great-grandfather's life.'

And then, as about him the others sat quietly in the trench and listened, Larn told them the same tale his father had told him in the farmhouse cellar on his last night at home.

He told them about his great-grandfather. About how his name was Augustus and he had been born on a world called Arcadus V. He told them about his being called into the Guard, and how sad he had felt at leaving his homeworld. He told them about the thirty years of service and his great-grandfather's failing health.

He told them about the lottery and the man who had given up his ticket. He told them it was a miracle. A quiet miracle, perhaps. But, a miracle all the same. Then, when he had told them all these things word for word the same as his father had told him, Larn fell quiet and waited to hear their reaction.

'And that is it?' Davir said, the first to speak after what felt to Larn like an age of silence. 'That is the proof you talked about? This tale your father told you?'

'It is an interesting story, new fish,' Scholar said, his expression ill at ease.

'Hah! Story is right,' Zeebers said, looking sarcastically down at Larn from up on the firing step. 'A fairy story, like parents tell their children to make them sleep. You believe that crap, new fish, maybe you should go tell your story to the orks and see if a miracle saves you then.'

'Shut up, Zeebers!' Bulaven snapped. 'You're supposed to be on watch, not flapping your lips about. And it is not as though anyone asked for your opinion. Leave the new fish alone.' Then, seeing he had cowed Zeebers to silence, Bulaven turned towards Larn again. 'Scholar was right, new fish. It was a very interesting story, and you told it well.'

'Is that all you are going to say?' Larn asked, surprised. 'You all sound like you think something is wrong. As though you don't believe what I just told you.'

'We don't believe it, new fish,' Davir was blunt. 'Granted, Scholar and Bulaven are trying to be soothing about it. But they don't believe it either. None of us do. Frankly, if the story you just told us is what passes your benchmark for a miracle, you are even more of an innocent than you look.'

'I would have expected you to say that Davir,' Larn said. 'You don't believe in anything. But what about the rest of you? Scholar? Bulaven? Surely you can see that what happened to my great-grandfather was a miracle? That it is proof that the Emperor watches out for us?'

'It is not a matter of believing you,' Scholar said, lifting his shoulders in a helpless shrug. 'It is just that even if we accept the details of your story are true, new fish, those same details are open to a variety of interpretations.'

'Interpretations?' Larn said. 'What are you talking about?

'He is saying you are being naive, new fish,' Davir said. 'Oh, he's doing it in that scholarly way of his, of course – just tip-toeing around the subject rather than coming right out and saying what is on his mind directly. But he thinks you are naive. We all do.'

'You have to understand our experience of life makes us see these things differently,' Scholar said.

'But how is there any different way to see it?' Larn said. 'You heard the story. What about the man giving my great-grandfather his ticket? Surely you can see that must have been the hand of the Emperor at work?'

'Far be it for me to shatter your illusions, new fish,' Davir said. 'But I doubt the hand of the Emperor had anything to do with it. No, likely the only hands involved in it at all would have belonged to your great-grandfather.'

'I... What do you mean?'

'He killed him, new fish,' Davir said. 'The man with the ticket. Your great-grandfather killed him and took his ticket from him. That's your miracle.'

'No,' Larn said, looking quietly from face to face in disbelief. 'You are wrong.'

'Course I can see how it could have happened,' Davir said. 'There's your great-grandfather. He's sick. Ailing. He knows winning the lottery is his only chance of making it out of the Guard alive. Then, when someone else gets the winning ticket, he realises only that one man's life stands between him and freedom. And he was a soldier. He'd killed before. *What is one more life in the grand scale of things*, he tells himself. It's a dog-eat-dog universe, new fish, and it sounds like your great-grandfather was a dirtier dog than most.'

'No,' Larn said. 'You're not listening to me. I'm telling you, you're wrong about this. You are sick, Davir. How could you even think something like that?'

'It is the name, new fish,' Scholar said sadly. 'Or the lack of one, I mean.'

'Yes, the name,' Davir said. 'That's what clinches it.'

'What are you... I don't understand...'

'They're talking about the name of the man who gave your great-grandfather the ticket, new fish,' Bulaven said with a sigh. 'It wasn't part of the story. And you must be able to see that makes all the difference? I am sorry to tell you this, but that is what proves your great-grandfather killed him.'

'The name?' Larn was floundering now, his stomach churning, his head dizzying as though the world about him had suddenly begun to turn strangely on its axis.

'Think about it, new fish,' Davir said. 'This man is supposed to have saved your great-grandfather's life. Your great-grandfather must have known his name. He was a comrade of his, remember? A man who had fought side-by-side with him through thirty years in the Guard? And yet, years later, when your great-grandfather tells the tale to his son he somehow neglects to even mention the name of the man who saved his life? It doesn't add up, new fish. Especially considering you told us your great-grandfather was a pious man. A man like that, if somebody does them a good turn they remember them in their prayers to the Emperor for the rest of their life.'

'It does have the ring of a guilty conscience about it, new fish,' Scholar said. 'Though, if it is any consolation to you, it also suggests your great-grandfather was not given easily to murder. If he'd been a more cold-blooded man, presumably he'd have just told his son the man's name and thought no more about it.'

'Not really, Scholar,' Davir said. 'Even though years had passed by then, he could've still been worried about his crime being found out. Maybe he thought it was better to let bad dogs lie, and never mention the name ever. Either way, it doesn't really make any difference. Your great-grandfather killed the man, new fish, and stole his ticket. That's all there is to it. So much for miracles.'

'No. You've got it wrong,' Larn said. 'There must be another explanation. One you haven't thought of. Surely you can see that my great-grandfather wouldn't have done anything like that?' But as Larn looked at them it was clear to him that was exactly what they did believe. Davir, Scholar, Bulaven, Zeebers. All of them. Looking at the faces of each man in the trench, Larn could see their minds were made up. There had been no miracle. No example of the Emperor's grace. To them, it was a simple matter. His great-grandfather had killed a man, then lied about it afterwards.

'No,' Larn said at last, hating how weak his voice sounded and way it wavered. 'No. You are wrong. You are wrong and I don't believe you.'

CHAPTER TWELVE

Sector Command and the Portents of a Coming
Storm – Larn Sulks – Davir at Last Finds a Reason to
be Cheerful – Meal Time in Barracks Dugout One –
The Culinary Arts as According to Trooper Skench – A
Discussion as to the Advantages of Artillery in the
Hunting of Big Lizards

'Here are the raw contact reports for the last half-hour, sir,' Sergeant Valtys said, holding out a sheaf of papers as thick as his thumb in his outstretched hand. 'You said you wanted to see them immediately, before they were collated.'

Sitting at his desk in his small office at Sector Command Beta (Eastern Divisions, Sectors 1-10 to 1-20), Colonel Kallad Drezlen turned to take the papers from Valtys and begin to read them. *There must be two hundred reports here at least,* he thought. *Each one recording a separate incident of contact with the enemy. Two hundred, when usually at this time of day we would expect to get no more than eighty or so in an hour. It looks like the orks are getting restless hereabouts and that is never a good sign. Something must be coming.*

'How bad is it, Jaak?' he asked, raising his eyes from the reports to look at the sergeant.

'Bad enough, sir,' Valtys replied, still standing ramrod-straight beside the colonel's desk as though he thought he was on a parade ground muster. 'Five of our sectors report coming under heavy shellfire from the orks. Another two report incidents of massed assaults. Then, we have received something like a hundred different reports from across all sectors of contacts ranging from raiding parties to an increase in the number of gretch snipers and scouts in no-man's-land. Looks like there's a real shitstorm brewing, colonel, if you pardon my language.'

'Hhh. You are pardoned, Jaak,' Drezlen said, looking up at the non-com's grizzled face with a quiet amusement born of long familiarity with his ways. 'What about Sector Commands Alpha and Gamma? Are they having the same problem with flying faeces?'

'No and I have to admit that's what put the wind up me, sir. Our neighbouring Sector Commands say they're having a quiet time of it. Too quiet, if you ask me.'

'As though the orks were planning something, you mean?' Drezlen said, his face serious now as he gave voice to the thought hanging communally in the air between them. 'Concentrating their forces here, as though they are about to launch a major offensive?'

'Yes, sir. Course, I know that's not supposed to happen. I know General HQ say the orks aren't smart enough to coordinate something like that. But I've got a metal pin in me, holding my left knee together from the time an ork shot blew a fist-sized hole in it. Ever since I got it, that pin has always started itching whenever the orks were up to something. And right now it's itching worse than a red-arsed monkey that's been sitting in a mound of firebugs.'

'I know what you mean, Jaak,' Drezlen said. 'My gut's the same way. All the same, I wouldn't want to go to General Pronan asking him to order an alert based on the combined evidence of your pin and my digestion. I'll need something a bit weightier than that. Get me the collated statistics and summaries for these contact reports ASAP. Then, I'll go see the general and see if we can get him to take some action.'

'Begging your pardon, sir, but the general's not on site. He still hasn't returned from the Staff Briefing at General HQ.'

'Spectacular,' Drezlen said, sighing in irritation. 'The one time we really need the old man he's off enjoying flatcakes and recaf with Grand Marshal Kerchan. All right, then. Looks like I'll have to be the one to put my head in the cudbear's mouth. Get comms to vox General HQ. Tell them Colonel Drezlen wants to put Sectors 1-10 through to 1-20 on Alert Condition Red.'

'You should try not to take it so much to heart, new fish,' Bulaven had said, going over to join Larn as he sat alone in a corner of the trench. 'So, your great-grandfather killed a man and stole his ticket. What of it? It hardly matters now, does it? It was a long time ago, after all, and anyone it might have been important to is long dead by now.'

'It is not as though we meant anything by it, new fish,' Bulaven had said then, once it had become clear Larn was not going to answer him. 'We were just talking is all. You have to find some way of passing the time in the trenches. So, sometimes we tell stories and afterwards everyone gives their opinion. You have to understand it is nothing personal.'

'Granted, maybe we should not have been so forthright,' Bulaven had said next, while Larn stared fixedly ahead and refused to look at him. 'Your story was important to you, I can see that now. We should have been kinder perhaps.'

'Perhaps you are right, new fish,' Bulaven had said at last. 'Perhaps it was a miracle and we are all full of manure. I am not a preacher. I don't know about such things. But really, new fish, it is making your own life hard on yourself if you just keep sitting there in silence.'

'Ach, leave him, Bulaven,' Davir had said. 'All your feeble-fabbling around the new fish is giving me a headache. If he wants to sulk, let him. Emperor knows, it'll be a damn sight more quiet around here without all his stupid questions.'

* * *

Time passed. Sitting alone in his corner of the trench while Zee-bers stood on watch and the others played cards, Larn found the heat of his anger had slowly cooled. With it, he became gradually aware of other things, sensations that until then had been masked from him by the intensity of the emotions boiling within him ever since the Vardans had defamed his great-grandfather's memory and ridiculed his story of the miracle.

Emperor's tears, but it is cold, Larn thought, suddenly realising he had been sitting in the same spot so long his backside had gone to sleep. Just as he was about to stand and stretch, to move about in the trench in the hope of getting his circulation working, some lingering residue of his anger stopped him.

If I get up and move now the others will think I have forgiven them, he thought, hating how childish the thought made him feel and yet at the same time helpless to resist it. *It would be like giving in*, he thought. *Like I was admitting I believed all the nonsense they talked before about my great-grandfather stealing the ticket*. Then, his anger re-igniting at the thought the others might think him weak, he resolved to sit where he was in silence a while longer.

Of course it doesn't really matter what they think, he thought after some further time had passed. *It doesn't matter if they think I have given in. It doesn't matter whether they think my great-grandfather stole the ticket or murdered anyone. All that matters is that I know those things aren't true. So long as I know that, they can believe whatever they like*. Still, he was not content. Something deep inside him refused to let him move.

They have all been in this place too long, he thought at last. *That's what it is. That is why they see dark motives in everything and can't accept the fact of miracles. Really, it is not even a matter of forgiving them. I should feel sorry for them. Not angry*.

Then, just as he had all but finally summoned the will to swallow his pride and move, Larn heard the sound of a shrill whistle that seemed to come from the direction of the dugouts.

'Ach, at last,' Davir said, as around him the other men began to stand and collect their weapons. 'It's about time. I have been getting so hungry sitting here I was beginning to think about eating Scholar's boots.'

'Really?' said Scholar mildly, checking to see if he still had his book with him. 'And there was perhaps some special reasons you were considering eating my boots rather than your own, Davir?'

'What, you think I should eat my own boots and risk getting frostbite?' Davir said. 'No thank you, Scholar. Besides, you have such big feet there would be plenty of boot to go around. Happily though, we seem to have averted that particular catastrophe. Time to get to the barracks and see what culinary pleasures are awaiting us.'

'Come on then, new fish,' Bulaven said, standing over Larn. 'If you are last to the mess line there won't be much left for you.'

'You mean it is meal time?' Larn asked.

'A meal, yes,' Bulaven said. 'And a two-hour rest-period as well. They rotate us off the line in groups of ten fire-teams at a time. One whistle means it is Barracks Dugout One's turn. Our turn. Now, come on, new fish. The food will be getting cold.'

'Yes, come on, new fish,' Davir said. 'Believe me, you think your day has been bad enough so far? Well, you haven't tasted Trooper Skench's cooking yet.'

After so long in the cold of the trench, the interior of Barracks Dugout One seemed warm and inviting to him now. So inviting, in fact, that Larn found he barely even noticed the stifling stench of smoke and stale sweat that permeated the air of the dugout. Inside, a line of Guardsmen had already formed up by the time they arrived. Waiting, with mess tins in their hands, as a lanky rat-faced Vardan trooper with only one arm dolefully served out portions of gruel from a battered and gigantic pot from on top of the stove.

'Ah, the inestimable Skench,' Davir purred as he reached the head of the line. 'Tell me, good friend Skench – what delightful delicacy are you attempting to poison us with today?'

'Hhh. It's gruel, Davir,' Skench said sourly. 'Why? What does it look like?'

'Between you and me, I wasn't entirely sure,' Davir said as he watched Skench ladle a steaming dollop into his mess tin. 'Gruel, you say? And you have followed your normal recipe, I take it? Sawdust, spittle, and whatever dubious organic refuse you could lay your hands on?'

'Pretty much,' said Skench, humourlessly. 'Though you can be sure I made certain you got an extra helping of spit in yours.'

'Why thank you, Skench,' Davir said, favouring the one-armed cook with his most irritating smile. 'Really, you are spoiling me. I must remember to write to Grand Marshal Kerchan and recommend you for a commendation. If you got a nice medal it would give you something extra to put in the soup.'

'Hhh. Always the funny man, Davir,' Skench muttered, watching Davir walk away. Then, turning back to see Larn standing next in line, he squinted at him in wary hostility.

'I haven't seen you before,' Skench said. 'You a new fish?'

'Yes,' said Larn.

'Uh-huh. You got something funny to say about my cooking, new fish?'

'Umm... no.'

'Good,' Skench said, dropping a ladleful of greasy brown gruel into Larn's tin, then nodding towards a pile of ration bars lying on a nearby table. 'Make sure you keep it that way. As well as the gruel you get to take a ration bar. *One* bar, mind, new fish. I've counted them, so don't try taking two. Oh, and if tonight you should have the runs, don't do what the rest of them do and come round here blaming me. There ain't nothing wrong with my cooking. We clear on that?'

'Uhh... yes. We're clear.'

'Good. Then get moving, new fish. You're holding up the line.

And remember what I told you. There ain't nothing wrong with my cooking.'

'This is disgusting,' Larn said. 'Really disgusting, I mean. I thought the food they gave us in basic training on Jumael was bad enough. But this is ten times worse.'

'Well, I did warn you, new fish,' Davir said, as he shovelled another spoonful of gruel into his own mouth. 'Such is Skench's extraordinary mastery of the culinary arts, he can make bad food taste even worse.'

Having collected his ration bar, Larn now sat with Davir, Bulaven and Scholar among the bunks inside the barracks. Meanwhile, still occasionally glowering at Larn as though to assure him his feelings of hostility had not waned, Zeebers sat alone and apart from them against one of the dugout walls. Though, while he still wondered at the source of Zeebers's strange antagonism towards him, Larn found he was more directly concerned at that moment with the small white shape he saw wriggling among the slop in his mess tin.

'There is some kind of maggot in my food,' he said.

'A Tullan's worm-grub,' Scholar said. 'They are quite plentiful hereabouts, new fish. And an excellent source of protein.'

'They add to the flavour as well,' Bulaven said. 'But make sure you chew up your food properly. If the grub is still alive when you swallow it they can lay eggs in your stomach.'

'Eggs?'

'Don't worry about it, new fish,' Bulaven replied. 'It's not as bad as it sounds. Gives you the runs for a couple of days, that is all. Course, if Skench cooked them properly, the grubs would be dead by the time they got to us.'

'Sweet Emperor, I can't believe you act like it is normal to eat things like this,' Larn said.

'Normal?' Davir said, mouth open to reveal a mashed lump of half-chewed gruel. 'In case you hadn't notice you're in the

Imperial Guard, new fish. And in the Guard you eat what you can get. Anyway, you think this is bad you should've seen the whipsaw grubs we had to eat on Bandar Majoris.'

'Actually, I seem to remember they were quite flavoursome, Davir,' Scholar said. 'Tasted a bit like ginny fowl.'

'I'm not talking about how they tasted, Scholar,' Davir said. 'I'm talking about the fact they were as big as your leg with a metre-long tongue covered in razor-sharp barbs. Not to mention they were strong enough to tear a man's arm off. And if you want know *how* we know that, new fish, just go ask Skench.'

'Don't listen to him. He is just fooling with you, new fish,' Bulaven said. 'It was an ork axe that did for Skench's arm right here in Broucheroc, not a whipsaw grub on Bandar Majoris. Though we did lose a lot of men to those grubs.'

'Do you remember Commissar Grisz?' Scholar said. 'Went behind a bush one morning to see to his daily bowel movement only to find he was squatting over a whole nest of the damned things. You could have heard his scream halfway across the planet.'

'Phah. Good riddance to bad rubbish,' Davir said. 'Grisz always was a pain in the arse. No pun intended.'

'You ask me,' Bulaven said, 'the thing I remember most from Bandar is Davir hunting the terranosaurs.'

'Ah yes,' Scholar said. 'You mean the wager.'

'Ach, you're not still going on about that, Bulaven,' Davir scowled. 'Emperor wept. Once a man wins a bet against you, you never forgive him.'

'You should have seen it, new fish,' Bulaven said, smiling. 'We'd been on Bandar a week maybe, at most. It is a jungle planet and there were these deathworlders. Ach, you tell it, Scholar – you always do a better job of it than me.'

'All right, then,' Scholar said, leaning intently forward. 'Imagine the scene, new fish. It is midday; the jungle is hot and humid. We have come back into camp after being out on patrol when we smell the most delicious and mouth-watering aroma. Following our noses we find a group of Catachans are roasting a metre-and-a-half long two-legged lizard on an open spit. Naturally, we enquire whether we can join in their feast. But, being Catachans, they refuse. "Go catch your own terranosaur," they say. Now, you thought that would have been the end of it. But Davir refuses to let matters rest. Soon, he begins bragging to us that he is more than capable of capturing a terranosaur just as the Catachans had. And, before you could say *small man, big mouth* we have agreed to enter into a wager with him on the matter.'

'He bet us he could hunt down a terranosaur, new fish,' Bulaven jumped in excitedly. 'He bet us a hundred credits he could hunt one, kill it, and bring it home for dinner.'

'So,' Scholar continued, 'armed with a lasgun, our intrepid, if diminutive, hunter goes alone into the jungle in search of his prey. Only to re-emerge two hours later, running back into camp in a panic as though he had a daemon on his trail!'

'Ach, you and Bulaven can laugh all you like,' Davir said, holding a hand high above his head like a fisherman describing the size of his catch. 'But nobody told me the one the Catchans killed was only a baby, and that the adults were ten metres tall when full-grown. Or, for that matter, that they hunted in packs. I tell you: I only got out of that damn stinking jungle by the skin of my teeth. And, besides, you have to admit I did what I said I'd do in the end. I did kill a terranosaur and I did bring it home for dinner. About three of them, in fact.'

'Only because you bribed someone in comms to let you call in an artillery strike against them!' Bulaven said, outraged. 'Then, after the batteries had been pounding that patch of jungle for an hour straight, you got a search party together and brought back the remains of all the terranosaurs that had been killed by the shellfire. That doesn't count, Davir.'

'Of course, it counts. What, you think I should have dug a pit trap like some idiot deathworlder and waited for one of the big dumb beasts to wander by and fall into it? I keep telling you, Bulaven: you should have been more specific about the conditions of the bet. You didn't say anything about not being able to use artillery.'

The argument continued: Davir and Bulaven squabbling comically about the details of the decade-old bet while Scholar attempted to act as arbiter. As he listened to them, Larn became aware of how different the three men's manner had become since the whistle had blown and they had come to the dugout. Here, they did not seem as gruff and intimidating. They seemed more relaxed. More at ease with themselves and their surroundings.

Looking around, Larn saw it was the same everywhere. All about him he could see Vardans talking, joking and laughing amongst themselves, their faces animated, their gestures more free and expansive. It was almost as though here in the dugout, for the moment at least, there were no orks. No constant threat of death. No Broucheroc. Here, the Vardans seemed almost like the people Larn had known back home. As though, momentarily released of the shadow of war and horror, they had reverted to their true selves.

As he watched them, Larn began to understand for the first time that each of the Vardans had once been like him. Each of them had been a green recruit. Each of them had once been a new fish and he realised there was hope for him in that thought. If each of these men had somehow learned how to survive the brutalities and privations of this place, then so could he. He would learn. And he would survive.

And then, comforted by that warm and happy thought, before he even knew it, Larn was asleep.

CHAPTER THIRTEEN

A Mosaic Coloured in Blues, Greens, and Reds – A
Dream of Home – A Bombardment Again – Zeebers's
Behaviour is Perhaps Explained – Sergeant Chelkar
Rallies the Troops – The Myth of The Big Push

'You ordered us to Alert Condition Red!' the general roared, his
voice so loud that the Guardsmen and militia auxiliaries seated
at their work stations around them in the Situation Room gave a
collective jump. 'Have you taken leave of your senses?'

'If you would allow me to explain, sir,' Colonel Drezlen said, his
expression tight as he stood facing the older man, fighting visibly to keep his own temper in check.

'Explain?' General Pronan thundered. 'What is there to explain?
You have grossly exceeded your authority, colonel. I could have
you court-martialled for this.'

'I had no choice, sir,' Drezlen said. 'We were faced with an
emerging situation, and you were elsewhere–'

'Don't try and lay the blame for this debacle at my door, Drezlen.' The general's cheeks grew florid with rage. 'You will only
end up making matters worse for yourself, you hear me? I know
very well I was away from Sector Command. I was at General
Headquarters, where fortunately I was made aware of your alert
order in time to quash it before all hell could let loose.'

'You... *quashed* it?' Drezlen said, appalled. 'You countermanded the alert?'

'Of course I did. Have you any idea of the fuss an alert order can cause? Troops are seconded from other sectors all across the city; extra supplies are sent up; reserve units are brought forward to the front. Sweet Emperor, man! Don't you know a sector has to be on the verge of being overrun before an order to go to Alert Condition Red is warranted? Never mind the fact that, by issuing an alert on your own authority, you violated the chain of command!'

'You countermanded the alert,' Drezlen said quietly, his face ashen. 'I can't believe it...'

'Yes. And by doing it I likely saved you from a firing squad,' the volume of the general's voice had fallen, his manner growing more composed as his anger abated. 'But you can thank me for that later, Drezlen. First, I want you to start giving me some answers.'

'Answers?' Drezlen was curt. 'Very well, general. Let me give you all the answers you could want.' He turned towards a nearby Guardsman seated beside a control panel covered in dials and switches. 'Corporal Venner? Activate the pict-display and bring up the current situation map for our sectors. Let us see if we can show the general exactly why I believed we had reached Alert Condition Red status.'

At the flick of a switch the large rectangular pict-display set into one of the Situation Room's walls suddenly hummed into life, a small white dot appearing in the middle of the black screen before expanding to cover its entire surface. Then, as Corporal Venner worked another series of switches, the situation map for Sectors 1-10 through 1-20 appeared on screen. A mosaic coloured in blues, greens, and reds: blue for the areas under Imperial control; green for the parts held by the orks; red for the territories whose ownership was currently being contested.

'I don't understand,' the general said, looking up at the pict-display in confusion. 'I don't remember seeing all this red on the board when I left for General Headquarters this morning.'

'Matters have developed considerably since then, general,' Drezlen said. 'As of fifteen minutes ago no less than *ten* of the eleven sectors under your command are currently being attacked by the orks. In each case, the pattern is the same: massed assaults preceded by lengthy bombardment by enemy artillery, as well as coordinated attacks on vital facilities by gretchin suicide bombers and ork troops. Currently, it is unclear how many of these assaults are the real thing and how many are intended only as diversions to put pressure on our resources.'

'Diversions? Lengthy bombardments? Coordinated attacks?' the general's expression was incredulous. 'Have you lost your mind, man? You're talking as though the enemy were working to some kind of coherent plan of action. For the Emperor's sake, these are orks we are talking about! They don't have the brains or organisational ability to put anything like that in motion.'

'Be that as it may, sir, it appears that is *precisely* what they are doing. So far, we are holding on by our fingernails. But if you want to see just how *bad* things here could get, take a look at Sector 1-13.'

'1-13?' the general said. 'What are you talking about Drezlen? The situation map says Sector 1-13 is blue.'

'Yes, sir. And what is more, it is the only sector that has yet to be attacked. And I ask you, leaving aside for a moment the fact that our enemies are orks, what does that suggest to you?'

'You don't mean?' the general blustered. 'But that is impossible, colonel...'

'Ordinarily I would agree, sir. But there seems to be a pattern here. And, given that pattern, we have to ask why would the orks launch a major offensive against every sector to the side of it and leave Sector 1-13 unmolested? Unless what we are seeing on the situation map are only the opening moves of a larger assault intended to tie up our forces and allow the orks a clear run at their *real* target. Imagine it, general: if the orks were to launch a full-scale assault on Sector 1-13 now, there would be precious little we could do to stop them achieving a sector-wide breakthrough.'

'But if that happened, our forces in other sectors would have to retreat or risk being cut off. It could turn into a rout. No. It is just not possible, Drezlen. They are orks. Savages. They are not clever enough to have...'

For a moment, turning to gaze intently at the pict-display before him the general fell quiet. Watching the old man's troubled face as he silently wrestled with all he had heard, Colonel Drezlen felt a sudden sympathy for him. General Pronan was an old school solider, thoroughly indoctrinated by his forty years in the Guard in the belief that all aliens were little better than animals. The idea he might have been outmanoeuvred by them, and by orks for that matter, would be hard for him to swallow but it was a matter of evidence. Slowly, Drezlen saw a grim look of resolve come over the general's face. He had made his decision.

'All right, then' the general said at last. 'Let us assume for the sake of argument your theory is correct. Can we reinforce Sector 1-13?'

'No, sir. As I say, all our forces are tied up fighting off the orks in other sectors.'

'What about our forces already inside Sector 1-13? Who do we have stationed there?'

'Company Alpha, the 902nd Vardan Rifles, commanded by Sergeant Eugin Chelkar.'

'A single company?' the general's voice was a dry whisper. 'Commanded by a sergeant? That's all we have? But, Holy Throne, if you are right and the attack comes–'

'Yes, sir,' Colonel Drezlen said. 'If that happens, then two hundred and something Guardsmen are all that stands between us and this entire map going green.'

He dreamed of home. He dreamed of spring: the earth of the fields wet and rich as the seeds were planted. He dreamed of summer: the sky blue and endless overhead as rows of golden wheat grew ripe below it. He dreamed of autumn: the same sky now thick with lazy smoke from the burning of the stubble after the harvesting was done. He dreamed of winter: the fields dizzyingly empty, the ground hard with frost. He dreamed, his dreams a jumbled montage of people, places, memories, recollections.

He dreamed of home.

He dreamed of the days of his youth. Of the change of the seasons. Of happiness, peace and contentment.

And then, he awoke to hell once more.

Starting awake at the sound of an explosion overheard, for an instant Larn had no idea where he was. Gazing blearily about him in confusion, he recognised the dugout and realised he must have fallen asleep on one of the bunks while the others were talking. Then, he heard another explosion much louder than the first and looked up to see a thin trickle of soil fall downwards through the gap between two of the wooden planks that made up the dugout's inner ceiling.

'That was a close one,' he heard Bulaven's voice say calmly. 'I wouldn't like to be above ground in the middle of this one.'

Becoming fully awake, Larn realised he had inadvertently fallen asleep on top of his mess tin. Wiping away a chunk of congealed gruel that had stuck to his uniform, he turned to see the Vardans were still gathered nearby. Bulaven sat in one bunk rubbing dubbing into his boots; Scholar sat in another reading his book; while, incredibly, despite the now continuous roar of explosions overheard, Davir lay in another bunk sound asleep.

'Ah, you are awake, new fish,' Bulaven said, gesturing up with his thumb toward the ceiling at the sound of more explosions overhead. 'I can't say I am surprised. They are making enough noise up there to wake the dead.'

'They are shelling us again?' Larn asked. 'Our own side, I mean?'

'Hmm? Oh no, new fish,' Bulaven said. 'It is the orks this time.

If you listen closely you can hear the difference, ork shells have a duller sound to them when they explode. Still, you needn't worry. These dugouts are built to last. We should be quite safe so long as we are in here.'

'Unless, of course, a shell scores a direct hit on the dugout's ventilation chimney,' Scholar raised his eyes from his book. 'Even if the shell doesn't break through it, the chimney is still likely to funnel the explosion down here.'

'True,' Bulaven said. 'Ach, but that hardly ever happens, new fish. You needn't worry about that. Anyway, this bombardment won't last long. The orks have no staying power when it comes to these things, you see. Chances are whichever ork is in charge of their big guns has become overexcited for some reason and has decided to let off a few rounds in celebration. Trust me, new fish, in ten minutes' time or so it will all be over.'

'How long has it been now,' Larn asked, listening to the muffled thud and whump of shells striking the ground above the dugout.

'About an hour, I'd say,' Bulaven shrugged, now busy cleaning the trigger mechanism of his heavy flamer. 'Maybe three-quarters. Looks like the orks must be very excited. Still, I wouldn't worry too much about it. Don't let it ruin your barracks time, new fish. They are bound to get tired of shelling us sooner or later.'

Finding himself far from reassured, Larn looked upward to see another trickle of soil falling from the gaps between the wooden planks of the ceiling. Remembering a dream of tattered crones standing around his grave as shovelfuls of earth hit his face, Larn felt an involuntary shiver run through him. *Those explosions sound close*, he thought. *What if one of the shells hits the dugout entrance and we are trapped down here? Would anyone on the surface be able to dig us out? Would they even try? Sweet Emperor, it might be better if what Scholar talked about happened instead and a shell hit the ventilation chimney. At least then it would be quick. You would be dead before you knew it. Not buried alive in this tomb of a dugout, waiting for your air to run out or to slowly die of thirst and starvation.*

Abruptly, realising his nerves were beginning to shred at the constant sound of explosions and the thought of what those explosions might cause, Larn begin to scan the interior of the dugout in search of something – anything – to take his mind from what was going on above them. Around him, the dugout had become crowded with men who had taken refuge from the shelling. Among them he saw Sergeant Chelkar, Medical Officer Svenk, and some of the men from Repzik's fire-team. While the din of explosions continued overhead, here life inside the dugout seemed to be proceeding just as it had before the shelling started. He saw Vardans eating, talking, laughing, drinking recaf; some of them even trying to sleep like Davir. Then, Larn noticed Zeebers was still sitting alone against one of the dugout walls, idly tossing a knife around in his hand to catch first the blade, then the hilt.

Watching Zeebers playing with his knife, Larn felt a sudden urge to have the answer to a question that had been gnawing at him ever since he had first met the man.

'Bulaven?' he asked. 'Before, remember when you told me that I shouldn't worry too much at the things Davir said? That it was just his way?'

'Of course I remember, new fish,' Bulaven said. 'Why do you bring it up?'

'Well, I was wondering about Zeebers...' Abruptly Larn paused, uncertain how best to broach the subject.

'Zeebers, new fish? What about him?'

'I think he has noticed that Zeebers has been showing a certain hostility towards him, Bulaven,' Scholar said, raising his eyes from his book once more to look at Larn. 'I am right, yes, new fish? That is what you were about to ask?'

'Ah, I see,' said Bulaven. 'Well, there is no great secret there, new fish. Zeebers just gets nervous whenever there are any more than four men in our fire-team.'

'Nervous?' asked Larn. 'Why?'

'It is a matter of superstition with him,' Scholar said. 'Apparently, on Zeebers's homeworld the number four is considered lucky. Then, when he first came to Broucheroc and joined us there were only three men left in our fire-team – Bulaven, Davi, and myself. Hence, Zeebers was the fourth man, lucky number four to his mind, and he has convinced himself that is how he survived his first fifteen hours – not to mention how he has survived ever since. So, you see, whenever they send us a new replacement and there are five men in the fire-team he tends to believe his luck has become endangered somehow. You remember before I said every man here has his own theory as to how he survived where so many others have died? Zeebers's beliefs are but another example of the same thing.'

'You see, new fish, no great mystery,' Bulaven said, before abruptly turning his head to look over at another part of the dugout. 'Hmm, looks like something is brewing.'

Following the direction of Bulaven's gaze, Larn saw Sergeant Chelkar standing deep in conversation with Corporal Vladek by the quartermaster's table in the corner of the barracks. Then, while Sergeant Chelkar walked away to talk to someone else, Vladek turned to open a wooden crate beside him and, one-by-one, began to carefully pull out a number of heavy demolitions charges and stack them on the table before him. As he did, Larn noticed that Bulaven's face had grown suddenly uneasy as though the big man had seen something in Vladek's actions to worry him.

'What is it, Bulaven?' he asked. 'What have you seen?'

'A bad sign, new fish,' Bulaven said. 'Between me and you, a very bad sign indeed.'

'We are at Alert Condition Red,' Chelkar said, his face grave as he addressed the Guardsmen standing before him while overhead the sound of explosions continued. 'Sector Command says we can expect an assault. A big one, probably timed to begin the moment this bombardment ends. Looks like the orks are going to hit us hard this time. Leastways, harder than any of the other attacks we've had to deal with today.'

A few minutes had passed and in the wake of his conversation with the quartermaster, Sergeant Chelkar had ordered the men in Barracks Dugout One to arm themselves and assemble around the iron stove for an impromptu briefing. Scholar, Bulaven, Davir, Zeebers, the other fire-teams, even Vladek and the one-armed cook Skench, stood in their battle gear listening intently to Chelkar's words, their expressions every bit as grave and serious as their sergeant's. Looking about him, Larn saw that the easy and relaxed manner with which these men had enjoyed their time in the barracks was gone now. They were soldiers once more. Guardsmen. They were ready for war.

'I won't lie to you,' Chelkar said. 'Things look grim. Every other sector in the area is under heavy assault and all reserve units are tied up elsewhere. Which means no there is no potential for reinforcements – at least not for several hours. Worse, Battery Command is already tasked to the limit, so we can't expect artillery support either. We still have our own mortars, of course, and our fire support teams but, other than that, we are on our own.

'Now for the good news. Sector Command has made it clear that if we lose here there is the danger of a major ork breakthrough into the city. Accordingly, they have ordered that we are to hold this sector at all costs. *Stand or die*, they say. No matter how many orks come at us or how hard they hit us, we are to hold on until we are reinforced, the ork assault fails, or the Emperor descends to fight alongside us – whichever one of those comes first. We hold the line. I don't care if hell itself comes calling. We hold the line no matter what. Not that we have much choice here anyway, you understand. You all know what happens if we retreat. The commissars don't even bother with a court martial any more: it's just a bullet in the back of the head and a place on the corpse-pyres. This is Broucheroc: between the orks and our own commanders, there's just nowhere else left for us to go.

'As for our plan of defence, I have ordered Vladek to distribute four extra frag grenades to each man and one demolition charge per fire-team. Once the assault begins we will hold the forward firing trenches for as long as possible, only retreating to the dugout emplacements when the situation there becomes untenable. Then, once we're at the dugout emplacements we will make a stand. That's as far as we go. After that, it's hold the line or die.

'Are there any questions?'

No one spoke. Silently, the Guardsmen stood gazing back at their sergeant with resolve and determination etched into every line of their faces. For better or worse, they were ready.

'All right, then,' said Chelkar. 'We have been in this situation often enough before to make saying anything else irrelevant. You all know what is ahead of us. I will say only this. Good luck to every one of you. And, fates willing, let us all see each other again when the battle is over.'

'Maybe it is The Big Push,' Larn heard one of the Vardans say as he hung the extra grenades Vladek had given him on his belt and went over to join the other members of Fire-team Three. 'Emperor knows, it was bound to happen sometime.'

'It can't be,' said another man nearby. 'General Headquarters would have told us.'

'Phah. You are fooling yourself,' a third man said. 'The damn generals refuse to even admit The Big Push exists. When it finally does come they'll be caught as much by surprise as the rest of us.'

The Big Push. By then Larn had heard the phrase used several times already, whispered amongst themselves by grim-faced Guardsmen as they stood in the dugout making final adjustments to their weapons and equipment as the bombardment continued above them. Each time he heard it, Larn found something in the tone of the way they said the phrase that made him uneasy.

It was a tone, he realised, of nervousness and quiet anxiety. *The tone of fear*, he thought with a sudden shudder.

'Bulaven?' he asked the big man beside him. 'What is The Big Push?'

For a moment the Vardan was silent, his usually affable manner replaced by the bleak and brooding expression of a parent who realises he can no longer protect his child from the dark realities of the world.

'It is a bad thing, new fish,' Bulaven said. 'A story you could call it, I suppose. Or a myth. You know when the preachers talk in church of the Last Judgement when the Emperor will finally step forward from His throne once more and judge humanity for its sins? The Big Push is like that.'

'It is something in the manner of a folktale,' Scholar said, standing next to him. 'The Big Push is the mythic apocalypse that every Guardsman in this city dreads. A Day of Judgement, as Bulaven puts it, when the orks will at last mount their long-expected final assault and the city of Broucheroc will fall. It is a nightmare, new fish. The one thing that the defenders of this city fear more than anything else. And, as such, I am not surprised you heard it mentioned. For the orks to launch so many assaults across different sectors at once and coordinate them with artillery bombardment is highly unusual. So unusual in fact that it is easy to see in it the portent of something larger.'

'The Big Push is bullshit, new fish,' Davir said. 'A story that the mothers of this city scare their children to sleep with, nothing more. Put it from your mind.'

At that, they became silent and, looking at the faces of his companions, Larn saw the same thing there as had been hidden in the whispers of the men he had heard discussing The Big Push to begin with.

He saw fear.

And he was not reassured.

CHAPTER FOURTEEN

Bookkeeping and the Tragedy of War – Matters of Tactics
while Waiting for an Eternity to Pass – Preparations
and Preludes in the Trenches – Holding the Line – Shot
in the Head and Saved by Davir – Last Stand by the
Dugouts – The Sound of Salvation

For Captain Arnol Yaab it had been a long and tiring day. A day
spent like every other day of the last ten years in a cramped win-
dowless office in the lower levels of the General Headquarters
building in the centre of Broucheroc, ceaselessly compiling the
twice-daily Imperial Guard casualty statistics from the reports
and logs of the various Sectors Command throughout the city.

Sector 1-11, he wrote in a neat and ordered hand in the pages of
the ledger before him. *12th Coloradin Rifle Corps. Commanding
Officer: Colonel Wyland Alman. Previous Strength: 638 men. Total
Casualties in Last Twelve Hour Period: 35 men. Current Adjusted
Strength: 603 men. Percentage Loss: 5.49%.*

Sector 1-12, he continued, carefully allowing the ink time to
dry so as not to risk smudging the previous entry. *35th Zuve-
nian Light Foot. Commanding Officer: Captain Yiroslan Dacimol
(Deceased). Previous Strength: 499 men. Total Casualties in Last
Twelve Hour Period: 43 men. Adjusted Strength: 456 men. Percentage Loss: 8.62%.*

*Sector 1-13. 902nd Vardan Rifles. Commanding Officer: Sergeant
Eugin Chelkar (Temporary Appointment). Previous Strength: 244*

men. Total Casualties in Last Twelve Hour Period: 247 men. Current Adjusted Strength: –3. Percentage Loss: 101.23%.

Abruptly, gazing down at the entry he had just written, Yaab became aware that there seemed to be some problem with his figures. *101.23%? That cannot be right*, he thought. *How can a unit have lost more than one hundred per cent of its original strength and be reduced to a current adjusted strength of minus three? It is an impossibility. How can you have minus three men?*

Pursing his lips in annoyance, Captain Yaab re-checked the figures in the Sector Command Beta casualty log. There, in black and white, the same statistic was confirmed. Out of a total strength of 244 men, the 902nd Vardan had somehow conspired to lose no less than 247 of their number in the last twelve hours. Then, just as deep in his pen-pusher's soul he began to fear he had made an error that would see him reprimanded – or worse – posted to the frontlines, Yaab noticed a sheet of paper clipped to the back of the log and realised he had perhaps found the source of the mistake.

It was a supplementary report, recording that a lander had crash-landed in Sector 1-13 at around midday and deposited an additional 235 Guardsmen into the sector. *Ah, now that would account for the discrepancy*, Yaab thought, making a quick series of mental calculations. *An extra 235 men would put the total strength of the sector at 479. Then, the loss of 247 men would leave us with a current adjusted strength of 232, constituting a percentage loss of 51.57%. All in all, a much more acceptable figure.*

Happy again, Captain Yaab adjusted his ledger in line with the new calculations only to find himself aggravated once more as he noticed the unsightly mess the alterations had made to the clean, well-ordered columns of his figures. Sighing as he returned to compiling his statistics, Yaab tried to take comfort from the thought that it could not be helped. It was the tragedy of his life that certain amount of unsightliness was to be expected.

War, after all, could be a messy business.

* * *

'Switch your comm-bead to our command net on frequency five,' Bulaven told Larn through the roar of shellfire shaking the ground above them. 'You will know we are about to go when the shelling stops. Then, when we get the order, we run back to our firing trench. No crouching or trying to stay in cover this time, new fish. You just sprint there as fast as you can. We have to be back in the trench and ready to shoot before the orks reach the kill zone at the three hundred metre mark.'

They were standing with the rest of the Vardans next to the steps leading from the dugout up to the surface. As his fingers fiddled to change the frequency of the comm-bead in his ear, Larn's mind turned to a lesson he had learned in his last battle. *This is the worst time*, he thought. *While you are waiting for the attack to start, before the battle even begins. Once the fighting is underway you are still afraid. But it is having time to think about what is coming that makes the fear worse. And the orks would seem to know it. They are giving us plenty of time to dwell on our fears. Right now, it feels like waiting for an eternity to pass.*

'All right, new fish,' Bulaven said. 'Now, I have told you everything you need to know about what we are going to do after that. I want you to tell it back to me now so I can be sure you have understood it.'

Can he see that I am afraid, Larn thought. *Is that it? Is he trying to keep me busy and take my mind off the fact we could all be dead in a matter of minutes? And if Bulaven can see it what about the rest of them? Are they all standing here watching me wondering if I am going to turn and run? Do they think I am a coward?*

'Our tactics, new fish?' Bulaven prodded. 'What are they?'

'Once we reach the firing trench we will hold it as long as we can,' Larn said, silently praying to the Emperor his voice did not sound as frightened and nervous as he suspected. 'Then, if it looks like we are going to be overrun, Scholar will set the demolition charge to buy us enough time to fall back. You will be carrying the flamer, I will be carrying a spare fuel canister for you, Davir and Zeebers will give us covering fire with their lasguns.'

'And if any of us are dead by then?' Bulaven asked. 'Or too badly wounded to move on their own? What then, new fish?'

'Then the three most important things are the demolition charge, the flamer, and the spare fuel canister, in that order. Other than that we will help the wounded if we can. If not, we will leave them behind.'

'Remember that one, new fish. It is important. Now, where will we fall back to?'

'To the sandbag emplacement above this dugout,' Larn said, repeating everything Bulaven had drilled into him while they waited for the shelling to stop. 'After that, it is like Sergeant Chelkar was saying. We do not fall back any farther. Once we are at the emplacements, we stand or die.'

'Very good, new fish,' Davir said sarcastically from the side of them. 'It sounds like you have got it.'

Abruptly, the shellfire stopped. The brief silence that followed it felt strange and eerie after so long a bombardment.

'Go! Go! Go!' Sergeant Chelkar yelled, as beside him Vladek threw open the door to the dugout and the assembled Vardans ran pell-mell up the steps toward the surface. 'Get to your trenches!'

Before he even knew it Larn was above ground, emerging blinking into the cold grey light of the sun outside to turn and sprint towards the firing trench with Bulaven and the others beside him as the rest of the Vardans spread out to run for their own positions. Then, with barely a few metres gone, he heard Corporal Grishen's voice in his ear through his comm-bead.

'Auspex reports activity in the enemy lines,' Grishen said, frantic through a squall of static. 'The orks are moving.'

Larn could already see them. On the other side of no-man's-land, a horde of orks had risen up and were now charging screaming towards them. For a moment Larn heard a still small voice in his head questioning what he was doing, running towards the orks when every fibre of his being told him he should be running away from them as fast as his legs could take him but he ignored it. Ignored it and raced instead towards the trench to take his place with the other members of the fire-team as they made ready to repel the assault.

'Five hundred metres,' Scholar said, already squinting at the oncoming orks through a targeter by the time Larn threw himself into the trench and took his place on the firing step beside Bulaven.

'Remember, new fish,' Bulaven said. 'When you hear the order to fall back, you grab a spare fuel canister and stay close to me.'

'Yes, new fish,' Davir said from across him. 'And while you're at it, don't go losing your lasgun again. I will let you into a secret: your helmet is for protecting your head, not for the hitting of gretchin. Now, get ready, puppy. Time to show the orks your claws.'

'Four hundred metres,' Scholar said.

Remembering this time to click off the safety catch, Larn hurriedly ran through his pre-battle ritual, silently reciting the Litany of the Lasgun in his mind before adding a quick prayer to the Emperor for good measure. Beside him he saw Davir, Scholar and Zeebers sighting in on the orks, while to the side of them Bulaven checked the pump pressure on his flamer. Then, from behind him, he heard the sound of mortars being fired and knew the battle was about to begin in earnest.

'Three hundred metres,' Scholar yelled. 'On my mark... fire!'

Lasbeams. Mortars. Auto-cannon rounds. Frag missiles. From all across the line the Vardans opened up with everything they had. All the while, as Davir, Scholar and Zeebers fired their lasguns from the side of him Larn fired with them, remembering to aim high for the orks as Repzik had once told him. And through it all, the orks kept coming.

There are more of them this time, Larn thought. *Ten times more at least than when I was in the trench with Repzik. Sweet Emperor! And we barely managed to hold out then!*

'One hundred and twenty metres,' Scholar said, the orks having seemed to cover the intervening distance between them with impossible swiftness. 'Change magazines and switch to rapid fire.'

The orks came closer. Some of them were already gruesomely wounded by the Vardans' remorseless hail of fire, all of them were red-eyed and eager in an apparently endless barbaric tide.

'Fifty metres,' Scholar's voice counted down calmly. 'Forty metres. Thirty.'

'Any time now would be good, fatman,' Davir said to Bulaven. 'Are you actually going to use that damn flamer, or just wait until the orks get close enough for you to try and fart them to death instead?'

In response, Bulaven lifted the nozzle of the flamer, extending himself to his full height to point the barrel over the trench parapet and unleash an expanding cone of yellow-black fire towards the closest enemy group. Screaming, the orks disappeared in a burning agonised haze while Bulaven sprayed bright fire at their comrades around them. Soon, all Larn could see directly ahead of him was a rising curtain of flame while the air grew thick with smoke and the sickly odour of burning *Xenos* flesh.

'Shoot to the sides, new fish!' Davir yelled. 'Bulaven can deal with the orks ahead of us – it's our job to stop the others flanking round them!'

Following Davir's lead, Larn began to shoot at the orks charging towards them from the right of the curtain of fire created by the flamer while Scholar and Zeebers shot at those on the left. For an instant, seeing the carnage inflicted on the orks, Larn thought he could see the beginnings of the greenskins' charge starting to falter. *We are winning,* he thought, exultant. *We have beaten them. There is no way for the orks to get past the flamer.*

And then, abruptly, the tongue of fire jetting from the flamer spluttered and died.

'Canister's empty,' Bulaven said, hands already at the fuel line. 'Reloading.'

'Grenades.' Davir yelled, his own hands at the grenades on his belt.

While Bulaven transferred the fuel line from one canister to another, the others threw two grenades each towards the orks. By the time the last of the grenades had exploded, the line was attached and Bulaven's flamer was once more spewing fire. More orks died but it seemed to make no difference. As though they had been given fresh impetus by the brief cessation in the flamer's attentions, the horde of orks crashed relentlessly nearer, some enveloped from head-to-toe in flame and yet still they kept coming. Thirty metres became twenty-five. Twenty-five became twenty. Twenty...

'Fall back!' Davir yelled. 'The bastards are right on top of us. Scholar, arm the demolition charge. The rest of you fall back.'

The retreat began.

Scrambling over the rear trench wall with his lasgun slung across his shoulder and dragging the heavy weight of a spare flamer canister behind him, Larn began to run for the dugout emplacement while Scholar threw the demolition charge at the advancing orks.

'Faster, new fish,' Scholar ran past Larn, his long legs eating up the distance. 'It's only a four second delay!'

Suddenly, Larn heard a tremendous explosion behind him as clods of earth flew past his head. For a moment, caught at the furthest edge of the blast, he stumbled and almost fell forward, only to be saved as the weight of the canister served as an accidental counterweight behind him. Then, as he tried to heft the canister on to his shoulder and pick up pace, he felt a painful blow at the back of his head, the jarring force of it sending him spinning towards the ground.

Landing in the frozen mud, Larn felt a warm wetness spreading across his scalp. Putting his hand to his head, when he brought it away again he saw red blood staining his fingers. He saw his helmet lying upside down on the ground before him – a large dent left in its side by whatever unknown missile had knocked it from his head. Incongruously, as he rose shakily to his feet, he wondered what would have happened to him if he had fastened his helmet strap instead of leaving it loose. Then, the guttural bellow of an alien war cry behind him put the thought abruptly from his mind.

Whirling to look, Larn saw an ork charging towards him with an enormous pistol in one hand and a broad-bladed cleaver in the other. The creature was huge; its body inhumanly and disproportionately muscled. Larn saw a jutting jaw, yellowed, sickle-shaped tusks, a line of three severed human heads hanging like grotesque spectators from a trophy harness above the monster's shoulders. He heard a bullet scream past him as the pistol fired. As though of its own volition his lasgun responded, the first las-blast flying wide over the ork's shoulder to hit one of the trophies.

Steadying himself, Larn fired again, hitting his enemy in the chest. Unfazed, the ork did not miss a step. Larn shot at it again, firing off a rapid series of blasts that hit the creature in the neck, the shoulder, the chest again, then the face. Until finally, just as Larn began to fear coming within reach of its jagged blade, the ork gave a last enraged bellow, collapsed, and died. Though whatever brief sense of elation Larn felt at his victory quickly evaporated as he saw more greenskins come charging towards him in the dead ork's wake.

'Get a move on, new fish!' he heard a voice yell behind him as a hand grabbed his shoulder. 'Damnation! Are you trying to take on the whole damn ork mob on your own?'

It was Davir. Firing his lasgun one-handed towards the approaching orks, Davir began to tug Larn in the direction of the dugouts. Realising he had dropped the flamer canister when he had fallen, his head still groggy from the blow, for a moment Larn tried to resist as his eyes scanned around in search of the canister.

'It is too late for that, new fish,' Davir shouted, pulling hard now at his shoulder. 'Leave it. I need that canister right where it is.'

Giving in, Larn turned to flee with Davir at his side, catching a last sight of the fallen canister lost among the legs of the screaming phalanx of oncoming orks. Then, turning briefly back as they ran towards the emplacements, Davir fired a snap shot toward it – the las-beam ruptured the canister's body and it exploded in a plume of orange flame, incinerating the orks around it and buying him and Larn time enough to reach their destination.

'You see there, new fish?' Davir said as the outstretched hands of eager Guardsmen helped them to safety. 'I *told* you I wanted the canister right where it was. Oh, and I saw you feeling at your head earlier? You needn't worry in that regard: it is still attached. Though for all that you seem to use it, you might as well have left it with the orks.'

'You came back for me...' Larn said incredulously. 'Even after what Bulaven said about leaving the wounded, you came back and saved me...'

'I wouldn't get too starry-eyed about it, new fish' Davir said. 'What I *really* wanted to save was the flamer canister – events just got ahead of me, is all. Now, shut up and start shooting. You have killed one ork. Only another twenty or so thousand to go.'

They were out of grenades. They had used the last of the flamer fuel. The auto-cannons, missile launchers and lascannons had fallen silent. Even the las-packs were running short. And still, no matter how many screaming greenskins died, the ork assault refused to falter.

Standing on the firing step along one wall of the emplacement, the barrel of his lasgun so hot in his hand now it burnt his fingers, Larn fired a las-beam into the face of an ork as it tried to climb over the bodies of the dead towards him. Then another, and another. Firing without thought or pause, barely even needing to aim so thick was the press of alien bodies charging towards him in wave after screaming wave. They were surrounded now, cut off from the other emplacements by vast throngs of orks; each emplacement a besieged and lonely outcrop amid an endless churning sea of savage green flesh.

From the corners of his eye Larn caught glimpses of the others around him. He saw Bulaven, a lasgun in his hands taken from another fallen Guardsman. He saw Davir. Scholar. Zeebers. He saw Chelkar, his expression cool and detached, working the slide of his shotgun to send round after round into the enemy. He saw Vladek. Medical Officer Svenk. The cook, Trooper Skench, a laspistol blazing in his one remaining hand as he stood beside the others. He saw their faces: Scholar drawn yet steadfast, Bulaven dutiful, Zeebers nervous, Davir spitting obscene and angry oaths at the advancing orks. He saw steely determination and a refusal to go easily to death. As he saw it, Larn felt a fleeting shame that he had doubted these men when he had first met them. Whatever their manner they were all what a Guardsman should be. Brave. Resolute. Unbending in the face of the enemy. These were the men on which the Imperium had been built. The men who had fought its every battle. Won its every victory. Today, they were hopelessly outnumbered.

Today, it was their final stand.

'I'm out!' Davir yelled, pulling the last expended power pack from his lasgun and flinging it towards the orks as his other hand went for the laspistol on his hip.

All about him, it was the same for the others. Around him, Larn saw the Vardans draw pistols or fix bayonets, while he wondered how many shots he had left in his own power pack. Five? Ten? Fifteen? Then, just as he rejected the idea of saving the last shot for himself, the question was answered as he pulled the trigger and heard a final despairing whine from his lasgun as it died.

This is it, he thought, his hands moving with nightmare slowness to attach his bayonet to the lasgun as an ork raised a bloodstained cleaver and charged towards him. *Merciful Emperor, please! It is so unfair. I can't die here. You have to save me.*

Abruptly, as though halted in its tracks by his silent prayer, the ork stopped and raised a bestial face to look up towards the sky. For an instant, Larn was left dumbstruck. Then, he heard a sound and suddenly knew what had given the ork pause. As from the sky above them, there came a cacophony of shrill and strident screams which at that moment sounded to Larn every bit as sweet as the voices of a choir of angels.

Shellfire, he thought, recognising the sound. *Hellbreakers. They are giving us artillery support at last! We are saved!*

'Into the dugout, new fish.' he heard Bulaven's voice beside him. 'Quickly. We have to get to cover!'

Racing to the entrance of the dugout with the Vardans, Larn stumbled down the steps to safety just as the ground began to shake with explosions. Breathing heavily and bolting the door behind them to prevent the orks from following, they stood there for long minutes of silence. Listening, as shells shrieked and roared and boomed above them.

'It makes a refreshing change don't you think, new fish?' Davir said, after a while as the bombardment continued. 'For our own side to be shooting at the orks rather than us, I mean. Now, assuming Battery Command keep this up long enough, I would say that is the last we will see of this particular ork assault.'

He was right. Hearing the shelling finally end after several minutes, the Vardans cautiously emerged from the dugout with Larn beside them to be greeted by the sight of a battlefield now left deserted save for the mounds of the sundered bodies of the dead. The orks had fled. The battle was over. Looking out at the scene of carnage and devastation before him, Larn felt a sudden dizzying sense of joyful exhilaration.

Against all expectation, he was still alive.

CHAPTER FIFTEEN

The Corpse-Pyres – Matters of Disposal and the Varied
Uses of an Entrenching Tool – To See a Perfect Sun

By necessity, he had long ago become inured to the stench of
burning flesh.

Sweating at the heat, Militia Auxiliary Herand Troil used the
hook of the long pole in his hands to push another ork body
into the enormous burning mound of corpses before him, then
stepped away for a moment to catch his breath. Finding it difficult to breathe through the charcoal-filled filtration tube of his
gas mask, he pulled it back from his face, opening his mouth
wide to gulp at the smoky air around him. Inadvertently swallowing a drifting fragment of ash he coughed, retching at the
taste as he tried to summon enough spittle to clean his throat,
before hawking up a greasy wad of brown phlegm and spitting
it towards the fire.

I am getting old, he thought. *I've only been working my shift
three hours now, and already I'm exhausted. Ten years ago I seem
to remember having more staying power than that.*

Ten years, he thought again. *Has it really been that long? Can it
really have been so long since I came to work on the corpse-pyres?*

Weighed down by a sudden sadness, Troil looked around him
at the place where he had spent virtually every waking moment
of his life since being press-ganged into service with the militia at the age of sixty. He was standing on a hillside, the ground

beneath his feet barren after so many fires, surrounded on all sides by tall mounds of burning ork corpses. Through the smoke and ash he could see other auxiliaries in masks tending to the pyres with long hooks, their figures little more than silhouettes through the burning haze. Looking at it, he was struck once more by grief. Grief not for the orks, but for himself. Grief for the life he had lost. Grief for his family and his loved ones long dead. Grief for his days spent working on the corpse-pyres. Most of all though, he felt grief for the city of Broucheroc and the horror the war had made of it.

It was a beautiful place once, this city, he thought. *Not beautiful as most people think of these things perhaps. But it was alive and vital with an energy, an industry, a character all its own. All that is gone now though. Gone and lost for good, taken away by the war. Now it might as well be a city of the dead.*

Sighing, finding his eyes starting to water at the smoke, Troil pulled his mask down back in place and began to walk towards the corpse-pyres to resume his labours. As he did, he spared a last glance down the hillside towards the endless lines of other auxiliaries dragging ork bodies up the slope towards him. He did not linger on the sight though because he expected it. The flow of bodies for the pyres never stopped. This was Broucheroc.

Here, there were always more corpses.

'You need to put your spade here, new fish,' Bulaven said, standing over the body of a dead ork and pressing the blade of his entrenching tool against its throat. 'Next, you draw the spade head back and forth a bit to cut through the skin. Then, you put your weight on it. Here, let me show you how it is done.'

Standing beside him, Larn watched as Bulaven stamped down to push the sharpened spade head partway through the thick muscles of the ork's neck. Then, occasionally wriggling the spade around to slice through the worst of the tendons and break the spinal vertebrae, the big man stamped down on the spade several more times until the creature's head had been completely severed.

'There. You see? Granted, ork skin can be tougher than reptile hide – especially on the big ones. But if you keep your spade head nice and sharp, and remember to let your body weight do the work, their heads come off pretty easy. All right, new fish. Now you try one.'

In the aftermath of battle came the clean-up. Around them, while other Guardsmen tended to the wounded or repaired the shell-damaged emplacements and militia auxiliaries carried in new ammunition and supplies to replace those expended in the fighting, Larn and Bulaven had been detailed to the task of beheading fallen orks. Dubiously, Larn picked an ork at random from the dozens of bodies lying nearby and placed the sharp end of his entrenching tool across its neck. Following Bulaven's earlier example he drew the blade back and forth, feeling the resistance as it cut through the skin and into flesh. Then, raising his foot he stamped down on the spade head, pushing the blade perhaps a quarter of the way into the ork's neck. Readjusting his position to put more force into it he stamped again, harder this time, then again, until at the fourth blow the ork's head finally came free to roll away across the frozen ground.

'That's good, new fish,' Bulaven said. 'Try to make sure you are standing right over the spade though when you stamp on it. That way you will put more of your weight behind it. It makes the work easier and takes less effort. We have a lot more corpses to do before our job is done.'

'But why do we need to do it?' Larn said to him. 'They are dead already, aren't they?'

'Maybe,' Bulaven said. 'But is always better to make sure with an ork, just to be on the safe side. They are tough bastards. You can shoot one in the head and think he's dead, only for him to suddenly get up and start walking about a few hours later. Believe me, I've seen it happen.' Then, noticing Larn casting worried glances at the bodies lying all around them, he smiled. 'Ach, you needn't worry about these ones, new fish. If any of them were capable of moving, they'd be trying to kill us by now already. We'll have their heads off long before any of them that are still alive have had time to heal. Then, the militia auxiliaries will take the bodies away for burning to get rid of the spores.'

'Spores?' Larn asked.

'Oh yes, new fish. Orks grow from spores. Like mold. Leastways, that's what Scholar says. I can't say I've ever seen it happen myself, mind. But I'm prepared to take his word for it. You should ask him about it later. He'll tell you all about it. You know Scholar, he loves telling people about things.'

Apparently satisfied that Larn now knew what he was doing, Bulaven turned away quietly whistling a cheerful tune to himself as he began to deprive more dead orks of their heads. In his wake, Larn set to the same task of decapitation. It was gruesome and tiring work, and Larn quickly found his boots and the spade head were stained black with viscous alien blood. Soon, he was sweating under his helmet; the salt of his sweat irritating the head wound he had sustained during the battle.

In the aftermath, telling him he was lucky and it was only a scalp laceration, Medical Officer Svenk had bandaged it for him while Corporal Vladek had supplied him with a new helmet – something for which Davir had been particularly scathing. *What is it with you and helmets, new fish*, Davir had said. *First, you use one to beat a gretch's brains in. Then, you go and get yourself shot in the head. What will you use the next one for? A soup bowl perhaps, or a planting pot for some flowers?* But, much to his own surprise, Larn found he was longer irritated by Davir's constant complaints and insults. He owed him a debt now. No matter how much the runtish trooper might protest to him that it had all been a mistake, even an accident, Davir had saved his life.

Then, pausing in his work to wipe the sweat from his forehead, Larn noticed a gathering redness in the sky. Turning to face the ork lines in the east, he saw the sun was setting. He saw it, and he was amazed.

It was beautiful. Extraordinary. More breathtaking and vivid even than the sunset he had seen on his last night at home. The sun that had so often seemed cold and distant above him had at last grown to become a warm red orb; the sky once grey around it had transformed and given way to a dazzling symphony in flaming shades of scarlet. Watching it, Larn found himself enraptured by awe. Moved to the very depths of his soul, he stood there transfixed. Hypnotised. *Who knew there could ever be such a sun*, he thought in wonder. *Who knew there could be such beauty here?* And no sooner had that thought occurred than it seemed to him it had all been worth it. All the things he had been through. The fear. The hardship. The danger. The isolation. All the carnage he had seen and all the horrors he had witnessed. All of them now seemed worthwhile. As though by right of his passage through hell he had paid the price that had allowed him this brief perfect moment of quiet and reflection.

'Are you all right, new fish?' he heard Bulaven say beside him. 'Is your head wound bothering you? You have been standing there a long time now, just looking at the sky.'

Turning, Larn saw Bulaven facing him and felt moved to tell him about the sunset. There were no words for his epiphany; no way to communicate what he was feeling to another. Unable to express his emotions, for a moment he was silent. Then, seeing Bulaven staring at him in concern and curiosity, Larn felt he should say something – anything – lest the big man should start to think he had lost his mind.

'I was just struck by how strange this place is,' he said, forced to retreat to more commonplace matters. 'To have a sun that sets so late in winter.'

'Winter?' Bulaven asked in good-natured confusion, looking around at the frozen corpse-covered battlefield around them. 'But it is summer hereabouts, new fish. Good thing, too. In winter, life in Broucheroc can really start to get nasty.'

CHAPTER SIXTEEN

A Visitor from General Headquarters – The
Reconnaissance Mission – Expressions of Disquiet
Among the Ranks – Into No-Man's-land – Alone in the
Darkness

'You have done well, sergeant,' Lieutenant Karis said. 'By holding out against that last assault you have delivered a crippling blow to the activities of the orks in this sector. And you may be assured your efforts in that regard have been recognised and will be rewarded. It is not official as yet, of course, but between you and me I understand you are to be decorated while your unit is to receive a citation.'

In reply, Chelkar was silent. Five minutes ago he had been supervising the repairs to the company's defences when Grishen had voxed him with the news an officer had arrived and was waiting to see him in the command dugout. Hurrying tiredly to meet him, Chelkar had found himself confronted with a fresh-faced junior lieutenant, all spit-shine boots and folded creases, a swagger stick poking out at a jaunty angle from beneath his arm. Though Chelkar had at first wondered if Sector Command had finally got around to sending them a new CO, it quickly became apparent the lieutenant had come here on behalf of General Headquarters. A situation that, to Chelkar's experience, was unlikely to bode anything but ill.

'Did you hear me, sergeant?' the lieutenant said. 'They are going to give you a medal.'

'I will have to remember to put it with the other ones, lieutenant,' Chelkar said, feeling so exhausted and bone-weary he no longer cared if his tone was properly diplomatic. 'But I am sure you didn't come all this way and dragged me away from my duties just to tell me that.'

Stung by his bluntness, the lieutenant's face briefly tightened into a look of displeasure. Then, abruptly, his mood softening and becoming patently false, he adopted a more conciliatory manner.

'You are right, of course, sergeant. And may I say what a pleasure it is to hear some plain speaking for a change. That is why I was so happy to get this chance to come to the front. Not that I find my duties at General Headquarters in any way irksome, you understand, but at GHQ one can so often forget the realities of frontline life in the Guard. We are soldiers, you and I. We don't do what we do for honours and medals. We do it selflessly in the name of duty and for the greater glory of the Imperium.'

I don't know what is more sickening, Chelkar thought bleakly. *The fact that someone has obviously told him an officer should try to strike up a rapport with the lower ranks, or the fact that he is so inept and insincere in trying to do it. Why is it whenever you hear one of these rear echelon heroes talk about selflessness you always know they are desperate to win a medal? This one's a glory hound, all right, you can see it in his eyes. He probably heard about some suicide mission at GHQ and volunteered right away.*

'Yes, lieutenant,' Chelkar said, hoping that at last the pipsqueak pedant before him might get to the point. 'And, talking of duty, I am assuming there is some matter with which you need my company's assistance?'

'Not the *whole* company, sergeant,' the lieutenant replied blithely. 'I just need some men to accompany me into no-man's-land on a mission towards the ork lines. A five-man fire-team to be precise. Of course, I leave it entirely up to you which fire-team to pick. Though I have always considered three to be a lucky number.'

* * *

'We will be going into no-man's-land tonight,' the lieutenant said, while Larn heard a sharp intake of breath from the other members of the fire-team beside him. 'General Headquarters wishes to know whether the orks' hold on their territory has been at all weakened by their recent losses. Accordingly, we are ordered to advance by stealth to within sight of their lines and scout out their defences and dispositions under cover of darkness. Then, we will return to our own lines before the orks are any the wiser. A simple and straightforward enough mission, I am sure you will all agree.'

Going about their duties as the clean-up proceeded outside, Larn and the others had been summoned to the command dug-out to hear a briefing from a stiff-necked young lieutenant called Karis. Now, standing before the sector map pinned to the wall behind him, the lieutenant pointed at something on the map with his swagger stick as the briefing continued.

'Let me make it clear this is strictly a reconnaissance mission,' he said. 'And, as such, it relies entirely on stealth. We are not to engage the enemy unless forced to do it by the direst circumstance. With that in mind we will maintain total light and noise discipline at all times and follow a route through no-man's-land designed to aid us in our attempts to stay unseen. If we are spotted by scouts or lookouts, we will attempt to dispose of them in as quick and quiet a manner as possible – only withdrawing from no-man's-land if it is clear our mission has become untenable. Now, I think that about covers everything. Are there any questions?'

No one answered and looking at the faces of the men about him – Davir, Bulaven, Scholar, Zeebers – Larn saw a subtle disquiet among them. As though they were every bit as uneasy at the prospect of a mission into no-man's-land as they had been earlier when it seemed The Big Push might be upon them. Watching them, Larn was gripped by a sudden revelation that he realised would have seemed quite commonplace to the others. In

Broucheroc the danger never ended; there were always new battles to fight. New ways for a man to get himself killed.

'Good,' Lieutenant Karis said when it became clear there were to be no questions. 'You now have twenty minutes to check your equipment and make your preparations. Zero hour is at 00.00 hours. We go into no-man's-land at midnight.'

'A simple matter, he says,' Davir grumbled afterwards. 'I tell you, someone should take that stupid bastard's swagger stick and shove it right up his arse.'

They were in the barracks dugout. In the wake of the briefing with the lieutenant, they had returned there to be issued with black dubbing and lasgun lubricant by Vladek. Now, their faces and all their equipment painted black, their knives and pistols oiled to glide silently from their sheaths, they made their final preparations while time counted down to midnight. As they did, Larn was suddenly struck by the thought he had been in Broucheroc almost exactly twelve hours. *Another three hours to go*, he thought, *and I will have made my fifteen.*

'You ask me, it is the new fish's fault,' Zeebers spat with sudden venom. 'He is unlucky. A jinx.'

'Shut up, Zeebers,' Davir spat back. 'Bad enough I have to go stumbling around no-man's-land in the dead of night, without having to hear you mewl and puke about luck and numbers like some halfwit gambler on a losing streak. Shut up, or after I'm finished shoving the swagger stick up the lieutenant's arse I'll stick my lasgun up yours.'

'How do you explain it then?' Zeebers said, defiant. 'We've had nothing but a bad day ever since the new fish got here. He's a jinx. You saw what happened to the men he came here with in the lander.'

'Shut up, Zeebers,' Bulaven rumbled. Then, while Zeebers fell silent and scowled at him, he turned to Larn. 'Don't worry about what Zeebers said, new fish. You're not a jinx. I only wish today *had* been a bad day. Fact is, every day in Broucheroc is pretty much as bad as this, one way or another. After a while you just get used to it.'

'But going out into no-man's-land at night is bad?' Larn asked, hoping the big Vardan could not hear the nervousness in his voice. 'Worse than usual, I mean?'

'Yes, new fish, it is worse,' Bulaven said. 'Especially after a battle. You remember I told you how sometimes a wounded ork will seem dead, only to get up and start walking about a few hours later? Well, right now, no-man's-land is full of the bodies of orks we shot during the battle. By now some of them could be healed already, just about ready to wake up and start killing again while we'll be right in the middle of them. Then, to make matters worse, we've got to worry about running into gangs of gretchin looking for spare parts as well.'

'Spare parts?'

'Orks are remarkably tough creatures, new fish,' Scholar said by the side of him. 'If one of them loses an arm or leg their surgeons will just staple the limb from another dead ork to them to take its place. After a battle such surgeries are in great demand – so they tend to send gangs of gretchin out into no-man's-land to cut undamaged limbs from the corpses. Of course, the real threat lies not so much in the gretch themselves, but in the danger of getting into a firefight in the middle of no-man's-land while the entire ork army is on top of us.'

'The short version, new fish, is that this whole damned business has the makings of a first class snafu from start to finish,' Davir said. 'So, this is what I say I we do. We will follow Lieutenant Arsehole's orders so long as there's no shooting. But the moment the shit starts to fly we get each other out of no-man's-land as fast as we can and to hell with his orders. Now enough talking and let's get outside. We need to spend at least ten minutes in the dark to get our night vision working. Considering what's ahead of us, I'd say we're probably going to need every advantage we can get.'

* * *

'Remember the signal, new fish,' Bulaven whispered quietly as they crouched in the darkness of one of the forward firing trenches with the lieutenant and the others waiting for the order for the mission to begin. 'We keep to comms silence. But if you make contact with the greenskins you squeeze the comm stud at your collar to create a squelch over the comm-link. You squeeze it three times. Three squelches. You understand? That way we'll know it's you. Now, tell me it again so I'll know you've got it.'

'We go quiet,' Larn whispered back, reciting the things Bulaven had already told him twice. 'Staying low and keeping together until we get halfway into no-man's-land. Then, while Davir and the lieutenant go forward to scout out the ork lines, the rest of us spread out into a wide diamond formation with you at the base, Zeebers on the left flank, me on the right, and Scholar on point. If any of us see or hear orks we squelch on the comm-line: one squelch for you, two for Zeebers, three for me, and four for Scholar – so that way the others will know where the orks are.'

'Noise discipline, troopers,' Lieutenant Karis whispered testily. Then, cupping his hand over the chronometer on his wrist as he pressed an illumination stud to briefly light its face, he gave the order. 'Zero hour. Time to move out.'

With Davir in the lead, they climbed over the lip of the trench and crawled out into no-man's-land. Then, at a hand signal from Davir showing the way before them was clear, they stood into a half-crouch and began to move slowly and quietly forward. Ahead, the night seemed impossibly dark, the stars dim and distant. Seeing no sign of a moon in the sky to guide them, Larn found himself wondering if the planet even had a moon or whether it was just hidden from his view. Whatever the case, keeping close to the others he followed them further and further into the forbidding wasteland between the human and ork lines. His every step wary, his senses sharp, his heart beating a tattoo of restless anxiety in his chest.

Around them no-man's-land was silent, made even more

threatening in the darkness now its flat and desolate surface was covered over with the shadowy foreboding shapes of so many bodies. There were corpses everywhere, strewn haphazardly across the landscape and fallen together so deeply in places the going was made treacherous with splayed limbs and uncaring torsos. Feeling the outstretched fingers of unseen hand touch his ankle, Larn looked down in sudden terror expecting the monstrous form of a wounded and reawakening ork to rise up before him. Only to see he had inadvertently brushed against a severed hand lying in the mud. Another dead hand like so many more around it.

They advanced further, slowly spreading out further apart from each other until they reached the centre of no-man's-land. Then, as Davir and the lieutenant disappeared from view to go scout the lines, Larn abruptly realised he could no longer see the others. For a moment he fought the urge to call to them on his comm stud. Then, he reminded himself they had been ordered to maintain vox silence: even if he did use the comm, no one would answer. Nor could he go in search of them. Robbed of all sense of direction by the darkness and the unfamiliarity of the landscape around him, it would take him a miracle to find anyone. Worse, hopelessly lost, he could easily stray into the ork lines. Terrified, Larn held his position and did the only thing he could.

Alone in the darkness, he waited.

Time passed and as he stood waiting, afraid that every shadow might belong to some subtle and stalking enemy, Larn realised it was the first time he had been on his own in weeks. More than that, here in no-man's-land, surrounded by corpses and barely within a stone's throw of thousands of sleeping orks, he felt more alone than he had before in his entire life. So alone now, in fact, he might as well have been the last man left in the entire galaxy.

Then, deep through the gathering haze in his mind of fear and loneliness, Larn heard a sudden sound that set cold fingers at his spine and turned his blood to ice. A single squelch on the comm-bead in his ear. Bulaven's signal. The signal that meant the big man had made contact with the enemy and from Larn's point of view it meant something worse.

It meant the enemy was behind him.

CHAPTER SEVENTEEN

00:37 HOURS CENTRAL BROUCHEROC TIME

Giving Aid and Comfort to the Wounded – As Hell Breaks
Loose Larn is Forced to a Decision – A Final Madness in
Zeebers's Smile – Unknown, a Bullet Finds its Mark

One of the orks was moving...

Standing alone in the darkness of no-man's-land, not quite
sure if it was only his imagination or if he had really seen a slight
movement in the legs of one of the corpses lying on the ground
before him, Zeebers decided it would be better to make certain
the creature was dead. Sliding his combat knife from its sheath
as he dropped to his knees beside the body, he quickly pulled
the ork's unresisting jaws open and silently stabbed the blade
up through the weak point in the roof of the mouth and into
the brain. Then, pulling the knife free, he glanced briefly at the
other corpses around him and wondered if he should do the
same with them as well.

I will do another three of them, he thought, wiping the blade
on his trouser leg as he crept towards a second body. *That way
I will have done four altogether. And I could do with some extra
luck, what with that bastard new fish being such a jinx.*

'Help me,' he heard a failing voice whisper in Gothic as he knelt
beside a second ork.

Startled, Zeebers turned to see an arm rise falteringly from
beneath a nearby pile of bodies. Going over to it, he saw a human
face peering out from among a nest of greenskin limbs. One of the

Guardsman from the lander he realised, mortally wounded and left for dead in no-man's-land but still clinging desperately to life.

'Please... help me,' the Guardsman said again, the weak voice was loud against the silence and forced Zeebers to clamp a firm hand over his mouth to keep him quiet.

Weakly, the Guardsman began to struggle, his free arm flailing and flapping around him. Feeling the man grab pleadingly at the edge of his greatcoat, Zeebers felt a sudden flush of disgust and anger to find yet another new fish was endangering his life.

It cannot be helped, he thought as he pushed down once more with his knife. *He is too far gone to live much longer anyway. And he will bring the orks down on both of us if I don't make him quiet.*

Seeing the arm fall and the Guardsman's spasms grow still, Zeebers pulled his knife free and turned to get back to the orks. The Guardsman did not count, he decided. He was not part of the pattern. Leaving Zeebers with another three orks to deal with if he was going to improve his luck.

Then, abruptly, he heard the signal. A single squelch over his comm-bead. The fathead Bulaven must have run into some trouble.

For a moment Zeebers considered leaving him to it. He did not like Bulaven, or any of the Vardans for that matter. It would be easy enough to slip back towards the line and claim he had lost track of the others in the darkness. Just as quickly he was forced to abandon the idea; if Bulaven or any of the others survived and thought he had left them to die they would frag him without even thinking. No, for better or worse, he had better go and try to save the fat man's hide.

Putting his knife back in its sheath, Zeebers turned to hurry in Bulaven's direction. Then, as he picked his way past a particularly large pile of ork corpses he saw shadowy movement at the corner of his vision and realised he had blundered upon a gang of gretchin harvesting limbs. Swinging his lasgun towards them while the gretchin were still dumb with confusion, Zeebers fired, hitting the nearest gretch in the chest. Swiftly, he fired again, unleashing another half-dozen las-beams, hitting two more gretch and causing the rest to flee. As Zeebers made to hurry once more on his way he heard something scraping wet and eager behind him followed by the whine of whirring motors. Turning, he saw a threatening shadow loom up in the darkness and knew the day he had feared for months was finally upon him.

Tonight, his luck had finally run out...

'Fall back! Repeat: fall back!' Davir's voice shouted forcefully in his comm-bead as Larn heard the sound of shots and all hell began to break loose around him. 'Everyone back to the trenches!'

Lost and still on his own, Larn turned to move quickly towards what was his best guess at the position of the human lines. Suddenly, he saw a staccato burst of white tracer lines in the distance to the right of him as somewhere in the darkness a lasgun fired.

'Help me!' he heard Zeebers yell in fear and agony over the comm-line. 'Sweet Emperor, it's got me! Someone help me.'

Unsure what to do, for the briefest instant Larn stood rooted to the spot. Then, as Zeebers's voice in his ear became a jumble of incoherent screams, he made a decision. Turning in the direction the las-fire had come from he ran towards it, jumping and stumbling over the ork corpses littering his path as he raced to help the pleading trooper. Seeing two shapes coming together in the darkness ahead of him, Larn ran closer, only to find a scene of horror. He saw Zeebers, arms flailing in useless spasms, belly ripped open and guts hanging out, held like a limp puppet in the hand of an enormous ork while with its other hand the creature used a whirring circular blade to further eviscerate Zeebers's screaming flesh. Then, tossing Zeebers's rag doll body aside, the ork turned to look at Larn and began to advance towards him.

It was huge, wearing a bloodstained apron across its body and a thick-lensed monocular over one of its eyes. Seeing the cruel curiosity written in the creature's monstrous inhuman features, Larn knew at once it must be one of the ork surgeons Scholar had mentioned. Instinctively raising his lasgun to ward off its advance, he fired, the first blast flying wide to hit one of the corpses lying on the ground behind it. Adjusting his aim, Larn fired again, hitting the monster in the stomach. Then again. The chest. Again. The shoulder. Again. The face; the las-beam briefly flaring brighter as it burned through the lens of the monocular. Tearing the melted mounting of the device away uncaring from the scorched socket of its now-blind eye, the ork kept coming no matter how many times Larn hit it. It seemed unstoppable; as inured to the pain of its own flesh as it was to the agonies of others. All the time, the whining blade in its hand grew closer and closer, as eager as its master to test its edge against the outlines of Larn's body.

Then, incredibly, salvation came from an unlikely source. As if from nowhere, Larn saw Zeebers appear in the darkness behind the ork and jump screaming onto the creature's back to wrap his arms about its throat. Horribly wounded, the spool of his intestines unravelled in the mud behind him, as the ork tried to pull him off, Zeebers briefly smiled towards Larn in pain-fuelled madness, before raising a hand above his head and letting out a bloody-mouthed and psychotic roar of triumph. Seeing the gleam of a half-dozen rings around Zeebers's fingers, Larn realised the madman must have pulled the pins from every grenade on his belt.

Knocked on his back as Zeebers and the ork disappeared in the roar and flash of the resulting explosion, Larn staggered to his feet once more and became aware the volume of firing about him had risen dramatically. All around him no-man's-land was alive with bullets as, fully roused now from sleep, the orks fired blindly from their lines in search of targets. A last glance confirming there was no more he could do for Zeebers, Larn turned to run for the human lines in the hope of safety. Only to trip, not realising at first he had been shot, before he could go even a dozen steps.

The sun was rising in the west, the first red fingers of dawn revealing the brooding and foreboding shape of Broucheroc on the
horizon. And still lying wounded in no-man's-land in the same
place where he had fallen, Larn looked up at the brightening
sky above him and knew he should fear the sun. With the gathering of the light soon the orks would be able to see him from
their lines. But where once he would have felt anxiety, even perhaps terror at that prospect, now all those things had left him.
Instead, he lay on his back watching the sun slowly rise and he
felt peace. He watched it and he knew contentment.

I have made it past fifteen hours, he thought, at last given answer
by the coming of the dawn to the question that had plagued him
throughout the night. *More than that even, now the sun is rising. And with it I have proved the others wrong. I have beaten
the odds. I have survived this place. I have passed the test. The
orks cannot kill me now. The laws that rule this monstrous city
will not let them.*

Certain now that his fate had been decided in his favour and it
was only a matter of time before someone came to rescue him,
Larn settled calmly down to wait. All the fear had passed through
him now. All the loneliness. The desperation. The despair. They
were gone, replaced instead by a growing sense of detached
serenity.

Over the last fifteen hours he had faced the worst this city could throw at him. It was over now and with it he was forever free. Free from doubt. Free from worry. Free from his fears. He did not even feel the cold any more. He felt safe and warm. He felt whole. He had survived his fifteen hours. He had lasted. He had proved himself. This place could no longer hurt him and with that last happy thought, Larn smiled and closed his eyes. Closed his eyes to drift away to dreamless sleep, the last shreds of his consciousness flying away from him like dead leaves on the wind as the relentless babble of his mind gradually gave way to silence. Drawing a last contented breath, his beating heart slowed and stilled.

Then, finally, there was only darkness.

KNEE DEEP

Mitchel Scanlon

The sewers of Broucheroc were a lesson in endurance. Granted, the hardships were not the same as in the city itself. Above ground, Broucheroc was caught in the merciless grip of another harsh winter. Blizzards hounded the city remorselessly. Shrill winds screamed through the desolate streets. The city's defenders huddled together for warmth, or else suffered miserably in icy foxholes. Only the dead did not feel the cold.

The sewers were different. The air in the tunnels was sharp and biting, but the temperature was above freezing. In the sewers, there were other hardships, other adversities.

In the dank dark spaces of the underground world, the damp was all-pervasive. Moisture gathered on the walls and dripped down to join the filthy river of sewage that ran throughout the system. The tunnels seemed endless. They burrowed deep into the earth, stretching outward for tens of kilometres in every direction. To walk them was to know the most ancient and primal of fears. Even with the advantage of a portable luminator, the darkness felt stifling. Shadows moved strangely. The slightest sound cast weird echoes that travelled back-and-forth across the tunnels. The sewers possessed an almost palpable sense of menace. It was as though they stood at the gates of the underworld, on the threshold between life and death.

'So this is hell?' Davir said, surveying the scene in the beam of the luminator clipped to the underside of his lasgun. 'Who could have guessed it would be so wet?'

Seeing that the way ahead looked clear, he raised a hand to signal down the tunnel and resumed trudging wearily through the knee-high waters. The other two members of Fire-team Three, his comrades Bulaven and Scholar, were beside him. Bulaven hefted the imposing bulk of a flamer while Scholar carried a hand-held auspex unit. The three of them were on point duty. The rest of a platoon of Vardans followed behind in single file. The men moved cautiously, keeping their lasguns at the ready and sweeping the barrels from side-to-side as they advanced through the tunnels.

'I don't like this,' whispered Bulaven.

'You don't like *what* exactly?' Davir countered.

He was in a bad mood, as ever, and the hulking figure of Bulaven made an easy target. They had only been in the sewers for a few hours, but it felt like days. Tempers were running ragged.

By common consent, sewer patrol was the worst duty in Broucheroc. The battle against the orks raged every bit as fiercely underground as it did on the surface. In order to prevent the enemy from gaining a foothold beneath the city, regular patrols were sent into the sewers on search-and-destroy missions to sweep them clear of ork infiltrators.

In the case of the Vardans, the new posting seemed doubly cruel. They had just served three times the normal rotation on the frontlines, facing multiple enemy assaults on a daily basis. By the unwritten law of Broucheroc, it was their turn to be assigned to less arduous duties in a more peaceful sector.

Instead, they had found themselves suddenly reassigned to the sewers on an emergency basis. Two patrols had vanished in the same section of tunnels. Much to their displeasure, the men of the 902nd Vardan had been chosen to follow the trail of the missing patrols to see what had happened to them. As an aid to the quest, they had been issued with an ancient, hopelessly outdated map of the sewer network. By common opinion, however, the map was next to useless.

'Is it that you don't like being in the sewers on an ork hunt?'

Warming to his theme, Davir sneered at Bulaven. 'Maybe you don't like the cold? The damp? You don't like getting your feet wet? Well? Spit it out. After all, we've already been given the worst available posting in this whole damned city. It would be the icing on the cake to have to listen to you complaining about it like some mewling infant. So, tell me, fat man. What is it that you don't like?'

'This is all wrong,' Bulaven said. 'We shouldn't be here in the sewers. We should be back topside. We should be looking for Larn.'

'Larn?'

'The new fish, Davir. He's only been missing for two days. You can't have forgotten him already.'

'I make it a policy to forget anyone I will never see again,' Davir scowled, but for once he took no pleasure in puncturing the fat man's illusions. 'The new fish is dead. You said it yourself. It has been two days. If he were coming back, we would have seen him by now.'

'You can't be certain that...'

'Yes, I can. The new fish is dead, Bulaven. It is better that you grow accustomed to the fact. Forget the idea of scouring no-man's-land for him. You'd only end up as dead as he is.'

'Davir is correct, you know. Statistically, the probability of someone surviving for two days in no-man's-land is nearly non-existent.'

Drawn by the discussion, Scholar had waded over to join them.

'It is a matter of facing realities,' he said, not without sympathy. 'Larn disappeared in one of the most hotly contested sectors in the city. That patch of ground has been fought over, blanketed with gunfire and subjected to artillery bombardment at least half a dozen times in the last forty-eight hours. It is the nature of the war here. Often, when two sides are in stalemate they struggle with ever-greater violence to achieve a resolution. Paradoxically, it creates a war where nothing of consequence ever happens, and yet men are constantly fighting and dying, giving their lives for as little as a few centimetres of territory. The militarist Hsu Chan discusses the irony in one of his tactical works, *The Book of...*'

'No. Stop right there,' Davir held up a warning hand. 'I have heard enough, Scholar. The day I need you to fight my battles for me, it will be because I have already been reduced to a drooling basket case. I don't care *what* the subject is – I don't want to hear another of your yammering, pointless lectures. I swear, between listening to you and Bulaven, it is a wonder I don't go skipping off into no-man's-land myself in the hope the orks will put me out of my misery. Whichever philosopher said that hell was other people, obviously he had you two in mind.'

'Frankly, I'd imagine he was talking about all *three* of you,' a voice said, behind them.

It was Sergeant Chelkar, the Vardans' leader. He had advanced forward from the rest of the platoon without Davir and the others hearing.

'I'm sure this is a fascinating discussion,' Chelkar regarded them coolly. 'But you will understand it is probably better left to another time. There is the small matter of the enemy. I'm aware the relevant manuals claim that orks have poor hearing, but I'd rather not trust our lives to it. The three of you were arguing loudly enough to forewarn the deaf. I want silence from now on. There are no complaints, I take it?'

Chastened, Bulaven and Scholar shifted uneasily. Only Davir did not give ground before the sergeant's gaze. It was not in him to accept discipline gracefully. He respected Chelkar like no other leader he had ever known, but it was Davir's nature to try to have the last word in every situation.

'Complaining? I wouldn't dream of it, sergeant,' Davir smiled sweetly, showing an ugly mouthful of broken and crooked teeth. 'I was merely remarking to my comrades that we are in a sewer, wading knee-deep through ork shit. If I was of a more poetic inclination, I might almost think of it as some form of extended metaphor for our lives here in Broucheroc.'

From the corners of his eyes, Davir saw Scholar and Bulaven goggling silently at him in disbelief. If he had spoken that way to an officer, a commissar or any other sergeant, he knew he would have faced a charge for insubordination – to likely later be flogged to death or shot, depending on the whim of the offended party.

Chelkar was not like other commanders, however. The sergeant was difficult to read, but at times, he seemed to find a dark humour in their situation. He was not a by-the-book soldier, nor a shrieking parade ground martinet. In contrast to most of the men who held authority of any kind in Broucheroc, the sergeant knew how to laugh. Sometimes, Davir supposed it was part of what had helped to keep Chelkar alive.

'A touching sentiment, Trooper Davir.'

A gallows smile twitched at Chelkar's mouth, confirming Davir's suspicions.

'Perhaps we should meditate on it at length later,' the sergeant continued. 'In the meantime, however, one of the advantages of a policy of operational silence is that I would hate it if the orks killed such an original thinker. It is better if they don't hear you coming. That way you can surprise them with such pithy comments when they least expect it. It is a widely known fact that nothing frightens an ork more than a well-constructed put-down.'

The sergeant made to turn away, before glancing back and tapping at the comm-bead in his ear.

'Oh, and a word to the wise. You may have noticed the comm-net has fallen quiet. It is the tunnels – they interfere with the transmissions. Our comms are as good as useless, so if you run into orks you will have to communicate with the rest of the platoon by more old-fashioned methods. I leave it to your discretion whether screaming or waving your arms is the better choice. Either way, it should serve to attract our attention.'

* * *

The first encounter with the enemy came a little over an hour later. By Davir's reckoning, it was at least four hours since they had entered the sewers. The members of Fire-team Three had reached a juncture where several tunnels met. In common with the other members of their platoon, they had left their great-coats at the surface, expecting to find them cumbersome while wading through the waters. Now, they keenly felt their loss as a vicious cross-draught blew through the junction, cutting through the relatively thin material of their uniforms and setting their teeth chattering.

'Contact!'

Suddenly, the auspex in Scholar's hands emitted a series of high-pitched beeps. In an instant, all the discomforts of the sewers – the cold, the damp, the claustrophobic closeness of the tunnel walls – were forgotten. Davir, Scholar and Bulaven readied their weapons, removing the waterproofed barrel smocks that protected their guns from corrosion in the wet environment.

'I'm reading multiple contacts ahead of us,' Scholar's face was given a ghastly glow by the green light of the machine's display screen.

He looked towards Davir, the most senior man in the fire-team and, technically, its leader.

'There's a lot of them. And the sensor traces look too big to be anything other than orks.'

'Which tunnel?' Davir asked as he waved a frantic arm to draw the attention of the other Vardans following them.

Ahead, the sewer branched off into three separate tunnels.

'The middle one.' Scholar's long fingers worked at the auspex's controls, calibrating the readings. 'They are directly ahead. I estimate the distance as no more than two hundred metres.'

Without warning, Sergeant Chelkar was beside them once more. The rest of the platoon had advanced to their shoulder. Instantly sizing up the situation, Chelkar signalled silently to the men around him.

With a firefight in the offing, a mood of grim seriousness had descended on the Vardans. They had been fighting orks for ten years, ever since they had first been posted to Broucheroc. They moved with a measured precision, as well ordered and disciplined in the face of potential combat as any more spit-and-polished unit.

The standard ten-man squads of Imperial Guard doctrine having long ago proven unwieldy in the close confines of the streets of Broucheroc, never mind its sewers, the Vardans were divided into a number of five-man fire-teams. At a series of hand signals from Chelkar, three fire-teams peeled off from the main group of the platoon – one to cover the Vardans' rear and the other two to guard the entrances to the tunnels on either side.

The remaining teams entered the middle tunnel in groups of four abreast, the selector switches on their lasguns turned ready for rapid fire. Davir, Bulaven, Scholar and Sergeant Chelkar were in the lead.

'We are getting closer,' Scholar said. The tunnel had widened, seeming to grow larger with each step as he counted down the distance to the enemy. 'I estimate contact in one hundred metres... Ninety metres... Seventy-five... Fifty... Thirty-five...'

'Where are they?' Chelkar said. 'We should be able to see them by now.'

The tunnel ahead was illuminated in the glare of more than a dozen lasgun-mounted light sources. It appeared to be empty of life.

'I don't understand it,' Scholar fidgeted with the controls of the auspex. 'According to these readings they are right in front of us. We should be face-to-face with them.'

'You must have read it wrong,' Bulaven said. 'Maybe they are not in this tunnel, but in the next one along.'

'These contacts. Are they stationary or moving?' Chelkar asked Scholar.

'Stationary, sergeant.'

Scholar advanced further down the tunnel, waving the auspex slowly from side-to-side. The beeping from the machine grew louder.

'It doesn't make sense,' Scholar gazed around quizzically. 'Unless... Wait a second... The display of the auspex can only show information two-dimensionally, as dots on a screen-map. But we are in a *three*-dimensional environment. Perhaps Bulaven is right. The orks could be in another tunnel, maybe directly below us. Or even....'

He paused, an expression of horrified understanding slowly dawning on his face.

'They could be *above* us...'

As one, the Vardans followed the line of Scholar's eyes in peering upward. Someone pointed a luminator at the ceiling of the tunnel, revealing the mouth of a vertical shaft, hidden in the shadows and rising in a diagonal line above them. Caught in the glimmer of the light, red eyes stared from the darkness. Dozens of orks hung like bats from the shaft wall, waiting to spring an ambush.

'Pull back!' Sergeant Chelkar yelled out as, all around him, the Vardans opened fire. 'Back to the junction! Don't let them get into close combat!"

It was too late. Releasing their hold on the shaft wall, the orks dropped among the Vardans with the guttural roar of alien battle cries.

Firing his lasgun, Davir scrambled to get out from under the avalanche of falling orks. He saw grotesque and muscular forms, glimpses of green skin peeking out from underneath layer upon layer of savage war paint.

The enemy were everywhere. Lost in the haze and confusion of battle, Davir barely had time to think as he fired a succession of las-blasts at the nearest ork. The noises of battle were deafening. He heard screams, the high-pitched whine of lasguns firing at full auto, the *whoosh* of Bulaven's flamer and the *thoom* of Chelkar's shotgun – all made more intense by the enclosed environment. Abruptly, one sound cut through all the rest. Davir heard a snarling war cry behind him.

Instinctively, he dropped forward into the sewer waters. The movement saved him as a blade whistled close by his head. Spluttering out a mouthful of rank and foul-tasting liquid, Davir twisted in the water and tried to bring his gun to bear. The ork was standing over him, an enormous cleaver raised in its hand.

Against a human opponent, Davir might have lashed out with the butt of his gun to break the target's knee. Ten years in Broucheroc had taught him the folly of trying the manoeuvre on an ork. He fought the urge to panic, taking careful aim at the greenskin's face. With the added force of a hotshot power pack behind it, he fired a single las-shot that burned through the creature's left eye and into its brains, the rear of its skull exploding in a blast of steam and red gore as the shot exited the head.

Even as the monster fell, Davir was back on his feet. Crouched up to his chest in raw sewage, he scanned the tunnels in search of another enemy to kill. He chose his targets carefully, conserving the punch of the hotshot pack for where it would have the most effect. He was no sniper, but he was cool and accurate under pressure. Experience had taught him that the man who panicked in combat was lost. It was one of the wisdoms of warfare he had learned in Broucheroc; a key, in its own small way, to his continued survival.

He fired his lasgun a half-dozen times, each one a headshot, each one another dead ork. The scrum and press of the melee between men and orks had begun to lessen. The skirmish had turned in the Vardans' favour. The last of the enemy were dispatched without mercy.

As quickly as the fight began, it was over. As ever, in the aftermath of battle, there was a moment of strange and eerie calm – a quiet instant of disbelieving silence as men struggled to come to terms with the fact of their survival.

'Davir?' Bulaven came splashing through the waters towards him. They had become separated in the fighting and he looked down in concern. 'It is you under that filth? Are you all right?'

'No thanks to you, pig face.'

Brushing at his uniform, Davir did his best to dislodge the worst of the muck he had inadvertently collected in his brief submersion in the sewer waters. It had not improved his mood.

'Where were you, fat arse? You realise I nearly had my head cut off by an ork with a meat cleaver? It is the whole point of being in a fire-team together that we are supposed to watch each other's backs.'

'We couldn't help it,' Bulaven gestured helplessly. 'Before we knew what was happening, there were orks all over us. There were more of them hiding further down the tunnel. They attacked at the same time as the ones from the shaft.' Bulaven reached over his shoulder to tap the fuel tanks on his back. 'If it hadn't been for the flamer, we'd have never been able to hold them back.'

'Excuses,' Davir snorted. 'It is always the same with you. "Oh, the greenskins attacked. Oh, I couldn't help it." Listening to you, you'd think you were the only one who ever had to fight an ork.'

His eyes narrowed as he glanced past Bulaven to see Scholar approaching.

'And you needn't look so pleased with yourself either, you long streak of grox piss. If you'd read the auspex better, I wouldn't have had to go for a swim in a river of shit.'

'I don't know why you're complaining, Davir,' Scholar said mildly. 'Swimming is excellent exercise. Certainly, it seems to have done wonders for your disposition.'

'Very funny, Scholar. You know, I think I like it better when you are giving lectures. It is true they are as dull as watching paint dry. But at least they are less of a pain in the spheres than your idea of humour.'

* * *

'We're six men down,' Chelkar said, a short while later. 'That's what you're telling me.'

Three-quarters of an hour had passed since they had driven off the orks and the sergeant had just received situation reports from the assembled fire-team leaders and the Vardan medic, Medical Officer Svenk. They stood a small distance away from the main body of the platoon so they could talk more freely. Despite the confines of the tunnels, and the dead bodies littered around them, the meeting had soon taken on the character of an impromptu briefing.

'Four men are dead,' Svenk replied. 'Another twelve are wounded.'

'But only two of them are injured too badly to continue,' Chelkar pressed the point. 'The others are walking wounded. That's what you said.'

'They should still be evacuated,' Svenk argued. 'In these unsanitary conditions it is almost a certainty that their wounds will become infected. And antibiotics are in short supply. Without them, a serious infection can easily turn out to be a death sentence.'

'All right,' Chelkar nodded. 'Pick four men from among the walking wounded to escort the non-ambulatory cases back to the surface. They'll have to improvise stretchers to carry them, if need be.'

Seeing Svenk about to protest again, he raised his hand to quiet him.

'That's the best I can do, Svenk. If I send all the wounded back, it depletes our numbers and endangers the rest of the platoon. You'd better make the arrangements. I want us underway again in ten minutes' time.'

Realising any further argument was useless, Svenk bowed his head and hurried away to organise the stretcher party.

Once the medic was gone, Chelkar turned to gaze at a trio of dead orks that had been propped against the sewer wall nearby for inspection. In keeping with standard procedure in Broucheroc, the Vardans had already beheaded the bodies to prevent any unexpected 'resurrections'. It was not unknown for a comatose ork, with a seemingly mortal wound, to suddenly spring to life several hours after the fight had ended. Accordingly, the city's defenders took the precaution of decapitating their defeated opponents after every battle.

'Well, I think we can agree we know what probably happened to the last two patrols,' Chelkar said, staring intently at the corpses. 'Obviously, the orks killed them. But that still leaves several questions to be answered.'

He looked up at the faces of Davir and the other fire-team leaders around him, before gazing down at the orks again. Together, the headless orks made a gruesome sight. They put Chelkar in mind of one of the traditions of his homeworld. On Vardan, it had been the custom for the authorities to display the lined-up bodies of executed criminals in public places on Imperial holidays, in order to serve as a warning to anyone contemplating breaking the law.

'They are poorly equipped, even by ork standards,' Chelkar said, thinking aloud as he nudged one of the corpses with his boot. 'We haven't found a single one of them with anything even approaching a firearm. They didn't have stick bombs, either. They were armed only with the most simple of weapons – spears, axes, clubs and the like.'

There was something puzzling, even unsettling here, Chelkar decided. In the breathless, dizzying, adrenaline surge of combat, he had hardly noticed that there was anything unusual about the enemy. Now, in the calm after the battle, it was clear they were different from the orks he had fought before.

The sewer orks seemed even more primitive than their normal brethren. They lacked any but the most basic technology. They did not even possess clothes or boots. They had gone to war naked, their bodies painted in vibrant colours and orkish symbols, wearing necklaces of human scalps, severed fingers and rat skulls as trophies. Even by greenskin standards, they seemed extraordinarily savage, as though some lost remnant from the very beginnings of ork history had somehow landed in the sewers of Broucheroc.

'Perhaps they are part of an outcast tribe?' a voice ventured, quietly.

Turning, Chelkar saw that Scholar had approached the meeting. Strictly speaking, as an ordinary trooper, he was not privy to command briefings – even at the platoon level. He hung back, staying to the edge of the half-circle of fire-team leaders who stood facing Chelkar.

A thin man, Scholar was taller than the other Vardans. Of the entire company, only the brutish Bulaven could match him for height. Alone of the men around him, Scholar was the only one who did not look down at the headless orks with either indifference or distaste. If anything, he appeared to find the dead xenos fascinating.

Chelkar had never known quite how to read Scholar. He was a strange bird, much given to random outpourings of facts and theories on almost any subject under the sun. Still, over time, Chelkar had learned to listen when Scholar offered his opinions. He found they were often of value.

'What is it, Scholar?' he asked, beckoning him forward. 'You have some insights?'

'I understand it is not unknown for ork war parties to be riven by religious schisms,' Scholar said, making no mention of where he might have gleaned such information. 'The orks who ambushed us might have been members of a tribe that has broken away from the main army. They might even be a form of ork heretic, come to hide in the sewers to elude their enemies. Perhaps they have adopted a primitive lifestyle as an attempt to return to the traditions of their orkish ancestors.'

'Perhaps,' Chelkar shrugged. 'But, who knows? There could be any number of reasons why they are so poorly equipped. The important issue is whether there are more of them down here somewhere.'

'With all due respect, isn't that a question for others, sergeant?' Davir asked. 'I mean, we have done our duty. We were sent to find out what happened to the other patrols. Our mission is accomplished. We have identified the culprits, searched them out and destroyed them. Frankly, I think it is time we returned to the surface for some hot recaf and medals all round. Not to mention some warm blankets and dry clothes. We are foot soldiers. Our place in the grand scheme of things is to follow orders. We should leave the bigger questions to the geniuses who command us.'

'Spoken like a true Guardsman, Davir,' Chelkar said. A smile ghosted across his face.

'However, I have never liked leaving a job half-done. Especially when it could be vital to see that job finished. If there are more of these feral orks about, they need to be located and destroyed. Otherwise, they represent a danger. If they manage to establish themselves permanently down here, they might destabilise our efforts to defend the city. It is bad enough Broucheroc is surrounded by orks on four sides. Imagine how much worse it would be if they gained control of the sewers. They could use the tunnels to penetrate our defences at will. The city would be under siege from below. We can't allow that to happen.'

'I suspect you are going to order us to do something noble, sergeant,' Davir's face wore a glum expression.

'Noble? Not really. We will continue through the sewers a while longer and see if we can find where the orks came from. Of course, given the problems with our comms, we won't be able to contact Sector Command to tell them where we're going. We also won't be able to call in reinforcements or heavy support if things get hot. The best I can do is send a message back with the wounded, apprising Command of our plans.'

'And if we run into trouble?' asked Davir. 'Not to seem a

pessimist, sergeant, but what happens if we find more orks down here than we can handle?'

'Then, we shall just have to fight our way through them,' Chelkar said. 'If that happens, and if we survive, you will probably get the medal you were talking about, Davir. Although, I can't promise to do anything about finding a hot cup of recaf. Not in Broucheroc.'

'I never thought I would agree with the arseholes who run this war,' Davir said, as they trudged through the tunnels several hours later. 'But, apparently, the generals are right when they tell us to shut up and follow orders. After all, look what happens when sergeants decide to start thinking for themselves and show some initiative. It's the poor, bloody Guardsman who suffers. That's what happens.'

He was back walking point at the head of the patrol with Scholar and Bulaven. According to the chronometer function on Scholar's auspex, they had been in the sewers for a grand total of nearly eight hours. As far as Davir was concerned, they were among the most miserable hours he had endured in his life.

He was cold and wet. He stank of sewage. His boots and trousers were sodden with water and, he was sure, other substances that were far more unpleasant. To make matters worse, the sewer waters had deepened as they pushed on into the tunnels. With his short, stocky build, Davir was now wading waist deep in water.

'And you needn't think I've forgotten your part in this, Scholar,' he said, viperishly.

'My part?' the other man blinked. 'I wasn't aware I had one.'

'No? "Perhaps they are part of an outcast tribe",' Davir said, mimicking Scholar's voice. He turned to Bulaven. 'You should have heard him, fat man. If he'd put his tongue any further up Chelkar's arse, we'd have had to surgically remove it. You couldn't just stay quiet, could you, Scholar? You had to open your slop-hole and send us all on this fool's errand, heading deeper and deeper into the sewers on the trail of an imaginary tribe of orks.'

'I was simply offering an opinion.'

'Well, *don't*,' he spat. 'In future, if you have any opinions, keep them to yourself. We'll all live longer that way. As it is, Chelkar will probably keep us wandering these damn tunnels until we get lost and die.'

'You know, you really should try to look on the bright side, Davir,' Bulaven said. 'After all, things could be worse.'

'The bright side? Do you see one hereabouts?' Davir gestured in annoyance at the sewer walls about them. 'I'll tell you what, you lumbering moron. If you can find a bright side to our situation, why don't you share it with us? We are in a sewer. We have been drenched to the bone with untreated sewage. In the next few days, we are undoubtedly destined to contract every deadly disease known to humanity. Assuming, of course, the orks don't kill us first. So, what is this "bright side" you were talking about? I can't wait to hear it.'

'Welllll...' For a moment, Bulaven seemed stymied. Either Davir's hectoring had put him off and he had lost his train of thought or, as Davir himself suspected, it was the first time the fat man had considered their situation in detail.

'Go on, imbecile. I'm listening. In fact, I'm on tenterhooks. What is the bright side?'

'Well,' said Bulaven, finally, 'it could be *colder*.'

'That's it?' Davir was aghast. 'After all this – the sewers, the orks, the shit-stink, the damp – that is the best you could come up with? "It could be colder". Truly, your idiocy holds no bounds.'

'Actually, Bulaven is right.' Abruptly, Scholar became animated, a familiar gleam of discovery shining in his eyes. 'It doesn't seem as cold now as it did an hour ago. I'd almost swear the sewers are getting *warmer*.'

Pausing to peer intently at their surroundings, Scholar suddenly handed the auspex to Davir and hurried over to examine a filth-encrusted section of the sewer wall. Pulling out his bayonet, he began to dig at the wall, removing an accumulation of mud and sewer residue to reveal a rusted metal pipe, bolted at about head height.

'We couldn't see it before under the layers of dried-out sewage,' Scholar said, pulling at the dirt with his hands to expose more of the pipe. 'It seems to run the length of the tunnel, bracketed to the wall. I would estimate it as about fifteen centimetres in diameter. It's definitely warm to the touch. I'd say it's some kind of heating system.'

'A heating system?' Davir squinted as Scholar excavated more of the area, revealing several similar pipes running in parallel. 'The smell in these tunnels must be getting to you, Scholar. Who would build a heating system to keep a sewer warm?'

'The function of the pipes is unmistakeable.' Scholar's voice was firm. He knocked on the surface of one of them with his bayonet, creating a hollow noise. 'The sound would be different if there were liquid inside. The system is obviously designed to funnel hot air or gases, warming the sewer tunnels. They couldn't possibly be serving any other purpose.'

'All right, Scholar,' Davir said, humouring him. 'So, these pipes are warming the sewers. If you insist on it, I believe you.'

Glancing behind him, he saw Chelkar approaching them, presumably eager to know what had caused this latest hold-up.

'But I leave it to you to tell the sergeant.'

'You were right, Scholar,' Sergeant Chelkar said. He waved a gloved hand in front of his face. 'Look. My breath is no longer frosting in the air. It is definitely getting warmer.'

Twenty minutes had passed since Scholar had shown him the heating pipes and explained their function. Initially, Chelkar had expressed the same disbelief as Davir. Deciding to test the matter, he had ordered the main force of the platoon to remain where they were, while he scouted further down the tunnel in the company of Fire-team Three. It had quickly become clear, however, that Scholar's theory had merit. Chelkar could not be sure whether the pipes were really a heating system, but it was beyond question that the temperature in the tunnel was rising.

'But what does it mean?' Bulaven asked, while Chelkar pulled out his map of the tunnels in an attempt to check their location. 'Why would anyone want to build a heating system for a sewer?'

'I don't know,' Scholar replied. 'But, looking at these tunnels and the pipes, the entire system could be centuries old. Perhaps even older. It could date back to when the city was originally founded. Who knows what secrets Broucheroc might hold beneath the surface?'

'Hnn. Listen to you,' Davir snorted in disgust. 'From the way you talk, Scholar, you'd think we'd found the secret of eternal youth or a treasure chest filled with gemstones. Ultimately, all we've discovered is that some idiots once built a central heating system for the express purpose of keeping their bodily motions warm. Frankly, I don't see it as any great cause for rejoicing. You ask me, it just demonstrates the extraordinary stupidity of the whole human race. I'd much prefer it if someone could find us some dry clothes and a good cup of recaf in this cesspit. Now, *that* would be a discovery worth celebrating.'

'You're missing the bigger picture,' Chelkar told him, refolding the map and placing it back in the pocket of his tunic. 'We've encountered two strange things since we entered the sewers. First, a group of feral orks armed only with primitive weapons. Second, a heating system for the sewers. I'm no savant, but I'd say they are likely to be connected. Either way, we need to check it out.'

He turned to Scholar.

'It only started getting warmer once we had pushed pretty deeply into the tunnels. Does it mean the heating system doesn't extend to the upper levels?'

'It could do,' Scholar nodded. 'Heat rises, so there would be a transfer of warmth up through the system even without the pipes. From what I've seen, however, the sewers appear to be designed to channel the waste downward. I can't be sure, but I suspect there's some form of treatment plant deeper underground. It was probably designed as a central collection point for all the city's sewage.'

'All right.' With a nod of his head, Chelkar turned to gaze into the darkness of the tunnel before them. 'We'd better go get the rest of the platoon and start moving. According to what I can decipher from the map, if we follow this tunnel it should lead us down to the lower levels. If the orks and these heating pipes are somehow connected, we'll find the answer deeper in the system.'

An hour passed. Soon, Scholar's theory that the pipes served as a heating system was proven beyond debate. As the platoon pushed onward, descending into a deeper section of tunnels, the sewers continued to grow warmer. Before long, it seemed remarkable this was the same environment which had once been cold enough to make them shiver. The surroundings began to feel almost balmy. If anything, having equipped themselves with the freezing temperatures of Broucheroc in mind, the Vardans found they were overdressed – even without their greatcoats.

The other hardships of the sewers remained. There was still the dampness to deal with; the thigh-high waters; the stench of raw sewage. After ten years spent freezing in Broucheroc, however, the warmth of the lower sewer levels made the rest of it feel almost bearable.

As the Vardans journeyed onward, the members of Fire-team Three had taken up their usual position walking point for the rest of the platoon. They were tired, but with the change in temperature, even Davir had found relatively little to complain about.

'Have you seen this?' Scholar said. 'Now, this is interesting.'

He drew the attention of the other members of the fire-team to a series of fist-sized fungal growths clinging to the tunnel wall over one of the heating pipes. Scholar prodded at the growths with his long fingers, showing all the enthusiasm of a child with a new toy.

'It's certainly some kind of fungi,' Scholar said. 'But I don't recognise the species.'

'Shouldn't you be careful with that?' Bulaven raised an eyebrow. 'Fungus can be poisonous, can't it?'

'Hmm?' Scholar did not appear to have heard him. 'Do you see how the heating pipes are already exposed here? In the other tunnels, they were buried under dried sewage. I think the fungus may be responsible for uncovering the pipe.'

He pointed at the green tendrils anchoring each fungal globe to the warm surface of the pipe.

'These anchor-roots must have absorbed all the nutrients and organic material from their surroundings, leaving the remaining inorganic detritus to fall away – hence, revealing the pipe underneath.'

Doing his best to look interested, Bulaven tried to follow Scholar's explanation. As ever, he found it hard going. In contrast to Scholar, whose learning covered hundreds of topics, Bulaven had been given only enough education to help him work in the foundries on his homeworld of Vardan – no more.

'It's amazing really,' Scholar stroked his fingers over the fungus almost lovingly. 'This may well be the beginning of a new ecosystem. The warmth from the heating pipes has created the conditions in which this fungi can flourish, allowing it to colonise the environment. At the same time, the presence of the fungus has effected the environment itself in turn – clearing the sewer residue from around the pipes and allowing them to heat the tunnels more effectively. I wonder where the fungi came from? It could be a new species, entirely native to the sewers of Broucheroc. If only there was some way for me to establish its identity...'

'I may be able to help you there,' Davir said. 'Although, I suspect you won't be thrilled with the answer.'

At some point, Davir had wandered away while the others were studying the fungus. Now, having scouted further down the tunnel, he returned. He walked toward them with an unhappy expression.

'While you two half-wits were gawking at the local life-forms, I decided to check what was ahead of us,' Davir said, his face grim. 'You'd better come and have a look. And fetch Sergeant Chelkar, as well – he'll want to see this. I have bad news, Scholar. Your fungus isn't a *new* species, after all.'

'You know something, Davir?' Bulaven whispered beside him. 'I thought you were only joking before, when you said this place was hell. Now, I am not so sure.'

They were lying on the ledge of an overflow outlet with Scholar and Sergeant Chelkar, peering cautiously over the edge to survey a scene that might have issued directly from the worst nightmares of every man, woman and child alive in Broucheroc.

The tunnel they were following had opened out into a broad atrium-like space where dozens of other sewer tunnels met. Davir had no idea who had built the city's sewerage system, but he was forced to concede the extraordinary scale of their design.

Considering they were underground, the size of the atrium where the tunnels came together was vast. It put him in mind of the Grand Basilica of the Imperial Light on the planet Solnar. Where the Basilica had been dedicated to the glories of the Emperor, however, the sewer atrium was like a gargantuan cathedral devoted to the disposal of human waste. For all that it took the breath away, though; Davir found his amazement at the atrium was overrided by more immediate concerns.

'You understand why I thought you should see it?' he said, for once ignoring the chance to snipe at Bulaven. 'Obviously, this is where the feral orks came from.'

The entire area of the atrium was covered in fungal growth, creating a weird alien landscape that was almost mesmerising in its strangeness. The predominant colour was green, but in places, Davir could see startling outgrowths and carpet-like patches in blue, red and purple. It was as though they stood on the edge of an altogether inhuman world, monstrously transformed in accordance with the needs of the *xenos*.

'It is the warmth from the heating pipes,' Scholar whispered. 'It created the perfect conditions for ork colonisation.'

Like the rest of them, he seemed caught between fear and awe. The Guardsmen spoke quietly, careful to keep their bodies low and stay out of sight. Dozens of orks could be seen moving in the fungal panorama below them. It was likely there were many more within earshot.

'This could well have started with just a single spore,' Scholar said. 'One spore, drifting down from the city above. In any other part of the sewers, it would have lain dormant. But, here, it found a warm setting in which it could thrive. The spore gave birth to an ork, whose body in turn released thousands more spores. They took root here as well, slowly changing the environment to make it more suitable for their needs. Now, it is like the whole area is an enormous nursery.'

All across the atrium, there were thousands of round globes of fungus – adhering to walls, suspended from overhanging pipes, or lying thick on the ground in clusters. They were like the examples they had seen earlier in the tunnel, but *bigger*. They ranged all the way up to several metres in width. Unlike the ones in the tunnel, the true purpose of the globes in the atrium was clear. On some of the larger specimens, the round outer skin of the fungus was pulled thin enough that shadowed forms could be seen within them.

Observing the scene, Davir realised he would have to revise his opinions. Long ago, Scholar had told him that orks grew from spores like mould or fungi. He had never believed it, instinctively rejecting the idea as a foolish fancy.

Yet, here was the proof. He could not argue against the evidence of his own eyes. Even as he watched, a muscular clawed arm emerged from one of the larger globes. Within seconds, the new ork had pulled itself free of its fungal chrysalis. Its skin still slick with amniotic fluid, it emerge eagerly into the world and threw its head back in an exhortation of triumph, before stumbling from the atrium in search of conquest – another ork born to plague a suffering, dying galaxy.

Davir could not be sure which was worse: the sight of so many orks waiting to be born, or the sound of their breathing. He could hear them, even from the ledge. The air of the atrium was alive with a constant susurrus. The skins of the larger globes rose and fell in time with the breathing of the horrors hidden inside them. The thought of it made Davir uneasy. He was standing no more than a stone's throw from an army of sleeping monsters, which might awaken at any moment.

'We will have to withdraw,' Chelkar said. 'Get back to the surface. There are too many of them for us to fight. We have to warn the city. Then, we can lead a larger force back down here to destroy the orks. Otherwise, if this colony survives, it could tip the balance of the war. We'd be fighting on two different fronts at once – above ground and below. Broucheroc could fall.'

Nodding in unspoken agreement, the four of them turned to retreat back down the tunnel to where the rest of the platoon was waiting. Instinctively, they knew Chelkar was right. After the ork ambush earlier in the day, there were barely twenty-five men left in the platoon – some of them wounded. The situation in the sewers was too big for them to deal with. For there to be any hope of success, they had to get back to the surface to warn the city.

Before they could move, though, the sound of shots came from further along the tunnel in the direction they were headed. Casting a wary eye at the atrium behind them, Davir saw the sudden disturbance had not gone unnoticed. He could see orks moving among the fungal landscape, alerted to the presence of intruders.

Suddenly, any prospect of an easy withdrawal appeared out of the question.

Afterwards, it would never be entirely clear who had fired the shots that had given the Vardans away. As far as anyone could work out, the men of Fire-team Six were the most likely culprits.

They had been assigned to stand overwatch on a subsidiary tunnel that ran off the main tunnel the Vardans were using. At some point, while Davir and the others were observing the atrium, the men of Six were attacked by a large group of orks.

It was unclear whether the orks had blundered into them by simple bad luck, or if the members of Six had given themselves away somehow. Whatever the case, it hardly mattered. By the time the dust settled, the five men of Fire-team Six were dead – as were over seven times their number of orks. More importantly, however, the fact there were humans in the tunnels was now known to every ork in earshot.

For Davir, the loss of the men of Fire-team Six was doubly troubling. He had known the fire-team's leader, Elias Yevgen, for years. They played cards together regularly, an activity of which Davir had been particularly fond, as Yevgen was perhaps the worst card player he had ever encountered. Money meant little in Broucheroc, not that the Guardsmen had it anyway, but it was a source of pride to Davir that he had beaten Yevgen so many times the man had been forced to offer the services of the next three generations of his family as indentured servants in order to pay off his debts. Yevgen had no children, so their contract was more theoretical than actual, but it was the winning that was important.

Sadly, the agreement had been rendered null and void by the bite of an orkish axe. Davir would never know what it was to own three generations of a man's family as slaves. Similarly, he would no longer be able to rub the fact in Yevgen's face every time they played cards.

More immediately, though, when Davir heard the sound of distant shots and saw that the orks in the atrium were now aware of their presence, his heart sank. He had a terrible feeling he knew what was coming next.

'Someone will have to hold the orks back and cover our retreat,' he heard Chelkar say.

'We understand,' Davir sighed, feeling resignation at something he knew was inevitable. As their commander, Chelkar was required to the lead the platoon to safety – meaning it fell to Bulaven, Scholar and himself to play the sacrificial lambs.

'We'll hold them as long as we can, sergeant.'

'Ten minutes,' Chelkar pulled the grenades from his belt and handed them to Davir. 'These should help. You have plenty of power packs? And, Bulaven? You have a laspistol for when the flamer gives out?' Seeing the three men nod, he continued. 'Give me ten minutes. It should give me time enough to get the rest of the men clear.'

'Ten minutes, sergeant,' Davir agreed. 'Although, I warn you, if you hear what sounds like a stampede in ten minutes' time, I wouldn't be surprised. It'll be the sound of me, Bulaven and Scholar running to catch up with you.'

'Ten minutes,' Davir shook his head once Chelkar was gone. 'Ten minutes, he says. Why not just ask for an hour and be done with it? For that matter, why doesn't he ask us to take on every ork on the planet, break the siege and save Broucheroc into the bargain?'

'It was you who told him we'd do it,' Bulaven said. 'In fact, you all but volunteered us...'

They were crouched in the tunnel, ready to make their stand. Bulaven had taken the fuel tanks of the flamer from his back and placed them on the ground. There had been no sight of the pursuing orks yet, but the thunderous rush of their stomping feet could be heard echoing down the tunnels.

'Can I help it if I am sentimental?' Davir shrugged. 'It was clear the sergeant was struggling with the unhappy duty of having to order someone to stay behind to face almost certain death. So, I took pity on him. I volunteered us. Don't tell me you would've done it any different, pig brain.'

'No, I wouldn't have done anything differently,' Bulaven said. 'Nor would Scholar. Sometimes, I think we are all as mad as each other.'

'Speak for yourself,' Davir checked the charge level on the power pack in his lasgun. 'I have a finely tuned mind and I intend to use it to survive this mess.'

'Perhaps you are thinking of painting yourself green and disguising yourself as a gretchin?' Scholar asked. 'You're certainly the right height.'

'Ho ho. If you were any more amusing, Scholar, I'd be afraid I might die laughing before the orks can get me. No, remember the plan I told you and everything will be all right.'

'This would be the plan to kill as many orks as we can, then run away?' Bulaven asked.

'Precisely.' Davir clicked off his safety. 'Now, shut up, both of you. The bastards are coming.'

It happened so quickly. Davir had been in combat on more occasions than he cared to count, but each time it was the same. It passed in a blur: minutes seemed like seconds, while seconds seemed like instants.

One moment, the orks were charging. Davir heard his own voice give the order to fire. He felt a wave of heat to the side of him as Bulaven triggered the flamer. In the tight confines of the tunnel, it was devastating. He saw orks burning, screaming. He and Scholar shot to the side of the flamer's expanding cone of fire, aiming for the orks at the edge of the inferno. He had spent ten years fighting orks in Broucheroc, but these creatures were hideous, terrifying. There was something about the war paint and the necklaces of bones. The orks seemed like savagery personified. If Davir had been created of less stern stuff, he might well have made water at the very sight of them.

All too soon, the flamer died. Where once there had been a fearsome torrent of fire, suddenly there were a few dying and fitful sparks.

'The canister's empty!' Dropping the flamer, Bulaven pulled at something on the fuel tank and then grabbed for the laspistol on his belt.

'Pull back!' Davir yelled. 'Run for it!'

As plans went, it was simple. Using the flamer, they had held off the orks for as long as they could. Once the flamer was empty, they had known they would need a diversion. It had been Davir's idea to strap every grenade they had – including the ones Chelkar had given them – to the flamer's fuel tank. The tank was empty, but even without fuel it made a useful source of extra shrapnel.

The grenades exploded with an impressive roar. The tunnel worked in their favour, channelling the blast and multiplying its power. Too much so, Davir realised as, unexpectedly, he felt the tunnel floor abruptly give way beneath his feet. For the briefest instant of time, he felt weightless.

Then, he fell into darkness.

'Davir! Davir!'

He awakened to a voice calling out his name as rough hands shook his body.

'Davir! Davir!'

For a moment, Davir wondered whether he was dead. Then, he opened his eyes, saw Bulaven's face looking down at him, and he knew he was not in the afterlife. At least, not any after-life he *wanted* to be in.

'Davir...'

'All right! If I answer you, will you stop rattling me like a rag doll? Didn't anyone ever tell you it's not a good idea to shake an unconscious man, Bulaven? For all you know, I could have a concussion.'

Taking his bearings, Davir looked around to find he was lying in another sewer tunnel. He couldn't see any orks.

'Where are we?'

'The floor gave way,' Bulaven told him. 'I think there must've been some kind of hatchway beneath us. When the grenades exploded, it blew open the hatchway and dropped us into a big overflow pipe underneath it.'

'So, basically, you're saying we fell down the drain? What about the orks? Didn't they follow us?'

'Not as far as I can tell. When we went down the overflow, a lot of water came down with us. Maybe they thought we'd been washed away. Either way, I haven't seen any orks since we landed.'

'Any idea how far we fell?' Standing up, Davir gazed at the tunnel ceiling. 'I wonder how far we are from Chelkar and the others?'

'I don't know. But I woke you because I was worried about Scholar.'

Bulaven moved aside and pointed to where Scholar lay unconscious against the tunnel wall. Going over to him, Davir saw a wound on Scholar's scalp. He checked his pulse.

'Well, he's alive,' Davir said. 'If you want a more informed opinion you'd have to find a medic. The head wound doesn't look too bad. We should probably just leave him to wake up in his own time.'

Davir turned and looked down the tunnel.

'Not to seem too exacting, Bulaven. But you did notice there's a light coming from the end of this tunnel, didn't you?'

'I did. Why? Do you think it's important?'

'Given that, for all we know, it's a torch-wielding mob of orks coming to finish us off? Yes, I'd say it could be important. You stay here with Scholar, while I go check it out. Oh, and you'd better keep your gun handy. Considering our luck so far today, whatever is causing the light, it's bound to be trouble.'

* * *

Following the light, Davir emerged into another cavernous underground space and was pleased to see there was no sign of a mob of orks – torch-wielding or otherwise – waiting to kill him. Instead, he saw a bewildering network of metal pipes that criss-crossed and came together at a squat, ugly metal building. Approaching it, he heard the sound of machines. He detected a distant rhythmic vibration through the soles of his boots.

'Finally, a delivery of personnel,' he heard a voice behind him. 'I was beginning to think our work here had been forgotten.'

Whirling in the direction of the sound, Davir found himself facing an old man in the faded robes of a tech-adept of the Adeptus Mechanicus. The ancient figure seemed as much machine as man, his body surrounded by fidgeting mechadendrites and his withered face barely visible from beneath the cowl of his robe. A half a dozen servitors trailed in his wake, as dutiful as dogs.

'I am Serberus, senior adept in charge of this pumping station,' the old man said. 'What is your designation?'

'Desig... Ah... My name is Davir.'

'Well, Layperson Davir, you can start by manually recalibrating the gas pressure in the methane feeds. The levels are still dropping, even with the temperature alterations in the sewer habitat. You have brought foodstuffs?'

'Food? Uh, no. Excuse me, did you say something about temperature alterations?

'Indeed,' Serberus nodded slowly. 'It is a pity about the foodstuffs. I have developed a method of processing the local lichens for their food value, but they are deficient in a number of vitamins.' One of his dendrites scratched absently at an ugly sore on the side of his head.

'Remember, we were talking about the temperature?' Davir prompted

'Hmm? Oh, yes. Methane production levels fell, so I redistributed some of the remaining supply toward heating the tunnels in order to encourage bacterial growth.'

'Bacteria?' This time, it was Davir's turn to scratch his own head. 'And why would you do that, exactly?'

The old man stared at him in incredulity for long seconds, before gesturing at the wide expanse of pipes and tunnels around them.

'Why, to perform my allotted task, of course. I can see your work instruction has been entirely deficient, Layperson Davir. The sewers of this city are a marvel of engineering, many thousands of years old. They are designed to be a self-sustaining system in which nothing of potential value is left unused. Human waste is converted into methane gas by the action of gene-sculpted bacteria bred specifically for that purpose. In turn, this methane is pumped to the surface to be used as fuel in some of the city's manufactoriums.'

'I see.'

Briefly, Davir considered the matter.

'So, if I understand this, you recently noticed the methane levels were falling? So you started heating the sewers, so the bacteria would create more methane. Is that right?'

'Indeed.'

'You do understand there is a war on?'

'Certainly,' Serberus gazed at him blithely. 'It is why we are short-handed. My fellow adepts in the sewers were transferred to other duties, years ago. I have been alone, with just these few servitors to help maintain the entire system. I will confess, Layperson Davir, I had even begun to wonder if my presence here had been somehow overlooked. But then, you arrived.'

'I'm not a coghead. I'm a Guardsman. As to the fall in methane production, I suspect that is to do with the war. At last count, more than four-fifths of the city's civilian population are dead. That's why your methane levels are falling. Less people means less shit, means less raw material for your bacteria to work on.'

In response, Serberus was silent. He stared at Davir with incomprehension.

'Don't you understand?' Davir asked him. 'Raising the temperature in the sewers was a mistake. In fact, it has put the city in danger. It has allowed the orks to infest the sewers.'

Still, the old man just stared at him.

'Are you deaf?' Davir said in mounting annoyance. 'I'm telling you that you've been wasting your time. Your work here is meaningless. Given the way that things operate in Broucheroc, there's every chance you've been forgotten. No one even knows you're down here.'

Suddenly, Serberus sprang to life. Screaming with incoherent rage, he leapt at Davir and tried to strangle him. Madness burned in his eyes. Catching his wrists, Davir fought to hold him back. Now they were standing so close, he could see the old man's skin was raddled with weeping sores. His gums were swollen and bleeding. Years of malnourishment had taken their toll. Despite this, Serberus was stronger than he looked. Insanity fuelled his strength.

As they struggled, the tech-adept's mechadendrites whipped into frenzy. Davir felt them scrabbling at his uniform, scratching at him. One of the dendrites gouged into his cheek, breaking the skin. He winced. Red with his blood, the dendrite withdrew and blindly stabbed at his face once more. Appalled, he realised it was trying to find his eyes, attempting to hook them from their sockets.

He felt a surge of anger. He had been trying to hold back so as not to hurt the old man, but it was time to end this.

Lowering his head like a bull, Davir butted Serberus across the bridge of the nose. As the pain made the old man shy away, the dendrites loosened their hold. Pressing home his momentary advantage, Davir twisted his body and levered Serberus over his shoulder. It was a demonstration of the effectiveness of the Guard's unarmed combat doctrine. Davir would not have cared to try it on an ork, but the tech-adept was a different story. Shrieking, the old man landed with a *thump* and was briefly still.

'Listen to me,' Davir said, holding out a placating hand as he saw Serberus stir back to life. 'Stay where you are. I don't want to hurt you.'

'Kill him,' the old man whispered, his voice as dry as dust and cracked with age. 'Kill him! Kill him! Kill him!'

For a second, Davir wondered who Serberus was talking to – until he heard the sound of heavy footsteps and saw the servitors lurching towards him.

They were hulking monstrosities, created from the union of machine and human corpse. There were six of them, each as old and poorly maintained as their master, Serberus: shambling, blank-eyed things that moved with the whirr of gears and the whine of motors.

Davir had seen servitors before. On some Imperial worlds they were relatively common, but he could never escape a feeling of horror when he looked at them. He understood enough to know they were not truly alive. For all that, the human parts still moved with the semblance of life, their owners were long dead, their bodies harvested and grafted to the machine for use as organic components.

Still, there was something unsettling about them, something sickening. The only reason that Davir did not give in to the impulse to flee in terror was that he was confident he could deal with them. He was armed, and they moved so slowly. Raising his lasgun to his shoulder, he sighted in on the lead servitor and drilled a las-blast through the centre of its forehead.

The abomination kept on moving.

Davir fired again. Another las-blast hit the servitor, destroying even more of its brain. It made no difference. The monster continued to advance towards him. They all did. Their slow, shuffling footsteps were like drumbeats, sounding his death-knell.

Realising the seriousness of his predicament, Davir looked around for somewhere to run. But it was too late. While he had been firing at the lead servitor, the others had moved to cut off every avenue of escape.

He fired his lasgun again, letting off a salvo of rapid shots in the hope of blasting his way through them. It was to no avail. No matter how much damage he did to their human parts, the servitors seemed indifferent to his efforts. When he fired at the machine parts, it barely dented them – the las-blasts were simply absorbed or deflected.

Trying to buy time, Davir retreated. His hand went to his belt in search of a grenade, only to remember he had used them all up against the orks. He switched his lasgun to full auto and fired off the remainder of the power pack in a matter of seconds. It achieved nothing. The servitors kept coming.

They had backed him into a corner. As one, the servitors lifted their arms towards him. In the background, he could hear Serberus still screaming at them to kill him. Horrified, Davir realised he was going to die.

'Adept! Desist immediately!' a strangely familiar voice called out in a commanding tone. 'Code command: epsilon beta nine-five, alpha seven-seven-seven omega! Adept! I am giving you an order!'

It was Scholar. Clutching at the wound on his temple, supported by Bulaven to the side of him, he advanced toward Serberus. The effect of his words was dramatic.

At a gesture from Serberus, the servitors suddenly stopped. Abruptly docile, the old man bowed to Scholar.

'Magos, I acknowledge your authority. I am yours to command.'

'Very good, adept,' Scholar said. 'Return to your duties. I will speak with you later.'

'I never thought I'd ever be quite so happy to see you, Scholar,' Davir said to him, once the tech-adept and the servitors had tottered away. 'Some day you will have to tell me just how you did that. In the meantime, however, with your help, I think perhaps I have a solution to all our problems...'

'Fire-team Three to Sergeant Chelkar. Are you receiving this, sergeant? Please respond.'

Chelkar was getting ready to make his peace with death by the time the call arrived. He did not intend to go quietly, but he could see no choice other than to accept the inevitable.

He had lost nearly half his men. It was all the remainder could do to hold off the orks. The enemy were everywhere. The Vardans were attempting to stage a fighting retreat, but it was hopeless. There was no way they could hold back the orks while making the long journey to the surface.

The call changed everything. Chelkar heard the comm-bead in his ear buzz into life, while a familiar voice came over the airwaves.

'Fire-team Three to Sergeant Chelkar. Are you receiving? Over.'

'Davir?' Chelkar voxed him back. 'Is that you?'

'Most definitely, sergeant. Listen, we have to make this quick. We're using some of the equipment down here to boost the signal and beat the interference from the tunnels, but Scholar says it won't take long for it to burn out. I have some directions for you. I know you outrank me, but you have to do what I say. Trust me. I have a way to pull your fat out of the fire.'

'It's called Tunnel Section A-92,' Davir had said, before giving him precise directions on how to reach it. Guiding his men toward it, Chelkar could only hope it wasn't some sick joke. Davir had promised him a miracle. He hoped he could deliver.

'Sergeant! This way!'

Leading his men down the tunnels with the orks in hot pursuit, Chelkar suddenly saw Bulaven ahead. The big man was gesturing frantically, urging the Vardans forward.

'Quickly! Quickly!' Bulaven shouted, herding them towards a place where the tunnel briefly narrowed before widening again. 'Scholar has jury-rigged the mechanism, but we don't have much time!'

Chelkar turned to ask what he was talking about, but when the last of the Vardans were past the section of narrowed tunnel, Bulaven gave a signal.

'Now! Do it! They're all across!'

A concealed metal shutter slammed down with the screech of rusted gears, cutting them off from the advancing horde of orks. Once the shutter came down, Davir and Scholar emerged from by the side of it.

'Not bad, eh, sergeant?' Davir smiled like a feline with a mouthful of cream. 'It is an old sluice gate. We saw it on the sewer schematics and knew it was just what we needed.'

'That shutter won't hold them back long,' Chelkar said. Already, he could hear the orks pounded against it from the other side.

'It won't need to,' Davir's smile widened. 'It only has to buy us the time to get back to the surface.'

He had lived in the sewers for so long. A lifetime, he supposed. Now, finally, it was over.

Deep below the city of Broucheroc, in the pumping station that had been his home for decades, Serberus stood in the main control room and felt an abiding sense of sorrow.

The feeling was unfamiliar to him. In many ways, so was every emotion. In order that he might better perform his labours, long ago his brain had been fitted with cybernetic implants designed to regulate and moderate his emotional responses.

He suspected the implants had begun to fail. Similarly, he was experiencing a curious malfunction in some of his organic systems. The ducts intended to provide lubrication to his eyes were overflowing. Tears stained his face.

For years, he had known nothing but duty. He had maintained the sewers, dedicated his every waking hour to ensure the system worked efficiently. It had been a constant losing battle, even more so since he had been left alone with only the servitors to help him.

Still, he had done what was expected. He had kept to his appointed task, foreswearing the half-remembered pleasures of friendship and human interaction. In the face of advancing age, and the progressive decline of his own augmetic systems, he had continued his labours.

He had not asked for thanks. As a servant of the Machine God, it was not his place to expect any honour for his work. In many ways, he was as much a component of the system as a bleed-valve or a humble restraining bolt. As with any component, ultimately he would wear down and need to be replaced. The only surprise was that he had continued in service as long as he had.

The news he was no longer needed had been unexpected. He had been told he was obsolete, as were the sewers. That last news had been the most surprising. With a single stroke, his entire life, every sacrifice he had endured, had been rendered meaningless.

He had been shocked, but there was no questioning his orders. They had come from the tall tech-priest – the one his bodyguards called 'Scholar'. He looked and acted strangely for a magos, but that was hardly an issue. His status was clear. He had spoken to Serberus in machine code, using all the correct commandments and overrides.

A tiny part of Serberus had wanted to rebel. He had wanted to refuse the order, but the impulse had quickly passed. He understood he was merely a small cog in the Great Machine. It was not his place to defy his superiors. The fact that he had even considered it was simply further proof of his growing malfunction. His life was no longer useful. It was time to put an end to it.

Moving his hands over the controls responsible for overseeing the sewers' function, Serberus adjusted the valves in the massive methane storage tanks beneath the pumping station. He raised the pressure in the tanks to critical levels.

He felt a tremor beneath his feet as the tanks struggled to hold together. He had pushed the system as far as it would go. His hand went to a red ignition switch, set under a protective plexiplast bubble in the centre of the control panel. He lifted the bubble, exposing the switch.

With a last prayer to the Machine God, Serberus followed the orders that Scholar had given him. He pressed the switch, sending a spark into the system, and welcomed oblivion.

The effect was spectacular. As the spark entered the system, the methane tanks ruptured as the gases inside ignited. Serberus was atomised by the blast, along with the pumping station.

A vast superheated cloud of burning methane exploded outward, expanding in every direction. Channelled by the tunnels, it moved at a speed faster than sound. By the time the roar of the explosion reached any given point in the sewers, there was nothing alive there to hear it – the fire cloud had already raced ahead, incinerating everything in its path.

In the ork-infested atrium, devastation came without warning. The weird fungal landscape of the birthing grounds was destroyed in an instant. Embryonic orks, yet to be born, burst into flame. Caught in the raging firestorm, every ork in the sewers was burned to ash. There were no survivors. The fire scoured the tunnels of life. Even ork spores could not withstand the inferno.

The fire cloud sped on. By the time it reached the surface the worst of the heat had dissipated, but sewer coverings were suddenly sent vaulting into the air all over Broucheroc due to the massive change of pressure. The ground beneath the city trembled. It was like an earthquake. Across the city, the pious made the sign of the aquila and prayed to the Emperor to stop the ground from rising to swallow them. Some wondered whether an angry god had awoken beneath their feet, a new horror to be added to the city's ills.

Briefly, the ground rumbled once more.

Then, it was quiet.

'We survived,' Chelkar said, afterwards.

He was standing in the shadow of a burned-out building, watching as the first glimmers of dawn touched the sky. Half an hour earlier, the Vardans had emerged from the sewers with hardly any time to spare. A few seconds, either way, and they would have been caught in the blast. As it was, they were still alive. Normally, it would have been a cause for celebration, but there were still other matters to which he needed to attend.

'Yes, we survived,' Davir said, standing beside him. He smiled, showing his bad teeth. 'Of course, I never had any doubt of it – that I would survive myself, you understand. Frankly, this city hasn't yet come up with the ork who can kill me.'

'Thank the Emperor for small mercies, then,' Chelkar said. 'It would be a shame to lose you.'

Nearby, the other survivors from the patrol were doing their best to recover from their ordeal. Men tended their wounds, or helped injured comrades. One of the Guardsmen had even managed to find fuel and a brazier. Troopers huddled around it for warmth. Ration bars were being handed around.

They had survived, but only at the cost of the lives of half the platoon. Chelkar hadn't lied to Davir when he said he did not want to lose him. He did not want to lose any of them.

'You realise, there will have to be a report made,' Chelkar told Davir. 'Probably a lot of them. General HQ and Sector Command will want to know about the orks in the sewers and where they came from. Most of all, they'll want to know how we destroyed the orks and we blew up the sewers. For that matter, I'd like the answer to it myself.'

'It is a long story, sergeant,' Davir shrugged. 'Though, suffice to say, I acted with extraordinary heroism throughout the entire business. Still, perhaps it would be better if you heard the story tomorrow. When we are both more rested.'

'When you have had the chance to come up with some convincing lies, you mean?'

'Precisely, sergeant.'

'Very well,' Chelkar agreed. 'Tomorrow, then.'

* * *

'Do you think we'll be in trouble?' Bulaven asked, later, once dawn had broken. 'For destroying the sewers, I mean?'

He stood around the brazier with Davir and Scholar, trying to keep warm. The balmy warmth of the sewers was a distant memory.

'I shouldn't think so,' Davir said. 'They were mostly derelict, anyway. If some general now finds his indoor plumbing no longer works, it is just tough luck. He can shit in a ditch like the rest of us. Besides, Chelkar will help cover for us. He's a good man, the sergeant. Of course, one thing still interests me.'

He turned toward Scholar and favoured him with a penetrating stare.

'I know you've always been a mine of information, Scholar. But I can't wait to hear your explanation for what happened in the sewers. Serberus may have been crazy, but it doesn't explain how you knew the codes the cogheads use. Well? I'm waiting.'

'It's been a long day,' Scholar said. 'Perhaps you will let me tell you tomorrow?'

Davir grimaced, looking out at the landscape of the city where he woke up every day knowing it could be his last. He shrugged.

'Tomorrow, then,' he said.

DEATH WORLD

Steve Lyons

CHAPTER ONE

As soon as he woke, Trooper Lorenzo knew there was something wrong.

He rolled to his feet, simultaneously drawing his fang. He crouched in silence, in the dark, ready to drive half a metre of Catachan steel into the heart of any man or beast that thought it could sneak up on him.

But Lorenzo was alone.

He turned on the light, suppressing a prickling, creeping feeling as he realised again just how close the walls of his basic cabin were. And beyond those walls...

Lorenzo's bed was undisturbed; he preferred the floor, though even this was too flat for his liking. He could feel the beginnings of a stiff neck. All the same, he had slept for almost five hours. Longer than usual. Warp space did that to him. Out there, beyond the adamantium shell of the ship that carried him, there was nothing. But the warp itself distorted space and time, and that played hell with Lorenzo's instincts – and his body clock.

His brain itched. He was tired, but he knew he wouldn't sleep again now. He cursed his weakness. His tiredness would make him less alert. In the jungle, it could mean the difference between life and death.

Lorenzo was safe here, in theory. No enemies of the Imperium lurked in the shadows. No predators to sneak up on him as he slept, unguarded. Only the warp itself to worry about, and the possibility that it might capriciously tear the ship and its occupants apart – and there was nothing he could do about that if it happened. Nothing anyone could do.

They said no one but the Navigators could look into the warp. They said it would drive a normal man insane. Still, Lorenzo wished he could take that chance. He wished the ship had windows, so he could face his enemy and, perhaps, begin to understand it as the Navigators did.

Lorenzo had been in the thick of a space battle once. He had sat inside a cabin like this one, gripping the side of an acceleration couch as he rode out the shockwaves of near misses and glancing blows, his knuckles white; his life, his destiny, in the hands of a ship's captain and his gunners – and of the Emperor, of course. He had hated that feeling of helplessness. He had prayed for the attackers to board the ship, so he could have met them face to face. When Lorenzo died, he wanted the comfort of knowing he had fought his best against a superior foe – and if he had his way, that foe would be no mere space pirate or ork, but something more worthy of his origins and training.

When Lorenzo died, he wanted to be able to salute his killer, and be buried in its soil.

He splashed a handful of water on his face, and ran a hand through his tangled black hair. He threw on his camouflage jacket, though it would be useless against the greys and whites of the ship's interior. He re-sheathed his knife, and was comforted by its weight against his leg; his Catachan fang was a part of him, as much as his limbs were. As unlikely as it was that an attack would come, he had learned always to be prepared. It was when you allowed yourself to get comfortable that death could strike unexpectedly.

Somewhere on this ship, he was sure that other members of the company would be awake. He could probably find a card game.

Lorenzo's booted feet rang against the metal floor as he left his cabin, tinny echoes returning to his ears. The air was recycled, stale, and it didn't carry sounds in the way that fresh air did. The artificial gravity wasn't quite the same as that of any planet he'd visited. And it was quiet – so deathly quiet. There were none of the sounds of nature to which Lorenzo was attuned, the subtle clues that mapped out his surroundings for him and warned when danger approached. Instead, there was only the faint throb of engines, the vibrations reverberating through the hull so their origin was untraceable.

There was something wrong...

Everything was wrong. Man wasn't meant to exist in this unnatural environment. None of its signs could be trusted, and this made Lorenzo uneasy. If he couldn't rely on his own instincts, what could he rely on? 'Fear not the creatures of the jungle but those that lurk within your head.' The old Catachan proverb came to him unbidden and he thanked the Emperor that his company had its next assignment. They were already on their way to a new world, a fresh challenge.

He didn't know the details yet. Still, he had no doubt of one thing. Soon – within days, he hoped – his squad would be fighting their way across hostile terrain and through hostile creatures, beset by threats from all directions. It was likely some of them would die. He would be in his element again, his destiny returned to his own hands.

He ached for that moment.

It was early afternoon, ship time, when Colonel 'Stone Face' Graves summoned his Third Company of the Catachan XIV Regiment to the briefing room.

The men of four platoons, their bandoliers slung across their backs, crowded into the small area. Four platoons, comprising twenty-two squads – including two squads of Catachan Devils, who stood near the front and around whom even the most hardened veterans left a respectful space. Then there were the hulking, low-browed ogryns, included in the briefing as a courtesy though they would most likely understand only half of what was said. So long as they were pointed towards the enemy and permitted to rend and maim, they would be happy.

Lorenzo felt comforted by the presence of so many compatriots – by the press of their bodies and the natural, earthy odours of dirt and sweat.

'Listen up, you soft-skinned losers,' barked the colonel. A howl of good-natured protest rose from the assembled company, but Graves's chiselled features remained harsh and rigid. 'Naval Command think you lot have had it easy too long, and I agree with them. I begged them: "No more milk runs. I want no less than the dirtiest, most dangerous job you've got. I won't have my Jungle Fighters turning into fat, lazy sons of acid grubs who wouldn't lift a hand to scratch their own arses!" So, ladies, last chance to pamper yourselves in your luxury quarters – because as of this evening, you'll be working for your keep.'

This pronouncement was met by a rousing cheer.

'Planetfall at 19.00 hours,' the colonel continued, his voice loud and clear across the tumult though he'd made no effort to raise it. 'Anyone not in full kit and waiting at the airlocks by 18.30 finds himself on punishment detail for a month!'

'*Yes, sir!*' came the answering swell from the crowd.

'Colonel,' someone yelled from the back. Lorenzo recognised the voice of 'Hotshot' Woods, from his own squad. 'You serious? Is this going to be a real challenge for us this time?'

'You idlers ever hear of Rogar III?' growled Graves. 'It's a jungle world, out in the back of beyond. Explorators found it a couple of years ago, decided it was right for colonising and strip-mining. Just one problem: They'd been beaten to it. That's why they called on us. We have Guardsmen down there fighting orks for the past year and a half, but they're starting to find it tough going.'

Lorenzo joined in the collective jeers of mock sympathy.

'They're crying out for someone to hold their hands,' added Graves, to a roar of laughter. 'You see, seems Rogar wasn't the walk in the park they thought it'd be. Three weeks ago, in response to reports from the front, the planet was re-categorised as no longer suitable for colonisation...' He left a long pause there, but every man present knew what was coming, and anticipation hung heavy in the recycled air.

'...on account of it being classified as a deathworld!' concluded the colonel – and this time, the cheer went on much longer and louder.

'It's a crock, that's what it is.'

Lorenzo was sharing a mess hall table with four other members of his squad. He looked down at his bowl gloomily, and let a dollop of over-processed grey mulch slide from his spoon. Another thing he hated: Imperial Guard rations. If he'd been planetside, he'd have found something – some herb or spice – to make them more palatable. Or someone would have hunted down some indigenous beast, and his squad would have feasted on meat.

Lorenzo considered not eating at all until he had made planet-fall. But on top of his disturbed sleep patterns, the last thing he needed was to let his energy levels dip. He gathered another spoonful, thrust it into his mouth and tried to swallow without tasting it.

'Stone Face got it right,' continued Sergeant 'Old Hardhead' Greiss in his gravelly voice. 'This is just another wet-nursing mission for a bunch of city boys who got in over their heads. You tell me, how can a planet go from being colony material one day to deathworld the next? It can't happen!'

'I don't know, sergeant,' said Brains Donovits, his thick black eyebrows beetling as his brow furrowed. 'I've been keeping an eye on the comms traffic, and the latest report from the commissars on the ground makes for pretty interesting reading. They've had some real problems out there.'

'Yeah,' put in Hotshot Woods, his blue eyes sparkling as he

suppressed a grin, 'and you know Command wouldn't send us in without good reason, sergeant. They know what they're doing.'

Greiss shot the young trooper a stern glare through narrowed eyes. It only lasted a second, though, before he dropped the pretence and let out a bark of laughter, slapping Woods amiably on the back.

'It'll be the same old story,' grumbled the grizzled sergeant as his good humour subsided. 'Things not going too well at the front, orks getting too close to Command HQ for the top brass's liking. The next thing you know, some officer's been stung by a bloodwasp or got himself a nettle rash, or... or...'

'Got his foot tangled in a poison creeper,' suggested Steel Toe Dougan in his usual laid-back tone.

'Suddenly, he's screaming "Deathworld"!'

'There has also been some mention,' Donovits continued undeterred, 'of abnormalities in Rogar III's planetary readings. The Adeptus Mechanicus went in to investigate, but found nothing. Nothing but orks, anyhow.'

'Ah, listen to Brains,' scoffed Greiss. 'Never happy 'less he's got his nose in some report or other.'

Donovits shrugged. 'It pays to be forewarned, sergeant.'

'And since when did Navy reports tell you anything worth reading? The only place you get to know your enemy, trooper, is down there on its surface, in the thick of the jungle. Man against nature.'

Lorenzo felt something stirring in his chest at Greiss's words. He'd been feeling less edgy since they'd dropped out of the warp into real space, for the final approach to their destination, but still he longed to escape this prison. It was almost worse, knowing that release was so close. Time seemed to have slowed down for him. Lorenzo knew the others were restless, too, chafing for action. He didn't know if they shared his sense of unease, if the warp had affected them as it had him, and he wouldn't ask. There were some things you didn't talk about.

'I don't know, sergeant,' said Woods. 'There were times on that last world I wished I *had* stayed curled up on a bedroll with a good book. Might have made for more thrills, if you know what I mean.'

'Got a point there, Hotshot,' laughed Greiss. 'I could almost have felt sorry for them... what were they called?'

'Rhinoceraptors,' prompted Donovits.

'Yeah, right. Few frag grenades under their hide plates, and boom! Didn't know what'd hit them. A couple o' squads could've taken out the lot of 'em. Hell, Marbo could probably have done it on his own.'

'He wouldn't have thanked us for wasting his time, though.'

'You're right there, Hotshot.'

'Of course,' said Dougan, quietly, 'they did get Bryznowski.'

Greiss sighed. 'Yes. They did get Bryznowski. Heard we lost a few of the ogryns, too.'

'And that rookie from Bulldog's squad,' said Dougan, easing himself back in his chair so he could stretch out his bionic leg. It had taken a hit a couple of worlds ago, and now it had a tendency to seize up if he didn't keep it exercised.

There was a short silence as the five soldiers remembered fallen comrades, then Greiss's craggy features folded into a scowl.

'Way things are going,' he grumbled, 'I'm going to end up dying in my damn bed!' He waved aside Woods and Donovits's well-intentioned protests. 'Come off it, you lot. I'm thirty-six years old next birthday. Leaving it a bit late for that blaze of glory. But that's okay. I made my mark. I just want to go out the right way, that's all. Been too long since I had a scrap I couldn't sleepwalk through. Long time since I faced a deathworld worthy of the name.'

'Maybe you should put in for a posting back home,' said Dougan, sympathetically. 'Back to Catachan. Stone Face will understand. He's coming up to the big three-oh himself.'

Lorenzo was aware that, by Imperial standards, Colonel Graves was a young man, and Greiss and Dougan only middle-aged. But then, most Imperial citizens didn't grow up on Catachan. Life there was shorter.

'Ah, I couldn't leave you jokers. But it's the youngsters I feel sorry for. Like Lorenzo here. How's he going to make a name for himself if he never sets foot on a world worth taming?'

Lorenzo looked up from his meal, to grunt an acknowledgement of the name check. He didn't reveal how much it smarted. Greiss would never have called Hotshot Woods a 'youngster', and Lorenzo was two years older than he was.

'I got a name for Lorenzo,' quipped Woods. 'Why don't we call him "Chatterbox" Lorenzo? Or "Never Shuts His Yap" Lorenzo?'

Lorenzo glared at him.

Greiss pushed his bowl aside, and hauled himself to his feet. 'All right, men,' he said, his voice suddenly full of confidence and authority. 'You heard what Colonel Graves said. Drop positions by 17.30 hours.'

'The colonel said 18.30, sergeant.'

'That's for the rest of those slackers, Donovits. *My* squad forms up at 17.30 sharp. Fifty deck reps, a few circuits of the deck – that should loosen up the muscles, get the adrenaline pumping. Then, when we get down to this "deathworld", we're going to tear through it like it was nothing, show those Guardsmen down there a thing or two. This time tomorrow, we'll be back in warp space, headed for somewhere worth the sweat!'

Lorenzo greeted the prospect with mixed feelings.

The whole of Third Company could have fitted into one drop-ship with room to spare. Instead, Colonel Graves had ordered them to split up, one platoon to a ship. That meant only one thing. He was expecting trouble on the way down. Better to lose a few squads and have the rest arrive intact than to risk losing all twenty-two to a lucky shot.

The five squads in Lorenzo's ship had separated to the edges of the troop deck, sitting in their own small clusters in the rows of narrow seats. It wasn't that they didn't get on, just that Death-worlders found it best to make no more attachments than they had to. They were too easily broken. Lorenzo had no friends, but he had something better. He had nine comrades, who would die for him in a heartbeat and he for them.

The shadowy spaces around the cramped seating area were empty, apart from a dusty Sentinel scout walker tucked into one. The Catachans carried little more equipment than would fit into their kit bags – and those bags stayed with them, nestled in their laps or deposited on an adjacent seat. Lorenzo pictured the four ships streaking towards the surface of Rogar III, blazing with the heat of re-entry, like meteors from the heavens. He wondered how many Guardsmen on the ground would turn their heads upwards and thank the Emperor for sending them such an omen. The thought made him feel good. It almost made him forget that he hadn't touched ground himself yet.

There had been a reallocation of troops a few days earlier. The commander of C Platoon, Lieutenant Vines, had disbanded one squad and reassigned its members to bring the rest up to strength. Greiss's squad had two new arrivals to complete its complement of ten – and old hands Myers and Storm were currently passing the time by quizzing one of them, a nervy youngster by the name of Landon.

Landon was eager to please, bragging about a time back on Catachan when he'd wrestled a blackback viper single-handed. Myers and Storm were pretending to be impressed, but Lorenzo knew they were poking fun at the rookie.

The other newcomer, Patch Armstrong, had an easier ride. It had taken an ambush by four ice apes on the frozen world of Tundrar to deprive Armstrong of his left eye – and even then he had snapped the spine of one beast, gutted two more and gunned down the fourth as it had fled. The patch he wore, and the crooked ends of the scar that protruded above and below it, were his badges of honour. Like Dougan's leg, and the plate in Sergeant Greiss's head.

The drop-ship was being shaken.

It had only been a little at first, but now it was growing stronger. Sharkbait Muldoon had rolled up the left sleeve of his jacket to paint his own, better, camouflage pattern directly onto his skin, layering on natural dyes with his knife; he let out a curse as the blade slipped and nicked his arm. Lorenzo said nothing, but his fingers tightened around the armrests of his seat.

'Must be one hell of a storm,' commented Woods. But Lorenzo observed that Greiss's jaw was set, his teeth clenched, his nostrils flaring, and he knew this was no mere storm.

Then, just like that, they were falling.

The drop-ship plummeted like a brick, like it had when it had first been launched from its mother. Lorenzo's stomach was in his mouth again; had he not been strapped in, he would have been slammed into the ceiling. Woods, cocky as ever, had loosened his own restraints, and now he was fighting to hold himself down as g-forces rippled the skin of his cheeks.

For eight long seconds, Lorenzo was facing his worst nightmare. Then the engines caught them and they were flying level again, but still buffeted, the deck lurching unpredictably beneath their feet. Behind the din of the protesting hull, the soft, artificial voice of the navigation servitor sounded over the vox-caster: *'Warning: extreme atmospheric turbulence encountered. Destination coordinates no longer attainable. Prepare for emergency landing. Repeat, prepare for emergency landing.'*

The first impact came almost as soon as the warning was issued.

Lorenzo had barely had time to get into the brace position, his chin on his chest, his hands clasped over his head. It felt like someone had taken a sledgehammer to every bone in his body at once. And then it happened again, with only marginally less force this second time.

The drop-ship was skipping along the ground, its engines

shrieking. Lorenzo was rattled in his seat, his straps biting into his chest. He concentrated on keeping his muscles relaxed, despite the situation, knowing that to resist the repeated shocks would do him more harm than good.

Then they hit the ground for the final time, but they were still barrelling forwards, and the scrape of earth and branches against the outer hull was almost deafening. Rogar III, as Donovits had taken pleasure in informing everyone, was blanketed in jungle. There were no open spaces in which to land, but for those cleared with axe and flame. Lorenzo pictured the scene outside the drop-ship's hull now, as it ploughed through tangled vegetation, the servitors straining to rein in its speed before it hit something that wouldn't yield to its considerable mass. Before it crumpled in on itself like a ball of paper.

And then, at last, they were still, the engines letting out a last dying whine as the drop-ship's superstructure creaked and settled. The lighting flickered and cut out, and Lorenzo could see nothing in the sudden total darkness. But he knew his way to the hatchway, and his squad was the closest to it.

The drop-ship had come to rest at an angle. The deck was tilted some forty-five degrees to the horizontal, so Lorenzo had to climb to reach his goal. He swung himself from one empty seat to the next, using their backs to keep his balance and his bearings. From all around, he could hear the sounds of buckles popping and men leaping to their feet.

He was almost there when he realised he had been beaten to it. The hatch had buckled a little and was sticking in its frame, but Woods managed to shoulder it open even as Lorenzo was about to lend him a hand. First a crack, then a rectangle of brilliant light blazed in Lorenzo's eyes, and he blinked to clear the patterns it burnt into his retinas.

In the meantime, Woods had clambered out onto the angled side of the ship. 'Hey,' he called down to the others enthusiastically. 'You've got to see this. It's a beautiful evening!'

Lorenzo frowned. The upturned hatchway offered him the familiar sight of a jungle canopy – but behind the greens and browns, the leaves and the branches, the sky appeared to be a perfect, deep blue, free from cloud. Woods was right. If there *had* been a storm, it had passed, impossibly, without trace. But then, what else could have tossed the drop-ship about like that?

It was there again: that sense of wrongness he had felt in the warp. He needed to get out into the open. The rest of the platoon were crowding up behind him anyway, so Lorenzo followed the sweet scent of fresh air, mingled though it was with the stench of burning. He gripped the sides of the hatchway and pulled himself up and out through it.

He had barely raised his head above the parapet and started to take in his new surroundings, when Trooper Woods pushed him down again, with a warning yell: '*Incoming!*'

Three plants were shuffling towards the drop-ship. They looked like the mantraps of Catachan, but taller. Three bulbous pink heads, surely too heavy for their stalks to support, split open like mouths. No teeth within, though. These plants were spitters.

Three jets of clear liquid plumed through the air. Lorenzo and Woods tumbled back into the drop-ship together. Woods had been hit, a thick gobbet of acid sizzling on his arm. He whipped out his knife – a devil claw, typically ostentatious – and half-cut, half-tore his sleeve away before it was eaten through. Still, the attack had left a livid red burn on his skin.

Somewhere, not far away, a carrion bird was screeching in delight.

'So, how's it looking out there?' asked Greiss – and Lorenzo realised that the sergeant was addressing him.

A smile tugged at his lips as he gave the traditional answer: 'Reckon I'm going to like this place, sergeant. It reminds me of home!'

CHAPTER TWO

The air outside the hatch filled with acid spray again, and a few drops made it inside the ship. The Catachans withdrew from the danger area, those at the front yelling at the others to get back. Lorenzo's bandolier was splashed – only a little, but enough to leave a steaming hole in the fabric.

Sergeant Greiss had shouldered his way up to Lorenzo and Woods through the crush. The platoon commander was only a few steps behind him. Lieutenant Vines was a quiet-voiced, unassuming man – but, because he had earned his rank, been elected to it by his fellow Catachans, they listened when he spoke. He asked the two troopers to describe what they'd seen, and Woods told him about the spitting plants. 'Three of them, sir,' Lorenzo confirmed, 'at two o'clock.'

'Who's your best marksman, sergeant?'

Without hesitation, Greiss answered, 'Bullseye, sir. Trooper Myers.' As he spoke, he seized the shoulder of a wiry, dark-skinned man, and pulled him forward.

'You know what to do, Myers,' said Vines.

With a nod of understanding, Myers drew his lasgun. He waited a few seconds to be sure it was safe, then darted up to the sloping hatchway.

As soon as he popped his head up into the open, there came another deluge. Myers let off two shots, then dived and rolled back under cover, landing at Lorenzo's feet. Lorenzo heard acid spattering the drop-ship's hull above his head. He looked down, and saw that the deck plates were bubbling beneath the droplets left from the previous attack.

Donovits was a second ahead of him, his eyes already turned upward. 'Do you think it can melt through adamantium?' asked Lorenzo.

'It's possible,' said Donovits, 'with the damage we must have taken on the way down. I'd keep an eye out up there. You see that ceiling starting to discolour, you find yourself a steel umbrella quick.'

'And that'd help?'

'For a few seconds, yes.'

'I've never seen plant acid so strong,' breathed Sharkbait Muldoon, 'not even back home.'

'Makes you wonder,' said Donovits, 'what kind of insects live on this world if that's what it takes to digest them.'

In the meantime, Myers had made his report to Lieutenant Vines: 'Three of them, sir, like Hotshot and Lorenzo said. I picked off the first, but I swear the second ducked under my shot. Got the measure of it now, though.' Vines signalled his approval with a terse nod, and Myers approached the hatchway again.

He was halfway there when the plants fired a fourth time.

This time, their two sprays were perfectly aimed. They collided above the hatchway, so that a sheet of liquid dropped into the ship with a slap. Myers let out a curse and leapt back. Several troopers were splashed, but those who had alkali powders in their kits – ground from the vegetation of their last deathworld – had readied them, and they quickly pressed them into service.

An acid river trickled down the angled deck, petering out as it sizzled into the metal. Still, Lorenzo wasn't the only trooper forced to climb onto a seat to escape its path.

'Cunning critters,' breathed Myers, almost admiringly. And then he was off, without awaiting instructions. He vaulted through the hatchway, the ship's hull ringing as his booted feet connected with it. Then he was out of sight, but Lorenzo could still hear, and feel, his footsteps overhead, and the crack of a lasgun, firing once, twice, three times, four times, then another spattering of acid, uncomfortably close to the point from which the last footstep had sounded.

Then there was silence.

Lorenzo held his breath, alert for any sounds from outside the drop-ship. Then he caught Sergeant Greiss's eye, and realised that Old Hardhead was smiling. A moment later, Myers appeared in the hatchway again, and he too was grinning from ear to ear. He blew imaginary smoke from the barrel of his lasgun. 'All clear,' he announced.

Four sergeants bellowed at once, ordering their respective troopers out of the ship double-quick. Lorenzo knew that whichever squad was last to form up outside would pay with extra duties for embarrassing their commander.

Fifty men rushed for the hatchway, but Woods reached it first. As Lorenzo climbed out onto the surface of a new world and looked for his squad, he felt a thrill of excitement. He was back in the jungle – back in his element. He knew that, whatever perils may lie in store for him on Rogar III, they couldn't be as discomforting as that stifling room with its single bed, up there in space.

The trees of Rogar III were generally tall, thin and gnarled, but they grew close together – too close, in places, for a man to squeeze between them. Their leaves were jagged, some razor-edged – and creepers dangled from their topmost branches, bulging with poisonous pustules. The undergrowth was thick, green-brown and halfway to knee height, the occasional splash of colour thrown out in the shape of a flower or a brightly patterned thistle or patch of strangle-weed. From a distance, it looked like any jungle Lorenzo had seen. He wanted to get closer, to inspect the peculiar shapes and patterns of *this* jungle, to begin to learn which shapes he could trust and which spelled danger – but, for now, it was not to be.

The drop-ship had gouged a great gash out of the planet. Undergrowth had been flattened, trees felled, branches shorn. Small fires were still burning, and creepers twitched like severed limbs in their heat.

Vines checked his compass, and received a navigational fix from the troop carrier in orbit. They were ten kilometres away from the Imperial encampment, he reported, and the quickest route to it was to retrace the trail of devastation to its source. It was also the safest route – for, although Lorenzo saw several more acid spitters among the ashes, most had been burnt or decapitated. When one plant did dare stir, and cracked open its pink head, it immediately became the focus of eight lasguns, and was promptly blasted out of existence.

The Catachans proceeded cautiously to begin with, and there was little talk. Each of them knew this was the most dangerous time: their first footsteps on a new world, not knowing the threats it posed, knowing that an attack could come at any second from any quarter. In time, they would become familiar with Rogar III – those of them who survived these early days. They would learn to anticipate and counter anything it could throw at them. Then this world would be no challenge any more and, Emperor willing, they would move on to another.

Lorenzo loved this time. He loved the feeling of adrenaline pumping around his body, loved the edge it gave him.

For the moment, though, the planet was nursing its wounds, keeping its distance. He heard more birds screeching to each other, but apart from a brief flutter of wings on the edge of his vision he never saw a single one. A jungle lizard skittered away as the Catachans approached. Lorenzo estimated it to be about twenty centimetres long, but without a closer inspection he couldn't tell if it was an adult or a baby.

It was almost as if Rogar III was watching the new arrivals, sizing them up just as they were sizing up it.

Bulldog Rock was the first to order his squad to double time, and Greiss and the other sergeants followed. Not to be outdone, another squad struck up a cadence call.

A scream of engines drew his attention to the sky, and he caught a glint of red as the rays of the sinking sun struck metal. Two drop-ships, ascending, from a point no more than a couple of kilometres ahead. He wondered what had happened to the third, and suppressed a shudder at the thought that one platoon may not have been as fortunate as his own.

Not long after that, they came to the end of their own ship's trail – the point at which it had hit ground. Lorenzo had looked forward to entering the jungle proper, but instead he found himself at the edge of an expansive clearing. It was man-made, about two kilometres in diameter, doubtless the product of many hours of toil by Imperium troops with flamers – and yet the vegetation at the clearing's edge was already showing signs of re-growth.

Without breaking step, the Jungle Fighters made for a huddle of prefabricated buildings in the clearing's centre, now little more than shadows in the twilight. As they reached it, the sergeants shouted more orders, and the Catachans formed up in their squads again and fell silent. Lorenzo was aware that their noisy arrival had turned the heads of several Guardsmen who'd been standing sentry. It had also given fair warning of their approach to the commissar who now came to meet them.

He was a young, fair-haired man with pale skin and ears that protruded very noticeably. The Imperial eagle spread its wings proudly on his peaked cap, and his slight form was almost swallowed by a long, black overcoat. Fresh out of training, Lorenzo thought. Even Lieutenant Vines, not a tall man, seemed to tower over the senior officer through presence alone. Lorenzo thought he could see a sneer pulling at Vines's lips as he folded his arm into a lazy salute and announced, 'C Platoon, Third Company, Catachan XIV reporting for duty, sir.'

'Not before time, lieutenant,' said the commissar tersely. 'I assume it was your drop-ship that screamed over our heads an hour ago, and almost demolished the very camp we've been fighting to defend?' He made it sound like an accusation, as if Vines had been piloting the ship himself. Before Vines could speak, however, the commissar raised his voice to address the assembled platoon. 'My name is Mackenzie. I am in command here – and as long as you are on Rogar III, my word is the Emperor's word, is that clear?'

A few of the Catachans mumbled a derisory, 'Yes, sir.' Most of them said nothing.

Mackenzie scowled. 'Let me make this clear from the outset,' he snapped. 'I don't like deathworlders. In my experience, they are sloppy and undisciplined, with an arrogance that far outstrips their ability. The Emperor has seen fit to send you here, and I concede you may have certain expertise that will hasten a conclusion to this war. But had the decision been mine, let me tell you, I would rather have fought on with one squad from the blessed birth world than ten from Canak or Luther McIntyre or whatever hellhole it was you lot crawled out from.'

'Catachan, sir!' hollered Vines, and a proud roar swelled from the ranks of his men. If Mackenzie had expected to get a rise out of the Jungle Fighters, he was disappointed. Most of them ignored him, not quite looking at him, undermining him with a wave of indifference. Woods said something under his breath, a few men laughed, and the commissar's eyes narrowed – but he hadn't quite caught the words and couldn't pinpoint their source.

'As you *are* here,' he continued, 'I intend to make the best of it. I'm making it my mission to whip you rabble into shape. By the time I'm finished with you, you'll be the smartest Guardsmen in the Imperium.'

Mackenzie turned on his heel, then, and snarled in Vines's direction, 'Your platoon is late for my briefing, lieutenant. Ten laps round the camp perimeter, double time. Last squad back does another ten.'

'With respect, sir...' began Vines, the look of contempt in his eyes suggesting that respect was the last thing he wanted to show.

'That includes you, lieutenant,' Mackenzie barked – and he marched away stiffly, into the largest of the buildings.

Vines took a deep breath. 'All right,' he said, 'you heard the man.'

The Catachans took their circuits at a leisurely pace, and with a cadence call that contained a few choice lyrics about senior officers.

By the time they got to the lower ranks' mess hall, there was only enough slop left for half rations, and it was cold.

About fifty Catachans and a handful of ogryns from A and D Platoons had taken over a generous area, perching on tables with their feet up on chairs, swigging from flasks and punching each other boisterously. They had broken out the hooch to celebrate their arrival; it had been brewed on the troop ship, and put aside for a special occasion. They filled the large space with their raucous laughter.

There were other Guardsmen here – they outnumbered the Catachans two to one – but they were finishing their meals in silence, along one side of the hall, looking very much like they'd been edged out by the newcomers. They wore red and gold, and were identified by their flashes as members of the 32nd Royal Validian Regiment. To Lorenzo's eyes, most of them looked tall and gaunt – but then, he was aware that Catachan had a higher than average gravity, which made its people more squat and muscular than most.

It didn't surprise him that the two groups had self-segregated. The Catachans were Jungle Fighters – elite deathworld veterans. The best the Imperium had to offer, they believed. The rank-and-file Guardsmen regarded them with a mixture of curiosity, admiration and, here more than in many places, outright resentment.

Lorenzo's squad picked up their meals and took over a table. Greiss joined them presently; he'd had the rookie, Landon, fetch his food for him while he'd pumped the other platoons for what they'd learned so far.

He threw a folded sheet of paper onto the table. Lorenzo saw the crudely printed header *Eagle & Bolter*, and needed to look no closer. Another propaganda broadsheet, doubtless full of consoling 'news' about how the war here was being won. 'Looks like we hit the jackpot this time,' said the sergeant happily. 'We got killer plants, man-eating slugs, poison insects, acid swamps, all the usual. On top of that, there's talk of invisible monsters – and ghosts, would you believe!' He saw that a couple of Validians were eavesdropping from the next table but one, and he added slyly, 'Course we only got the word of a few rookie Guardsmen for that. Probably jumping at their own shadows.'

'Ghosts?' echoed Donovits, interested.

'Yes: ghosts, lights, whatever. Supposed to appear at night, lure men into the jungle – and those crazy enough to follow them don't come back.'

'Speaking of which, sergeant,' said Armstrong, 'any news on B Platoon?' The one-eyed trooper made the question sound nonchalant, but Lorenzo knew Armstrong had belonged to the missing platoon before his recent transfer.

'Not yet,' said Greiss. 'They had the same trouble we did on the way in, but it looks like they set down further away. They're out there somewhere.'

'Lucky for them,' said Woods. 'They don't have to put up with Commissar Jug-Handles throwing his not considerable weight around.'

'It must've been some storm,' remarked Donovits.

'Blew up out of nowhere,' said Greiss, 'by all accounts. One second, the sky was clear; the next, our drop-ships were drawing strikes like lightning rods. Then clear blue again.'

'Still think Naval Command were exaggerating, sergeant,' asked

Woods with his characteristic cheeky grin, 'about this place turning into a deathworld?'

'Can't see this place ever having been anything but,' commented Bullseye Myers. 'I don't know why it took 'em so long to admit it.'

'Maybe it was Mackenzie,' considered Dougan. 'You heard what the man said. He doesn't want us here.'

'Yeah,' said Woods – and in a passable impression of the commissar's nasal whine, he continued, '"I don't like deathworlders. I'm making it my mission to whip you lot into shape. You hear me, Greiss? On your knees and lick my shiny black boots. And when you're done with that, you can kiss my–"'

'If I were you,' snarled a voice from behind him, 'I'd be careful what you say about an officer of the Imperium.'

Woods didn't even glance back to see who was talking, though Lorenzo could see that it was a broad-shouldered, square-headed Validian sergeant. 'Don't care what his rank is,' said Woods offhandedly, 'he's still a damn idiot.'

'You want to repeat that to my face?'

Greiss's eyes narrowed. 'Stand down, sergeant,' he growled. 'I'm in command of these men. You have a problem with them, you bring it to me.'

'Mackenzie was right about you deathworlders,' the Validian sneered. 'You've no discipline, no respect.'

'Where we come from,' murmured Muldoon, idly sharpening his night reaper blade on a piece of flint, 'respect is earned, not given.'

'You come charging in here, all gung-ho, badmouthing our people, thinking you can just take over.'

'And here I thought you begged us to come,' said Woods, 'because your lot couldn't do your jobs properly. What's the problem – sun too hot for you?'

'We've been here eighteen months,' snapped the Validian, 'and we're winning this war. We've driven the orks right back; there hasn't been an attack on this encampment or any other in three weeks. If you wanted to help, you should have been here when we were cleansing areas, holding the line, facing ambushes day and night. But no, true to form, you glory hounds show up in time for the mopping up and claim all the credit.'

Greiss was on his feet, his lip curling into a dangerous snarl. 'Have you quite finished, sergeant?'

Woods stood now, too, on the pretext of clearing away his half-empty bowl. 'It's okay, sergeant,' he said, 'just a bitter old man letting off some steam – and can you blame him? Can't be many Imperial Guard regiments have had to go crying for reinforcements against a few trees and flowers.'

The Validian's eyes bulged and his face reddened. He pulled back his fist, but Woods had anticipated the move. He sidestepped the sergeant's blow, and simultaneously took hold of his attacker, using his own weight to flip him onto his back on the table.

The move had the effect of bringing the rest of Lorenzo's squad to their feet, as they leapt to avoid flying cups and bowls. Two tables away, the Validian's fellows were also pushing back their chairs and standing. Their downed sergeant tried to right himself, but Woods was keeping him off-balance. The sergeant kicked out, and Woods danced out of the way of his boot. As the sergeant swung his legs over the side of the table and made to stand at last, Woods head-butted him – the fabled 'Catachan Kiss' – and his nose splintered in a fountain of blood.

The first two Validians came at Woods, but Armstrong and Dougan intercepted them. It looked like Steel Toe was just trying to calm things down, even at this stage, but his efforts were futile: as a Validian took a swing at him, he responded with a punch to the jaw that laid him right out. Another six Guardsmen surged forward as one, and Myers and Storm leapt onto the table and stood back to back, lashing out with fists and feet.

In just seconds, an all-out brawl had broken out. No guns

or knives were drawn, but nor were any punches pulled. Even Landon joined in with gusto, pummelling away at the stomach of a man two heads taller than himself until he staggered and passed out through sheer inability to draw breath.

A pug-nosed, unshaven sergeant came at Lorenzo with a chair raised over his head. Lorenzo ducked under the makeshift weapon, and threw himself at its wielder. His head impacted with the soft tissue of the sergeant's stomach, and they went rolling end over end on the dirt-streaked floor.

The violence was spreading like unchecked fire. Other squads were pulled into the fray, taking sides according to regimental loyalty. Validian reinforced Validian, Catachan reinforced Catachan, until the entire hall had erupted into a cacophonic mass of screams and yells and crashes and the dull smacks of fists and feet against flesh. Out of the corner of his eye, Lorenzo saw two ogryns ploughing into the melee, picking up men by the throat two at a time and knocking their heads together.

He had managed to get on top of his opponent, surprising the sergeant with his litheness. He pinned him with a knee to his chest, and drove his knuckles repeatedly into the sergeant's face – until two Guardsmen seized him from behind, and tore him away. Lorenzo had seen them coming, but in the midst of such chaos it was impossible to avoid all the possible threats. Still, he was prepared for this one. He thrust his elbows back, catching his would-be captors off-guard, and threw himself into a forward roll, wrenching their hands from his shoulders. He dropped into an alert stance, expecting the Validians to come at him again, but they had other problems. Greiss had just waded into them.

The sergeant planted his hand in one man's face, and pushed him back with enough force to send him sprawling. Then he concentrated his efforts on the other, his expression feral, a zealous gleam in his eyes as he laid into his victim with a barrage of punches so fast and furious that their sheer force kept him upright for a second after he was knocked cold.

Dougan was in trouble. He was surrounded, and it looked like his artificial leg was playing up again, slowing him down. Lorenzo flew to the older man's assistance, but two more Validians rose up in his path. He transferred his momentum to his fist, and drove it into the first man's skull. The second made a grab for Lorenzo's throat, and simultaneously knocked his legs out from under him. For an instant, he was suspended in midair, choking. He managed to plant his hands on his attacker's shoulders, and bring up his feet, kicking at the Validian's chest. They both fell, but Lorenzo spun and hit the ground on his feet, and was ready for the first Validian as he came at him again.

In the meantime, Muldoon had come to Dougan's aid, letting out a war cry as he bowled into the men surrounding his comrade and scattered them. Dougan got his second wind, hoisted one foe by the scruff of his flak jacket and hurled him, arms and legs thrashing furiously, into another. The ogryns were still cracking skulls, the Validians now realising what they had taken on, almost trampling each other to get away from the misshapen creatures.

One particularly hapless specimen backed into Lorenzo, eyes wide with fear, just as the Catachan finished putting down his own two opponents. In the heat of a terrified moment, the Validian broke the unspoken rule, by drawing his lasgun.

Lorenzo was on him before he could aim it. The gun dropped from the Guardsman's grasp as Lorenzo seized his arm and twisted it until the bone snapped. The Validian let out a yelp and fell to his knees, but he had foregone any right to sympathy or mercy, and Lorenzo knocked him cold with a spinning kick to the head.

His keen ears caught the sound of a whining voice, straining to be heard across the tumult. Commissar Mackenzie had just strode into the hall, and he was demanding calm, to no avail. At his heels, however, was Graves – and when the colonel spoke, Catachans and Validians alike fell still.

'Just what the hell is going on here?' Graves roared, his voice resonating in the sudden guilty hush.

CHAPTER THREE

'I said, what the hell is going on? What do you think you're doing?'

Colonel Graves strode deeper into the mess hall, his blazing eyes darting from Catachan to Validian to Catachan, sharing around the force of his scorn. 'I've seen acid grubs behave with more dignity. You're meant to be on the same side!'

Mackenzie scuttled after him. 'Do you see?' he fumed. 'This is why I was opposed to bringing Jungle Fighters into this campaign.' He raised his voice to address the hall. 'I want – no, I *demand* – to know who the ringleaders were behind this disgraceful display. Names and ranks!'

A few eyes were cast down, a few feet shuffled, but the Validians were no more willing than the Catachans were to tell on their own. In the face of their intransigence, the commissar's face grew steadily redder.

'Sergeant Wallace!'

The unlucky Validian who the commissar had singled out snapped to attention, and reported, 'My apologies, sir, I didn't see how the incident started. My men and I only acted to calm the situation when it seemed to be getting out of hand.'

Mackenzie got the same story, almost verbatim, from his next two sergeants.

Lorenzo sensed a surreptitious movement behind him, and he turned to see that the sergeant whose nose Woods had broken was being helped to his feet, a piece of cloth clasped to his bloodied face. He was glaring venomously at the cause of his woes, but Woods returned his gaze with a smug grin and cracked his knuckles into his palm.

It was this look that Commissar Mackenzie caught, and he bustled over to the pair, his nostrils flaring with self-righteous zeal. 'Enright?'

The bloodied sergeant shrugged helplessly, using his cloth as a shield from interrogation. Mackenzie clicked his tongue in impatience, then dismissed Enright and the two Guardsmen who were supporting him with an impatient hand movement. The trio made their way to the door, and no doubt to whatever medical facility this camp offered.

Mackenzie fixed Woods with a shrivelling glare, which he then turned upon the Catachans around him until he saw the sergeant's stripes on Greiss's arm. 'Perhaps *you* can shed some light on this matter, sergeant?'

'Greiss, sir.'

'Sergeant Greiss. You seem to have had a ringside seat for the worst of it.'

'My apologies, sir,' said Greiss in a faintly mocking tone, 'I didn't see how the incident started. My men and I only acted to calm the situation when it seemed to be getting out of hand.'

One of the Catachans let out a harsh laugh, but Mackenzie wasn't amused. He cast another distasteful look at Woods, and snapped, 'It seems clear to me, Sergeant Greiss, that you and your squad were responsible for this outrage, and I intend to make sure you regret it. How would you feel, Greiss, about sleeping out in the jungle tonight?'

Greiss's eyes lit up. 'Delighted to, sir.'

That wasn't the answer Mackenzie had been expecting, and he seethed impotently. 'Let me tell you, Sergeant Greiss, what happens to Guardsmen who disrespect their senior officers.'

'I'm all ears, sir,' growled Greiss.

Mackenzie flushed. 'We bury them. Let me tell you what it's

like, Greiss. It's too small for you to stand, too narrow for you to sit down. You'll spend the night – as many nights as I choose – in the most uncomfortable position you can imagine, until you think your spine will crack. You'll feel spiders gnawing at your feet; you'll be at the mercy of the jungle lizards. And during the day – in the daytime, when the sun's beating down on you and you don't have the room to lift an arm to shade your eyes – in the daytime, Greiss, let me tell you, you'll start to wish you were dead.'

Graves had moved silently to the young commissar's side. He cleared his throat now, and murmured, 'May I remind you, sir, that we need these men fresh and active for duty in the morning? I don't see much point in pursuing this matter. Especially–' and he laboured this point particularly heavily '–with no evidence to lay charges against any individual. No harm done, I'd say. In fact, it's probably best for all sides they got it out of their systems.'

Mackenzie said nothing for a moment – and Lorenzo expected him to snap at the colonel the way he had at Lieutenant Vines. Instead, he seemed to accept the quiet wisdom in Graves's words. He turned and marched stiffly out of the door, the tension in the hall diffusing in his wake. People began to pick themselves up, to collect scattered bowls, chairs and tables and to tend to their wounded, Catachans and Validians working together to restore order.

'For any of you girls who were fretting,' announced Colonel Graves, 'B Platoon have voxed in. They've had some casualties – lost eight men – but most of them are still standing, and they're making their way to us, ETA 11.00. In view of this delay, Commissar Mackenzie has decided not to wait. All Jungle Fighters are to assemble in the briefing hut in twenty minutes.'

Lorenzo slept under the stars that night, on a bed of leaves picked from the edge of the jungle and carefully tested for hidden spines and poison sap. Basic quarters had been provided for the Catachans, but there weren't enough bunks for all of them – and most would have chosen to sleep outdoors anyway. It had been too long.

The sounds of the jungle at night brought a feeling of calm to Lorenzo. The rustle of a breeze in its leaves, the caws and cackles of nocturnal predators, the gurgle of water – or some other liquid – carried from far away. He wished he could be deeper inside it. The area cleared out by the Validians had an acrid burnt scent to it. Lorenzo was used to having a canopy of green above him – but tonight it was black, and freckled with the white points of distant suns. The night sky was crystal clear, the air warm. It was as if Rogar III was showing him its good points, its aesthetic qualities. As if it wanted to lull him into a sense of security by hiding its true, savage beauty from him. Lorenzo wasn't fooled. He looked forward to the morning, to testing this world's mettle.

He thought back to Mackenzie's briefing, and suppressed a thrill. The commissar had been furnished with a list of the Catachan squads, and had assigned them to various missions. B Platoon had drawn the short straw in their absence; they would arrive at the encampment to find that their comrades had moved out and left them to reinforce the security details here. If they were lucky, the orks would provide a distraction or two to break up the monotony.

The rest of the Catachans were to do what the Validians could not: take the fight to the orks themselves. Which meant, of course, fighting the jungle too.

'I know what you're all thinking,' Colonel Graves had added to Mackenzie's speech. 'It's a jungle world, maybe even a death-world, nothing you haven't seen before. Well, believe me, Rogar III *is* different. The commissar here tells me that, a year ago, this place was a little green corner of paradise. Well, I don't know what's happened, and to tell the truth I don't much care – but as you ladies can see, this isn't paradise any more.'

Later, Donovits had tossed around a lot of phrases like 'climate change' and 'axis shifts' – but Lorenzo hadn't cared much.

He'd been more interested in hearing how the Imperium's attempts to expand its encampments had met with failure. It was a full-time job for a squad of Guardsmen to maintain this one, small though it was. For every jungle creeper they burnt away, two more seemed to replace it – and their rate of growth was prodigious.

'When the Explorators came to Rogar,' Graves had said, 'they recorded some weird energy signature.' Of course, Lorenzo had already known that, thanks to Donovits. 'Now, I'm not saying there's anything in that – just warning you hotheads not to get too cocky. We don't know what this deathworld has to throw at us, but we do know a couple of hundred Guardsmen have died trying to find out.'

Mackenzie had displayed a rough map of the area, and pointed out the known ork strongholds. He was planning an attack on one of these; intelligence suggested that it was lightly defended, the orks depending on the jungle itself to protect them. A derisive snort had gone up from the Catachans at this point.

The whole of A Platoon, ogryns and all, was committed to this offensive, while two of D Platoon's four squads were to set traps and lay in wait for reinforcements from the other ork camps. Other squads would target supply lines – hit and run tactics, to divide the enemy's attention.

Lorenzo's squad had been the last to learn its assignment – and its ten men had let out a cheer when Mackenzie had explained that it was the most vital, and most dangerous, of all. The commissar had shouted at them to be silent.

'One particular ork has been giving us trouble,' he had said. 'Their current warboss in this region. You know how it is – we take out one, another takes its place. But this one has a few more brain cells than most. The troops have taken to calling him Big Green. He's actually got the beasts organised, to an extent. Their last few raids on us were almost well planned. And this ork has a keen sense of self-preservation. Most warbosses lead from the front; this one stays behind the lines. He's become a legend to the orks, if only because he's lasted longer than his predecessors. He's good for their morale. Too good. I want him dead!'

According to the commissar, the Imperial Guard had been close to finding the warboss's hideout when, in his own words, 'the jungle became impassable'. They knew its general location, but the lair itself was well concealed. The Catachans' job was to find the ork warboss and do the necessary deed. A stealth mission; a single assassination. Sounded simple, Lorenzo thought.

Then, Mackenzie had thrown a spanner in the works.

'Given the importance of this mission,' he had said, 'I will be leading it myself. *Silence!*' he bellowed in response to the Catachans' howls of protest.

Sergeant Greiss, who a moment earlier had sported a broad grin on his face, now looked as if he had been slapped. 'With respect, sir,' he had growled, 'you aren't a Jungle Fighter. Better if the men take their orders from someone used to-'

'Contrary to popular belief, sergeant,' Mackenzie had sneered, 'they do teach us to do more than sit around and drink amasec in officer training. I am fully qualified in jungle warfare – and more importantly, in command. Now, I'm sure your style of leadership is adequate for charging at the enemy with your bayonets fixed – but this is to be a precision strike. For that to work, I need...' He raised his voice to speak over the growing grumbles of dissent. 'I need a well-drilled, efficient squad of men, who know what's expected of them and will comply without question or complaint. *With respect*, sergeant, I doubt you can provide that.'

Lorenzo wasn't looking forward to serving under Mackenzie. Still, he wouldn't have swapped this assignment for any other. He felt proud at the thought that Colonel Graves might have recommended his squad above all others – although he wasn't kidding himself. He knew that, if they *had* been recommended, it would have been for Greiss's experience or the distinguished war records of Dougan and Armstrong. Chances were, the colonel didn't even know Lorenzo's name. Anyway, it seemed more likely that Mackenzie had made the choice himself, probably just for the opportunity to laud it over Greiss.

The Catachans had insisted on providing their own night watch, to the chagrin of the Validians already standing sentry over the camp. Lorenzo had volunteered for the duty, but he hadn't been quick enough. He slept soundly, knowing he was safe in the charge of his comrades – until, in the dark hours of the morning, some inbred danger sense woke him.

He opened his eyes, instantly alert, to face a yellow stare.

A jungle lizard, just a little larger than the one he had seen yesterday. Somehow it had slipped by the Guardsmen of two regiments, and crept up on him. Its eyes stared into his eyes. It was perfectly still, its trailing body propped up by two legs like miniature tree trunks. Tiny nostrils quivered as it breathed, slowly and calmly. Its mouth was a thin line, perhaps a little upturned at the edges. As if it was mocking him, gloating.

Lorenzo had seen lizards that could breathe fire and spit poison, or eviscerate a man with their claws in seconds. He had seen one burrow into a man's stomach and attach itself to his nervous system, working him like a puppet. He had no idea of the capabilities of this one, but he didn't doubt that it was deadly. Deathworlds bred no other type of animal. And it had the drop on him.

He lay still as a rock, staring into those yellow eyes, looking for the slightest glimmer of intent, the warning that the lizard was about to strike.

Slowly, painfully slowly, so slowly that his muscles screamed in protest, Lorenzo's fingers worked their way down his leg. Toward his Catachan fang.

The lizard made its move.

Its mouth gaped open, impossibly wide, almost larger than its head – and during the briefest split-second that followed, Lorenzo got the impression of a coiled red tongue with a glistening needlepoint end. He snatched his knife from its sheath, tried to roll out of the way, but he knew there was no time.

Something flashed through the air. Something metal.

Then there was blood – thick, green blood – and Lorenzo was up and armed, but only because the expected attack had not come.

A Catachan fang was buried up to its haft in the lizard's head. Its blade had passed through the creature's mouth, pinning its tongue, and into the scorched earth beneath it. An ordinary man might have thanked the God-Emperor for sparing him, but Lorenzo had long since learned there was no divine intervention in such matters. He thanked good comrades instead.

'Sorry 'bout that, pal,' said Myers, reclaiming his knife from the dead lizard's head and casually wiping off its blood and brain matter with a leaf. 'These critters are like chameleons; they can change their scale patterns to blend in with their surroundings.'

As usual, Myers was accompanied by Wildman Storm – a muscular, bearded Catachan who often looked like he would tear off your head as soon as look at you, until his features broke into a dazzling grin. 'We've picked off a few tonight,' he said, 'but we didn't hear this one until it was already past us. Took a minute to find it.'

'No problem,' said Lorenzo, adding a grateful nod for the rescue.

No longer pinned, the lizard had toppled onto its side. Its ruptured tongue lolled out of its mouth, leaking venom and blood. From above, no longer eye to eye with it, it seemed small and insignificant. It was easy to forget the real threat it had posed just a few seconds earlier. Lorenzo wondered what its poison would have done to him – weakened him, paralysed him, killed him outright?

'Do you suppose these are the "invisible monsters" they talk about round here?' asked Storm.

Lorenzo shrugged.

'Hope not,' said Myers, as he re-sheathed his knife and sauntered away. 'I was hoping for something more of a challenge.'

Breakfast for the Catachans was a vegetable broth, brewed by Dougan from local plants. It was the best meal Lorenzo had tasted in weeks – made even more so when Storm dropped a hunk of lizard steak into his bowl. The men were in high spirits, looking forward to their missions. The only shadow on the horizon was that of Commissar Mackenzie – and Greiss in particular was taking the usurpation of his position badly.

'You tell me what the Imperium is even doing here,' he grumbled over his soup. 'We're out at the rear end of nowhere, there aren't any minerals here worth a light, and as for colonising, forget it! I'll tell you this much: if the orks packed up tomorrow and left Rogar III, we wouldn't be too far behind 'em. Seems to me the only reason we're here is because they are, because the Emperor's armies can't be seen to be turning their backs on the enemy. The only reason the orks won't leave is because they won't turn their backs on us, so we just keep fighting.'

'Hey, steady on, sergeant,' said Woods. 'You're starting to sound like a heretic!'

'Hell, don't get me wrong,' said Greiss, 'I'm as up for a scrap as the next man. I'd just rather orks and Guardsmen alike moved their backsides out of here and left us to it. Jungle Fighters against the jungle, the way it should be.'

'Yeah, I can get on board with that,' grinned Woods.

'Course,' sighed Greiss, 'ours is not to reason why. We just move where we're told to move, fight who we're told to fight, jump when we're told to jump.'

Lorenzo remembered what the sergeant had said back on the ship, how he wanted his blaze of glory. He was unlikely to get it with Mackenzie calling the shots. He told himself there'd be other chances for the grizzled sergeant, but he could see it in

Greiss's despondent eyes: he'd convinced himself that this would be his last hurrah. Lorenzo had seen what happened to men who began to think that way. It was a thought that tended to become a self-fulfilling prophecy.

The hall was beginning to empty when a Validian approached Lorenzo's table, and took a seat beside him. He was in his thirties, but still baby-faced. He wasn't exactly fat, but then nor were his muscles exactly toned. He was beginning to grow jowls. Sizing him up in a second, Lorenzo concluded that he'd never have reached half his present age on Catachan.

Greiss looked up from his meal. 'You're at the wrong table, boy,' he growled, although the Validian couldn't have been much younger than he was. 'Your lot are over that side of the hall.'

'I know that, sergeant,' said the Guardsman. 'I wanted to introduce myself before we set out. Braxton.' He held out a hand, which Greiss ignored. 'Commissar Mackenzie's adjutant – and I report for the *Eagle & Bolter*. Didn't anyone tell you? I've been attached to your squad. I'm coming with you this morning.'

'Like hell!' snapped Greiss, and he pushed his bowl aside and stormed out of the hall. Woods shot Braxton a mocking sneer, then followed. Myers and Storm, further down the table, were absorbed in their own conversation, which left Lorenzo effectively, awkwardly, alone with the newcomer.

'Don't mind Old Hardhead,' he said. 'He's had his nose put out of joint by your boss.'

Braxton nodded. 'The commissar does seem to have a talent for that.' The Validian and the Jungle Fighter shared a brief smile. 'I just thought you ought to know we aren't all like him,' said Braxton. 'Or Enright.'

'Enright?'

'The sergeant who started the trouble yesterday. Talk about noses being out of joint! Or if it wasn't before the fight, your trooper over there sure saw to it... Enright and his cronies can't face the fact that we need your help. They think we should be able to handle a few orks by ourselves.'

'But the orks aren't the problem,' Lorenzo pointed out.

'I know,' said Braxton. 'Rogar III has changed. I think I've noticed it more than some of the others, because... well...' He shifted in his seat. 'Since I got this assignment, I haven't seen much action, you know? But last week, I went out there, into the jungle, for the first time in a while, and...'

Lorenzo's ears pricked up, eager for some hint of what was to come.

'I swear,' said Braxton, 'those jungle lizards had doubled in size since the last time I'd seen one – and they'd never been so vicious. They used to run for cover when we got within ten metres. We used them for target practice. Now, they're getting bolder, sniffing around the camp itself. One of them stung Marks. The veins in his neck, and then his face, they turned black, throbbing. He was screaming, begging us to put him out of his misery. We had to do it. He'd have brought the orks down on us.'

'I just wanted to say,' said Braxton, 'that it's good to have the experts here.'

'Not according to Mackenzie,' said Lorenzo.

'I know – and if it were up to me, we'd leave you to do your jobs. We're only going to slow you down out there. But the commissar – he's young, he wants to prove himself. I think he wants to be the one to tame the famous Jungle Fighters. And deal with Big Green, of course.'

'And you just go where Mackenzie leads, huh?'

'My job is to report his glorious victory – if I'm lucky.'

Lorenzo regarded Braxton with a newly sympathetic gaze. It occurred to him that he was only obeying orders, like anyone – and that, in his own milieu, he was probably an able fighter. But, like most Guardsmen, he would have been conscripted at the age of sixteen or seventeen, already an adult. Lorenzo had been taught to defend himself with a knife before he could walk. By the age of eight, Catachan children were expected to be able to tame a wild grox; a harsh lesson that some did not survive, but such was the nature of life on a deathworld. You could be forged in its jungle heat, or you could wither and die in it.

Beneath Guardsman Braxton's words was an unspoken plea for help. But the men of Lorenzo's world – like those of all deathworlds across the Imperium – obeyed only one law: that of the jungle. Survival of the fittest.

CHAPTER FOUR

It was another clear day. The sun blazed bright and hot, the morning temperature far in excess of that of the previous evening, the air bereft of breeze. Most of the Validians had been forced out of their stuffy huts, and some were evidently finding the heat uncomfortable. The Catachans, however, revelled in it. It opened Lorenzo's pores and invigorated him.

The clearing was full of sweaty bodies, moving in time to barked commands. Jungle Fighters were forming up in their squads and moving out. The men of A Platoon were arming themselves with autocannons and heavy bolters, and tuning up the three Sentinels that would precede them into battle.

Mackenzie was in the thick of the activity, dispensing words here and there to the sergeants, complaining repeatedly about the Catachans' lack of a formal uniform. 'Uniforms get damaged,' Colonel Graves told him, 'when you're out in the jungle.' But it didn't seem to calm Mackenzie's ire.

Greiss would normally have had his squad doing circuits or squat-thrusts by now; instead, he sat with his knees to his chest, and snarled at anyone who dared come near him. Muldoon had acquired the dyes of some indigenous plants, and was adapting his body camouflage to the local shapes and colours. A few other Catachans had followed his lead, Myers and Storm among them, glad to let the sun caress their skin. Lorenzo, however, was no artist; he would have to make do with his heavy jacket, and with a few streaks of dubbin across his face.

Mackenzie was annoyed to find the squad not standing to attention, awaiting his inspection; he made his displeasure known to Greiss, who shrugged and climbed to his feet in his own time. The Catachans fell in sloppily, making their feelings for the young officer clear. In turn, Mackenzie griped about the absence of regulation shoulder guards with identifying numbers, but there wasn't much he could do about it at this stage. He gave a stern speech that was mostly a reworking of the previous day's – 'whip you rabble into shape', 'smartest Guardsmen in the Imperium' and so forth – with a few clichés added: 'When I say "jump"...' '...expect you to crawl on your bellies over broken glass...'

'We're facing a four-day journey together,' concluded the commissar. 'Eight days, for those lucky enough to make the return trip. It'll go much easier if we all pull together.' He produced a sheet of paper, then, and began a roll call. 'Sergeant Greiss.'

'Yes!'

'Yes, *what*?'

'Yes, sir!' said Greiss with a sneer.

'Trooper Armstrong.'

Patch Armstrong answered to his name, and Mackenzie went through the others, giving each trooper in turn an appraising look as he committed his face to memory. Dougan, Storm, Myers, Donovits, Muldoon, Woods; finally, Lorenzo and Landon.

Braxton, of course, was already well known to the commissar. The Validian had found an ill-fitting camouflage jacket in the stores, and was looking uncomfortable. Mackenzie was in camouflage too, though he had retained his peaked cap. It was a little too large for him, but his jutting ears kept it from sliding down. 'Do you think it's a good idea to be going into this with an eagle-shaped target on your head, sir?' Greiss asked, with measured disdain.

'It's a symbol of authority, sergeant,' snarled Mackenzie. 'You'll learn. By the time I'm finished with you, you'll all learn.'

They moved out, at the commissar's insistence, at a quick march in two ranks of five, with Greiss leading the way. Mackenzie brought up the rear, occasionally shouting orders.

They broke step, however, as they crossed the tree line – and Lorenzo noted that Mackenzie worked his way into the centre of the group, so that there would always be a Catachan between him and any potential threat. The commissar had a rough sketched map, which he kept to himself, and a compass. He kept the squad moving on a bearing of approximately twenty-five degrees. 'We're taking a circuitous route,' he explained when questioned, 'to avoid a small ork encampment to the north-west of here.'

'I'm sure we could take 'em, sir,' offered Woods.

'I'm sure we could, trooper,' said Mackenzie icily, 'but as I explained at the briefing last night, this is a stealth mission. A single ork gets wind of our presence in this area and lives to tell of it, and we may as well pack up and go home – because our chances of getting within shooting distance of their warboss will be zero.'

'I still say we could take 'em,' muttered Woods resentfully. But Mackenzie was right, and he knew it.

The jungle closed in above them, sparing them the fiercest of the sun's rays, though the air was still sweltering. Braxton was sweating, wiping his damp forehead with his sleeve every few steps. The burnt odour lingered, and the Catachans' feet crunched on dead, blackened leaves. This area had been torched – and recently – but with little effect. Some of the plants and trees seemed to have been growing here for years.

Their progress was punctuated by cracks of las-fire, whenever a jungle lizard was sighted. Myers and Storm had warned everyone of the creatures' chameleonic properties, and Lorenzo had added the information he'd received from Braxton, so the whole squad was on the alert. Out loud, each man swore he would never end his days like Braxton's ill-fated friend, pleading for the mercy of a quick death. Privately, Lorenzo knew – as the others must have known – that stronger men than he had been broken by such pain as only a deathworld could inflict.

In time, the discharges became less frequent, as if the lizards had learned from their mistakes and were keeping their distance. Lorenzo didn't imagine for a second, though, that they had seen the last of them.

That burnt smell was fading. The jungle grass was growing taller and the trees more closely together, letting less sunlight in through their branches. A pink-headed, acid-spitting plant reared up beside the Catachans without warning, but Myers blasted it to pieces before it could open its mouth.

Lorenzo felt goose bumps on his flesh, but it was a pleasant feeling.

He seemed to have been waiting a long time for this: to plunge into the darkest heart of the jungle. To face Rogar III on its own turf.

They were about two hours out when Braxton reported to the nearest Jungle Fighters – Myers and Storm – that he thought they were being followed. Their only response was a pair of knowing grins, so Braxton called out to Commissar Mackenzie. 'Sir! Sir, I think we're being followed.'

The young officer called a halt, and the squad stood silent for a minute or two. Mackenzie frowned. 'Anyone hear anything?'

'No, sir,' murmured the Catachans.

'It was up there, sir,' said Braxton, pointing, 'in the trees.'

'You're imagining things, Braxton,' decided Mackenzie, though his voice betrayed a doubt.

Lorenzo caught an aside from Storm to Myers: 'Looks like the commissar's radar dish ears are just ornamental, then.'

'Actually,' said Sergeant Greiss, with no little satisfaction, 'there *is* someone stalking us. The rest of us have been aware of it since we left the clearing.'

Mackenzie turned pink. 'What? Then why didn't you speak up?'

'Because he's on our side. In fact, we're honoured to have him watching our backs.'

The commissar looked none the wiser, and fumbled with his list of names. 'There's no one missing,' he said.

'This man works alone,' said Dougan.

Mackenzie scowled. 'That is not acceptable. This offensive has been planned to the last detail, and I will not have those plans jeopardised by a maverick.' He shouted into the jungle: 'You, trooper. Come here, now!'

Dougan cleared his throat. 'Should you be yelling like that, sir? If there are ork patrols or gretchin in the area–'

The commissar ignored him. 'Trooper, my name is Commissar Mackenzie, and I am in command here. I demand you show yourself immediately. You have ten seconds. If I can't see your face by then, you will be facing court-martial!'

The echoes of his words were soaked up by the foliage. In the distance, a bird took flight. There was no other sound.

'Could be out of earshot by now, sir,' offered Myers.

Mackenzie rounded on the Catachans, clenching his fists. 'If anyone sees or hears a trace of that man again, I wish to be informed of it immediately, do you hear me? Immediately!'

They moved on.

Dougan dropped back in the marching order until he was alongside Braxton. He gave the Validian an approving nod. 'Mostly, if Sly Marbo doesn't want to be seen or heard, he isn't – sometimes not even by those of us who know he's around. I'm impressed.'

An hour after that, the jungle became so dense that the Catachans had to draw their knives and cut their way through. Armstrong and Muldoon took point to begin with, Armstrong's devil claw and Muldoon's sleek, black night reaper hacking at stinging plants and thick purple creepers.

All of a sudden, Muldoon let out a warning cry, and a cloud of insects blossomed from the undergrowth at his feet. Each was the length of one of Lorenzo's fingers, with hairy black bodies and gossamer wings. Armstrong hopped out of the way of the swarm, but it latched onto Muldoon, following him with an angry, high-pitched whine as he tried to back away from it. He swung his arms furiously, flattening several insects against the nearest tree, his blade slicing through two more.

The rest of the squad had withdrawn out of reach. Lorenzo brought up his lasgun, squinting along its sights until he knew he could fire without hitting Muldoon. His las-fire fried several insects, as did simultaneous shots from Greiss, Woods and Donovits. But there were too many of them. The cloud seemed hardly to have lessened in size.

Myers and Storm had flung their packs to the ground, and they pulled out the constituent parts of a heavy flamer. They clicked them together, then Storm steadied the bulky weapon while Myers aimed it at the swarm. The first explosion of fire singed the ends of Muldoon's hair, and lit up one flank of the insect cloud, sending them streaking to the ground as dying embers. Muldoon hurled himself face-first into the undergrowth, giving Myers a clearer second shot that took out the bulk of the remaining swarm.

There were still more than a dozen insects crawling over Muldoon, but he rolled and crushed those that couldn't take flight in time. The others rushed to stamp on the rest, or to skewer them with blades. Myers and Storm aimed one final, precautionary blast of flame at the ground from which the swarm had risen. Then the Catachans surrounded Muldoon where he lay on his back. He blinked up at them, flushed and chagrined, his face pimply with insect bites.

'What the hell do you think you're doing, Muldoon?' barked Greiss without sympathy. 'You know better than to disturb an insect nest. You didn't see it?'

'I saw it, sergeant,' said Muldoon. 'I was giving it a wide berth, but the bugs came out fighting all the same.'

'They must be sensitive to vibrations in the ground,' guessed Donovits. 'Or to body heat – though that's less likely in this climate. But why would they attack if their nest wasn't directly threatened?'

'Just antisocial, I guess,' said Greiss, reaching down to help Muldoon to his feet. 'You feeling all right, Sharkbait?'

'Like a walking, talking colander,' said Muldoon ruefully. 'They took chunks out of me all over. I got them in my boots, under my backpack, in my collar...'

'Show me,' rapped Greiss.

The sergeant spent the next few minutes examining Muldoon's bites. Lorenzo knew why. On Catachan, there was a creature known as the vein worm, which burrowed into its victim's flesh and laid its eggs in his bloodstream. Greiss intended to make sure these alien insects had left no similar surprises in his trooper. When he'd satisfied himself on that count, he asked Muldoon to tell him how many fingers he was holding up, checking for toxins that may have begun to cloud his senses. Muldoon answered correctly, and Greiss rewarded him with a grim smile, and clapped him on the arm. 'You'll live,' he concluded. 'Probably.'

'Do you think we can get on now?' asked Mackenzie, impatiently.

They proceeded more cautiously after that, with Woods and Donovits taking over cutting duty up front. As soon as Woods sighted a second nest in among the creepers, they all fell back, and Myers and Storm readied the flamer. 'What are you waiting for?' cried Mackenzie. 'Just torch the damn thing!' But the troopers turned to Greiss for confirmation of that order, and the grizzled sergeant shook his head and reached for a stick.

He flung it at the hive, and once again a cloud of black insects darkened the air. Myers's finger twitched on his trigger, ready to unleash a stream of fire should any man be threatened. The insects, however, didn't seem to have detected the watching Catachans. They buzzed around for a while, finding no one upon whom to expend their wrath, and then settled resentfully back into their disturbed home.

'What the hell was the point of that?' demanded Mackenzie. 'You just wanted to provoke those things?'

'To observe 'em,' Greiss corrected him. 'Anyone else see what I saw?'

'The red flower over there,' spoke up Donovits. 'The insects were giving it a wide berth.'

Greiss nodded. 'Let's find out, shall we?'

He followed Donovits's pointing finger to a delicate red flower sprouting from the trunk of a tree. It had eight perfectly formed petals, and it was quite the most beautiful thing Lorenzo had seen on this world so far. That left him in no doubt that it was dangerous.

Greiss found another stick, and poked the head of the flower with it. Immediately, its petals snapped shut like a vice, gripping the stick so strongly that he couldn't pull it free. He tried to uproot the flower with a yank, but its hold on the tree behind it was just as tenacious. It was crying, letting out a shrill wailing sound that, after a few seconds, bored into Lorenzo's ears like a drill.

Greiss whipped out his fang, and sliced the head of the flower from its stem. Immediately, the wailing ceased and the red petals flopped open. Greiss turned, and displayed the decapitated head to the others. 'Doesn't seem too dangerous on its own,' he commented, 'but watch one of these things doesn't grab your ankle. It might just hold you still long enough for something bigger to come along.'

A flutter of wings drew everyone's attention upwards. A shadow flitted between the trees, and was gone. A bird of prey, Lorenzo surmised, answering the flower's alarm call, put off by the number of strangers present and by the fact that none of them were immobilised.

'Now,' said Greiss. He flipped the flower head onto the insect nest, and withdrew to safety again. This time, there was a distressed quality to the displaced insects' humming – and a definite direction to their flight. Within a minute, they were all gone, deeper into the jungle.

Donovits nodded. 'They didn't like that. The flower probably preys on the insects, so they've learned to detect its scent and avoid it.'

'All right,' rapped Greiss, 'everyone spread out, look for more of these flowers.'

Mackenzie's nostrils flared. 'I think you're forgetting who's giving the orders here, sergeant.'

'If you've got a better idea, commissar,' Greiss shot back. 'Now's the time to speak up.'

'Sergeant,' protested Hotshot Woods, 'you expect us to wear flowers in our hair now?'

'In your hair, in your lapel, down your trousers,' growled Greiss, 'I don't care what you do with 'em, Hotshot, just as long as you wind up smelling right.'

As he joined the search, Lorenzo noticed that Muldoon was looking a bit woozy. The trooper pulled himself together when he saw he was being observed, and he smiled grimly. 'Dizzy spell,' he said, apologetically. 'I think those damn bugs sucked a few pints of blood out of me. I just need a minute...'

Lorenzo kept an eye on Muldoon after that, and realised he wasn't the only member of the squad to be doing so. He was usually more zealous than any of them, with the possible exception of Woods – always scouting ahead with a gleam in his eye, a feral smile on his face and his night reaper in his hand. Now, however, he lagged behind, finding the going tough. They all had plant tendrils grasping and tearing at their heels, of course – but Muldoon was the only man particularly troubled by them. He lost his footing a number of times, and almost fell, but Lorenzo knew better than to offer assistance where it wasn't requested.

Muldoon was swigging too freely from his bottle, too; the other

Catachans were taking it steady, not knowing when they might find fresh water.

'You're worried about him, aren't you?' said a low voice beside Lorenzo. It was Braxton.

He shrugged. 'What do you think? You ever come across bugs like that before on Rogar? Seen a man bitten by one?'

'A few times, yes. Didn't seem to do any lasting harm. I've never seen a swarm attack like that, though.'

Lorenzo nodded. 'Bugs carry diseases,' he said knowledgeably. 'Sharkbait might get lucky – or he might get sick. Real sick, real soon. Or real dead. That's why Old Hardhead had us take precautions.' They had all teased sap from the stems of the red flowers, rubbed it into their faces and hands. 'New world, new rules – and there's only one way to learn what they are. Sharkbait knows that as well as the rest of us do.'

'Why do you call him Sharkbait?'

'Before my time,' said Lorenzo.

Dougan fell into step beside them. 'Poseidon Delta,' he grunted. 'We had to cross a swamp, but there was a catch. The mother of all marsh sharks. It hunted by radar, could detect a ripple on the surface from ten kilometres. The span of its jaws was wider than you are tall. Sharkbait – he was just Trooper Muldoon then – took a Sentinel in. You saw them at the camp: armoured hunter-killer machines. Chainsaws, flamers... We use them when we don't exactly care about being subtle. But this Sentinel got its leg jammed in the mud, came crashing right down. And the marsh shark was there, of course, peeling back the outsides of the crew compartment like a tin opener. It got Reed, swallowed him whole. But Muldoon...

'We were firing our lasguns from the bank. The shots just glanced off this monster, gave it no more than a bad case of sunburn. Muldoon was lying there, pinned by the wreckage, going under, and this shark was rearing over him, coming in for the kill. We thought he was a goner. Then, calm as you like, he just reached *into* its mouth, slung a whole pack of frag grenades down its throat.

'We didn't even hear the explosion; the damn thing's hide was so thick. But suddenly, it was thrashing and groaning like it had the worst case of bellyache in history. Then it went down. Greiss and me, we went in and pulled Muldoon out of the mud. He was lucky not to have lost an arm – or a head. If that shark had snapped its teeth shut just a fraction of a second sooner... I don't recall a discussion. We all knew "Sharkbait" Muldoon had earned his name, that day.'

'That's important to you people, isn't it?' said Braxton. 'Earning your name. I've heard Hotshot, Old Hardhead – and they call you Steel Toe, right?'

'Another story,' said Dougan, 'for another day.'

'And "Sly" Marbo?'

'Never been quite sure about that one,' Dougan confessed, 'if it's an earned name or a given name or just something he's picked up along the way. Seems to suit him fine, though. What's with all the questions, son?'

'*Eagle & Bolter*,' said Braxton. 'Just wanted a bit of background info for my piece. Everyone knows what you Jungle Fighters do, but no one really knows all that much *about* you. I thought, if I could tell them what life's like where you come from – Catachan, right? – there might be a few less, uh, misunderstandings.'

Dougan nodded. 'A word of advice, son. Not everyone likes to talk. Oh, stick around long enough and you'll hear all the old war stories, all right – but you start probing someone like Old Hardhead about his past, and he's liable to probe you in return. With his bayonet, in your guts.'

Braxton fell silent for a time, after that. But it wasn't long before he turned to Lorenzo, and asked the question the Catachan had been dreading.

'So, what's *your* earned name, Lorenzo?'

'Don't have one,' Lorenzo said. Not that he had anything to be ashamed of. 'Not yet.'

Armstrong was the first to hear them. He froze, listening, and the others did the same one by one.

Footsteps, crashing through the undergrowth. A guttural grunt that could only have been formed by a larynx. There was somebody nearby. Several somebodies – and not bothering to hide their presence. Braxton turned to Lorenzo, and mouthed silently, 'Marbo?' Lorenzo shook his head.

A second later, the Catachans had melted into their background – and Lorenzo saw the confusion in Braxton's face as he turned to find himself standing alone. Lorenzo himself had slipped behind a tree trunk and was hugging its contours. Muldoon had chosen the same hiding place, and was crouched down beside him. From close up, Lorenzo could see that Muldoon was running a fever. His bandana was soaked with sweat, and his breathing was hoarse and ragged.

Storm lay flat on the ground nearby. He had arranged a few creepers across himself, breaking up the lines of his body so that its patterns blended perfectly with those of the foliage. From any further away, and most other angles, he would have been invisible. Indeed, to Lorenzo, the rest of the Catachans *were* invisible. He could make out only one other outline – that of Commissar Mackenzie, trying to conceal himself behind a blossoming nettle plant.

Guardsman Braxton caught on, and ducked under cover himself.

More footsteps, and the rustling of leaves. Whatever was out there, they were coming closer. Eight or nine of them, Lorenzo now estimated. Too small, too nimble, to be the muscular, lumbering orks. Gretchin, most likely. Genetic cousins to the orks – smaller, weaker, subservient, but far more cunning. If they realised they were outnumbered, they were likely to scatter and run, take word to their masters.

There was no urgency to their movements. Chances were, they didn't know they had enemies nearby. The gretchin were probably just out foraging – but they might get lucky. Thick as the jungle was, they wouldn't see the Catachans' trail of severed tendrils and uprooted plants unless they stumbled right onto it. It sounded to Lorenzo, though, like they were within a bloodwasp's length of doing just that.

Suddenly, somebody slammed into him from behind.

Lorenzo was taken by surprise, winded. No mean feat – but then this attack had come from the last direction he'd expected. From a comrade; a man he'd entrusted with his life countless times, and who was now bearing him down into the dirt, eyes ablaze with madness, a black knife raised to strike at Lorenzo's throat.

Muldoon was trying his best to kill him.

And he was screaming with incoherent fury as he did so – a sound that could hardly have failed to reach the gretchin's ears.

CHAPTER FIVE

Muldoon was bigger and stronger than Lorenzo, and certainly heavier. Lorenzo was pinned to the ground by his weight, the jungle grass now growing above his head, rough against his neck and his cheeks. His right arm, and his Catachan fang in its sheath, were trapped under Muldoon's knees. All he could do was strike out with his left elbow, knocking his attacker's knife hand aside.

Muldoon's night reaper was smaller than Lorenzo's fang, but just as deadly. Its blade was triangular, shaped to leave a large entrance wound that wouldn't clot – and knowing Muldoon it was almost certainly poisoned. Probably with the venom of a jungle lizard. He was always the first of the Catachans to turn a deathworld's threats to his advantage.

Lorenzo kicked out with both feet, trying to unseat Muldoon, but Muldoon knew too well how to spread his weight to maintain his balance. That knife hand was coming around to strike again. Muldoon loomed over Lorenzo, his unshaven features crazed with blind fury, his eyes wide, white, unblinking. There was no point talking to him, in appealing to reason. He was too far gone. There was no way to know what was going on in Muldoon's head, what those insect bites were making him see, but Lorenzo would have laid odds he didn't even recognise his old comrade right now. He was fighting his own daemons.

He couldn't afford to hold back. He found Muldoon's face with his free hand and dug his fingernails into his eyes. Momentarily blinded, Muldoon threw back his head and let out an uncharacteristic howl of pain and rage. Lorenzo pulled his right arm free, twisted out of the path of a badly aimed knife blow and seized Muldoon's wrist in his left hand. He tried to shake Muldoon's grip on his weapon, but his fingers were locked around its haft. As Muldoon lashed out again, Lorenzo guided his thrust and buried the night reaper's blade in the ground beside his head.

If Muldoon had been in his right mind, he would have abandoned the knife until it was safe to retrieve it. Working on primal instinct, however, he only knew the night reaper was a part of him, his most important possession, and he all but forgot about Lorenzo as he struggled to reclaim it from the unyielding earth. Lorenzo crawled out from beneath him, and tackled him side-on. He hurled blow after blow at Muldoon's head, praying each time that the next one would be the one to put him down, knowing he was made of sterner stuff than that. He was afraid he wouldn't be able to stop him without inflicting a lasting injury.

Lorenzo could have drawn his own knife. He could reach it now. Against any other foe, he would have done it. He would have ended this.

Blood rushed in his ears, dulling his senses. He could hear, though, that the rest of his squad had broken cover. They were slashing and beating their way through the jungle, regardless of the danger from hostile flora or more insect hives, toward the gretchin. The creatures couldn't help but hear them coming, and they turned and fled back up the path they had cleared for themselves.

Muldoon must have been in pain, near senseless, but he was fighting back. Lorenzo would have expected no less from him. Fortunately, his fever slowed his reaction time, and Lorenzo ducked the worst of his punches.

Help came, at last, in the form of Dougan. The older trooper knew his bionic leg slowed him down, and so it was natural that he should have been the one to stay behind. Dougan came up behind Muldoon, and tried to restrain him while Lorenzo knocked the wind out of him with a double jab to the solar plexus. He remembered head-butting a Validian Guardsman the previous day, finding his stomach soft and yielding; in contrast, hitting Muldoon was like driving his knuckles into rock.

Muldoon let out another animal roar, and broke Dougan's hold. Lorenzo held back for an instant, waiting to see what he'd do. Muldoon looked wildly from one of his comrades to the other, realising he was surrounded. His eyes flicked towards his night reaper, still buried in the ground, but it was too far away. Muldoon reached into a pouch of his bandolier and pulled out a demolition charge.

With a quick flex of his thumb, he popped out the charge's pin.

Lorenzo and Dougan hit him at the same time, from opposite sides. Dougan was trying to wrestle the charge out of Muldoon's hand, but his grip was as resolute as that on his night reaper had been. Lorenzo's survival instinct was telling him to dive for shelter, but he wasn't about to abandon Muldoon while there was the slightest chance he could be saved. He added his strength to Dougan's, taking one of Muldoon's fingers in each fist and forcing them open.

The demolition charge dropped out of Muldoon's hand.

Lorenzo had to dive for it, cradling his palms to give the explosive device the softest landing he could. In so doing, he left himself exposed, and Muldoon punished him with a brutal kick to the face. Lorenzo felt his lip splitting. He rolled with the blow, and was back in the grass again, his own blood on his tongue. But Dougan was keeping Muldoon busy, keeping him from pressing his advantage, and Lorenzo had the charge with – he estimated – less than a second to spare before it went up.

He hoisted himself onto one elbow, took a fraction of that second to orient himself, to check where the others were, then he put all the strength he had into an over-arm throw. The demolition charge seemed to have barely left his hand, arcing towards the treetops, when it burst and showered him with hot shrapnel.

Dougan had locked an arm around Muldoon's throat, and was holding on despite his kicking and screaming. Lack of oxygen had an effect on the frenzied trooper at last, and Muldoon's eyelids fluttered and closed. Dougan waited a moment longer before he relinquished his grip. A flicker of regret crossed his face as Muldoon's legs buckled beneath him and he crashed into the undergrowth.

Lorenzo and Dougan drew their Catachan fangs, cut down a couple of thin vines and bound their unconscious comrade's wrists and ankles with them. Lorenzo yanked the night reaper out of the ground, and respectfully returned it to its sheath. Even with Muldoon in this state, he couldn't deprive him of his knife – though he ensured that his tied hands couldn't reach it.

Lorenzo could hear las-fire through the foliage, and he knew the rest of his squad were close on the heels of their prey.

Myers and Storm were the first back from the gretchin hunt. They were followed by Donovits and Armstrong. 'How is he?' asked the one-eyed veteran, nodding in Muldoon's direction. He must have seen the start of the fight, and deduced the reason for it.

Dougan shrugged. 'Hard to tell. His fever's broken, so he could be all right. Best leave him to sleep it off, and hope he's seeing things more clearly when he comes to. How'd it go with the gretchin?'

'We got 'em,' said Storm, baring his white teeth. 'They won't be taking any tales back to their greenskin masters.'

Commissar Mackenzie came crashing through the foliage then, Guardsman Braxton at his heels. 'What the hell was all the screaming about?' the young officer demanded to know. 'And who let off a bomb? Where's the point in our chasing down gretchin left, right and centre if some idiot just broadcasts our position to every ork on the planet?'

'Couldn't be helped, sir,' said Dougan.

'And the jungle would have deadened the sound of the explosion,' added Donovits. 'I'd say it couldn't have been heard more than, say–'

'I don't want to know, trooper!' snapped Mackenzie. 'This operation is turning into a shambles. Where's Greiss?' He turned, and jumped to find that the sergeant had appeared noiselessly at his shoulder. Recovering himself, he snarled, 'Sergeant Greiss! Is it too much to expect you to exercise a modicum of restraint over your men? God-Emperor knows, I wasn't expecting much – but so far I'd have been better leading a squad of orks into the jungle. At least they have some semblance of self-control!'

Greiss glared at Mackenzie as if he was an acid grub he'd just found eating into his boot. The rest of the Catachans – somehow without seeming to move, just shifting their stances – formed into a vague circle around the commissar. No words had been spoken, but something had definitely changed.

Lorenzo caught Braxton's eye. The Validian didn't know what was happening – but he couldn't have been more aware at that moment that this was Catachan turf, that he and the commissar were the outsiders here. Instinctively, he shrank back against Mackenzie. He looked pale.

Mackenzie himself appeared to keep his cool, but Lorenzo could see the apprehension in his eyes.

Sergeant Greiss broke eye contact, took a half-step back, and just like that the threat was dissipated. 'Well done, men,' the sergeant barked. 'A bit of bad luck, Sharkbait here going crazy when he did – but it couldn't have been helped, and you dealt with it well.'

Greiss wasn't normally so effusive with his praise – it wasn't usually needed – so Lorenzo knew his words hadn't been for the Jungle Fighters' benefit. Mackenzie looked irritated, but he didn't protest.

It was only when Greiss detailed Woods to pick up the unconscious and bound Muldoon that the commissar broke his silence with an outraged splutter. 'What the hell are you thinking, Greiss?

That trooper has given us away once already. We can't afford to let it happen again.'

'And it won't,' Greiss promised. 'I'll see to it.'

His tone left no room for argument, but Mackenzie didn't take the hint. 'That man is diseased. He might be infectious. Even if he isn't, what can we do for him out here?'

'You got anything at the camp that could help him?'

'No,' said Mackenzie emphatically.

'Then Muldoon comes with us,' said Greiss with equal force, 'until I'm sure there isn't a cure for him.'

'You think you can drag him all the way to the warboss's hide-out and back? You think you can guarantee he won't wake up along the way and bring the orks down on us? No, sergeant. No, no, no. I don't like doing this – but I'm ordering you to abandon this trooper for the sake of the mission!'

'Sorry, sir,' said Woods, who by now had slung Muldoon over his shoulders and was carrying the bigger man effortlessly. 'Isn't the sergeant's decision no more. Sharkbait is my buddy. You want me to drop him now, and leave him here for the lizards and the birds, you'll have to shoot me.'

With that, Woods turned his back defiantly and set off into the jungle once more. The rest of the Catachans wasted no time in joining him, leaving Mackenzie standing. The commissar turned to Greiss as if for support, but recoiled at the malicious half-grin on his face. So he took the only course open to him at that moment. He lapsed into a judicious, if sullen, silence.

They moved on.

It was as the evening closed in that the birds launched their attack.

The sky, where it could be seen, was still a light shade of blue – but with the sun having surrendered its efforts to pierce the trees, the shadows had free rein down here. The canopy had captured much of the heat, but it was beginning to evaporate.

The Catachans were used to jungle nights, of course, and their eyes adapted well to the gloom. The same could not be said of Mackenzie and Braxton. After stumbling one too many times, Braxton had made to light a torch, but Greiss had hissed at him to put it away. 'You want to draw every critter in the jungle to us – and blitz our night vision while you're at it?'

They were caught by surprise, because they hadn't heard the birds massing. This in itself was unusual. It suggested a level of coordination unprecedented in such creatures, in Lorenzo's experience – that the birds had appeared in such numbers, so quickly.

The beating of their wings was like oncoming thunder, except that it sounded from all directions at once. Their bodies were a storm cloud, drawing with it a darkness even the Catachans couldn't penetrate. And then they were there, the birds, plummeting through the leaves like hailstones – but hailstones that, when they hit, burst into screeching, scratching darts of fury.

Lorenzo had just had time to draw his Catachan fang and lasgun. He was wielding the latter one-handed, keeping his knife hand back to protect his face. He fired repeatedly, aiming up above the heads of his comrades. It felt like the air was full of whirling blades, scratching, cutting, pecking at his flesh. He could barely see to take aim through the tumult of black wings – but as a particularly large bird flew up before him, claws outstretched, beady eyes trained upon him, Lorenzo saw his chance and struck. He felt his bayonet punching into the soft tissue of the bird's heart, and he smiled grimly as blood welled onto his fingers. The bird had been skewered, and Lorenzo didn't have time to remove it, so he fired the lasgun again and swung it like a club, knocking a few of his avian attackers from the sky, hopefully stunning some. The dead bird's corpse split, lost its grip on the bayonet, and hit Lorenzo's boot with a wet slap.

A sharp beak had clamped onto his ear and was tugging at it, so he sideswiped its owner with his fang, which left his face exposed for a split-second and gave another bird the chance to swoop in and jab at his eye. Lorenzo twisted his head aside in time, but they were tugging at his hair, clawing at his scalp. The birds had torn away his bandana, and drawn blood. He was pumping las-bolt after las-bolt through feathered bodies, but for each one that dropped two more seemed to replace it. And, unexpectedly, they had his gun, their claws scrabbling at its furniture, working in concert to yank it from Lorenzo's grasp. They didn't quite have the strength, so instead they piled their weight on top of it, forcing its barrel down until he couldn't pull the trigger for fear of blowing off his own foot.

The gun was useless to him now, a dead weight in his hand, so he sacrificed it. He flung it to the ground, taking several startled birds with it. He delivered a vicious kick to one as it struggled to right itself, and sent it sprawling. Then he brought his boot down on another, and snapped its neck.

Was it his imagination or was the flock thinning at last? Lorenzo could focus on individual birds now, rather than being overwhelmed by their mass. They were indeed, as first impressions had suggested, jet black, from their wingtips to their claws, even their eyes. There was no expression in those eyes – no rage or satisfaction, just a matter-of-fact blankness. Their wings were short, flapping furiously to keep their squat bodies aloft. Their black beaks came to wicked hooked points.

Lorenzo found a tree and backed up to it, denying them the chance to come at him from behind. He kept his fang in motion, slashing at any bird that ventured too close. They had become less bold with fewer numbers, keeping their distance, giving the impression of watching, waiting for an opening, although their eyes were still glassy. Lorenzo feinted, drew one of them in, and tore open its stomach with his blade, showering himself in its guts.

Another tried to blindside him, but he caught it by the throat, squeezed, felt its bones popping between his fingers and thumb. Its body joined the growing pile at his feet – and then, something in that pile nipped his ankle. At first Lorenzo thought it was just one bird, crippled, unable to fly but still single-minded in purpose. He raised his foot, tried to kick the wretched creature away – but there were more of them down there, scratching and pecking. The air around him seemed to have darkened with their bodies again. Reinforcements?

A bird shot up from below and got past Lorenzo's defences, latching onto his face and hugging it, and he would have let out a cry if he hadn't bitten his tongue in time. He was blinded; he could barely breathe for the bird's sticky, bloodied feathers in his mouth and nose. He clawed at it, but its brethren were pecking at his knuckles, biting his fingers, keeping him from getting a grip, and his tormentor's claws were like nails raking his cheeks. He dropped into a protective crouch, closed his fingers around the creature on his face at last, and tore it away from him, taking too much of his own skin with it. He saw it properly for the first time as it struggled in his hands – and although Lorenzo had seen much in his short career as a Jungle Fighter, the sight that greeted him now caused his mouth to gape in surprise.

The bird's neck had been cut almost through. Its head flapped lifelessly against its wing until, as Lorenzo watched, it detached itself at last and plopped into the long grass. But the body was still moving – and not just the uncoordinated twitching that could follow death in some species, but a deliberate and almost successful attempt to squirm free from him. With a shudder of revulsion, he dashed the bird against the nearest tree, with enough strength that his hand cracked through its body like an egg. It didn't move again.

Then Lorenzo felt them, saw them clawing their way up his legs: more bird corpses, some nursing broken legs, wings, backs, some eviscerated. Some of them had been dead a long time before this battle had begun. Putrid flesh slid from their gnarled bones; the stench that hit Lorenzo's nostrils would have been sickening to someone less familiar with it.

The first few skeletons had climbed as far as his lap, and they sprang for his throat, falling short, their wings too tattered and rotted to catch an air current. Lorenzo tried to brush them off, but they were tenacious. He mimicked Muldoon's earlier actions, rolling on the ground, feeling a satisfying crunch of bones beneath him. One skeletal bird hopped onto his face, and he stabbed at it with his knife. The blade passed through its empty eye sockets, and he lifted the undead creature off him, its legs pedalling the air, wing bones cranking uselessly. He flicked it away.

And then, suddenly, he was unmolested, the last of the birds around him finally still in death. His own survival assured for the moment, Lorenzo's thoughts went to his comrades. He was relieved to see that each of them had won or was winning his own battle. He joined them in shooting, slicing and bayoneting the few remaining birds. Without their superior numbers, they were easy prey, and soon the Jungle Fighters were jumping and stamping on hundreds of small corpses.

Then there was silence.

They regrouped, and took stock of their injuries. Landon was the worst, his face red with his own blood – but nobody had escaped harm, apart from the unconscious Muldoon. Lorenzo's comrades all sported crazed scratch patterns on their arms and faces, and he could tell from the prickling pain in his cheeks and forehead that he looked no better than any of them. His jacket sleeves were gashed and ragged, one trouser leg also torn.

Guardsman Braxton appeared to have held his own, though he was exhausted. He leaned against a tree trunk for support, flushed and out of breath. Storm was looking particularly irked that the birds had taken great clumps out of his beard. Dougan's bionic leg had been gummed up with feathers, which he was picking out of its joints ruefully.

Woods was the first to find his voice. 'Well,' he said, 'that was interesting. Who's up for seconds?'

Mackenzie was in no mood for jokes. 'What the hell just happened?' he demanded. 'I've been on this world a year, and never seen the birds behave like that.'

Greiss frowned. 'No?' And, for a moment, their animosity was softened in the face of a shared concern.

'I mean, don't get me wrong,' said Mackenzie, 'they were always vicious – but after a few initial sorties, they kept their distance. They knew they were no match for us.'

'They made no attempt to retreat,' Donovits mused, 'even when it became obvious they couldn't survive. As if they had no choice but to fight us.'

'Even in death,' grumbled Mackenzie.

'Some of those birds had been dead for months,' said Donovits. 'There was no tissue left holding their skeletons together. What was animating them?'

There was silence for a long moment as everyone pondered that question. Lorenzo suppressed a shudder, and his eyes involuntarily flicked towards the crushed and splintered bones at his feet, as if they might yet somehow spring to life again, repair and rebuild themselves.

Greiss made an attempt to diffuse the tension. 'You ask me, it was sheer bloody-mindedness!' he said, as if that might explain everything. 'We probably stumbled into their territory. How about it, Brains? Think they could have been protecting something down here? Eggs, maybe?'

Mackenzie shook his head. 'There was nothing here a few weeks ago. I sent a squad to reconnoitre this area, and they reported nothing like this.'

Greiss raised an eyebrow. 'This area? You sure about that, commissar?'

'Of course I'm sure, sergeant. What are you suggesting?'

'Well, I know the jungle can be good at covering tracks – but I'd swear that, till we turned up, there hadn't been anyone come this way in a long time.'

That sent the commissar scrambling for his sketch map. In the meantime, his adjutant had recovered his breath, though he still looked pale. 'I guess that could have been worse, right?' said Braxton – and Lorenzo looked at him, and tried to work out what he really wanted. Some reassurance that the Catachans had everything under control? Or that things *couldn't* have been worse, that he'd just survived the best this jungle had to throw at him? He couldn't give the Validian either.

'I mean, most of us escaped with superficial cuts. Unless–'

'Unless?'

Braxton's eyes flickered towards Muldoon, and now Lorenzo understood.

'Relax, city boy,' drawled Woods. 'If the birds had poisoned us, we'd know about it by now. You feeling ill? Because I've never felt healthier in my whole life. Raring to go!'

'Muldoon didn't know,' said Braxton quietly.

Lorenzo and Woods glanced at each other, and Lorenzo knew they were both thinking the same thought: that Muldoon *had* known, that he'd felt the sickness creeping up on him, even fought off the first of the hallucinations. He had known, but he had been too proud to speak up.

'You want to worry about something,' said Woods, 'you worry about those "superficial cuts" – because out here, there's no such thing. Any cut can be deadly. Jungle worlds breed diseases – and not all of them are carried by insects and vermin. Most, you can't see – but they're around us all the same, in the air. And they're just looking for a way into your bloodstream!'

Woods wiggled his fingers, miming the action of a bacteria creeping its way under Braxton's flesh. Then he closed his fist with a clap, and Braxton jumped.

He laughed, but Lorenzo didn't join in. Woods had seemed to enjoy tormenting Braxton – but the threat he described was real, to all of them. Maybe, he thought numbly, that had been the point of the birds' attack all along.

CHAPTER SIX

Mackenzie was all for setting up camp there and then, the fight knocked out of him, but Greiss insisted on moving on. 'This place stinks of death,' he growled, kicking out at a fresh bird corpse that, despite having lost its wings and its head, had crawled out from a bush to make a feeble attack on his ankle. 'God-Emperor knows what that might attract here tonight. Bigger birds, maybe.'

Lorenzo knew there was one other reason. The Jungle Fighters' mood had darkened since the attack. They were quieter now, and more apprehensive. They spoke few words as they treated their wounds with sterilising fluid and synth-skin. Even Woods, now he'd had time to reflect upon what had happened, seemed subdued. They had faced greater threats – Braxton had been right about that – but none like this. The way their attackers had fought on beyond death – that was different. The men of Catachan lived by the laws of Nature, and tonight those laws had been violated. Greiss wanted to get them away from the scene of that violation, from the broken bones, to give them something else to think about.

'Five minutes, troopers,' he growled. 'Finish up what you're doing, then we're getting out of here!'

Landon's left eye was bleeding. One of the birds must have found it with its hooked beak. Myers and Storm had sat the rookie against a tree, cleaned his face with swabs from their first aid kits, and now they were applying a field dressing to the injured area.

'Look at you,' Storm tutted good-naturedly, 'this is, what, your first, second, time out in the field, and you're trying to get yourself scarred permanent-like. What, you bucking for your earned name already?'

'Can't be that, Wildman,' said Myers. 'Even a rookie wouldn't be stupid enough to let those birds go for his eye, knowing we got a "Patch" already.'

'Yes,' said Storm, nodding with mock gravity, 'can't have two of those.'

Landon smiled, but the smile turned into a wince. Lorenzo felt ice in his stomach. He knew Myers and Storm were only joking, trying to keep up the youngster's spirits – but just for a second there he'd feared Landon *would* get his earned name before he did. He chided himself for that thought. A comrade was hurt. Would he rather it was him sprawled in the dirt, wondering if he would see out of both eyes again?

Armstrong sported a nasty gash on his arm, where it glistened amid the knotted tissue of old scars. He was sewing it up with a needle, biting on a stick to control the pain. When Greiss gave the word, however, he – like all the others – clambered to his feet and hoisted his pack, fresh and ready to go.

Mackenzie didn't question the sergeant's decision. He knew he was right. But Lorenzo could read the commissar's eyes. He resented the way the Catachans deferred so readily to their sergeant over him. That was going to mean trouble.

Ninety minutes later, in a less dense part of the jungle, Greiss came to a halt and called for silence. He listened for a moment, then declared this as good a spot as any. Braxton shucked off his pack and sank to the ground with a sigh – but he scrambled guiltily to his feet and joined in as the Catachans got straight to work. They identified any flora that could be classed as dangerous and cut it down. Donovits found an acid spitter behind a tree, almost as if it had been deliberately hiding there. They thinned out the undergrowth, and Myers unearthed a jungle lizard. It sprang at his crotch, its legs propelling it higher than Lorenzo would have thought possible. Myers flashed his knife, and bisected it in midair.

'I think we should light a fire,' said Donovits, addressing his sergeant rather than the commissar.

Greiss nodded his approval, and Mackenzie opened his mouth to object. 'Worth the risk, I'd say,' Greiss interrupted sharply. 'The men fight better with a hot meal inside 'em. And it's going to get dark around these parts pretty damn soon. Don't know about you, but I like to be able to see what's creeping up on me – and in the jungle, there's a whole new menagerie of critters come out at night.'

'Apart from anything else, sir,' said Dougan in his usual polite manner, 'it's always good to know which of those creatures are afraid of fire.'

'And which ones aren't,' added Greiss under his breath.

'Where's Sly Marbo?' asked Braxton. 'Is he joining us?'

Nobody answered him. The truth, Lorenzo knew, was that none of them had a clue where Marbo was now. They hadn't glimpsed or heard him in hours. He might have been present for the bird attack, perhaps firing in from the sidelines; in the chaos, Lorenzo could have missed him. Or he might have gone scouting ahead, maybe encountered orks and found a good sniping position in which he would wait for hours or days – as long as necessary. One thing, Lorenzo did not doubt: wherever Marbo was, he could look after himself. He would be back.

The Jungle Fighters broke into their standard rations, because they were tired and because none of them had the spirit to go hunting or gathering anything better. Anyway, their trust in what they knew about this jungle had been shaken, and no one was especially keen to sample its wares right now.

The night brought with it the fluttering of leathern bat-wings, the soft chittering of a new type of ground-based insect, and – at one point – the footfall of something bigger and heavier, which never-theless slipped away before it could be seen. The fire drew curious moth-like creatures – and, although they seemed non-aggressive, Armstrong pointed out their barbed fangs and the Jungle Fight-ers took to swatting them when they could, just in case.

There were snakes, too. Storm found one, about a metre long, slender and black, coiled around a tree trunk, slithering its way down towards the roots. He glared into its slit eyes, challenging it, and the snake glared back. It hissed and struck, and – hav-ing ascertained that it was hostile, as if there had been much doubt – Storm caught it by its head, squeezing its mouth shut with his fingers. He yanked it from its perch, swung it over-arm and smacked its body hard into the ground like a whip. Lorenzo glimpsed a distinctive silver triangular pattern on the snake's back. Then Storm casually tossed its lifeless body to Donovits, who would probably spend his watch teasing venom out of its glands for analysis.

Lorenzo was loath to lie down, to close his eyes on an environ-ment about which he still knew so little. But he had no choice, and he trusted his comrades to protect him. So, he lay down on the damp earth and slept.

He was woken by Trooper Storm.

He reached for his fang, and started to push himself to his feet. Storm clapped a steadying hand on his shoulder, and a bright grin broke through his now ragged-looking black beard. 'Easy, trooper,' he laughed. 'There's no fire. It's time for your watch, that's all.'

Lorenzo nodded and relaxed. He glanced at the small patch of sky immediately above him. It had been pitch black when he'd gone to sleep, but now it was showing just the earliest signs of lightening. If Rogar III had a moon, Lorenzo hadn't seen it yet. He threw on his jacket and his bandolier, and checked that his lasgun was locked and loaded.

The only other light source in the Catachan-made clearing was the embers of the fire. They popped and cracked as Myers poked them with a stick, keeping them alive but torpid. There was a slight chill in the air, and Lorenzo drew closer to the glowing coals, to soak up their scant warmth.

'Steel Toe was right, by the way,' said Storm. 'The lizards really don't like fire. Even this is enough to keep them away, though we've heard them hissing out there. You want steak for breakfast this morning, you're going to have to go get one.'

Dougan greeted Lorenzo with a nod. They were to share the last two-hour watch. Typical of Greiss, thought Lorenzo, to pair him up with a veteran, as if he still needed watching over. The rest of his squad were shadowy mounds in the darkness – though he could identify the sergeant by his quiet but distinctive snore, like a grox breaking wind. Presumably, it was Braxton who was twitching in his sleep and sometimes letting out a quiet whimper – while Muldoon, of course, was the one tied to the tree. 'Keep an eye on him,' advised Storm, nodding toward their unconscious comrade. 'Woods says he woke during his watch, muttered all kinds of gibberish about daemons and monsters. Hotshot had to slug him one to put him back under.'

Lorenzo was disappointed to hear it. He'd hoped that time, or maybe one of the herbal remedies Donovits had forced down Muldoon's throat, may have dispelled his hallucinations. For all that Greiss and Woods had said to Mackenzie, the Catachans knew they couldn't lug Muldoon around with them indefinitely. There would come a time when they'd have to accept that he was lost.

Myers and Storm lay down, and soon their heavy breaths joined the sleeping chorus around Lorenzo. He sat on a tree stump, left behind after Armstrong had unpacked a machete and made firewood. It was a little too small for him, and he was uncomfortable – but then comfort was hardly desirable when the lives of your comrades depended on your staying alert.

Dougan knew that too, and he was circling the camp slowly. His soft footsteps were barely audible, but Lorenzo could tell that his artificial foot fell a little more heavily than the real one. Dougan didn't like to sit on duty. He didn't like to take the risk of his leg seizing up at a critical moment.

It was about forty minutes later that Lorenzo saw the light.

He wasn't sure what it was at first: a faint blue glow, somewhere between the trees, lasting just an instant. He couldn't pinpoint its location; he had no idea how far away it had been. He had been sharpening his Catachan fang, but now he froze – and Dougan, though he was somewhere behind Lorenzo on his latest circuit, picked up on his body language and did likewise.

It could have been a trick of the approaching dawn. The sky was now a deep indigo. But no, there it was again. Too soft, too muted to be a torch, it wasn't the kind of light you could see by. And yet too wide, too sustained to be an accidental glint off a weapon or a suit of powered armour.

Lorenzo grabbed for a stick, and brushed it across the embers of the fire, smothering them in their own ashes.

The blue light was clearer to him now, but still maddeningly undefined, still seeming to lurk at the edge of his vision, never quite in focus. One second, it was at ground level; the next, it glimmered through the branches at head height, and every time he moved his eyes to find it, it slipped away from him. Some sort of glowing creature, Lorenzo wondered? What was that word Brains had once used? 'Bioluminescence'. He wondered if he should wake the others, but he pictured their faces if he did and they found he'd been spooked by a swarm of fireflies.

Anyway, the light was coming no closer.

He watched it a moment longer.

It blinked out.

A second ago, there had been a wisp of smoke coiling up from the ashes of the campfire. Now, it was gone. The sky was a little lighter – wasn't it? Lorenzo frowned, and crouched by the ashes.

He touched them tentatively. They were still warm, but cooler than they ought to have been. His mind was struggling to catch up with what his senses were telling him: that some minutes had passed without him knowing it. It took some time for the message to get through – but when it finally did, Lorenzo stiffened in horror.

The light had hypnotised him, dulled his mind. Anything could have happened while he'd been distracted. Anything could have crept into the camp, and dragged his comrades away while they slept.

There *was* something. A shape at his shoulder. Lorenzo whirled around, but it was only Dougan. 'It's all right, son,' the veteran assured him in a whisper. 'We zoned out for a minute or two, that's all. Everyone's all right.'

'Old Hardhead said something,' Lorenzo recalled, 'in the mess hall yesterday.' Why was it so hard to remember? 'Something about... about ghosts. Lights that lured Guardsmen into... ambushes, I guess. I didn't realise... I didn't feel it, but that thing must have got inside my head.'

Dougan nodded gravely. 'I'm going out there,' he announced.

'But–'

'We need to know what we're facing. Don't worry. We've seen what it does now, and we've shaken it off once. It won't fool me again. It's just a question of focus. It won't even see me coming.'

'You're right.' Of course he was right. Lorenzo wished he had realised it sooner, then he could have been the one to volunteer, to have gone out there alone. To have made a name for himself, perhaps. 'I'll come with you,' he offered.

Dougan shook his head. 'You need to stay here, watch the camp. Could be this light's meant to lure us away while something worse creeps up from behind.'

'I can wake one of the others.'

'No need to panic them just yet. It's best I go alone. You could be right about there being an ambush. Any trouble out there, I'll shout a warning. *Then* you can wake the others, and point them in my direction. I'm counting on you, Lorenzo.'

Lorenzo shook his head. 'I'm coming with you.'

Dougan laid a hand on his shoulder, and looked him right in the eye with an unnerving intensity. 'Let me do this,' he said. 'I *need* to do this!'

Lorenzo was left in no doubt that he did. He nodded glumly, and Dougan smiled and clapped him companionably on the arm. Then he slipped away into the jungle, in the direction in which the blue light had last been sighted. After only a few seconds, Lorenzo could neither see nor hear him.

Why did Dougan need to do this?

He'd had his share of glory. Why couldn't he have let someone else have a taste of it, this once? Why had Lorenzo accepted what he'd said? Why hadn't he spoken up, persuaded Dougan that his need was greater?

He had picked up a stick – and as resentment welled in his chest like a living thing, he felt the wood snapping in his clenched fist, driving a splinter into his palm. How could he ever prove his worth?

He pulled himself together, horrified by what he had been thinking. He admired these men, trusted them more than anyone or anything else. He surveyed the sleeping bodies around him, tried to remind himself of that – but that feeling in his chest was back, and he hated them, all of them, for keeping him here. He hated Old Hardhead Greiss and Hotshot Woods, hated Steel Toe Dougan most of all.

The light was back. Lorenzo noted its presence with a numb feeling of acceptance, because somehow he knew it had been there all along. It was brighter than before – and behind him, this time. In the opposite direction from the one in which Dougan had gone. And closer. Almost close enough to touch, it seemed. For a second, just a second, Lorenzo's dulled mind grasped the idea that the blue light was fooling him, playing with his thoughts and feelings – but then that revelation slipped away and was forgotten.

It might not have seen him, he thought. It didn't know he was here. It probably thought he had gone off with Dougan, fallen for its lure. It probably thought it could move in now, for the kill – but the light had underestimated him.

A few steps. A few steps into the dark, that was all it would take. Lorenzo could be the hero for once, the man who had captured the light itself.

To his credit, he did hesitate. He tore his eyes away from the light and shook his head to clear it. He understood that the light had been clouding his thoughts, though he certainly didn't appreciate the extent of its influence. He remembered what Dougan had said. A question of focus. So he focused on what he knew, his comrades, and reassured himself with the knowledge that they were real and tangible. He tested his senses one by one, listening, breathing, feeling, and found each of them as sharp as he remembered.

Then Lorenzo turned back to the blue light, and found it waiting.

He should have called out to Dougan, but he didn't want to scare the light away. He should have woken the others, but the light made him think they would steal his glory. He shouldn't have abandoned them, sleeping, helpless, relying on him to keep them safe, but it was only a few steps and he was in control.

Just a few steps.

Then a few steps more.

The jungle closed around Lorenzo, but that was all right because he hadn't come far. He *knew* he hadn't come far, because he hadn't reached the light yet, and he knew the light hadn't moved. He knew that, if he looked back, he would still see the camp. His comrades would hear him if he called.

Not that he was likely to call. He didn't need them. In his mind, Lorenzo had left the jungle of Rogar III for a different jungle altogether: that of his home world. He was leading a group of children – some of them *his* children, probably – on a hunt, and they were hanging on his every word of advice, looking at him with awe in their eyes. A man who had earned his name, and more. One of Catachan's greatest heroes, and yet still humble enough to spend time with them, to pass on his wisdom.

Lorenzo pointed out a deadly spiker plant lurking in the foliage, and they gave it a wide berth. He heard snuffling ahead, and he held up his hand for silence. He crept forward, pushing aside the vegetation with his lasgun. There it was, in the centre of a small clearing, basking in the sunlight: The most fearsome of his world's predators, near legendary throughout the Imperium. The beast after which his own regiment had been named. A Catachan Devil.

They were downwind of it, and it hadn't scented them. Lorenzo beckoned to the children to come forward, to take a look at the beast. They obeyed, and let out hushed gasps of fear and wonder. Lorenzo recalled how, at their age, he had been afraid too, and he resolved to prove to them that there was no need, that Man could always triumph over Nature. If he was the right man.

At their age...

He laid his gun aside. This would be a fair fight. Lorenzo drew his knife – a devil claw, the finest of all Catachan blades, over a metre in length – and he pounced. The creature reared up on six bristling legs, opened its mighty claws, and whipped its spiny tail around to sting him. It was fast. He had almost forgotten how fast. Or perhaps it was just that he had slowed down with age. How old was he now, anyway?

He could still take it.

Lorenzo landed in the spot where the creature had been, his knife raised to strike. But the Devil was no longer there. He whirled, disoriented, but saw no trace of it. How could it have escaped from him? From... from... what was his earned name, anyway? He felt confused, standing in that clearing alone.

Confused and humiliated. He thought he could hear the children laughing at him.

Then Lorenzo glimpsed a spiny tail a short distance ahead of him, and he knew what had happened. The Catachan Devil had simply wandered away, in search of a better light. A soft blue light. He could see it through the trees, and though he didn't know what the light was, he didn't wonder. The light was safe. Everything made sense again. Except...

How had he got so old?

Lorenzo knew what the children said about him behind his back. They said he couldn't be a hero as he claimed, because he had survived the war when all the real heroes had died. They called him a coward, said he'd never taken a risk, never distinguished himself. Never earned his name after all. He could hear their taunts now. He tried to blot them out, tried to focus on the creature in the blue light ahead of him. He couldn't see it any more, but he could see the light, and he approached it with increasingly urgent steps. In that light, he would prove them all wrong about him. *'I don't know but I've been told, Jungle Fighters don't grow old...'*

This wasn't what Lorenzo wanted.

Even if it had been, he knew it was an impossible dream. Few Jungle Fighters ended their days like this, and he had never expected to be one of them.

It wasn't real.

It wasn't real.

With that sudden knowledge, he snapped back to the present, to Rogar III. It hit him between the eyes like a smack of cold air, and he was on the bank of a stagnant lake, one foot poised over its surface. He pulled back, and sent loose dirt skittering over the side. As it hit, it evaporated in a cloud of white steam. Acid.

The blue light was hovering in the centre of the lake – but now, as if it knew its ploy had failed, it blinked out again and left Lorenzo in the dark. Alone. Without his lasgun.

In a part of the jungle he had not seen before.

CHAPTER SEVEN

Lorenzo was afraid.

It was a feeling to which he wasn't accustomed. But then, nor was he used to being alone, separated from his squad – to having abandoned them. It was their lives he was afraid for, not his own.

He didn't know where he was, nor where Dougan had got to. He didn't know how far he had walked, mesmerised by the blue light. He just knew he had to get back to the campsite. He crashed through the jungle, following a trail he didn't remember leaving, cursing himself for his weakness.

It wasn't as if he hadn't been warned. He could see it clearly now. The light had been inside him all the time, a more subtle presence than he could have imagined. It had heightened his desires and his fears, whatever it had taken to lead him where it had wanted him to go. To his death. He had been lucky. It hadn't been strong enough. Somehow, he had found the will to focus, to snap himself out of its spell.

The only thing he wanted right now, the total of his hopes and ambitions, was to find his comrades alive. He remembered what Dougan had said; how he'd suspected that the blue light was trying to lure them away. What if there had been an attack in his absence? What if they were all dead, and it was his fault?

Dougan. Suddenly, Lorenzo could hear his voice again, and see the intensity in his gaze. *'Let me do this... I need to do this!'*

He hadn't questioned him, hadn't seen that the light had cast its spell over Dougan too.

He stumbled to a halt. Somehow, impossibly, his trail had petered out.

He was lost for a moment, scrabbling in the undergrowth, looking for something – a snapped twig, a crushed leaf – anything to show he had passed this way before. There was nothing. Until, just as he was beginning to give up hope, wondering if he should risk calling out to the others, Lorenzo's fingers brushed against something. Something cold, hard, smooth, angular. Wood and metal.

His lasgun. He had to tear it from the clutches of weeds, as if it had lain here for weeks, been claimed as the jungle's own. He felt another stab of anxiety. He didn't feel as if more than a few minutes, maybe a half-hour, had passed, and the pre-dawn sky supported that theory – but in the blue light's embrace, time hadn't meant a great deal. His comrades' corpses could be rotting already.

He tried not to think about it. No point in worrying about what he couldn't change. Just get back to the campsite, and deal with what was real.

A pair of yellow lizard eyes blinked at Lorenzo from under a flowering plant. He fried their owner with a las-round, just to test that his gun wasn't clogged.

A faint breath of air caressed his face, and made his scratches sting. So, he hadn't been entranced long enough for them to heal. He remembered stalking an imaginary Devil, standing downwind of it. He had to hope that this part of the fantasy, at least, had been real. He closed his eyes and oriented himself at the spot where he'd found the lasgun, tried to transport himself back to that Catachan clearing and to mentally retrace his steps towards it.

When he opened his eyes again, he knew which way he had to go.

* * *

Lorenzo heard movements through the trees – and was that the sergeant's voice?

He broke into a run, and came up short when two familiar figures loomed before him, Armstrong and Landon.

'What happened?' asked Armstrong and Landon at the same time.

'We've been searching for you,' said Armstrong. 'Where–?'

'Is everyone–?'

'We thought something must have dragged you away. We were lucky Sharkbait woke when he did, and started yelling. Landon here had a lizard on his neck; we only just got it off him in time.'

'I'm sorry. I didn't mean to–'

'Where's Steel Toe? Is he with you?'

Lorenzo felt as if his blood had just frozen. 'You haven't seen him?'

He swallowed, and told Armstrong everything, burning with shame beneath the veteran's one-eyed gaze. Before Lorenzo's story was done, Armstrong was leading the way back to the camp. En route, they were joined by Myers and Storm, both bursting with questions. Armstrong filled them in brusquely, and Lorenzo pointed across the ashes of last night's fire to where he had last seen Dougan. Myers and Storm went straight off to resume their search in that direction. Armstrong mimicked the screeching call of a Catachan flying swamp mamba, and the rest of the Jungle Fighters answered his summons, appearing two by two to hear the news and to have their own efforts redirected.

Sergeant Greiss cast an appraising eye over Lorenzo, and asked if he was all right. Lorenzo nodded, and Greiss crooked a finger in his direction and growled, 'You're with me, trooper.'

Lorenzo fell in at the sergeant's heels, avoiding his gaze. He knew what he must have been thinking.

The search went on for another hour, aided by the reappearance of the sun. Donovits and Woods found a partial trail, and Donovits identified the uniquely heavy indentation of Dougan's bionic leg – but as with Lorenzo's trail earlier, it led them nowhere.

Greiss was about ready to give up, Lorenzo could feel it. Until he gave the order, though, there was still hope. He found a path they hadn't searched, because it was so overgrown, and he started to hack at the vegetation with his knife. Greiss regarded him for a second then, to his immense gratitude, the sergeant drew his own Catachan fang and joined him.

They hadn't gone far when a figure dropped out of a tree in front of them. It was a lithe man in camouflage fatigues and the customary bandana, with tanned skin and dark hair like Dougan's. Lorenzo's heart leapt – and it stayed in his mouth as he recognised this new-comer, not as the man they were looking for but as Sly Marbo.

He had never been this close to the legendary one-man army before. In other circumstances, he might have felt honoured – but Marbo seemed hardly to have seen Lorenzo. His face was taut, denied so much as a flicker of emotion, and his eyes were white and penetrating but dead inside, as he addressed Greiss. 'You won't find your trooper this way.'

Greiss accepted the pronouncement without question. 'Have you seen him?'

Marbo shook his head. 'This jungle has a way of hiding things, and people. Haven't worked it out yet.'

Greiss sighed, and called out, 'Right, let's call it a day. Reassemble at the campsite.' There was no response, but Lorenzo knew that one of the others would have heard, and passed the message on.

'One more thing,' said Marbo in his deep, throaty voice. 'There's an ork encampment forty kilometres from here, twenty-two degrees. A big one. Don't think the Validians know about it – but your course will take you right through it.'

Lorenzo didn't question how he could have scouted so far ahead. He was Sly Marbo.

'No way round?'

'Not unless you want to go wading through an acid swamp – or adding four days to your journey.'

Greiss expressed his gratitude with a curt nod – then Marbo was gone. Just gone, in the time it took Lorenzo to blink, leaving not the faintest ripple in the foliage. Sergeant Greiss turned to retrace his steps too, but Lorenzo stopped him with a hand on his shoulder. 'No. You can't... Trooper Dougan, he could still be...'

Greiss raised an eyebrow. 'You heard what Marbo said. Steel Toe's gone. Accept it and move on.'

'But what if the light still has him? If he's been hypnotised... He could be out there!'

'You say this light of yours tried to give you an acid bath.'

'Yes, but I broke free...'

'And if Steel Toe had done the same, he'd have found his way back to us, like you did. What's up with you, Lorenzo? You've lost comrades before.'

Lorenzo didn't say anything. How could he articulate the pain he'd felt, like a body blow, when Greiss had called off the search? That terrible moment when his last hope had been snatched from him. The sergeant was right, he *had* lost comrades before – you couldn't fight the Emperor's war, nor grow up on Catachan, without seeing death on a regular basis, becoming inured to it almost. But it was different this time. Different, because he could hear Dougan's words in his head: *'I'm counting on you, Lorenzo.'*

He had let Dougan down. He had let them all down. Lorenzo had been given his chance to be a hero, at last, and he'd failed. He had seen what happened, just a couple of times, to Jungle Fighters who lost the trust of their squad. It was as if they weren't there, as if they didn't exist. And he had felt no sympathy for those wretches. In this environment, if you didn't have the trust of your comrades, you had nothing. Lorenzo would be as invisible to the others as he had been to Marbo.

'I can't help wondering,' said Sergeant Greiss as they trudged back to the campsite empty-handed, 'how you did it.'

'Did what?' asked Lorenzo.

'Broke the spell. Brought yourself to your senses before you took the big plunge. I mean, no disrespect to Steel Toe, God-Emperor rest his soul, I'd have said he was as strong-willed as any of us – but you're the one who made it back.'

'I don't know, sergeant. I just don't know.'

'Must've taken some force of mind. You know, some of the others and me, we were talking – figured you were about due your earned name.'

'No!' said Lorenzo, firmly. 'Not for this, sergeant.'

Greiss nodded, and Lorenzo suddenly realised that the grizzled sergeant knew what he was feeling, and understood. He hadn't lost the sergeant's trust. Quite the opposite – Greiss didn't blame him for losing Dougan *because* he trusted him, because he knew Lorenzo had done all he could and that few among them could have done better, not even a veteran of Dougan's experience.

Lorenzo felt ashamed, now, for not trusting *him* – for believing that his squad would turn their backs on him, when he should have known them better. He swore he'd make it up to them. His tread felt just that little lighter as he and Sergeant Greiss walked on.

They wouldn't talk about it again.

The commissar was in a foul mood.

He hadn't recognised Armstrong's Catachan call, so he and Braxton had been searching alone in the wrong area all this time. Mackenzie blamed Armstrong personally for this, but Woods had leapt to his defence and a row had broken out. As Lorenzo and Greiss arrived, Mackenzie was jabbing a finger into Woods's chest, yelling almost hysterically about how he had almost died because of the Jungle Fighters' negligence.

'I was attacked out there – by the biggest jungle lizard you've ever seen! It dropped from a branch, right onto my shoulder. It's only because of Braxton's quick thinking and keen aim that I'm here to tell the tale.'

Lorenzo hid a smile, imagining Mackenzie's expression as his adjutant was forced to shoot the lizard from his shoulder. Woods was less polite, and just laughed. Armstrong turned to Braxton and congratulated him. 'I'm not sure I could've hit such a small target.'

The commissar was already scowling, but before Mackenzie could give vent to his anger again, Greiss marched forward, his fists clenched, a scowl on his face. 'I'll tell you what I told your sergeant back at the encampment, commissar,' he growled. 'You have a problem with my men, you bring it to me.'

Mackenzie squared up to him, his nostrils flaring. 'And what good would that have done, Greiss? You've demonstrated repeatedly that you can't keep your squad in line. We've wasted the best part of the morning looking for two of your men – contrary to my explicit wishes – because they decided to go for a stroll in the night.'

'And I suppose your Validians would have stayed put?' sneered Greiss.

'My Guardsmen know better than to follow pretty lights into the jungle, sergeant. That's because they've been taught self-control! If Trooper Dougan couldn't hold himself in check, then we're better off without him.'

Greiss's voice was low, but the threat it carried was unmistakeable. 'Don't push me, commissar. I've just lost a good man, who deserved better than to be taken down without a scrap. I'm in no mood for this right now.' He handed his lasgun to Woods, who received it without comment.

Mackenzie's eyes bulged. 'Well, I don't have to wonder where troopers like Woods and Armstrong here learn their impudence!' he stormed. 'I've had enough, Greiss. I've had enough of this attitude of yours – of having my every order questioned by you. As far as I'm concerned, you aren't fit to lead a squad of dung beetles, and I'll be saying as much in my report!'

Greiss drew his Catachan fang, weighed it in his hands for a second, then handed it to Woods.

'In the meantime,' Mackenzie continued, 'you will consider yourself demoted to the rank of trooper. Guardsman Braxton will be my second-in-command for the duration of this operation.'

It was obvious from the paling of Braxton's face that he was anything but happy with this sudden promotion.

Greiss shucked off his pack and rolled up his sleeves, slowly and deliberately. Mackenzie was still ranting as if he hadn't seen what was coming. It occurred to Lorenzo that, had he been here, Dougan would have been the one to step in, to defuse the situation. But then, Dougan had always known what needed to be said, and how to make it sound polite and reasonable. No one would have thanked Lorenzo for interfering, so he held his tongue.

Greiss's first punch took the commissar by surprise. It snapped his head around, staggered him and almost made him lose his balance. It wasn't that Mackenzie hadn't seen the signs, Lorenzo realised – it was just that he'd hardly been able to conceive of a subordinate actually striking him. Even now, his first thought was for his lost dignity. He was steadying himself, pulling himself up to his full, unimpressive height, drawing breath to remonstrate with Greiss, when a second fist connected squarely with his jaw.

This time, Mackenzie fell, flipping almost head over heels to land on his back, losing his peaked cap. Greiss planted his boot on the commissar's chest and leered down at him. 'That's for what you said about Steel Toe!' Then he took his foot away and turned his back in a gesture of utmost contempt.

Lorenzo thought it was over – until Mackenzie did the last thing he had expected. He sprang to his feet, and with a speed and ferocity that Lorenzo would never have credited to him, he leapt at Greiss.

Greiss heard him coming and half-turned, as Mackenzie cannoned into his side. Jungle Fighters danced out of their way as they careened back and forth, shifting their grips on each other, each looking for a clear shot at the other. Greiss found one first, and delivered a punishing blow to Mackenzie's stomach, which doubled him up and brought his chin within striking distance. Woods let out a passionate 'Yes!' as a two-fisted uppercut left the commissar stunned and reeling. Greiss bore his opponent down into the dirt, but Mackenzie recovered and planted a foot in the sergeant's stomach, flipping him over and away from him. Woods winced as Greiss landed hard – and then Mackenzie was on top of him, and it was all Greiss could do to fend off his punches.

The rookie, Landon, looked to Armstrong with concern in his eyes, but he just shook his head: *No. We stay out of it.*

Greiss had caught Mackenzie's wrist in his left hand. He planted his right arm across the commissar's throat, protecting his head from Mackenzie's free fist with his elbow. He pushed up with both knees. Mackenzie's eyes were almost popping out of their sockets as he fought to retain his position. He was good – far better than Lorenzo would have imagined – but Greiss was better. He knew his body, every muscle in it, like he knew his Catachan fang. He knew when to tense, when to push, when to shift unexpectedly so that Mackenzie reacted to an absent force and unseated himself.

Slowly, inexorably, Greiss gained the advantage, and their positions were reversed. Greiss had the commissar pinned now, his arm resting across Mackenzie's windpipe, his eyes blazing with ruthless zeal as he pressed down hard. Mackenzie kicked and scrabbled at the arm that was choking him, but Greiss wasn't giving a millimetre. 'Braxton,' the commissar spluttered.

Braxton had almost started forward once already, but he'd been frozen by a glare from Storm. Now, he took Sergeant Greiss's arms in a nervous grip, glancing over his shoulder as if he expected the rest of the Jungle Fighters to stop him. He was able to tear the sergeant away from his opponent only because Greiss chose not to resist him. He let Braxton haul him to his feet, then threw off the Validian's hands and brushed himself down, glaring at the prone Mackenzie as if challenging him to a second round.

Mackenzie was having enough trouble trying to breathe. As soon as he could, he lifted a trembling finger to point at Greiss – a feeble attempt to assert some authority – and he wheezed, 'I'll have you court-martialled for this, Greiss. If you thought Trooper Dougan died an undignified death, just you wait. You'll end your days in front of a firing squad! If we weren't on radio silence, I'd be voxing a squad of Validians to come and collect you right now. And the rest of you... You just stood there and watched while this man assaulted a senior officer. You'll pay for this, all of you. When I make my report, you'll pay dearly. You'll be an example to every damn Jungle Fighter in the Imperial Guard!'

Mackenzie picked himself up and marched into the jungle, with a curt order to the Jungle Fighters to follow him. Braxton looked around as if he wanted to say something, then thought better of it and hurried after his commissar. The others gathered their equipment, Myers and Storm hoisting Muldoon between them, and set off in their own time. Lorenzo caught the looks that passed between the others – Greiss and Woods in particular – and he suppressed a shiver.

Somehow, he doubted the commissar would ever make that report.

The going was easier than it had been the day before, and the squad made good progress though they were in sullen spirits. They were starting to get the measure of Rogar III. They knew which plants to avoid – and the flower sap they'd been careful to reapply to their skin kept the biting insects away. More jungle lizards tried to pounce on them from the trees, like the one that had attacked Mackenzie – evidently, this was their latest trick – but the Catachans were forewarned, and it became a sport to them to pick off the creatures with las-fire in midair. Myers was the champion of this game, of course.

Braxton broke the silence to express his admiration at the speed with which the Jungle Fighters had adapted to their new environment. It was an attempt to build bridges, but it fell on stony ground.

If there were any birds left in the vicinity, they were keeping a low profile. Lorenzo didn't hear a single call. But the memory of the creatures that had pressed their attacks beyond death hung over the squad like a pall.

There was some good news, though. Muldoon had come round again, and this time he was quite lucid. Myers and Storm continued to support him for some time after he'd started to complain that he could walk unaided. They fed him simple questions until they were sure he was in control of his faculties. Muldoon had no memory of anything after he'd disturbed the hive, so Storm had to fill him in about his attack on Lorenzo.

'I can't have been trying too hard,' he commented. 'I seem to have left him in one piece.'

Lorenzo turned to him with a grin. 'You're just lucky I was going easy on you, because you were an invalid.'

'Ha! If I hadn't been holding back, I'd have dropped you before you knew I was coming.' He was certainly back to his old self. He turned to Myers and Storm. 'Seriously – Lorenzo here knocked me out all by himself?'

'Well,' said Myers with a grimace, 'he did have help.'

Lorenzo's stomach knotted as he remembered how Dougan had come to his assistance. 'Yes,' he said numbly. 'I had help.'

It was about twenty minutes after that, trailing a short way behind the others, deep in thought, that Lorenzo got the feeling he was being followed. He whirled around, and thought he saw a shape through the trees. A humanoid figure, just standing, watching. But as he brought it into focus, it slipped away like a shadow. Like last night's blue light. Was he being tricked again?

He called out a challenge, which alerted his squad and brought them to a halt. He hurried up to where he thought the figure had been, his lasgun trained on a thorny bush behind which it could have taken cover. There was nobody there.

'Sorry,' he said. 'False alarm.' The others accepted his apology, and moved on.

For Lorenzo, it wasn't so simple. This *wasn't* like last night –
when, having snapped out of the blue light's trance, he had seen
so clearly what had been real and what had been an illusion.
Perhaps something like the light was still working on his senses,
because this time, he was certain that there *had* been something.

No, not just something. Some*one*...

He knew it didn't make sense. He knew that, even without
external provocation, the mind could play tricks. Especially the
grieving mind. Especially the guilty mind. But, just for a moment
as he'd glimpsed that figure, Lorenzo had been sure – as sure as
he'd been of anything in his life – that he had known it.

He was sure he had recognised Trooper Dougan.

CHAPTER EIGHT

The jungle seized Trooper Woods without warning.

The red flowers were particularly prevalent in this area, and Lorenzo and his squad had been treading carefully. Woods was sharing a joke with Greiss, who was in a surprisingly sanguine mood, when his feet were yanked out from under him. The Catachans went for their weapons as their comrade dropped. Woods was on the ground, in the long jungle grass, and the red flowers were all screaming.

Lorenzo's first thought was that he had been careless, stepped too close to the flowers – though he had to admit, that didn't sound much like Hotshot. But Woods, he realised, wasn't just being held, he was being *dragged*.

It wasn't the flowers' heads that had Woods, it was their roots. They had burst out of the ground, tangled themselves around his ankles – and they were grasping now for his wrists. They were coiling and writhing around him like living things, like serpents, striking when they sensed an opening. The closest troopers – Muldoon and Landon – had dropped to their haunches, knives drawn, but the roots were thick and tough. By the time Landon had drawn sap, and Muldoon had cut his first root through, ten more had erupted from the undergrowth to replace them. And the wailing flower heads were snapping at the would-be rescuers, straining at their stems.

Woods was pulled out from under Landon. The rookie lunged

after him, desperate not to lose the root he had almost severed – and a flower head caught his finger. Landon fought to free himself, but the red petals held him as tightly as they'd held Greiss's stick the previous day. Landon redistributed his weight, tried to gain leverage, and another flower opened its petals wide and clamped itself onto his left ankle. He was immobilised.

Muldoon had fared better, snatching his hand away from a similar attack – but by the time he and his night reaper resumed their work, Woods had been pulled another metre toward uncharted territory. The nearest roots had relaxed their grips now, having passed their captive on to those behind. They were rearing up, twitching from side to side as if on the lookout for fresh prey.

Woods had one hand free, and he was clutching at the undergrowth, at anything that might anchor him. After pulling up a third clump of weeds, he abandoned this plan and reached instead for his devil claw. As he tried to manoeuvre it through the living bonds that held him, a flower caught the blade and wrenched it from his grip.

'Hey,' called Woods, the strain in his voice belying his forced jovial tone, 'a little help would be appreciated, you know?'

The entreaty was unnecessary. Most of the Jungle Fighters were on him, or struggling to reach him through the minefield of grasping vegetation. They were cutting, tearing, hacking, but Woods was still being pulled away from them. A root caught his free arm, and pinned it to his side like the other one. Now he was trussed up good and proper, like a fish in a net, hardly able to even struggle any more.

Mackenzie was shouting, 'Don't just stand there, do something! Cut him loose!' as if it might help. Lorenzo was just watching, thinking... looking for a way, a safe path, to reach Woods through the press of bodies that surrounded him, realising that even if he could find one he would only be joining a losing battle...

He remembered the acid lake, and it occurred to him that the roots might be pulling Hotshot *towards* something...

Lorenzo bounded past his comrades, drawing his lasgun. He was surprised to find that Guardsman Braxton had had the same thought. They stood side by side, and scanned their surroundings, fingers uneasy on their triggers.

Lorenzo saw it first: an acid spitter, lurking in the heart of a flowering bush, almost totally concealed. It stiffened, as if sensing eyes upon it, and opened its mouth. He was sure it was too far away to reach him with its deadly spray – but instinct made him leap aside anyway, and push Braxton with him.

The spitter's aim was perfect, its liquid plume sluicing into the dirt at just the spot where they had been standing. A few seconds later, and Woods's head would have entered its range.

A dual burst of las-fire destroyed the acid spitter. Then, without having to confer, both Lorenzo and Braxton pointed their guns at the undergrowth in Woods's path, and began to blast the flowers that waited there. The flowers' siren wail went up an octave, becoming louder, more intense, more painful, and Lorenzo's head began to throb. He could see black spots at the edge of his vision, and he knew the rest of his squad was affected too, because they were starting to reel and shake their heads and put their hands to their ears.

He kept on firing, because it was the only way to end it. Each time he incinerated a red flower head, its roots thrashed for a few seconds longer and then fell limp, but that dreadful sound never seemed to ease.

Lorenzo had to cease firing when he was too blind to aim properly, when the remaining flowers were too close to the prone Woods for safety. He was going nowhere now, the roots around him dead and blackened, but he was still firmly entangled. The other Jungle Fighters followed Lorenzo and Braxton's lead, targeting the flower heads rather than their roots. They seized them by the red petals, holding their 'mouths' closed, and sawed them from their stems. With each flower that died, more of Woods's bonds fell loose, and finally he was able to tear himself free and stand, evidently in pain from the continuing screaming.

Mackenzie was feeling the worst of it, though. He was practically on his knees, his hands clasped over his ears, and Lorenzo was alarmed to see blood trickling through his fingers.

With Woods out of the danger area, however – and Landon freed now, along with Woods's knife – lasguns could be employed again, and it wasn't long before the final red flower was blasted to a cinder. Lorenzo closed his eyes and let out a long, shuddering sigh as he was soothed by a blessed silence.

'Well, that seals it,' muttered Greiss, when their ears had finally stopped ringing. 'There's something seriously nuts about this place.'

Donovits was sitting on the ground with his knees drawn up to his chest, his forehead shiny with sweat. 'It's as if evolution has been speeded up here,' he considered. 'The red flowers couldn't catch their prey any more, because the insects – and we – had learned to keep out of their way, so they evolved a means of bringing their prey to them. Likewise for the spitters; they've learned how to spit further. The different species are even working together – but all this should take generations. Instead, it's happened in a few days. I'd say it was impossible, but we're seeing it with our own eyes.'

Lorenzo felt that chill of the unnatural playing about his spine again. He didn't want to hear this, didn't want to believe, but he had no choice. 'That's why the birds and the lizards have been growing more hostile,' he said in a hollow tone.

'And changing their tactics,' Donovits confirmed.

'And why they only started calling Rogar III a deathworld a few weeks ago,' said Armstrong.

'I'd guess,' said Donovits, 'that it was the arrival of the orks and the Imperium that upset the ecological balance here. Since then...'

'Rogar has been evolving ways to combat them,' Armstrong concluded the thought grimly. 'Now, it's evolving ways to combat *us*.'

It took a moment for that to sink in, for the consequences to register with everyone, before Greiss put them into words.

'That means we can't take a thing for granted,' he said glumly. 'Soon as we think we know what a creature or plant can do, it's likely to up and develop a whole new set of offensive capabilities. You need to stay on your toes, troopers.'

Mackenzie had been leaning against a tree, hands on his knees, getting his breath back, licking his wounds. Now he pushed himself up to an unsteady vertical. 'You're forgetting, Trooper Greiss, you don't give the orders around here any more.'

'Will do, sergeant,' said Woods as if the commissar hadn't spoken.

'Too right, sergeant,' said Myers.

'Whatever you say, sergeant,' said Storm.

Mackenzie just scowled, and ordered them to get moving. He was no longer so keen, though, to lead from the front as he had been doing. He instructed Woods to take point in his place, and fell back to his more accustomed position among the troops. He saw that Greiss was regarding him through hooded eyes, and he said curtly, 'I'm watching you, Greiss. One misstep and I'll have you in chains.'

'With respect, commissar,' Greiss growled, 'you might be better off watching your own back. The jungle's a dangerous place – and if you get dragged away like Hotshot just did, you don't want to be relying on an "undisciplined rabble" to save your scrawny hide, now do you?'

He bared his teeth in a cruel smile.

They reached the river early in the afternoon.

Mackenzie looked pleased about this, as it suggested he had kept his squad on course despite Greiss's reservations. 'Five minutes, everyone,' he said magnanimously. 'Fill your water bottles, wash up, whatever you feel you need to do. Just remember, this is the last known fresh water between us and the warboss.'

'You're assuming it *is* fresh water,' said Greiss.

'I told you before, Greiss, my men reconnoitred this area. We tested the water for all known poisons and diseases.'

'We might know a few you don't,' suggested Armstrong.

Mackenzie's voice rose in indignation. 'That water is perfectly safe. I've drunk it myself. Or did you think we'd been sitting on our hands for the past year just waiting for the almighty Jungle Fighters to show up and rescue us?'

'Just saying I'd like to see for myself,' growled Greiss. 'Sharkbait?'

'Aye, sergeant.' Muldoon tore up a handful of weeds and approached the riverbank. The water, a short way below him, was impossibly clear and fast flowing. It was six metres wide, and it sparkled hypnotically as it caught the sun. Lorenzo shared the sergeant's suspicion: it looked too good to be true.

Muldoon cast his weeds into the river. It hissed and bubbled where they hit, and Lorenzo could see that the water was eating into the vegetation, even as the current swept it away in a telltale cloud of vapour.

Mackenzie blanched. 'It... The reports... My men assured me... Why would they...?'

'Just a guess, commissar, sir,' said Greiss with a crooked grin, 'but perhaps your men just don't like you much.'

Braxton hurried to offer a kinder explanation. 'It must be as Donovits said, sir. The planet is adapting to our presence, finding new ways to fight us.'

'Maybe,' agreed Donovits, 'but this goes beyond evolution, accelerated or not. If this really was a freshwater river – if it's become so highly acidic in a matter of weeks – we're talking about a sizeable ecological shift.'

'Could it be the orks?' asked Braxton – and he wasn't the only man present, Lorenzo sensed, who wanted to think that – to cling to a rational, *knowable* cause for their woes. 'Could they have poisoned the water somehow?'

'Maybe,' conceded Donovits, though he sounded doubtful.

'Don't underestimate these orks,' muttered Mackenzie. 'I told you, this new warboss is smart!'

'Yes, well,' said Greiss. 'Right now, the important thing isn't what may or may not have happened in the past – it's what we do about it in the here and now.'

Mackenzie had been staring into the acid river. Now, he snapped to attention as if remembering his responsibilities. 'Right. I hope I don't have to tell you people to conserve supplies from here on. In the meantime, we have a more pressing problem.'

'Don't tell me,' said Greiss wryly. 'We have to cross that thing.'

They began by sending Woods up a tree.

He shinned up to its topmost branches, until its leaves hid him from view. He disturbed a bird – the first the squad had seen all day – but instead of attacking him it squawked in terror and took flight.

From his new vantage point, Woods scanned the length of the river in each direction, looking for a natural crossing. No one was really surprised when he returned with the news that there was none. That would have been too easy.

Armstrong had brought rope, so the rest of the squad stood back as Myers tied a lasso, swung it over his head and let the looped end fly. It soared across the acid river to the opposite bank, and caught hold of a tree branch. Myers tugged at it to confirm it was secure. The rope came loose, and there was a collective wince as it slapped into the river and was dissolved in an instant, before he could even think about reeling it in. Myers was left with just the two-metre length that had been coiled in his hands.

The Jungle Fighters tested a few creepers, but found them brittle, dried out by the relentless heat. Muldoon suggested they dig up some snapper flowers, and Greiss approved the idea. Mackenzie grumbled something under his breath, but he didn't object – so soon, they were working in a heavy silence, weaving a replacement rope from the flowers' hardy roots. They knotted several short strands together, and finally they were ready for Myers to try again.

This time, the lasso caught and held. Myers tied his end of the rope around the sturdiest tree he could find, and Mackenzie asked for a volunteer to be first across. Lorenzo's was the second hand in the air, as usual. The first belonged to Landon.

'You sure about this?' Greiss quizzed him.

'Makes sense, sergeant,' said the rookie. Lorenzo could see how nervous he felt about saying this, but he was saying it anyway. 'Someone's got to go over there and tie the rope up securely, and I'm the lightest. I'm the most likely to make it.'

Greiss accepted that, so Muldoon set about tying his remaining two metres of rope around the volunteer's waist, passing it between his legs and finally over the knotted plant roots to act as a safety harness. To this, he attached the end of another length of roots, which would pay itself out as Landon went across.

Then the Jungle Fighters watched in tense silence as Muldoon hoisted Landon up until he could grip the precarious root bridge with his hands and feet. The rookie had left his heavy pack behind, but his lasgun was slung across his back; he never knew what he might encounter, alone on the far side.

Landon made his way across quickly, hanging upside-down from the makeshift rope like a squirrel. He only slowed as he neared the middle of the river, where the slack brought him down almost to its level. If he'd made a slip there, he would have been dead before his harness could catch him.

It was at this moment that Myers's lasso, straining to cope with Landon's additional weight, lost its grip on the branch.

Mercifully, it snagged again, only a centimetre further along. Almost a centimetre too far. Lorenzo, watching, sucked air between his teeth, knowing he could do nothing as his youthful comrade dropped – as he was caught an instant later, holding on for his life to his shaking, swaying lifeline. The acid river lapped against Landon's lasgun, but as far as Lorenzo could see, Landon himself was unharmed.

When the rope had steadied, he resumed his crossing, hugging more closely to the rope than before until it had begun to rise again, to lift him out of danger. Then he struck out more confidently towards the far bank, and set foot on dry land at last.

Landon untied himself from his harness, and made a quick check of the area for immediate threats. He inspected his lasgun and discarded it; evidently, the acid had rendered it useless. Then he knotted the rope he had carried across with him around a tree. He retrieved the end of the first rope from its branch, and tied it around a different tree nearby, making sure he pulled it good and taut. Then he turned to his comrades, and gave them a thumbs-up sign.

Mackenzie sent Woods across next. The other Jungle Fighters had almost made enough root rope to construct a harness for him, but he didn't bother waiting for it. The crossing was less fraught for him than it had been for Landon; Woods had two ropes to cling to, and he knew both were firmly anchored at each end. He reached the other side of the river in seconds.

Armstrong was more prudent, waiting until his safety rope was prepared and in place, attached to both crossing ropes, before he set off at a perfectly measured pace. Once he'd set foot on the far bank, he hurled his harness, and Landon's, back to the others, so Myers and Storm were able to follow him in short order. Donovits was next; once he'd crossed the river, he called back a warning that the first rope was beginning to fray in the middle. 'Best keep most of your weight on the second,' he advised.

Braxton had been watching the Jungle Fighters closely, and when his turn came he tried to mimic their actions. Only a third of the way across the ropes, however, he missed a handhold and fell. His harness brought him up short, but for a moment he was bouncing and flailing in midair.

That was when the second rope snapped, its loose ends flopping into the acid to be eaten away. Braxton scrabbled for the remaining rope, and held onto it with white knuckles. A minute passed before he felt confident to proceed further. He made one more slip, but his harness saved him again and he was quicker to recover this time. Lorenzo let out a breath of relief – and realised he had been holding it – as Braxton joined the others. Mackenzie had been rigid with worry, too. Who'd have thought the commissar cared about his adjutant as anything more than a human shield?

Greiss and Muldoon, on the other hand, had been conferring in low whispers, ignoring the drama playing out over the river. As the threat to Braxton passed, and Mackenzie's attention turned back towards them, they parted smoothly – but their eyes met for a second, and Lorenzo thought he saw something ominous in that gaze. A flicker of a resolution made and confirmed.

Mackenzie ordered the three remaining Jungle Fighters to begin work on another rope. 'Waste of time,' opined Greiss. 'We don't need two ropes. The second was a backup, that's all.'

'A safety precaution,' said Mackenzie stiffly, 'that turned out to be entirely necessary.'

'Only because your Guardsman didn't know what he was doing,' countered Greiss. 'If he'd followed Brains's advice–'

'I'm not trusting my life to–' Mackenzie began.

Greiss interrupted with, 'There's only four of us left to cross, and Muldoon and Lorenzo here aren't crying about it. That rope's held up just fine so far. Better to take a chance than spend another hour sitting around here doing craftwork. We're already behind schedule.' And with that, he hoisted Landon's pack on his right arm, and slipped his own onto the left to keep himself balanced. Then he hauled himself up onto the remaining rope and, emulating Woods, began to swarm across it without a harness.

'Come back here, Greiss!' roared Mackenzie. 'I'm warning you, if you don't come back here this instant, I'll... I'll...'

'Way I see it, sir,' said Muldoon nonchalantly, 'there isn't much more you can threaten him with.'

'I'll be adding this to the list of charges against you, trooper!' the commissar yelled after the departing Greiss. 'Muldoon, what do you think you're doing?'

Muldoon had beckoned Lorenzo forward, and was tying a rope around his waist. Mackenzie pushed Lorenzo aside, and announced, 'I'll be going across next. I don't trust Greiss and Woods over there unsupervised.'

'I'm sure Guardsman Braxton can keep an eye on them, sir,' said Muldoon, tongue-in-cheek. Mackenzie just glared at him, and said nothing.

Muldoon tied Mackenzie into his harness, then gave him the nod that he was ready to go. He didn't help him up to the rope as he had most of the Jungle Fighters, he just watched as the commissar scrambled up to it himself. He took hold unsteadily, and eyed the acid river below him.

Then the commissar began to cross, moving hand over hand and foot over foot at a confident, unhurried pace. That was when Lorenzo caught that glint in Muldoon's eye again, and he felt his heart miss a beat.

He had heard that the attrition rate of commissars assigned to Catachan squads was many times the Imperium average. These losses were officially dismissed as accidents, of course – a natural consequence of sending non-deathworlders, no matter how high-ranking, how well-trained, into an environment to which they weren't suited. It was rarely acknowledged that there might be anything more to it than that – at least, it hadn't happened within Lorenzo's earshot. But everybody knew – or at least suspected – the unspoken truth.

The deathworlds of the Imperium bred men who were independent, proud, and loyal only to those who had earned their respect. That went double for Catachan.

'He's doing well,' murmured Muldoon, watching the commissar's progress with obvious resentment, 'for a city boy. Too well.'

He reached up to the end of the root rope, still tied to the tree beside him, and he looked at Lorenzo as if he was challenging him to say something, to stop him – and it did occur to Lorenzo that maybe he should, maybe it was the right thing to do, but his throat was dry and the words wouldn't come, and anyway this was nothing to do with him and even if it was, his loyalties lay with his own kind, didn't they?

Didn't they?

Too late. He was always too late.

Muldoon wrapped his fingers around the end of the rope and, with a smile of grim satisfaction, he gave it a good tug.

Lorenzo watched as the vibrations travelled the first half of the rope's length, to where Mackenzie was clinging on. There wasn't time to shout a warning, even if he had wanted to. The rope jerked itself out of the commissar's hands, simultaneously flipping him so that he was on top of it. He flailed, caught by surprise, trying to find fresh purchase, slipped, plummeted to the extent of his harness's slack – and then the harness gave way, as Lorenzo had known it must. A simple slipknot.

There was nothing holding Commissar Mackenzie now.

He was in freefall.

CHAPTER NINE

Lorenzo didn't want to look, but he couldn't turn away.

There was no time, anyhow. Mackenzie would hit the acid before he could blink.

Unless, somehow, impossibly, the direction of his fall was reversed.

Unless he had managed to reach up and, with a last desperate lunge, catch the rope above his head and ride it back up as it bounced.

The commissar's grunt of pain was loud enough to reach Lorenzo's ears, even over the rushing of the river. He was clinging, one-handed, to a rope that was still bucking, trying its best to shake him. The way he had dropped, the way he'd arrested his fall, the way he was hanging now, his feet pedalling the air – Lorenzo was sure Mackenzie must have dislocated his shoulder. It must have been a supreme effort of will for him to hold on at all, as the pain spread to his fingers and numbed them. But hold on he did – and more than that, he managed to lift himself, find the rope with his other hand, and finally grip it between his knees.

Lorenzo was impressed despite himself. Muldoon looked like he could hardly believe his eyes. Then his expression darkened, and he reached for the end of the rope again.

Lorenzo put out a hand without thinking, and caught his comrade's own. Muldoon looked angry, and Lorenzo didn't blame him; he wasn't sure of his own motives for intervening, so how could he expect Sharkbait to understand? He held his gaze, and shook his head: *Enough!* But he knew he was going to blink first.

To Lorenzo's surprise, Muldoon gave a nod of acceptance. He took his hand away. He turned so that Lorenzo couldn't see his expression.

The rope began to tremble again. Lorenzo didn't look, but he knew Mackenzie must be back on the move. A moment later, the rope gave a little jerk as it was relieved of the commissar's weight, and Muldoon turned to catch the remaining harness as Myers flung it back to him.

He said nothing as he tied the rope around Lorenzo's waist. As Muldoon hoisted his comrade into position on the crossing rope, however, their eyes met, and Lorenzo thought they shared a moment of mutual respect.

Then Muldoon turned away again, and Lorenzo was alone, concentrating on the rope between his hands and feet, the muscles in his arms and legs, and the rushing acid river below his dangling head.

Halfway across, it occurred to him that if he *had* upset Muldoon, he was probably about to find out all about it.

When Muldoon stepped onto the far riverbank, the last of the squad to cross, Mackenzie was waiting for him.

Braxton had reset the commissar's shoulder, and fixed him a makeshift sling, but he was obviously in pain. Still, he greeted Muldoon with a left-handed punch to the jaw that was fast, accurate and powerful enough to knock him off his feet.

Muldoon lay sprawled in the undergrowth, wiping the blood from his lip.

Mackenzie stepped back and straightened his jacket, glaring down at the trooper.

The Catachan rubbed his chin ruefully and conceded, 'Alright. I deserved that.' He got to his feet and dusted himself down.

'And a damn sight more,' hissed Mackenzie. 'If you wanted to join Greiss on Death Row, you couldn't have thought up a better way of doing it, Muldoon.'

'Hey,' said Muldoon, all injured innocence, 'you can't blame a trooper for a simple accident.'

Mackenzie's nostrils flared. 'Accident my–!'

Greiss interrupted, 'You want to be careful, commissar, accusing a good man of attempted murder when you've no evidence, especially in front of his squad. Muldoon says it was an accident, that's good enough for me.'

Mackenzie ignored him. He was glaring at Muldoon. 'I want him restrained,' he said icily. *'Silence!'* he bellowed at the chorus of protest that greeted the order. 'I want this man stripped of weapons, and his hands tied. Braxton!'

Braxton started forward, seeming almost relieved when Greiss barred his way with an outstretched arm. 'You can't do that, commissar,' he snarled. 'You make a man defenceless in the jungle, you're as good as killing him, without a trial, without nothing.'

'What do you suggest I do, Greiss? Muldoon has proven himself a danger to this mission – to me personally. I have the authority to execute him on the spot. Is that what you want?'

'It was an accident.'

Lorenzo had surprised himself again, but he felt he owed Muldoon something. He was committed now; everyone had turned to look at him.

'I was right there,' he said. 'I saw it all. A bird flew at Muldoon. One of the black ones, from yesterday. It came right out of the tree above his head. It startled him. His arm jolted the rope.'

'That's right,' Woods spoke up. 'I saw it from here. Sharkbait slashed at it with his reaper, injured its wing I think, and sent it flapping away.'

A couple of the others gave nods and murmurs of agreement.

Mackenzie looked from one of the Jungle Fighters to another, evidently not believing a word of their story. 'My harness–'

'–must have been frayed,' said Muldoon. 'I'm sorry. I should have checked it more closely. I should have seen the damage before I sent you off. Sir.'

Mackenzie glared at Muldoon for a long moment. Then he turned to Braxton. 'I still want him bound,' he said. 'To ensure there are no more "accidents".'

This time, both Myers and Storm stepped forward, placing themselves between Braxton and Muldoon, their arms folded in defiance. Woods drew his devil claw, the glint of it catching the commissar's eye and giving him pause for thought.

'I don't think you're hearing us, Mackenzie,' growled Greiss, stepping forward until he was nose to nose with the slighter man. 'You may be Mr High-and-Mighty Commissar back in your comfortable quarters, surrounded by a thousand Guardsmen ready to bow and scrape and lay down their lives for you – but you're on a deathworld now. This is our territory – that's why we're here! Until you start to wise up and do things our way, "accidents" are going to keep on happening, you get my drift?'

'Are you threatening me, Greiss?' demanded Mackenzie. 'I have witnesses.'

'You have Braxton.'

'If anything happens to me, anything at all–'

'It'll be in his report. Yes, I worked that out. If he ever gets to make one, that is. Like I keep telling you, Mackenzie, accidents happen out here.'

Mackenzie's ears were still red, but the rest of his face had turned very white indeed. He'd got the message, at last.

'He's a good man, you know.'

Lorenzo's attention had been focused on the jungle. There had been more lizards stirring in the foliage, and he'd that feeling of being followed again although he could see no proof. He hadn't noticed Braxton until he had spoken, hadn't seen that he'd dropped back in the marching order to be at Lorenzo's side. Briefly, he felt irritated that the Validian always seemed to come to him. Lorenzo didn't feel like talking right now, least of all about what had happened by the river.

But Braxton was determined. 'The commissar, I mean,' he continued. 'You'll see that when you've worked beside him for a while.'

Lorenzo raised a sceptical eyebrow.

'I know he's been tough on you all. He's fresh out of training. Maybe he's trying too hard to prove he can do the job.'

'His problem,' said Lorenzo curtly. 'We can't afford to carry him. On Catachan, he'd have been dead twenty years ago.'

'Thank you, anyway,' said Braxton.

'For what?'

'For stopping Muldoon. I saw you.'

'You were too far away. You're mistaken.'

'You must agree with me – that the commissar doesn't deserve to die.'

'I agree with my comrades,' said Lorenzo, 'that Old Hardhead doesn't deserve what Mackenzie has planned for him; that Steel Toe was a good soldier, who didn't deserve what Mackenzie said about him.'

'There has to be a way–'

'It's him or Greiss.'

'You know, if it comes down to that,' said Braxton, 'I... I have to...'

Lorenzo nodded. He knew.

They said no more. There was nothing more *to* say.

They rested in an area lush with what Muldoon and Donovits judged were water-bearing vines. They snacked on purple berries that Muldoon had picked and tested earlier. Then Lorenzo drew his Catachan fang, took a vine in his hand and scored a thin cut in its skin. The vine bled clear, and Lorenzo positioned his near-empty bottle to capture the precious drops of liquid, of which there were all too few.

Within twenty minutes, the Jungle Fighters had drained the vines of all they had, replenishing their supplies just a little. As Lorenzo returned his bottle to his pack, he heard low voices, and realised that Greiss wasn't with them.

He could just make out Sergeant Greiss through the jungle. He was talking to somebody else: a man whom Lorenzo couldn't see at all, so easily did he blend into his surroundings, but he knew it could only have been Sly Marbo. He couldn't make out what was being said – but as Greiss turned and trudged back to the others, it was with slumped shoulders and a dark, brooding expression.

He gathered the Jungle Fighters around – and to Lorenzo's surprise, Mackenzie didn't object, he just joined them and listened. Greiss told the squad what Lorenzo already knew: that there were orks ahead – and Mackenzie raised his eyebrows and frowned at his sketch map but again said nothing. 'Marbo's scouted a path for us,' said Greiss, 'that'll take us around the greenskins, but still too close for my liking. Now, the commissar here explained why we can't blow our cover, but here's another reason for you: Marbo figures, from the size of this camp and the number of huts, that the greenskins outnumber us about thirty to one. Even Hotshot can't take down thirty orks on his own!'

'Oh yeah?' grinned Woods. 'Lead me to 'em, that's all I'm saying.'

'So the only way we're getting through this one,' Greiss continued, 'is by stealth.'

'How far is this camp?' asked Donovits.

'Another five kilometres,' said Greiss, 'before we start running into patrols. I say we make up that ground, then break early for the night. We get some food, some shuteye, then make our move in the small hours.'

There was a general murmur of assent, and the Jungle Fighters were starting to get to their feet, to retrieve their packs, when Greiss stopped them. 'One more thing. Any of you felt like you're being followed? Since Lorenzo's little outburst, I mean.'

Nobody spoke up. A few of the Jungle Fighters exchanged

uncomfortable glances. Greiss's eyes narrowed. 'I don't hear any of you denying it.'

Unexpectedly, it was Mackenzie who spoke up. 'I thought I heard something. Footsteps, about an hour and a half ago. When I looked, there was no one there. I assumed it was Marbo.'

'I saw something,' offered Donovits, 'more recently. I didn't speak up because... Sergeant, it was just a flicker in the corner of my eye. A trick of the light. A... a feeling, more than anything.'

'Wildman and me, we dropped back without telling the rest of you,' said Myers, 'checked out a bush where I thought I'd seen something move. It would've been about the time the commissar said.'

'But there was no one there,' Storm took up the story, 'and believe me, if there had been, there was nowhere he could've gone without us seeing him.'

Greiss took all this in with a grim nod. 'Marbo reckons there *is* something. He's caught glimpses of it, like the rest of us, reckons it's stalking us. But whenever he gets too close, it disappears. It leaves no tracks, no nothing.' With a smile, he added, 'Marbo says it's almost as good as he is.'

'Ghosts!' said Braxton.

Everyone turned to look at him.

'That's what the Validians have been saying. I reported on it for *Eagle & Bolter*, our broadsheet. The same story, from four different squads. They all had the feeling they were being followed, but there was no evidence of it. I thought it might be connected to the blue lights; the jungle playing tricks on their minds.'

'Hallucinogens in the atmosphere?' mused Donovits. 'Could be put out by one of the plants. They could even be in the berries we've eaten.'

'I didn't eat any berries,' said Myers, 'at least not till after I saw that... thing.'

'This could be serious,' grumbled Greiss. 'First Sharkbait goes off the deep end, then Steel Toe and Lorenzo go wandering in the night, now this. If this jungle gets us so we can't trust our own senses...'

'You said Marbo saw this "ghost", said Donovits. 'He saw it following *us*. If the jungle were affecting him, making him – making all of us – paranoid, then surely he'd have thought the ghost was following *him*. That makes sense, yes?'

'Then it has to be real,' said Lorenzo.

'We need to know for sure,' said Armstrong.

'Maybe we should leave well enough alone,' said Braxton. 'I mean, there's no record of these "ghosts" attacking anyone.'

'Yet,' said Armstrong. 'You should have learned by now, that could change in a heartbeat. I say we search.'

Greiss nodded his agreement, and the squad separated, each man taking a sector of the jungle around them, though each was sure to stay within sight of two others at all times. They kicked and cut their way through the undergrowth, beat bushes, shook trees and even shinned up some to search their leaf-shrouded upper branches. The Jungle Fighters checked all the places where *they* would have hidden. Finally, they regrouped, having covered an area some three hundred metres in radius and found nothing. No one. No sign that anyone had been here, other than the Jungle Fighters themselves.

There was nothing they could do after that but go on. It was only a few minutes later, however, that Lorenzo had that feeling again, like a prickling on his neck.

He wasn't the only one. As he whipped around to inspect the foliage behind him, Storm and Braxton did the same. And this time, Lorenzo was sure of it. There was something there. He could just make out a shape between the trees. A head and shoulders. He drew his lasgun and stepped forward, not wanting to move too fast, not daring to blink, to take his eyes off the shape. His other senses told him that Storm and Braxton were beside him, and the rest of his squad not far behind. Lorenzo took another step. The head moved, shifting just a fraction, in a very human gesture.

He was only a few metres away from the shape when it changed. It seemed to metamorphose – or, more accurately, to come into focus – in front of his eyes. The shape resolved itself into a cluster of thistles. Thistles that had always been there; the rest, Lorenzo had imagined. He started as Storm shot the thistles anyway, and fired into the surrounding undergrowth a few times for good measure. 'In case this thing is a shape-shifter,' he explained. But he disturbed nothing more than a few black insects, which smelt the flower sap on the Jungle Fighters and buzzed away.

The whole squad was on the alert after that, on edge. Lorenzo had to force himself not to jump at every shadow he saw, every distant sound that came to his ears. He thought about what Greiss had said, about losing trust in their own senses. The others hadn't seemed too worried, probably didn't believe it could happen to them, but he remembered the blue light. He remembered how real its lies had seemed.

Landon had approached Greiss, and Lorenzo was just close enough for his keen ears to pick up their hushed conversation. 'I've had an idea, sergeant,' said the rookie. 'Why don't I hide in a tree and let the rest of you go on a way? If we are being followed, I'll soon find out.'

'I don't know,' said Greiss. 'We're talking about someone or something that's given Sly Marbo the slip – and that isn't easy.'

'Maybe he knew Marbo was around. Maybe he heard us talking about him. I'm the smallest of us, sergeant, the one he's least likely to miss if he *is* watching us. The rest of you could gather around, block his view for a second, and I'll be gone. Next time our "ghost" sees me, he'll be passing right under me, and I'll raise the alarm.'

Greiss raised a cynical eyebrow. 'That a promise? Swear on your blade? Because you've been pushing yourself forward today, Landon – and that's good, don't get me wrong, we'll make a fine soldier of you, maybe even a sergeant one day – but this isn't the time for grandstanding, hoping to hog some glory for yourself.'

'Soon as I see a thing,' Landon promised, 'I'll yell my lungs out.'

Greiss considered the proposal, and finally nodded. By the time he passed it on to the rest of the squad, however, two men at a time, in a quiet growl, he'd made a few alterations. He approached Mackenzie last – but by this time, the commissar had heard what was afoot. 'If you're asking for my permission to proceed, Greiss,' he remarked acidly, 'then consider it granted.'

A short time later, they came to a mournful-looking tree with branches that sagged almost to ground level, dripping with water-bearing vines. It was almost too perfect. They gathered round and set to work with their knives, teasing out what liquid they could. Lorenzo stopped Braxton from putting his thirsty lips directly to a vine, pointing out that the skin was probably poisonous.

After a few minutes of this, Landon worked his way to the centre of the group, and was handed a lasgun by Donovits to replace the one he had lost in the river. He stepped onto Muldoon's cupped hands and was hoisted onto the tree's lowest branch, his camouflage uniform and dubbin-streaked face immediately lost among its leaves. Lorenzo heard the faintest of rustles above his head as the rookie climbed higher, and he resisted the urge to look up.

'Right, men,' announced Greiss, in what was maybe a slighter louder voice than usual, for the benefit of any eavesdroppers, 'time we made a move. We've still got lost time to make up.'

As the squad set off again, the Jungle Fighters spread out more widely than they would normally have done, yet contrived to cross each other's paths frequently. An observer would have been hard-pressed even to count them, let alone to work out which of them might be missing. They also moved more slowly than before – because, although nobody said anything, each of them was reluctant to leave his inexperienced comrade too far behind. Indeed, the further they strayed from Landon's position, the slower, the more reticent, their steps became – and Lorenzo noticed a certain amount of jostling for the rearmost position, the man who would be able to respond first to the alarm call when it came. Woods, of course, came out on top.

Lorenzo had been counting out a minute in his head. As he reached sixty, Greiss gave a nod, and Muldoon disappeared into a bush. Myers provided a distraction, this time, by yelling 'Jungle lizard!' and firing into the undergrowth before professing, with mock sheepishness, to have been mistaken.

They proceeded at length, expecting Trooper Landon to reappear before too long, at which point somebody else would slip into hiding. After twenty seconds had passed, though, Lorenzo saw that Greiss was getting worried. Another five, and he came to a halt, and drew breath to give the prearranged signal that would call off the operation.

That was when Landon yelled out, at last.

Only this wasn't a yell of discovery. It was a yell of fear.

Lorenzo was running before the echoes had subsided. They *had* come too far, because Landon was still all the way back where they had left him, and Lorenzo was pushing his muscles as hard as he could, willing himself forward, and yet still the path to his comrade seemed to stretch a near-infinite distance. He concentrated on what he could do: pumping his legs, faster than he could think, so fast that he was sure only sheer force of will kept him from falling. There were sounds ahead – ugly sounds, full of foreboding – but they were almost drowned out by his heartbeat, by the crashing footsteps of comrades around him and of Woods in front.

Every second counted. Every fraction of a second.

And there weren't enough of them.

Landon yelled again: a terrible gurgling scream, which was cut off in mid-flow and could only have meant one thing.

He came into sight at last, limp and no longer struggling in the grip of a figure that was humanoid in shape but a mockery of a human in its aspect.

The monster was caked in dirt, centimetres thick, and it bristled with grass, dead leaves, living flowers and the severed roots of larger plants as if a whole section of the planet had been scooped up and wrapped around its frame. Lorenzo thought the monster *was* flora, at first, but he could make out patches of suntanned skin, and human fingers around Landon's neck. Woods had already charged it, a lasgun fanfare presaging his arrival. Lorenzo had brought up his weapon but hadn't fired, fearful of hitting the monster's captive – but Woods had seen what he hadn't, or rather accepted what he didn't want to accept.

It must have waited for Landon, he realised. It was right under the tree in which the Guardsman had concealed himself – but he wouldn't have come down from there unless he was sure it was safe. The monster had discovered the Jungle Fighters' trap, and set its own in return.

As Woods hit the monster, it dropped Landon, and he fell to the ground, his head coming to rest at an acute angle to his body. Lorenzo was halfway to him when he realised there was no point. He changed course and leapt at the monster instead, along with Myers and Storm, whose howl of rage echoed in Lorenzo's ears. Woods could probably have handled the monster on his own – and he would have enjoyed bragging about it later – but Lorenzo wasn't thinking about that right now. He was thinking about Landon.

The monster, it turned out, was stronger than they had expected. It dislodged Woods and Myers, and sent them flying with a sweep of its arm. As the two troopers fell, however, Muldoon and Greiss appeared in their places. The monster was borne down under the combined weight of four Catachans, but showed no sign of slowing or weakening as they pounded at it with their fists. Lorenzo drew his fang, and plunged it into the monster's heart with a snarl, but the blade came out encrusted with muck and no blood, and still the monster fought on.

It shifted beneath his knees, and he realised with a start that it was *sinking*... as if the monster lay in quicksand, though the earth around it felt as hard as it ever had to the touch of Lorenzo's foot. He was scrabbling at the monster, desperate to stop it, to hold it here, because all he could think was that it was getting away – it had killed Landon and it was getting away – but the pull of the earth was inexorable, and the monster was gone, leaving Lorenzo with only two handfuls of mud and an empty feeling in his heart.

He staggered to his feet, and stepped back from where the monster had been, from the spot where the jungle grass still grew as if it had never been disturbed – and he looked at Greiss, with bewilderment in his eyes, as he realised that the sergeant had claimed a souvenir, wrenched it free from the monster's mass even as it went under. He was just staring at it, the first time Lorenzo had seen him speechless, as the rest of the Jungle Fighters gathered round.

Greiss held up his find, and one by one they realised what it was, and then they had no words either.

It was a bionic leg.

CHAPTER TEN

Lorenzo couldn't sleep.

This was highly unusual – at least when he was planetside, out in the jungle.

They had set up camp before the sun had gone down. They were resting in preparation for their passage by the ork encampment – a trial in which the night would be their ally. Lorenzo could feel the distant sun on his face, and its red glow penetrated his eyelids – but he was used to that. He was used to making the best of sleep whenever, wherever and for however long he could grab it. It wasn't just the sunlight that kept him awake.

Nor was it just the death of a trooper he had hardly known, to whom he didn't remember saying a word; a young man who could have become a good comrade, even a hero, had he lived to earn his name.

The monster – Lorenzo couldn't think of it as Dougan – could sink into the ground, and rise from it as silently. Little wonder, then, it had proved so elusive so far. Little wonder Landon hadn't seen it coming.

Lorenzo was feeling the same discomfort, the same restless itch, as he had on the carrier ship. That creeping realisation that the world around him didn't bow to the edicts of nature, to the physical laws he had thought inviolable. The feeling that nothing made much sense any more.

'It couldn't have been Steel Toe,' Woods had insisted, in the aftermath of the brief fight with the monster, manifestly ignoring the proof that had been there for all to see, in Greiss's hand. 'I don't care what happened to him, what this planet did to him, he wouldn't have... He wouldn't have. Not Steel Toe.'

'Sorry, Hotshot,' Greiss had said gloomily, 'we have to face facts. I'd recognise this hunk o' metal anywhere. See under the dirt here? Scorch marks from where Steel Toe was bitten by that critter on Vortis. It shorted the circuits, sent a lethal shock across its own mandibles. Steel Toe couldn't walk for a fortnight, till we got the leg fixed, but he saved our bacon that day.'

'It *wasn't* him,' said Donovits firmly. 'It may have been his body, but it wasn't Steel Toe. He's dead!'

Myers had rubbed his chin where the mud-encrusted monster had hit him. 'Well, he was sure taking a long time to lie down.'

'Brains is right,' said Muldoon. 'What we just fought wasn't Steel Toe. It wasn't alive. It was some kind of a zombie. I looked into its eyes – and I'm telling you, Steel Toe wasn't in there.'

Greiss, as usual, had turned the topic to the future, to what they did next, not letting his troopers dwell on what they couldn't explain. 'Right, men,' he had announced, 'that means we have a problem.'

'I can't see that thing coming back, sergeant,' said Myers, 'not minus its leg.'

'Not what I meant, Bullseye. There's something on this planet can bring the dead back to life.'

'Not exactly bring them back,' Donovits had corrected him, 'just reanimate them. Without getting a closer look at Steel Toe's body, I couldn't tell you if it was host to some parasite, or...' He'd tailed off as he had followed Greiss's gaze.

They'd all looked down at Landon's body.

Lorenzo let out a sigh, now, and rolled onto his back, accepting that he was awake for the duration – until he could calm the raging thoughts that filled his head to bursting. He listened to Myers, who was on watch, humming a quiet tune as he cleaned

his knife. He stared, almost sightlessly, at the plastic sheeting that
Muldoon and Donovits had tied around the leafiest branches of
the surrounding trees, collecting condensation for the squad's
water bottles. He listened to Braxton's breathing, beside him,
and he knew the Validian was awake too.

Rogar III was winning. It was beating them – and the fact that
it could only do so by changing the rules was cold comfort to
Lorenzo.

He had wanted a challenge. He had wanted to earn his name.
But his squad was already two men down, and they hadn't seen
a single ork yet. There would be more casualties; of that, he was
certain. More chances to prove himself. Or die trying. Not that
Lorenzo was afraid of death, but he thought about the rest of his
company, by now no doubt engaged in fierce battle. He wondered
if they had scratched the surface of Rogar yet, if they'd learned
its secrets – or if the planet was concentrating its forces on this
one small squad, the twelve men who had dared try to penetrate
its dark heart. Ten men, now. He wondered what those fellow
Jungle Fighters would think, upon completing their missions, if
they found their bravery had all been for nothing – if there was
no word from the squad that had been entrusted with the most
important assignment.

No, Lorenzo wasn't afraid of death. But he *was* afraid of failure.
And of going to an unmarked grave, with no one left to remember his name or to tell of his heroism at the end.

They hadn't been able to cremate Landon. They were too close
to the orks now to risk lighting a fire. Myers had expressed the
dubious hope that their fallen comrade's broken neck might prevent his resurrection by the force that had animated Dougan. But
Donovits had just shaken his head.

Greiss had done the deed himself, in the end. He hadn't let
anyone else help; he'd roared at Woods when he'd tried to ignore
that order. He had told them to remember Landon as he was in
life. Still, Lorenzo couldn't shake the image from his thoughts:

Old Hardhead, driving the butt of his lasgun down into the dead rookie's arms and legs, over and over again. Until his body was no more than a fleshy sack for the fragments of his shattered bones. Until no force in the Imperium or beyond could have made Landon's limbs support his weight.

The sound of a shovel striking the earth had seemed to repeat forever. Greiss had reappeared, at last, with his face dirt-streaked and red. He had reported, in a hollow tone, that it was over, that Landon could rest in peace.

Lorenzo drifted into a fitful doze, haunted by nightmares in which he was fighting his own comrades, and the bony hands of Dougan and Landon were grasping at his ankles, trying to pull him down into the earth to join them.

He could hear low voices.

He opened his eyes, catching his breath at a lingering vestige of some dream horror already fading in his memory. The night had swooped in when he hadn't been looking. It was dark, and the huddled shapes around him were stirring, preparing. It was time, already.

He scrambled to his feet, still unsettled by the dream but trying not to show it. He pulled on his jacket and bandolier, checked his pack. Few words were spoken, the Jungle Fighters all concentrating on what lay ahead of them, knowing its import. Mackenzie and Braxton looked especially tired, and Lorenzo realised that each must have slept only half the short rest period. Neither had been placed on the watch rota, but the commissar probably hadn't dared close his eyes without his adjutant to look out for him. He didn't trust anybody else.

Lorenzo hadn't been placed on watch either. A part of him wondered if it was because Greiss didn't trust *him*. Despite his pretence to the contrary. Because of last night. The sergeant's briefing soon quelled that fear, though.

Greiss spoke quietly and didn't say much. Sounds carried

further at night. Anyway, the Catachans knew what was expected of them, and Mackenzie and Braxton would just have to follow their lead. He reminded the squad of the importance of stealth: 'One ork or gretchin gets sight or sound of us and lives to tell of it, and we've not only blown our mission, we won't be around to explain to Colonel Graves what the hell we thought we were doing.' Then he made the pronouncement that caused Lorenzo's heart to leap.

'Lorenzo takes point,' said Greiss. 'That's because we might have more to contend with than just greenskins. Remember, people, those blue lights come out at night. I want you to pair up, keep an eye on your opposite number – first sign he shows of going misty-eyed, you give him a slap. Lorenzo, I'm trusting you upfront alone because you've shaken off the effects of the light once. If it comes back, you can resist it, right?'

'Right, sergeant.'

Greiss outlined their proposed route, and Lorenzo felt a swell of pride when he turned to him in particular and asked if he was clear on it. He confirmed that he was, and Greiss drew him to one side, and clapped him on the back. 'I know I don't have to tell you to go slow and careful. Hell, if you're as quiet out there as you are around us half the time, those orks will never hear you coming.'

Then Greiss gave the order to move out, and Lorenzo drew his Catachan fang and slipped into the jungle, quickly but quietly, staying low, in cover. He used his lasgun to part the vines and creepers in his way, surveying the ground for predators and other hazards. He advanced cautiously, doing his best to leave no trail. The foliage yielded to his soft but firm touch, but closed in again behind him until he felt like he was travelling in his own green cocoon. He knew his comrades were behind him, but all he could hear of them was an occasional rustle that might have been a lizard or a whisper of the night breeze. They were keeping their distance, in case Lorenzo made a misstep, set off an ork trap and blew himself to pieces. He was alone now, to all intents and purposes. In the most dangerous position, but that was all right. He wanted that responsibility.

The danger focused Lorenzo's mind. It sharpened his senses. It blew away the doubts of a few hours earlier, like a strong, fresh wind.

He maintained a good pace for the first hour or so, but slowed when he knew the encampment was near. He saw no evidence of its presence yet, but he fancied he detected a hint of greenskin stink on the air. Something stirred in a bush beside him, and Lorenzo froze, hoping his camouflage would hide him – but it was only a snake. One of those with the silver triangles on their skins.

He crept on – but, a few minutes later, he spotted another triangle-backed snake in the undergrowth, and this one had seen him. Its head reared up. It bared its tiny fangs and hissed, but it made no move to strike Lorenzo. It appeared to be watching him.

He remembered how the birds had stalked the Catachans, how he'd kept spying them out of the corner of his eye before they launched their attack. He remembered Braxton saying that the lizards had done something similar, poking around the edges of the Validian camp for a few days before they'd dared enter it. The silver-backed snake didn't appear to be a threat right now, but as Armstrong had said, that could change in a heartbeat. Particularly if it wasn't alone, and especially if a concerted attack on the Jungle Fighters drew the orks' attention.

Lorenzo took a step forward, fingers twitching on his knife. The snake tensed, watching him. A lasgun would have done the job more efficiently, but with too much noise. Lorenzo stooped down, holding out his free hand as bait. The snake backed away a centimetre, suspiciously. Lorenzo took another step.

The snake struck. From further away than he'd expected. As if its coiled tail had acted as a spring to propel it out of the grass. It jabbed at the proffered hand, and Lorenzo snatched it away and decapitated the snake with his fang before it could land and reorient itself. He stamped on its severed head, exploding it in a mass of black blood. He grabbed the twitching body, wrung it until it was still, and tossed it aside into the dark. A quiet, discordant hiss of alarm told him that his message had been received by multiple unseen onlookers. The jungle grass swayed and rustled in a dozen thin paths away from him.

It was shortly after that that he came across the first trap.

Lorenzo had known it was imminent, because the undergrowth in this area was flattened, plants and branches broken. The orks had been here, and recently.

The trap was crude and obvious, like most of their constructs: a cord stretched between trees at knee height, connected to something hidden in the lower branches of one. A grenade, most likely. Still, a Guardsman in a hurry might not have spotted it. It was more evidence of the warboss's cunning, spreading to his followers.

Lorenzo stepped over the tripwire carefully, and waited. Thirty seconds passed before Muldoon's head peeked out of a bush a few metres behind him. He saw Lorenzo, and an inquisitive expression crossed his face. Lorenzo indicated the wire; Muldoon would probably have seen it anyway, but better safe than sorry. Muldoon nodded, then waited for Lorenzo to regain his lead.

Alone again.

The second tripwire was higher, and better placed. To its right, the jungle was dense with poison creepers – and Lorenzo knew that that way lay the acid swamp of which Sly Marbo had spoken. To the left: a cluster of red snapper flowers, through which he could see no safe route. Again, his inability to use his lasgun narrowed his options. Bad enough to be grabbed by those intractable petals – but the greater peril would be the flowers' alarm wail, certain to attract attention.

He approached the wire, and stooped beside it gingerly. It was too high to step over. He could disarm the trap: cut the wire or retrieve the grenade from the tree. The risk in so doing would be minimal, but actual. If an ork or a gretchin came this way after the Jungle Fighters had passed, it would know they had been here.

No. Far better, far safer, to take no chances. To go under.

Lorenzo lowered himself onto his stomach, noting that the ground was a little soft, a little wet. He removed his pack and his lasgun from his back, to reduce his prone height, and pushed them under the wire before him. Then he dragged himself through the mud on his elbows, keeping his head down.

He had plenty of clearance. So long as nothing unexpected happened, so long as he didn't get careless, he had nothing to worry about.

So long as nothing unexpected happened...

The blue light snapped on like a shipboard lighting panel, just ignited into a glowing ball ahead of him, a few centimetres off the ground. Lorenzo felt his stomach tighten as he craned his neck to look at it without raising his chin. He sensed that it was calling to him, urging him to stand and approach it, and he felt the muscles in his arms and legs tensing to obey.

He stopped himself, before his back could brush the tripwire.

He closed his eyes, and immediately felt better. His head was clearer. Lorenzo listened to his own breathing, and he felt the cold of the mud against his stomach. He thought about Steel Toe Dougan. He knew the blue light was still out there, but he was certain it hadn't entered his mind. He was certain that it couldn't, so long as he didn't look at it.

But what if the blue light wanted that? What if its purpose, this time, was to blind him to something else? To something creeping up on him...

...something rustling in the undergrowth beside his head...

Lorenzo opened his eyes, as breathless and disconcerted as he had been after his nightmare. He looked around quickly, but saw nothing. Nothing but the blue light, drawing his eyes in like it was the only thing in the world. The only thing that mattered, anyway. It occurred to Lorenzo that it was closer than it had been last night, that this time he really could catch it, catch whatever it was that was generating it. End its threat. Save his comrades.

In the blue light, Lorenzo saw Sergeant Greiss's approval, so rarely bestowed. Yet, in his memory, he heard his voice: *'I'm trusting you up front alone... If it comes back, you can resist it, right?'*

Greiss was counting on him.

'Right?'

Lorenzo remembered how determined he had been to prove himself worthy of Old Hardhead's trust, not to let him down again. He knew the only way to do that was to obey his orders, to do what he'd promised he would do...

'Right?'

'Right, sergeant.'

To resist. That was Lorenzo's greatest ambition, what he wanted most at this moment, and so – as a part of him was only dimly aware – that was what the blue light showed to him, and in so doing it defeated itself. Lorenzo blinked, and the light was still there, but suddenly it was just a light, and it had no hold over him.

Still, he stayed where he was for a moment longer, exploring the crannies of his mind, ensuring there was no trace of the blue light left in there. Ensuring that he wasn't being tricked again. He concentrated on what he remembered, what Greiss had told him – and he reassured himself that, as long as he heeded those words, those explicit instructions, he would be doing the right thing.

Lorenzo dug his elbows into the mud and pulled himself forward again, until he was clear of the ork tripwire, then he climbed to his feet and collected his belongings.

The blue light was gone. Blinked out. As if it had sensed it had no power here any more. Somehow, Lorenzo knew it wouldn't be back. Not for him.

He realised something else too: that his hands were stinging.

He looked down, saw that his palms were red and beginning

to blister. He had been so wrapped up in his thoughts, in the light, that he hadn't noticed. The wet ground. Acid. It must have seeped from the nearby swamp. The knees of his trousers had almost burnt through, and the soles of his boots had begun to melt. Not much harm done yet, but in time...

Lorenzo cleaned his hands on a leaf, and waited for Muldoon to appear again. This time, once he'd pointed out the tripwire, he beckoned him forward. Greiss came too, holding up a hand to halt the troopers behind him.

'I think we need to bear a little further north,' whispered Lorenzo, displaying his damaged boots.

'That'll take us closer to the orks,' Muldoon pointed out.

But Greiss looked down at his own feet, and scowled. 'Lorenzo's right. No point our finding Big Green if we're all walking on bloody stumps by the time we do.' Then, with grudging admiration, he conceded, 'Mackenzie was right about that greenskin. Building his camp on the edge of the swamp, making the best of the natural defences – he's a clever bastard, all right.'

The encampment was even closer than Lorenzo had estimated.

Almost as soon as he changed his course, he found himself at the edge of a clearing, a little smaller than the Imperial Guard's, crammed with ramshackle buildings of metal and wood.

He lay and watched it for a while, scrutinising each shadow until he was sure of its nature, until he knew it wasn't an enemy waiting in ambush. He studied the ork huts, familiarising himself with their layout, with every blind corner from which an ork or a gretchin could spring out at him as he passed. He saw no sentries – which worried him, because he knew there would be sentries. Somewhere.

At last, Lorenzo glanced behind him, saw his squad waiting, gave them a thumbs-up signal and moved on. He moved on slowly – almost painfully so, knowing that stealth was more imperative now than ever. A single thin line of trees separated him from the orks. He had to make maximum use of the scant cover he had – and he had to be sure he didn't make the slightest sound.

It seemed to take an age for him to reach that first danger point, that first gangway between two huts, to be able to edge forward and peer down it, to reassure himself that it was empty. It seemed to take an age – although he knew it had only been a few minutes. But Lorenzo wasn't impatient. He lived for moments like this.

There was something in the trees ahead of him.

He froze.

It was taller than a man, but hunched, enormous arms hanging down to its knees, its shoulders broad and muscular. It was wearing dulled armour – and, although the darkness made it difficult to pick out colours, the skin that showed through the metal plates had a decidedly green tint.

The ork didn't seem to be trying to hide. Lorenzo wondered, for a heart-stopping moment, if it was searching for him, if it had heard something. Any closer, and he feared it might catch his scent.

Then it turned away from him, grunting as it fumbled with its protective metal layers, and he realised it had only come out here to relieve itself. Lorenzo would never find an enemy more exposed, more helpless; he could attack it from behind, wrap a cord around its throat and strangle it. But orks were a sturdy breed, and it would certainly have struggled loudly as it died. Reluctantly, he let it be – and when it had done its business, the ork shuffled away and faded into the shadow of a metal hut.

Lorenzo crept forward again. He stepped over another tripwire, and waited to point it out to Muldoon. Glancing ahead, he saw that he was almost there, almost past the camp. Maybe they'd call him 'Sneaky' Lorenzo. No, he wasn't sure he liked that. 'Shadow' Lorenzo? 'Sly' Lorenzo?

Voices.

They were hushed – but against the muted sounds of the night, they sounded unnatural, harsh and as loud as las-fire discharges.

He thought one of the voices belonged to Greiss. There was an urgent tone to it, almost a plea. Lorenzo looked to the ork camp, certain that the voices must have carried that far, but nothing was stirring. Not yet. He ached to know what was happening, but he knew he ought to maintain his position. He sheathed his knife and fingered his lasgun, ready to draw it if necessary.

The explosion caught him totally unawares.

The night erupted into daylight, too quickly, too shockingly, for Lorenzo to avert his gaze, to protect his night vision. He was half blinded.

But, as the echoes of the explosion died away and his deadened ears popped, he could hear movement and grunting from the encampment just a few footsteps away. And the shadows, the only things he could make out now, were shifting.

Lorenzo's mind raced. Had his comrades blundered into a trap he had missed? Had something else found them? Was it his fault?

There had to have been casualties, he realised, his throat drying at the thought. The explosion had been centred right at the spot where he'd heard Greiss's voice. It had sounded like a frag grenade.

The shadows were converging on that spot now, orks snarling and roaring with battle lust as they rushed to defend their territory.

A wave of despair passed over Lorenzo as he realised it didn't matter now which of his comrades were alive or dead. The orks knew where they were – and as Greiss had said, the orks outnumbered them thirty to one. They had nowhere to run, trapped between the encampment on one side and the acid swamp on the other.

There was no doubt about it. They were all dead.

CHAPTER ELEVEN

The orks were an oncoming mass, one indistinguishable from the next, at least to Lorenzo's compromised sight. The air was filled with noise, and the ground shook to the staccato flashes of more explosions: makeshift grenades, hurled over the heads of the orks' front ranks by those in the rear.

In response, las-fire barked out of the jungle, striking the foremost orks and passing through them into their comrades. Lorenzo felt like cheering. At least five, six, seven of his fellow Catachans were alive and fighting back – and the next explosions blossomed in the heart of the orks' own ranks. The Jungle Fighters' frag grenades were more effective than the orks' bombs, because the greenskins were packed so closely together, each of them more likely to take a shrapnel hit. Their armour, and their thick hides, would protect them from the worst of it, but many would be injured, some badly. Some were knocked off their feet by the concussive force of the blasts; as Lorenzo's eyes cleared, he saw orks stumbling over each other, trampling on the fallen, pushing each other aside – and yet still advancing.

They didn't know where he was.

As the orks closed in on Lorenzo's squad, he realised they were passing him by, in his solitary position ahead of the others. The others were dead anyway. He had a chance to save himself, to sneak away, maybe take a report back to Lieutenant Vines so that the next men sent out here would know what lay ahead of them.

He didn't consider it for a second.

Lorenzo broke cover, letting out the loudest, wildest war cry in his repertoire, his finger locked around the trigger of his lasgun so that it fired repeatedly into the enemy mass. He didn't care how accurate his shots were; chances were they'd find a few orks wherever he aimed them. He just wanted to draw attention to himself. Maybe – with luck – convince the greenskins that he was more than one trooper, that their enemies had surrounded them in a pincer movement. The more of them he could distract from his squad, the better their chances would be; the worse his own chances.

He was dead anyway, he told himself. They were all dead. But the longer the Jungle Fighters survived, the more orks they could take down with them. The more orks they took down, the greater the chance there'd be stories told of them back home. Assuming that, by some miracle, this story made it back home at all.

The nearest orks responded with alarm and confusion to Lorenzo's attack, took a moment to pinpoint the source of it, and aimed their weapons: crude, solid-shot guns. They were too slow. Lorenzo had already dived into the sheltered gap between two huts, and he was still running as bullets pinged off metal behind him. He heard grunts and howls and footsteps, and he knew he'd succeeded in drawing the attention of a few dozen orks. Now he just had to survive the consequences of that success.

He ducked and weaved and twisted between huts at random. The longer he could keep his pursuers searching for him, the fewer orks the others had to contend with in the meantime. But he couldn't disappear completely, couldn't flee back into the jungle, because the orks might just abandon their hunt in frustration and return to the combat. Lorenzo let out a whoop and fired his lasgun three times into the air, drawing his foes further into their own camp. He rounded another corner and disturbed a knot of gretchin, who screeched and jabbered in their own crude, incomprehensible tongue, and came at him.

Lorenzo brought up his lasgun, fired, downed several targets – and then the rest were upon him, or streaming around to attack him from behind. They were kicking and scratching, squealing for their masters. He swung his lasgun like a club, dislodging two of them. He kicked and punched at the others; he reached over his shoulder, seized a gretchin that had clung to his back, and slammed it into the ground. He tried to run, kicking more of the creatures out of his path, but they dogged his heels. He spun around, fired, claimed two more kills, and the rest of the gretchin scampered out of sight. They emerged again as soon as Lorenzo had turned his back.

Their cries drew the orks, as he had known they must.

The first of them appeared ahead, and barred Lorenzo's path. It snarled at him, as if to intimidate him with its presence. That worked, he had heard, against some men; the ork, with its sloping brow, its jutting jaw and its recessed, baleful eyes, cut an imposing figure – and his eye line was level with its fearsome tusks and its slobbering lips. To a man who had faced down a Catachan Devil, though, a single ork was nothing special. It might walk and talk, but to a Deathworlder this green-skinned monster was just another thing to be killed.

Lorenzo snapped off a round, the shot narrowly missing the ork though the flash sent it howling and reeling in pain – but he'd pay for the second's distraction it had caused him. The ork's comrades had found him too, and they came at him, rounding the ramshackle buildings from all directions. More than one of them mimicked the Catachan's earlier actions, kicking aside the gretchin that had summoned them. The pathetic, stunted creatures slunk away, their job done.

Surrounded and outnumbered, Lorenzo concentrated his fire in one direction, hoping to clear an escape route for himself. His one advantage was that the greenskins couldn't use their guns without hitting each other – though, given the speed at which they were coming, that wouldn't keep him alive for long. He finished off two of them, but the lasgun's power pack whined and died as the third bore down on him. He tried to impale the ork on his bayonet, but it wrestled his gun away and tossed it aside. Another ork smacked into Lorenzo from behind, and he rolled with the blow, drawing his knife as he hit the ground and twisted out of the way of a descending axe blade. It sliced into the earth a whisker from Lorenzo's ear. Its wielder wasn't far behind it, choosing not to retrieve its weapon but to leap instead on its fallen prey and rend him with its bare hands. Lorenzo threw up his knife so the ork's own momentum forced the blade through the roof of its mouth and into its brain.

Its dead weight smacked onto him, winding him, pinning him down, but providing him with cover and a moment's respite. By the time two other orks had hoisted their dead comrade aside, Lorenzo was ready to act. On hands and knees, he slipped between the legs of one of his attackers, and tripped it in the process. The orks fumbled and stumbled and generally fell over each other in their eagerness to apprehend the slippery, squirming Catachan – but any green hands that found him were rewarded with a slash of Lorenzo's fang.

Then, joyously, he was through them all, open space looming ahead of him, and he was pushing himself to his feet, snatching his stolen lasgun, reaching for a fresh power pack from his bandolier and a meaty hand grabbed him by the back of his jacket and pulled him back, twisted him around, slammed him into the metal wall of a hut, and while he was still trying to get his breath back from that, a giant ork fist pounded into his stomach and Lorenzo coughed up blood and felt his legs giving way.

He managed to block another axe thrust with his lasgun – the last time it would save him. The blade embedded itself in the gun's furniture, and came free with a cracking and a splintering and a last sullen fizz of energy. Lorenzo found an ork snout with his bayonet, drawing blood and making the creature squeal and fall back, but then he let the gun go and it was just him and his

Catachan fang, and he knew that at best he'd be able to kill one more ork before they killed him.

He focused on doing just that. He picked his target, pushed himself away from the wall behind him, ducked beneath a pair of flailing green arms. He locked himself into a deadly embrace with the luckless ork, denying it the chance to swing its axe or raise its gun. He buried his knife in its stomach, twisted it, cutting through the ork's guts, feeling its blood spilling out, soaking into his own clothes; at the same time, its fingers closed around his neck, cutting off his oxygen, fading his surroundings to black. A deadly dance from which neither partner would ever break.

Lorenzo wasn't sure at first if the pops and cracks he could hear as if from the end of a long tunnel were those of his own bones breaking – but the orks were reeling in confusion again, and the grip on his throat was loosened, and he thought he could see a lithe, dark-haired figure hurling grenades from the roof of a nearby hut, although he might have imagined it.

He raised his fang to make the most of his reprieve, thinking he might claim another ork life, but the world was still darkening and the commands from his brain didn't seem to be reaching his muscles... and now Lorenzo was sliding to the ground, falling in slow-motion but still too fast to put out a hand to save himself. He was lying facedown, and his back was showered first with hot shrapnel and then an ork body landed on top of him, hiding him, and he just lay there, clinging to consciousness, his face sticky with blood but he didn't know whose.

A long time after that, it seemed, Lorenzo heard the orks moving away from him. They were turning their attention to a new enemy, leaving him for dead, and he couldn't have said for certain that they were so wrong. It was only after a long minute had passed and he was still breathing, his heart still beating and his head clearing as his lungs heaved precious oxygen into his bloodstream, that he knew he would fight on. Only then that Lorenzo breathed a grateful prayer to the God-Emperor for sparing his life, until he recovered his wits and realised he ought to thank Sly Marbo instead.

He didn't know why Marbo had chosen to save him, above the others. Maybe he'd just been lucky – in the right place at the right time. Knowing Marbo, it was possible he'd been on that roof all night, waiting for his moment. Whatever the reason, Lorenzo was determined to return the favour, or to pass it on.

Marbo, he decided, had the right idea. Find high ground.

He pulled himself up onto the roof of the nearest hut, finding plenty of handholds in the old, pitted metal but almost falling as his muscles protested at being put to so much effort so soon. He'd half-expected to find Marbo up there, but he had moved on, of course. Lorenzo lowered himself onto his stomach, and craned his neck to see over the edge of the building without being seen in return.

Much of the fighting had now moved out of the encampment. The Catachans had drawn their more numerous foes into the jungle environment they knew best, though with the acid swamp at their backs they had precious little room to manoeuvre. From here, Lorenzo couldn't see any of his camouflaged comrades – but he guessed, by the positions of the orks, that they'd separated along the perimeter line, making themselves harder to find. The orks, in turn, seemed to be everywhere, shaking trees, firing into bushes, doing everything they could to beat their foes out of hiding.

There were more of them, of course, among the buildings, searching for the long-gone Marbo, liable to find Lorenzo instead.

His eyes alighted upon one building in particular: a small metal structure, built with a little more care than most, no windows cut into its walls, its door secured by thick chains. Ammo store, he guessed. He strained to reach his backpack, unfastened it, and rummaged out the two demolition charges with which he'd been equipped. They weren't really for combat use – the Catachans employed them to clear hard-going areas of the jungle when they were in a hurry and stealth wasn't such an issue – but they were just what he needed now.

The first charge landed with a plop beside the chained door, when no orks were looking that way. Lorenzo set the second to detonate only two seconds after, and he felt his palm sweating as he held the cold sphere in his hand, counting down.

He let the second charge go even as the first explosion shook the buildings around him. By the time its vibrations overtook him, he was running, but they made him mistime his leap to the next hut across. Lorenzo pedalled empty air, desperate to propel himself that vital centimetre further, and somehow he caught the protruding edge of the roof as it passed him, and almost yanked his fingers out of their sockets as they caught his falling weight.

There were two orks below him, and they turned their guns upwards. Before they could squeeze their triggers, they were knocked off their feet – and Lorenzo felt it simultaneously: a furious shockwave of heat and sound, like a hurricane raging around him, in which it was all he could do to grit his teeth and maintain his hold on the parapet while his back was peppered with debris.

The hurricane lessened, and he strained and pulled himself up, attaining his new perch at last. He rolled onto his back, breathless, but raised himself on his elbows because he couldn't resist the chance to inspect his handiwork.

It looked like the sky was on fire. The building he had just leapt from had collapsed, along with several others, and Lorenzo could see the burning, smoking hole where the ammo store had been. Evidently, he'd guessed right about its contents. His first charge had blown off the door; the second must have bounced neatly through the resulting aperture. Its detonation had sparked a chain reaction, just as he had planned. The sturdy walls had absorbed much of it before they had given, else he would have been dead. To his satisfaction, several orks – presumably reacting to the first explosion, too late to stop the second – *had* perished, their burnt corpses twitching and steaming in the midst of the devastation.

Dozens more orks were turning from the jungle, streaming back into the camp, looking for the enemy that had penetrated their home. Lorenzo couldn't have hoped for a bigger distraction – and it had certainly been well timed for at least one Jungle Fighter. He saw a blur of activity, heard the howls of stricken orks, and then Muldoon came streaking out of the foliage, his lasgun firing. From this distance, Lorenzo couldn't see what had happened, but he could guess. One of Muldoon's favourite tricks: he would gather up a cluster of deadly creepers, secrete himself in a tree and, when the enemy got too close, let the creepers go. Lorenzo could see orks dancing and twisting as they fought to disentangle themselves, as the creepers stung them and burst their poisonous pustules in their grotesque faces.

But he was exposed now, left with nowhere to run but out into the open where his painted skin couldn't camouflage him. Like Lorenzo before him, he raced for the shelter of the ork huts, miraculously untouched by a hail of bullets – but one great brute of an ork had avoided his trap, and it came charging after him, and cannoned into him from behind.

Lorenzo was on his way before Muldoon hit the ground. He leapt onto the sloping roof of the next hut, almost lost his footing on its slick surface, righted himself and jumped again. His fingers hovered over his bandolier, over the pockets that held his frag grenades – but unless more orks moved in, unless they formed a living shield between Lorenzo and Muldoon as they had between him and Marbo, a grenade could do more harm than good. His lasgun was gone. That left him with his knife.

He launched himself from the last roof, at the ork's broad back, and he let out a cry – enough for it to hear him coming and half-turn its head, not soon enough for it to bring around its gun and pick him off in midair. Enough for it to take its eyes off Muldoon for a moment. The ork jerked backwards, easing its weight off its fallen prey, as Lorenzo's fang sliced down between its shoulder blades – and in that same moment, Muldoon drove his night reaper up into the ork's throat.

The ork took a long, long second to die – but at last it toppled like a felled tree, and Lorenzo fancied he could feel the ground shaking with the impact of its heavy corpse. Or with something else...

Something was coming. Something big. Lorenzo didn't have to look, didn't have to waste the half-second it would take him, to know it was bad, that they had to take cover. But Muldoon was slowed, having trouble standing, and Lorenzo saw that his head was cut, his eyes glazed over. Concussion.

He reached out a hand, and Muldoon laughed giddily as he took it, as Lorenzo hauled him to his feet. 'Looks like... like I owe you my life,' he giggled. Then, suddenly earnest, he gripped Lorenzo by the arms and stared into his eyes as if he had the most important information in the Imperium to impart. 'Hey, Lorenzo, you noticed? There isn't... isn't half as many of the greenskins as Greiss said there'd be. Thirty... thirty to one, my eye! More like ten to one. And we can take down ten orks apiece, right? Hell, I must've killed five already.'

That noise was getting closer... The rumbling of an engine. Lorenzo looked now, and he saw it – saw its piercing light first, through the drifting smoke of the battlefield, and then the shape of the behemoth behind it.

It was black, daubed with crude paintings of human skulls and bones – ramshackle in appearance, but bristling with armour plating and weapons. Lorenzo had seen vehicles like this before. It was the ork equivalent of a tank – a battlewagon, they called it – manned by a greenskin mob. They howled and strained forward on the back of this unnatural beast as they saw their two exposed foes. The pilot trained the vehicle's searchlight upon the Catachans, and wrestled its great wheels around.

Muldoon's mood had changed again, and suddenly he looked distant and extremely pale, apart from the livid red gash across his head. 'Trouble is,' he said to himself in a hollow voice, 'they got Brains. I saw him go down. So, we have to take out a few more orks each to make up his share.'

Lorenzo couldn't allow himself to react to this news. There would be time for mourning the dead later, when the act of so doing wouldn't add to their numbers.

The battlewagon had two guns, like eyes on stalks protruding before it. The one on the right flared, and Lorenzo pushed Muldoon aside as a shell whistled by and thumped into the dirt, and filled the world with light and sound again. His comrade sagged in his arms like a dead weight, and Lorenzo slapped him across the face, hoping to shock him back to alertness. More gunfire – the right-hand gun again – but the searchlight had lost its targets and the smoke from the first impact was swirling around them and ork weapons, mostly lashed together from spare parts, were notoriously unreliable anyway. Still, the impact almost knocked Lorenzo off his feet.

Muldoon blinked as blood seeped into his eye, and coughed as smoke crept into his throat. Lorenzo tried to drag him toward the huts, but there came another explosion from that direction and they were thrown back, back into the open, and the searchlight had rediscovered them and there were more orks coming, silhouettes through the haze, from the encampment, from the jungle.

Muldoon was pressing his lasgun into Lorenzo's hands, saying, 'Here – you can make better use of this than I can.'

'What... what are you–?'

He wouldn't have had to finish the question, even had the smoke not robbed him of speech. He could see the answer. Muldoon was rummaging in his bandolier, finding a demolition charge with each hand – and although Lorenzo's first instinct was to stop him, to save him, he held himself back because his comrade was grinning at him now. 'You saved my life. That makes it my turn. And besides, I count nine greenskins on that tank. Add them to the other five, and that's my share and a few for Brains to boot.' Looking into his comrade's ashen face, Lorenzo saw the pain he was holding at arm's length, the darkness lurking at the edges of his eyes, and he knew then as Muldoon surely did that this was how it had to be.

Then he was gone, tearing himself from Lorenzo's grip before he could think of a word to say. He was racing into the light – and before the orks knew what was happening, he was too close for them to train their gun upon him, but not too close for them to bring their other weapon – the one on the left – to bear...

It was a flamethrower. That explained what this single wagon was doing out here, thought Lorenzo, why the orks had assembled it in the depths of a jungle that would only impede it: they'd been using it for clearance operations. A fierce jet of flame licked around Muldoon now, and although he seemed to avoid the worst of it, and though Lorenzo's vision was obscured by smoke and by the battlewagon's glaring light, he was certain that Muldoon had been winged, that he'd been burnt, and yet like the relentless orks themselves he kept going.

He vaulted over the guns onto the front of the tank, planting his feet and his fists into the faces of the orks at the triggers. Those behind saw the threat to them and, snarling, drew their own guns, and one of them leapt at him but he turned its momentum and its weight against it, and threw it over his shoulder and off the moving vehicle. The others fired, and Muldoon's body twitched and jerked as their bullets ripped into him, and Lorenzo feared that he too would fall and die in a splatter of mud and blood, but he was *climbing* – climbing onto the back of the battlewagon as if animated by willpower alone, and he fell into the midst of the ork mob and they leapt upon him and tore him apart, but by then his final goal had been achieved.

The charges blew the battlewagon apart from the inside, and eight orks died screaming.

By that time, Lorenzo had replaced the depleted pack in the lasgun his comrade had given him, and he was firing at the shapes that loomed about him, making sure he kept moving, an impossible target amid the sensory chaos. He felt a grim sense of triumph as he claimed his tenth kill of the night, and he thought of Sharkbait Muldoon and knew he would have been proud.

But he also knew he was surrounded, and the orks were homing in on him now, closing him down. They came at Lorenzo from all sides, moving in to close combat as usual, trusting in their greater strength and numbers against his greater dexterity. This time, he knew, he had no right to expect a reprieve, no Marbo to save him. He had used up all his luck. So he dropped his gun and hurled the last of his grenades, and he thought about how bravely Muldoon had died – and Donovits too, he didn't doubt – and he drew his Catachan fang.

And finally, Lorenzo ran to greet his enemies, with his trusty knife in his hand and a defiant roar in his throat.

CHAPTER TWELVE

The fighting seemed to have gone on forever.

Lorenzo remembered the first tint of sunlight touching the sky, remembered how amazed he'd been that only one night had passed because it seemed so long since he'd thought of anything but blood and smoke and fire. Yet when he looked back on that time, much of it was no more than a blur of sneering ork faces and knife thrusts and death. Lots of death. He thought that, at one point, he'd stood back to back with Sergeant Greiss, but he couldn't be sure. Once they'd moved into hand-to-hand combat, he'd had no choice but to surrender himself to his instincts. Otherwise he'd have thought about the tiredness in his muscles and the aches from his bruises and the still-overwhelming odds against him, and he would have lain down and died. Or, worse still, he'd have thought about dying.

He *could* have died, and he'd probably have known nothing about it. Just wound down like a spring, from a wound he hadn't yet felt, and that wouldn't have been so bad, would it?

Lorenzo was fighting in his sleep, muscle memory twitching his arms in response to an imaginary parade of blood-crazed enemies. Somewhere in the back of his mind, he thought he must have wondered if he would ever wake up, or if he would fight this nightmare struggle forever.

Yes, it had been a glorious battle.

And it was made all the more so by the fact that, in the end,

Lorenzo felt sunlight touching his face, and he opened his eyes and knew that he had *lived*.

It took him a moment to work out where he was. The light was bright, but his surroundings seemed dim. He realised that the light was streaming through a small window, to be swallowed by the dust and the dirt in here.

An ork hut. Lorenzo was lying on a makeshift bunk, really no more than a pile of junk draped with rags, and he was swaddled in stinking furs. He was hot, burning up. It crossed his mind only briefly that the orks themselves might have brought him here, as a hostage. That wasn't their style. The fact that he *was* here meant his small squad had achieved the impossible. They had won. But at what price?

Lorenzo felt a stiffness in his side, and sent a tentative hand under his bulky coverings to investigate. His questing fingers found a hard knot of synth-skin, between the ribs in his right side, and he winced at the sudden white hot memory of an axe blade scything through his flesh. His memories were disordered, still vague, but that pain, he felt sure, was among the most recent of them. He sighed regretfully. He would have liked to be found standing, at the end.

'Hey, Lorenzo? You moving under all that lot?'

The familiar voice drew Lorenzo's gaze to his left, to the next bunk, where lay Woods. He must have been injured too, though Lorenzo wouldn't have known it from the cocky grin on his face. ''Bout time too,' said Woods. 'Been lying here awake on my own the past couple of hours, while you've been snoring away. What's the point in winning the biggest damn scrap this squad's ever seen if you can't jaw about it with your buddies afterwards, huh?'

'We... did win, then?'

Woods raised an eyebrow. 'I'll put that down to your being flak happy. Of course we won, Lorenzo!'

'What I mean is... I heard about Brains.'

Woods pouted. 'Yeah. We lost Brains. And they're starting to give up on Sharkbait, too. Been looking for him all morning.'

Lorenzo's mind's eye flashed up a picture of Muldoon racing into the light of the ork battlewagon, and he felt a pang in his stomach. 'They won't find him,' he said numbly. Woods fixed him with an inquisitive, almost needy gaze, and Lorenzo realised that it was up to him to tell Sharkbait Muldoon's last story, to keep it alive. He had that honour, and that responsibility. So he took a deep breath, closed his eyes for a moment as he picked his words, and he told it.

He emphasised how brave Muldoon had been. He mentioned the gash in his head, because it made him seem all the more heroic for having overcome such an injury – and he exaggerated the number of orks on the wagon, that he had killed, because after all it had been dark and there'd been so much smoke and there *could* have been fourteen or fifteen of them, and Lorenzo didn't want to sell his comrade short. Woods listened to the story with growing admiration, and when it was done he breathed in through his teeth and agreed that Sharkbait had died well. Lorenzo felt an odd sort of pride at having been there, at having seen something so inspiring, but most of all at knowing he'd done justice to his fallen comrade's memory, and somehow everything seemed a little brighter then.

'A couple of the others saw how Brains went,' Woods related in return. 'There were a few of them together, and the orks were searching the jungle, and they hadn't had time to find a proper hiding place what with everything going to hell so fast. They say Brains let the greenskins find him, because a couple more steps and they would've stumbled right onto Wildman and maybe Bullseye. He gave his own life to buy the rest of us time. Course, he came out firing. I have to confess, sometimes I didn't have much time for old Brains, thought he yapped too much when he should've been getting on with it – but the way the others tell it, he would've done Marbo proud last night. Took on ten, twelve orks by his lonesome, and stayed standing long enough for the others to retrench, to start fighting back.'

'What happened?' asked Lorenzo. 'What started it, I mean? We were almost there, almost past the encampment, and then...'

'Oh yeah,' said Woods, screwing his face up into a scowl, 'I almost forgot you were up front, missed it all. I bet you can guess, though. I bet you can guess who was brainless enough to step on an ork trap, blow himself right up.'

'Mackenzie?' Lorenzo hazarded. The disdain in Woods's voice and expression had been something of a giveaway.

'Mackenzie,' he confirmed. 'The commissar.'

'I wouldn't have thought even he–'

'It was the blue light. Came up on us all unexpected like. I felt it in my head for a bit – just a second – like it was scanning me, reading my mind, then it moved on. Mackenzie... I figure what happened was, the light picked on the weakest of us. Mackenzie got up, started walking towards it like he was in a trance or something. The sergeant tried to stop him – brought up his lasgun, told Mackenzie he'd shoot him dead if he took another step, though I don't know why he cared; can't say I'd have shed a tear if Mackenzie had gone on, if he'd sunk into the swamp and never come out again. But Old Hardhead seemed to be getting through to him. Mackenzie just froze, and he was looking at Old Hardhead, and at the blue light, all confused – and it was Bullseye, I think, who saw the wire.

'Mackenzie was standing with one foot in front of it, one foot behind. God-Emperor knows how he hadn't tripped it already. Old Hardhead, he motioned to the rest of us to get back, and he kept talking to the commissar, all quiet and calm. Mackenzie, he was listening, he could see the sergeant was making sense, but he still wanted to go to that light, you could tell. He kept asking why he should trust any of us. He talked about what happened at the river, and he accused the sergeant of wanting him dead. I knew we were in trouble right then, knew he'd bring the orks down on us eventually even if he didn't trip that wire. Old Hard-head was whispering, trying to hush the commissar, but he was getting hysterical.'

'That's what the light does to you,' said Lorenzo sombrely. 'It plays on your hopes, your fears. And Mackenzie was already so afraid...' He fell silent as he realised what he'd said. He'd admitted to a weakness, in front of Woods of all people – a soldier who, if he'd ever feared anything, would certainly not have confessed to it.

It didn't seem to matter. 'Makes sense,' said Woods. 'I think, deep down, Mackenzie maybe *wanted* to believe – he wanted to be convinced – but that light was just too damn strong for him.'

'What about Braxton?'

'Give him his due,' Woods conceded, 'he tried. He crawled forward, put himself in the danger zone, just so he could talk to Mackenzie, back up what Old Hardhead was saying. But as soon as he opened his mouth, Mackenzie, he just... it was like he freaked out good and proper. He accused Braxton of betraying him, said he was alone now and he wasn't going to listen to anyone any more. He closed his eyes, put his hands over his ears, like he was in pain, and he was screaming for everyone to stop talking, to leave him alone, to let him think.

'Well, it was all over then, of course. Braxton started forward – I don't know why, like maybe he thought he could drag Mackenzie to safety or something – but the commissar had made up his mind.'

'Or rather,' Lorenzo murmured, 'the light had made it up for him.'

'And the rest, like Commissar Mackenzie, is history.'

'And Braxton?'

'Oh, he's all right. Old Hardhead grabbed hold of him, pulled him back, damn near got himself killed in the process. Now, that – that *would've* been a tragedy!'

'I shouldn't have stopped him,' said Lorenzo. 'Sharkbait. At the river. He would've killed Mackenzie, but I thought... I don't know what I thought. If I'd kept quiet, if I'd let him... Sharkbait would still be alive. And Brains.'

'Doesn't work like that,' said Woods, with more understanding than Lorenzo would have expected from him. 'No one made Sharkbait do anything he didn't want to do. You made him think, is all. He let Mackenzie off the hook for the same reason any of us would've done it: because when the commissar's harness went and he grabbed for that rope and he held on, he surprised us all. You were right, Lorenzo. You can't deny a man a second chance after proving himself like that.'

'Even so...'

'If the light hadn't got Mackenzie,' said Woods, 'it would've worked its influence on someone else. Braxton, maybe. Or... or... I told you, Lorenzo, I felt it in my head. I felt it calling to me – and in that second, I think I would've done just about anything it told me to do.'

That sealed it. This wasn't the Woods that Lorenzo knew. He turned to his comrade with a new anxiety prickling at him, and he said, 'You never told me about yourself. How you ended up... I mean, how you went on. Last night.'

'Hey, don't worry about me,' said Woods cheerfully. 'I did okay. Really. Just tired myself out, is all – and you know Greiss: he likes to think he's looking after us. He said if I didn't come in here for a lie-down, he'd knock me out himself.'

'Right,' said Lorenzo, not quite buying it. He was just starting to realise how pale his comrade seemed where the daylight fell across him. Sweat beaded his brow, as if he was feverish – or perhaps he too was just hot in his ork furs.

'Seriously,' said Woods, 'you think this looks bad, you should see the ork that did it to me. I should say, the twenty orks!' And he launched into a detailed and bloody account of every punch he had thrown, every shot he had fired, every thrust of his devil claw against the ork hordes.

Lorenzo stopped listening after a time. He tuned out the words, and strained to catch the distant, muffled sounds beyond the hut's walls: footsteps, scraping, the odd snatch of conversation. He felt as if he had been lying in this bed for an age, and he longed to feel fresh air on his face, to catch up with the comrades he had thought he would never see again. To see what fresh challenges had arisen in his absence.

He knew he should wait. He didn't know the extent of his injuries. He didn't *feel* too badly hurt, but then his head was muzzy and he could have been in shock. He could have been infected. But normally, the person to tell him that – the man who ought to have been at his bedside with his revolting herbal cures – was Brains. Lorenzo couldn't bear to wait any longer.

Woods had fallen silent. Lorenzo realised he was asleep.

He peeled off his bed coverings and tested each of his limbs, trying his weight on them, before he levered himself to his feet. He swayed a little, and felt sickness rising in his throat but suppressed it. Morning air breezed in through the window, and prickled his skin like pins and needles. He crept over to Woods and put his hand to his forehead, finding it hot like a simmering pan. He located his clothes and backpack in a pile in the corner, with Muldoon's lasgun laid out almost reverently across them.

His jacket felt heavy and grimy against his skin, its insides caked with his own dried blood. It was only when he saw his water bottle that he realised how dry his throat was, and how cracked his lips. He gulped from the bottle greedily, and had to stop himself before he emptied it. There had to be fresh water somewhere in the camp, he reasoned. The skin around his patched-up wound had evidently been cleaned. He longed for a pool to bathe in, though a bit of dirt didn't usually bother him.

Finally, Lorenzo approached the door to the outside world – and thought it was locked at first, as it jammed in its frame. He put his shoulder to it, and tried to pretend that the effort hadn't made stars explode in front of his eyes. He stumbled out into the sunlight, unsteady and blinking, and walked straight into Sergeant Greiss.

Somewhere, there was a fire burning, and Lorenzo caught a glimpse of Myers and Storm lugging an ork corpse between them.

Then Greiss was guiding him back into the hut, telling him to take it easy in his gentlest growl, and Lorenzo tried to throw off his hold, tried to prove he could stand unassisted, but before he knew it he was sitting on the bunk again, just grateful that the room wasn't spinning any more. Greiss took Lorenzo's head in his callused hands, peered into his eyes, and nodded, satisfied. 'You'll live.'

'We did okay – right, sergeant?'

'Yes, Lorenzo. We did okay. We did more than okay. We've been tossing ork bodies on the flames all morning.' Lorenzo didn't question that statement. He knew the Catachans didn't burn their enemies' corpses for the sake of their souls. Orks were renowned for their regenerative properties; it was common for one thought dead to rise from a cold battlefield in search of revenge. On Rogar III, he realised, there was even more reason to take precautions.

'Sergeant!' Lorenzo's fellow patient was awake again. Lorenzo found himself wondering if Woods's voice had sounded so weak, so subdued, the last time he had spoken. Perhaps it had, and he just hadn't noticed. 'Lorenzo tell you about Sharkbait?' asked Woods. Greiss replied that he hadn't, and Woods repeated the story as the sergeant listened patiently. This time, there were twenty orks on the battlewagon, and Muldoon had to hack his way through four more to reach it, but Lorenzo didn't bother to correct the details. Woods's version made a better story, and Muldoon deserved his glory.

'We ready to move out yet, sergeant?' asked Woods, when the story was told.

'Not yet, Hotshot,' said Sergeant Greiss. 'Still cleaning up behind ourselves. We've taken apart all the comms we can find, but you can bet a few gretchin would've made a run for it when they real-ised they were beaten.'

Woods grimaced. 'Sooner or later, they'll find more greenskins, and then the whole planet will know we're here.'

'If we're lucky,' said Greiss, 'the orks won't put two and two together in a hurry. For all they know, this camp could've been our target all along.'

'Yeah, 'specially when they hear about the attacks on their other camps.'

'But they'll know we're closing in on their warboss – whether they believe we know it or not – and if Big Green has half the brains Mackenzie reckoned he had, he'll be doubling his personal guard about now. Our dear, departed commissar just made getting to our target about ten times harder than it ever was.'

'I thought as much,' said Woods. 'But, we just came through against thirty-to-one odds. Shouldn't think there's a whole lot can stop us now, yeah?'

'Funny thing about that,' Greiss growled. 'There aren't half as many dead orks about these parts as there ought to be. I think we got lucky, Hotshot. I think our job was half-done before we got here.'

'You think Rogar's been as hard on them as it's been on us?'

'About the size of it, yes.'

'Now you're wondering what happened to the orks it killed. And how long it took the survivors to work out that any bodies they leave intact...'

Lorenzo didn't remember lying down, but he was staring at the ceiling. He didn't remember discarding his backpack and jacket, but he was unencumbered by them. He had been thinking about Dougan, or rather about the mockery this deathworld had made of his memory. About the skeletal birds that had refused to lie down. And now, about a hundred, two hundred, dead orks, in varying stages of decay, clambering from the ground all over the planet...

'Should make for an interesting few days,' murmured Greiss.

'Nothing we can't handle though,' said Woods, 'right, sergeant?'

Lorenzo drifted into a dreamless sleep, then, and opened his eyes only once in the next few hours to find himself on the cot again, and Greiss in the doorway of the hut. He must have been leaving, waking Lorenzo as he shouldered the sticking door out of its frame. But something had stopped him. He was looking at Woods, and with the sunlight behind him casting his face into shadow, Greiss seemed weighed down by every one of his thirty-five years, older and more tired than Lorenzo had seen him before.

When next he woke, Greiss was there again, standing over him, shaking him, and from the quality of the light through the window he guessed it was early afternoon. 'Time you dragged yourself out of that pit, trooper,' he said. 'We got a lot of ground to make up if we still want a chance of catching the warboss by surprise. You up to it?'

'Yes, sergeant,' said Lorenzo, getting to his feet, relieved when his body didn't make a liar of him. He still felt weak, drained, and his side hurt like hell, but his senses were clearer now. Catachan men healed quickly. He donned his jacket and his backpack again, picked up the lasgun that he supposed was now his, and made for the door. He stopped when he realised Greiss wasn't following. He was sitting on the bunk Lorenzo had vacated, staring into space, a lasgun laid across his lap. Not his own gun: that was slung under his pack as normal. Lorenzo felt a knot forming in his stomach as he was finally forced to face an unpleasant truth.

'What about Hotshot, sergeant? Aren't you going to wake him?'

'In a minute,' the sergeant said.

Lorenzo looked at Woods. His skin was whiter than ever, drenched in perspiration. His breathing was ragged, and his face twitched with emotions that Lorenzo had never seen writ there before. Every few seconds he let out a low moan, almost a whimper. He seemed to be having the mother of all nightmares. The young trooper looked surprisingly, awfully small.

'Is he...?' Lorenzo ventured.

'Hotshot managed to find a sniping position,' said Greiss, 'up a tree. He was cutting down those greenskins like dummies on a shooting range. But one of 'em got lucky – happened to be looking the right way when an explosion went off and the light glinted off Hotshot's lasgun. He couldn't get down in time. The orks surrounded him, started firing up into the branches. Hotshot took a bullet in the leg, was grazed by two more, but nothing critical; he knew how to make himself small, use his backpack and the tree trunk to protect himself – and with his camouflage and all, the greenskins didn't know where they were aiming. Hotshot was firing at 'em, dropping grenades on their heads – he must've taken out a dozen or more. But you know what orks are like. They don't give up easy. They were swarming up that tree, and Hotshot was shooting and slashing down at 'em, but even he couldn't stay put forever. He made a jump for it, sailed right over their heads.' There had been a touch of admiration in Old Hardhead's voice, but now it faded, and his shoulders slumped. Lorenzo knew how fond he had always been of Woods.

'He didn't make it.'

'If it hadn't been for that damn slug in his leg...' Greiss was silent for a moment, then with pride in his voice, he continued, 'He kept fighting. Even though he'd shattered his spine, he was on the ground, and the orks were piling onto him... I should've got there sooner.'

'No, sergeant!' Lorenzo protested automatically.

'Don't give me that,' Greiss growled. 'If any of us had to end his days a cripple, better it be an old warhorse with no fight left in him. Better it be someone who's had his day, whose story's been told.'

Lorenzo was still digesting the full import of what Greiss was saying. '...end his days a cripple...' They were on a stealth mission, without backup, unable to vox for an airlift – and even if they could get Woods back to an Imperium facility, it would certainly have been the last thing he wanted. It was unlikely a medic could do much for him. The only person who could save him now from a fate worse than death was Greiss. Lorenzo's gaze strayed to the spare lasgun on the sergeant's knee.

'He'll be remembered,' was all he could think of to say. It seemed to cheer Greiss up a little.

Then there was an awkward silence as Lorenzo realised there was nothing more he could say, and eventually turned to the door again.

The last thing he saw as he left that hut, as he left another comrade behind forever, was Greiss leaning over Woods, shaking him gently awake, telling him it was time and pressing the lasgun into his hands. And Woods's smile – not afraid, but relieved. Grateful, even.

Just one of those things. Lorenzo had learned to accept it. He walked away from the hut, and ignored the part of him that wanted to break into a run, to get away from there before he had to hear...

He thought about his promise: '*He'll be remembered.*' He walked, and waited. And thought about his comrade, relating his last story, and he wished he'd known, wished he'd been more attentive. He thought about the dangers that still lay ahead, all his depleted squad still had to do, and he told himself they'd come through somehow.

Lorenzo pretended not to hear the dark voice in the back of his head. The voice that said: *Yes, Hotshot Woods will be remembered. Sharkbait Muldoon will be remembered. They will all be remembered.*

But for how long?

CHAPTER THIRTEEN

The rain came early in the evening.

The Jungle Fighters had seen the clouds, felt the cool, fresh breeze that presaged the outburst – but the speed and ferocity with which it broke defied their expectations.

The rain was acidic. Guardsman Braxton winced as the first drop splashed off his cheek, and Lorenzo threw a hand to his neck as the skin there began to smart. The acid, fortunately, wasn't strong, not like that from the spitter plants – but with prolonged exposure, it could do as much damage.

They found some shelter beneath the spreading branches of a huge tree. Lorenzo listened as the rain beat down on its roof of leaves, and he looked gloomily at the cascade of redirected liquid like a waterfall around him. He wondered how long it would be before the leaves were burnt through, and he couldn't help but feel that even this downpour was deliberate. It was as if the planet was so determined to destroy them that it would sacrifice a part of itself.

They debated the wisdom of turning back, of scavenging sheets of metal from the ork camp, but Greiss in particular was reluctant to lose ground. 'Aside from which,' he growled, casting a wary glance back over his shoulder, 'we don't know what might be behind us.' They all knew what he meant. Ever since they had set off, they had all been aware of ghosts dogging their footsteps again.

It had been inevitable, of course. Still, Lorenzo had hoped for at least some respite. He wasn't the only one of the six remaining men in his squad – half their original complement – to have been injured in the previous night's battle, nor to feel profoundly tired. Armstrong's left arm was useless, the nerve tendons in his shoulder severed by an ork axe, and Braxton hadn't said a word all afternoon and looked like he could drop at any moment. Their lasguns were low on energy, too; Myers wore a belt of strung-together power packs, letting the dwindling sunlight do what it could to recharge them until they could build a fire to do the job properly. But the nature of their mission – and Greiss, now firmly back in command – had required they press on, and not one of those six men was prepared to admit defeat.

Their map had been incinerated along with Mackenzie, but Armstrong knew where they were and was sure he could remember the location of the warboss's lair from the briefing. He could get them close, at least.

They broke out the alkaline powders from their backpacks, rubbed them into their exposed skin and hair. As they worked, the ghosts began to gather, in the corners of their vision. This time, they had attracted more than one stalker. Many more. And these creatures, it seemed, were trying less hard to conceal their presence.

Or maybe it was just that they were bigger and clumsier than Dougan, less able to hide. Ork corpses, as the Jungle Fighters had anticipated. This close, there was no denying the stink of death that rose from them; it had been wafting past Lorenzo's nostrils for the past few hours, whenever the breeze was right. Some of these orks had been dead weeks or months, but now they were a part of the planet itself, cocooned in its substance and animated by its mysterious energy.

It had taken six Jungle Fighters to send one monster into retreat. A smaller monster. Six Jungle Fighters, relatively refreshed and ready for battle.

For now, the zombies seemed content to keep their distance, to watch. Greiss moved his squad on quickly anyway, worried that if they stayed put too long they might be surrounded. They moved through the rain at a faster-than-normal pace, with their packs over their heads, hugging the trees. Fortunately, they knew enough about Rogar now to avoid its more obvious traps – though Lorenzo remembered what Donovits had said about this world's rapid evolution, and he eyed even the safest-looking flowers with suspicion.

He twitched at another rustle from the foliage. It was closer than usual, to the left of the squad rather than behind them. He brought his lasgun around but didn't dare fire lest he start something they couldn't finish. Another ork shape was clearly outlined, watching him with unblinking eyes, one of which had slid half out of its socket on a slagheap of dried blood. As Lorenzo watched, it withdrew and sank silently into the ground.

'They're watching us,' he announced. 'We've survived everything else Rogar has to throw at us, so it's got its zombies watching us, looking for a weakness.'

'I'd almost rather they made their move,' murmured Braxton, 'and got it over with.'

'Careful what you wish for,' Storm cautioned him grimly.

'When you people first arrived,' said Braxton, 'and you were talking about Rogar like it was a – I don't know – a living thing, an enemy, like an ork or something, I didn't know... I mean, I'm starting to see it now. I'm starting to feel like this planet *is* alive, like it's intelligent, like it really wants us dead.' He sounded as if he wanted somebody to contradict him. No one did.

The jungle had started to close in again. Greiss had sent Myers and Storm ahead to clear the way, and the squad's pace had dropped to a crawl.

And the ghosts were gathering at their backs.

'Maybe we should send a few las-shots their way,' suggested

Armstrong, worriedly, hefting his gun in his good hand as if to reassure himself he could still operate it. 'Discourage them a little.'

'Don't know if it'd work,' murmured Greiss.

'Hotshot fired at...' Lorenzo began, then was unable to say Dougan's name. '...the first one. It didn't seem to react at all.'

'They don't feel pain,' said Greiss. 'You remember what Brains said. We've got to stop thinking of these things as living creatures. They're less than that – less than orks, even. They don't have hearts – or if they do, they sure aren't beating any more. No internal organs, no nerves, no pressure points, and I doubt their brains are getting much use. They're plants, no more than that. Part of the jungle – the planet itself – just wrapped around the remains of the dead.'

Lorenzo stole a quick look at the collecting shadows, searching for one that was shorter and thinner than the others, hoping he wouldn't find it. If the God-Emperor had any influence at all here, so far from his Golden Throne, he would see to it that Dougan could rest in peace.

'Then we deal with them like we would any hostile plant,' reasoned Armstrong.

'Can't tear 'em up by the roots,' growled Greiss. 'They're up and walking about already.'

'Shred 'em?' suggested Storm, his fingers twitching over his knife hilt.

'Take too long with the knives,' said Greiss. 'Way I'm thinking, those things will keep going till you get to the skeleton and can take it apart.'

'We've got to do something,' said Braxton, 'before they attack!'

'Boy's right,' said Armstrong. 'We need a show of strength, give them something to think about. If they *can* think, that is.'

'If they can't,' muttered Myers, 'looks like something does it for them.'

'How much ordnance do we have left between us?' asked Lorenzo.

'Couple of shredder mines,' offered Storm.

'Still got my demolition charges,' said Myers.

'Save 'em,' said Greiss, with a gleam in his eye, 'for a special occasion. I got a better idea.' He and Armstrong spoke as one: 'Burn 'em!'

Lorenzo and Braxton took over clearance duty as Myers and Storm assembled the flamer again. Greiss wielded it himself, straining under the weight of the device as he lugged it a few steps closer to the watching zombies. Then he pulled the trigger, and simultaneously swept the flamer around in a wide arc.

It was like a dozen explosions had gone off at once, plants and trees erupting as if they'd just combusted from within. The zombies – those Lorenzo could see – they were burning too, starting with the parts of them that were the most flammable: the clumps of weeds and grass embedded in their bodies. They reeled in apparent confusion, their arms pumping in futile slow-motion, patting themselves down, trying to extinguish themselves, succeeding only in setting fire to their hands or bumping into each other and spreading the flames to their comrades.

Lorenzo was amazed at the severity of the reaction, until he remembered that Rogar III had felt fire before – from the Jungle Fighters' small campfire of two nights ago to the all-out attempts by humans and orks alike at deforestation. It knew what fire could do to it, and – Lorenzo knew this didn't make sense, but he was suddenly sure of it, more sure than he'd been of anything his instincts had told him of late – it was afraid of it. The deathworld itself was afraid, and in its fear, it chose to attack the creatures that had hurt it so much, while it still had the means to do so. And it sent its soldiers forward...

The Jungle Fighters drew their lasguns as six flaming zombies – those that could still walk – came stumbling towards them, trailing smoke, like a small army of infernal daemons. They let off a fusillade of shots, to no effect, and Greiss sent another blast of fire the zombies' way in the hope of hastening their demise, before abandoning the flamer and leaping aside, not an instant too soon. A zombie hurled itself at him, and hit the ground where Greiss had been, setting light to the undergrowth. It tried to stand again, but scorched earth was sloughing from it like dead skin, withering to ash, and the bones of its purloined skeleton were beginning to show through and it could no longer lift its own weight.

The rest of the squad dropped their packs and tried to scatter, but they couldn't go far, confined to the narrowed corridor their knives had cleared. The same couldn't be said of the zombies: their movements were slow and awkward but unhampered, the foliage itself seeming to part for them. They separated too, each choosing a target. Lorenzo found himself side by side with Braxton, both trying to press themselves back into the jungle, thorns tearing at their jackets and their hair, nettles stinging their hands, as two flaming zombies homed in on them.

He heard a yell, 'Aim for their kneecaps!' and he followed Armstrong's suggestion and tried to shoot the nearest zombie's leg out from under it. He got in four shots before it was upon him. It raised a ponderous fist, and Lorenzo wasn't sure who its target was – him or Braxton – but then the fist came down towards him, and he ducked, and he tried to scramble past the zombie's leg, but his hand recoiled from a flaming footprint in the grass. The zombie swung around to follow him but a bone snapped, and its leg buckled, and Lorenzo knew his las-shots had done some good after all.

The zombie was falling – but it managed to turn its fall into a lunge, and Lorenzo couldn't get out of the way in time as the creature, now little more than a burning skeleton, plummeted towards him. For an instant, he was staring into its hollow eye sockets – piggy ork eye sockets – and they seemed to be mocking him. A tusked mouth gaped in a rictus grin. Lorenzo brought up a foot, planted it in the zombie's stomach and tried to fling it over him. It fell apart with the impact of his boot, and though the bulk of its mass passed safely over his head, Lorenzo was showered with bones and mud and burning leaves.

He rolled, to put out any flames that may have taken hold of his clothing. Then he sprang to his feet, lasgun in hand, to find that the other zombies had suffered the same fate as his. The combination of flames and las-fire had destroyed their cohesion, and they were collapsing at the feet of the relieved Jungle Fighters. Two skeletons were relatively intact, and as Lorenzo watched they were drawn into the ground. Storm reached one before it could vanish, and drove his gun butt into its spine, breaking it. The other – the skeleton of the monster that had attacked Greiss – escaped.

The Jungle Fighters relaxed and regrouped in the sudden silence, dozens of small fires flickering around them until the rain extinguished them.

'Think that's the last we'll see of them, sergeant?' asked Myers.

'I hope so, Bullseye,' growled Greiss. He cast a disparaging eye over the discarded flamer. 'Because this thing's just about on empty.' Myers and Storm packed up the device anyway, in case they were being watched – although for the first time in two days, none of the Catachans felt as if they were.

'There were more of those things out there,' Armstrong pointed out to Greiss. 'You only burnt the front ranks of them. There were at least a dozen more behind – they escaped into the ground when they saw the flames.'

'Not to mention all the other orks that must've died on Rogar these past few years,' said Lorenzo.

'And Guardsmen,' said Braxton quietly.

Greiss nodded. He knew.

'Do you think they can move underground, sergeant?' Braxton asked. 'Or will they have to resurface where they went down?'

'I don't know,' said Greiss. 'What're you thinking?'

'That it might be the right occasion to break out those mines.'

Greiss studied Braxton for a moment, then a grin tugged at his lips. 'I like the way you think, Guardsman. Right, troopers, all the shredders you have, hand 'em over. Patch, you're with me. You saw where some of them walking corpses disappeared, right? Well, the next time they try climbing out of their graves, they'll have a nasty shock waiting for 'em. Lorenzo, Braxton, you get back to clearing the way. Once these babies are laid, we're going to want to get out of here real quick.'

'Yes, sergeant,' said Lorenzo.

Greiss had half-turned away when a thought occurred to him and he looked back at Braxton. 'Let me see your knife,' he demanded. Braxton showed him the small, blunt blade he had been using, and Greiss expressed his contempt for what he called an 'Imperial pig-sticker'. Lorenzo had noticed that he had been wearing two knives today, and he'd guessed where the second had come from. Still, he felt his eyes widening as the sergeant drew Woods's devil claw – at over a metre long, more a sword than a knife – and handed it to the Validian. 'Here,' he grunted, 'you should find it easier going with this. It's only a loan, mind.'

Braxton accepted the claw, and turned it over in his hands. He admired its well-honed edge, and gauged how light and well balanced it was thanks to its hollow blade, half-filled with mercury. 'Yes, sergeant,' he said, in a voice full of awe.

'I can see now why you think so much of him,' said the Validian, when he and Lorenzo were alone together. Greiss and Armstrong were still some way behind, laying mines, and Myers and Storm had taken this opportunity – while their progress was impeded – to fall back and hunt jungle lizards and anything else they deemed edible. Lorenzo and Braxton were left with the repetitive and wearying work of swinging their knives, forging ahead – though Lorenzo had to admit, it was going a lot faster now that Braxton was properly equipped.

'Who?' he asked.

'Sergeant Greiss.'

'Of course we do. He wouldn't have that rank if he hadn't earned the respect of all of us.'

'I didn't realise. At first, he seemed – I don't know – surly, I guess. Distant. Disapproving.'

'If you're looking for a soft approach,' said Lorenzo, 'I'm afraid Catachan doesn't breed 'em like that.'

'I guess not. But now I've seen Greiss in action – the way he leads from the front, keeps this squad together, keeps us focused on the mission. And the way he... I mean, he really does care about his troopers, even if he doesn't always...'

'He'd give his life for us,' said Lorenzo simply, 'as we would for him. Your point is?'

'I'm used to sergeants who do things by the book, that's all. Same with the commissar. If Mackenzie had survived, if he could see Greiss now...'

'If he'd been willing to look,' said Lorenzo pointedly.

'Yes. I just think, Mackenzie, he was like most of us. We don't know till we see for ourselves. I can't imagine what it must have been like for you, for Greiss, for all of you, being brought up on a world like this. A deathworld. But I'm starting to understand, and Mackenzie – I think he would have understood too, in time.'

'You don't think he'd have filed his complaint against Old Hardhead? You don't think he'd have had him shot?'

'We'll never know,' said the Validian. 'Best thing, I think, is to let it lie. I certainly won't be saying a thing.'

Lorenzo was about to agree when he spotted something. A triangle. Silver. He could easily have mistaken it for an exotic leaf, lying flat against a branch, had the pattern not connected with something in his memory. A warning. Braxton's knife hand was moving towards it, and Lorenzo batted it away even before his conscious mind remembered what the pattern represented. The triangle wrinkled, as a snake head jerked out from beneath it and made a stab at where the hand had just been.

'I think we should both talk less,' said Lorenzo, 'and pay more attention to where we're going.'

Braxton nodded. But it wasn't long before he spoke up again. 'I just wondered,' he said, 'if I should say something. To the others. Let them know. That they can trust me, I mean.'

Lorenzo smiled tightly. 'They know. Old Hardhead in particular.' He indicated the devil claw in Braxton's hand. 'Trust me, he knows.'

Then Greiss and Armstrong came pelting towards them, sweeping Myers and Storm along in their wake. They had barely come to a halt when a series of explosions from behind them rattled the ground and shook leaves from their branches. The trap had been sprung. Greiss's cruel grin exposed his teeth and flared his nostrils. They all waited for a minute, listening for the shuffling footsteps of zombies, squinting through the rain for the shape of an ork, but there was nothing.

And, a few minutes after that, Braxton found a trap. A snare in the undergrowth, ready to tighten about the ankle of an unwary traveller and hoist him into the trees. A sign, Lorenzo agreed when the Validian pointed it out to him, that orks had been here. Crafty orks. Then he inspected the snare more closely. It was fashioned from creepers – but, far than having been knotted together by hand, it seemed to have grown into its unnatural shape.

'Rogar's still learning,' he murmured as Braxton used his devil claw to slice through the snare. 'It's learning from us.'

They forged on well into the night, making up for their late start, until Lorenzo's body wanted nothing more than to shut down. He'd been running on adrenaline, but now even this was spent. The acid rain hadn't let up, and despite his precautions Lorenzo's face and neck were red raw. The wound in his side felt like it was ablaze. He had begun to wonder if Sergeant Greiss would ever call a halt to this torture, though of course he would never have complained.

At last, Greiss accepted that even his squad needed rest. He warned, however, that they didn't have much time. He intended to move out early in the morning – and until then, the Jungle Fighters would have to keep watch in three shifts of two in case the blue light returned.

For the first time, Lorenzo didn't volunteer for first watch. Greiss detailed Myers and Storm to that duty, and Lorenzo was grateful to be placed on the third and final watch with Armstrong, possibly in deference to the fact that both were wounded. Only as they set up camp – positioning their plastic sheeting not to collect water tonight but to deflect the rain – did he realise how tired the sergeant himself looked.

They built the biggest, hottest fire they could, despite the risk that it might be seen. They did it to spite what they now saw to be their real enemy: Rogar III.

Lorenzo was asleep almost before his head touched the ground. But it seemed like his eyes had only been closed a minute when the shouting began.

He thought he was dreaming again, at first. That dream from the previous night, before the ork camp, when dead comrades had pulled him down into the earth to join them. Only this time it was real, and it was the earth itself that pulled at him. Lorenzo was already half-buried; he tried to stand, to tear himself free, but he couldn't gain leverage and the pull of the earth only increased.

Quicksand? He was sinking, though the ground had been perfectly firm when he had lain down on it. He fought the urge to lash out, because he knew he would only go down faster. Somebody was shouting his name, yelling at him to wake, and the rain was still drumming on the plastic sheets above his head, searing them brown.

This was worse than quicksand. Lorenzo knew how to deal with quicksand, knew how hard it was to actually drown in it, but this – this was Rogar III itself, grasping at him, drawing him to its heart. His first instinct was to unsheathe his Catachan fang, though he had no use for it yet, because if his legs went under he didn't want to lose it with them.

With a supreme effort, he raised his head. The whole campsite was a quagmire. Armstrong and Myers had been caught sleeping too, and were being sucked under. Greiss and Braxton were standing but buried up to their knees; it must have been their watch when the planet had struck. It was Braxton who had shouted, presumably unable to see from where he was that Lorenzo had already woken. There was no sign of the campfire: it must have been pulled under and smothered.

Storm was doing better than any of them. He was on his hands and knees in the mud, but pulling himself along with his powerful muscles, almost swimming, his teeth clenched, face red with exertion, until he came to the edge of the Catachans' small clearing and his flailing hand caught a tree branch. He had something to hold on to now, and he could begin to haul himself upright.

Lorenzo was determined to follow Storm's example. But suddenly, the earth beside him seemed to explode, and he recoiled and sank a little further as a figure erupted from beneath it. A large, hunched figure with tusks protruding through a matted layer of plants and dirt. An ork zombie.

And there were more of them, bursting from the ground all across the clearing, outnumbering the Jungle Fighters and surrounding them. In contrast to their floundering targets, they waded easily through the mud, their ponderous gait now seeming only too fast.

The nearest zombie loomed over Lorenzo, and raised both fists above its head as it prepared to strike him dead.

CHAPTER FOURTEEN

Lorenzo brought up his right hand, his knife hand, to protect his head, and tried to do the same with his left, but the earth had it. He pulled at it, and brushed something below the surface: a familiar shape. He wrapped his fingers around it, feeling like he was squeezing cold slime until they closed around hard metal. With a gut-wrenching effort, he brought his hand, and his lasgun, tearing out into the open and braced the weapon in both hands above his face.

The ork zombie's blow landed, hit the gun, and Lorenzo felt the vibrations juddering through his bones and thought he'd lost another lasgun, thought it would snap in two, but somehow it remained intact. He realised that his shoulders were in the earth again, the impact and his own efforts driving him downwards.

The zombie was preparing to strike again, and Lorenzo turned the lasgun around and pulled the trigger, but it jammed. Mud in the barrel. He could just reach the zombie's leg with the tip of his knife, and he slashed at it, scoring a groove, but it didn't react. The quagmire was sucking at the back of his head, caressing his ears with cold tendrils.

He couldn't beat the monster. The best he could hope for was to keep it from killing him long enough for the planet to take him, to fill his nose and mouth with its substance and suffocate him.

He couldn't beat the monster. So he stopped fighting it.

A clump of flowers protruded, ridiculously, from the zombie's thigh, and Lorenzo strained to reach them, trusted them to support his weight as he hauled himself up, mud slurping and sucking at him but losing the contest of strength. With both hands full, holding his lasgun, his knife and the flowers, he couldn't defend himself against another double-fisted blow to the back of his stooped head. He took it with gritted teeth, blinded for a moment as he almost blacked out. He felt as if his skull must have cracked. Then he felt the flowers give way, their roots torn clean out of the zombie's earthen flesh.

Lorenzo was falling back, and he couldn't shift his trapped legs to steady himself, but he threw out his arms and found the zombie's legs, and he hugged them tightly, holding on for his life. This had the useful side-effect of unbalancing the zombie, which reacted too slowly, toppled, and splashed into the quagmire on its back. Lorenzo was scrabbling, clawing at its cold, wet mass, using it like a log in a river. He climbed onto it, dragging his legs after him; he pulled himself along the zombie's length, yanking dead leaves from the vegetation that coated it, simultaneously trampling the zombie further down.

He hauled himself upright as the zombie's head sank underground. He used its chest as a springboard, pushing off it, leaping for the edge of the clearing. He landed with both feet in the mud, and was instantly buried up to the waist again, but as the top half of his body fell forwards, he was able to grab at a branch and, like Storm before him, use it as a lifeline.

He glanced over his shoulder, to see that the zombie was thrashing about, resurfacing and beginning to stand – and that another was heading his way. There wasn't time to free himself completely from Rogar's grip. He settled instead for dragging his backside up onto the dry ground beyond the clearing, his legs still in the mud but his shoulder hooked behind a tree, bracing him, allowing him to resist the suction force from below. He plunged his fingers into his lasgun barrel and scooped out as much mud as he could. Then he dug the butt into his shoulder, aimed for the second zombie and fired. The gun whined and let out a feeble light. The second zombie lurched closer. Lorenzo pumped the trigger again, and on his fourth attempt, the lasgun finally coughed up dirt and struck true.

He had aimed for the knee again; it took four shots to penetrate through to the bone, and then the oncoming creature collapsed like a puppet with its strings cut, and disappeared below the surface.

By that time, the first zombie had somehow managed to right itself and was bearing down on him. This one took six shots, and fell less than a metre from him, hands reaching for him. He thanked the God-Emperor for the creatures' sluggish reflexes: if this one had only shifted its weight onto its good leg, it could have stayed upright long enough to wrap its fingers around his throat.

In no immediate danger now, Lorenzo took a second to scan the battlefield. Myers and Armstrong were engaged in their own struggles, each beginning to gain the upper hand – but Braxton was in trouble.

Three zombies had surrounded the Validian, overpowered him, and pushed him headlong into the mud. His face was buried; he couldn't breathe.

Greiss had seen what was happening, and was just finishing up with his own opponent. Astonishingly, he had whittled into it with his Catachan fang until he had exposed its spine, which he had then seized and yanked right out of its body. He tossed the wretched creature's remains aside, with a sneer, and began to wade towards Braxton, but the mud was up to his stomach and his progress was slow.

Storm was firing in from the sidelines, and as Lorenzo watched, the first of Braxton's attackers fell beneath his las-fire at last. Storm switched targets, and Lorenzo joined him; their shots converged on the back of the second zombie's knee and burnt through it in seconds.

The third and final zombie swung around to greet Greiss with a hefty punch, which the grizzled sergeant dodged. His face was level with the creature's stomach – with its greater bulk, it looked like it could crush him with its thumb – but he drove the butt of his lasgun into its leg and, to Lorenzo's amazement, shattered it. The bone must have been old and brittle. But this zombie's reflexes were better than most. Instead of falling, it swayed on one leg, and looked down to where its other leg hung loose, still attached to its body by muddy tendrils.

Then Greiss laid into it with his gun butt again, roaring like an animal, and slowly, as if it was fighting gravity itself, the zombie fell and was gone. Greiss's path to Braxton was clear – but the Validian was gone now, too.

There was nothing Lorenzo could do for him, no chance of reaching him. He shifted his attention to the zombies still standing, supporting Myers and Armstrong's efforts with his las-shots. But his eyes kept flicking to the patch of mud where Braxton's head had gone under, and he found himself holding his breath as Greiss propelled himself towards that spot and plunged his hands into the shifting earth.

Myers was free of ork zombies, but his struggle had cost him. He was sinking fast. Storm leapt back into the quagmire, and waded to his comrade's aid. He reached Myers and gripped him beneath the arms. He tried to drag him free, but for every two centimetres the pair gained, the quagmire reclaimed one, and Myers was buried up to his neck now.

Lorenzo concentrated on freeing his own legs. When the planet let go, it did so suddenly, and he fell back into a bush and lost vital seconds disentangling his vest from its thorns. He raced around the edge of the quagmire, to the point at which Storm had re-entered it. He could reach him from here, by placing one foot in the mud while leaving the other braced behind him. He caught Storm's reaching hand, and pulled at it with all his strength.

Across the clearing, to Lorenzo's relief, Greiss pulled Braxton, coughing and spluttering, to the surface – but the effort had cost him, and now they were both treading mud, only their heads visible, helpless.

Armstrong's las-bolts despatched the final zombie, and he was in trouble now too; he wasn't too far from the edge, but with his useless arm he had no way of reaching it. Lorenzo gritted his teeth and pulled harder, and at last Storm stumbled onto the bank beside him, and they took one of Myers's arms each and dragged him up after them.

Myers was trying to bring something with him. He strained and pulled, and the earth released its grip on his muddied backpack. Lorenzo had lost his, along with his jacket and his bandolier. Myers was rummaging in the pack before his legs were even out of the quagmire, and Storm grinned behind his black beard as his comrade produced a rope. He must have woven it himself from plant roots, after they'd lost the others at the river.

Myers made the throw, of course. The end of the rope slapped into the mud a centimetre or two from Greiss's head, but was absorbed before he could free an arm to reach for it. Both Greiss and Braxton strained to move their submerged limbs, to find their sinking lifeline, and Braxton's chin went under and he spluttered again as he took a mouthful of earth. Then, a tense moment later, the Validian yelled out, 'Got it!' and Myers and Lorenzo pulled for all they were worth.

Storm, in the meantime, had found a branch that jutted out over Armstrong's position. He climbed up to it and swarmed along it, the branch bending beneath his weight. Armstrong raised his good arm, and their fingers strained to find each other.

At last the struggle was won, and six muddy, exhausted soldiers lay on dry land and looked mournfully at the swamp that had been their campsite, thinking of the precious kit they had lost to its embrace, and of how much more they could have lost.

They had just three half-filled water bottles between them now, Lorenzo's, Storm's and Armstrong's having gone down with their backpacks. The flamer could never be assembled again without the parts Storm had been carrying. They were just grateful that Myers still had the power packs for their lasguns.

But Lorenzo felt most sorry for Armstrong, because his devil claw knife had been snatched from him. The veteran Jungle Fighter looked devastated about that, far more hurt than he'd been by his shoulder injury. Braxton offered him Woods's old devil claw, but he just shrugged the Validian away. It wasn't the same.

'I hate to say this,' announced Greiss, 'but we need to move on before we can bed down again.'

'You think there's anywhere safe on this damned planet?' asked Armstrong, sullenly.

'I'm gambling it takes a good while for Rogar to turn an area like this into a bog,' said Greiss, 'else why would it have waited till now? In future, we're just going to have to move between two or three campsites a night, grab our sleep a few hours at a time.' They all saw the sense in that, though it was a disheartening proposition.

In the event, they moved only a few hundred metres before Greiss gave the order to start clearing the ground again. Lorenzo and Armstrong took their watch while the others slept. Armstrong was poor company, sitting on a tree trunk and stared at his own feet. Lorenzo, fortunately, had slept long enough to feel relatively refreshed. He hoisted the protective plastic sheets over his comrades' heads by himself, though shortly after he had done so the rain subsided at last.

A few silver-backed snakes hissed in the undergrowth – but to Lorenzo's relief, the rest of the night passed without incident.

The next morning, the Jungle Fighters had an unexpected visitor.

The figure stepped out of the trees as they were making to move out – and instantly, six lasguns were drawn and aimed at it. The figure made no threatening move, however.

Lorenzo peered at it curiously. It was humanoid in shape, about his height and build – and to an extent, it resembled one of the ork zombies, fashioned as it was from Rogar's vegetation. But this figure was wearing a jacket woven from varicoloured leaves, and a branch slung across its back where the Jungle Fighters kept their lasguns, and it even seemed to have a face, wide-eyed and grinning, though this was just a pattern formed – accidentally? – by the twisted stalks and plants that ran through its rough, sculpted head. A thatch of straw was perched atop that head, like a mop of blond hair.

It grinned at the Jungle Fighters for a minute or more, as they watched it warily. Then the figure let out a bizarre, inhuman noise: a series of guttural clicks and warbling vowel sounds. Then it turned, and with a clumsy, rolling gait like it might shake itself apart, it moved away from them, in the direction they intended to go, until its path was blocked. Then it brought up an arm, jerkily, and sliced it down, then up and down again.

'What the hell is it meant to be?' breathed Myers.

'Best guess?' growled Greiss. 'It's meant to be one of us. Look at it, Bullseye! Pretending it's cutting its way through the jungle like we've been doing.'

'I think it was trying to talk,' Armstrong said. 'It was trying to sound like us, imitate the noises we make, but it doesn't understand language.'

'You think we're supposed to be taken in by that?' asked Lorenzo, not sure if he should be amused or disturbed by the idea. 'We're supposed to think that's one of us, let it join us, and – then what?'

'I vote we don't give it the chance to show us,' said Myers.

'I'll second that,' said Greiss.

Six lasguns converged on the unlikely doppelganger – and it whirled around to face the Jungle Fighters, and if Lorenzo hadn't known better he could have sworn it seemed surprised. Then the figure exploded.

Hidden spines shot out from its chest and mouth, like slender darts, and the Jungle Fighters leapt for cover, and fortunately had kept enough distance between them and the twisted effigy to avoid being struck. Lorenzo raised his head to find a dozen spines embedded in a tree beside him. More lay in the grass, and he noted that their needle points dripped with poison. Of the effigy, there was no trace at all now. It had fallen apart, returned to its constituent components and reclaimed by the jungle, and Lorenzo couldn't tell which of the leaves and plants that strewed the ground before them had belonged to its mass.

The second effigy showed itself almost four hours later, just stepping out behind the Jungle Fighters into the path they'd cut, greeting them with its incoherent warble. It didn't last a second before it was gunned down, falling onto its back and shooting its poisonous payload into the sky. Lorenzo had barely set eyes upon it before it was gone – but he was left with the distinct impression that this doppelganger had been more sophisticated, a far more accurate likeness of its template, than its predecessor had been.

It was about then that they all felt the first tremor.

It had been a quiet day by the Jungle Fighters' standards. They had dealt with routine attacks by jungle lizards, snakes and spitter plants, but nothing that had really challenged them. Since the incident with the second effigy, they'd had no sense of being followed, so it seemed that – for now at least – they were safe from zombies.

As they had progressed, so too had their spirits lightened. Lorenzo had started to feel like they had finally got the measure of this deathworld, like Rogar had run out of new ways to torment them and accepted their mastery of it. It was a good feeling. A reaffirming feeling. It made their sacrifices worthwhile.

They didn't speak about the tremor. With luck, it had been an isolated incident – and the more time passed without a recurrence, the more likely this seemed.

Then, as the daylight began to die, the jungle opened up again, and they were able to sheathe their knives as their passage through it eased. Shortly thereafter, they uncovered gretchin footprints and knew they were close to their goal. They withdrew a short way, and found a secluded spot in which they could rest for a time. The last time, they all knew, before the culmination of their mission. Find the ork warboss and take him out. They were starting to look forward to it again.

Greiss agreed to let them light a cooking fire, because the canopy was thick here and a small amount of smoke would likely go unnoticed. Anyway, they were low on standard rations, but they did have the lizards Myers and Storm had caught, along with a few handfuls of Rogar's choicest spices. Myers tasted each one before he added it to the pot, in case its nature had changed since the last batch he'd gathered. In case the planet had brewed up a new poison to surprise them.

They knew there was a small chance that foraging gretchin would happen upon them, so Lorenzo helped Armstrong set up a few traps. Any creature that came within earshot of them would be strung up in a net, unable to raise an alarm.

They ate, and their conversation turned to the usual subject: to comrades gone but not forgotten. They spoke of Hotshot, Sharkbait and Brains's defiance of the ork hordes. They had all heard the stories by now, of course, but it helped to reiterate them. It comforted them, and ensured that they had the details right, for the next time the stories were told. They talked of Landon's bravery, and of the heroic fight Steel Toe Dougan had no doubt put up against the blue light. In time, their conversation turned to earlier exploits, and they found these stories were even more worth the telling because Armstrong and Guardsman Braxton were new to their squad and hadn't heard them before.

Greiss recalled how, as an eager young rookie, Hotshot Woods had rushed an ork sniper that had pinned the squad down, miraculously reaching it without a scratch and wrestling it from its emplacement. Myers and Storm took it in turns to relate how

Brains Donovits had survived an encounter with a stranded
Chaos Space Marine, simply by outthinking it, and were pleased
when Braxton asked questions and made expressions of admiration in all the right places. Then they all listened attentively
to Armstrong's fresh tales of heroes from his former squad, and
expressed a collective wish that they could have known these
great men and witnessed their deeds.

Myers followed that with the tale of how Old Hardhead had
earned his name. It was a story from before Lorenzo's time, of
course – before Myers's, for that matter – but they had both heard
it often enough. Trooper Greiss, as he had been then, had been
part of a single platoon that had taken down a Chaos Dreadnought. He had lain some of the snares into which it had walked,
and planted a mine on its leg as it had struggled to free itself.
Unfortunately, he hadn't been able to outrun the explosion that
had ripped the Dreadnought apart. Or maybe it hadn't been
fortune but fate that had lodged a sizeable hunk of shrapnel in
Greiss's skull. The surgeons had reportedly written him off, but
his strength of character had buoyed him to a full recovery. 'Without that metal plate they put in his head,' Myers concluded, 'he
wouldn't be the cantankerous old sod we know today.'

'Knock it off, Bullseye,' growled Greiss, 'unless you want latrine
duty when we get back to civilisation.'

'You wait till you're splashed over the front page of *Eagle &
Bolter*, sergeant,' said Myers. 'We got their star reporter in our
midst, you know.'

'Yes, that's right,' remembered Storm, turning to Braxton.
'Didn't I hear you were working on a story about us?'

'We give you enough material yet?' put in Myers.

'Ease off, you two,' said Greiss. 'You know what those rags are
like. The higher-ups wouldn't let Braxton print any of this stuff if
he wanted to. They're only interested in their own truths.'

'I wish I could argue with that,' said Braxton, 'but you're right,
yes. I always wrote what I was told to write – about successful

missions, and ground that we'd gained. I don't think half of it was even true. I didn't ask.'

'Never saw a broadsheet that was any different,' remarked Myers.

'And I thought that was all right,' continued Braxton, 'because it was all about morale. That was what Mackenzie always said, and the commissar before him. Put the best possible spin on it, they said. Tell the troops about the overall campaign, about the Imperium resisting its enemies, and remind them why they're doing it. Don't let them dwell on the details, how people like them – like us – are suffering and dying for the cause. Your story would have been no different. Just a few lines about your great victory, maybe a name check for the commissar. They'd never have let me write about Woods or Dougan or the others.'

'All the more reason for us to make it back alive,' said Storm. 'Because if we don't tell those stories, who will?'

'I will,' swore Braxton. 'One day. I'll tell them how it is with you – how you make sure that everyone matters, every life counts for something.'

'Keep talking like that,' said Greiss, 'and your next commissar will probably boot you right out on the first suicide mission to cross his desk.'

Braxton grimaced, but took the joke in the spirit it was intended.

They were all still smiling when the ground shook again.

This tremor was worse than the first one. It lasted longer, felt deeper and more destructive, although the only visible signs of it above ground were a slight blurring of the trees and the dislodging of a few leaves and fruits. The tremor died down with no harm done, but Lorenzo could see his apprehension mirrored in the other Jungle Fighters' eyes, because they knew what it might presage.

Maybe Rogar III hadn't conceded defeat after all. Maybe it was just waiting, planning, and building up to its biggest offensive against its interlopers yet.

CHAPTER FIFTEEN

'Sergeant – you've got to see this.'

As the Jungle Fighters had ventured deeper into ork territory, they had switched to stealth tactics, as they had by the encampment. This time, it was Myers who had the task of scouting ahead for traps. He had already guided the squad around several trip-wires and a concealed pit. Now he came scurrying back to them, face flushed.

They followed him through the foliage, all too aware that they were moving parallel to a path worn down and churned up by footprints. Lorenzo could hear clinking and clunking and the guttural sounds of ork voices ahead, and he moved as carefully as he could, disturbing hardly a leaf.

A light spilled into the jungle, and Lorenzo feared at first that it was the mind-altering blue light. It was white, though, far more harsh, and it seemed to emanate from many sources. The Jungle Fighters were careful to stick to the shadows, not to let the light reveal them.

Then, with a cautious touch, Myers parted a cluster of spiny fronds, and Lorenzo saw what the excitement was about.

The orks had set up a mining operation. They were working well into the night. A clearing was illuminated by lanterns strung up in trees, turned inwards, their light bleaching out all but the faintest hints of colour. Across the clearing, the ground rose steeply, and a tunnel had been dug into the side of this hillock. A square wooden frame propped up its entrance – and as the Jungle Fighters watched, another light appeared in the tunnel's depths. An ork emerged, the light streaming from a battered helmet that was balanced atop its misshapen head. It was wheeling a lopsided barrow overloaded with rocks, which it dumped unceremoniously onto one of several heaps dotting the area.

Four gretchin were sorting through this heap, giving each rock a cursory glance before they tossed it onto a discard pile. Nearby, two orks quarrelled over a pickaxe – and ten more stood sentry at regular intervals around the clearing, with one stationed to each side of the mine entrance. A few more gretchin were scampering about, fetching and carrying, offering their ork masters food and drink.

'What do you suppose they're looking for?' asked Armstrong, after the Jungle Fighters had backed up a safe distance.

'Isn't much worth digging up on Rogar,' said Wildman Storm, 'at least not according to Brains – or did I hear that wrong?'

Greiss shook his head. 'You heard right, Wildman. But remember what else Brains said – about this world's energy signature. There's something here, something the explorators couldn't identify. I'm guessing the greenskins are after it.'

'How?' protested Lorenzo. 'If the explorators couldn't find it...'

Greiss shrugged. 'You know orks. Bloody-minded. Likelihood is they got nothing, know nothing, but they'll just keep on looking on the off-chance that there's some miracle rock down there they can mine and use against us. Probably hollow out this whole planet before they admit defeat.'

'Emperor help us if they do find something,' murmured Armstrong.

'So what now?' asked Storm – and Lorenzo recognised the impatient gleam in his eyes. 'The odds are way better than they were two nights ago, and this time we have the advantage of surprise. We come out firing, we'll have half those greenskins down before they know what's hit them.'

'I don't care about "half those greenskins",' growled Greiss.

'We're here for one reason, and one reason only – and I didn't see anyone out there answering Big Green's description.'

'There were no huts,' Braxton realised. 'Where do these orks live?'

'Another encampment, somewhere nearby?' hazarded Myers.

'Your job to find out,' said Greiss. 'When I give the word, you take a scout round that clearing, see if there's any wheel tracks or evidence of orks tramping to and fro. My guess is, there won't be. I reckon these greenskins have taken their equipment and their beds underground, into the mine itself.'

'So, getting to their boss won't be as easy as it sounded,' added Myers.

'He's got to show his face on the surface sometime,' opined Braxton.

'Has he?' said Armstrong, cynically.

'Normally, I'd say wait,' said Greiss. 'Set up sniper positions, sit it out for a few days, let our target come to us. But this is Rogar III. We sit around here too long, we don't know what it's going to throw at us.'

'If we go into that mine with all guns blazing,' said Armstrong, 'Big Green will know about it – and I'm betting, if he's half as smart as Mackenzie reckoned, he won't let himself be cornered in there.'

'Something else for you to keep an eye out for, Bullseye,' said Greiss, 'on your reconnoitre: a back way in – though if there is one, it's probably kilometres away, and well hidden. No, I've a feeling in my old bones: the only way we're getting in sniffing distance of our man is if we barge in the front door. Question is, how to do it without tipping off the warboss that we're coming?'

Twenty minutes later, Lorenzo was lying flat on his face in the grass, having mud slapped onto his back by his comrades – some of them, he thought, with a little too much relish. He protested as Storm tried to tie a branch into his hair with clumsy fingers, but succeeded only in poking him in the eye.

Finally, Sergeant Greiss suggested he try standing, and Lorenzo did so, helped to his feet by Braxton. A heap of vegetation crashed to the ground around his feet, and he looked at Armstrong, upon whom similar indignities had been heaped, and stifled a laugh.

It took another ten minutes' work to achieve anything like the effect they wanted. Lorenzo and Armstrong remained standing for this final stage, and Lorenzo watched admiringly as his comrade disappeared beneath layer after layer of dirt. Much of it didn't stick, and even now some patches of Armstrong's skin showed through, but that didn't matter so much. A garland of plants had been knotted together and draped around Armstrong's shoulders; from a distance, it might have looked like the leaves were growing out of him. The likeness wasn't perfect, but even Lorenzo had to suppress a shudder, staring now at a figure that reminded him of the zombies that had almost killed them all. Of course, although he couldn't see it, didn't dare tilt his head for fear of dislodging its dressings, he knew he had undergone a similar transformation.

Greiss cast an appraising eye over his two troopers, and announced that they were ready. 'At least,' he added, 'I'd say we've done as much as we can with you. I suggest you stick to the shadows at the edge of the clearing, and – I don't know – try and puff yourselves up a bit, stick your shoulders out. You're supposed to be orks under all that muck. Pair of scrawny buggers like you two, you'll be lucky to pass for grtechin.'

'So long as the greenskins don't pick 'em as Catachans, eh, sergeant?' said Myers. He had surprised everyone by producing two ork guns from his backpack; now he pressed one into Lorenzo's hands, and the other into Armstrong's. 'Here, this should help keep up the illusion.'

'You got any more of them, Bullseye?' asked Greiss.

'Afraid not, sergeant. Just picked up two at the encampment, for a rainy day. I loaded 'em both up, though.'

'Rest of us will have to make do with lasguns, then. We let Patch and Lorenzo start firing first, and with a bit of luck the orks won't think about it in the confusion.'

It sounded like a risky plan. For a start, the Jungle Fighters were relying upon the likelihood that the orks had had their own encounters with the plant zombies. 'When they start falling,' Greiss had said, 'we want them to think that that's who's behind it: their own living dead. So, no heroics. We're just going to pick off a few sentries, narrow the odds against us and fall back, no more than that.'

Greiss, Myers, Storm and Braxton slipped away to their positions then, and left Lorenzo and Armstrong standing, looking at each other. Lorenzo hoped that Armstrong, with all he'd been through, was up to this – but when Greiss had expressed a similar sentiment, the veteran had snapped that he had lost an eye and an arm, not the use of his legs or his brain.

They waited two minutes as arranged, then began to shuffle toward the lights and the sounds of ork voices. It was easier than Lorenzo had expected to replicate the zombies' stiff, unnatural gait: it came naturally to him, so worried was he about shedding his disguise before it was even put to use.

They split up as they neared the clearing, Armstrong going right, Lorenzo left. He saw no sign of his other comrades, but he knew they were nearby. He drew in a deep breath and stepped out into the open, stopping just short of the footprint of the nearest lantern. The nearest ork sentry was a little closer than he'd anticipated, and he squeezed the trigger of his gun and sent a hail of bullets its way. Somewhere to Lorenzo's right, the chatter of a second ork gun echoed his own.

The ork was coming at him, snarling, foaming at the mouth. It must have known it was dead, but it was using its body as a shield, giving its fellows time to react to the intruders in their midst. There was every chance that if it could cling to life long enough to reach Lorenzo, it could do some real damage. He took a step back, but he couldn't display too much speed or agility for fear of exposing his deception. All he could do was keep shooting, and pray.

Then the ork fell, and the clearing was full of answering fire, then the whines of las-bolts shooting in from positions unknown, and there were four more orks coming Lorenzo's way and it was time to get the hell out of there.

It took all the self-control he could muster not to duck or run – to turn his back and to shamble away, hearing ork feet pounding ever closer, making himself a clear target for an agonising second. A bullet whistled by his ear; another blew a clump of mud from his shoulder and grazed his skin. Then Lorenzo rounded a bush, passed out of his enemies' sight, and abandoned all pretence.

He left a trail of debris behind him as he raced through the jungle; he just hoped his pursuers wouldn't recognise it for what it was. He put as many obstacles as he could between him and them. The orks were snarling and howling, and letting off gunfire in random directions, so he knew they wouldn't hear him; as long as they didn't see him either, they should assume he had sunk underground like Rogar's other zombies. In theory, at least.

The explosions came in quick succession – two of them. The orks had run into their own traps, the positions of the tripwires changed by Greiss and Myers. Some of them would have died. It was still too early to tell, though, if the rest of the plan – the important part – had succeeded.

There was mud in Lorenzo's eyes and mouth, but he had reached his rendezvous point with the rest of his squad. He was the first there. He clawed great handfuls of dirt from his face, breathed deeply of the warm night air and coughed up a leaf. He was recognisably Lorenzo now, but a film of the planet's substance clung to him like a second skin. He didn't think he would ever feel clean again.

Somebody spoke, and he jumped; he hadn't heard anybody approaching. Then he recognised Greiss's voice, and saw the familiar figure of his sergeant out of the corner of his eye, though he couldn't make out what he was saying, so bunged up were his ears. He started to clean them with his fingers, as Greiss padded up to him and laid a hand on Lorenzo's shoulder.

That was when he saw his mistake.

Lorenzo's head snapped up, and he looked into the hollow eyes of an effigy. A better effigy, far better, than the first two; Rogar had sculpted Greiss's craggy features perfectly, even found plant tendrils to match the iron grey of his hair. And that voice – it had possessed exactly the right gruff tone, even if, Lorenzo now realised, it hadn't been saying a thing. He muttered a curse, aimed at himself for not having paid attention, as he pushed the effigy away from him and dived at the same time, but knew it was hopeless.

The effigy exploded, and Lorenzo felt his ears popping, felt its spines stabbing into him before he hit the ground, his left side feeling as if it was on fire.

He rolled onto his back, raised his left arm, and saw four spines protruding along its length, three more embedded between his ribs. He yanked them out quickly, some tearing his skin and sending more lances of pain through him. Most of the spines, he was grateful to see, still dripped poison and therefore hadn't pumped the whole of their doses into him. Seven spines, though... He was bleeding through some of his wounds, and this too was good because it meant he might bleed some of the poison out. He twisted his arm around until he could reach two of its punctures with his mouth, and he sucked at them, his tongue recoiling at a strong, sour taste.

His heart was hammering, his head light. The first effects of the poison – or of his own fear? He didn't want it to end like this. Not through his own carelessness. Not without a name by which his comrades could remember him.

He searched his pockets, found the capsule of herbs that Donovits had given him some months ago. A generic antitoxin, he had called it – though he had warned it wouldn't work in all situations. Deathworlds, Donovits had said, had a habit of evolving poisons faster than men could combat them – and, Lorenzo supposed gloomily, he would have said that went double for a world like Rogar III.

He gulped the herbs down anyway, taking hold of all the lifelines he could. He clambered unsteadily to his feet as Armstrong burst through the jungle behind him, followed by Storm, Greiss and then Braxton.

Lorenzo told them what had happened to him. He had no choice: he had to warn them in case Rogar tried the same trick on them. He downplayed his injuries, though, claiming to have been hit by only three spines and professing a false confidence that he had sucked most of the poison out of his bloodstream. Greiss gave him a sceptical look, but Lorenzo was able to return it with clear, focused eyes. Maybe, he thought, he would be all right after all?

Myers returned a few minutes after that – having stayed to view the aftermath of the Jungle Fighters' incursion – and Lorenzo could tell from his broad grin that he had the news they wanted to hear. 'We gunned down three greenskins altogether,' he reported, 'and wounded a few more. They lost another three, and most of the gretchin, to their own traps.'

'They called for replacements?' asked Greiss.

Myers shook his head. 'Just spread their sentries more thinly. 'It worked, sergeant. Judging by the way they're looking around and pointing guns at the plants, they think the planet did this to them.'

'How many orks left?' asked Armstrong, performing a quick mental calculation. 'Six?'

'Five,' said Myers. 'One went and stood itself right next to my bush. I caught a jungle lizard creeping up on me. I couldn't resist it. I gave it a flick with my lasgun, catapulted it onto the greenskin's shoulder. The lizard stuck the ork's neck with its tongue before it could move. It was on the ground, thrashing and howling, when I slipped away.'

'Five orks,' said Greiss, 'and how many gretchin?'

'I reckon about four. Five, maybe,' said Myers.

'Not bad,' mused Armstrong. 'We got the greenskins down to less than half strength, and they don't even know they're under attack yet.'

The Jungle Fighters' next step was to make their presence well and truly felt.

They synchronised their assault, bursting out of cover from six points simultaneously, their lasguns flaring. Lorenzo, Braxton, Greiss, Armstrong and Storm took an ork each, though Armstrong had grumbled under his breath about being assigned one that was already injured. As Lorenzo fired repeatedly at his target, he was aware of gretchin scampering away towards the mine, intent on taking a warning to their warboss. That was Myers's job: to stop them.

Myers's las-bolts struck the stunted creatures unerringly, often finding the best angles from which to penetrate two or three of them. Two gretchin fell, and the remaining three were deterred from their course, giving Myers the chance to get between them and the mine tunnel. The single ork that had been guarding the entrance had been lured away by Greiss; now it hesitated, glancing back, not sure whether to press its attack against Greiss or to tackle this new foe. In the event, it was spared that decision. One of Greiss's las-bolts passed through the ork's thick skull and fried its brain.

Lorenzo's ork was thundering towards him, weakened but not defeated. He dropped his gun, pulled his Catachan fang, and greeted his opponent with a well-aimed slash to the throat. The ork was dead, but still fighting. Lorenzo avoided its clumsy grasp, but almost fell as it rammed him with its shoulder. The ork toppled, catching him off-balance, and bore him down with its weight. Its left hand was trapped beneath it, but it seized his throat with its right, and Lorenzo grabbed a chunky green finger in each hand and strained to pry them apart.

The ork ran out of strength, and its eyes rolled back into its head as it heaved its final breath. Lorenzo pulled himself out from under it, in time to see Sergeant Greiss gunning down the last of the gretchin. The rest of his squad were already pulling ork corpses into the foliage, hiding them, and Lorenzo followed suit. None of their targets had survived to spread word, but it was possible that the sounds of battle had carried into the mine.

Lorenzo waited, crouching silently, watching the tunnel entrance, the blood of his dead enemy seeping into his boot. After a minute or so, something stirred down there, and Lorenzo tensed at the sight of an oncoming light.

It was another barrow-pushing ork. Evidently, it hadn't heard anything amiss, because it strode right out into the clearing and stood there, blinking in the harsh light of the lanterns, just beginning to register the fact that it was alone.

It dropped its barrow, which teetered and upturned itself, spilling its contents. A look of confusion, tinged with fear, began to spread across the ork's face – and froze there as multiple las-bolts stabbed out of the darkness to impale it.

The Jungle Fighters emerged into the clearing again, and Greiss jabbed the fallen ork with his toe to check that it was really dead, that it wouldn't spring up and surprise them. Myers asked if they should burn the bodies, to prevent the planet from making use of them. Greiss concluded, reluctantly, that they had no time, that their work here could be discovered at any moment, and that they would just have to take that chance.

They headed into the mine tunnel, in single file, Storm taking point wearing an ork miner's helmet, lighting their way through the darkness. Myers was behind him, then Armstrong, Braxton, Lorenzo and finally Greiss, his knife drawn, ready for anything that might try sneaking up on them from behind.

They had taken only ten steps, hardly left the lights of the clearing behind them, when they came across another ork with a barrow. Its helmet beam dazzled Lorenzo – but Storm's beam blinded the ork in turn so that, for a fateful moment, it didn't recognise the intruders for what they were. Sergeant Greiss had decreed that lasguns should only be used now when strictly necessary – not just because they were low on ammo, but because who knew how far the sound would carry through these tunnels – so Storm leapt at the creature with a muted snarl and his Catachan fang raised and, impressively, he gutted it before it could raise much more than a whimper.

Storm took the dead ork's helmet and passed it back along the line to Greiss, who turned off the helmet's light but placed it on his head for future use. Then they crept on downward, the slope of the tunnel becoming more pronounced until Lorenzo judged that they were descending below ground level.

He eyed the precarious wooden struts – most of them just branches chopped to size, still sprouting offshoots and leaves – that were wedged into the passageway, supporting the increasing weight of the earth above their heads. He didn't trust them.

The ground shook again then, as if to underscore his fears, and Lorenzo swallowed as the makeshift struts rattled fiercely and a shower of loose soil fell about his ears. He couldn't tell if this tremor was lighter or heavier than the first two; he only knew that it felt more ominous down here, where it wasn't just below him but around him and above him too, and where he knew there would be nowhere to hide from a more severe quake, no way to avoid being buried alive.

'You realise,' said Braxton, putting Lorenzo's own thoughts into words as the tremor subsided, 'if this place caves in, we'll have come all this way for nothing. Rogar will have dealt with Big Green for us.'

'Maybe,' grunted Greiss, 'and maybe not. Maybe he'll just slip away through his escape tunnel, wherever that is, and maybe it'll take us a year to find him again. No, I don't care if this whole damn world blows itself apart around us – I for one am not backing out of this on a "maybe". Far as I'm concerned, that brute's still alive until I clap my own eyes on his stinking corpse!'

Lorenzo became aware of a sick ache in his stomach, and he fought down a surge of bile in his throat. His skin felt hot, prickly, and he was short of breath. The symptoms came from nowhere, and at first he thought the tunnel must have caused them, this unfamiliar, claustrophobic environment.

Then he remembered the effigy, and its spines.

His precautions had done him no good. Rogar III's poison was coursing through his veins. He knew he should tell the others, warn them in case he went crazy like Muldoon had, became a threat to them. But then they would probably have left him behind, to die on his back like Woods, and he couldn't face that. Not when they were so close to their goal. Not when he was so close to a chance to earn his name, at last.

He *would* earn his name. Lorenzo swore that to himself. He didn't know how – but if he couldn't find a way down here with a world against him, then where could he? A way to surrender his life for his squad, for his cause, for a chance to be remembered, and he knew he wouldn't hesitate this time. Because, this time, he had nothing to lose. This time, he was dying anyway.

Might as well go out in a blaze of glory.

CHAPTER SIXTEEN

Sergeant Greiss swore under his breath.

The orks' mine tunnel had opened into a cave – and Lorenzo could see, from the lack of wooden props and the uneven texture of the rock where Storm's light fell upon it, that it was natural. Passages snaked from the cave in all directions – ominous black holes in the walls.

'Looks like the greenskins have bust their way into a whole underground complex,' Greiss grumbled. 'Could spread for kilometres.'

'What do we do now, sergeant?' asked Braxton.

Before Greiss could answer, Myers let out a 'Ssshh,' and held up his hand for silence. A second later, they all heard it: lumbering footsteps, echoing from the walls until there was no way of knowing which direction they came from.

Storm snatched off his helmet, snapped off the light, and the Jungle Fighters dispersed, navigating by memory in the total darkness, finding nooks into which they could squeeze. Lorenzo found himself in the mouth of a narrow, twisting passageway, and feared for a moment that it was along this very route that the orks were approaching. Then the footsteps – two sets, he estimated – seemed to move around him, and he saw the bobbing beam of a helmet light, and then there were two hulking shapes in the cave, striding toward the exit tunnel.

Then the Jungle Fighters were upon the orks, Storm reaching

them first, leaping onto the back of the nearest and drawing his blade across its throat. Greiss and Braxton crashed into the second creature, staggered it, and Lorenzo lent his shoulder to their efforts and it fell, three knives plunged into its chest and stomach.

'You notice something?' asked Armstrong, as the others confirmed their kills. 'These two were going up to the surface, but they don't have barrows. No pickaxes, no spades, just guns.'

'You think they suspect something?' murmured Greiss darkly.

'I think Big Green's maybe starting to wonder what's been happening to his barrow boys. Or maybe the sentries up top were supposed to report in. Either way, I'll bet these two were coming to investigate.'

'When they don't come back either...' breathed Myers.

'Alright,' Greiss nodded. 'We've got – how long would you say? – a few minutes before all hell breaks loose down here. Meantime, we need to make inroads into these caves, make sure the warboss can't go nowhere without getting past us first. Anyone else hear that? Sounds like digging?'

Myers reported that he did hear it – and, screwing up his face in concentration, Storm agreed. Lorenzo didn't hear a thing, and he scrabbled at the insides of his ears in frustration, evacuating more of Rogar III's mud. The effort disturbed his equilibrium, and his brain performed a lurching spin. The sickness in his stomach made another surge for his throat, and he swallowed it down.

Greiss and Myers followed the digging sounds to the right-hand side of the cave, and Myers located a tunnel that was wider and straighter than the others, its floor a little smoother. 'I'd say there's been a few barrows pushed up this way, sergeant,' he reported – and, standing at the tunnel entrance, even Lorenzo could now hear the distant clink of metal against rock from somewhere below.

'Right,' sighed Greiss, 'this is how it's going to have to be. We split into three teams. Patch and Lorenzo, you follow this tunnel here. Braxton, you're with me – we'll take the passage those two orks came up from. Bullseye, Wildman, you wait around here a while, stick to the shadows. Chances are, there'll be more green-skins along soon, and I'm betting once they find their buddies' corpses littering the place, they'll send word back to the big boss.'

'We can follow 'em,' concluded Storm. 'Right, sergeant.'

Everyone seemed happy with that plan, and Lorenzo didn't want to be the one to object. Still, he felt numb. His chances of being the one to find the warboss had just been slashed by two-thirds. He pictured himself dying quietly in a dark tunnel somewhere, while Greiss and Braxton, or Myers and Storm, stumbled upon their target and grabbed all the glory. He wouldn't let that happen.

Greiss handed him the miner's helmet from one of the dead orks, and Lorenzo jammed it onto his head and practically dragged Armstrong away, down the tunnel towards the digging sounds. 'Steady on,' whispered Patch in his ear, 'you'll run straight into the greenskins at this rate.' But Lorenzo wasn't listening. He'd had a lifetime of being too cautious. All he cared about now was covering as much ground as he could. More ground than the other two teams could cover. Being the first to find the ork warboss. Earning his name, before it was too late.

There were lights up ahead – harsh, like the lanterns outside. Lorenzo switched off his helmet beam and crept forward, Armstrong at his heels.

The tunnel they were following took a sharp dip, its gradient so steep that they were half-walking, half-sliding. The sounds of picks and shovels were unmistakeable now, and there was something else. The squeak of a wheel. Armstrong tapped Lorenzo on the shoulder and indicated a side passageway, narrow and level, also well lit. Lorenzo nodded, and they slipped into it, and pressed themselves against its walls so the light wouldn't cast their shadows across the junction.

An ork appeared, grunting as it strained to push a loaded barrow up the slope. Lorenzo's hand moved to his lasgun, knowing that if the creature saw them their cover was blown. It only had to yell out. To his relief, it moved on. Let Myers and Wildman take care of it when it reached them, he thought.

They moved further down the side passageway, until the right-hand wall fell away and they were in a natural gallery, looking out across a vast cavern. Its floor lay some ten metres below them; its far wall was four times that distance. The cavern was swarming with orks, hefting tools, battering at the walls, breaking off chunks of rock that gretchin gathered and piled into waiting barrows. The area was lit by six lanterns, squeezed into niches at varying heights, connected by tangles of thick cabling. There was a lantern beside the Jungle Fighters, on the gallery, lying on its side – and they crouched behind it so any ork that glanced their way wouldn't see them behind its intense light.

Lorenzo scanned the throng with his eyes, fervently hoping to find an ork with cleaner, better armour than the others; an ork that was giving the orders; an ork perhaps a little larger than its fellows. He was disappointed.

'Another nine, ten passageways off this chamber,' breathed Armstrong. 'This place is like a maze!'

'I don't know,' Lorenzo muttered. 'Most of those tunnels, I think the orks dug themselves – and I think they're still digging them. See how the gretchin keep coming back along them with more rubble. I'm betting most of them are dead ends.'

'Doesn't mean we won't find Big Green's quarters down one of them.'

Lorenzo conceded the point, but nodded towards a wide tunnel entrance below them to the left. 'Seems to be a lot of coming and going through there,' he remarked, 'and the passageway we're in heads in that direction. I think it's worth a look.'

'Your call,' said Armstrong.

They crept on, until rock closed in around them again and their passageway dipped and narrowed and came to an abrupt end. Its floor didn't quite meet the wall, however, and Lorenzo peered through the gap thus created and saw another passageway below. Even as he watched, an ork passed along it; he could almost have reached down and touched its head. He listened a moment, but the only sounds he could hear came from the main chamber behind and below them. He glanced at Armstrong, who nodded – and Lorenzo lowered himself through the hole, until he was hanging from his fingertips, then let himself drop.

The world gave another spin as he hit the ground, and he lost his balance and fell. He picked himself up quickly, humiliated, and gestured up to Armstrong that he was all right. He had guessed right. This tunnel sloped back down to the main chamber in one direction, climbed more gently into darkness in the other. He could only see a short way in the lantern light that bled up from below, but it was enough to see that the tunnel walls were riddled with openings.

At Lorenzo's signal, Armstrong joined him, hampered by his dead arm but still affecting a more graceful landing than his comrade had managed.

Two orks were coming their way. Quickly, they ducked into the nearest of the openings, and found themselves pushing through a tattered curtain. Beyond this, a small cave was littered with skins and debris, and Lorenzo realised that orks had been sleeping here. Fortunately, there were none present at the moment.

A little further up, the tunnel levelled out and split into three, and they followed the left-hand branch. They found more quarters, some rumbling with the grunts and snores of sleeping residents, some apparently empty. Some had lights within, spilling around the edges of their curtains – and in one, the curtain was pulled aside and four orks sat around a flat-topped boulder, playing with knuckle dice. Lorenzo and Armstrong didn't dare risk passing that cave, so they backtracked and chose another path from the three-way junction.

Lorenzo felt angry. What the orks were doing here – it was wrong.

At least, when the men of Catachan tamed a deathworld, it was a fair fight. They didn't burrow under its skin, try to destroy it from within like a virus. The thought of it made him itch, made the sickness rise in his stomach... He wasn't sure why, didn't know where these feelings were coming from, because it wasn't as if the Imperium had never strip-mined a world. Maybe just not a world like Rogar III...

They came across a particularly large entranceway, and Lorenzo hesitated, wondering if this could be the cave to house the warboss. He didn't want to poke his head around the curtain, though: he'd have been unlikely to see anything in the dark and he might have disturbed somebody. Anyway, he could hear at least three different snores from within – and it was probable, he thought, that the orks' warboss had a cave to himself.

A moment later, however, more footsteps – shuffling unexpectedly from an unseen tunnel, little more than a fissure in the rock – forced the two Jungle Fighters to duck into another cave. And this one was occupied.

Lorenzo held his breath, and not just because of the stink of ork bodies around him. He could just make them out: three festering lumps crammed together on the floor. He had almost stepped on one as he'd entered, and he eased his foot away from it. For a moment, he thought he had left Armstrong behind outside, so silent was he – but then he saw the glint of a single eye in the darkness, and was comforted.

The footsteps shuffled up to the cave entrance, and for a moment Lorenzo feared he might have had the bad luck to have taken cover in the wandering ork's own quarters – but then the moment passed and the footsteps were receding. Heading for the main chamber, he guessed.

But there was still something wrong – badly wrong – if only he could put his finger on it. Lorenzo's spine prickled with dread.

He realised what was about to happen a second before it did, and he knew that his luck had turned bad after all. As bad as it could have been.

The tremor shook the soles of his feet, then seemed to rise through the walls and meet again above his head. One of the sleeping orks stirred instantly, and Lorenzo was trapped. He didn't think it had seen him or Armstrong yet, but that could change in an instant, if they moved – and the footsteps outside the cave had come to a halt, so where could they have gone anyway?

The waking ork was fumbling for something, and Lorenzo wondered if there was a chance, a tiny chance, that he could reach it and muffle it before it yelled out, plant his hand over its mouth and his knife in its throat. But that tremor wasn't subsiding – and as he took his first step, the earth bucked underneath him and he fell, put out his hands to catch himself, ended up sprawled across one of the two sleeping orks. Which, of course, was awake too now.

The first ork had found a miner's helmet, and it snapped on the light, shining it around the cave. Armstrong let loose with a las-bolt volley, which kept the ork pinned down but didn't prevent it from letting out an alarm howl.

So now the third ork was clambering to its feet, blinking, reaching for its weapon, and Lorenzo was still trying to avoid the flailing grasp of the second. It caught him by the arm, and he was trying to pull away from it, dragging it to its feet after him, its fingers digging painfully into him. He turned, braced his shoulder against the ork's chest and tried to throw it. It was too heavy, shifting its weight to counter his move, but in so doing it relaxed its hold, and Lorenzo wrenched himself free from it, though it felt like he had lost a handful of his flesh.

Then he and Armstrong were running, as the third ork found its gun and fired – in entirely the wrong direction, confused by the shifting shadows and its wounded fellow's dancing beam of light. The Jungle Fighters burst out into the passageway, where the ork they had been hiding from was waiting, its gun raised. Lorenzo lowered his head, rushed it, and a bullet pinged off his helmet, then he cannoned into the ork and it gave a few paces but braced itself. They were fighting for the ork's gun, and Lorenzo feinted, let the greenskin have the weapon but unbalanced it in the process. It stumbled, and fell onto his freshly drawn knife, impaling itself. Planting his foot in the ork's stomach, he pulled the blade free. It was still alive, but he didn't have time to finish the job.

There were more orks in the passageway, pouring out of the openings on all sides, reacting to the clamour, and the only thing that kept Lorenzo and Armstrong alive was the fact that the earth was still shaking, and with increasing ferocity, confusing the issue, giving the orks more to worry about than just them. Armstrong made to flee back the way they had come; Lorenzo's impulse was to go deeper into the mine, find the ork leader, and they both came up short as they realised they were pulling in opposite directions.

Lorenzo knew, just *knew* they were in danger, and he threw himself at Armstrong, barged him into the wall as the roof caved in. They were coated in soil, disturbed dust tearing at Lorenzo's throat, making his eyes water, but they had avoided the worst of it and the orks were reeling around them, and Lorenzo grabbed Armstrong by the hand and pulled him along, guiding him through the chaos by instinct, at a loss to explain where that instinct had come from.

The tremor was more than a tremor now. It was a fully-fledged earthquake – and Lorenzo knew, with a gut-wrenching certainty, that this was only the beginning. The tunnel was shaking so fiercely, it felt like he had double vision; cracks were opening in the walls, the floor was churning itself up, tossing him about like a wild grox, and the roof was groaning and grinding and collapsing in stages. Rogar III was taking its revenge on the orks that had defiled it, driving them out of itself or just burying them. Lorenzo had lost all sense of direction, but he was moving broadly with the ork flow, and he knew that this meant he was headed back to the main chamber, and from there to the mine entrance. As if the planet itself was herding him that way. What hope did he have now of finding the ork warboss? What hope for him at all in that lantern-lit clearing, with a hundred evacuated green-skins waiting for him? Even assuming he could make it that far.

He was looking for another option, a way to cheat his fate, when an ork reared up in front of him, a spade levelled at his throat like a knife. Lorenzo swung his fang, but the quake made the ork appear to be in ten places at once, and his thrust passed through its ghost image. He didn't know which of its ten spades to avoid.

But then, with a tremendous crack, the wall behind the ork split, and Lorenzo caught his breath in the face of an explosion of fire.

Molten lava, bright red with its own luminescence. It burst through the sundered rock, broke over the ork's back, and the creature let out a howl of incandescent pain. Lorenzo didn't stop to ask how it was possible, how the planet could have pumped its own lifeblood so close to its surface. This was Rogar – and he could feel the lava's heat scorching his face even before it reached him. He kicked out at the scalded, screeching ork, and landed his boot dead centre where all its images combined. It staggered, fell backwards, and its bulky form all but plugged the fissure as Lorenzo had planned. The ork's screams were quelled, its body shuddered and fell still, as liquid fire crept over its shoulders and between its legs.

Lorenzo and Armstrong had a moment's respite. Many of the orks behind them had held back, or tried to back up along the narrow tunnel, when they'd seen the lava. They were colliding with each other, knocking each other down. From the chorus of screams that suddenly rose from up there, somewhere in the darkness, Lorenzo guessed that another lava spring had just opened behind them.

The Jungle Fighters ran – but Lorenzo dragged his comrade to a halt as, suddenly, he saw where they were. Above them was the hole in the roof through which they had dropped: the one that led up to the natural gallery. A way to circumvent the main chamber and all the confused, frightened, angry orks within.

He gave Armstrong a boost, and the veteran shouldered his way up through the narrow opening, attained the ledge above, then turned and reached down with his good arm for his comrade. As Lorenzo took it and scrambled up after him, an ork came roaring out of nowhere and swung its axe at his dangling legs. The shifting earth threw off its aim, and Lorenzo stamped on the ork's face and pushed himself up the final section of his climb. He fired his lasgun down the hole behind him to discourage pursuit, then turned and followed Armstrong along the narrow passageway – to find, to his horror, that it came to an abrupt end.

The gallery, their route to freedom, had crumbled away. They were looking out of a hole in the side of the main chamber, at another hole too far to reach by jumping, the intervening expanse of wall too sheer to climb along even if it hadn't been shaking madly. Lorenzo's foot touched something: the lantern they had passed earlier, still on its side, wedged into position by a stubborn outcrop. He followed its light beam, and on the floor of the chamber he saw a molten river.

The chamber had split down the middle, and its halves were divided by a roiling, bubbling lava flow. Dozens of orks had been trapped on its far side, and panic had broken out. An ork tried to leap the stream, but fell short, howling as its legs were dissolved, the rest of its body sinking after them until only a thin wisp of steam remained of it.

Lorenzo had his own problems. An ork head popped up through the hole in the floor behind him. He and Armstrong fired at it – and, holding on with both hands, there wasn't much it could do to defend itself. Even in death, though, it kept coming, the head followed into the passageway by a pair of broad shoulders, then a green-skinned torso. Lorenzo realised that the corpse was being pushed up by more orks below, shielding them as they followed it. The muzzle of a crude ork gun appeared over the hole's edge and fired blindly. Bullets ricocheted around the confined space, and Lorenzo drew a sharp breath through his teeth as his shoulder was nicked.

'We're easy targets up here,' muttered Armstrong. 'We can hold off these greenskins for a while – but our backs are exposed to the main chamber. Once the orks down there see us, we'll be caught in a crossfire, dead meat.'

He was saying nothing Lorenzo didn't know. He cast around for something, anything – and his eyes found the lantern. It was trailing tangled cables in each direction around the great cavern; clockwise, the next lantern still clung to the wall, but anti-clockwise, the nearest two had been wrenched free from their moorings and were hanging suspended. Lorenzo pulled at the cables in that direction, and found plenty of slack.

Armstrong glanced at him, saw what he was thinking and nodded his approval. 'That might get one of us out of here,' he said. 'Go. I'll buy you some time.'

With that he was off, before Lorenzo could stop him – back down the passageway, leaping onto the first ork as it hauled itself up out of the hole, taking it by surprise, forcing it back down but falling with it, toward the bloodthirsty pack that Lorenzo knew must have gathered below. His instinct was to go after his comrade, to do what he could to help him – but not only was it hopeless, he would have been doing him a disservice. Armstrong had sacrificed himself to save Lorenzo, to give him a chance at least – because Lorenzo had let him, because he hadn't spoken up first, because he hadn't told his comrade that his life was over anyway, that if the orks and the quake didn't finish him the poison would.

Armstrong was relying on Lorenzo to tell that story – which was all that kept him going now as he yanked on the lantern, tore out the taut cables from one side of it and gathered the loose ones to the other. He looked for a safe landing spot, clear of orks and lava and falling rocks.

That was when he saw it. Amid the chaos below, a great brutish ork, trapped on the far side of the lava stream but walking taller, more confidently, than its fellows. It was surrounded by an entourage seven-strong – one of which was festooned with bizarre totems and carried a staff.

As Lorenzo watched, two of the guards seized another gretchin, and bore it face-first into the lava. First the larger ork then the shaman used it as a stepping-stone, hopping onto its back and across to safety before it boiled away. Then the big ork turned and shouted impatient curses at its guards, and they tried to follow but without any such assistance. Four of them made the leap; two did not.

Lorenzo didn't care about them. He had eyes only for their master, with its tough, leathery skin and its gleaming new axe, twice the size of the other orks' weapons and with ceremonial trappings. He had no doubt that this was him. The warboss. Big Green. He even knew, with a flash of insight, what the strange-looking ork with the staff had to be, why it was getting preferential treatment. The source of Big Green's vaunted intelligence. An ork psyker – a weirdboy!

Everything he had ever wanted. His blaze of glory...

Lorenzo wrapped his hands around the entwined cables, calculated the trajectory of his swing. The ork leader was facing away from him, at the edge of the lava flow. One kick between the shoulder blades, with enough weight behind it, would send him reeling. Hit him at the right angle, and the weirdboy might even go with him. And the fact that Lorenzo would doubtless follow both orks into the fire – well, that was good too. A fitting end for a hero.

Only, he realised, with a pang of despair, who would see it? Who would tell the story of this, his greatest moment? He hesitated.

Which, in turn, made him angry with himself. Not this time, he thought. His last chance to count, to make his life mean something. At least *he'd* know.

So, Lorenzo pushed himself off from the rock, and his heart leapt as he saw that his path was true, that even the quake hadn't shaken him off-course. He saw his destiny rushing towards him, and in that moment he *knew* that someone, somewhere, would tell a story about this some day.

Even if it was only the orks themselves.

CHAPTER SEVENTEEN

Everything had changed in an instant.

Lorenzo was on the ground, fighting unconsciousness, not sure how much of the violent, lurching motion around him came from the earthquake and how much from inside him. He tried to put together the pieces of what had just happened.

He had seen it lain out before him: the rest of his life. His heroic death. The ork warboss, growing larger and closer until there was nothing else in the world, nothing else that mattered. Only the warboss, and the river of fire.

Only Big Green, somehow, had heard him coming, or maybe a follower had shouted a warning or his psyker had muttered a prediction, because he had turned – and, with no time to swing his axe nor to sidestep, he had *leapt* instead, and met his oncoming attacker head on. His muscular arms had encircled Lorenzo's legs, and they had hit the ground together but the warboss had landed on his feet while Lorenzo had been smacked down onto his back.

He expected to die a failure – until he realised that the warboss had staggered, at least. He had taken a step back to brace himself – and his foot had slipped into the lava stream. The psyker let out a panicked chittering sound at his master's peril and hobbled away. Lorenzo held his breath but the warboss's self-control was incredible. He triumphed over what must have been searing agony, to keep his balance – and he loomed over the Catachan with his axe raised high, though one of his legs now tapered to a dripping, cauterised stump at the ankle. Lorenzo still didn't know what to do, because he hadn't planned for this situation, hadn't planned to survive this long.

So it was just as well that his instincts took over – and he kicked out at the warboss's intact leg with all his might, and he managed to fell him but not backwards as he'd hoped. Lorenzo scrambled on top of the huge ork, still hoping that somehow he could roll them both into the lava – but Big Green was too heavy and unyielding, and Lorenzo was seized from behind by two of his four remaining bodyguards.

He kicked and yelled as he was dragged from his foe – as more orks streamed towards him from all directions, disregarding their own peril in the face of his threat to their leader. Rarely had he seen such a display of loyalty from the greenskins. Now a curtain of snarling faces closed in front of Lorenzo, and he couldn't see the ork leader any more, and he knew it was all over.

The sounds of las-fire seemed distant at first, as if they came from a world that was no longer his concern. It was only when the orks began to scatter, when one of those that held him was hit and loosed its grip, that Lorenzo realised a new element had entered the equation. Or rather, two new elements. Sergeant Greiss and Braxton. Lorenzo didn't know where they'd come from – a tunnel opening beneath the collapsed gallery was his best bet – but they had bought him another chance when he had thought he was out of chances, and he wasn't about to waste it.

He tried to throw his remaining captor, but failed. Again, his instincts came to the rescue, predicting the patterns of the quake, telling him when the ground would buck beneath the ork's feet, which way to push when it did. The greenskin squealed as it fell, surfed the shifting floor on its back and wound up with its head in the lava.

Lorenzo drew his gun, and immediately found a target. The greenskin psyker. He had thought it long gone, but it must have run into the new arrivals and reversed its flight. At least, he thought as he killed it, that was the end of the warboss's advantage. He was just a normal warboss now. But his squad's orders hadn't been to kill the psyker, they'd been to kill Big Green himself, and he intended to do just that.

The warboss couldn't have gone far – not with only one foot. Indeed, there he was, just a few metres distant, being helped along by two guards. But Greiss was closer, and Lorenzo could see the familiar gleam in his sergeant's eyes, knew he had spied an opening and would take it, heedless of the cost to himself. While Lorenzo's path was blocked again, and he couldn't clear it in time – though he ploughed into the orks anyway, lasgun flaring, fang flashing, and he wasn't sure if the red mist he could see was a product of his own unreasoning anger or his poisoning or just an afterglow from the lava stream.

All he knew, in that desperate moment, was that he had to reach the warboss before his sergeant did. He couldn't help himself. Greiss was tired of life, wanted to go out on a high – but he had earned his name. Weren't there enough stories told of him already?

Greiss was wading through orks like they were nothing. They'd given up trying to shoot him, because it was hopeless aiming through the quake, and they were throwing themselves at him to be hurled aside or gutted or just trampled as they mistimed their rushes and fell at Greiss's feet. Lorenzo was so busy watching this performance that he was barely aware of his own actions, moving on autopilot, stabbing at an ork throat here, reacting to the whistle of a descending axe there. It was only as a substantial chunk of the chamber's roof fell, as Lorenzo danced out of its way and a dozen orks were crushed, that he realised what he'd been doing: drawing his foes to him, bunching them together, setting them up for a fate no man could have predicted... could he?

Dust billowed black around him, rubble made his footing treacherous, and the last of the lanterns toppled from its high perch, smashed and died. The only light now came from the lava – and Lorenzo almost plunged into it as, scrambling to find the warboss, he slid on a layer of scree. Then the earth cracked again, and suddenly the molten stream had a hundred narrow tributaries, crazing the cavern floor. Lorenzo vaulted them two at a time; he knew where he was going, almost as if he could sense his prey's ponderous, one-legged footsteps through the ground itself.

There he was – stranded on an island, only one guard left at his side, the lava flows around him thin and shallow but impassable to one with his disability. As Big Green saw Lorenzo, his eyes widened with fear and hatred, and he yelled and gesticulated to his guard, ordering it to lay itself down as a bridge for him. The ork signalled its refusal by swiping at the warboss's neck with its axe; evidently, loyalty had its limits, especially when an ork sensed that its leader's day was done.

But Big Green had earned his position for a reason. Some warbosses had been known to go toe to toe with Space Marines. Displaying the same lightning reflexes with which he'd met the Jungle Fighters' first attack upon him, the warboss caught the axe's blade between both hands, a centimetre from his slavering sneer, and twisted the weapon right out of his startled guard's hands.

Lorenzo was firing frantically – but like the orks, he found his shots knocked astray. the warboss had his traitor guard by the neck, had wrenched its arm up behind its back, and was pushing it down, and it looked like he was about to get his bridge after all, so Lorenzo sprang for the warboss's back.

He timed his leap just right, to benefit from an upsurge beneath his feet; Big Green whipped around and swung his giant axe, but Lorenzo was higher than he could have expected, and the blade passed beneath his feet – and then he was on the warboss's shoulders, and he plunged his knife into the ork's eye and tried to work its point up into his brain.

Big Green howled and threw back his arms, trying to swat the Jungle Fighter from his back. Lorenzo held on as long as he could, but between the warboss and the quake it was like trying to straddle three grox at once. He pulled his knife free and jumped before he could be thrown, landing nimbly on his feet.

He parried an axe thrust with his knife, and simultaneously kicked out at the warboss's injured leg, making him howl again. But Big Green didn't fall. He barely even flinched – and Lorenzo had been counting on at least a momentary respite to drop back into a defensive position. The axe blade whistled toward him again, and the flat of its blade struck a resounding blow against his wrist, splintering bones, and his knife flew out of his grasp.

It was spinning towards the lava, and Lorenzo leapt after it without thinking, dropping his lasgun, catching the knife with his off-hand in midair, twisting to avoid a scalding death himself. He landed on his back, winded as the ground rose up to meet him. The warboss lunged, and Lorenzo barely brought up a foot in time, tried to kick the warboss away, but the ork batted it aside. Then he was on Lorenzo, the sharp points of his tusks almost touching the Catachan's face, dripping drool onto his cheek and blood from his punctured eye, and Big Green's axe haft was pressed down across Lorenzo's throat, crushing his windpipe.

All Lorenzo could do was take that haft himself, try to force it upwards, away from him, but the warboss was too strong, and he could feel the breath being choked out of him. His lungs were empty, burning, and his head felt light. He held on, because every fraction of a second he could keep Big Green here dealing with him was a further delay to the warboss's escape. Lorenzo may have failed to kill this monster, but he could be the hero who engaged it in single combat, kept it trapped long enough for the earthquake to finish it. A forlorn hope, he realised.

Then, suddenly, the pressure on his throat was released, and Lorenzo tried to see what was happening, but without him knowing it his eyes had closed and he couldn't open them because they were prickling with tears and his entire body was preoccupied with just trying to breathe. His stomach convulsed as he heaved in air, and spluttered on its gritty texture.

By the time he could look again, he knew what he would see: Sergeant Greiss, wrestling with the warboss. Greiss had landed a few good blows, too – the warboss had a livid scar on his cheek to add to the one Lorenzo had left across his eye. But he was fighting on, as if nothing would ever stop him.

Lorenzo's legs were too weak to stand, so he contented himself with hitting his opponent low, the combination of his efforts and Greiss's, and Big Green's missing foot, flooring the big ork again. They piled on top of him, fists and knives flying, but they couldn't still his axe – and its blade swung and impacted with Greiss's head, cleaving his miner's helmet in two, cutting into his scalp and, with a resounding clang, hitting the metal plate just below the surface. Greiss fell back, blood matting his grey hair as Lorenzo used the momentum of the warboss's swing against him, and with a tremendous, last-ditch heave, tipped and *rolled* him into one of the narrow streams. The ork leader was facedown in the lava but still thrashing, and Lorenzo placed his good hand on the back of the warboss's head and, releasing a strangulated roar of utter hatred from the back of his throat. He pushed down...

Then he was scrambling towards Greiss, though he didn't know what he could do for him. The sergeant was bleeding freely, but all Lorenzo could see in his face was a malicious satisfaction at the death of an enemy. And maybe, when he looked at Lorenzo, a hint of approval?

Then, a sudden change of expression – a warning glint in Greiss's eyes. Lorenzo whirled around and the warboss was standing, molten lava streaming from his face, most of the skin burnt away, but he was coming at them again...

Greiss was firing at him, pumping las-round after las-round into the warboss's chest, and Lorenzo didn't think it would be enough – but then there was las-fire from behind Big Green too, and a bedraggled, soot-blackened figure emerged through a haze of dust – and even as the ork leader reached his targets, as he made to bring his axe down, it was one of Guardsman Braxton's rounds that finally sizzled through his skull and put out the feral light in those eyes once and for all.

Lorenzo had thought he'd feel different when the ork leader died at last. He had expected to feel... something. Relieved, perhaps. Or dismayed, that another man had delivered the killing blow. Somehow, he had thought there would be silence, and time to reflect – but as another great chunk of rock was dislodged from the cavern roof to thunk into the ground beside him, he knew it was not to be.

Braxton helped Lorenzo to his feet, and they both turned to give Greiss a lift, but the grizzled sergeant waved them away stubbornly. 'We've got to get out of here, sergeant,' insisted Braxton as Lorenzo retrieved his gun and slapped a new pack into position. 'This place won't hold up much longer. Most of the orks have already run for it. Where's Patch?'

Lorenzo shook his head. 'Bullseye and Wildman?'

'Dead,' said Greiss, flatly. 'Me and Braxton, we stumbled across their bodies on our way in. Looks like they found Big Green before we did, more's the pity.'

'I'm sure they put up a good fight,' said Lorenzo, almost automatically. 'I'm sure if it hadn't been for them, if they hadn't weakened–'

'Time enough for eulogies later,' growled Greiss. 'Looked like the greenskins were mostly headed back up to the clearing, but we found another way out.' He nodded in the direction from which he and Braxton had appeared. 'We take that, chances are we'll run into less opposition along the way. That is, if the whole tunnel hasn't collapsed by now.'

'Let me lead the way,' said Lorenzo.

Greiss snarled. 'Like hell! In case you hadn't noticed, trooper, I am not dead yet – and I'm still in charge of this squad, what's left of it.'

'That's not what I meant, sergeant. I've been having a... a... I don't know how to describe it, some kind of an instinct about the quake. Like I know how the earth's going to move, where it's safe to step, where...' Lorenzo tailed off, embarrassed at how implausible the words sounded out loud.

But Greiss just regarded him coolly for a moment, then nodded and grunted, 'Step to it, then.'

Lorenzo set off sure-footedly, affecting confidence while inwardly he half-expected his luck to run out at any moment. Then, there it was again: that indefinable feeling, that tug in a certain direction. Greiss indicated a tunnel mouth ahead of them, but Lorenzo balked at a direct approach, and picked out a circuitous path towards their goal instead. His caution was rewarded as a lava stream bubbled and spat its contents straight up like a geyser.

The Jungle Fighters hugged the wall, keeping just out of range of burning droplets, until they reached the tunnel and stumbled gratefully into its stale but cooler embrace. After that, their progress was a little easier, because there were no lava streams up here and because they could lean on the walls for support. To some extent, anyway. A particularly violent shudder pinballed the trio from one side of the passageway to the other and back, and made Greiss curse and demand to know why Lorenzo hadn't felt that one coming.

Darkness enveloped them, and Lorenzo snapped on his helmet light, which luckily still worked. They passed several junctions, with Greiss bellowing directions at each one – and they found their path strewn with crushed ork bodies, and had to squeeze their way around more than one partial cave-in.

It was Braxton who first voiced the feeling that they were being followed, though when Lorenzo shone his light behind them they could see nothing. Greiss urged them on, and eventually he directed them into an upward-leading passageway that was smoother and straighter than the others, obviously worked, like the one they had followed down from the clearing.

The first set of wooden struts they came across had slipped and buckled but, miraculously, held; they climbed past them gingerly. The second had broken into splinters, but fortunately the roof was staying up by itself.

It was just past the third that their luck ran out.

Lorenzo heard the orks ahead of them before he saw them. There were a half-dozen of them, jabbering in panic as they tried to dig through a pile of rubble that had completely blocked the tunnel. They were succeeding mostly in getting in each other's way: as the Jungle Fighters watched, one ork accidentally embedded its pickaxe in the skull of another.

They were sitting ducks for a volley of las-fire, the narrow confines ensuring that even through the quake most of the Jungle Fighters' shots found a target. The orks, in turn, didn't seem to be armed – and, taken by surprise, they jostled with each other in their haste to close with their attackers, more than one of them stumbling in the melee and being manhandled aside. A single greenskin made it within knife range – and this, Lorenzo made short work of with his Catachan fang.

As he yanked his blade out of the ork's chest, he stumbled, brushed the tunnel wall with his bare arm and recoiled from its unexpected heat. Greiss had felt it too, and he gave Lorenzo a quizzical look. 'Lava,' he confirmed. 'It's all right – it hasn't built up enough pressure yet to cause a burst. We've got a few minutes.'

Greiss nodded, and asked, 'How far to the surface?'

'Almost there. Just the other side of that cave-in.'

'Guess the orks had the right idea, then,' said Greiss – and the Jungle Fighters rummaged amid the corpses of their enemies to retrieve their pickaxes and spades, and set about the blockage with gusto and a great deal more efficiency and teamwork than the greenskins had demonstrated.

Lorenzo was worried about Greiss. He had retied his bandana like a bandage over his head wound – but the bleeding showed no sign of abating, red rivulets rolling down his cheek. None of this seemed to lessen the zeal with which he swung his pickaxe, but then Lorenzo had learned to expect no less from him.

'Looks like you were right, Braxton,' Greiss murmured – and Lorenzo swung around, and this time his light beam *did* pick out something. A lot of somethings, no longer bothering to hide.

Ork zombies, shuffling up the tunnel behind them. They could only fit two abreast with their broad shoulders, but their ranks extended further back than Lorenzo could see – and, at their heart: the chilling sight of an even bulkier creature that could only have been the warboss himself, his skull half-caked with mud but stripped to the bone beneath this.

There was still too far to dig, no way they could escape in time. There were too many sources of fresh corpses for Rogar to use against them, even discounting those orks that had been melted in lava or whose bones had been shattered. Lorenzo found himself averting his gaze from the oncoming army – not through fear of their strength and numbers, but lest he glimpse the familiar shape of a lost comrade among them.

'Looks like this is it,' growled Greiss.

'No, sergeant,' protested Lorenzo – though he knew it was hopeless too. 'Not now. Not when we're so close!'

'I didn't mean the end for all of us. Just me. About damn time!'

'What… what are you…?' Lorenzo began – but Greiss hefted his pickaxe, and Lorenzo saw that gleam in his eyes, saw where it was focused, and suddenly he knew what the sergeant was planning. And, impulsively, he laid a restraining hand on his shoulder and he said, 'Let me.'

'What's wrong with you, trooper?' snapped Greiss. 'That's twice you've questioned my orders, and I'm telling you, I don't like it!'

'You've taken worse hits than this, sergeant. I know you have. You aren't going to let some dumb ork get the better of you, are you?'

'Too damn old,' grumbled Greiss. 'This was always going to be my last outing. And you, Lorenzo, you got a job to do. You're the only one who can tell Patch's story. I'm only sorry I won't be around to hear it.'

'I... I'm dying too, sergeant. Poisoned.'

Greiss looked Lorenzo up and down, and said curtly, 'You look all right to me.' Lorenzo couldn't argue, because Greiss was right – because, exhausted and hurt though he was, he realised only now that the effects of the effigy's venom, the nausea and the dizziness, had receded.

Then Greiss clapped him on the arm and smiled grimly. 'Live for me. Tell everyone I did it, got my blaze of glory. And don't be so damn impatient for yours. Way I see it, you got a lot of stories in you yet; you only just earned your name.'

He turned and, before Lorenzo could say anything else – before he could think what *to* say – he was charging at the front rank of zombies with a bloodcurdling scream. As he reached them, as they grabbed and clawed at him, he smashed his pickaxe into the wall beside them, again and again, until the first crack began to show... and to widen... and *explode*.

A deluge of lava crashed into the passageway, and surged downhill. It subsumed Sergeant Greiss and the zombies, swept them away, and Lorenzo knew that this time there wouldn't be enough left of any of them for Rogar to reanimate. He turned away, couldn't watch, concentrated on the blockage in front of him, swinging his pickaxe in time with Braxton's, driving himself on, ignoring the pain in his fractured wrist, not letting himself think about anything but the task at hand because if he did think about it, what had happened to Greiss and Armstrong and Myers and Storm and all the others, if he really *thought* about it, he might have been overwhelmed by the unfairness of it all. Why them? Why them and not him?

Lorenzo thought about their sacrifices, and his greatest fear was that they would all be for nothing.

His pickaxe rose and fell, and he could feel the heat from the lava at his back and the rock walls closed in around him, and his pickaxe rose and fell, and there were tears in his eyes but that might have been the dirt. He remembered the ship, out in warp space, so long ago now, and that feeling of being trapped, surrounded by hostile forces, helpless to influence his own fate, and he longed for the open air but feared he would never breathe it again.

Lorenzo's pickaxe rose and fell, and he felt as if he had been doing this forever, getting nowhere. He could sense the planet, his enemy, a living presence in his thoughts, and he knew it had won, defeated him, that he would never find his way out from inside it – that Rogar III would bury him as it had buried the rest of his squad. Just swallowed them up, left no trace of them. No one to tell their stories.

No one to remember...

CHAPTER EIGHTEEN

Daylight.

Lorenzo hardly registered it at first, couldn't bring himself to believe in what might have been a cruel trick on the planet's part. It was only a pinprick, after all, not enough to make out any details of what might be out there. But it was daylight, nonetheless, and its touch invigorated him.

His right wrist was bruise-blackened, stiffening, and he couldn't wield the pickaxe any more without suffering a lance of pain up his arm. But he and Braxton had chipped most of the bigger pieces of rock away, and Lorenzo's knife was now sufficient to whittle at the packed soil that remained. To make that pinprick wider.

Finally, thankfully, after what seemed like an age in the dark, they pushed their way through a curtain of loose earth and emerged, stumbling and choking, into the dew-pregnant morning. Only a few hours, Lorenzo calculated from the height of the sun, since they had entered the ork mine – but what a difference those few hours had made.

The earth had stopped shaking; Lorenzo didn't know when. Maybe Rogar III had expended its energy – or maybe it was just content with its fresh kills, for now. Nothing stirred in the jungle – and, after so much noise, the silence felt eerie. It heightened Lorenzo's creeping sense of loneliness.

There was a shape in the undergrowth. An ork, lying face-down.

He thought it was sleeping at first, but on closer inspection it proved to be dead. He recognised the multiple scorched entrance wounds of las-rounds on its green skin. A short way from it, he discovered another two greenskin corpses, and a gretchin that had evidently tried to run and had been cut down from behind. They must have escaped the mine before the tunnel collapse, he thought, to find a greater peril waiting outside. He was grateful. In his current condition, even a trio of orks, if they had taken him by surprise, might have proved too much.

Lorenzo sensed, rather than heard, movement behind him, and he knew it could only be one man. He turned to greet Sly Marbo with a cool nod.

The legendary Catachan stood just a few metres away, but Lorenzo could hardly make him out against the greens and browns of his background. He recognised his dead, white eyes, though, and his deep voice, empty of emotion.

'Did you get him?' asked Sly Marbo.

'Big Green?' said Lorenzo. 'Yes, yes, we got him.'

Marbo nodded. He had heard what he needed to know. He left without a footstep or a rustle, seeming to melt into the jungle without moving at all. For a moment, Lorenzo fought the discomfiting feeling that he *hadn't* moved, that he was still there, watching with his white eyes. But that was just paranoia, he knew. Marbo was gone – and it was unlikely Lorenzo would see him again.

Braxton, meanwhile, had sagged to the ground, and was sitting with his back to a tree, knees up to his chest. 'I could sleep for a week,' he moaned.

'Go ahead,' said Lorenzo, checking for jungle lizards in the grass before he sat down beside him. 'For an hour or two, anyway. I'll keep watch – but I think it's safe. I think it'll take Rogar a while to gather its strength, to be ready for its next move.'

'How can you know that?' asked Braxton.

Lorenzo shrugged. 'I just do. It's like I can feel it in the back of my brain. Like I could feel, underground, when the earth was going to move, where the lava was flowing... I've been feeling it ever since the effigy poisoned me.'

'You told Sergeant Greiss you were dying.'

'I thought I was. But this was something different. A part of the planet in me. I think it was trying to... In some weird way, I think it wanted to... communicate.'

'Didn't stop it trying to kill you,' remarked Braxton. 'Or any of us.'

'No,' agreed Lorenzo. 'I think – I *feel* – it didn't have much choice in that.'

'And I expect it'll try again.'

'I expect it will.' It felt strange to say the words, to accept something that a few days earlier he'd have sworn was impossible. If Brains had been here, he reflected, he'd probably have been able to make it all sound rational. As it was, there was only one way Lorenzo could make sense of all he'd been through. 'Remember,' he said, 'when the zombies were stalking us, you said something about the planet itself being intelligent.'

'It seemed that way, at the time.'

'Yes, it did. To all of us. But I'm not sure that was quite right. No, I don't think Rogar III *is* intelligent as such – not in a calculating way. It's more like... like it's just been reacting. To what's been happening on its surface. To the orks. To us. To the fighting. Like it can't help it.'

'Like some kind of an allergy,' suggested Braxton. 'The more we fight, the more we harm the planet, the more deadly the defences it evolves. New plants and animals, springing up on its skin like rashes. Or antibodies.'

'Yes. Like that. And whatever it is, whatever's caused this, I doubt it's something that can be mined. The orks are wasting their time.'

'That's what Rogar wanted you – wanted all of us – to understand,' said Braxton. 'We're all wasting our time.'

Lorenzo looked at the Validian, and he remembered the nervous, apologetic adjutant who had joined their squad four days ago, the stranger whose intrusion he and the other Catachans had so resented. 'You did well,' he said. 'I mean, really well. All the men, good men, who died trying to see this mission through to the end – but you're the one who finished it. You struck the killing blow.'

Braxton waved aside the compliment. 'I did nothing. It was a team effort. You took on the ork leader by yourself, and crippled him. And Sergeant Greiss – if it hadn't been for him, we'd both be dead. I just blundered along at the right moment.'

'You made it this far,' said Lorenzo, 'when most didn't. I guess that makes you one of us, after all.'

'It isn't over yet,' said Braxton. 'We've got a four-day trek ahead of us, if we're to make it back to the encampment.'

'Even if we don't,' said Lorenzo, 'Marbo will. They'll know we did our job. They'll know Big Green is dead.'

'Maybe,' said Braxton, 'but they ought to know more than that. They ought to know about Old Hardhead and the others, what they did for us – what they did for everyone. Don't suppose I'll get to write that story, though.'

Lorenzo grinned. 'You could always try. You get drummed out of the Imperial Guard, I'm sure the Jungle Fighters would have you.'

They sat there, side by side, for a long time, warmed by the sun, exchanging no words but sharing a deep bond of comradeship forged in the fires of their mutual experience. Eventually, Braxton got up and searched the dead orks, finding a water bottle and taking a long swig from it before he passed it to Lorenzo. The Catachan hadn't realised how thirsty he was, and the cold liquid felt blissful against his parched throat.

'So, what do I call you now?' asked Braxton, sitting beside him again.

'I don't know what you mean,' he lied.

'Now you've earned your name. I heard what Greiss said.'

'He didn't want me sacrificing myself instead of him. He wanted his blaze of glory. He was just telling me what I wanted to hear.'

'You really think?' Braxton raised an eyebrow. 'Maybe I didn't know Old Hardhead as well as you did – but tell me this: in all the time he led your squad, did he ever once just tell anyone what they wanted to hear?'

Lorenzo let out a bark of a laugh, and conceded, 'Suppose not.'

'So, what do I call you?'

He sighed. 'Lorenzo, still. Just Trooper Lorenzo. A Catachan's earned name – it's given to him by his comrades. It's like a mark of their respect, a sign that they accept him. And I've got no comrades left.'

'Maybe, when the other platoons hear–'

'Maybe. But hearing about it isn't the same as being there. I'll probably be assigned to another squad, with men who don't know me, and they won't care that my old sergeant *meant* to give me my name if he'd been able to think of one, if he hadn't been too busy charging to his death. I'll have to prove myself all over again. Anyway, what *are* they going to call me? What did I do that was so special? I wanted to... I wanted to be the one who held off the orks so Patch could escape, but he got there first. I wanted to be the one who took out Big Green, but I wasn't strong enough. I wanted to stop the zombies, but Old Hardhead...'

'Sounds to me,' said Braxton, 'like you got a suicide wish – like you think you can't prove yourself unless you die in the process. What was it you just said to me? *"You made it this far..."'*

'By not being brave enough,' Lorenzo muttered.

'By taking everything this planet had to throw at you,' countered Braxton. 'Birds, acid plants, lights, zombies, the earthquake... By facing all that and surviving! You think that was dumb luck? I've been watching you, Lorenzo, and okay, maybe you aren't always the first to stick your head in the lion's mouth, but that's because you think about things, assess the situation, then deal with it – not in a showy way, not looking for glory, but efficiently. You get the job done. You were the first person to give me a chance, to look beyond the fact that Mackenzie had foisted me on you. Maybe it took the others too long to appreciate that; maybe they took you for granted. But I'll bet that's what Old Hardhead Greiss realised at the end there: that you were always there, for him, for all of us, that you were the most dependable man on this squad. I'll bet if he were here now, he'd find a name for you to say all that. Something like... like... "Long Run".'

'"Long Run"?'

'"Long Run" Lorenzo. What do you think? Got a ring to it?'

'I don't know. I...'

Braxton grinned. 'You've got to accept it. You just told me, I'm one of you now.'

'You enjoy throwing my words back in my face, don't you?'

'So I've a right to give you your name. The name you've earned. And I like the sound of Long Run.'

Lorenzo sat back, turned the words over in his head, tried to find an argument against accepting them, and smiled. 'Yes,' he said. 'I like it too.'

'So,' said Braxton, 'what do you say, Long Run? Ready to move off?'

'I thought you wanted to sleep.'

'I feel okay now. More than okay. I think we should get some distance under our belts, while things are quiet.'

Lorenzo nodded. 'Maybe Rogar hasn't covered over the paths we cut through the jungle yet. We're not likely to run into any more orks for a while. I reckon we can make this return trip in three days – less, if we hustle.'

'I guess that depends,' said Braxton, getting to his feet, 'on how hard Rogar III tries to stop us.'

'Whatever it does,' said Lorenzo, straightening his bandana, 'we'll deal with it. We have to. We've got a story to take back. The other squads, the other platoons, they'll be back from fighting orks by now, probably razed a few settlements. They'll want to know how we got on, if any of it was worth the sweat. We have to warn them about Rogar. We have to tell them what it is, what they're doing to it.'

'You think it'll change anything?' asked Braxton.

Lorenzo shook his head. He remembered something Old Hardhead had said, on the morning they'd set out from the encampment. 'Best thing we could do now would be to leave this world alone. That's all it wants. But the Imperium won't leave as long as the orks are here, and the orks won't leave until we do. Neither side can afford to turn its back on the other, so we'll just keep fighting.'

'Over nothing,' said Braxton.

'Over nothing,' Lorenzo agreed. 'And in the meantime, our violence will breed violence in turn. They only started calling Rogar III a deathworld a month ago. You have to wonder, what will it be like in another month? A year? A decade?'

'I don't know,' said Braxton, 'but I'm counting on being around to find out.'

Lorenzo grinned. 'Look forward to it.'

Then, like Sly Marbo before them, they disappeared into the jungle together, in near-total silence. They left only the faintest footprints to suggest that either of them had ever been here. And, a few minutes later, the deathworld had erased even them.

BETTER THE DEVIL

Steve Lyons

When Lorenzo came round...

He was blindfolded, bound and sinking. He could feel the burn of the Catachan sun on one side of his face, the sting of its mud on the other, and the creepers that tied his hands and feet were contracting as they dried, pulling him into an unnatural hunch, his spine already aching with the increasing pressure.

And that wasn't the worst of it.

The smell was like rotten fruit and vinegar, sickly and acidic at the same time. It tripped some primal alarm in Lorenzo's head, made his every nerve scream out.

He shifted, strained, tried to work out how much give he had. Not much, he concluded. Dry shoots cracked beneath his weight and released a fresh vinegar wave. Lorenzo rarely questioned his own senses, but he did so now. He asked himself if he could be hallucinating, if the drugs he'd been force-fed could be fuelling his paranoia, making him imagine his worst fear – because otherwise, if the smell was indeed real, then why wasn't he dead yet?

He *wasn't* dead. That was all he needed to know. At least, so his upbringing told him. It was only a matter of time, though, before that changed. He'd be snapped in two; most likely living out his final minutes a sightless, helpless cripple until the mud claimed him. An hour from now, there'd be no trace he had ever been here.

Lorenzo focused on that immediate test, tried to think past the fear. It was a test not so much of skill, he realised, but of resolve. His bonds had been tied well, as he would have expected; they entangled his body beyond all hope of escape – unless he could change his body's shape.

The fear worked for him now, the need to be free blotting out all other considerations. Lorenzo wasted no time on preparing himself, in anticipation of what was to come. He worked his left shoulder out of its socket, and the lancing pain brought tears to his eyes, almost made him black out, but he clenched his teeth and he breathed through it. The creepers slackened, almost imperceptibly but enough for his needs. He squirmed his way free of them, as the bones in his shoulder ground and crunched and popped. And he snatched the blindfold from his face – to find, to his gut-wrenching horror, that the worst had indeed happened.

Lorenzo reached for his knife, his trusty Catachan fang, and his palm moulded itself to the handle as if it were a part of him, an extra limb. In his own mind, it was. He had carved the blade himself when he was seven, spent the intervening ten years honing it to perfection. It only occurred to him now, with hindsight, that the men who had drugged him, brought him here, might have taken it from him – but no, they would never have dared break that bond.

He hacked at the remaining dry creepers, haste rendering his strokes imprecise, costing him time despite his best efforts to find focus. He freed his feet, at last, and hauled himself out of the sucking mud into an unsteady standing position. His lungs were heaving, partly from exertion, partly from panic at the thought of where he was, of what they had done to him: dumped him in a *den*.

Half-chewed reeds clung to his clothes and his skin, coating him in their stink. His right foot had been resting against a knee-high pile of droppings, which had burnt through the sole of his boot – and he'd just stepped back onto a skull of some kind, which caved in beneath his heel. Many more bones festooned the area, most of them picked clean. The majority of them came from small jungle creatures but more than a few were distinctly human. The fact that the den was empty came as small comfort. Lorenzo's eyes searched the trees for a spark of intelligence, a shuffle of movement, any sign of its occupant's return. Why *wasn't* he dead?

Don't question it, he told himself. Your one chance now is to run, to pray you are faster than it is, because it is certainly stronger, more cunning, more vicious, than you are. But which way? Can't see it, can't sense it. Where is it waiting?

He couldn't believe this was happening, couldn't believe he had been left like this, at the mercy of a monster. The most deadly of predators on this most deadly of worlds.

Lorenzo had seen a Catachan Devil laid low only once, and it had taken four men, each older and far more experienced than he was, to achieve that feat.

He didn't stop to think. He ran, heedless of the many and varied perils about him, the traps they set for the unwary. He ran, trusting to good fortune to keep him safe although good fortune was rare in the jungle. He ran, not pausing to reset his shoulder, letting his left arm hang numb by his side. And he knew that running would do him no good, because it was already too late.

Lorenzo had the Devil's scent on him now – and no distance would be far enough to keep it from hunting him down.

He had to go back.

He couldn't go back.

He had no choice. He had no idea where he was. He had to get back to the Tower, back the way he had come – back the way he had been brought, rather. He had to follow his captors' tracks, the ones they must have left after they had abandoned him. He had to go back to the den.

Lorenzo felt sick at the thought, and his nerves were screaming again.

He couldn't stay here much longer. The surrounding vegetation, dark, dense and twisted, had begun to react to a human presence, to orient itself towards him. It reached out with its branches and its shoots, and some plants had even begun to shuffle in his direction. The movement was slight, too slight to see yet, but Lorenzo could sense it. He could also hear the drone of an insect swarm, and something even closer: a slither, a rustle, a hiss.

The snake, rearing up on its tail, was almost six paces tall, its scaled armour a jet black in hue, a spiky hood flaring about its triangular head as its mouth gaped open. A flying swamp mamba. It must have sensed Lorenzo's preoccupation and used it to get close, hoping for an easy kill – but he'd seen it now, faced it with his blade in hand, and it was suddenly less sure of itself. The mamba swayed slightly, fixing him with its poisonous yellow eyes as if it thought it could hypnotise him. He knew, if he blinked, it would be on him, at his throat. But maybe it could help him too.

Lorenzo shifted his stance a fraction, to suggest tiredness. The snake fell for his feint, and its head stabbed towards him. Its fangs were the length of his hands, drooling clear venom. He sidestepped the lunge and drove his blade toward the exposed back of its head, but pain from his shoulder shot through him, threw his balance, and he did no more than dislodge a few scales.

Living up to its name, the flying mamba shot itself into the air with a casual tail flick, and Lorenzo gasped as its coils whipped around him. His dead left arm was pinned, but he managed to keep the right free and lashed out once more, half-blindly. The snake's head had been coming for his throat again, and he cut a deep gash across its left eye. The head withdrew, but the body increased the pressure about his ribs, attempting to crush him into submission.

Lorenzo's fang went back to work, sawing at the snake's armour until green, viscous blood welled onto his hand. His chest felt as if it would crack, each breath a feat of heroism, and he didn't know which could endure the longer, he or his foe – but the mamba lost its nerve first, its head darting back into striking range in a last, desperate attempt to claim victory. Lorenzo drove his knife between its fangs, up through the roof of its mouth into its tiny brain, and its coils fell limp.

An unexpected weakness rushed to his legs, and he almost fell atop the snake but willed himself to remain upright. Brief as his skirmish had been, it would have attracted attention. The eyes of a dozen creatures, some invisible to him, some lurking on the periphery of his senses, were upon him, looking for a sign that he had been weakened, that now was a good time to chance their own luck against him.

The snake's blood still flowed freely, and Lorenzo bathed his hands in it, rubbed his clothes in it and smeared it across his face before it dried up. The stench of it made him gag, but it masked the far more dangerous smell of the den – at least to Lorenzo's nose. It was unlikely that the keener senses of a Catachan Devil would be fooled – but they might at least be momentarily confused, and that was something.

He approached the den from downwind, hoping this too might give him some small advantage. His shoulder still throbbed with the ghost of the agony he'd felt as he had braced himself against a gnarled tree and pushed it back into place. Lorenzo trod as lightly as he could and kept his breathing shallow, almost silent, although it was still deafening to his ears.

Reaching a suitable vantage point, he teased aside thin, whip-like branches and peered through the gap thus created. He allowed himself a faint sigh of relief as he saw everything as he'd left it, the den trampled and broken from his intrusion but nobody and nothing else present. Maybe, he thought, its owner was dead. Maybe his captors had found the den empty and decided to use it to play a joke on him. It was unlikely, though. Not much could keep a Devil from returning to its lair to die – and 'Barracuda' Creek hadn't seemed like a man with a sense of humour.

Lorenzo circled the den, keeping a wide berth to get no more of its scent on him than he already had. The first trail leading from it, he uncovered in short order – but his instincts told him it was too obvious, and he carried on searching.

The second trail was better hidden, every care taken not to disturb the undergrowth, but there were signs for the trained eye; a broken twig here, a branch pushed aside there, an unnatural smoothness to the ground where footprints had been brushed out. It was this trail, then, that he followed. And he knew he had made the right decision when, some twenty minutes later, he came upon a body.

It was lying facedown in a patch of weeds; a young man, like him, squat and powerfully muscled even by their people's standards. Lorenzo couldn't see what had killed him at first – he couldn't get too close until he had ruled out infection; some jungle-borne diseases killed at a dozen paces – but then he saw the puncture wound between the man's shoulder blades, and his blood chilled.

The Devil must have crept up on him, driven the poisonous barb of its tail into its victim's back before he could turn. And it could only have happened a few hours ago, because the body was intact, not yet stripped to its skeleton by the jungle's plants and its smaller scavengers.

The man was holding something: an improvised spear with a sharpened stone head. It was crude, evidently assembled in a hurry. Crouching by his side now, Lorenzo prised the weapon from his cold, stiff fingers. He had no compunction at all about so doing: the spear was no use to this fallen soldier any more, but it might save Lorenzo's life. The dead man's fang, on the other hand, he took as a mark of respect, hoping that one day he could return it to his clan for burial. He tucked the blade into his boot and returned to the trail.

He thought he knew now what Creek had done, had had his men hogtie the Catachan Devil, at insane risk to their own lives, and haul it away from here. A few kilometres would have been far enough, then they would have set the monster loose and run for it. Denied an immediate chance of revenge, the Devil's first thought would have been to find its way back home – where by now it must have found a vandalised den and the culprit's inviting scent trail waiting for it.

It was behind him. Lorenzo didn't know how far behind, but it was there. A short head start was all he had been given. A chance of survival, but a slim one.

He couldn't fight it. He couldn't imagine doing such a thing – and if it came to it, he would certainly need more weapons than he had to even try. Nor could he outpace it, not while he was following in his tormentors' too-faint footprints.

All he could do was wait for it. Wait for the Devil, watch for it in every shadow, listen for it in every sound. Wait for the Devil, and hope to be better prepared for its attack than his predecessor had been... The last man to take Creek's test, to travel this route... The man whose pain-contorted corpse would remain a vivid image in the space behind Lorenzo's eyelids for some time to come.

It was almost a relief when the waiting ended and terror struck.

Lorenzo had been right about his stalker: it was stealthy. Had he not known it was coming, he might have blamed the rustling sound behind him on a creature far smaller than it was, might have missed the faint but familiar scent on the air. Even with those warnings, he barely had time to turn, to drop into a defensive crouch, to raise his fang, as the Devil came at him.

It was an old one, too. A big one. Big and nasty. At least twenty pairs of legs. It thrust its maw into Lorenzo's face, its mandibles click-clacking, acidic drool spraying his cheeks, and looking down its throat was like staring into an infernal pit. The Devil's front claws were gigantic, snapping at him, attempting to gain purchase. Lorenzo pushed his newly-acquired spear into one of them, jamming it open, and he braced an arm across the creature's thorax, using his leverage to force the head up, away from him. At the same time, he fended off the second claw with his fang, but its blade glanced off an armoured carapace and the Devil succeeded in gouging a chunk of flesh from his right calf, eliciting a hoarse yell from him. It was too strong for Lorenzo, too heavy, bearing him to the ground, and he still had its tail to worry about.

He saw its shadow over him, felt the downdraught of its approach, and he knew he had to time his next move perfectly. He shifted his weight, ducked, rolled beneath the Devil's front section, even as its tail smacked into the ground where he had just been and buried itself. The Devil was off-balance, but not for long. Lorenzo made a run for it, impulsively lashing out at a blood-wasp hive so that its occupants swarmed out into his attacker's path. They were no threat to it, not like they would have been to him, but Lorenzo prayed they might blind it for a second before they realised what they'd taken on and abandoned their home forever.

He didn't dare look back to check, knew he couldn't spare the instant it would take him to do so. The Devil was probably reaching for him, bringing up its tail to strike him down, and like its last victim he wouldn't even see it coming.

But the killing blow never came, and Lorenzo was clear, he could no longer sense his bulkier, slower pursuer at his heels. He had escaped it. For now.

The whole encounter had taken less than ten seconds from start to finish. Lorenzo was astonished, and proud of himself, that he had lasted so long.

He maintained a punishing pace for the next few hours, though he didn't know where he was going: the trail was well and truly lost now, and Lorenzo didn't dare go back to search for it again because he knew what would be waiting for him. Instead he looked for higher ground where he could, and hoped to come across a hilltop or cliff edge from which he could survey the surrounding terrain.

He had been heading in roughly the same direction – north-north-west – since he'd left the den, but he wouldn't have put it past Creek and his men to have led him this far only to double back on themselves.

For the time being, however, orientation was the least of his problems.

It would take a while for the Devil to catch up to him, but catch up it certainly would. Its breed was nothing if not tenacious – and though, when Lorenzo was at his best, the Devil couldn't match him for speed, he couldn't be at his best all the time. Already, his wounded leg was beginning to tell, to slow him down, and he was tiring. He tried not to think about how long it had been since he had last slept. Slept properly, that was, because the drug-induced coma of the morning had hardly recharged him.

When he felt safe to do so, he slowed down and started to look for plants from which he could tease water, leaves with antiseptic properties that could dress his wound. Neither of these tasks were simple: on Catachan, the flora was more likely to kill than to cure, and Lorenzo needed all his concentration, couldn't afford the slightest slip, if he was to sift what little good there was from the downright fatal.

Lying on his stomach, he reached between the branches of a brainleaf for edible berries, knowing that the slightest breath of air would alert the plant to his presence; cause it to fire its tendrils into him. If that happened, he would no longer be Lorenzo, no longer be a man at all, but the brainleaf's unthinking meat puppet. This ought to have been a two-man job: one to obtain the berries while the other kept watch over him. Were the Catachan Devil to appear now – if so much as a heretic ant were to happen by, for that matter – it would be the end of him.

The operation was successful however – moderately refreshed, his leg newly bandaged with strips of his own shirt, Lorenzo moved on.

Nightfall changed the character of the jungle, while making it no less dangerous. The creatures of the daytime retired, and the air was filled with the chirruping and the hissing of their nocturnal counterparts. The thick canopy kept in much of the sweltering heat of the day, but the shadows grew deeper and more numerous so that lurking threats were far harder to detect. Some plants curled up their blossoms and slept, while others awoke to dance in the darkness.

Lorenzo had been following the rushing sound of a river, and he came to its bank now. The water was clear, glistening, inviting, and his dry throat tensed in anticipation of relief – but the algae on its surface was of a toxic type, and one known to spawn a flesh-eating virus. There would be no relief here.

He shinned up a tall tree, careful not to damage its bark and unleash the poison spores beneath it. From up here he could see a small patch of sky and identify its stars, thankful that the night wasn't overcast, that acidic clouds weren't gathering. Lorenzo knew now, at last, where on Catachan he was, and where he had to go – and fortunately, the blind wanderings of the evening had not brought him too far off course. He could still reach the Ashmadia Tower before he dropped, he figured. If he could stay alive that long.

For the hundredth time, he let his thoughts drift back three days, to a room on the Tower's mid-level and his first – his only – face-to-face meeting with Sergeant 'Barracuda' Creek. He ran their conversation through his mind, trying to work out what he'd said, what he had done, to raise the other man's ire, to make him think he deserved this, deserved to have a monster put on his tail.

'I don't think you're ready,' Creek had told him bluntly.

'But I've done all the training,' he'd protested. 'I've passed your tests. I've done everything you asked of me.'

'Oh yeah, you've gone through the motions well enough – but I want more than that, Lorenzo. I want to know there's fire in your belly.'

'Fire' was one thing, but this... No one could have expected him to deal with this, to outfight a Devil alone. Not at his young age. *Not at any age...* And a fierce resolve swelled in Lorenzo at that thought: a resolve to prove himself. To slay the Devil after all, and to march up to the Tower with its tail slung over his shoulder, its carcass dragged behind him. He imagined Creek's face when he did so: the surprise and the grudging admiration in that spiteful son-of-a-grox's sunken black eyes.

Then his thoughts returned to reality. He remembered burning spittle on his face, the *whoosh* of a death-dealing tail against his back, and the mental picture faded.

Lorenzo's wounded right leg chimed in with a mournful throb. He could feel it stiffening. He thought it might have been infected, but there was no point removing the dressing as there was little he could do about it anyway, out here. He could no longer focus through the pain, no longer keep up his accelerated pace, which meant that the Devil – for he knew it was still following him, even if he had detected no sign of it for hours – would be starting to close in.

Lorenzo thought long and hard before he eased himself into the river. It was another way of masking his trail, of delaying his pursuer, but it would also expose him to untold other dangers, dangers he would be less able to detect in the waist-high water. He knew that reptiles and aquatic rodents concealed themselves in the cracks of the riverbed, and that some types of weed could drag him under in a heartbeat if he stepped on them. And indeed, he had only been wading for a few minutes when he disturbed a small nest of leeches.

Fortunately, only four younglings were at home, and Lorenzo's Catachan fang despatched three of them in two strokes, the second thrust lopping off two heads at once. He cursed, however, as he realised that the fourth leech had sunk its circular jaws through the threadbare leather of his damaged boot. He pulled himself onto the bank, and tore the bloated creature painfully from his right heel. He smacked it into the ground so that it burst and showered him with his own stolen blood.

It was about an hour later that Lorenzo saw the first sign of an altogether more worrying presence. Not that he could have missed it. A moment ago, the foliage around him had grown thick and high, crowding each side of the river; now, suddenly, it fell away to leave him wading through a large, open area.

Immediately, he knew this was no natural glade, nor had it been cleared by human hands or tools. The ground was coated with a glutinous brown slime: plant and animal life had once thrived here, but all had been reduced to this. The stench of decay hung heavy in the air – and, underpinning it, a subtler burnt odour.

Lorenzo had seen devastation like this before, more than once. He had been just three years old when his mother had shown him the devolved remains of a Catachan fortress, much like the one in which they lived and none too distant from it. It had probably taken just one slip, she'd said, one small misstep, to bring about the end. The hapless culprit had probably never even known what he'd done, hadn't lived long enough to realise he had disturbed a barking toad.

The galaxy's most poisonous creature, and one with a unique defence mechanism. Uniquely explosive, that was.

Lorenzo hauled himself out of the water, knowing that for the next few kilometres he would have to proceed with extra caution, needed to know exactly where he was stepping. The toad that had blown itself up here had been a small one, its blast diameter less than two hundred metres – but still, Lorenzo knew that nothing would ever grow in this area again.

And, where there had been one barking toad, there were bound to be others.

Sure enough, he had barely crossed the dead zone and re-entered the trees when he heard a distinctive cough-like cry from ahead, to his right, from the river – then an answering call from the left, too close by for comfort. Lorenzo's stomach tightened at the thought of the peril before him – and of how it would slow him down, and make him far easier prey for the one still closing in from behind.

But perhaps, he thought, there was some hope after all – some way in which he could set one imminent threat against the other, and come out on top of both.

It wasn't long before he found what he was looking for. The barking toad was deceptively small and fragile-seeming – and, unlike most of the creatures of Catachan, it didn't appear remotely resentful of a human presence. Lorenzo supposed its kind was well used to being left alone. He followed it for a little over ten minutes – from a distance, of course – during which it hopped about without apparent aim, as if it were playing with him. Then it sprang into a patch of weeds, and was lost.

Lorenzo searched again, and this time he had more luck. A second toad led him back to the river, where he was just in time to see it slipping into a nook in the bank. He could tell from the guttural sounds that greeted it that there were three or four more toads in there: a family unit, he supposed. Perfect for his needs.

He gathered creepers from the surrounding trees, started to twist and to knot them together. It was fiddly work, and time-consuming, and Lorenzo's tired eyes began to blur. He found a sizeable enough boulder, threaded his makeshift rope about it, and hauled it onto his good shoulder, and from there into the V-shaped crook of a stout tree. By now, he feared very much that he had been still too long, that the Devil could appear at any moment – and as before, that fear only slowed him further.

At last, though, his work was done, and he stepped back to inspect the results. He had rigged his tripwire high so as not to be triggered by anything too small – but in the darkness, even he would have been hard-pushed to see it without forewarning. Anyway, as a rule, Catachan Devils didn't tread carefully. They had no need.

At least, Lorenzo was banking on this particular Devil believing that, on it walking confidently into his wire, yanking the boulder from its tree. The rock would smack right into the toads' burrow like a wrecking ball – and its four or five occupants would react in the only way they knew how. Even if some of them could contain themselves, he only needed one to panic, to spark a chain reaction...

Would it be enough? Lorenzo didn't know. He had to believe it might be. The armour hadn't yet been forged that a cloud of barking toad poison couldn't liquefy in a heartbeat – and this cloud would be four or five times normal strength. But then, no man-made armour was as strong as the natural plating of an elderly Devil – and the flesh beneath those plates was almost as tough.

He moved on, parting company with the river now as it bent toward the north, and he waited and listened and prayed to the God-Emperor that his plan would succeed, because he didn't know what else he could try if it didn't.

The explosion came sooner than he had anticipated. It rocked the ground beneath him, almost threw him off his feet. Lorenzo fought down a lump in his throat as he turned to find a thick green cloud blossoming behind him, vegetation wilting in its embrace, and he knew if he had been a fraction slower, taken a minute longer over the setting of his trap, he would have been caught in that cloud himself.

But he hadn't been slower, he told himself. He'd survived. Again. And this time he had done more than that. He had – could this even be possible? – he had triumphed over his foe. Done what few men had achieved. He, Lorenzo, just seventeen years old, single-handedly, had faced down and killed – *killed* – a Catachan Devil.

...maybe...

He didn't know what to do, then. He stood and watched as the green cloud settled, and a part of him longed to go back, once it was safe to do so, to find the Devil's remains and to verify his kill. Images of a triumphant return, a hero's welcome, played in his mind again – but what if there *were* no remains? What if the Devil had been reduced, as everything in its vicinity must have been, to sludge? Every second Lorenzo spent in the jungle, alone, wearying, increased the risk to his life – was it wise to prolong his time out here for what was, at best, a small chance of glory?

And what if the Devil was still alive? What if it was waiting for him?

It was with reluctance, then, that he tore himself away from that spot. It was with a sense of shame, too, because he felt he had made the wrong choice, the cowardly choice, and he was sure that 'Barracuda' Creek would delight in telling him so.

The sky was beginning to lighten, the first insects of the morning striking up a low, growling hum while other, bigger creatures stirred in the undergrowth. Through his growing fatigue, Lorenzo heard the screeches of carrion birds as they woke to discover his recent handiwork, now a few kilometres behind him. Not that the barking toads would have left them too much to feed on.

He climbed another tree to take a final bearing from the fading stars – and found to his relief that he could see his destination. The Ashmadia Tower was by some way the tallest structure on Catachan – conceitedly so – and the Imperial Eagle still gleamed at its black tip, despite the best efforts of the elements to erode it.

He had disturbed a retiring bat, which flew at him and tore at his face and hair. With his fang, Lorenzo impaled it against the tree trunk – but a dizzy wave crashed over him, and he almost fell from his perch. He longed to close his eyes, to sleep – but he knew that if he did, alone out here, he wouldn't wake up again. He buoyed himself with the knowledge that his trial was almost over. If only his temples weren't pounding so, and his muscles so weak from dehydration...

He dropped from the tree, but his bad leg gave way and he landed heavily on his backside. He forced himself to stand, to march on, making himself focus on nothing more than that endeavour. Scan the ground ahead, left foot forward, drag the right foot after it, repeat... and he thought about the Catachan Devil, and convinced himself that he must have killed it, that Creek would be able to verify that fact, that he'd get his hero's welcome after all – and Lorenzo wasn't about to miss that, couldn't bear to have come so close, achieved so much, to fall at this final hurdle.

He saw the patch of spikers just in time. They were laid out in a thin band, as tall as he was, spreading into the trees to each side of him, and he couldn't guess how long it would take him to go round them.

He fell back on an old Catachan trick instead: he flushed a small lizard out from a nearby hole, and swiped at it with his fang as it spat venom at him. He left it alive but wounded, blocking its attempts to flee past him until it had just one way to go.

The spikers shot their payloads, and Lorenzo leapt for cover. The air was suddenly thick with black, needle-thin, thorns, and his protective tree trembled with the thuds of their multiple impacts. As soon as those impacts had ceased, he made a run for it.

He ploughed through the denuded plants, moving as fast as his leg would allow him. Already, the spikers' leaves were bristling anew, and he flung himself to the ground as he drew clear of them, only just ahead of their second discharge.

Hundreds of fresh thorns sprayed over him, but they'd been aimed too high from too far away, and they covered his back without piercing his skin. He picked himself up, breathlessly, and shook the thorns off him. And his eyes alighted upon the luckless lizard, now wandering confused and already sprouting the first prickly leaf of its own. Soon, there would be one more spiker in this patch: an unusually small one.

He gathered up some thorns, and carefully broke a few open, dripping their poison onto the tip of his blade. A dozen more, he bundled together and held at arm's length, gingerly, ensuring that none could scratch him. The Devil may have been dead – oh, please, let it be dead – but there were other creatures out there.

He was being followed again.

He hadn't been sure at first. Tiredness was making his head swim, and Lorenzo's senses had started to deceive him, made him see threats in the random shapes of the foliage, made him fear he might be too distracted to see the real threats when they came. He jumped at every shifting shadow cast by the rising sun, every slight sound borne on the morning breeze – and he had blamed his own sleep-deprived paranoia for piecing those subtle signs together, unreliable though they were, to paint a nightmare picture for his mind's eye.

That was what he had thought at first. Not now.

He hadn't yet clapped eyes on his pursuer. It was animal, though, not vegetable, as he knew that none of Catachan's plants could have kept pace with him for so long. It was big, too: Lorenzo could tell this from the force with which twigs snapped beneath its feet, from the pattern of displacement of the bushes in its path, though he had barely glimpsed this latter. Too big to be one of Creek's men, presenting him with one final challenge. Almost big enough to be...

Don't think that!

...a razor-tusk? But no, a razor-tusk wouldn't have had the intelligence to stalk a man, to remain unseen, and this thing could certainly do that. Even when Lorenzo slipped behind a bush and held his breath and the creature couldn't have heard or seen him, it fell still and silent too, and almost made him think it wasn't there after all...

...until he resumed his trek, at which point all those subtle signs returned.

Why was it hiding from him? If this creature was so big, so smart, then it must have known it was more than a match for Lorenzo in his current condition. Unless...

The only thing that makes sense. It has to be... No, it can't be!

Unless the creature was tired and hurt too, too weak to risk a full-frontal assault and yet so stubborn, bloody-minded, that it couldn't bring itself to abandon the hunt. Unless it had been compelled to change its tactics, to watch and wait for the moment of maximum advantage, for its prey to make a mistake. Unless...

He didn't have far to go now. Ashmadia Tower was little more than an hour away. If Lorenzo could grit his teeth and ignore the throbbing pain in his leg, if he could concentrate for just that short time, sort the real threats from the imaginary ones, if he could keep up a good enough front that his pursuer might think it not worth engaging him and a brisk enough pace that it couldn't reach him anyway... if Lorenzo could do all that, and if in addition he didn't run into any more surprises... maybe then, just maybe, even though he had failed this test, he could at least survive it.

He cursed himself for his pride, for having allowed it to lead him to here. Why had he had to confront Creek? Why hadn't he been content with domestic duties, until he was ready for more? So, most of his friends had been shipped out already; so he'd feared what people would say about him if he was kept behind... They would say those things anyway, now. Creek had been right about him all along, he thought. No fire. He must have pitted him against that Devil in order to prove that very point. He would probably be glad to be rid of an under-achieving trooper.

Something shifted beneath Lorenzo's foot – and he could almost have wept as he realised what he'd done: allowed his mind to wander again, let his gaze lose focus. Blundered into a mantrap, a full six paces across. It had felt his weight, and its edges were already curling, about to snap shut. He tried to leap from it, but too late, and he was far, far too slow.

The plant swallowed his trailing right leg, pain slicing through him as its teeth dug into his wounded thigh. It was all Lorenzo could do to keep from being yanked off his remaining foot. Almost reflexively, he wielded his fang and began to cut through the mantrap's tough outer shell: he knew from experience that he could free himself before it could digest much more than his trouser leg and the top layer of his skin – under normal circumstances, that was.

His stalker was no longer trying to hide.

The Catachan Devil was suddenly, shockingly, *there*, as if its shape had formed out of the trees themselves, and it was barrelling towards him with a cry that was half-roar, half-screech, and this time he couldn't dodge it, couldn't run from it. It pounced on Lorenzo, knocking him backwards so his left foot floundered in the air and only the mantrap's hold on his right leg kept him from falling. He was watching for its tail, knowing that off-balance as he was he wouldn't be able to avoid it this time – and a claw slipped by his defences and clamped itself to his right arm, numbing his fingers so he could no longer feel his fang though he clung to it doggedly.

The other claw came for him, and he twisted his left arm out of its path but could do no more than that. The claw bit into his ribs, puncturing the skin, and Lorenzo knew he had only a second to live, that the Devil was about to rend him apart.

With his left, free hand, he was still clutching spiker thorns. It was all he could do to thrust them in his attacker's direction, the whole bundle, but somehow he got lucky. He had expected their points to snap against armour; instead, they pierced something soft. And the Catachan Devil howled. It actually howled.

Its claws flopped open, and it reared away from him, Lorenzo managing to give the thorns one last, savage twist before they were ripped from his hand.

It was only now that he got a good look at his foe, really took in what he was seeing – as it writhed in pain, its head down, its many legs twitching and thrashing.

It was injured – badly so. There was certainly no doubt that, when Lorenzo's barking toad bomb had gone off, the Devil had been at ground zero. Toad poison had eaten into its carapace, apparently causing whole patches of it to melt, to be sloughed off like an old skin. It was through one such hole that Lorenzo had been able to strike, and his spiker thorns still protruded from it, heads buried in the leathern, dark flesh beneath. They had drawn blood: thick, black, vinegar-stinking Catachan Devil blood. He didn't think he had seen that before.

The poison had gotten into one of the Devil's eyes, causing it to distend, to run like a half-fried egg – and a number of its legs were also mottled and twisted, some tapering to fused stumps. Its tail seemed intact but badly burnt, and it trailed across the ground limply as if its nerves had been destroyed – which, Lorenzo thought, would explain why the Devil hadn't employed it against him this time.

It could only have been a few knife thrusts away from death. He had done that to it. And he could finish the job right now. He could take it.

If only he could reach it.

The Devil was visibly rallying, throwing off the effects of this latest dose of venom. By the time he could escape the mantrap's embrace, Lorenzo knew it would be on him again, back in a position of strength. But the force of the Devil's attack had had an unintended consequence; its feet had churned up mud, exposed the plant's roots and hacked into them, weakening them. The mantrap's hold on Lorenzo remained firm; its hold on the earth was less so.

His hands trembling, he put his blade to work in a sawing action, weakening that hold further, his own tiredness forgotten in the adrenaline high of the moment. First one green strand

and then two more parted, but the shape of the Devil was always lurking in his peripheral vision – and as it began to recover its composure, to draw itself up to its full height again, Lorenzo knew that, ready or not, he had to act now.

He threw himself at the creature, his right arm fully extended, pulling the mantrap after him, elated as its roots clung and strained and tore and gave just – *just* – enough for him to be able to drive his fang, his still poison-tipped fang, into the Devil's gaping mouth. It roared again, struck out blindly, caught the side of Lorenzo's head and almost snapped his neck with the force of the blow.

For a second he couldn't see anything, just black stars exploding. Then he blinked away his dizziness, and he saw the Catachan Devil looming over him...

...for a second, then it let out an agonised shudder and its legs splayed out beneath it and, with a resounding crash, it flopped onto its stomach.

Lorenzo leapt onto its back, found an exposed patch of flesh and focused all his attention upon that, upon bringing his knife arm up, down, up, down, stabbing away and just praying he could dig his way down to something vital. A claw came grasping for him, but he batted it away and he kept on cutting, cutting, cutting, establishing a mechanical rhythm until there was nothing left in the world but him and the slab of warm meat beneath him and his fang and the black blood in which he was steadily becoming coated, and he wasn't even sure the Devil was alive, didn't dare stop to check, but he knew he had beaten it. He could taste his victory.

And then all he could taste was mud, because the Devil had found a last vestige of strength and it had bucked and thrown him, and he tried to stand but he could feel the mantrap on his leg reasserting itself, and he let out a scream of frustration as he was dragged away from his nemesis, watched it slip through his fingers.

Then it was gone, swallowed by the surrounding jungle as quickly as it had emerged from it, and Lorenzo was alone and bloodied and caked in dirt and his trapped right leg was stinging, and he hammered his fists into the ground and he screamed out again and again, because he had been so close this time, so close to achieving what he had once thought impossible.

So close. Not quite close enough.

When Lorenzo came round...

He was lying on his back in a clean, white bed, staring up at bright lights in a black ceiling, and the first thing that rushed back to him was a feeling of shame. They must have carried him into the Tower, Creek's men, after he had... had...

He was starting to remember, through a fog of confusion: half-walking, half-crawling, dragging himself across the tree line, and Creek had been there... hadn't he?... and Lorenzo had been determined to meet him on his feet, to look him square in his black eyes, but he'd been too weak...

He was not alone.

His heart leapt at the realisation, and he scrambled onto his elbows, tried to sit to attention, but he couldn't quite make it. He felt nauseous – anti-plague drugs, he guessed – and he could taste the chalky residue of water tablets on his tongue.

Sergeant 'Barracuda' Creek patted him on the shoulder in a curiously paternal manner. 'Easy there, trooper,' the old soldier growled, 'you've had a tough time of it, so I hear; it cost us three cans of synth-skin just to fix up that leg of yours.'

'I... I almost had it, sergeant,' he stammered. 'I was so close, but it ran from me and I couldn't... Let me try again. Next year. I can train harder, *try* harder.'

'You know the problem you've caused me, don't you? The mess you made of that Devil – I hear it's cowering in its den right now, gonna be laid up a whole lot longer'n you are. Means I'll have to break in a brand new critter for the next initiation test.'

'One more try,' Lorenzo pleaded. 'I can beat it next time. I know I can.'

'I don't think you're hearing me, trooper,' said Creek. 'I wasn't too sure about you, didn't think you were ready to go off-world, not yet. But you did a good job out there. Real good. In fact, a whole better'n most. In the long run.'

Lorenzo tried to say something, but no words came out. He didn't dare *let* the words out, didn't dare believe what he thought he was hearing.

'What,' said Creek, his lips curling to expose a row of small, pointed teeth, 'you thought you had to kill that thing? I wouldn't have expected that from a vet, let alone from a newbie. You didn't have to kill the Devil, Lorenzo. You just had to survive.'

And then the half-smile faded, and Creek straightened up, very much the dour, brusque military man of a few days earlier again. 'You ship out in seventy-two hours,' he barked. 'The medics say you'll be fit by then, or I'll want to know the reason why. You're going to war now, Trooper Lorenzo – and if you think I've been tough on you... well, let's just see how you cope with a real challenge!'

REBEL WINTER

Steve Parker

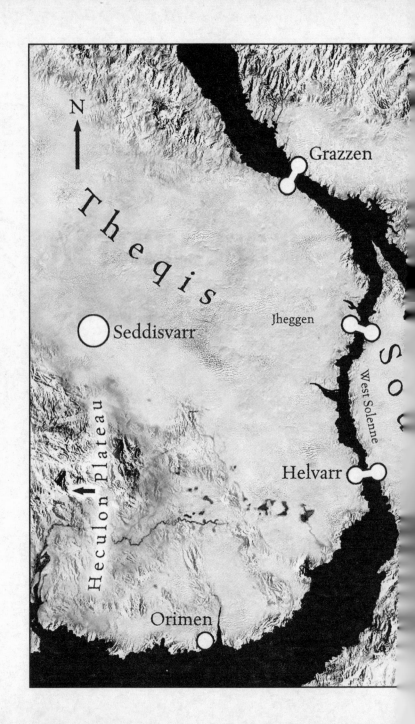

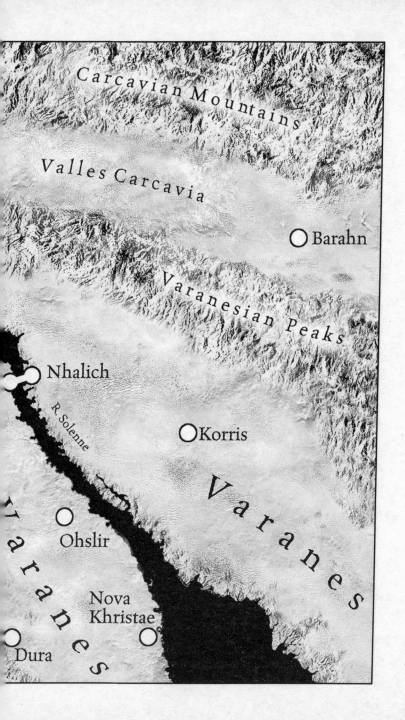

'Secession – let a single rebel world go unpunished and countless more will rise up, all clamouring for those religious and economic freedoms better known to loyal citizens of the Imperium as heresy and ingratitude.

'On Danik's World, the seeds of rebellion were planted in the deep snows of an ice age that ravaged the planet for two thousand years. It began when volcanic eruptions on the southern continent filled the atmosphere with debris and plunged the land into darkness. The sudden climatic change wiped out over half the human population and reduced planetary productivity to almost nothing. On countless occasions in the years that followed, one loyalist governor after another begged the Administratum for aid. Eventually, the Administratum approved the deferment of Imperial tributes, but more direct aid in the form of food and technologies was repeatedly denied. Imperial coffers, the Danikkin were told, were being drained by anti-xenos campaigns throughout the segmentum.

'When Danikkin scientists finally announced the beginning of a slow return to warmer temperatures, the population had climbed to two-thirds of its pre-catastrophe figure. An estimated ninety-three per cent of that population supported open revolt against the Imperium. The central figure behind this movement was Lord General Graush Vanandrasse, High Commander of the Danikkin Planetary Defence Force.

'Vanandrasse had spent his life rising through the ranks of the PDF, finally attaining absolute command at the age of sixty-one. Mere months after his accession, he led his forces in a bloody coup against troops loyal to the Planetary Governor. He celebrated victory by renaming his force the Danikkin Independence Army. To ensure absolute loyalty to his vision of planetary independence, he established a brutal organization of elite officers called the Special Patriotic Service.

'Agents of this so-called Special Patriotic Service publicly executed the legitimate Planetary Governor and his family, and sent a formal notice of secession to the Administratum.

'Two years later, in 766.M41, Lord Marshal Graf Harazahn of the Vostroyan Firstborn – then charged with overseeing all ground operations in the Second Kholdas War – relented before pressure from the Administratum and agreed to send a small punitive force to Danik's World. Twelfth Army was formed for this purpose and deployed under the leadership of General Vogor Vlastan – a man for whom Harazahn allegedly bore little genuine respect.

'Twelfth Army's orders were to crush the Danikkin rebels, restore order, and return to action in the Second Kholdas War with all due haste. As the old adage goes, however, few plans survive first contact with the enemy.

'The climate and the rebels were bad enough, and Twelfth Army underestimated both. But there was another force present on Danik's World for which General Vlastan and his Guardsmen were unprepared – a force that would claim all too many of Vostroya's firstborn sons.

'The old foe, you see, had got there first.'

Extract: *Hammer and Shield: Collected Essays on the History of the Second Kholdas War*, eds. Commissar-Colonel (Ret.) Keisse von Holh (716.M41-805.M41) & Major (Ret.) Wyllum Imrilov (722.M41-793.M41)

A TRIAL BEGINS

The Exedra Udiciarum Seddisvarr was a grand place indeed, as grand and dark as an Imperial mausoleum. The ancient court had stood for millennia, echoing with the sounds of innumerable trials, both military and civil. Stylised images of the God-Emperor and His saints stared with unblinking eyes from great stained-glass windows, weighing the souls of the innocent and the guilty.

Tapestries hung from the dark marble walls, their fading colours struggling to contrast the aura of the room: here, an image of Tech-Magos Benandanti, who'd rediscovered the Kholdas Cluster in M37 and restored it to its rightful place in the Imperial fold; there, Saint Hestor, who'd led loyalist forces against the dread armies of the Idols Dark, which had spilled from the warpstorm at the cluster's centre in M39. Around these worthy historical figures, pre-Winter Danikkin iconography spoke of better days, days before the people had turned from their God-Emperor's light.

Had the faith of these people remained unbroken, the Vostroyan Firstborn might never have set foot on Danik's World. Dead men might yet live. Then again, thought Captain Grigorius Sebastev, as well to die on this world as on some other, so long as one dies well.

As commanding officer of the Firstborn Sixty-Eighth Infantry Regiment's Fifth Company, Sebastev went where his Emperor needed him. It was as simple as that. For now, he stood patiently in the dock, awaiting the beginning of his trial, uncomfortable and self-conscious in his ill-fitting dress uniform.

He was a stocky man, short for a Vostroyan, but thickset and powerful. In the days since his return to Command HQ in Seddisvarr, with solid meals and little to do in his cell but practise the forms of the *ossbokh-vyar*, he'd quickly regained the size and strength he'd lost since being posted to the Eastern Front. His bright red jacket, piped with shining gold brocade, strained to contain the thick muscles of his chest and back.

He'd have given anything for the familiar comfort of battle fatigues and a greatcoat. Strutting and posturing like the high-born officers had never interested him. Sebastev was a fighter, a brawler. His men called him the Pit-Dog, though rarely to his face since it tended to ignite his temper.

A dozen servo-skulls drifted overhead, carrying braziers filled with hot coals, but the air would hardly be warmer by the time the judges took their seats. That would set them in foul spirits from the outset. No matter. His future was in the Emperor's hands, as it had always been.

Sebastev shifted his gaze to the most central of the hall's windows and looked up at the glowing image of the Emperor. 'Light of all Mankind,' he said, uncaring that the bailiffs behind him would hear, 'I've lived my life on the battlefield, serving your will. Let me die doing so.'

Someone coughed off to Sebastev's right, and echoes chased each other up the stone walls to the shadowy reaches of the high ceiling. Sebastev turned.

'Really, captain,' said a man sitting alone on the observers' benches, 'must you be so gloomy this early in the morning?'

It was the commissar. He looked well rested, healthy. A few days away from the fighting had taken the sunken look from his cheeks. His oiled black hair shone as it had when they'd first met. The ubiquitous cap, the symbol of the man's rank, sat neatly on the bench by his side.

'Commissar,' said Sebastev with a nod. He was surprised to note a feeling of comfort at the man's presence. No matter what transpired during this hearing, the commissar had been right there in the thick of things. He'd played his part and knew the truth. But how would he testify? For all they'd been through together, the man was still something of an unknown quantity to Sebastev. He was brave enough, yes, and had demonstrated his dedication and loyalty to the Emperor, but he was also *chevek,* an outsider, a non-Vostroyan. The minds of such men were frustratingly difficult to comprehend.

A flicker of movement on the balcony above the benches caught Sebastev's eye. He lifted his gaze from the commissar and saw a curious duo sitting in the balcony's front row. Two figures diametrically opposed in bearing stared back at him, a man and a woman, though the term 'man' seemed hardly adequate to describe the former.

The woman sat hunched, almost drowning in the black folds of her robe. Her back was bent, her body twisted with age. She appeared no larger than a child of ten, but from the shadows of her cowl, her eyes shone with wisdom and a sharp intellect.

Was she Danikkin? An off-worlder? The sight of her made Sebastev uncomfortable, but he couldn't fathom why.

Next to the crone, dwarfing her utterly, sat a man who seemed nothing less than a statue cut from living marble. His skin was the white of daylit snow, and his spotless robes did little to mask the gargantuan body beneath. He was absolutely hairless, reinforcing the illusion of stone construction, but that illusion was shattered when Sebastev met the man's gaze. His eyes were blood-red, even where they should have been white.

Sebastev had never seen such a figure, so ghostly and yet so overwhelmingly solid, in all his travels across the Imperium of Man. Who were these people? And what in the blasted warp were they doing at this trial?

He might have asked them had the silence not been shattered

at that moment. Doors banged as they were thrown open, and the air filled with the tumult of booted feet on marble flooring. A mixed crowd of Munitorum staff and Vostroyan military personnel poured into the room, chattering loudly as they took their seats.

Sebastev scanned the crowd for familiar faces, but could find no sign of his men. He wasn't surprised. In all likelihood, *Old Hungry,* or General Vogor Vlastan, as the bastard was more properly known, had forbidden their presence among the spectators. Sebastev turned his eyes from the crowd and faced forward, just in time to see the door of the judges' chambers crack open. A wash of warmth and orange light spilled into the hall. The general's military judiciary entered slowly and in single file.

Sebastev couldn't keep a scowl from his face as his eyes tracked the bloated figure of the general. He was a ruin of a man, confined to a multi-legged mechanical chair wired directly to his nerves via data-plugs at the base of his skull. The chair carried him to his place at the judges' bench with smooth, spider-like movements.

Sebastev raised his right hand to his brow in a sharp but grudging salute.

'In the name of the Emperor,' called the court secretary, 'all rise!'

The people on the spectators' benches clattered to their feet, and the trial of Captain Grigorius Sebastev began.

CHAPTER ONE

Morning at the Eastern Front began, as it most often did, with the dark sky shifting from midnight blue to slate-grey. Down on the ground, everything turned a brilliant white. Only regular clearance work prevented the heavy snow from filling the Vostroyan trenches. Out here, eight kilometres east of the town proper, the only true shelter to be found was in the dugouts that the engineering teams had cut into the frozen earth. If Sebastev lived through this campaign – and the odds were against it, given the wretched state of things – he was sure he'd remember it, not for the fury of the warp-damned orks or the desperation of the filthy rebels, but for the relentless assault of the Danikkin deep winter.

Icy winds gusted down the firing trench, catching the snow as it fell, and hurling it against his men with a fury that was almost human. Fur hats and cloaks became coated on their windward side. But the Vostroyan Firstborn had weathered worse in their time. It would take more than the Danikkin ice-age to shake their commitment to the fight. Vostroyan pride was at stake here.

Sebastev moved up to the firing step, raised his head over the lip of the trench and peered out between coils of rusting razor wire and sandbags frozen hard as rock. The deep winter had pulled powdery blankets over yesterday's dead, and there was little evidence of the violence that had shaken the earth. Only irregular mounds of snow on the otherwise level battlefield hinted at the multitude of dead xenos that lay beneath.

Given the uniform white that lay before him, it was hard to believe a battle had been fought here at all: no scorched ground, no smoking craters. Yet, barely twenty hours ago, Sebastev had led his men in a bloody defence of these very trenches.

Here he was again, called back from the warmth of his bunk after First Company scouts had alerted the regiment to a massing of enemy forces beyond the tree line to the east. Tired as they were, those off-duty had quickly reassembled to face the inevitable attack.

The orks, damn them all, seemed impervious to the deep winter.

On either side of Sebastev, the trenches snaked off north and south into the snow veiled distance, filled with men in greatcoats of deep red, cinched under plates of polished golden armour. These were his men, the men of the Sixty-Eighth Infantry Regiment's Fifth Company. They stamped their feet on the frozen planking of the trench floor, and rubbed gloved hands over their weapons to keep the mechanisms from freezing. Their pockets bulged with lasgun power packs waiting to be loaded at the last minute so that the cold of the open air wouldn't leech their valuable charge.

There were three hundred and thirty-eight men at the last count, spread across five platoons. He'd started with four hundred. Twenty-two had been lost since the last reinforcements had come in. Those same reinforcements accounted for most, but not all, of the recently deceased. That was the way of things in the Guard, of course. Those with the right stuff lived to fight on. As far as most officers were concerned, the rest were just cannon fodder.

Sebastev pulled his scarf down for a moment, so he could scratch his face where the coarse hair of his moustache was itching. The bitter air nipped at his exposed skin. Every face around him was covered against the cold, some with warm scarves, others with rebreather masks that offered better protection against the elements, but reduced peripheral vision. Sebastev had always allowed his men a certain amount of freedom in the way they configured their gear. Each man knew himself best, after all. Even so, he'd have welcomed the chance to read their expressions as they readied themselves for the inevitable ork assault.

Stand strong, he thought. You're tired, cold and hungry, I know, but in three more days, we've a duty rotation. Hold fast until then.

He knew there would be mistakes brought on by exhaustion, and decided to order extra checks on cold climate discipline. Pneumonia and frostbite were constant threats on this world. The deep winter stalked every man, waiting for simple mistakes, for chances to claim the lives of the careless.

Early in the conflict, the youngest and greenest Guardsmen in the Twelfth Army had suffered in depressingly high numbers. Frostbite: for some it was lips or noses, for others it was fingers or toes. The flesh became numb, then shrivelled and turned black. If the dead flesh didn't fall away first, the medics would cut it off. Many of the afflicted didn't need scarves and goggles now. They wore permanent masks, expressionless machine faces screwed into the bone of their skulls by the regiment's tech-priests and the chirurgeons of the Imperial Medicae.

Twelfth Army Command had since made instances of frostbite a capital offence, but flogging men for losing a finger or two didn't sit well with Sebastev. He preferred to omit the mention of it from his reports. Since Fifth Company had yet to be assigned a replacement commissar, Sebastev dealt with most infractions in his own way. For frostbite, it meant the confiscation of alcohol or tabac. For other offences, it meant a stint as his sparring partner.

Sebastev tried to gauge the mood of the men around him. Despite their being covered from head to toe against the razor winds, it wasn't all that hard to sense their agitation. Their bodies were in continuous motion, keeping their joints loose and their blood pumping in readiness for combat. It kept them warm. Many were veterans who, like Sebastev, had opted to serve beyond their ten years of compulsory service. Such men would have sensed the coming storm of battle just as he had.

He raised his magnoculars and squinted into the lenses, picking out the tree line just over a kilometre east of his position. The heavy curtains of falling snow hampered his view, but the shadows beneath the trees stood out as a dark border in all that white, marking the far edge of the killing fields. As he adjusted the magnification, bringing the wall of pine into sharper focus, he thought he glimpsed motion between the black trunks.

Lieutenant Tarkarov was right, he thought. We should have cut the trees farther back. We've no idea just how many are massing there.

After watching for another minute with no further sign of movement, Sebastev returned his magnoculars to the case on his belt.

The foothills of the Varanesian Peaks lay beyond the great pine forest, hidden today, as on most days. On those rare occasions when the cloud cover broke and the sky shone bright and blue, the mountains were visible, rendered in sharp detail, the land displaying a rare beauty. It was everything Sebastev's home world might have been were it not covered from sea to poisoned sea in gas belching, city-sized manufactories.

We may not have the same grand vistas, Sebastev thought to himself, but at least Vostroya is no traitor world.

He turned at a muttered curse from behind him. His comms officer and adjutant, Lieutenant Kuritsin, was crouching by the rear wall of the trench, adjusting the frequency dials on his vox-caster back and forth in tiny increments. His motions betrayed a mild frustration.

Still, thought Sebastev, you've a lot more patience than I have, Rits. I'd have blasted the damned thing to pieces by now.

Long-range comms had been unreliable since they'd landed on the planet. Some two thousand years after massive volcanic eruptions in the far south had kick-started this Danikkin ice age, tiny particles of volcanic debris in the high atmosphere still played hell with signals over distance.

Short-range vox, at least, was somewhat less affected.

'Captain,' said Kuritsin as he joined Sebastev on the firing step, 'that was a message from the colonel's office.'

'A full message?' asked Sebastev doubtfully.

'I'm afraid not, sir. The last half was mostly static.'

'Sometimes I feel guilty for making you carry that bloody thing, Rits. Just give me what you've got.'

'Yes, sir. Lieutenant Maro just wanted to let us know, sir. A Chimera left Korris HQ a few minutes ago, heading for our current position. It shouldn't take long to arrive.'

Not an inspection, thought Sebastev. The colonel knows better than to trouble us at a time like this, and Maro wouldn't have warned us if it was good news.

Sebastev frowned under his scarf and said, 'I don't suppose you know who's riding it?'

'I'm afraid we didn't get that far, captain. Would you like me to keep trying?'

Sebastev was about to answer when the vox-bead in his ear crackled. It was Lieutenant Vassilo, commander of Third Platoon. 'Vassilo to company leader. Movement among the trees. Lots of movement.'

'No, Rits,' said Sebastev to his adjutant, 'it'll have to wait. It sounds like we're about to have our hands full.'

Sebastev keyed the company command channel on his vox-bead, cleared his throat and said, 'Captain Sebastev to platoon leaders. I want all squads on full alert. Wake up, gentlemen. Expect a charge from the tree line any minute. I can bloody well smell them coming.'

Sebastev's officers broke through the static with brief confirmations.

'Rits, get a message off to First and Fourth Companies. Tell them we've got activity at Korris East, grid-sector H-5. Make sure they get the message, and keep Korris HQ updated on our status.'

'Yes, sir,' said Lieutenant Kuritsin.

As Sebastev raised his magnoculars again, Kuritsin transmitted his message to the company commanders in the neighbouring sections of the trench. Each Guardsman wore a vox-bead. The devices didn't have much range, maybe five kilometres on a good day, just one or two as standard on Danik's World, but they were absolutely vital for coordinating operations. Anything over that range required a heavy vox-caster set like the one Kuritsin carried around, strapped to his back. Every company and platoon leader in the Sixty-Eighth had a comms officer beside him.

Sebastev didn't have the faintest idea how vox worked, but that was the Imperium for you, he supposed. If the Priests of Mars understood it, they guarded the knowledge jealously. No matter. So long as everything worked as it was supposed to, that was enough. Sebastev's own regular obeisance to the machine-spirits seemed to keep his equipment in working order.

He flexed his fingers. That feeling had descended on him again, the tightness in his muscles, in his gut, as if he needed to piss. He knew it was partly the cold, but it was more than just that. He pulled the folds of his thick, white cloak tighter around his body, glad of its protection from the worst of the winds, and for the tall fur hat that warmed his head.

Slow adrenal increase. He always felt it before they came. Another tide of violence was building, about to spill over, to shatter the relative silence of the deep winter. The feeling was so strong it left little room for doubt.

How many will I lose this time, he wondered? Twenty? Thirty? By Terra, let it be less.

If he worked smart, and if the Emperor was with him, maybe he could keep the numbers down. It was what he excelled at, so Colonel Kabanov had told him. Sebastev hoped the old man wasn't just blowing smoke up his backside. Good men still died under his command, and bad ones, too.

He keyed his vox to the company's open channel and addressed his troops. 'Ready yourselves, Firstborn. Check your kit. Follow your platoon leaders.'

Up and down the line, he could sense the men preparing themselves, switching mental gears at the sound of his voice. These were the times he missed his old friend and mentor, Major Dubrin, the most. The man had always been ready with an inspirational phrase or quote to bolster the troops. Conscious of this, Sebastev struggled for something to say. 'Ask for the blessings of the Emperor. Do your duty without hesitation, free of all doubt, and when those ugly green bastards come charging over the snow, drop them with a las-bolt to the brain, and buy us all another day of righteous service in the Imperial Guard!'

That'll have to do, thought Sebastev. I've never been much of a speechmaker. You should be standing here, Dubrin, girding these men for battle. An old grunt like me has no business in officer's clothes. Any blue-blooded bastard in Twelfth Army Command can tell you that much. If it weren't for my damned promise...

Lieutenant Kuritsin spoke from behind him. 'Captain, First and Fourth Companies report movement all along the line, sir. Looks like a big one.'

As if on cue, an all too familiar sound erupted from the distant trees: the rage-filled battle cry of an ork leader. If the sub-zero temperatures of the Danikkin day weren't enough to chill a man's blood, an alien roar like that would do it. More sub-human roaring sounded on the air, racing over the white drifts to the ears of the anxious Guardsmen, signalling the start of the battle.

Sebastev tapped a finger on his adjutant's vox-caster and said, 'Monitor the regimental command channels for me, Rits. Keep me updated on the status of the First and Fourth. I'll need to know what's going on in their sectors. We don't want any surprises.'

'Understood, sir,' replied Kuritsin, 'but transmissions are really starting to break up between here and Korris HQ. I think the weather is worsening.'

Sebastev looked up at the sky. The snowfall was getting heavier, but the gusting winds had eased a little. He spoke again on the company's command channel. 'Ready yourselves, Firstborn.'

Lasgun charge packs were drawn from pockets all along the trench, and clicked into place under long, polished barrels.

'Maintain fire discipline. Power settings at maximum. Choose your targets. I want redundancy minimised. Remember, all of you, that temperature, visibility and the nature of our opponent have reduced lethal range to approximately one half. Any trooper wasting bolts on long shots will immediately forfeit his *rahzvod* allocation. You don't fire until I bloody well say so.'

Despite the usual groans from nearby soldiers at the thought of losing their alcohol, Sebastev knew he hardly needed to warn them. He was proud of them, his Fifth Company. Their discipline was rock solid. Most of his men were as dedicated and faithful as a commander could have wished for, committed to a life of fighting for the honour of Vostroya and the glory of the Imperium of Man.

Faith is the armour of the soul, thought Sebastev. That's what Commissar Ixxius used to say.

Commissar Ixxius was another friend and mentor who'd been lost to the campaign. The man had been a pillar of strength to Sebastev's company after Dubrin's death. He'd been a fine speaker, too.

In scholas and academies across the Imperium, officers and commissars were taught how to tap that faith. There were entire study programs dedicated to battlefield oration, but that didn't help Sebastev, because his was a field-commission. Everything he knew about leadership had been learnt the hard way, through blood, sweat and tears shed on battlefields from here to the Eye of Terror.

For better or for worse, litanies and the like were firmly the province of Father Olov, Fifth Company's aging and slightly insane priest. Sebastev hoped that the men at least drew some strength from his insistence on fighting alongside them, shoulder-to-shoulder, in these freezing trenches or anywhere else the enemies of the Imperium dared to show themselves.

As if summoned by the thought, they showed themselves now, bellowing their challenge as they broke cover. They crashed from between the trees, a thunderous green tide of muscle-bound bodies, kicking up great sprays of snow as they raced over no-man's-land towards the Vostroyan lines.

Orks.

'Mark your targets,' ordered Sebastev. 'First volley on my order. Not one shot till we see their breath misting the air. Let them extend themselves. Grenades and mortars on dense knots only, please. I *will* be watching you. Your platoon leaders *will* be taking names.'

From the bead in his right ear, he heard his officers acknowledge.

'Sir,' said Kuritsin. 'First and Fourth Companies both report enemy charges in their sectors.'

Sebastev raised his right hand to his chest and the holy icon that lay beneath his clothes. An image, rendered in Vostroyan silver, hung from a cord around his neck. It felt cold against his skin. It was a medallion given to him by his mother some thirty years ago on the day he'd left to begin his term in the Guard: the Insignum Sanctus Nadalya, the holy icon of the Grey Lady, Vostroya's patron saint.

He mumbled a quick prayer for the Lady's favour and drew his gleaming, handcrafted bolt pistol from its holster. 'Let's see what they're made of, eh Rits?' he said.

Lieutenant Kuritsin slammed a power pack into position on his lasgun. 'Aye, sir. On your order.'

Sebastev felt his adrenaline surge as he watched the enemy speed towards him, signalling his body's readiness for the fight. The cold lost some of its bite. His fatigue faded and all his long years of training and experience rose to the fore.

Along the trench in both directions, men made ready to fire at the tide of charging orks. 'On my mark,' Sebastev voxed to them.

He raised his pistol high above his head. Out on the snowfield, the green horde swept closer.

That's it, you snot-coloured xenos scum. Keep coming. We're not going anywhere.

Bestial roars filled the air, pouring from mouths filled with jutting yellow tusks. The wall of monstrous green bodies closed with frightening speed. All too quickly, with their oversized feet eating up the distance to the Vostroyan trenches, the orks came into lethal range.

Sebastev fired a single bolt into the air and voxed the words his men were waiting for. 'Open fire!'

A searing volley of las-bolts blazed from the trenches, each shot slicing through the air with a distinctive *hiss-crack*. Scores of charging greenskins howled in agony and fell clutching their faces. Massive pistols and cleavers were flung aside as grotesque bodies tumbled to a lifeless heap. But for all those that fell, there were hundreds more that hadn't been blinded or crippled. They kept charging, their hideous faces grinning with bloodlust.

The Vostroyan heavy bolters opened fire, filling Sebastev's ears with deep machine chatter. Pillboxes and gun-platforms up and down the line laced the rough ork formations with enfilading fire, sending fountains of dirt, snow and blood high into the air.

'Fifth Company, fire at will,' voxed Sebastev. 'They do not get to the trenches. Do you hear? Fire at will!'

Enemy slugs, solid rounds as big as a man's fist, bit great chunks of frozen dirt from the sandbags on the trench lip. But the greenskins, despite their obsession with battle, were notoriously bad shots. They represented a far greater threat in close combat. Sebastev had to make sure the charging mass didn't breach the Vostroyan defences, at least not until their numbers were manageable.

'Take those bastards down, Firstborn. The Emperor demands it!'

A knot of massive orks charged straight towards Sebastev's

section of the trench. Perhaps they'd marked him out by his white cloak, or by the gold Imperialis insignia on his hat, but it was just as likely that the monsters sought their kills at random.

Troopers to left and right opened up on the orks as they sped nearer, carving black wounds into the wall of green flesh. Lieutenant Kuritsin scored a masterful headshot that put one of the monsters straight down. But, while all this las-fire would have obliterated an army of men, the ork charge barely slowed. Las-bolts could cut and char, but they lacked the raw kinetic punch of solid rounds. The orks shrugged off anything that wasn't crippling. The battle-lust burned bright in their red eyes.

Sebastev brought his bolt pistol to bear on a massive ork charging straight towards him. He slowed his breath, took aim, and squeezed the trigger.

The gun kicked hard, and hot blood misted the air where the monster's head had been. The heavy body ran on, legs still pumping, muscles executing the last orders from an absent brain. Sebastev watched the headless body snag on a tangle of razor wire, ripping open with a red spray before it tumbled down into the trench.

Both Sebastev and Kuritsin stepped neatly aside. Steaming fluids poured from the corpse, freezing quickly on the trench floor. Even through his scarf, Sebastev could smell the pungent fungal stink of the ork's insides. But this was no time to stand gaping. More greenskins boiled towards the Vostroyan defences. Sebastev turned his bolt pistol on them.

Solid firing discipline and Vostroyan accuracy were taking their toll on the orks. Out on the open drifts, the first charge broke. Stragglers turned and sped back towards the trees to join up with the second wave.

The angry rattle of the heavy bolters ceased.

'Good work, Firstborn,' voxed Sebastev, 'but there's no time for smiles and back-slaps.'

Another green tide had already broken from the trees.

'Second wave,' he called. 'Ammo counters and charge packs, all of you.' He pulled a fresh bolt magazine from his greatcoat pocket and slammed it home.

If the first wave of orks had looked large and fierce, they were mere youths compared to the dark-skinned brutes that now swarmed over the snows. Their overlong arms bulged with muscles swollen to unnatural proportions. Some wore crude suits of armour strapped or bolted together from plates of scrap metal and leather. Barring a direct headshot, a lasgun wouldn't do much damage to them, short of making those plates scalding hot. But orks didn't care about superficial burns when the battle-lust was on them. It just made them mad. They'd come straight through, soaking up las-fire until they were right on top of Fifth Company.

Emperor above, prayed Sebastev, give us strength.

'I want heavy bolters to concentrate fire on those armoured bastards. Leave the rest to mortars and lasguns. Is that clear? Flamers, wait for your range. No wasted shots. Mortars, I want focused fire at mid-range, centred on dense knots, as before.'

Heavy weapons teams readied themselves up and down the line.

Sebastev turned to Kuritsin. 'Where's Father Olov?'

'Just north of us, sir, fighting alongside Second Platoon today.'

Somewhat reluctantly, Sebastev voxed, 'Father Olov, a reading if you please. Draw the Emperor's attention to us. I think He might enjoy this.'

And for Throne's sake, he thought, make it uplifting for once.

The priest's gravelly voice came back over the vox a moment later. 'Something to strengthen our souls, captain. Volume II of *The Septology of Hestor*, I think. Ruminations on the Divine Ecstasy of Holy Service at Magna Garrovol is a particularly invigorating piece.'

'A fine choice, I'm sure, father,' replied Sebastev dubiously. He could hear Kuritsin groaning under his scarf. 'Begin at your convenience,' he told the priest.

The second ork wave was closing fast, shooting wildly in the general direction of Sebastev's men.

Lucky for us, thought Sebastev, they couldn't hit the hull of a battleship at point-blank range.

Even as he thought this, a trooper a few metres down on his right was thrown against the rear wall of the trench with bone-splintering force. He slumped dead to the wooden planks of the trench floor. Fully half of his head was gone, as if something had taken a great bite out of him.

Within seconds of each other, two more Guardsmen fell further along the trench, fatal head wounds spraying the rear wall red. The blood froze before it could even run down the wall.

'Gretchin snipers!' voxed Sebastev. 'Keep your heads down.'

They must've moved up under cover of the first assault, he thought. But where the khek are they?

Father Olov's voice sounded in Sebastev's ear as the priest began his reading. 'Saint Hestor dedicated victory at Magna Garravol to the Emperor, as always. Blood was spilled on both sides that day, and many lamented the passing of good men. But he rejoiced in their sacrifice, since paradise belongs only to the righteous.'

'I need spotters,' voxed Sebastev, breaking through the priest's oration. 'I want those snipers taken out, now. Fifth Company, pick your targets. Prepare to fire.'

Someone to the north of Sebastev's position fired off an early shot, hitting a massive ork in the throat. At closer range, the shot might have been fatal, but this far out, the monster just stumbled, regained its footing and continued to charge. A crude banner snapped in the freezing wind above its head: a poorly painted serpent with three heads, its yellow body coiled on a field of black, the mark of the Venomhead clan.

'Damn it, who was that?' roared Sebastev. 'Maintain fire discipline. That's an order.'

Olov continued his reading unperturbed. 'A messenger appeared before Saint Hestor in a dream, and said, "This is your path. There can be no turning from it. False hope fathers forgiveness. Forgiveness lays open the naked heart. There can be no forgiveness for the enemies of our great Imperium. Destroy the forces of the Idols Dark and you will live forever by the Emperor's side".

Sebastev held his pistol in the air again. 'Steady, Firstborn. Steady. On my mark...'

The musty stink of unwashed ork bodies pushed ahead of the charging mass. An ork round whistled past Sebastev's head, punching into the frozen dirt of the trench wall behind him. Then the second wave came into lethal range.

'Now!' he voxed.

All along the trench, the sharp report of the Vostroyan lasguns drowned out the alien battle cries. From foxholes and pillboxes up and down the line, heavy bolters resumed fire, beating a deep tattoo that resonated in Sebastev's lungs. Mortars sent a deadly explosive hail at any cluster of orks that held together for even a moment. The explosions hurled massive bodies into the air, spinning them end over end, and breaking them open.

Gouts of blood splashed to the snow, the only rain these frozen lands had known for two millennia. But the death of their fellows did nothing to stop the horde. The orks trampled the bodies of their dead and kept coming.

As much as Sebastev detested them, he couldn't deny a grudging respect.

'Hestor led his people across the plains,' droned Father Olov over the vox, 'thirsty and tired, but hungry no more for the knowledge he had sought. The fate of the cluster was clear to him. His hands, stained with blood, carried chalice and censer. Behind him marched the faithful, dedicated to glory, and to a worthy death in the final battle.'

A deep voice broke through the priest's reading. 'Second Platoon to Company Command. We've located two grot sniper teams lying low in the drifts.' It was Sergeant Basch.

'Good work, sergeant,' replied Sebastev. 'Lieutenant Vassilo, did you hear that? Second Platoon has co-ordinates for you. I want Third Platoon mortars on those grot sniper positions now. Sergeant Basch will advise.'

'Understood, sir,' Vassilo voxed back.

Sebastev turned his attention back to the killing field. He fired bolt after bolt into the disordered ranks of the orks as they neared, felling a few with carefully placed headshots. But there were just too many. It was clear to him that the second wave was about to breach the trenches.

When that happens, thought Sebastev, we're–

His bolt pistol gave a loud click. The magazine was spent. The orks came on, waving their massive chipped blades. No point reloading, things were about to get very close and very bloody.

Sebastev knew he had to give the call his men dreaded. 'Fix bayonets!' he yelled over the vox. There was no escaping it. This battle would be won or lost at close quarters.

He holstered his pistol and grasped the hilt of the power sabre at his left hip, but when he moved to draw it, he found the sword frozen in its scabbard. Cursing loudly, he tried to tug the blade free.

He could hear his officers calling for courage as the orks leapt over the banks of razor wire and sandbags. Some of the orks became snagged. Others simply trampled over them, using their backs as bridges over the vicious barbs.

'Everyone back to the cover trench,' yelled Sebastev. 'The firing trench is lost.'

As the first of the orks leapt down into the trenches, the Vostroyans turned and raced off down the communications trenches that led to their fallback positions.

'I want flamers at the trench mouths,' voxed Sebastev. 'We can burn them as they follow us in.'

Sebastev, Kuritsin and the others from his section sprinted along the passage that led back to their secondary defensive positions. He didn't need to turn round to know just how close the orks were. He could hear their heavy boots thundering on the frozen planks as they gave chase.

Trench walls flashed past him as he ran a few metres behind his adjutant. Then, suddenly, the walls on either side ended, and Sebastev found himself in the cover trench, surrounded by his troopers. He spun around and yelled, 'Get me a khekking flamer, now!'

Trooper Kovo of Fourth Platoon stepped across Sebastev's field of vision just as the pursuing orks rounded the last bend. Sebastev's eyes went wide as he saw the enemy. They were monstrous, even for orks, towering hulks of savage muscle far bigger than even the largest of Sebastev's men. He only saw them for an instant before Kovo opened fire. A jet of blazing promethium blasted down the passage, searing away the flesh of the enemy. A moment later, the only evidence that the orks had ever existed was the molten metal that had been their armour, boots and weapons.

'More coming down on us,' yelled Trooper Kovo over his shoulder. 'I'm down to a quarter tank. Get ready.'

He loosed another jet of flame. Sebastev could hear ork screams over the flamer's roar, but they were cut off as the burning promethium consumed all.

Then, with more orks pouring down the passage, Kovo's fuel ran out. 'Incoming,' he shouted as he darted out of the way. Lasgunners moved in to take his place.

'Listen up, fighters,' barked Sebastev over the vox. 'We've got them in bottlenecks. The trenches are too narrow for them to fight properly. I want lasguns on them until they get within bayonet range. You know what to do after that. Hold the line, and remember the Emperor protects.'

Shouts filled the air all along the trench. 'The Emperor protects!'

The greenskins were charging straight down the communications trench. With a last hard tug, Sebastev's power sabre came free of its scabbard. He thumbed the rune that activated its deadly energy field just as a trio of massive orks barrelled forwards, howling in rage as Vostroyan las-fire strafed their bodies. Agony didn't slow them. They slammed troopers aside with ease as they broke into the cover trench.

One of the beasts lunged straight at Sebastev, laughing madly as it raised a huge cleaver above its head. The trench didn't offer any room to avoid the engagement, but that suited Sebastev fine.

As the crude blade came whistling down towards his head, propelled by green arms as thick as his torso, Sebastev darted forward into the blow, throwing his left arm up at the last moment. The ork's wrists clashed with the golden bracer that shielded his arm. The impact was bone-jarring, but Sebastev weathered it. Thanks to the bracer, his arm didn't break. The instant he caught the blow, he rammed his power sabre up into the ork's unprotected sternum.

The effect was immediate, but less than Sebastev had hoped for. The monster's expression shifted from delinquent glee to abject hate and rage, but it didn't die. Instead, it dropped the huge cleaver and wrapped its arms around Sebastev, pulling him into a crushing bear hug. It was a bad move on the ork's part, the motion forcing Sebastev's blade deeper inside its body. Howling in pain, it craned its head forward and tried to snap at him.

Sebastev gagged on the beast's stinking, rotten-meat breath, and reared his head back just in time. Massive yellow tusks slammed together scant centimetres from his face. Making use of the distance he'd created to gain momentum, Sebastev rammed his head forward with all his strength, smashing the metal insignia on his hat straight into the ork's nose.

As the monster reeled backwards, it loosened its grip. Sebastev yanked the hilt of his power sabre hard to left and right, causing massive internal injuries to his foe. Reeking gore poured out over his greatcoat. When the ork's misshapen face finally went slack, Sebastev pushed free and kicked the big body from the end of his blade.

There was no time to revel in the victory. He heard screams and calls for aid from nearby. Close combat raged all around him. Sebastev spun, looking for his adjutant, suddenly aware that they'd been separated.

There! There was Kuritsin, ten paces further up the trench, thrusting his gleaming bayonet at the face of an ork that had just cut down a trooper from First Platoon. Sebastev ran to join him, and began hacking at the ork's wide back. The broad wounds he carved in the dark green muscle steamed in the freezing air.

Assaulted on two sides, the ork was swiftly overcome, and went down with a final bestial scream. 'Thank you, sir,' said Kuritsin, 'but there's no time for a breather.' He pointed over Sebastev's shoulder. More orks were pushing their way into the cover trench, hacking at Sebastev's men as they came, stomping the bodies of those that fell. Sebastev and Kuritsin both rushed forward to engage, calling others nearby to assist.

'You're not going to horde all the glory for yourself, are you, captain?' someone shouted.

Sebastev looked in the direction of the voice and saw a black figure standing on the lip of the trench, looking down into the mayhem below.

'For the Emperor and Holy Terra!' yelled the stranger. He launched himself into the trench, crashing into Sebastev and barrelling him from his feet. There was a flash of gold at collar and sleeve as the figure spun to face the orks. Sebastev heard the greedy purring of a chainsword before it buried itself in green meat, stressing the motor, changing its pitch.

Sebastev leapt back to his feet with a growl.

'Your wait has ended, captain,' yelled the stranger as he hacked the orks apart with deadly efficiency. 'Your new commissar is here at last. Now, secure the area behind me, for Throne's sake.'

Sebastev's first instinct was to cuff the man, once for knocking him down, twice for his verbal audacity. But there was no time for that. The trench was choked with orks and men fighting on every side. Kuritsin was helping First Platoon troopers to push back the orks attacking from the northern end. The southern end was likewise choked. There was nothing else for it, Sebastev would have to go up and over if he wanted to help his men. Sheathing his blade for a moment, he hauled himself out of the trench. The instant he scrambled to his feet, however, he found himself in trouble. To his right, a large slobbering ork with a black eye-patch had been looking for a place to jump down into the fray. On seeing Sebastev, it changed its mind, bellowed a challenge and stomped straight towards him, hefting a massive axe.

Sebastev drew his blade and hunkered down into his fighting stance, knees bent, sword ready in his lead hand.

The ork's opening move was a sweeping lateral backhander aimed at Sebastev's head. Sebastev ducked under the whistling blade with practiced ease, but the edge of the axe lopped a chunk from the top of his hat. Freezing air rushed into the hole, chilling his scalp. He didn't wait for the second attack. His power sabre flicked out and sliced through the tendons of the ork's thick wrist. Its fingers went limp and the axe spun to the snow. The ork gaped for the briefest moment, surprised and confused by the sudden uselessness of its hand. Sebastev took the opening without hesitation.

He stepped in with a powerful diagonal cut. The humming, crackling power sabre bit into the ork's right trapezius muscle with such force that it passed straight through, exiting the beast's torso below the left armpit.

The ork rolled quietly to the snow in two, lifeless pieces. Steam boiled up from a spreading pool of blood.

'Son of a grox!' cursed Sebastev to himself. *Maro should have warned me there was a new commissar. That's the last bloody thing I need.*

He heard Lieutenant Vassilo's voice over the vox, issuing orders to the men of his platoon. 'The orks are packed in tight. Get up on the trench lip. Fire down into the bottlenecks.'

Behind Sebastev, dozens of men pulled themselves up onto the snowfield and raced along the trench lip, stopping to pour fire down onto the trapped greenskins.

With their numbers cut by the charge over open ground, and their close combat abilities hampered by the narrow trenches, the orks had fared badly once again. Sebastev thanked the Emperor that they didn't learn quickly from their mistakes. But how long could it last? Sooner or later, the greenskins would surprise them.

Sebastev thumbed his power sabre off, giving thanks to the machine-spirit of the weapon before returning it to its scabbard.

Well done, my fighters, he thought. Let's hope it's the last attack before the rotation. But how many did we lose? Will I still call this a victory when the headcounts come in?

It seemed unlikely that the orks would launch a third wave. It wasn't their habit to hold forces in reserve, and they'd waited too long to take advantage of any confusion or cover that the second wave might have offered. Still, it was hard to fathom the workings of the alien mind. From an official standpoint, it was heretical to even try. In all Sebastev's experience with them, ork behaviour was rarely as simple and predictable as Imperial prop-aganda made it out to be.

Returning to the cover trench, Sebastev sought out his adju-tant. He found him standing over the dismembered corpse of a fallen Firstborn.

'Bekislav,' said Kuritsin simply. 'He got himself blindsided.'

Sebastev bowed his head. Bekislav had been a good man. He'd served with Fifth Company for almost eight years.

Lieutenant Kuritsin bore only a few shallow cuts and scrapes, nothing serious. The vox-caster on his back, however, looked a little worse for wear. It bore a number of fresh dents.

Sebastev tapped it with a finger and said, 'This thing still working?'

'About as well as before,' replied Kuritsin, 'so far as I can tell. It's temperamental, but it's tough. A little bit like–'

'Fine,' said Sebastev, cutting him off. 'Check in with the other companies. Tell them our sector is secure, and make sure the ork bodies are burned quickly. You know the drill.'

Left unattended, the ork corpses would shed their spores. They'd probably begun to do so already. It was best to burn them all as quickly as possible.

As Kuritsin voxed the order over to the platoon leaders, Sebastev walked on, surveying the results of the carnage. It was a grim picture. The red fabric of Vostroyan greatcoats peeked out from beneath the heaped bodies of the foe.

Sebastev looked down at himself. His own coat was drenched with splashes of ork blood. He'd have to get inside soon. He was losing too much heat through the hole in his hat. Maybe he could stuff it with something in the meantime.

Warp damn this place, he thought. We can't last like this. If Old Hungry doesn't mobilise us soon, we'll die out here for nothing. We can't afford to play a numbers game with the orks, not with so few men.

Sebastev heard booted footsteps behind him and turned, expecting Kuritsin. But the man who faced him wasn't his adjutant. He wasn't even Vostroyan.

'You, captain,' said a tall, dark figure with a very distinctive cap, 'are an absolute bloody mess.'

CHAPTER TWO

With the orks repulsed, the men of Fifth Company set about tending to their wounded, salvaging equipment from the dead, and repairing their defences. The snows abated for a while, and the air was filled with the black smoke of burning xenos corpses. Commissar Daridh Ahl Karif followed Captain Sebastev through the winding maze of communications trenches to the man's dugout.

The captain's sour mood was all too apparent to the commissar, and he resisted any attempts at conversation while they walked. Despite reminding himself not to judge the captain too swiftly, Commissar Karif couldn't help it. First impressions hadn't been good.

Moving south along the supply trench, they arrived at a flight of steps cut into the frozen earth. Captain Sebastev descended the steps and tapped a four-digit code into the rune pad on the door-frame. With a hiss, the door opened and the captain went inside.

Karif didn't wait for an invitation. It was far too cold to observe such niceties. Instead, he hurried in after the captain, closed the door quickly behind them, and slapped the cold seal activation glyph on the door's inner surface. When he turned, he found himself in a dimly lit room of dirt walls, with shabby furniture and a ceiling of wooden beams so low that they scraped the top of his cap.

The stocky Vostroyan had no such trouble. As the captain removed his damaged fur hat, Karif saw for the first time just how short Captain Sebastev was. The top of his head barely reached Karif's shoulders. At just under two metres, the commissar would have been considered a fairly tall man on most worlds, but he'd met enough Vostroyans to know that Sebastev was below average height for his people. It seemed that this dugout, with its preposterously low ceiling, had been constructed with his exact proportions in mind.

Sebastev's dugout may have been too small by half, but it was infinitely cosier than the freezing trenches outside. A quartet of small thermal coils, one in each corner, hummed as they struggled to take the chill from the air.

Both men removed their cloaks and scarves, and hung them on pegs hammered into the frozen, dirt wall. Karif felt so much lighter without the heavy fur cloak weighing him down, but he'd been glad of its warmth and protection in the open air. Not for the first time since planetfall, Karif cursed this world and the personal disaster that had brought him here.

Damn you, old man, he thought, remembering the gloating look on the face of Lord General Breggius as the man had informed him of his reassignment. I wasn't to blame for your son's death. You must've pulled some long strings to get me posted out here, but I'm determined to make the best of this. There must be some glory to be had in this campaign.

Captain Sebastev moved across the room and dropped himself onto the edge of a simple wooden bunk. 'Sit if you've a mind to, commissar,' he rumbled as he began unfastening the clasps of his blood-covered boots.

Karif drew a rickety, wooden chair from beside a small, central table and sat down carefully, half-expecting the thing to collapse under him. When the chair had accepted his full weight, he placed his black cap on the table's grubby surface and pulled a shining silver comb from his pocket. As was his habit whenever he removed his cap, he ran the comb through his oiled black hair, sweeping it back behind his ears.

Captain Sebastev grunted when he saw this.

Karif didn't consider himself a vain man, but he believed that a position of authority brought with it certain requirements of appearance. It was a matter of self-respect. And if such an appearance happened to appeal to a particular class of lady, so much the better.

It was unfortunate that his appearance had also appealed to the Lord General's son. He'd been a charming boy with great potential as an officer, but he'd misinterpreted Karif's friendship as something... deeper. Karif hadn't expected his rejection to lead to the boy's suicide.

Clearly, Captain Sebastev would never suffer such difficulties. The man was almost beast-like. Then again, Karif supposed as he watched Sebastev remove his carapace armour, his breeding hadn't given him much to work with. Compounding the captain's limited height, he was so disproportionately thick with muscle that, had he been painted green and set loose on the snowfield, his own men could have mistaken him for an ork... albeit a very short one.

The captain's black moustache was unkempt, clearly in need of waxing, and his hair was little more than coarse stubble. His leathery face was split by an ugly diagonal scar that ran from his forehead, across his left eye, all the way down to his jaw-line, tugging one side of his mouth into a permanent snarl. All in all, Karif decided, without the accoutrements of his position, the commanding officer of Fifth Company would be all but indistinguishable from an underhive thug.

Being a field commissioned officer, rather than an academy man, thought Karif, he may well have come from the underhives. But I'm hardly catching him at his best. He must have some worthy qualities. By all accounts, his fellow officers in the Sixty-Eighth Infantry Regiment rate him very highly. Time will tell.

'Have you anything to drink, captain?' Karif asked hopefully, thinking a little alcohol might take some of the chill off. The room's thermal coils seemed inadequate to the task. 'Amasec, perhaps? I'll even take caffeine if there's any going.'

'Rahzvod,' said Sebastev, indicating a cabinet behind the commissar with a nod of his head. He didn't get up.

Whatever his qualities are, thought Karif, he needs a damned good lesson in manners. A skunkwolf would be a more gracious host.

'Perhaps later,' said Karif, masking his irritation. 'First, let me congratulate you on today's victory. It was most exhilarating to get my hands dirty after such a long trip through the empyrean. A fine introduction to serving with your company, yes?'

Sebastev growled and shook his head. 'Nineteen dead on my section of the trench, commissar. An unacceptable loss, and one that hardly warrants your congratulations.'

Nineteen men didn't sound like a lot to Karif. In fact, given the ferocity of the fighting he'd seen earlier, it sounded incredibly low. He'd served in conflicts where the daily tolls ran into the thousands. But it was clear from his tone that the captain was genuinely angry about the day's losses. Did he blame himself?

'I'm surprised by your reaction, captain,' said Karif. 'I'd have thought the tally would please you. An ork assault of that size repelled with Guard losses in only double figures? You should be expecting a decoration.'

Sebastev laughed, if the short, sharp bark that issued from his mouth could truly be called a laugh. 'I'll be dead before that ever happens, commissar,' he said, 'and so will you, most likely. It's clear you've no idea how bad things are out here. Weren't you briefed on the way in?'

Karif frowned. 'Perhaps you'd better enlighten me, captain, since you clearly feel the officers at Seddisvarr haven't done an adequate job.'

'Bloody right they haven't,' said Sebastev. 'What does anyone at Twelfth Army Command know about the realities of the Eastern Front? Damned little, that's what. Whichever bigwig you angered knew what they were doing when they posted you out here. You're right in the middle of it, commissar. We're outnumbered, ill-equipped, and so badly supported you'll wonder if the Munitorum isn't just a figment of your imagination. It's only my faith in the Emperor and in the strength of my men that gives me any hope.'

'I haven't angered anyone that I know of,' Karif lied, 'except perhaps you. I was sent here because your company needed a replacement commissar, and it galls me to hear such words from an officer of the Imperial Guard. I've little tolerance for fatalism, captain. In fact, I'm a strong believer in the might of the common man. With good leadership and morale, there's nothing the Guard can't achieve. Be careful not to let me hear you speak thus in front of your men. I'm sure I don't have to remind you of my commissarial remit.'

Sebastev simply stared back at Karif, unflinching, until finally he said, 'Fear won't work for you out here, commissar. I tell you this because you're clearly a man used to being feared. But don't mistake a lack of fear for a lack of respect. I'll admit I wasn't pleased at the thought of a new man coming in. Your predecessor, Commissar Ixxius was a great soldier and friend. We won't see his like again. If he proved anything, it was that the right man can make a great difference. There is a place for you here among the Firstborn, if you're such a man. It'll take time, perhaps, but once you've earned the respect of my fighters, you'll see what a force they can be. Maybe this conflict could use a fresh pair of eyes to assess it.'

Sebastev stood up, crossed to the cabinet in his bare feet and poured two shots of clear liquid into a pair of dirty glasses. 'Rahzvod,' he said for the second time, placing one glass down on the table next to Karif.

I confess I've never approved of the idea of field commissioned officers, thought Karif, and this one justifies all my prejudices: ill-mannered and contentious, unmindful of his appearance and the protocols of Imperial society, and yet, the man's lack of sophistry is refreshing. He's ugly, brutal and direct, it's true, but if men like me are the surgical scalpels of the Imperial Guard, perhaps men like Sebastev are the sledgehammers. The Emperor has a use for both, I suppose.

He raised his glass to his lips and said, 'For the Emperor.' The liquid ran down his throat, searing the walls of his gullet. He almost spluttered, but caught himself. His cheeks grew hot and he knew they must be flushing.

'For the Emperor and Vostroya,' replied Sebastev, raising his own glass into the air before knocking back the bitter liquid. He sighed happily, as if he'd been waiting all day for that drink.

In the momentary silence, Karif took another look around the little room.

Ill-mannered or not, Sebastev was clearly a pious man: aquilas on every wall, an image of His Divine Majesty set into an alcove there, several holy texts stacked by his bunk, and even a small altar to the female saint they loved so much. That, at least, was gratifying to see.

Sebastev, looking up from his empty glass, followed the commissar's gaze towards the little altar and said, 'Are you familiar with the Grey Lady, commissar?'

Karif nodded and said, 'I read the Treatis Elatii once, the story of her ancient crusades. But that was many years ago.'

'Still,' said Sebastev, 'that's something in your favour. Commissar Ixxius could quote the text from memory. It made a great difference to the men during hard times. I'm afraid Father Olov, much as we revere the man, is a far better fighter than he is a preacher of the Holy Word. If you've any skill in oration at all...'

'Yes, well, I'll keep that in mind, captain, but I didn't come here to replace the regiment's priest. Battlefield oration is–'

Karif was interrupted by a loud knock at the door.

'Come in,' barked Sebastev.

The cold seal hissed and the door cracked open with a sucking sound. Bitterly cold air rushed into the room, causing Karif to pull his coat tighter around him. The promethium lamp on the ceiling swung in the gust, sending the room's shadows into a dance. A Vostroyan with lieutenant's stripes at his collar and cuffs stepped in and quickly sealed the door.

The newcomer had to stoop under the ceiling, and not merely because of his fur hat. The man was almost as tall as Karif. Like many Vostroyans, he was well built. The gravity on Vostroya was slightly higher than on Karif's homeworld.

Throne preserve us, thought Karif as he watched the man stoop, did they fashion these dugouts for children? My own accommodation had better not be like this. I won't spend this campaign bent double like an old ape.

Even as the thought crossed his mind, Karif had a sinking feeling that his fears on the matter would be realised. Cutting trenches into permafrost was hard enough, but Twelfth Army engineers would have taken as many shortcuts as they could while working in the bitter cold.

'Sorry to intrude, gentlemen,' said the lieutenant. He gave a sharp salute before removing his hat and scarf.

Now here's a proper officer, thought Karif. The contrast between the lieutenant and Captain Sebastev was stark. He had a handsome face, a well-groomed moustache, and good, noble bearing. He was an academy man, for certain. How could he stand to serve under this glorified grunt?

Sebastev didn't stand, but he gestured from his bunk and said, 'This is my adjutant and comms-officer, Lieutenant Oleg Kuritsin. Rits, this is Commissar Daridh Ahl Karif from... Sorry, commissar, I didn't catch where you were from.'

'I never said, captain,' replied Karif.

'Tallarn?' guessed Lieutenant Kuritsin with a smile.

Karif wasn't quite fast enough to hide a flash of irritation.

Why does everyone I meet assume that, he thought angrily? Do all men with black hair and a deep tan have to come from that wretched place?

'Delta Radhima actually,' he said, recovering his composure and standing, or rather stooping, to shake the lieutenant's hand, 'but I attended the Schola Excubitos on Terrax.'

Let's see what that does for them, he thought.

He watched the name register with the lieutenant, though Captain Sebastev's grim features didn't change at all. The schola on Terrax was infamous for producing some of the strictest, most militant commissars in the history of the Imperium. Karif didn't care to mention that he'd been considered one of the more liberal graduates.

'Forgive my ignorance, commissar,' said Kuritsin with a short bow. 'I hadn't heard of Delta Rhadima until this moment. In any case, welcome to Fifth Company.'

'Something to tell me, Rits?' interrupted Sebastev.

'An urgent message from Colonel Kabanov's office, sir. The colonel's calling an assembly in the war room. He'll be arriving at nineteen hundred hours.'

'The war room?' asked Sebastev. 'Our war room?'

'Yes, sir,' said Kuritsin, 'at nineteen hundred hours.'

'Is that unusual, captain?' asked Karif.

'Yes,' said Sebastev.

Lieutenant Kuritsin explained. 'Colonel Kabanov usually holds his briefings at the regimental headquarters, commissar. With the scale of today's attack, he may feel he can't pull his company commanders away from the front. In any case, he's chosen our war room, and that means something has happened.'

'Are there any reasons for optimism, gentlemen?' asked Karif. 'Before you arrived, lieutenant, the captain was telling me all sorts of things about poor supplies and the like. The latest reinforcements, at least, must be welcome news.'

'Reinforcements?' asked Sebastev.

'Sorry, sir,' said Kuritsin. 'I forgot to tell you. Some shinies came in with the commissar.'

'Shinies?' asked Karif.

'Aye,' said Sebastev, 'new conscripts, fresh off the assembly line: shinies. How many did we score, Rits?'

'The regiment as a whole, sir? Or Fifth Company?'

'Fifth Company, of course.'

Kuritsin glanced at the floor as he said, 'He's waiting outside, sir.'

Karif suppressed a grin at the look on the captain's face.

'He?' spluttered Sebastev. 'You mean–?'

Kuritsin turned, opened the door, and called out into the icy air.

Answering the lieutenant's call, a Vostroyan of unusually slim build stepped into the dugout, clumps of snow falling to the floor from the top of his hat and armoured shoulders. The lieutenant sealed the door behind the newcomer and ordered him to remove his scarf.

The trooper's face was blue-eyed, red-cheeked and innocent. There was more of the choirboy about him than the battle-ready Guardsman. He looked barely halfway through his adolescence, though he'd have to be at least eighteen years old to be posted to a regiment. His face bore none of the scars from basic training that most new conscripts were so proud of.

Karif recognised the boy immediately. They'd ridden together with a handful of others in the back of a Chimera from the town to the trenches, though he couldn't remember his name.

Captain Sebastev was staring at the youngster with a mixture of disgust and disbelief.

'What the khek is this?' he growled. 'The new company mascot? This one's never old enough for duty. What's your name, trooper? And where's your damned moustache?'

Clearly feeling sorry for the nervous boy, Lieutenant Kuritsin answered on his behalf. 'This is Danil Stavin, sir. His papers say he's eighteen. He came down on the last boat with the commissar and about three hundred others. The Sixty-Eighth was assigned about forty in all. We got this one.'

'Well then,' said Captain Sebastev, 'he must be some kind of Space Marine, by the Throne. Is that right, Stalin? Are you a Space Marine?'

'It's Stavin, sir. With a "v", sir,' said the boy. His voice was little more than a nervous whisper.

The 'boat' Lieutenant Kuritsin had referred to was the Imperial Naval cruiser *Helmund's Honour*. Rather than raise new foundings like most Imperial Guard regiments, the Vostroyan Firstborn was reinforced in the field, a peculiarity that was, according to some, the result of an ancient debt about which no one living seemed to know a great deal. If they did know, they weren't talking.

The newest levies from Vostroya had already settled into the passenger holds when Karif stepped aboard the ship at Port Maw. In the months it took the ship to navigate the warp, Karif had watched the young Vostroyans train, readying themselves for action in the Second Kholdas War. Since Danik's World was considered little more than a backwater with minimal tactical importance to the war effort, those unlucky enough to be earmarked for the Twelfth Army had suffered the taunts of the others. The real glory was on the cluster's spinward side, where those on the Kholdas Line fought to hold back the massive ork armada from the Ghoul Stars.

On the journey out to the Eastern Front, Karif had enjoyed impressing the new conscripts with tales of his battlefield exploits. He told them of his experiences facing the inexplicable eldar. His stories of the terrifying tyranids had drawn gasps of awe from the young men. Karif's ego had been well fed. What did it matter that he'd embellished a little? Karif grinned at the boy as he remembered, and was rewarded with a broad smile in return.

'What are you so happy about, trooper?' growled Sebastev. 'The deep winter'll soon knock that smile off your face.'

Stavin's cheeks glowed and he dropped his eyes to the floor.

'Rits,' said Sebastev, 'who took the most hits today?'

'That would be Fourth Platoon, sir, though not by much.'

'Right. Stavin, I'm assigning you to Fourth Platoon. Your commanding officer is Lieutenant Nicholo. Understood?'

Kuritsin suddenly looked uncomfortable. 'Actually, sir, Lieutenant Nicholo took an ork blade in the shoulder today during the second wave. He's at the field hospital.'

Sebastev loosed a string of curses, the likes of which Karif had never heard. Some of the images they conjured were deeply unpleasant. 'How bad is it?'

'He lost an arm, sir, his left. Full augmentation from the shoulder down, so I'm told.'

The captain was quiet for a moment, visibly disturbed by the news. Then he caught Karif assessing him. His face quickly reverted to its previous snarl. 'Nicholo's a solid man. He's in good hands. Our medics are the very best in the Twelfth Army, commissar.' He turned his eyes to the boy. 'Right then, Stavin, you'll report to Sergeant Breshek in the meantime. He'll get you sorted out.'

It's a fact, thought Karif as he looked at the young trooper, that most new arrivals to the battlefield don't survive their first skirmish. Those that do survive tend to be born fighters, bullies, killers, sociopaths. There are occasionally others, the quick studies. Some of them make it. They learn the hard way. This one doesn't look like a fighter. Is he a quick study, I wonder?

'Excuse me, captain,' said Karif, 'I'd like to present a proposal of sorts regarding Trooper Stavin here.'

'Very well,' said the captain. 'Out with it.'

'You appreciate that newly assigned commissars often experience a regrettable amount of culture clash. It makes things difficult for all concerned. So, in order to help me adjust to Vostroyan ways, I'd like to request an adjutant. Since Trooper Stavin is, in your own words, a shiny–'

'I see where you're going with this, commissar,' said Captain Sebastev. 'I certainly can't assign a more experienced man to spit-polish your boots for you. Very well. Trooper Stavin, you'll serve as the commissar's adjutant. Do as he says except when I tell you otherwise. A commissar's adjutant you may be, but I'm in charge. Make sure you don't forget it.'

Stavin saluted the captain and said, 'Yes, sir. I won't forget.'

'Good.' Sebastev faced his own adjutant and said, 'Rits, take the commissar and his new aide to their dugout. D-fourteen is free, isn't it? Get them settled in. And make sure the relevant people know about the briefing in the war room later. Tell them Colonel Kabanov won't stand for any tardiness, clear?'

'Like good rahzvod, sir,' said the lieutenant with a sharp salute.

The commissar rose from his chair, forced to stoop again, and placed his cap on his head. He lifted his cloak from its peg, fastened it over his shoulders, and joined Kuritsin and Stavin at the door.

'Make sure you're at the briefing, commissar,' said Sebastev. 'You can be sure the colonel has something damned important to say.'

'Naturally, captain,' replied Karif. In truth, his mind was firmly fixed on the weather outside. He was disturbed to find just how much he dreaded re-emerging into the freezing cold. He was somewhat concerned, too, by his impulse to take Stavin under his wing.

Careful, Daridh, he told himself. It was your kindness to Breggius's boy that got you shipped out here in the first place. Where does it come from, this need to look after them? Who looked after me when I was that age? Ah, but perhaps that's it.

Lieutenant Kuritsin hit the cold seal rune, opened the door of the dugout, and ushered the commissar and his new adjutant out into the cold. Karif threw the captain a salute before he stepped out into the howling wind and snow. He drew his cloak tight around him, sinking his chin into the thick fur. Lieutenant

Kuritsin stepped out last, closing the door of the dugout behind him. Karif heard the hiss of the cold seal as it re-activated.

So that's Grigorius Sebastev, he thought. That's the man to whom my fate is bound. Emperor above, did you have to make him such a bad-tempered little grox? I'm eager to see how he interacts with other officers at the briefing.

'Follow me, commissar,' shouted Kuritsin over the noise of the wind. 'Let's double-time it so you don't catch your death.'

Karif nodded, and he and Stavin fell into step behind Kuritsin, moving north up the trench with some haste. They bent almost double against the whipping snow, eager to get to shelter as soon as possible.

CHAPTER THREE

Cold air scythed through the war room as the door was flung open. Lieutenant Maro of the colonel's personal staff limped through, and pulled his scarf down to reveal a round face with a clipped brown moustache. His cheeks had been pinched red by the cold. 'Stand to!' he called. The pistons in his augmetic leg hissed as he stepped away from the door.

The assembled men pushed their chairs back from the long, central table and stood, snapping to attention with crisp salutes.

Colonel Kabanov hurried inside, his shape lost in the thick folds of his white fur cloak. He stamped the snow from his boots and shook it from the top of his hat. 'At ease, all of you,' he said after a brief but sincere salute of his own. Then he shuffled forward, moving straight towards the nearest of the room's thermal coils. 'Talk amongst yourselves while I get some heat back into me.'

A stream of officers and command-level personnel entered the room behind him, eager to get out of the punishing winds. Last to enter were the servants of the Machine-God. Tech-priest Gavaril and Enginseer Politnov swept into the room like shrouded ghosts, and sealed the door firmly shut behind them. The machinery that sustained their ancient bodies clicked and hummed as they turned their cowled heads to greet the others.

The newly arrived officers from regimental HQ hung their hats and cloaks on wall pegs and took their seats. Soon, Colonel

Kabanov was the only man still wearing both his hat and his cloak.

I suppose I'd better take them off, he thought.

Turning from the heat of the coil, still rubbing his hands together, he said, 'I don't suppose there's a pot of ohx' on, is there? I could use a cup.'

He grudgingly removed his outdoor gear, revealing a pristine formal jacket of bright Vostroyan red trimmed with white and gold. In truth, the jacket was far too ostentatious for the occasion, but it was well made and warm and, for these reasons alone, he'd put his modesty aside, adding another valuable layer of insulation against the deep winter.

Captain Sebastev's adjutant, Lieutenant Kuritsin, stood from his place at the table and moved to a cabinet in the far corner to fix a steaming mug of ohx' for the colonel.

'If there's any going about, lieutenant,' added Kabanov, 'you might put a little shot of rahzvod in it. Do an old man a favour.' The men chuckled. More than a few drew Guard-issue flasks from their pockets and offered them to the lieutenant, but Kuritsin had already unscrewed his own flask. Kabanov saw him pour a generous measure of the strong Vostroyan liquor into the mug.

Good man, he thought. A dash of that will do the trick.

The war room filled with low chatter as officers from different sections of the trenches discussed the day's defensive actions. Two men were notably absent: Lieutenant Nicholo of Fifth Company and Lieutenant Vharz of the Tenth. Nicholo looked set to recover given time, but Vharz had met his end. As the uninformed were told of this, the tone of the conversation changed, and the mood in the room became sombre.

It will get a lot worse before I'm through, thought Kabanov. May the Emperor help you in particular, Sebastev, because you're going to need it.

Lieutenant Kuritsin crossed the room and presented Kabanov with a mug. 'Thank you, lieutenant,' said the colonel with a smile.

'There's nothing like a hot drink on a night like this, eh? So long as there's a drop of the liquid fire in it.'

Kuritsin grinned. 'You're not wrong, sir.'

The ohx' was thick and salty, just as it was meant to be. The drink's proper name was *ohxolosvennoy*, but no one ever called it that. It was a staple on Vostroya, cheap and easy to make. In its dry form, it was simply powdered grox meat with a few added stimulants and preservatives. Workers in every factorum on Vostroya swore by ohx'. It was the only way to get through double shifts. On Danik's World, the Firstborn drank prodigious amounts of the stuff.

Kabanov sighed happily as the hot liquid warmed his belly. Low enough not to be heard over the general hum of conversation, he said, 'Fifth Company did well today, soldier, holding back the greenskin filth. You and your men did the regiment proud. The late major's faith in the captain is vindicated once again. Don't tell the captain I said so. His head will swell and his hat won't fit anymore.' The two men shared a quiet laugh, while Sebastev, busy conversing with other officers around the table, sat oblivious to them.

Kabanov nodded towards the far corner of the room where a small group of commissars conversed around another of the room's thermal coils.

Not one of them had removed his black cap.

The shadowy group reminded Kabanov of nothing so much as a flock of giant crows, the kind he'd seen gather to feast on the dead in the aftermath of so many battles. He immediately felt a twinge of guilt at the comparison. Commissar-captain Uthis Vaughn, the regimental commissar, was a close personal friend. Despite the man's intimidating public persona, Kabanov knew him to have a wonderful sense of humour, a deep appreciation of art in its many forms, and a frustrating talent for the game of regicide. He was the best player Kabanov had met in all sixty-eight years of his life. But it wasn't Vaughn the colonel was concerned with. 'How about the new man, lieutenant?' he asked Kuritsin. 'How are you getting on with Ixxius's replacement?'

Kuritsin shrugged and, with his voice barely more than a whisper, said, 'It's early days yet, sir. The man seems to be a fearless fighter, at least. He literally threw himself onto the orks today. Unfortunately, he threw himself onto the captain first. He's lucky the orks took the brunt of the captain's rage. I'd say they're not off to a very good start.'

'And you expect more trouble between them?' asked Kabanov reading the lieutenant's expression.

'I'd say they have very little in common, sir. The commissar seems a very proud man, a man of fine breeding and aristocratic ancestry. I'm sure that the reputation of the Schola Excubitos on Terrax is well earned, but that'll carry little weight with the captain. You know what he's like with the proud ones, sir.'

Kabanov frowned and stroked his long white moustache. 'Perhaps you could caution the captain, lieutenant. He mustn't underestimate Commissar Karif. Commissar-Captain Vaughn considers his posting to Fifth Company a most perplexing turn of events. The man is an unknown quantity.'

'How so, sir?' asked Kuritsin. 'Didn't the commissar-captain request a replacement after Ixxius was lost?'

'He did, but, at the last possible moment, the postings were changed. Commissar-Captain Vaughn was expecting another man entirely.' Kabanov leaned close and added, 'According to Vaughn, Karif's record is conspicuously impressive. He's been decorated for success in some very high profile campaigns. Foremost among his achievements, so I'm told, is the Armoured Star for a pivotal action on Phenosia.'

If Kabanov remembered rightly, and it was difficult to be sure after a lifetime of trying to stay current on the Imperium's countless wars, Phenosia had been won back at great cost from the forces of the dreaded Traitor Legions.

'If that's true, sir,' said Kuritsin, 'it begs the question: why has the man been shipped out here, of all places? And to a mere company-level commission? It seems most irregular, sir.'

'I'd hazard a guess that our new commissar recently made a powerful enemy, lieutenant.'

'I hope it's just that, sir.'

Kabanov raised a querying eyebrow. 'What do you mean?'

'I wouldn't like to think that it was anything more sinister, sir. Captain Sebastev isn't very popular with Twelfth Army Command.'

I know, thought Kabanov. If General Vlastan didn't owe me his life twice over, he'd have bounced Sebastev back down to sergeant the moment Dubrin breathed his last. The idea that some grunt from the Barony of Muskha, of all places, has been given a company command... Now it seems the general's patience has run out. He's been listening to the wrong people. I can't shield the captain any more. The politics in Seddisvarr are out of hand, but if they think I'll just drop the man like a hot ingot, they don't know the White Boar, by Terra.

Colonel Kabanov realised with a start that he'd drifted off into his own thoughts. The lieutenant was staring at him, waiting patiently. 'Sorry, lieutenant, old men like me have these moments.'

'Not so old, sir,' replied Kuritsin with a grin and a shake of his head, 'and still the best of us by far.'

Kabanov was caught off-guard by the look of admiration in the lieutenant's eyes. Hero worship: he'd never gotten used to it, though he'd had to endure it since winning his first regimental combat tournament. He'd earned his nickname during that contest.

By the Throne, he thought, that was fifty years ago.

At least his time away from the frontlines didn't seem to have impacted on his reputation among his men. Clearing his throat, he put a hand on the young officer's shoulder and said, 'It's time we got this briefing started. Call this lot to order for me, lieutenant.'

'At once, sir,' said Kuritsin. He turned to face the crowded table and called out, 'To order, Firstborn. Colonel Kabanov will begin the briefing.'

The younger man moved off to take his seat, and Colonel Kabanov stood alone, scanning the faces of his patient officers.

No more procrastinating, Maksim, he told himself.

Sebastev was glad he was sitting down when the colonel gave them the news, because he could hardly believe what he was hearing. The words stunned him. It was a bloody disaster. That was the only way to put it. Twelfth Army Command's gross mismanagement of the Danik's World campaign had now cost them an entire regiment of men and a vital beachhead in the north-east. The Vostroyan Firstborn 104th Fusiliers had been decimated. Over two thousand souls had been lost defending the city of Barahn against the concentrated might of the Venomhead clan. Warp blast and damn the orks.

But if the news itself was grim, the implications were even worse.

Someone a few seats to Sebastev's left banged a fist on the table. The hololithic projector studs set into the surface jumped, and bands of static rippled across the ghostly green projection of the Danikkin landscape that floated before them. Sebastev's eyes were fixed on the glowing three-dimensional representation of Barahn. Even now, as the officers of the Sixty-Eighth sat in silence with their jaws and fists clenched, hordes of filthy orks were ransacking the city, stripping it of anything they could use to fabricate their shoddy war-machines, enslaving or murdering anyone they found alive.

Sebastev had seen what ork slavers would do. Though the ork intellect was universally denigrated, he'd worked enough reconnaissance in his past to know better. He'd seen greenskins threaten to devour captive children, forcing their parents to work themselves to death. He'd watched laughing gretchin torture innocent men and women to instil fear and obedience in the enslaved. He remembered, too, the Marauder air strikes he'd guided in to deliver the Emperor's justice. He'd known that, given the choice, the enslaved would gladly give up their lives to ensure the destruction of their captors.

Old memories mixed with fresh anger and made his blood surge. He fought to stay in control.

Most of the officers in that room were looking at the map, giving thanks for the range of high mountains, the northernmost extents of the Varanesian Peaks, which separated the fallen city from the town of Korris by almost three hundred kilometres of difficult terrain.

So far, the Sixty-Eighth had only ever had to contend with roaming bands of ork scavengers or, like today, warbands that spilled over the mountains from the battle in the north-east. Even so, the number of orks in the region and the frequency of attacks had been increasing. Despite the losses they were surely taking, it seemed as if the ork horde was actually gaining in size, strength and ambition. It didn't make sense.

Since taking Barahn in the opening stages of the Twelfth Army's eastern push, the 104th Fusiliers had suffered the brunt of the ork attacks. Twelfth Army Command had believed the city's defences to be far beyond the greenskins' siege capabilities. What fools! Sebastev would have wagered every bottle of rahzvod in Korris that the men assembled tonight felt the same guilt that he did twisting their guts.

'Now that the orks have pushed through our northern line,' said Colonel Kabanov, breaking the silence, 'the entire Valles Carcavia is open to them, from its easternmost mouth all the way to the outskirts of Grazzen in the west.'

The colonel lifted a light quill and inscribed a small circle on the projector's control tablet. A circle of light appeared on the shimmering holomap, circling a riverside city about one hundred and fifty kilometres west of Barahn.

'There's no doubt,' continued the colonel, 'that General Vlastan's tactical staff will be expecting to stop the ork advance at Grazzen. The Thirty-Fifth Mechanised Regiment is stationed there. They need only fall back to the west bank and destroy both the city's bridges to prevent the orks from advancing into Theqis. The river Solenne is over two kilometres wide at its narrowest point, and runs so fast and deep that even our Chimeras can't ford it. Without the bridges here and here, the orks will have no way across.'

'Meaning that they'll turn southwards and crash down on us like an apocalypse,' said a gruff voice. Sebastev looked across the table at Major Galipolov, commander of First Company. 'When they hit the banks of the Solenne and find themselves checked, they'll turn and follow it all the way down to Nhalich, isolating us and cutting off our supply lines. Isn't that right, colonel?'

What supply lines, thought Sebastev bitterly? With things the way they are out here, would we even notice?

Colonel Kabanov nodded, his face grim. 'I'd call that a certainty, major. With these changes to the campaign map, Korris sticks out like a grot's nose. But I'm afraid the orks are only half of the problem. It pains me to say it, but I've more bad news. Listen up.'

All eyes rose from the holomap and fixed on the colonel as he said, 'At daybreak this morning, armour columns from the traitor-held towns of Dura and Nova-Kristae laid siege to the town of Ohslir. The 212th Regiment fought back, but their defences were overcome. This is the first direct offensive action taken by the Danikkin Independence Army in over a hundred days, and the timing can't be a coincidence. The possibility that they received real time intelligence from observers at Barahn is something I find both significant and disturbing, especially since our own comms have proven so damned unreliable.'

The colonel suddenly looked over at the attending members of the Cult Mechanicus. He bowed by way of apology and said, 'Of course, I meant no offence.'

'None taken, colonel,' said Tech-priest Gavaril. His voice crackled from a sonic resonator sunk into the pale flesh of his chest. 'We are in agreement.'

'The machine-spirits are discontent,' added Enginseer Politnov. Unlike Tech-priest Gavaril's, the enginseer's mouth moved as he spoke, but the sound was exactly the same, toneless and electronic. 'More obeisance must be made. More obeisance!'

'Indeed,' said Colonel Kabanov. 'We ask much of the Machine-God.'

'Wasn't any support sent out from Helvarr?' asked the Eighth Company commander, Major Tsurkov. 'Surely the 117th were sent east to flank the rebel armour? Didn't Major Imrilov send out a call for emergency support?'

The question had occurred to Sebastev, too. Tank columns from Helvarr could have reached Ohslir in just a few hours, but had they been sent out to help?

'No support was sent,' said Kabanov darkly. 'From what I understand, storms over Theqis prevented Twelfth Army Command communicating with our bases in the south until it was too late. We didn't receive news of the attack until the relay station at Nhalich was finally able to boost the signal to our array. The 212th took heavy losses, but I've been told that a few companies did manage to escape under the leadership of Major Imrilov. As far as I know, they've joined up with the 117th at Helvarr.'

Old Hungry will have a fit, thought Sebastev. I wouldn't want to be Imrilov the next time they meet.

On the hololithic map, Kabanov again drew a small circle of light, this one marking the town of Ohslir. 'With the campaign map altered so dramatically, we are extended well beyond our lines of support. With Ohslir under their control, it's a fair bet the Danikkin Independence Army will strike out for Nhalich next. So, if the orks don't cut Korris off, the rebels will certainly try.'

Major Galipolov leaned forward on his elbows, tugging a waxed end of his grey moustache, and said, 'It's a classic pincer, only each claw belongs to a separate beast. If the dirty xenos were anything but orks or tyranids, I'd suspect some kind of collusion with the rebels. The timing of this DIA push can't be a coincidence, but, given that we're talking about orks here, the notion is preposterous.'

'Speculation won't get us very far,' said Captain Grukov of Third Company. 'We need action.' Refusing to meet Major Galipolov's furious stare, he addressed Colonel Kabanov directly. 'What's to be done, sir?'

'The decision has been made for us, gentlemen,' said Kabanov. 'The Twelfth Army's tactical council have assessed the situation. I received new orders this afternoon.'

Colonel Kabanov's expression told Sebastev he wasn't going to like what he was about to hear. The old man's face betrayed his disgust, as if he'd bitten into a piece of fruit only to find it riddled with Catachan pusworms.

To Sebastev's mind, the smart answer was to move companies from the 117th across from Helvarr to engage the rebels at Ohslir. Then flank the enemy on its north side using companies from the 701st at Nhalich. While the orks were engaged with the Thirty-Fifth at Grazzen, the Sixty-Eighth could move up to flank them from the south. If they were lucky, there might be a chance to take the orks out permanently.

Of course, it would mean abandoning Korris, but, in Sebastev's opinion, Korris's only strategic value was as a launching point for Vostroyan assaults on the rebel-held hive-cities in the south-east. Such an action didn't look likely. The discovery of the Venomhead presence on Danik's World had brought a swift halt to the Twelfth Army's original plans.

The colonel cleared his throat and said, 'The Sixty-Eighth Infantry Regiment has been ordered to pull back to Nhalich. When we arrive, we're to join up with the 701st and assist them in readying their defences against a possible siege from the south. Our redeployment is scheduled to begin at first light, two days from now, preparations to start immediately.'

Redeployment, not retreat: retreat was practically a curse word to many of the Vostroyan Firstborn. Sebastev had never liked it much, but he didn't try to deceive himself now. It *was* a retreat. The Twelfth Army had suffered a devastating double blow. They had to consolidate their forces, and that meant pulling back, at least for now. It wasn't how Sebastev would have fought the war, but at least it made some kind of sense. That was more than he'd expected from Old Hungry and his advisors.

Major Galipolov, on the other hand, was typically direct in voicing his displeasure. 'So we're to just up and leave?' he asked. 'After two years of hard-fought occupation? Does General Vlastan know how many of my men died holding this place? This doesn't sit well with me, colonel. It doesn't sit well at all.'

'Noted, major,' replied Colonel Kabanov.

Captain Grukov added his voice, saying, 'I can't stomach the idea of just letting the damned greenskins roll right in here. The least we can do is leave a few surprises for them, wouldn't you say? What's to stop them following us to Nhalich and attacking at the same time as the Danikkin rebels?'

Colonel Kabanov frowned. 'Now that Barahn has fallen, General Vlastan is betting that the orks will stop crossing the Varanesian Peaks to attack Korris. As a buffer of sorts for our forces at Nhalich, Twelfth Army command has decided that a single company will remain behind in Korris to continue our occupation of the town.' The colonel paused. 'Captain Sebastev's Fifth Company has been selected for this honour.'

'By the Throne!' exclaimed Grukov. 'With respect, sir, you can't be serious. A single company?'

'Honour indeed,' said Major Galipolov, banging the table. 'It's a bloody death sentence!'

Others spoke up, eager to voice their protests. Only the members of the Commissariat and the Cult Mechanicus remained silent, masking their reactions well, if they had any at all.

Sebastev was unsure what to think or feel. A single company, even his outstanding Fifth Company, might hold off a minor assault if they could stomach the heavy losses, but an ork charge like today's...

So, thought Sebastev, the blue bloods have finally made their move. I knew it would come sooner or later.

Not for the first time, Sebastev wished he'd never made his promise to Dubrin, but his friend had been dying. How could he have done any less than swear, on the Treatis Elatii no less, that he would lead Dubrin's company to glory and honour? That he would get them through this wasteful mess of a campaign? And, because some men cared about things like lineage and Vostroyan military politics, and Throne knew what else, Sebastev's whole company had been ordered to hold the line or die.

The other officers were talking over each other. There was such a cacophony that no single voice could be made out.

Colonel Kabanov rose to his feet, toppling his chair to the cold, wooden floor. His fists struck the tabletop so hard they cracked it. 'Silence, all of you!' he bellowed. 'I'm not finished, Throne damn it!'

The protests stopped dead. Sebastev, Galipolov and the rest of the assembled officers gaped at their leader. His eyes blazed from under his thick, white eyebrows, and he seemed to crackle with power. This was Maksim Kabanov, the formidable White Boar and the most decorated man in the Firstborn Sixty-Eighth, former combat champion in the regimental games, and master exponent of the ossbohk-vyar. One ignored or disrespected him at great risk.

Colonel Kabanov stared each man in the face, daring him to open his mouth.

Silence gripped the war room, broken only by the buzzing of the overhead strip lights and the soft humming of the field-cogitator banks by the rear wall.

'Fifth Company will not be holding Korris alone,' said the colonel through gritted teeth. His eyes settled on Sebastev.

'Commissar-Captain Vaughn and Major Galipolov will be taking joint command of our main force during the redeployment.

'I, Colonel Maksim Kabanov, will be staying to lead Fifth Company.'

CHAPTER FOUR

DAY 686

KORRIS – 10:39HRS, -17°C

The town of Korris, half-ruined and abandoned but for the presence of Fifth Company, basked in a wash of rare sunshine. Overhead, the yellow globe of Gamma Kholdas crossed the blue sky in a lazy arc, turning the snowfields that surrounded the town into an endless blinding carpet of white light. Sebastev's men patrolled the town's perimeter in pairs, wearing dark goggles to prevent snow-blindness, their booted feet cutting deep channels in the glittering landscape.

Many of the old buildings were little more than angular piles of black rubble, having collapsed under heavy burdens of snow during the last two millennia of the Danikkin deep winter. Metal beams jutted at all angles from the ruins, turned red with rust, flaking away or crumbling to powder in the frequent gales. The corners of those buildings that remained intact were rounded and smooth, as if sandblasted. Particles of ice driven by gusting winds had scoured away all but the most subtle signs of the decorative carvings that had once graced many of the structures.

Here and there, the rough outline of an Imperial eagle could still be seen over some of the doorways. The Danikkin had pulled out of Korris at the start of the deep winter, long before the current rebellion had erupted across the planet. No rebel had defaced the Imperial icons, only time.

Today, the air was still, and visibility was better than it had been

for weeks. Fifth Company had moved back from the trenchworks
to occupy the town. There were simply too few of them to hold
the trenches against any kind of attack. Colonel Kabanov had
posted scouts out there to watch the foothills of the Varanesian
Peaks for any sign of an ork advance, but so far, Old Hungry's
supposition that the orks would stop crossing the mountains
seemed to be holding true.

Sebastev was far more comfortable with the prospect of fighting
in an urban area. The Vostroyan Firstborn were quite probably
the finest city fighters in the Imperial Guard. They were bred for
it: trained in close quarters combat from a young age, and taught
to fight from cover in the ruins of the old factorum complexes
that dotted so much of their home world. Korris suited Sebastev
and his men fine. It almost didn't matter than Old Hungry had
ordered them to remain out here.

For the last two years, Colonel Kabanov's home had been the
abandoned councillor's mansion that stood just north of the
town's central market square. The building had served as regimental headquarters since the arrival of the Sixty-Eighth. It was
a natural choice, its superior construction having allowed it to
weather the very worst of the winter storms with only minor ero-
sion. The regimental engineers had easily restored the mansion's
interior to a habitable condition, but despite their best efforts, it
was still too cold to be called comfortable.

It was in this building, in Colonel Kabanov's spacious office,
that Sabastev now stood, still dressed in his full winter kit, facing his commanding officer.

Colonel Kabanov sat behind a broad desk carved from dark
Danikkin pine. The surface of the desk was covered with a dis-
orderly arrangement of rolled maps and message scrolls. On
either side of him, placed close to offer maximum warmth, two
thermal coils hummed softly, casting a red tinge over the colonel's face that made him look almost healthy.

'Three days,' grumbled the colonel. 'Three days since the regiment departed, and the third day in a row that you've come to me to register a formal protest.' He scowled at Sebastev. 'Am I to suffer this every day, captain? I'm not logging these protests, you know.'

'I'll continue regardless, sir,' said a frowning Sebastev, 'at least, until you see sense and ship out.'

Kabanov shook his head. 'By the Golden Throne, you're stubborn, and insolent too, damn it. That's Dubrin's doing. You get more like the old scoundrel every day, Throne bless him.'

'I thank the colonel for his compliment.'

'It wasn't a compliment, blast you,' said Kabanov, but a grin twitched at his moustache nevertheless. 'Good old Alexos, eh? Arrogant, proud, cocky. Then again, one might suppose the same is true of all Vostroyans, damn our pride. I'm a victim of it myself, I expect.'

'Am I to understand from that statement, sir,' said Sebastev stiffly, 'that pride is the reason for your insistence on staying here with us?'

Colonel Kabanov didn't answer. Instead, he lifted a hand to stall any further questions while he coughed wetly into a handkerchief. Then he folded it, and returned it to his pocket.

When he'd composed himself, he leaned forward on his desk, stared Sebastev in the eye and said, 'I attached myself to Fifth Company because it's what I wanted to do, captain. I've never been in the habit of explaining myself to my subordinates, and I'm not about to start now. I'm your commanding officer, so you'll just bloody well accept it. Now, let this be an end to it.'

There was an uncomfortable pause. When the colonel spoke again, his tone was less contentious. 'In all your time under my command, have I ever done anything to betray the faith my fighters have placed in me? Have I ever put myself above our men? Never, not in all our time serving the Imperium together. Stop these daily protests, captain. If a simple request is not enough, you may take that as a direct order.'

Sebastev bowed his head, resigned.

Colonel Kabanov sat back in his chair and sighed. 'I do hate clashing blades with you, Grigorius. Are we not friends as well as comrades? Thirty years have seen us struggle through some hard times together, after all.'

'You honour me by saying so, sir,' said Sebastev. He meant it, too.

Urgent knocking sounded on the room's broad double doors. Colonel Kabanov sat forward again. 'Enter,' he called out.

Lieutenant Maro walked awkwardly into the room, his metallic foot clattering on the marble floor with every other step. He was gripping a sheet of parchment in his right hand and looked anxious.

'What's wrong, Maro?' asked the colonel. 'You look like you sat on a spinefruit.'

'A communiqué from Nhalich, sir, from Commissar-Captain Vaughn: It just came through this minute.' Maro moved across to Kabanov's desk and handed him the parchment. The colonel quickly unrolled it and scanned it with his eyes.

As Sebastev and Maro waited for Colonel Kabanov to finish reading, Maro threw Sebastev a meaningful look that told him the message wasn't good news.

Colonel Kabanov finished reading, loosed off a few curses, rolled the parchment up, and sat tapping the surface of his desk with his knuckles.

Sebastev's lack of patience finally got the better of him, and he cleared his throat. Colonel Kabanov looked over at him. 'Captain,' he said, 'the message states that the Danikkin Independence Army has moved into position around Nhalich. There's a lot more to it than that, however. Saboteurs have attacked Vostroyan vehicles and supplies there, and the men of the 701st seem to be suffering from some kind of illness. The commissar-captain says he has tried everything to make contact with Twelfth Army Command. Nothing is getting through to Seddisvarr. Damned storms again, it seems.'

'Attacked from within by civilians?' asked Sebastev.

'These people are desperate,' said Kabanov, 'desperate and doomed. Assemble the men. We're the closest assistance on offer. Since Command HQ is still unreachable over the vox, I'll have to take the matter into my own hands. Fifth Company must ride to the aid of our regiment. I want all our transports ready and waiting on the western edge as soon as possible. Since I'm in command, the decision is mine to make. I'll answer to the general later.'

It was suddenly clear to Sebastev that Kabanov had been expecting this all along, possibly even counting on it. He'd known the chance to withdraw from Korris would come all too quickly. He'd probably ordered Galipolov and Vaughn to request aid at the first sign of trouble.

You knew I wouldn't pull the company out, thought Sebastev. No matter how I feel about Old Hungry, orders are orders.

'I'll order the transports assembled at once, colonel.'

Sebastev saluted the colonel and turned to leave, his mind fixed on the task of organising his men. But just as he was crossing towards the door, sound poured into the room, stopping him in mid-stride. The air filled with a terrible ululating wail. It was so penetrating that it made the thick stone walls seem like paper. Sebastev had been dreading that sound. The timing couldn't have been worse.

'Raid sirens on the east towers,' he shouted over the din. 'Orks, sir!'

His vox-bead burst to life with a dozen frantic voices. Reports came flooding in from his scouts. Orks were pouring over the snow from the east. They'd already reached the abandoned trenchworks. The scouts were heading back to the town with all the speed they could manage.

Fifth Company was in trouble.

Colonel Kabanov had established procedures for repelling enemy assaults on Korris back when the Sixty-Eighth Infantry Regiment had first moved in to occupy the town. Of course, those plans had been built around command of an entire regiment, so they were mostly useless now. Instead, his strategy for holding Korris with only Fifth Company under his command relied in no small part on the colonel's many previous experiences with orks. In Kabanov's opinion, the greatest advantage one had in fighting the greenskins was that they were particularly easy to bait. That knowledge was being put to use right now by the squads of men tasked with drawing the oncoming orks into a trap in the market square.

Kabanov stood with Captain Sebastev and Lieutenants Maro and Kuritsin, around a table covered with a large tattered map of the town. Kabanov didn't intend to occupy the place for long, but this building, the remains of a once grand, three-storey hotel overlooking the market square from its eastern edge, was well suited to his current needs. The construction of the old hotel was solid. Thick stone walls offered reassuring cover for the men stationed at shattered windows on each floor.

Vox traffic was still heavy. Snipers were calling in the movements of the orks. The baiting squads were in constant contact as they drew the orks in. Enginseer Politnov and his small staff of Mechanicus servants had assembled Fifth Company's vehicles, a few Chimeras and heavy troop transporters, outside the town on its western edge.

Kabanov tapped the map with a gloved finger and said, 'Squads are waiting at these intersections, ready to converge on the square once the orks are in. We've got heavy bolter nests set up here, here and here to provide enfilading fire. And you've ordered snipers onto rooftops and balconies at these points. Is that right, captain?'

'As ordered, sir,' said Captain Sebastev.

'Good,' said Kabanov. He traced a street to the point where it opened onto the square and said, 'When they reach this point, our men stationed around the square will have visual contact. I want everyone to wait for my order. No firing until the orks have

Sarovic had always considered himself a fumbler where the opposite sex was concerned. With no real idea of how to secure a willing partner, he'd attached himself to a group of troopers that were going to one of the more notorious entertainment districts not far from the base.

He hadn't had much luck at first. It was getting late. Most of the others had paired off with women who seemed very keen to accept the honour of Firstborn seed. Sarovic's lack of confidence was letting him down. The only thing he was confident about was his skill with a sniper rifle. He'd already been singled out for special training. He'd almost given up on meeting anyone, when a skinny girl staggered drunkenly through the door, tripped on her own feet, and spilled her drink over his good, clean uniform.

He'd been livid, and had chewed her out immediately. But rather than cower before his anger, the girl, unremarkable but for her big brown eyes, had shouted right in his face, telling him to shut up, sit down, and get over himself. Sarovic still didn't know why he'd done exactly that. Maybe basic training had conditioned him to take orders on reflex.

A few moments later, she reappeared from the bar, slamming two drinks down in front of him. Without waiting to be invited, she dropped herself into the chair next to his, and began to ask him about himself. Sarovic couldn't remember even the smallest snippet of the conversation, only that he'd thought over and over again that her perfume smelled nice. Before he knew it, they were back at her scruffy little hab, thrashing around on the bed together as if every second counted.

In the morning, when Sarovic woke up, he'd been confused by his surroundings. Then he'd seen her standing over a blue flame, cooking breakfast. He'd thrown her a smile. She didn't smile back.

Shalkova: cold and silent and deadly. She never missed.

He racked the slide, chambering his next bullet.

He'd never understood why the girl had turned nasty on him. From the moment he got out of her bed, she'd attacked him with a vicious critique of his efforts at lovemaking the previous night. Her taunts were cruel, and her laughter, more so. The breakfast she cooked was hers. He could buy his own or go hungry. She didn't care. She'd chased him from her door, his uniform stained and in disarray, her taunts following him along garbage filled alleyways as the Vostroyan sky brightened overhead.

Did she bear me a son, he wondered? A daughter? Anything?

He'd asked himself a dozen times, but he supposed that it didn't really matter. He would never know for sure. She represented a single wonderful, terrible night in his life. Her touch had thrilled him. Her words had been as cold and cruel as bullets, fired to inflict maximum damage. So, he'd named his rifle after her.

He pressed his right eye to the scope and adjusted the zoom to bring his target into clear focus. Range, about six hundred metres. Wind, negligible.

Snipers from other companies tended to favour the long-las. It was a fine weapon, highly accurate, but its bright beam gave the shooter's position away. On the orders of the late Major Dubrin, Fifth Company snipers employed hand-crafted, Vostroyan-made rifles that fired solid ammunition. It was a harder weapon to master than the long-las, but a sniper with good cover could take down target after target without giving himself away.

Shalkova was fitted with flash and noise suppressors. Sarovic enjoyed friendly competition with another sniper from First Platoon called 'Clockwork' Izgorod. Each man had made a wager on who would rack up the most kills throughout this Danikkin Campaign. So far, old Clockwork was in the lead, but his numerous augmetics gave him something of an advantage.

Sarovic centred his sights on the target. It was a massive, dark skinned ork in the front ranks of the charging horde. The monster wore a necklace of severed human hands strung on barbed wire.

Emperor above, thought Sarovic, these beasts are foul.

He breathed out slowly as he squeezed Shalkova's trigger. There was a whisper of rushing air. In the scope, he saw the ork's head jerk backwards. The fiend sank to the ground with a neat black hole punched in its skull. The other orks trampled over the body, hardly noticing it.

Another deadly word from the lips of Shalkova, he thought. You never tire of killing, do you, my love?

Sarovic imagined he could smell perfume. He racked the slide and chambered another bullet.

The square was full of them now, orks of every shape and size stumbling over each other in their eagerness to engage the Vostroyans. Hundreds, maybe thousands more, were still trying to push their way forward. Retreat for the orks trapped in the square was impossible, such was the crush at their backs. Kabanov watched it all play out as he'd known it would. In the course of his career, he'd seen them make the same mistakes time and time again.

The greenskins just couldn't control their urge to fight. If they'd landed here on Danik's World to find a lifeless rock, they'd have simply fought amongst themselves.

Kabanov leaned from the window and loosed another shot down into the orks. He'd already lost count of his kills and the battle had been raging for mere minutes. He pulled the trigger of his hellpistol again, but nothing happened. The power pack was spent. As he drew a fresh one from a pouch on his belt, he remembered other scenes just like this one. The press of orks out there in the square was almost as dense as it had been on the bridge at Dunan thirty-five years ago. It had been the same in the canyon on... where was it again? There had been so many battles.

He slammed the fresh power pack into the pistol's socket and resumed firing. With the orks bunched so tight down there, every single shot found a mark. Green bodies crumpled to the ground clutching the black pits the pistol burned in their chests and bellies. The hellpistol, a House Kabanov heirloom, still performed with lethal efficiency despite over three centuries of service.

From positions of cover, both high and low, Firstborn troopers fired again and again into the mass of enemies. There was so much las-fire it hurt Kabanov's eyes, but the orks were fighting back. Some began throwing grenades at the windows from which Kabanov's men fired.

Most of the grenades clattered off the walls, falling to the snow below or bouncing back towards the orks at the fringes. They detonated noisily on open ground, causing welcome greenskin casualties, but a percentage of the grenades found their mark, gliding through the openings they'd been aimed at.

Muffled booms echoed over the square, and black smoke billowed from old habs. Tumbling red forms plummeted from some of the smoking windows, to land in unmoving heaps on the snow.

'Men are dying out there!' barked Kabanov. 'Where are my flanking squads?'

On the colonel's right, Captain Sebastev was pouring shots down on the horde from a smashed window, his bolt pistol barking aggressively. There was a feral look on the man's face as his finger squeezed the trigger again and again. 'We need some fire on those black, battle-scarred ones,' said Sebastev. 'They're leading the charge.'

Kabanov scanned the green mob and found the individuals in question, three of them standing in the centre of the horde. These ork leaders bellowed orders to their kin in the inscrutable series of grunts and snorts that constituted the ork language.

'Colonel,' said Captain Sebastev between shots, 'I'd like to send an order to First Platoon's snipers to take them out.'

'Do so at once, captain. The enemy is pressing uncomfortably close to the east edge of the square. I'm still waiting for my bloody flanking squads.'

'They're on their way, sir,' reported Lieutenant Kuritsin, 'but Third Platoon reports contact with orks sneaking through the backstreets. They're engaging them now.'

'Sneaking?' said Captain Sebastev. 'Orks don't sneak, Rits.'

'Lieutenant Vassilo was very specific about it, sir. He reported a squad of orks employing something almost like stealth tactics, sir.'

Captain Sebastev turned to look at Kabanov and said, 'If our flanking squads are engaged before they get to the square, sir, we're in a lot of trouble. The orks are still pouring in. We need those squads here. The crossfire must hold until the sappers are done!'

'We've got to be on our way,' said Kabanov. 'What's the word from our demolition squad?'

Lieutenant Kuritsin voxed an update request to Fifth Company's sappers. The men under the command of Sergeant Barady of Fifth Platoon had been given a special mission of their own. Like most Danikkin towns, Korris had been built around a geothermal energy sink. The massive structures generated tremendous amounts of electrical power. Barady's sapper team was charged with denying the orks this valuable energy source. Enginseer Politnov had advised the sappers how the charges might be set to cause a significant explosion, one that would level most of the town. With Colonel Kabanov personally ordering a full withdrawal, Fifth Company had one final chance to deal devastating damage to the orks that had troubled them for the last two years.

'Our sappers report a problem, sir. They're proceeding to rig the charges, but they're under fire. Sergeant Barady says he'll need twice as much time to complete his mission if his men keep having to defend themselves.'

'Damn it,' barked Kabanov, 'it's all going to hell. There is no more time.'

Just as he spoke, however, the orks began falling back to the centre of the square, desperate to escape a sudden and massive increase in las-fire from the avenues to the north and south.

'Our flanking squads are here, sir,' reported Captain Sebastev. He began firing again from his position at the window.

Kabanov saw the full might of Fifth Company hit the orks. It was a wonderful sight, reminiscent of so many old victories, proud Vostroyan Firstborn marching in ordered rows from the openings on north and south sides, loosing well-ordered volleys into the desperate alien foe.

The square was being covered, metre by metre, under a growing carpet of dead orks. Ork blood had turned the snow into a dark red slush.

'Outstanding,' said Kabanov. He turned to his adjutant, Maro. 'Now that's a wonderful sight, wouldn't you say?'

'Wonderful, sir,' said Maro.

'Sir,' said Kuritsin. 'Squad Barady is again calling for urgent assistance. What is your response?'

Kabanov quickly assessed the situation in the square. The orks were being murdered in great numbers. They returned fire and tried to charge the Vostroyans with cleavers held high, but Vostroyan discipline was unbreakable and, no matter how great the difference in numbers, the enemy rabble was faltering in the face of it.

'Very well, lieutenant,' said Kabanov turning, 'order Squad Breshek to break from the attack on the market square and divert to the power plant. The sooner we get that thing rigged to blow, the sooner we can pull out and leave Korris to the orks and their doom.'

Sebastev spoke from his position at the window. 'Commissar Karif looks to be enjoying himself.'

The commissar was down in the streets, alongside Sergeant Grodolkin and his men. The commissar's gleaming chainsword was raised aloft, and he seemed to be orating to the squad as they fired volley after volley at the massed foe.

I'd like to hear what he's saying, thought Kabanov. I notice Father Olov is conspicuously quiet. I wonder if he's wary of broadcasting a reading with the new commissar around to hear it.

At the thought of Fifth Company's battle-hardened priest, Kabanov scanned the square and saw him almost at once. He stood out clearly in his tan robes, brightly chequered at the hem and sleeves, yelling at the top of his voice to the men of Squad Svemir. He swung his massive eviscerator chainsword again and again, hewing apart the luckless orks that came at him.

Half-mad he may be, thought Kabanov, but what a fighter.

One of the squads on the north side, Squad Breshek, broke from the battle in the square and pounded north, racing to the aid of the beleaguered sappers. The other squads tried to cover the gap this created, but the orks noticed the absence of pressure from that quarter and immediately moved to take advantage.

Without waiting for Kabanov's approval, Captain Sebastev ordered Squads Ludkin and Basch to spread out, cutting off any chance of an ork pursuit of Squad Breshek. Sergeant Breshek would have enough to deal with at the power plant without having to worry about orks at his back.

Kabanov felt momentarily irritated by Sebastev's presumption, but the order was exactly the one he would have given, had he been quicker off the mark. Sebastev must have sensed his colonel's irritation, because he stopped firing briefly, turned to his superior officer and bowed. 'My apologies, colonel. It was wrong of me to... usurp your authority.'

'Less talking, more firing, captain,' said Kabanov, realising how foolish it was to damn the man for his quick thinking. If anything, the speed of Sebastev's reflex had prevented the other officers from seeing just how slow Kabanov had become. 'You're used to leading these men in battle, and they are used to you. I'll have no apologies for that. In my own way, I'm the usurper here.'

Sebastev straightened. 'Never that, colonel. This company follows the White Boar.'

Kabanov grinned, and then turned and resumed firing.

Sometimes your behaviour drives me to distraction, captain, he thought, but at other times, you're an exemplary officer. Let's have more of the latter.

The greenskins' next action disgusted Kabanov, highlighting the fact that orks lacked even the least comprehension of honour or pride. Pinned down without adequate cover, they began to haul the carcasses of their dead into piles to be used as shields. They pulled the heavy corpses up and over their bodies. It was something the proud Vostroyans would never have stooped to, but it was immediately effective. The shields of dead meat soaked up las-fire and bolter fire alike, giving the orks the protection they needed to rally.

Grenades exploded. Orks armed with cleavers and axes darted forward. More Vostroyans began to fall from their positions in the smartly ordered lines. Kabanov could hear increased vox-traffic, officers and sergeants calling for order and courage among the men.

'Two of the ork leaders are still standing, captain,' said Kabanov. 'Where in the warp are my snipers?'

Even as the colonel barked at Sebastev, the largest and darkest of the orks rocked on its feet, and collapsed, its skull perforated by a masterfully placed shot.

'Trooper Sarovic reports a successful kill, sir,' said Kuritsin.

Out in the square, the monstrous form of the last ork leader crumpled soundlessly, a sniper's bullet cutting a neat hole in its chest, punching an exit wound in its back as large as a man's head.

'Corporal Izgorod also reports a successful kill, sir.'

'My compliments to both men. It's time we started pulling back. What news from our sappers?'

Lieutenant Kuritsin checked in with Sergeant Barady, but it was another member of the sapper squad that answered in his place. Kuritsin reported to the colonel. 'Squad Breshek is at the power plant, sir. They're engaging the orks. I have reports that Sergeant

Barady has fallen, sir. As have three others from his squad. The remaining men... what? Please confirm that.'

'What is it, Rits?' asked Captain Sebastev, moving from his position at the window to stand before his adjutant.

'Our sappers confirm that the charges are set, sir. We've got twelve minutes to evacuate the town before the power plant blows. The blast will reach our current position.'

'Then we'd best be away from here,' said Kabanov. 'Lieutenant, broadcast the order. I want our men to fall back to the transports in a well-organised relay. Pull squads Breshek and Barady out first, and then the squads on north and south. I want the heavy bolters to cover the final retreat.'

'Understood, colonel.'

'Very good,' said Kabanov. He faced Sebastev and said, 'Let's get ourselves down to ground level and ready to move out, captain. We want to be as far away as possible when the power plant blows. I expect the blast will make a proper mess of things here.'

'No doubt about that, sir,' said Sebastev with a wicked grin. 'The bloody orks won't know what hit them.'

Things immediately looked different to Sebastev from the open street. As he raced from the old hotel's side entrance with the colonel and the men of First Platoon, he glanced left towards the market square. From behind the heaps they'd made of their dead, ork mobs raced swinging their blades, only to be cut down before they could engage the Vostroyans at close quarters.

The Vostroyan squads had been ordered to fall back, but as they did so, they were forced to keep the pressure on the orks by utilising a staggered retreat formation that made pulling out far slower than Sebastev would've liked. Just as he was turning from the scene, ready to race west to the transports with Kabanov and the others, the ground began to shake. Great piles of snow slid from the rooftops around the square, and rubble began to topple from the tops of half-shattered walls.

'What the Throne is going on?' asked a wide-eyed Maro. 'An earthquake?'

It was a fair guess given the amount of regular seismic activity that Danik's World endured, but this was no earthquake. The shuddering of the ground was different somehow. It was rhythmic and regular, like giant footsteps.

'Get moving, now!' barked Sebastev. But the others stood transfixed as a building on the far side of the square exploded outwards into spinning, tumbling chunks of broken masonry.

The orks turned to look, and were showered by a hail of flying fragments. Some of them were crushed to death, rendered little more than smears on the snow by the passage of the largest tumbling blocks. The others ignored the casualties, and began to hoot and cheer. As the great cloud of dust and debris slowly settled in the still winter air, a monstrous silhouette appeared from within, the massive form of an ork dreadnought.

Thick black fumes boiled up from its twin exhausts as they coughed and chugged. The sound of its engines was a throaty, bass rumble that vibrated the plates of Sebastev's armour.

It was absolutely huge – even taller than a sentinel and far bulkier. A moment ago, the powerful bodies of the orks had looked formidable to Sebastev, packed with dense slabs of muscle that could tear a man apart. Now they looked small by comparison.

As soon as the dreadnought stomped into the middle of the square, the orks swarmed around it, seeking shelter between its gleaming piston legs. Vostroyan las-fire continued to slash across at them from the mouths of alleys and streets, a few beams licking harmlessly across the dreadnought's armour.

For all its size, the killing machine looked as if it had been slapped together in the most haphazard way. Its bucket-like torso was covered with thick plates of metal that looked as if they'd been stripped from security doors or tank hatches, and bolted to it at all angles. Massive twin stubbers sat fixed above its thick piston legs.

From either side, long steel arms extended outwards, covered in snaking cables and powerful hydraulics. The bladed pincers at the end of each arm clashed together restlessly, eager to tear weak, fleshy beings to bloody tatters.

A ragged banner of black cloth with a familiar image painted in bright yellow hung from the top of the machine. It was the three-headed snake of the Venomhead clan.

'By the Throne,' gasped Kabanov, 'we'll need more than heavy-bolters to take that out.'

'The power plant explosion should do the job, sir,' said Sebastev, 'but let's not stick around to find out. We've less than six minutes to get clear of the blast radius.'

Even as he spoke, the dreadnought turned towards the retreating Vostroyan squads on the south side, and Sebastev's stomach lurched. 'Rits,' he shouted, 'tell our lads to move it. Forget the covering fire. Retreat at speed! That thing's going to–'

A deafening staccato beat tore through the air. Fire licked out from the fat barrels of the stubbers, illuminating the whole square in stark, flickering light. A blizzard of large-calibre bullets spewed forth, stitching the front of the south-side buildings, ripping through the walls, and pounding the thick stone construction into so much dust and stone chips. The upper floors of the ancient habs, untouched for two thousand years, tumbled to the ground in billowing clouds of dust.

Sebastev could hear yelling over the vox. His officers were calling their men to cover. 'Throne damn it,' voxed Sebastev to them, 'forget cover. I want a full-speed retreat, now! Get yourselves out of there. Head to the transports at once. That's an order!'

The order came a little too late for some. Firstborn were getting slaughtered under the dreadnought's devastating hail of fire. If the rest lingered even a moment longer, the orks would take their chance to rush forward and engage them at close quarters before they could escape west.

Sebastev saw Colonel Kabanov looking at him. He realised that, for the second time today, he'd bulldozed his superior officer, trampling on the colonel's authority. But there wasn't time to offer another apology. They had to get moving. Sebastev figured he'd face the consequences later.

'Colonel,' said Sebastev, 'we should run now, sir.'

'First Platoon,' said Colonel Kabanov, 'get us safely to the transports, please.'

Lieutenant Tarkarov immediately ordered his men into a defensive formation around the command staff officers. At another word, they took off down the street at speed.

As Sebastev ran, he noticed that the colonel was struggling to keep up. Kabanov was pushing himself hard to match the speed of the others, but his age had eroded his former athleticism. Maro, on the other hand, had mastered a kind of loping run that negated the disadvantage of his augmetic leg.

In the square behind them, the thunder of the dreadnought's heavy footsteps had been joined by others. More of the ramshackle, red killing machines lumbered into view between the ruined habs. The orks roared and cheered as they raced forward in pursuit of the retreating men.

Sebastev saw that the colonel was gasping hard, but there was no time to stop. They were almost at the western edge of the town. Then the assembled heavy transports and Chimeras came into view, waiting patiently in a snow covered field. Their engines idled noisily. Their exhausts, like those of the ork dreadnoughts, spouted dark fumes into the air. The men of Fifth Company who'd already reached the site were hurriedly loading their gear onto the vehicles.

As First Platoon and the command squad emerged from the avenues of buildings, Sebastev saw more men in red and gold running up ramps and into the bellies of the heavy transports. There wasn't time for any kind of accurate assessment, but at a glance it looked to Sebastev as if Fifth Company hadn't fared too badly.

As the command squad slowed to a trot, and then a walk, Kabanov scrambled in his pocket for a handkerchief. He raised it to his mouth and gave a series of hacking coughs that made him hunch over. On the colonel's behalf, Maro faced Lieutenant Tarkarov and said, 'Thank you, lieutenant. You and your men should board your transport now. Prepare to move out at once.'

Tarkarov nodded, though it was clear from his face that he was concerned, and perhaps a little shocked, by the state of Colonel Kabanov. Throwing a quick salute, he spun and led his men away.

Maro ushered Colonel Kabanov up the ramp and into the colonel's command Chimera. Sebastev hesitated for a moment. He and Kuritsin looked at each other unhappily.

'It seems the colonel isn't a well man, sir,' said Kuritsin.

'You're not joking,' said Sebastev.

More Vostroyans raced from the edges of the town, sprinting towards the safety of the waiting vehicles. The orks could be heard from between the buildings, their grunts and roars getting louder as they closed.

'We need to get moving, captain.'

'There must be more to come, Rits.'

'You know there isn't, sir. Anyone who hasn't made it here by now isn't coming.'

'Father Olov? The commissar?'

Kuritsin quickly voxed a call out for the priest and the commissar, and received prompt answers from Second and Third Platoon lieutenants.

'Third Platoon reports that Father Olov is safe with them in transport three. The commissar has apparently decided to travel with the men of Second Company. Our drivers await the colonel's order to move out.'

The first knot of ork pursuers emerged from the edge of the town, firing their pistols in Sebastev's general direction. Sebastev turned and marched up the ramp into the back of the rumbling Chimera, Kuritsin following a pace behind.

Inside the cramped rear compartment, Kuritsin hit the control rune to raise the ramp. Kabanov was already strapped in, covered with a thick blanket, drinking rahzvod from a silver flask. Sebastev had expected the man's face to be red from his exertions, but it was ghostly white.

'May I give the order for all transports to move out, sir?' asked Kuritsin.

'Do so at once, lieutenant. Get us away from this accursed place.' The colonel's voice was scratchy and subdued. He lifted the flask to his lips and took a deep draught.

Kuritsin voxed the order, and the rumbling of engines intensified outside. Lieutenant Maro gave two sharp knocks on the inside of the hull and, with a jolt and a shudder, the command Chimera accelerated away from Korris, leaving the frenzied orks and their monstrous contraptions behind.

Sebastev and Kuritsin strapped themselves into their seats, a quiet look passing between them. No one spoke. A minute later, a flash of bright light poured through the Chimera's firing ports, followed by a distant boom that rocked the vehicle.

Colonel Kabanov managed a small grin, perhaps imagining the utter devastation the explosion had wreaked on the orks. Sebastev took the colonel's reaction as a cue. He leaned forward, stared the old man straight in the eye, and said, 'No more grox-shit, colonel. It's high time you levelled with me.'

CHAPTER FIVE

The setting sun painted the land in hues of reddish gold before it slid from the sky. Cold, dark evening descended. The stars glittered overhead, a billion icy pinpricks of light, and the Danikkin moon, Avarice, rose fat and glowing.

Over the moonlit snows, a column of rumbling vehicles charged west with all available speed. It wasn't much, the unbroken drifts averaged over a metre deep. Fifth Company's Chimeras were forced to run slow, matching the speed of the massive, Danikkin-built troop transporters that moved up front, carving broad channels through the snow with their huge plough blades.

The local machines, called Pathcutters, had been sequestered from captured depots throughout Vostroyan occupied territory on Danik's World. They were ponderous compared to the smaller, better Imperial machines, but they hadn't been built for speed. Instead, their design stressed large capacity and a ruggedness that could handle the very worst of the Danikkin terrain. The troop compartment at the rear could accommodate over thirty personnel and was split into upper and lower decks. The chassis sat high on twinned pairs of powerful treads, well clear of the ground and any obstacles the vehicle might encounter. The height of the troop compartment called for a long ramp that dropped from the vehicle's belly rather than from the rear like most other APCs.

Commissar Karif had opted to travel in one of these relentless giants, committed to his belief that a commissar should provide a role model to the rank and file. So, as the Pathcutter juddered and forced its way through the deep snow, he moved along the rows of seated Vostroyans, using the handgrips that hung from the ceiling to maintain his balance. Everyone else was strapped into their seats.

'What's your name, soldier?' Karif asked, stopping to look down at a thick necked man with a waxed, brown moustache and piercing, grey eyes.

'Akmir,' replied the man. 'Trooper Alukin Akmir. Third Platoon, sir.'

'Good to know you, Akmir,' said Karif with a nod, 'and how many of the foe did you slay back there in Korris?'

'Not enough by half, sir,' said Akmir. There was a quiet anger in his voice. He turned his eyes down to his hands and rubbed at them, feigning preoccupation with some invisible mark. He didn't seem the talkative type.

Karif wasn't finished. 'How long have you served in this regiment, Akmir?'

The trooper paused before he answered, perhaps gauging just how open he should be with this newcomer to the Sixty-Eighth. After a moment's thought, however, he threw the commissar a lop-sided grin and said, 'Long enough to know when things are properly khekked, sir.'

Karif was about to ask for specifics when another trooper spoke from behind him.

'He's not wrong, commissar. We've all served long enough to know that those cosy bastards in Seddisvarr left us out to dry.'

There were grunts of agreement from soldiers sitting on either side of the compartment. 'Old Hungry,' hissed one. 'I never thought he'd finally do for the captain like that. Leastways, not so overt.'

'Emperor bless the White Boar for taking command and pulling us out like that,' said one. More grunts of agreement sounded over the rumble of the engine.

'All credit to the White Boar,' added another. 'The Pit-Dog's a great man, but I reckon he'd have stood his ground to the last. One's life for the Emperor and all that.'

'The Pit-Dog?' asked Karif in some confusion.

'That'd be Captain Sebastev, sir,' offered Trooper Akmir. 'Only, he doesn't like the name much, so I don't recommend using it to his face.'

Interesting, thought Karif, and appropriate.

Voices rose in heated conversation, and Karif listened carefully, eager to discover more about the men's mood. They continued to surprise him. While they'd been somewhat stony and indifferent towards him during the first few days, these Vostroyans now seemed surprisingly open and unguarded. The change was remarkable. Perhaps it was due to his fighting alongside them in Korris. He'd heard it was the way with the Firstborn.

'Madness,' growled a loud voice. 'One bloody company to hold the Eastern Front!'

'Not madness,' answered another, 'just plain, old-fashioned treachery!'

Others agreed, adding their anger and their disbelief to the cacophony. But then the voices were joined by a new sound, a rhythmic clanging that cut through all the noise. Karif turned with the others to face its source. A grizzled old sergeant, scar-faced, grey-haired and built like a Titan, was striking the steel floor at his feet with the gilded wooden stock of his lasgun.

When he had everyone's attention, and their silence, he looked Karif in the eye and spoke. His was the kind of voice, quiet and controlled, that forced other men to listen. 'You must forgive these lads, commissar, speaking out of turn like that. They mean no disrespect to the captain, the general or anyone else. But you must understand our frustration, sir. It's not easy to walk away from Korris. We fought near enough two years just to hold it. A lot of good men died for it. It's hard to watch the old foe just roll in. Vostroyan pride, see? In the end, it'll kill more of us than winter, orks and rebels put together.'

Karif let his eyes linger on the sergeant's stripes until the man took the hint.

'My apologies, sir,' said the sergeant with a short bow. 'Sidor Basch, sergeant, First Platoon.'

'Daridh Ahl Karif,' replied Karif with a smile and a bow of his own, 'commissar.' Aware of the attention on him, he added, 'Proud to serve with the Sixty-Eighth.'

Basch thumbed for a young trooper opposite to vacate his seat. Karif sat down. The compartment remained quiet while the rest of the troopers listened in.

'How long have you served with the Sixty-Eighth?' asked Karif. 'Twenty years? Thirty?'

'Thirty-five, sir. Longer even than Captain Sebastev, though he's twice the man.'

Karif wasn't foolish enough to express his doubts about that remark, not while these men were being so frank, at least. But he still couldn't reconcile himself with the boorish captain's solid reputation, so he said, 'General Vlastan doesn't seem to think very highly of the captain. Why such bad blood between the two?'

Basch grinned and said, 'That's a hard one for a chevek, sir. No offence intended.'

'Make me understand,' replied Karif with good humour, 'and I'll forgive the mild insult.' Glancing at the seated men, he saw some of them stifling a laugh.

'There are a lot of reasons why the general doesn't like our Captain Sebastev, sir. The obvious ones are the biggest. Vostroya's class divide is a proper chasm, and the higher ranks were always the province of the aristocracy. Most of them would like to keep it that way. Major Dubrin... well, it was the major's dying wish that Captain Sebastev take over company command. Colonel Kabanov honoured that wish. Since General Vlastan owes the colonel a life debt from their early years of service, I guess he felt obliged to let it be, at least for a while. General Vlastan probably figured life on the frontline would be short for the captain, that it wouldn't require any direct intervention on his part. Obviously it didn't work out like that.'

The old sergeant shook his head. 'Like the men were saying, Captain Sebastev wouldn't have pulled us out of there without direct orders. We still draw breath because the White Boar stayed behind to save us. It's not the first time he's done something like that. The general will spit fire when he hears about it. It's a right mess. Mind you, for us grunts, none of that should matter a damn.' The sergeant threw a pointed look along the rows of listening troopers. 'There's little else should occupy a good trooper's mind than orders, kit and the Emperor's blessing.'

Karif found himself quickly warming to the man. It seemed that Sergeant Basch had all the qualities of discipline, dedication and honour upon which the mighty Firstborn reputation was built.

'Well said, sergeant,' said Karif. 'Well said, indeed. I'm gratified to find that the ardour of the Vostroyan Firstborn is no myth. Solid discipline, martial skill and good old-fashioned grit: where these things abound, there is nothing we can't achieve in the Emperor's name.'

'For the Emperor and for Vostroya!' called one of the troopers. The rest immediately took up the cheer. Basch leaned out from his seat and said to Karif, 'It seems you have a way with words, commissar.' When the cheer died down, Basch addressed a young trooper at the far end of the row. 'Let's have a tune, Yakin,' he said, 'something to stir the blood a bit.'

The trooper, Yakin, began digging through his pack. After a moment, Karif saw him pull out a long, black case. He drew a seven-stringed instrument and a bow from it, and the troopers around him began making requests. It wasn't long before notes filled the air, clear and high over the rumble of the Pathcutter's fuel-guzzling engine.

Sergeant Basch smiled, sat back, closed his eyes, and nodded his head in time with the tune. 'Have you an appreciation for the *ushehk*, commissar?'

To Karif's ears, the music sounded like the screeching of a wounded grot. It grated on his nerves, and he was forced to stop himself from wincing openly. 'I hadn't heard it until this moment, sergeant,' he replied. 'I'll have to assume one grows to appreciate it over time.'

The skin at the sides of the sergeant's eyes wrinkled as he laughed. 'A very politic answer. Our Yakin isn't the most talented player, but he's better than nothing.'

That's debatable, thought Karif.

The Vostroyans linked arms where they sat and stamped their booted feet on the floor in time with the music. Their earlier anger had been chased away for the moment by the musical reminder of their kinship and their home world.

Karif found himself infected by the camaraderie they displayed. Despite himself, he began tapping a foot in time with their stomps. He might even have joined in but for the sudden change in Basch's expression. It caught Karif entirely off-guard, and that was a rare thing. The sergeant leaned close and said, 'Now that they're occupied, commissar, perhaps you'll be kind enough to tell me what in the blasted warp is really going on? All that stuff about orders and kit is right enough for the troopers. They needed to hear it. But any man with two stripes or more needs to know what he's leading his men into. Are we heading straight for another fight, or did the White Boar pull us out on a simple pretence? If you know which, don't keep me in suspense.'

White Boar this, and Old Hungry that, thought Karif. And the Pit-Dog? What is it with Vostroyans and nicknames? Throne help the man who christens me with anything less than respectful.

'It's no secret, sergeant,' Karif replied. 'Nhalich is under siege. The Danikkin Independence Army has made its push and there have been attacks from within the city, either by agents of the secessionist movement or by sympathetic civilians. Commissar-Captain Vaughn reported heavy fighting before comms were lost. We've heard nothing from Nhalich since then. Perhaps the relay station was struck in the fighting. We'll know soon enough, I suppose. How a mere planetary defence force can hope to stand against the might of the Emperor's Hammer, with or without its damned civilian militias, is quite beyond comprehension. Are they mad?'

'We were fools who once believed so, sir' said Basch. 'Again, I mean no disrespect, but two thousand years of carving a life out in the deep winter, of struggling for survival without any aid from the Imperium... It changed these people. The Danikkin are a hard folk. That lord-general of theirs, Vanandrasse, is as black hearted and vicious as the winter night.'

Karif's jaw clenched. 'The man is no lord-general, sergeant. He has turned his people from the Emperor's light and doomed them to oblivion. Hard as ice, they may be, but the Emperor's Hammer will shatter them. To that end, I will be unrelenting in my duty, and so will all of you.'

Karif's righteous fury had done for him what the Vostroyan music could not; his blood surged and he felt his pulse beat in his clenched fists and at his temples. He longed to personally smash aside the traitors on this world. Orks were foul, benighted things, and must be decimated utterly, but they had never known the Emperor's light and never would. To know it and to turn from it was the greatest crime in the Imperium, and the mere thought of it sickened Karif.

The worthless apostates, he thought, they've brought death down upon themselves.

Sergeant Basch nodded and raised his hands to his chest, pressing them there, splaying his fingers in the sign of the aquila. 'Inspiring words, commissar! They could have come from the lips of Commissar Ixxius himself.'

That was all it took, a few simple words, poorly chosen, to

shatter the bridge Karif had felt building between himself and these men. He stood quietly from his seat, holding back his irritation and disappointment.

'Damn it, man,' he said to the confused sergeant through clenched teeth, 'I am your commissar now. I won't be constantly measured against the dead. Mark my words well, and tell your men.'

Then Karif walked away, steadying himself against the juddering motion of the Pathcutter with the overhead grips as he moved. Sergeant Basch stared after him, dumbfounded.

At the far end of the compartment, nearest the cockpit section, Karif hauled himself up the steep metal stairs to the top deck.

Trooper Yakin brought his tune to an end with a final quivering note.

Since leaving Korris, Stavin had been kept busy on the top deck of the transport while the commissar mingled with the men on the lower deck. He turned his head for only a moment when the music first began drifting up from the deck below. The Eyes of Katya, he thought with a smile. Someone's playing The Eyes of Katya.

'Focus, boy,' snapped Sergeant Svemir. 'I need you to put pressure here and here. Hold that in place while I stitch this up.'

Sergeant Svemir was a medic with Fifth Company's Second Platoon. His head was round like a melon, and covered with grey stubble that looked so coarse you could light a match on it. The line of his jaw was likewise covered, but the waxed ends of a long, salt-and-pepper moustache hung over it.

The first thing Stavin had noticed about the man was the absence of two fingers on his left hand. He tried not to stare. At least the loss of those fingers didn't seem to hinder the sergeant while he worked.

Though his eyes stayed on his wounded patient, Sergeant Svemir talked as he worked. 'I don't mean to snap at you, son. I appreciate you helping out, but you need to keep your eyes on your work. These brave fighters need our help.'

The upper deck of the Pathcutter transport was currently functioning as a rather inadequate surgery. Commissar Karif had loaned his adjutant to the sergeant, remarking that Stavin needed 'exposure to the grim realities of life in the Guard.' Stavin didn't mind. These bleeding men had fought bravely against the xenos. They deserved to live. If he could do something to help them, he would.

Sixteen of them, with wounds of varying seriousness, lay on bedrolls spread across the floor. It was no small relief that they were quiet now. The anaesthecium injections administered by Sergeant Svemir had really kicked in, bringing a welcome end to the groaning and the cries of pain. A few had needed flesh clamps, but most, according to Svemir, would get by with simple stitches. Stavin watched the sergeant carefully tug a long, black piece of shrapnel from a trooper's arm. Then he lifted a curved needle and deftly stitched the wound shut.

'This one got too close to a greenskin grenade,' said Svemir. 'That's a hard one, boy. Do you throw it back, or do you dive for cover? Half the time, the damned things are duds anyway.'

Stavin didn't take long to answer. 'If it was just the one, sir,' he said, 'I'd try for the return.'

Svemir looked up, having finished stitching. 'You're a strange one, shiny. The accent is from Muskha, but the looks say you're from The Magdan.'

There it was again: *shiny*. Stavin wondered how long they'd call him that. It didn't bother him all that much, but it was another barrier between him and acceptance. It was common knowledge that new things needed breaking in before they worked properly.

Then again, he thought, I don't really want their acceptance. I want to go home. I don't belong here at all.

'My mother is a Magdan, sir,' said Stavin. 'My father was Muskhavi. I grew up in Hive Tzurka.'

It was the first time he'd mentioned anything of his family since leaving Vostroya. No one had asked, not even the commissar. But something about Sergeant Svemir made Stavin want to open up. There was a strange comfort in the presence of a man who worked to save lives rather than take them. Stavin realised then that he was desperate to talk to someone, though he also saw the danger in that need.

It was dangerous because Stavin was a keeper of secrets, and his greatest secret was that he had come to Danik's World under false pretences. Basic training might have made him a soldier, but he'd never be true Firstborn on account of his older brother, the brother whose name he'd taken when he joined the Guard.

'Hive Tzurka, eh?' said Svemir, shuffling across to the side of his next patient. He waved Stavin over beside him. 'What was that like? I'm from Hive Ahropol in Sohlsvod. Never got out as far as Muskha.' He gestured for Stavin to raise the woozy trooper's leg so that the blood drenched bandages could be replaced.

Stavin wasn't sure how to answer. Words didn't seem adequate to the task of expressing the misery of existence in Tzurka's slums. So he pretended he hadn't heard the question, and tied off another fresh bandage in silence, noting how sticky his hands had become with the drying blood of other men.

Sergeant Svemir interpreted the young trooper's silence for himself. 'That bad, huh?' he said. 'I'd heard Hive Tzurka was rough. Trouble with anti-Imperial dissidents a while back, wasn't there? I heard they took over a bunch of old munitions factories. You know about that?'

Stavin nodded. His father had been a Civitas enforcer seconded to the local Arbites at the time. He'd been killed in the fighting. It was the turning point in Stavin's life, the dark, pivotal moment that had thrown his family into poverty and desperation. But these were private pains. Stavin bit back on them and said simply, 'That was eleven years ago, sir. They got them all in the end.'

'Good to know,' said Svemir with a nod, 'can't have bastards like that running around on Vostroya. Though I admit the home world's a fading memory to me these days. You'll get like that before long. Fighting on so many worlds... after a while, the battles all merge together. You feel like you've been fighting your whole life without a break. Makes it easier to keep going, I suppose. The regiment becomes home.' His voice grew quieter. 'Lost some good friends out here, sitting in the snow, waiting to finish this business. I'll be glad to get off this rock when the time comes.'

Stavin didn't like all this talk of long years in the Guard. It made him anxious to be away, eager to return to the mother and brother he'd had to leave behind. They'd watched helplessly as the Techtriarchy's much-hated conscription officers had dragged him off to their truck. It was for the best. They would have taken his brother, the real Danil Stavin, if they'd known about the switch of identity cards.

Then again, thought Stavin, maybe those officers didn't care who they took, so long as the numbers added up.

Iador Stavin, that was his real name, had a brother just two years older who'd been born with a learning disability. Life in the Guard would have been brutal and short for Danil. For years, Stavin had endured nightmares about Danil being mistreated at the hands of xenos, heretics, or even other troopers. Neither he nor his mother could bear it. So Iador had become Danil, and Danil had become Iador.

Now I fight the monsters from those dreams, thought Stavin. I don't regret it, but I must find some way home. I must get back to them, one way or another.

Sergeant Svemir had been lost in his own thoughts as he worked on. He emerged from them now and ordered Stavin to fetch a box of ampoules from the medical case he called his *narthecium*. Some of the men were coming round from the effects of their anaesthecium injections and would need to be administered a second dose.

As he raised his injector pistol, Sergeant Svemir said, 'Twenty whole years in the Guard. Time pours through a man's hands, by the Throne.'

Stavin must have looked horrified, because the sergeant laughed and said, 'You think that's a long time? You think I should have left after my ten?' He shook his head. 'You're fresh, son. Your memories of home are still sharp. Give it time. Ten years from now, when the papers come through, you'll tick the second box just like I did. When you've given such a chunk of your life to the Emperor's service, it doesn't take much to sign over the rest of it. A little guilt will do it. I could never have left knowing my brother Firstborn fought on. Retiring from the Guard is the coward's way out.'

Stavin's jaw clenched.

I'll never tick the second box, he promised himself. If that's what the Emperor asks of me, he can bloody rot on his Golden Throne. They can call me a coward as much as they like but, one way or another, I'll find my way back to Vostroya.

'My family, sir,' said Stavin. 'I'll want to return to them. When my term is up, I mean.'

Sergeant Svemir was readying to dispense another injection, but he stopped and met Stavin's gaze as he said, 'Family is important to a good Vostroyan. It's good that you feel this way. Think of the honour you do your family. What Vostroyan mother could be anything but proud to have her son serve with the finest regiment in the Imperial Guard?' He waved a hand over the wounded men that surrounded him and said, 'They all left their families behind. They all made the same sacrifice you did. After twenty years of service, the Sixty-Eighth is my family now. It's yours, too, though you're too fresh to know it yet.'

No, thought Stavin, I'm not like them. I'm no Firstborn son. My family is back in Hive Tzurka.

Footsteps rang on the metal staircase to the lower deck, and Stavin knew before he turned that Commissar Karif was ascending. A moment later, the familiar black cap appeared, followed by the rest of the tall, dark form as the man pulled himself up the metal railing and stepped onto the top deck.

For a brief moment, Stavin caught a look of cold fury in the commissar's eyes. Someone or something on the lower deck had made him angry. But the moment Sergeant Svemir looked over at him, the commissar masked his discontent. He threw the sergeant a half-smile and said, 'I hope my adjutant is proving his worth, sergeant.'

Svemir nodded, and then winked at Stavin. 'Rest easy, commissar. The lad has been most helpful. It'll take more than the sight of shed blood and broken bones to shake this one up. In fact, we're always short of medics, perhaps with some additional training–'

'Nice try, sergeant,' replied the commissar, 'but young Stavin has quite enough to do as my adjutant.'

That's right, thought Stavin, don't bother asking me what I think. He talks as if I'm not even here.

Stavin had thought he was getting used to the commissar's incredible arrogance, but it still irked him now and then. The man was mercurial, to say the least. At times, he was surprisingly friendly, almost parental in his level of concern. At others, he was ice-cold, with an absolute disregard for the feelings of others.

Still, Stavin supposed, there are worse things to be than a commissar's adjutant, I'm sure. I could be cleaning latrines somewhere.

'And what of these men?' asked Commissar Karif. He looked around at the men lying bandaged on the floor. 'How many can we count on should we find the battle at Nhalich still raging?'

Sergeant Svemir's face darkened. 'These are badly wounded men, commissar,' he said. 'Colonel Kabanov will receive my strong recommendation that none be called upon to perform in battle. If their wounds were to re-open...'

'I see,' said the commissar. 'However, sometimes even the wounded must fight. Let's hope the town is secure by the time we arrive.'

The transport suddenly lurched hard, almost throwing the commissar off his feet. His hand caught the steel banister at the top of the stairs, saving him from a fall. A number of the wounded groaned as their bedrolls shifted on the floor.

'We've stopped,' said Svemir. 'Something must be wrong. We can't be at Nhalich already.'

Commissar Karif raised one hand for silence and pressed the other to the vox-bead in his ear. His eyes widened. 'Stavin,' he said, 'get cleaned up. We're returning to the colonel's Chimera.'

Stavin nodded and rose to his feet.

'What's going on, commissar?' asked Sergeant Svemir.

Karif was already halfway down the stairs, his boots clanging on metal, but he paused before his head disappeared below the deck. 'Contact, sergeant,' he said. 'The colonel's driver just spotted las-fire in the woods up ahead.'

CHAPTER SIX

The moment the Chimera's hatch crashed open, Sebastev felt the night air stabbing at his skin. He pulled his scarf up over his nose and stepped out, his boots crunching on the snow. Lieutenant Kuritsin followed a step behind him.

Low clouds muddied the sky, moving up from the south-east at speed, swallowing the bright stars as they came. The landscape had turned from moonlit silver to dark, icy blue. Bitter winds were picking up, driving north-west from the Gulf of Karsse.

All around, the air was filled with the impatient rumble of idling vehicles. The Chimeras had moved up on Colonel Kabanov's orders, arranging themselves in a tight wedge formation with autocannons, multi-lasers and heavy bolters aimed out into the night, ready to protect the more vulnerable Pathcutters.

The Pathcutters held back, arranged in a single column that extended out behind the Chimeras like the shaft of an arrow. The Danikkin machines were light on both armour and armaments. They'd never been intended for a frontline combat role. Maximum load capacity was their strongpoint.

Fifth Company's officers descended the ramps of their respective vehicles. All interior lights had to be switched off before they opened the hatches. Nhalich wasn't far away. It wouldn't do to be spotted. For that same reason, the vehicles had been pushing west all night without the benefit of headlights. The snow was bright enough, even now, for them to see where they were going.

Sebastev watched the silhouettes of his officers as they kicked their way through the snow towards him. Soon, he was surrounded by expectant men. In the darkness, the figure of Commissar Karif stood out from the others, his commissarial cap distinct among the tall fur hats.

Sebastev gestured for the men to step close, and they formed a huddle with their backs to the night air. 'About three minutes ago, Sergeant Samarov reported seeing lights up ahead,' he told them. 'Possible las-fire at a distance of about three kilometres. Nhalich is about twenty kilometres west of here. According to our maps, it should be visible from the next rise. It's possible that Samarov's lights were Vostroyan, but since there's been no further contact from Nhalich, I'm not counting on it.'

'You expect the worst, captain?' asked Commissar Karif.

'I'd say we've every reason to do so, commissar. Something should have gotten through to us by now. This lack of vox-chatter...'

The men were silent as they considered the implications.

'Regardless,' said Sebastev, 'our immediate objective is to investigate the lights that were spotted in the woods up ahead.' He turned to the First Platoon leader and said, 'Lieutenant Tarkarov, I want you to organise a reconnaissance. Draw scouts from each platoon and have them sweep in twos. The moment they find anything, I want to know about it. The rest of you, go back to your vehicles and prep your men for combat. We'll know what we're up against soon enough. Colonel Kabanov will let us know how he wants to play it.'

'I don't want to believe, sir,' said Lieutenant Severin of Fifth Platoon, 'that our own company might be all that remains of the Sixty-Eighth.'

'I don't want to believe it, either, lieutenant,' said Sebastev, 'but I won't lie to you. We have to consider it a possibility. The colonel always planned to pull us out of Korris. It's why he stayed. But

I don't think he was expecting this. We'll proceed with all caution. Lieutenant Tarkarov, let's get those scouts out there. I want vox-chatter kept to a minimum. And one more thing: get your snipers up front with your drivers. I want our best eyes searching the darkness, not sitting in the back with the others.'

Before the men turned to disperse, Commissar Karif asked them to wait. With hands pressed to his chest in the sign of the aquila, he said, 'Emperor, grant us your blessing. Let us be the hammer in your hand, as you are our lantern in the dark. This, we beseech thee. Ave Imperator.'

'Ave Imperator,' replied the officers. Their tone was subdued. Sebastev could tell just how worried they were. The mood was grim as they moved off.

For a moment, he watched their shadows disappear up ramps and into hatches. Then, as he turned to re-enter the colonel's command Chimera, an unwelcome image came upon him: his officers walking, not into the hatches of their vehicles, but into the hungry mouths of a dozen crematory furnaces.

Troopers Grusko and Kasparov moved into the cover of the trees. A wide road cut through the woods, but it was well-buried under the drifts. Before the deep winter had come, the road had been a busy highway, well-used by trucks carrying Varanesian goods to the docks at Nhalich for export to other Danikkin provinces.

Only the biting winds travelled this road regularly now.

Grusko and Kasparov had been skirting the woods together when a noise – was it a human cry, or just the wind? – made them stop. They split up, intending to advance on the source from two different directions. They were close to the area in which Colonel Kabanov's driver, Sergeant Samarov, had glimpsed the lights, but there were no lights visible now.

Overhead, the wind whipped at the tops of the Danikkin pine, dislodging snow, and sending a rain of frozen flakes down to the carpet of fallen needles below.

Grusko was glad of the wind in the branches. It masked his footsteps as he pressed forward. Both he and Kasparov had been issued with low-light vision enhancers. The old goggles didn't offer true night vision, the best kit was always earmarked for the regiments that served on the Kholdas Line, but at least Grusko could see where he was going despite the all-consuming darkness of the woods. As he moved cautiously from trunk to trunk, he caught movement up ahead. The goggles showed him the figure of a man leaning against a tree with his lasgun raised. He was aiming at something on the ground a few metres away from him.

The man was dressed in a long, padded coat, with a light pack strapped to his back, and seemed to be wearing night-vision apparatus of his own. Unusual headwear, tall and pointed, sweeping backwards like the crest of a strange bird, immediately identified him as a member of the Danikkin Independence Army.

DIA filth! cursed Grusko. What the hell is he pointing his lasgun at?

Kasparov was nowhere to be seen. He should have been approaching from the left. Had he already spotted this figure? Grusko pressed forward, lifting his own lasgun, and taking careful aim.

By Terra, he thought, if I could just take the man alive...

Grusko stopped. Another shadow was moving towards the rebel soldier from the right. The thick woods made the approaching figure difficult to discern. Is that Kasparov, he wondered, or another rebel bastard?

He continued forward, but even slower now, placing each foot with a careful shifting of his weight. The second figure had almost reached the first, and Grusko still couldn't be sure if it was Kasparov.

As the mysterious figure finally emerged by the side of the first, Grusko saw that both men were, in fact, rebel soldiers. They began talking in hushed voices, but he could clearly make out the sound of harsh Danikkin consonants. So where in the warp is Kasparov, he asked himself? If I attack on my own, I'll have to kill both of them. I'm sure the colonel would appreciate the chance to interrogate one.

The first figure still held his lasgun steady, barrel pointed towards something that Grusko couldn't make out from his current position. From their posture and the smug, taunting quality of their laughter, Grusko felt sure they'd caught themselves a prisoner.

Emperor above, it must be Kasparov, he thought.

Grusko considered trying to circle around, get closer and find out, but any more movement at this range might cost him the element of surprise. There was nothing for it. He'd have to take the shot, and it would have to be a clean kill, because the moment he fired, the remaining rebel would know exactly where he was. If the rebels' prisoner was indeed Kasparov, Grusko hoped he'd have the sense to scramble for immediate cover.

He eased himself down onto the carpet of needles, careful to make as little noise as possible. The wind continued to cover what noise he did make. Once he was settled, he sighted along the barrel of his lasgun and slowed his breathing.

Right between the eyes, he told himself. One shot, one kill.

He placed his gloved finger on the trigger and gently began to squeeze it.

A single crack sounded in the night, echoing from the black trunks. The woods lit up momentarily with the flash of a single las-bolt.

The man with the raised lasgun fell to the ground, as suddenly limp and silent as a discarded marionette. The other stood stunned, gaping at his comrade's body. Grusko drew a bead on him, but the rebel soldier's training kicked in. He threw himself behind the nearest tree before Grusko could fire.

Grusko scrabbled to his feet, his heart pounding in his ears. He raced forwards, using the trees for cover as he moved. 'Surrender, rebel dog!' he called out.

There was a grunt of pain some metres off to his left. It was the prisoner the rebels had been taunting.

'Kasparov?' hissed Grusko. 'Is that you? Are you hurt?'

He was answered with more groans of pain.

'Hang in there, Firstborn,' said Grusko, trying to pick out the shape of the wounded man among all those trees and shadows. Then the wounded man moved, and Grusko saw him, lying on his back with one hand pressed to his stomach. The smell of blood and burnt flesh was strong on the air.

It wasn't Kasparov.

Fifth Company scouts rarely deployed with carapace armour. The heavy golden plates confounded any attempt as stealth. This wounded man wore full Vostroyan battle-gear.

'Another Firstborn,' said Grusko. 'Who are you? Can you talk?'

The soldier might have answered, but Grusko never heard it, because the surviving Danikkin rebel chose that moment to open fire. The first bolt seared the air just centimetres from Grusko's head and caused him to duck back down into cover.

'Damn you!' he yelled. 'Throw down your weapon in the name of the Emperor, Danikkin scum.'

More las-fire followed, carving deep black lines in the trunk that protected Grusko. But the firing stopped quickly, replaced by a chilling scream that echoed through the woods.

What now, thought Grusko? Is this a trick?

'Nice try, traitor,' he called, 'but I've used that one myself.'

A familiar voice came back at him from the same direction as the scream. 'Who are you calling traitor, Grusko, you grox-rutting *zadnik*?'

'Kasparov? Is that...?'

'Well it's not Sebastian Thor,' replied Kasparov, poking his head out from behind the thick, black trunk the rebel had used for cover. 'You can relax,' he said. 'This one has gone to answer before the Emperor for his treachery.'

Grusko stepped out and saw Kasparov tug his knife free from the rebel's corpse. 'Damn it, Kasparov,' he said, shaking his head. 'Couldn't you have taken him alive?'

Kasparov shrugged and wiped his knife on the dead man's coat. 'He was a traitor, you said it yourself. He didn't deserve to live. Besides, you weren't doing so great. You're lucky I was here.'

Through the lenses of his goggles, Grusko could see that the dead rebel was drenched in blood from a multitude of gaping wounds. Still shaking his head at the missed opportunity for a capture, Grusko turned and walked over to crouch by the groaning Vostroyan soldier. The steaming hole in the soldier's belly said he wouldn't be alive for much longer. 'We've got us a survivor here, Kasparov, but only just. We need a medic, fast.'

Kasparov came over and stood looking down at the wounded trooper. 'By the Throne!'

'We're out of vox-bead range. Get back to the vehicles and get old Svemir down here,' said Grusko. 'Sprint, damn it! Go now!'

Kasparov didn't waste time arguing. He turned east towards the transports and raced off into the darkness to get help.

Grusko rose and fetched the padded coats from the bodies of the dead rebels. He had to keep the soldier warm. He had to keep him alive. Colonel Kabanov, Grusko knew, would have important questions for this man.

Lieutenant Tarkarov led Captain Sebastev and Lieutenant Kuritsin through the trees, risking the light of a torch on its lowest setting. Here, where the snow rested on the canopy overhead rather than on the ground, the men could move at a decent pace. Tarkarov and Kuritsin were long-legged men, but they carefully paced themselves so as not to overtake the captain. Up ahead, the low amber light of a hooded promethium lamp marked the clearing where Sergeant Svemir was already tending to the wounded man.

As the trio of officers drew closer, they saw two other figures moving about in the light: First Platoon scouts Grusko and Kasparov. Their restless pacing betrayed their agitation. Grusko was the first to see Sebastev coming, and marched forward to greet him.

'Sir, I'm sorry. We couldn't take the rebels alive.'

Kasparov moved up to stand by Grusko's side. 'It was my fault, sir,' he said. 'I got a bit carried away.'

Sebastev looked them in the eye. 'Did they have comms equipment? Did they get a vox-message off?'

'No, sir,' said Grusko, 'not to our knowledge. Neither man was carrying a vox-caster unit.'

'And neither of you were injured?'

'No, sir,' said Kasparov.

Sebastev nodded and pushed past them, saying, 'Never apologise to me for killing traitor scum. You did fine.'

The scouts saluted, but Sebastev didn't notice. He'd already turned towards the wounded man on the ground.

'Get back to the transport,' Lieutenant Tarkarov told his scouts. 'Get some hot ohx' down you. No rahzvod. I need you to stay sharp. Are we clear?'

'Clear, sir,' replied both men. They saluted their platoon leader, turned and jogged back towards the waiting vehicles.

'What have we got here, sergeant?' Sebastev asked the medic.

Sergeant Svemir was bent over a Vostroyan dressed in full battle-gear. The man's breathing was shallow, and his eyes were closed, but he continued to grip his lasgun tightly with one hand. Svemir lifted away the edges of two Danikkin coats to show Sebastev the extent of the man's wounds.

Sebastev grimaced when he saw what lay beneath. The armour that was supposed to shield the trooper's stomach had been melted through. It looked to Sebastev like the result of a full power lasgun blast at very close range. Beneath the hole in the man's armour, the flesh was burnt black and cratered. Steam rose from the wound.

As Sebastev got down on his knees, the soldier opened his eyes and looked straight at him.

'Hang on, Firstborn,' said Sebastev, 'our man will do what he can for you. Just hang in there, son.'

'This one's Eighth Company,' remarked Lieutenant Kuritsin. He pointed to the bronze motifs on the trooper's hat and collar, 'One of Major Tsurkov's men.'

The trooper's eyes shifted to Kuritsin. 'That's right, sir,' he croaked. 'Bekov, Ulmar, trooper, Eighth Company, Second Platoon.'

'Well met, Bekov,' said Sebastev, 'but don't talk, man. Save your strength.'

Sergeant Svemir turned and threw Sebastev a meaningful look. 'I think it would be all right if Trooper Bekov talked to you for a while, captain,' he said. 'You'll have to listen carefully, of course.'

Sebastev understood. There would be no saving Bekov. The man was dying where he lay. If he had anything to pass on to Fifth Company, it had to be spoken right here, right now.

'Trooper Bekov, my name is Captain Grigorius Sebastev, Vostroyan Firstborn Sixty-Eighth Infantry Regiment, Fifth Company. We're from the same regiment, son. I know Major Tsurkov well.'

'The Pit-Dog?' asked Trooper Bekov.

Sebastev winced. He hadn't had his nickname spoken to his face like that for quite some time. Most of the men knew better than to say it within earshot of him, but this man, dying slowly on the floor of these night-shrouded woods, had nothing left to fear.

'Aye,' said Sebastev, 'the Pit-Dog. You know me then, Bekov. You've got to tell me what happened, son. Where is the rest of Eighth Company? Where's Major Tsurkov?'

Bekov coughed. It was a harsh, rasping sound. His face creased in pain. Sebastev turned to Sergeant Svemir and raised an eyebrow.

'Very well,' said Svemir. 'I'll give him one more dose, but another and you won't get any sense out of him.' The medic slid a brown ampoule into his injector pistol and pressed it to Bekov's neck. With a sharp hiss, the liquid emptied into the trooper's veins.

Bekov's creased brow soon smoothed, and his breathing became a little easier. When he opened his eyes again, they were glazed, but he was better able to talk. Sebastev asked him again what had happened to the rest of Eighth Company.

'We hit Nhalich three days ago, sir,' said Bekov. 'No one was happy about leaving the Fifth back in Korris. You should know that. The Sixty-Eighth don't go anywhere without the White Boar. Major Tsurkov was livid. Said it was grox-shit, sir.'

Suddenly, something occurred to Bekov and he gripped Sebastev's arm. 'The colonel, sir. Does the White Boar live?'

It was Kuritsin who answered. 'Have no fear on that count, trooper. The White Boar still leads us. It will take more than filthy greenskins to beat him, by Terra!'

'Bekov,' said Sebastev, 'we need to know about Nhalich. The rebels: what's the situation?'

'The rebels!' gasped Bekov. 'Mad with hate for the Imperium, sir. There were spies in Nhalich from the start. The DIA hid people among the loyalist refugee caravans from the south-east. Don't know how they got past our checks. Once they were in they sabotaged our armour, our stores, everything. It was the bridge that hurt us most. We lost a lot of men on the bridge. Still, I'd rather have died in the Solenne than suffer the fate of the 701st.'

Behind Sebastev, Lieutenant Tarkarov cursed and struck a tree with his fist.

'What happened to the 701st, Bekov?' asked Sebastev.

'Blind, sir. The bastards got into their stores somehow. Tainted their food, their water. The troopers from the 701st couldn't see a thing after that. There was chaos at the barracks. Major Tsurkov ordered us back onto Guard issue meal bricks. No local food. The Danikkin armour had already engaged us by then. We tried calling Seddisvarr for help, but we couldn't get through. Nothing. And there was no answer from Helvarr or Jheggen. Some said they were jamming our vox.'

'Jammed?' asked Kuritsin. 'Could it be that we've blamed atmospheric conditions all this time, while the rebels...?'

A breath snagged in Trooper Bekov's throat and he began coughing. Blood flecked the sides of his mouth. His face screwed up with the pain.

'He's fading,' said Sergeant Svemir. 'You'll need to be fast, captain.'

'Not yet, son,' said Sebastev. 'Soon, but not yet.'

Bekov tried to smile through the pain. 'I'm trying, sir,' he said, 'but I reckon I can hear the Emperor's angels singing.'

'The White Boar,' said Sebastev, 'he needs to know about Nhalich. How many are there? What's the condition of the bridge?'

'It's gone. We tried to pull back across the bridge when the west bank fell to the enemy, but they came up from the south-east too.' He coughed again, blood bubbling on his lips. 'They caught us right on the bridge. Ordered us to surrender. Old Tsurkov wasn't having it. Galipolov, neither. Not to bloody rebels, sir. So the enemy shelled the bridge.'

If Sebastev had thought things could hardly get worse, that nugget of information proved him wrong. The bridge was gone, and with it, the company's most direct route back to Vostroyan territory.

'A handful of us–' Bekov's words were broken off as he began choking on his own blood. It ran freely from his mouth, soaking into his moustache. He gripped Sebastev's arm tight.

Bekov kept fighting to speak through the blood, and finally managed a few words, spoken more to himself than to those around him. 'The Pit-Dog,' he gurgled. 'Imagine that.' Then his lungs rattled and his chest sank for a final time.

The silence of the woods roared in Sebastev's ears. Gently, he pried the trooper's hand from his arm, and rose to his feet. 'Thank you for your efforts, sergeant,' he said to Svemir. 'Let's get a flamer out here to cremate the body, and make sure you bring his tags and lasgun back to the transports with you. I'll want to apply for a posthumous commendation on his behalf when we get back to Seddisvarr.'

Svemir bowed his head and replied, 'I'll take care of it, captain.'

'Good. Gentlemen.' Sebastev walked past Kuritsin and Tarkarov, heading back to the waiting vehicles. His lieutenants turned to follow him.

So it's true, thought Sebastev. Fifth Company may very well be all that remains of the Sixty-Eighth. What a burden to bear! We must survive at all costs. By abandoning us at Korris, Old Hungry unwittingly spared us to resurrect the regiment. Thank the Throne Colonel Kabanov stayed with us.

With their long strides, Kuritsin and Tarkarov caught up to Sebastev easily. As the three men stepped from the forest, back out onto the open snow, Sebastev looked up at a night sky thick with storm clouds. They stretched from horizon to horizon. The day was still some hours off, but it would bring the snows with it when it came.

'I'll never understand why you don't just embrace it,' said Kuritsin, and Sebastev knew immediately what his old friend was talking about.

'It is an insult,' he snapped. 'It was created to be such, and so it remains.'

'You're wrong. That snotty officer from the Thirty-Third may have intended it to be such, but our men use it as a term of great respect. It's a strong name, and it suits you. What does it matter who coined it? I've used it on occasion myself. Would I do so if I thought it was an insult to you?'

Sebastev didn't answer.

'Names have power,' continued Kuritsin. 'The White Boar revels in his. The men rally to it. Will you not let them rally to yours, also?'

Sebastev was occupied with far greater and darker matters. He didn't have time for this. 'Let them continue to rally behind the White Boar, damn it,' he growled. 'That has always been good enough for me.'

He put an extra burst of speed into his step.

This time, Kuritsin and Tarkarov let him pull ahead.

In a mood like this, the Pit-Dog was best left alone.

Colonel Kabanov didn't try to soften the blow. There was little point, the truth was the truth. Nhalich was in the hands of the Danikkin

Independence Army. The 701st and the Sixty-Eighth, with the exception of this very company, were all but wiped out. The bridge over the Solenne lay as rubble beneath its deep, black waters.

To make matters worse, thought Colonel Kabanov as he looked at the anxious faces of his assembled officers, there's all this talk of rebel jamming abilities. We should have suspected it from the start. There's no doubt the Adeptus Mechanicus spoke the truth when they told us the atmosphere would interfere with our comms, but we should never have assumed all our problems stemmed from a single source.

Danik's World had never been known for technological developments. Up until the dawning of the deep winter, it had been a rather average world, civilised and fairly self-sufficient, but with little to distinguish it from a million other worlds in the Imperium. Then the eruptions on the southern continent had changed everything, plummeting the world into two thousand years of ice and snow. The people that had survived fled to the warmth of the hive-cities, hoping their descendants, at least, would one day be able to return to the land.

How would these people come by jamming technology? Some officers had commented on the possibility of outside support for the rebels. Trade with pirates and arms smugglers was typical of all rebel worlds. The idea that they might even be colluding with xenos sickened Kabanov, but couldn't be ruled out. Without proof, however, all of these things remained mere speculation.

In any case, thought Kabanov, such things are for others to attend. We've got enough trouble up ahead. Right now, these men need briefing.

Since this briefing required all officers, commissioned or otherwise, to attend, Kabanov had been forced to hold it in the belly of a Pathcutter transport. The men on the upper deck were being treated by a Second Company medic and couldn't be moved, but that was fine. The injured men had as much stake in the coming events as everyone else.

Let them listen if they wish, he thought.

Kabanov turned to Captain Sebastev, sitting on his right, and said, 'About the trooper in the forest, captain, were the rites observed?'

Sebastev nodded. 'They were, sir. Father Olov has formally commended the man's spirit to the Emperor.'

'Very good, captain,' said Kabanov. 'We must focus our attention on the fate of the living. There's a time to honour our fallen, but it's at the conclusive end of a crisis, not in the middle of it.'

Kabanov saw Captain Sebastev sit up a little straighter. 'It is as you say, sir,' he answered. But there was something in the man's eyes that Kabanov hadn't expected: anger. It wasn't anger against the enemy, but at Kabanov himself. Had Sebastev misinterpreted his colonel's words?

Perhaps I shouldn't have been honest with him, thought Kabanov. He didn't take it as well as I'd expected. I may be dying slowly, but I was sure he'd guessed as much for himself. It seems I was wrong. And this anger... Perhaps he blames me for the pressure he feels, knowing that the future of the regiment will soon pass into his hands. What a time to receive that responsibility! While I've still got some fight left in me, I'll do what I can to see this company through. But Sebastev, you'll have to face up to the truth soon.

Kabanov glanced at his adjutant and said, 'If you would, please, Maro.'

Maro called the men to order.

'Thank you, gentlemen,' Kabanov said when they had quieted. 'I want to start by making sure we're all on the same page. A young soldier from Eighth Company was found mortally wounded in the woods. Before he passed away, he was able to inform Captain Sebastev of the situation we face up ahead. I'm afraid his message was dire indeed. I can say with grim certainty that Fifth Company faces its greatest test yet. This company is all that remains of our proud regiment.'

Some among the officers shook their heads in denial, unwilling to believe that their fellows in the other companies were gone.

Twelfth Army Command had underestimated the Danikkin Independence Army, and the rebels were punishing them for it, but Vlastan's tactical council needn't shoulder all that blame themselves. Lord Marshal Harazahn and Sector Command were as guilty as anyone else. Proper reconnaissance could have made all the difference. If they'd only known that the orks were here.

The rebel leader, Vanandrasse, had played things surprisingly well for an ex-PDF upstart. He'd ordered his men to back away from the Vostroyans, fostering a belief among the Imperial forces that the orks represented a far greater threat. Then the rebels had watched and waited, and marshalled their strength. Their strike had been well planned, well executed, and superbly timed. Kabanov could admit that much.

'Nhalich is in enemy hands,' he continued, 'that much is certain. The hows and whys remain somewhat unclear. Trooper Bekov reported poisonings, sabotage of Imperial vehicles, and the advance of rebel armour columns on both sides of the Solenne, not just on the west. That means the second column slipped up behind us as we occupied Korris. Regardless of communication difficulties, our preoccupation with the orks is unforgivable. It has cost us dearly, and I intend for us to make amends during the coming day.'

The officers were silent, knowing better than to interrupt Kabanov, but perhaps also unsure of what to say given the enormous gravity of their situation. Kabanov let the silence hold for a moment. His throat hurt and he indicated to Maro that he required water. Maro handed him a canteen from which Kabanov gulped down a few mouthfuls. The cold liquid soothed his throat.

Commissar Karif, who was standing against the back wall, uncrossed his arms and raised a black-gloved hand. 'Yes, commissar?' said Kabanov. 'You wish to ask something?'

Karif touched a finger to the brim of his cap by way of apology for his interruption, and said, 'From the sound of it, colonel, you're committed to entering Nhalich, despite the fact that we almost certainly face an overwhelming force.'

'I dislike the word "overwhelming", commissar,' said Kabanov. He scanned the faces of his men as he spoke. 'We have little idea of the true size of the force entrenched in the town, save that it was large enough to overcome our kinsmen. A straight fight would have seen different results, I'm sure. From the words of the trooper we found in the woods, it's clear the rebels employed every bit of shameless trickery at their disposal. They fought without honour or pride. That will come back to haunt them, I assure you. As far as actual numbers are concerned... yes, we can expect heavy resistance, but the enemy on the west bank no longer concerns us. When they shelled our forces on the bridge, they cut themselves off from this side of the river. That was a big mistake. Whatever strength they have on the far bank will be staying on the far bank. We face only those units entrenched on this side. That evens things out a little, I'd say.'

Though not by much, he thought to himself.

'It's also a certainty that our brother Firstborn from the Sixty-Eighth and the 701st inflicted some damage on the invading force before they succumbed. We can be sure they took some of the bastards with them. We ride to deal with the rest. Fifth Company will have vengeance. Are you with me?'

They responded in the affirmative, strong but still unsure. It wasn't enough for Kabanov. The fires in their bellies had to be stoked. It was time to make them remember just who led them. He still held Maro's canteen. Lifting it high into the air, he hurled it at the metal floor of the transport and shouted, 'I said are you with me, warp damn it?'

The sudden motion caused pain to flare under his ribs, and his ears filled with the sound of his pounding heart, but he couldn't let it show on his face. Instead, he glared at each of them with all the intensity he could muster.

Every man in the back of that Pathcutter sat up straight under the burning stare of the White Boar. 'Yes, sir!' they shouted back at him.

Kabanov turned to Sebastev and said, 'I don't know what the hell's wrong with Fifth Company today, captain, but it'd better get sorted out fast. I'm the White Boar, by Terra, and my Firstborn are supposed to be the toughest damned killing machines in the Imperial Guard. This company will live up to its reputation. The Emperor demands it!' He turned from Sebastev, to face the rest of the assembly. 'If we die, we die in the Emperor's name. This company will not go down without a fight. Every man left in my regiment will do his duty. Is that understood?'

The voices were much louder this time, and filled with the kind of fire that Kabanov had needed from them. 'Yes, sir!'

As the men answered, Kabanov fought to hold back a fit of coughing. His lungs felt as if they were full of pine needles. He suddenly wished he hadn't thrown Maro's water on the floor. There was another flask, one containing rahzvod, in the adjutant's pocket, but it wasn't strong alcohol that his body needed, it was rest.

When he'd overcome the need to cough, he addressed them again. 'That's better,' he said. 'Every day you've spent serving in the Guard, all of it, comes down to what you do now. The regiment mustn't end with us. We have to smash our enemies, live through this and rebuild. It won't be easy. With the bridge gone, we may be stuck out here, cut off completely from our own lines. The Solenne is too fast and too rough to be forded by Chimeras. The orks will be assaulting Grazzen in the north, in which case both of that city's bridges will have been destroyed, too. The ports to the far south are located in the rebel heartland, so a sea crossing is out. For now, at least, it looks like we're stuck on this side of the line, no matter what we do.

'I believe the biggest difference we can make is right here at Nhalich. I want the relay station and, if it exists, I want the

Danikkin jamming device. If we can capture it, we can counter it.' He looked over at Enginseer Politnov, sitting at the back of the transport beside Commissar Karif and Father Olov. 'Is that not so, enginseer?'

Politnov lifted his head, hooded as always, and said, 'Obtain the device and the Machine-God will reveal its secrets to us. We need only observe the proper rituals.'

Kabanov nodded. 'I have absolute faith in that, and I don't need to tell you the difference we could make to this campaign by restoring full communications to the Twelfth Army. What a worthy task! If the damned thing is in Nhalich, Fifth Company are going to go in there and get it for me, aren't you?'

This time, Kabanov thought he felt the transport tremble at the sound of their voices. He couldn't fight the grin that spread across his face. He raised a hand to his long, white moustache and stroked one end. 'Excellent,' he said, 'that's what I thought you'd say.' Turning to Captain Sebastev, he said, 'It's time I turned the floor over to you, captain. Tell these fine officers just how we're going to dispense the Emperor's justice.'

'Aye, sir,' said Sebastev as he stood.

And I'll sit down, thought Kabanov, before I fall down.

CHAPTER SEVEN

In better days, Nhalich had been a hub of commerce, and a vital link between the Danikkin nations of Varanes and South Varanes. The city's massive bridge, straddling two and a half kilometres of deep, rushing water, was the primary conduit for trade between the two neighbouring countries. Vast loads of fruit and vegetables from the temperate south moved eastwards through the town, while timber and ore moved west. The citizens enjoyed life, gave weekly thanks to the Emperor in the local cathedral, and looked forward to many more years of the same.

Nhalich had been a bright, comfortable place to live back then.

None among its people had imagined that two thousand years of winter would destroy everything they knew, but it had. The Nhalich of today was a dead place. The streets and alleyways were choked with snow. Habs lay derelict, their doors and windows hollow and dark like the eye sockets of human skulls.

It was not, however, completely dead. Ghostly figures moved in pairs, slipping between the buildings, little more than shadows sketched on the dark canvas of the hour before dawn: Vostroyan shadows.

Sebastev's hand-picked team of saboteurs infiltrated the town, moving quickly and quietly, committed to the mission objectives that Colonel Kabanov had assigned them. Their first priority was to de-fang the snake: to cripple any rebel armour and render it useless prior to Fifth Company's imminent charge.

A freezing mist had risen as night gave ground before the coming day, aiding them in their work. Sebastev saw the Emperor's hand in it. The mist was a divine gift, cloaking his men from the eyes of the enemy as they worked to even the odds. Maybe his regular prayers were finally paying off.

The mist had also forced the Danikkin soldiers to rely on promethium lamps to light their way as they patrolled the town's perimeter, making it easier for Sebastev's men to avoid them. Defences seemed light, as if the rebels believed their east flank was secure now that the Vostroyan presence in the town had been eliminated. They hadn't counted on the arrival of Fifth Company.

Since the operation called for both stealth and technical knowledge, Sebastev had paired scouts with those troopers who had anti-vehicle experience. Since he qualified on both counts, having served as a scout in his early years and taken out his fair share of vehicles in later ones, he'd insisted on deploying, despite the protestations of Lieutenant Kuritsin. But there was another reason he'd included himself in the operation; by engaging in direct action, he hoped he'd be able to drown out the darkest of his thoughts. The sense of doom that had descended on him as the company had travelled from Korris was heavy, and he knew he had to shake it off.

Sebastev focused on his anger and on his hunger for the Emperor's justice, as he lay on his back under the chassis of a rebel Salamander. Cold seeped into his body from the frozen ground as he fixed small, high-yield melta-charges to points that shielded vital wiring and control mechanisms. The Salamander was a scout variant, but it shared much of its construction with the Chimera on which it was based. The underside was vulnerable. The charges would burn straight through when the time came, and another machine would be rendered useless.

He cursed silently as he worked against the clock. Who knew

how old the Salamander was? It was certainly a former PDF machine, a leftover from the days of Danikkin loyalty, shipped from a nearby forge-world, probably Esteban VII, to serve in the Emperor's name. Perhaps its venerable machine-spirit had known great honour before it had been turned against the Emperor's forces.

Such a waste, he thought, a machine like this in the hands of fools. Mankind has enough enemies among the stars without these idiotic secessionist wars. Division weakens us, leaving us open to xenos attack. It has to be stamped out.

Sebastev dug another melta-charge from the pack lying at his side. It was the last of them. He'd already rigged two rebel Chimeras and a Leman Russ Demolisher to blow when the timers hit zero.

Even from under the tank, he could see that the mist was growing lighter as day dawned in the east. The greater part of the enemy forces would be waking soon. There would be civilians, too.

Most refugees that passed through the Vostroyan-held towns were loyalists eager to escape persecution by Lord-General Vanandrasse's agents. They numbered in the millions. They usually went west to the so-called *contribution camps* established by Old Hungry in the territories south of Seddisvarr. Once there, they were fed and housed, and put to work making coats, blankets and the like for the Vostroyan forces.

Since the camps were filled to bursting, the decision had been made to allow refugees to stay in the garrisoned towns, but the price of that decision was becoming all too apparent. Sebastev couldn't be sure how many non-combatants remained in Nhalich. If they stayed out of the coming fight, they'd live through the day, but if they insisted on joining the battle, Sebastev's men would cut them down without remorse.

Civilian or not, those who turned their back on the Emperor deserved no quarter.

The killing of misguided civilians was a grim duty, true, but it was hardly new to the men of Fifth Company. As Sebastev set the timer on the final charge, memories returned of the war on Porozh some thirteen years before. It had been a beautiful, lush world, warm with sunshine, covered in bright fields and orchards. On the face of it, the differences between Porozh and Danik's World couldn't have been greater. The women on Porozh had been so pretty, small and delicate like finely sculpted dolls with skin the colour of rich honey and hair the colour of chocolate. He remembered one, a young woman, her hat covered in flowers, who'd brought his men fruit while they patrolled the borders near her family's orchards. She had danced as she moved, smiling brightly as she handed each man a gift from her basket. Even the most jaded old veterans had smiled back, eyes alight as they followed her, taking in the swell of her hips and breasts, and the light playing on her hair. They thanked her and bit into the succulent fruits she dispensed.

She'd finally stopped in front of Sebastev, beaming at him and holding up a juicy local fruit called a *vusgada*. He'd accepted it from her with a nod of thanks. The bright yellow fruit was almost at his lips when one of his troopers began retching. Then the trooper began vomiting mouthfuls of blood onto the grass.

The girl didn't stick around to watch. She immediately threw down her basket and broke into a run. More of Sebatev's men fell to the ground around him, groaning, clutching their bellies and puking blood.

He'd turned and killed her, of course, without even thinking about it: a single shot to the back of her head at about sixty metres. All that beauty, all that light, extinguished with a crack of his bolt pistol. The flowers on her hat burst like little fireworks, scattering pink petals on the warm afternoon air. Her body hit the ground so hard it flipped over. Sebastev remembered feeling hollow and confused.

Under all that beauty and light, he thought, Porozh was as sick and faithless as Danik's World, as all rebel worlds. Scratch the surface and they were all the same, dead the moment they turned from the rest of the Imperium.

Of the men who had bitten into the poisoned fruit, three died that day and six were permanently injured, requiring augmetic organs. The rest received medical treatment in time to avoid long-term damage. No one ate local food again.

The girl's family was burned to death for treachery. Commissar-Captain Vaughn had seen to that. Over the years, Sebastev had wondered about the girl. Had she even known the fruits were poisoned? He hadn't given her a chance to say.

New regulations on interacting with the local populace had come after that, but for many Guardsmen, it was too late. Thousands had caught terminal diseases from the local women. An official investigation concluded that the prettiest Porozhi had deliberately infected themselves before sleeping with as many of the occupation troopers as they could entice.

What a campaign that was, thought Sebastev. Those people turned everything they had against us. Why do all these traitors and heretics insist on sacrificing themselves for the ideals of madmen like Vanandrasse?

Sebastev had never forgotten the young woman's face, the pretty smile as she handed him her deadly gift, the way her wounded head blossomed in the air like a crimson flower.

'Are you done, sir?' hissed a voice from the side of the Salamander. 'The patrol will be returning any second.'

Sebastev finished up and slid out from under the vehicle. Trooper Aronov stood close by. Fifth Company scouts were generally small, lithe men, but Aronov was huge. He towered over Sebastev, turning his head this way and that, scanning the mists for any sign of trouble. 'Don't you think you're cutting it a bit fine, sir?'

'We're done,' whispered Sebastev. 'Think you can get us to the rendezvous point?'

'You know it, sir' replied Aronov. He tapped a finger on the side of his head. 'Pictographic memory. It's all in here. I figured that's why you partnered with me.'

Sebastev shook his head. 'Not a bit of it, trooper. I just needed the biggest, dumbest human shield I could find.'

'Pfft! Whatever you say, sir,' said Aronov. 'Let's move.'

They headed west through the back streets, still well-cloaked by the mist, but holding to the shadows regardless. There were only minutes left before Nhalich got a very special alarm call. Sebastev was surprised at how fast Aronov moved, and how quietly.

Damn it, he thought, this is what my commission has done to me. There was a time when I moved like that. Now I'm slowing this one down. By the Golden Throne, if I live through this...

They reached the corner of an intersection when Aronov suddenly dropped into a crouch. Sebastev halted immediately. With a blur of hand signals, the big scout indicated a patrol up ahead. From the mist, three men emerged, armed with lasguns, moving south to north along the street that bisected theirs. With more sign language, Aronov asked Sebastev how he wanted to proceed.

We can't wait for them to pass, thought Sebastev. We should get to the rendezvous point on the east bank before the charges blow, but if we attack and one escapes to raise the alarm, Colonel Kabanov will face heavy resistance on the way in.

Aronov's gestures became more urgent. The rebel patrol was getting closer.

How good is this trooper, Sebastev wondered? How good am I?

He made his decision. His hands cut three quick gestures in the air: *Take them out.*

'This is close enough, sergeant,' said Colonel Kabanov to his driver. 'I can see lantern lights at the edge of the town. Any closer and our engine noise will give us away. Lieutenant Kuritsin, order the others to hold position.'

'Aye, sir,' said Kuritsin. He lifted a speaking horn from the wall beside him, using the Chimera's vox-caster rather than his own. He keyed the appropriate channel and said, 'Command to all units. Hold position on this ridge. Ready yourselves to charge on the colonel's order.'

Fifth Company's Chimeras ground to a halt in the snow. The Pathcutters pulled up into horizontal formation behind them, ready to disgorge their payloads of vengeful Guardsmen when the time came to storm the town. Fifth Company simply didn't have enough resources to launch attacks from multiple angles, so Kabanov had decided that they'd charge forward in a wedge formation, punch through the rebel line and engage them in a city fight. Urban warfare was a Firstborn speciality, after all.

'Let's hope the captain can ease our way in as planned,' said Commissar Karif.

The colonel turned to look at him. 'Have no fear on that count, commissar. Captain Sebastev's effectiveness is not to be doubted. By the time we descend on the rebel filth, there won't be a working piece of enemy armour on this side of the river. Not that their infantry will be a pushover, of course.'

'There it is again, colonel,' said Karif, 'a certain respect for the strength of the rebels. It's a stark contrast to the attitudes that seem to prevail in Seddisvarr.'

'Twelfth Army propaganda, commissar,' said Colonel Kabanov. 'They'd have you believe we're fighting hapless fools. I wouldn't put too much stock in it, if I were you. Good for morale, of course, but the greatest mistake a man can make is to underestimate his foe. The deep winter has made the Danikkin a hardy people. That they occupy the town up ahead should be ample proof of that. They're not constricted by any sense of honour or piety. They fight with desperation. It gives them strength. Perhaps our own desperation will do the same for us.'

'Perhaps,' responded Karif, 'but honour and piety will prove greater in the end. I expect Fifth Company to uphold both. A commissar can accept no less.'

The colonel nodded as he said, 'Honour means a great deal
to the men of this company. You needn't worry about that. But
their survival means a great deal to the future of the regiment.
I believe that sometimes, in order to serve the Emperor better,
honour must occasionally be sacrificed. Had we served Captain
Sebastev's sense of honour and duty at Korris, Fifth Company
would have fallen before the orks. You and I would both be little
more than frozen bodies. Despite everything, Captain Sebastev
wouldn't have disobeyed General Vlastan.'

Karif remembered the words of the troopers in the back of the
Pathcutter. 'Which is, of course, why you stayed with us, is it not,
colonel? Through your insistence on taking command, you managed to preserve both the company and the captain's honour, at
least in the meantime.'

'That's your interpretation of events, commissar,' said the colonel testily, 'and you're welcome to it. But the Danikkin Campaign
is not a simple one. Few men outside the Twelfth Army's tactical
staff, including myself, have anything more than a rough idea of the
whole picture. I can tell you this much: a man would have to look far
back in the annals of the Sixty-Eighth to find days as dark as these.'

Colonel Kabanov flexed his fists as he continued. 'The history of the regiment is a chain unbroken for thousands of years.
Despite countless wars and untold losses, there have always been
survivors around whom the regiment could be restored. But the
Danikkin... their hatred is a powerful thing. They don't take prisoners, commissar. Enemies of their secessionist movement are
killed at once. I believe that Fifth Company is the last remaining seed from which the regiment might again grow. The coming
day will bring one of two things: either the breaking of our proud
tradition, or another victory to add to it.'

Karif sat quietly, digesting the colonel's words for a moment
before he said, 'With your permission, colonel, I'd like my adjutant to man the heavy bolter as we ride in. The boy needs such
experiences if he's to become a well-rounded soldier and aide.'

'No objections here,' replied the colonel. 'Send him up front. Sergeant Samarov will make good use of him.'

Stavin moved up as ordered. Karif heard Sergeant Samarov welcome the young man into the driver's compartment.

Lieutenant Kuritsin, sitting opposite Karif and next to Father Olov, lifted a gold-plated chronometer from his coat pocket and looked at it. 'Saints be with the captain. He should be at the east bank by now. We'll have our signal soon.'

Father Olov's gravelly voice sounded from under the matted tangle of his long, white beard. 'Rest easy, lieutenant. The Grey Lady watches over that one. You should know that well enough.' He looked over at Karif and said, 'Saint Nadalya, commissar. Patron saint of Vostroya. The captain is a man protected by his faith, mark my words.'

Karif grinned at the old priest and said, 'I know who she is, Father, but your words have reminded me of a matter I wished to discuss with you. I hope you won't think it presumptuous on my part.'

'Which means it is presumptuous,' grumbled the old priest, 'but go ahead, commissar.'

Olov's beard was so long that he could have tucked the end of it into his belt. Beside him, sheathed in a covering of brown leather, was his preferred weapon, the mighty eviscerator chainsword favoured by many a battlefield priest. Years of wielding it in practice and in battle had given the priest a broad physique. Karif hadn't missed the hints of thick muscle beneath Olov's robes.

'I confess to feeling a certain kinship with you, Father,' said Karif. 'We're both men of the Imperial Creed. Granted, our roles differ, but I hope you feel the same kinship in your own way. With that in mind...'

'Spit it out, man,' rumbled Olov.

Once again, Karif found the Vostroyan manner a source of no small irritation. He had to keep reminding himself that it was a cultural trait, one that clearly extended to both the officer class and members of the Ecclesiarchy. Suppressing a retort, Karif said, 'Very well. I'd like to make a battlefield reading to our men during the coming fight. I'm sure I can fortify their spirits and lend them some divine strength. What say you, Father?'

Olov's brow creased and his eyes narrowed. 'I handle the readings, commissar. That might not have been explained to you properly. Have done for almost eleven years with this particular lot.'

And from what I've heard, thought Karif, you've made a fine mess of it. The Septology of Hestor? It may be officially approved by the Ministorum, but it's widely held to have been written by madmen. It's time this regiment had a proper reading that will gird them for battle.

Karif didn't think it prudent to mention that Captain Sebastev had asked him to consider orating in the priest's place. Would the priest have believed him anyway?

Instead, Karif said, 'This company is lucky to have you, Father Olov, and they know it well enough. But as a newcomer, I'm eager to strengthen my presence among the men, get them acclimatised to me, as it were.'

Colonel Kabanov spoke up from his seat near the driver's compartment. 'I can see the logic in that, commissar' he said, 'but the decision lies with you, Father Olov. Would you have our new commissar try his hand?'

If Father Olov was at all influenced by the colonel's words, it didn't show on his face. 'What would you read, commissar?' he asked, still scowling.

It was time for Karif to play his ace. He drew a small blue tome from an inside pocket and raised it for the others to see.

Lieutenant Kuritsin's eyes flashed. 'Have a care, commissar,' he hissed. 'If you've taken that book with anything less than his express permission, he'll have your head, and all laws be damned.'

'Do you mean to say, lieutenant,' spluttered Kabanov, 'that the book is Captain Sebastev's own copy?'

'It is, sir,' said Kuritsin, 'unmistakably so.' He faced Karif. 'That book is the last memento the captain has of his father, commissar. I'm sure you didn't know, but perhaps you should give it to me. I won't tell him of this. It would be better for all concerned that he never find out.'

Colonel Kabanov nodded. 'That sounds best.'

Karif grinned, shook his head and returned the book to his pocket. 'I suppose I should be terribly offended, gentlemen, but you're reaction amuses me. Captain Sebastev insisted I read the book. I can assure you that I carry this copy with his express permission. I'd like to give a reading from it during the battle, provided the honourable father has no objections, of course.'

Olov's scowl had softened, but the man still looked less than friendly. 'The very worst orator in the Imperium could motivate Firstborn with a reading from the *Treatis Elatii*. It's a safe choice, commissar, unoriginal, but safe. Go ahead with my blessing. I'll listen with interest.'

Karif bowed his head in mock gratitude. Conceited old grox, he thought.

Was it possible that the old man didn't know his own reputation? The men of Fifth Company thought him a far better soldier than a priest. His kill count was impressive and his faith in the Emperor inspirational. It was just a shame, said some, that Olov had been born a second son, rather than a first. He'd proven to them on the battlefield many times that he would have made an excellent sergeant.

Karif knew all this from his time among the troopers. The words of the officer class alone rarely painted accurate pictures. It was only by listening to the conversations of the rank-and-file that one could learn the truth as seen from ground level. He was confident that his reading would be well received, earning him a little more acceptance among the men. Today would be hard on all of them: a single company against Throne knew how many. Karif's chest swelled as he thought of it.

Commissars are made for these kinds of odds, he thought. Glory abounds on such days. Victory may bring decorations, medals and promotions. With luck, I'll receive the kind of recognition that will see me returned to a higher station, a station befitting my past achievements. Breggius may blame me for the shame his son brought upon him, but all his scheming will have been for nothing if I can restore my former status.

'...reading?'

Karif shook himself, realising that the colonel had addressed him. 'I apologise, colonel. I'm afraid I didn't catch that.'

'I asked, commissar, whether you believe you'll be able to fulfil your other duties while giving a battlefield reading.'

'Oh, without question,' said Karif with a broad smile. 'I won't be reading from the actual pages. I've already committed the entire volume to memory and made some preliminary selections. I'm sure you'll be satisfied.'

Father Olov's scowl deepened, but he didn't meet Karif's eyes. The priest was probably damning him for a braggart and a fool. So be it. Karif had indeed memorised the text using techniques of mental imprinting taught to commissars in scholams throughout the Imperium. He could hardly be blamed for the Ecclesiarchy's failure to promote such skills among its own servants.

Lieutenant Kuritsin mumbled something to himself, drawing Colonel Kabanov's eye.

'If you've something to say, lieutenant,' said the colonel, 'share it with the rest of us.'

Kuritsin's face reddened. 'Sorry, sir. I was just thinking that, in all my years serving with Fifth Company, I've never known the captain to let someone else handle his treasured book. I confess that it's got me in something of a spin, sir.'

Kabanov grinned. 'Dare we hope that Captain Sebastev is finally maturing? I don't mean as a man, of course, but as a commanding officer. Dubrin always insisted that it would happen eventually. Our current crisis may have been the catalyst he needed.'

'Change can be a painful thing,' said Father Olov. 'Captain Sebastev has always struggled with his responsibility for the company. I think he regrets his promise to the late major. But it's about time he stopped wishing he could be a simple grunt again.'

Lieutenant Maro, a man Karif had noticed was prone to quiet observation, surprised everyone by speaking up. 'Let's hope his acceptance of the role doesn't jeopardise the very qualities for which Dubrin selected him.'

Colonel Kabanov nodded. 'Sebastev can be bad-tempered, even for a Vostroyan, but Dubrin knew what he was doing. I'd trust Sebastev's instincts before I'd listen to any tactician in Seddisvarr.'

They do flap on about him, thought Karif. There are hard men on worlds throughout the Imperium. I wonder what they see that I don't.

Lieutenant Kuritsin again lifted his chronometer from his pocket. 'Sir,' he said, addressing Colonel Kabanov, 'the melta-charges should be just about–'

Explosions sounded from the direction of the town, a deep stutter so rapid it sounded like stubber fire. The walls of the Chimera trembled.

'That's our cue, gentlemen,' said Colonel Kabanov. 'Lieutenant Kuritsin, you know what to do.'

'Yes, sir,' said Kuritsin. He pulled the horn of the Chimera's vox-caster from the wall and said, 'All Chimeras, advance! Hold formation until you hit the streets. Follow your designated routes. Gunners are to provide continuous covering fire for our infantry squads. Visibility is low. Use caution. Friendly fire incidents will be logged and passed to Commissar Karif. Ride out, for the Emperor and the Sixty-Eighth!'

Colonel Kabanov's Chimera gunned forward. Within minutes, the sound of las- and bolter-fire erupted all around. The Danikkin rebels had awoken to the sound of explosions and the growl of advancing Chimeras. They were already firing out into the mist.

Sergeant Samarov shouted back from the driver's seat, 'Nothing to worry about, sirs. They're trying to zero their fire on engine noise. They can't see us worth a damn.'

'Maro,' said Kabanov, 'get onto that multi-laser and give our lads as much cover as you can. Trooper Stavin,' he called up to the front of the vehicle, 'make that bolter work for us. Bring the Emperor's punishment down upon them.'

Lieutenant Maro leapt from his seat, moved forward, and climbed up into the chair of the Chimera's turret.

As they raced nearer the rebel defences, Stavin opened fire on the rebel positions. The deep barking of the bolter began reverberating through the Chimera's frame. The sound was soon joined by the hum of the charging multi-laser.

'As soon as we reach the perimeter, gentlemen,' said Colonel Kabanov, 'this will become a street fight. And let me tell you, commissar, no one loves a street fight more than the Firstborn!'

Sebastev and Aronov threw themselves down the snow-covered bank as a drum roll of explosions ripped through the town. Shouting immediately sounded on the freezing air. Sebastev could hear rebel officers barking orders to their men in their harsh Danikkin accent. From some of the habs by the river, those boasting windows and cold- sealed doors, the muted cries of frightened civilians could be heard. They should have left when they had the chance, thought Sebastev. If they stay inside, they might just live through this.

He looked out into the mists. He could hear the rushing waters of the river close by. As he moved down the slope towards the sound, shapes resolved themselves. For a moment, Sebastev was sure he'd been misinformed. Hadn't Trooper Bekov said the bridge was shelled to rubble? He could see thick steel girders reaching out into white space. They looked undamaged. But as he moved closer, more of the framework revealed itself. The straight spars became twisted and then completely broken.

It was true; the bridge over the Solenne was gone.

'Captain,' hissed Aronov, 'over here.'

Sebastev walked over to the big scout's side. There was movement in the shadows under the bridge's truncated stump. Lieutenant Tarkarov was waiting there with the other saboteurs. 'Glad you finally made it, sir,' said Tarkarov with a grin.

'Are you saying I'm slow, lieutenant?'

'Perhaps we can settle on thorough, sir?'

There was a chuckle from some of the men. Sebastev managed a smile and said, 'We had a bit of trouble with an enemy patrol, but not much.'

Tarkarov gestured at Sebastev's greatcoat. 'I can see that, sir. What did you do, mop the blood up after you killed them?'

Sebastev looked down. Every fight seemed to end with him soaked in blood these days. 'Damn it. I'll have to give Trooper Kurkov an extra bottle of rahzvod.'

Kurkov of Third Platoon was the only man in the regiment of a similar stature to the captain. Since Sebastev's own coats boasted a little too much gold for stealth operations like this one, he'd borrowed Kurkov's. It was unadorned, and far better suited to the task. The men around him were likewise dressed in only the most basic kit. Their carapace armour remained with the rest of the company. With the exception of Sebastev, who'd brought his bolt pistol, each man carried a lasgun slung over his shoulder and a standard issue, Vostroya-pattern long knife sheathed at his waist.

For Sebastev, the knife had already proven its worth. When he and Aronov leapt on the surprised Danikkin patrol, Sebastev had rammed the cold, black blade straight up under the jaw of the nearest rebel, punching through the roof of the man's mouth and into his brain.

Then, with no time to yank the knife free, Sebastev had flown at the second man, grasping the collar of his quilted Danikkin coat, hoisting the man's body over his hip and slamming it hard to the frozen ground. The man's neck had twisted awkwardly as he landed. The sickening snap announced a quick end to the fight.

Aronov had choked the third man, holding him until his brain was starved of oxygen. Sebastev had watched the man's eyes roll up into his head. Then, they'd hidden the bodies and dashed west to the rendezvous at speed. Their melta-charges had ruined a great deal of rebel armour, and the Danikkin forces on this side of the river would be in utter chaos.

Colonel Kabanov was about to descend on them, and that meant it was time for Tarkarov, Aronov and the rest of the saboteurs to move into phase two of the operation.

'Right you lot,' said Sebastev, 'you know what you've got to do. Get into your squads. Lieutenant Tarkarov will take his squad and deploy at the rebels' backs. You'll give them a nasty surprise while they're engaged with our main force. Make sure our boys know exactly where you are. Save your surprises for the Danikkin scum. I don't want to hear the words "friendly fire".'

'Don't worry, sir,' said Tarkarov. 'We'll make sure our lads know exactly where all the help is coming from.'

Sebastev turned to the squad he'd be leading. 'While we've still got this mist to cover us, let's make the most of it. Our objective is the comms relay station south-west of the old cathedral. I want that building, Firstborn. Possible heavy resistance there, so you need to stay on top of things. Aronov knows the way, don't you Aronov?'

Aronov tapped the side of his fur hat with a gloved finger.

'Good,' said Sebastev. 'Let's move out. It's time we take our revenge for the Firstborn who died here.'

Fires blazed in the eyes of his men when they heard those words. Sebastev turned back to Lieutenant Tarkarov and said, 'Best of luck to you, lieutenant. Don't disappoint the White Boar.'

Tarkarov gave a sharp salute. 'I've no intention of doing that, sir. Best of luck with the relay station. I'll see you when it's over.'

'Yes, you will,' said Sebastev with conviction.

Tarkarov marched his men out from under the shadow of the broken bridge. Within moments, their forms melted into the mist.

Sebastev turned and nodded to Aronov. 'Lead the way, trooper.'

As his squad moved out, Sebastev heard the sounds of heavy fighting from the east. Colonel Kabanov had engaged the enemy. The battle for Nhalich raged.

CHAPTER EIGHT

DAY 687

NHALICH, EAST BANK – 07:38HRS, -26°C

Karif held on tight as Colonel Kabanov's Chimera smashed through the rebels' outer defences, lurching over the rubble of shattered walls, and easily bridging old trenches that hadn't been manned since the Vostroyan frontline had moved east to Korris two years earlier. The colonel's driver, Samarov, held his speed steady so the vehicle didn't pull away from the infantry squad it was shielding. Each of the Chimeras was followed by a squad on foot, pounding the snow packed hard by the broad treads of the thirty-eight tonne behemoths.

Karif peered out from a firing port in the Chimera's rear. It was difficult to properly assess the strength of the rebel defences in the glowing mists, but it was clear to him that the enemy hadn't expected any kind of assault on their east flank. Between the rebels' overconfidence and the weather, Fifth Company had caught the so-called Danikkin Independence Army completely off guard.

Lethal beams of energy cut bright ribbons in the mists, and the air resounded with the staccato of cracking lasguns and chattering bolter fire.

Damn it all to the warp, thought Karif. Now that we've breeched the town, I wish the mist would lift. If I can't see the enemy, how can I be expected to kill him?

Colonel Kabanov called out to Maro and Stavin as the Chimera shuddered and jounced. 'Don't waste ammunition firing blind. Trace their fire back. Give them something to think about before our infantry breaks cover.'

Sergeant Samarov shouted something from the driver's compartment. Karif had to focus hard to catch his words over the angry buzz of the Chimera's multi-lasers.

'Colonel, sir,' called Samarov, 'this is as far in as I can take you. There's tank wreckage all over the road. It looks like armour from the 701st, sir.'

'Understood sergeant,' said Kabanov. 'Maro, stay on the multi-laser. Cover our men as they move forward. Try to keep the enemy's attention on the Chimera. The rest of you, get ready to deploy. Lieutenant Kuritsin, inform Squad Breshek that I will be joining them. Make sure they're ready when I drop that ramp.'

Lieutenant Kuritsin immediately relayed the message to Squad Breshek.

Karif fastened his black fur cloak over his shoulders. Apart from his usual robes, Father Olov's only concession to the biting cold was a pair of brown leather gloves that he tugged over his hands. Karif eyed him incredulously.

'Should you not don something more substantial, Father?' asked Karif.

'I'm cloaked in my faith, commissar,' rumbled the old priest. 'It's always been enough.'

'Is that so? Then perhaps the fires of your holy zeal are warming you from within.' Karif's tone was snide.

'Almost certainly true, commissar,' rumbled Olov. 'Speaking of holy zeal, I'll be listening closely to your reading.'

'Then I'll be sure to give my best.'

Lieutenant Kuritsin finished helping Colonel Kabanov ready himself to lead the men. The colonel presented a striking image of Vostroyan military nobility. Under the white fur, Karif saw shimmering golden carapace armour that was finely embossed with images of the Imperial eagle, the winged skull of the Imperial

for a moment. Each man lay in a pool of dark blood frozen mirror-smooth. The steam from their wounds had stopped. The bodies were quickly freezing solid. He knew he'd lose more before the relay station was firmly back in Vostroyan hands.

'Ulyan!' said Sebastev. 'Gorgolev! Get your backsides up here.'

Two troopers shuffled forward, eager not to step out too far from the safety of the wall. Ulyan was the older of the two. He was grey-eyed, slim, and a damned good shot with a lasgun. Gorgolev, on the other hand was brown- eyed, broad-faced and mean: a troublemaker. That made him a good choice for what Sebastev had in mind.

'Get yourselves into cover on the other side of the target. Use the back alleys to get there. Don't let the stubbers draw a bead on you. When you're in position, I want you to unleash hell on the station. You don't need to hit anything specific. I just need you to draw the rebel guards away from this side. They need to believe a concentrated attack is coming from the east. It shouldn't be too difficult. The rebels defending the base are militia, I'm sure of it. Feel free to engage them once they move to your side of the building. Are we clear?'

'A feint, sir,' said Ulyan.

'Count me in, sir,' grinned Gorgolev.

'Good,' said Sebastev. 'What are you waiting for? Go.'

The two troopers moved off to begin their circle to the other side of the relay station. Sebastev faced the others and said, 'The rest of you know what we've got to do. It'll be a dangerous sprint over open ground. Spread out. Find cover along this side and be ready to run like the warp. The signal to move will be a single shot from my bolt pistol. Understood?'

'Yes, sir,' replied the men.

'Go,' said Sebastev. He watched his men scatter.

May the Emperor smile on us, he thought. With numbers like these, there was no such thing as acceptable losses.

* * *

Karif moved through the streets with Squad Breshek, his boots crunching on the snow between tall tenement-habs of blue-grey stone. His eyes flashed to every shadow and cranny as he pressed forward.

Almost every building they passed showed some degree of damage from the conflict of the previous day. Stone pillars had spilled halfway across the road from a colonnade that had collapsed, blasted by stray cannon-fire. Hab walls on either side of the street had been ripped open by artillery. Dark, gaping wounds with ragged brick edges testified to the power of each impact.

The roads themselves were littered with twisted, black wrecks. A small number of machines still blazed, pouring black smoke into the air above. These machines were casualties from Captain Sebastev's sabotage operation. Karif couldn't help but be grateful for the thoroughness of the captain's men. Thus far, not a single enemy vehicle had rolled out to challenge them. But rebels kept appearing among the rubble to fire their lasguns at the advancing Vostroyans.

Colonel Kabanov organised Squad Breshek into two fire-teams in order to flank enemy positions. This way, Squad Breshek managed to gain ground quickly.

In the lee of two barely recognisable Leman Russ battle tanks, the men took a moment to reload. Danikkin rebels continued to pour fire at them from further up the street.

Karif looked down at the young man crouching on his right. 'How are you doing, Stavin?'

'Fine, thank you, sir,' replied Stavin. Steamy breath rose from the adjutant's scarf where it covered his mouth. 'But I can't really see well enough in this mist to fire effectively, sir.'

'Just do as the colonel suggested,' said Karif. 'Trace our enemies' fire back to them. Exercise your judgement. Don't waste ammunition if you've no shot. The air is definitely clearing. Now that we're pushing deeper and the streets are getting narrower, the pace of the battle is sure to change. Things will get close and bloody. How many charge packs have you got?'

'Two in my pockets, sir,' said Stavin. 'One up the spout with the counter reading half.'

'That's plenty for now,' said Karif. Beneath the warm fabric of his muffler, he grinned.

I don't mind admitting, he thought, that this lad's aptitude for war has genuinely surprised me. His diffidence and youthful appearance belie a fighter's constitution. I should have expected as much. The Vostroyans, by the very nature of their curious conscription system, must prepare their children for war from a very young age.

Karif felt a hand grip his upper arm. He turned and saw Colonel Kabanov beside him, breathing hard. 'I'd say it's about time, commissar, that you started your oration. Our men are right in the thick of things. Give them some words to fight by, as you said you would.'

'Yes,' barked an impatient Father Olov from the corner of the burnt-out tank. 'Get to it, commissar. I would've started by now. Let's see what the Schola Excubitos taught you about oration.'

The wild old priest had been in a foul mood since they'd left the Chimera. There was a blood-thirsty quality in his eye that Karif found unusual for a Ministorum man. Zeal was one thing, but animal savagery? Olov had, as yet, been unable to make use of his massive chainsword. This was still a fire fight for the moment. His patience was clearly being tested.

'You're right, of course,' said Karif. 'It's time I began.'

Karif raised a finger to his vox-bead, keyed an open channel, and said, 'Hear me, Firstborn sons of Vostroya. This is your commissar, Daridh Ahl Karif. I fight beside you in the name of the Emperor, and for the Imperium of Man. Our lives for the Emperor! Let these words from the Treatis Elatii of Saint Nadalya inspire you to victory over our wretched and unworthy foe.'

Even as Karif said the words, fresh waves of las-fire slashed out from the rebel held hab-stacks, hissing and sending up steam where they laced the snows. The volley was answered a second later by Vostroyan retaliatory fire. Karif dedicated part of his awareness to his memory of the text. 'Have faith in the Emperor, said the Grey Lady, and you may abandon fear. Abandon fear, she said, and you may do your duty unhindered. By this alone will you earn your place at the Emperor's side.'

Screams sounded from rebel positions in the street to the south as Squads Severin and Vassilo moved up to flank entrenched enemy infantry.

'The Grey Lady did not stay long on Vostroya,' continued Karif, 'but she set foot in each of the seven states, and their capitals swelled to bursting with those that wished to gaze on her.'

Colonel Kabanov addressed Squad Breshek as Karif gave his reading. 'Move up. I want two pairs of sweepers clearing each building as we go. Leave nothing alive to fire on our backs.'

'There are civilians in some of the habs, sir,' replied Sergeant Breshek as his squad moved out from behind the shelter of the ruined tanks.

'I said leave nothing alive, sergeant,' barked the colonel. 'The rebels will have already killed those who joined our brother First-born in defending this place. Those still alive are either traitors, or bystanders that did nothing to prove their loyalty. Apathy and cowardice are as bad as treachery in my book. The Emperor will judge their souls. We send those souls before him.'

Over the vox, Karif continued. 'On the day of her leaving, the lady blessed the Techtriarchy with a gift. Into the air, she released a great two-headed eagle, symbol of the Imperium, and told them that the Emperor would watch Vostroya through the eagle's eyes. Toil hard in the factorums, she said, for where would the Imperium be without its machines? Fight hard on the battleground, she said, for where would the Imperium be without the endless sacrifice of its sons?'

Heavy bolters and stubbers added to the las-fire. The rebels had built a hasty barricade on the road ahead and were bringing out their heavy weapons. Sandbags and razor wire stretched across the street, from one corner to the other, and the colonel's men were forced into the shelter of the side alleys.

In the middle of his reading, Karif heard a Danikkin sergeant shouting orders from nearby. Three rebels rounded the corner of a building on his right, clearly intending to flank the Vostroyans while their fellows provided suppressing fire. Before Karif had time to mentally process what he was seeing, his hand rose of its own accord and fired off a lethal hail of laspistol shots.

The first of the Danikkin flankers was knocked from his feet, his face a smoking black oval.

Trooper Stavin slew another with two solid hits to the chest in rapid succession. He hit the last man in the shoulder, enough to spin him and cause him to scream out, but not sufficient to kill him. Karif remedied that by rushing forward with his chainsword raised high. He swept the man's head from his neck.

Lasguns cracked all around as Squad Breshek returned fire on the roadblock ahead, but it did little good. From the other streets, screams and shouts filled the freezing air. Karif returned to his oration.

'The lady left Vostroya with one hundred regiments of Firstborn in her charge. Many said she favoured her Vostroyan fighting men above all others, for they were grim and hardy, and they sold their lives dear for the honour of their world and for the Imperium they had sworn to serve.'

While Kabanov and his squad were pinned down, more rebels moved up, eager to make the most of the Vostroyan loss of momentum. High above the street, the Danikkin announced themselves by shattering ice encrusted panes of glass. They began firing down on the Vostroyans from tenement windows. Stavin loosed a trio of shots into the shadows of a high window on his right. Seconds later, a lifeless rebel body tumbled from the empty sill. It hit the street below with a crunch of breaking bone.

Members of Squad Breshek turned the muzzles of their lasguns upwards and pushed the rebels back into cover, but it was becoming too dangerous to hold their position. Colonel Kabanov opened the command priority channel on his vox. It meant his words would cut across Karif's reading, but it was necessary. No man who offered battlefield oratory expected to do so free of interruption.

Kabanov's voice sounded in the ears of every man in Fifth Company. 'Use your grenades on occupied buildings. We mustn't lose momentum, and someone flank that damned roadblock up ahead.'

It was easier said than done. A squad of Danikkin rebels, ten heads by Karif's count, charged round the left- hand corner, firing wildly at the Vostroyans as they ran. Karif dived for cover as las-bolts slashed the air around him. A derelict hab on his left offered the most immediate respite. 'Stavin,' shouted Karif as he threw himself through the door, 'to me, boy. To me!'

Stavin didn't wait around. He darted through the gaping doorway just as another searing volley strafed the walls. Someone screamed outside: one of Breshek's men, cut into burning chunks by enemy las-fire.

The hab interior was absolutely black with shadow. Karif's feet kicked broken furniture as he moved to peer from a broken window. He could see Colonel Kabanov, Lieutenant Kuritsin and the others. They were completely pinned down in the shelter of a broken wall that wasn't going to offer cover for much longer. The enemy heavy bolters began rattling, chewing the wall apart.

'We're out-flanked, warp-damn it!' roared Colonel Kabanov. Even from across the street, the colonel's rage was palpable. Karif saw Father Olov stand up, eviscerator in hand, as if readying to rush the rebel positions single-handed. But the powerful form of Sergeant Breshek wrestled the crazy old priest back into cover.

'Damn it, Stavin,' spat Karif. 'Those rebel flankers are getting ready to move up. Squad Breshek has nowhere to go. They'll be massacred.'

Stavin scrabbled to his feet in the dark. 'Maybe there's a back door, sir. I'll check.'

Karif had been looking outside where the snow was bright. When he turned to face Stavin, he couldn't see a thing, but he could hear frantic movement in the back of the derelict hab. 'Damn this all to hell and the warp,' he growled. 'Stavin, are you all right? What have you found back there?'

There was a crash and cold daylight spilled in from the rear. 'I found it, sir,' chirped Stavin. 'There's a narrow alley running all the way along.'

'By Terra!' exclaimed Karif. 'A chance to make a difference. Good work, trooper. We move.'

Karif joined Stavin at the back door and poked his head out to scan for activity. 'You weren't joking about it being narrow,' he said. 'We'll have to move sideways. Follow me.'

They moved out from the doorway, heading south, lifting their feet high to clear the deep, hard snow. Stavin tried desperately to keep his armour from scraping the walls, but it couldn't be helped. The sounds of battle were softer between the high walls of the old tenements. By contrast, every noise they made sounded unusually loud to the commissar's ears.

They soon reached the corner where the narrow alley opened onto the street. Karif peered around the corner and raised a hand for Stavin to halt. About twenty metres up the street, leaning out from their positions of cover to loose barrages of las-fire, Karif could see the rebels that had moved up to flank Squad Breshek and the colonel's men.

'Two against ten,' he told his adjutant in hushed tones. 'It won't do to engage directly. Hand me one of your grenades.'

'Yes, sir,' nodded Stavin. He plucked a frag grenade from the fixings on his belt.

Karif took the grenade with a grin. 'This is the Emperor's work, by Throne! How's your throwing arm, Stavin?'

'I'm sure it's not as good as the commissar's, sir.'

'Patronising, but well said. Let's find out. I'd say two of these ought to clear those fools right out. Think you can put one right in amongst them?'

'You point, I throw, sir.'

'Right then,' said Karif. 'Pull that pin and get ready. Throw on three.'

Stavin nodded. Both men pulled the pins from their grenades. 'One...'

Side by side, they stepped out of the alley and into the street. 'Two...'

Karif leaned back, careful not to tense, but to keep his muscles loose. 'Three! Damn all traitors to the warp!'

Whipping their arms forward, Karif and his adjutant hurled their grenades towards the unwary enemy squad. Some of the rebel soldiers spotted the motion, but it was too late. Both grenades landed within metres of each other, close to the enemies' feet.

'Good throw,' said Karif as he shoved the young trooper back into cover. The grenades detonated with a sharp boom, sending a shower of snow and icicles down on them from the rooftops above.

Loud screaming filled the air. Those few rebels who hadn't been killed outright by hot shrapnel fell to the snow with gushing wounds. 'Move up,' said Karif, and he broke from cover to sprint towards the wounded men.

'No mercy, boy,' he called over his shoulder. 'The graveyards are full of merciful men.'

Stavin pounded up the street after the commissar, skidding to a stop when they reached the wounded rebels on the ground.

Together, the commissar and his adjutant fired las-bolts into the writhing bodies at their feet. Each shot silenced another howling man.

It was murderous work. Karif couldn't deny it. He wondered how Stavin felt about it. To the young soldier's credit, he'd done exactly as ordered at every turn.

'Don't you dare pity these men, Stavin. They turned from the Emperor's light. They put themselves above every other man, woman and child in our great Imperium. Never forget that.'

Stavin nodded silently.

Karif turned from the smoking bodies and looked up the street to where Kabanov's squad still huddled behind their covering wall, harried by the bolters and stubbers at the roadblock on their west side. The colonel was poking his head out, trying to see just what the hell was going on, but his tall fur hat confounded him, announcing his every movement.

'Colonel,' voxed Karif, 'your south flank is secure, sir.'

'About bloody time,' the colonel voxed back. 'Now move up that street and flank that khekking roadblock, if you would, commissar.'

'You're welcome,' grumbled Karif to himself. 'Come on, Stavin. It seems even the famous White Boar needs someone to save his backside now and then.'

So far, so good, thought Sebastev.

The diversion had begun. Repeated las-fire sounded from the far side of the relay station, answered by the chatter of the east-facing heavy stubbers. As Sebastev had fervently hoped he would, the rebel sergeant became flustered. Loud booms joined the sounds of las- and stubber-fire. Troopers Ulyan and Gorgolev were using the few grenades they carried to draw the attention of the relay station's defenders.

It worked.

At the sound of the explosions, the rebel sergeant became convinced that the Vostroyan attackers had circled east and were throwing themselves into a full assault against the east side. He ordered all but two of his men to follow him and took off at a run.

'You ready, scout?' Sebastev asked Aronov.

'Ready, sir. First man to the door gets a case of the good stuff, right?'

'Right,' said Sebastev as he raised his bolt pistol. 'I'll pay for it myself when we get to Seddisvarr.' All along the street, hidden behind stone walls, his squad crouched ready to rush the building.

Sebastev's pistol barked and spat a brass shell casing, and the Vostroyans exploded from their cover, zigzagging as they ran forward, desperate to throw off the guns.

Sebastev sprinted hard, not daring to glance left or right to see how his men were doing. He saw muzzle flashes flicker out of each of the dark apertures positioned high in the relay station walls. 'Khekking run!' he yelled at his men. He put everything he had into pumping his legs, powering forward as fast as he could. His muscles started to burn, and the cold air rushed into his lungs, making them feel like they were on fire.

The stubbers sent a blizzard of shells whipping down around him, but nothing hit. There was no pain, no battering impact. Then someone to Sebastev's left cried out. Sebastev couldn't look round. Pausing for just a moment meant certain death.

'Keep moving!' he bellowed. In his peripheral vision, he saw a number of troopers moving forward, outpacing him in their race to the safety of the relay station's walls.

Torrents of lead continued to pour from the stubbers. Bullets churned the snow and bit into the frozen rockcrete beneath. Some of the shells punched into living meat. Screams sounded from Sebastev's right. Someone behind him shouted, 'No!'

Five metres! Four... Three...

Sebastev passed under the stubbers' field of fire, moving so fast he couldn't stop. He threw himself down onto his right side, skidding to a stop just as one of the remaining rebel guards fired off a las-bolt at him. The bright beam scorched the air above him, missing by centimetres. Sebastev looked over in time to see Aronov impale the offending rebel on his long knife. The man was still screaming when the big scout hoisted him into the air with his free hand and yanked his knife out. That cut the scream short.

The crack of a lasgun marked the death of the other rebel that had been left to guard the entrance. Sebastev rose to his feet and brushed the snow from his coat. He looked back at the street they'd just crossed. Two fresh bodies lay bleeding on the snow. One of them was still moving, still groaning, calling out weakly for help. It was Blemski, a young trooper from Fourth Platoon.

Trooper Rodoyev, also from Fourth Platoon, followed Sebastev's gaze and saw his comrade lying wounded out on the street. He dropped his lasgun and made to rush to his friend's aid, but Aronov's massive hand caught him by the wrist. 'Don't be a fool, trooper,' hissed the scout.

'Aronov's right,' said Sebastev. 'The guns will chew you up the second you run out there. Blemski wouldn't want that, and I can't lose another man. Think about it.'

'But he's not dead, sir,' said Rodoyev through gritted teeth.

Perhaps Blemski heard those words because, at that moment, he struggled to his knees, fighting the agony of the horrific injuries he'd sustained. The movement was enough for the rebel stubbers. They spat another stream of shells. Blemski's body shuddered as it was chewed apart by a score of impacts. Then it fell forward on the blood spattered snow and lay perfectly still.

Rodoyev howled. His face reddened and his eyes bulged. He snatched up his lasgun. 'Where are they? I'll kill them. I'll kill them all.'

Sebastev grabbed him by the collar and hauled him downwards so that they were almost nose to nose. 'Pull yourself together, Firstborn. I need you in control of yourself. If you can't give me that, you're no damned–'

Sebastev broke off in mid-sentence. He could hear orders being shouted from the other side of the relay station. The rest of the rebel guards were coming back.

'To the corners, all of you,' he hissed, letting go of Rodoyev. His men rushed to either edge of the building, some following

Sebastev to the north-east corner, the others moving with Aronov to the south-east.

When the rebel guards appeared, the Vostroyans gave them time to commit themselves. When the rebels were halfway around, beyond easy reach of any solid cover, Sebastev gave the order to open fire.

Bright beams stabbed out, punching holes in the thick, quilted coats of the rebels and cutting deep, charred pathways into their flesh. Screams filled the air. Bodies crumpled to the snow, some thrashing in pain from wounds that weren't immediately fatal.

'Move up and put them out of their misery,' ordered Sebastev. He threw Rodoyev a pointed look. 'Remember that you are Firstborn, not torturers. You're here to represent the Emperor. I want the wounded rebels dispatched quickly. No toying with them. Firstborn fight with honour.'

As his men moved forward to do as he'd ordered, Sebastev walked back around to the west entrance of the relay station. It was sealed tight from the inside. He was standing in front of the door when Aronov joined him.

'Are they dead?' asked Sebastev.

'Aye, sir.'

'The door is sealed. Any melta-charges left?'

'I haven't got any,' said Aronov, 'but I think Rodoyev and Vamkin are still carrying, sir.'

'Rodoyev... is he all right?'

'They were good friends, sir. He took Blemski under his wing when the lad joined Fourth Platoon. Both men were from Hive Slovekha.'

Sebastev thought of Dubrin and Ixxius. He remembered watching Dubrin's life ebb away as he lay on a stretcher. He remembered seeing Ixxius's body disintegrate in a burst of shrapnel from an ork grenade. 'Understood,' he said to Aronov, 'but the time for mourning is after the battle. Words from the White Boar himself.'

Aronov nodded. The others joined them at the entrance. There was a fierce look in their eyes, a look of absolute focus on the work in hand. It was just what Sebastev wanted to see.

'Get a melta-charge on this door,' he told them. 'Once we're in, we move in pairs, sweeping each level. The gunners are still inside. We'll make them pay, by the Throne. But there may be others, comms officers and the like. Keep your eyes open. They know we're coming in, so no mistakes. Watch each other's backs. Are we clear?'

'Clear, sir,' said the troopers.

'Like good rahzvod, sir,' said Aronov.

CHAPTER NINE

Kabanov stood in Reivemot Square. It was a terrible sight. The corpses of good men, men of the Sixty-Eighth and 701st, lay in heaps like stacked timber. The Danikkin rebels had stripped them of anything useful and piled them up. Now the bodies were frozen together, as cold and hard as blocks of ice. His heart filled with anger and regret as he looked at them. He ordered Sergeant Breshek to organise a search of the corpses, looking for Commissar-Captain Vaughn and Major Galipolov. He was sure they lay somewhere in the square, but it was still hard to believe that these uncompromising men were truly dead.

The remains of a statue that had once been dedicated to the Emperor stood in the centre of the square. Who knew what it was supposed to be now? It stood headless, limbless, wrapped in razor wire and splashed with vivid red paint. A dedication, perhaps, to that misguided notion of independence that had brought war to this world. Some damned fool rebel had written *DIA – No Emperor, No Slavery* in the same red paint on the base of the statue.

The occasional crack of lasguns still sounded in the air as Fifth Company troopers continued to discover and eliminate rebel stragglers hidden in buildings on this side of the town, but the greater part of the fighting was over. Nhalich East was back in the hands of the Firstborn, for now. Kabanov could do nothing about that part of the town that sat on the west bank.

No matter what we achieved today, he thought, the DIA has taken control of South Varanes, the orks are dominating in the north-east, and Fifth Company has little hope of getting back to the relative safety of our own lines. By Holy Terra, have Lord-Marshal Harazahn and Sector Command completely forsaken the Twelfth Army? General Vlastan may be unsuited to this campaign, but one can hardly lay all the blame at his feet. In his own way, he must be struggling as much as we are.

Vostroyan squads moved through the town, herding frightened groups of Danikkin civilians into temporary containment facilities. They'd be locked up until it was decided what to do with them. Many had been killed during the battle, but there had been little need for more slaughter once the town was properly secured. The survivors simply had nowhere else to go. Nhalich might be a battle zone, but it was the only shelter for many kilometres. The nearest town had been Korris until Fifth Company sappers had razed it.

Kabanov wondered how much damage the power plant explosion had done to the orks. How many had survived? Would they follow Fifth Company out here?

With the losses we took today, he thought, we couldn't hold this town for a full hour. The headcount isn't in yet, but I saw enough men fall in my proximity to know the numbers aren't going to be good. We won, and the regiment lives on, but only just. If there are over a hundred men left by the time the headcount comes in, I'll be genuinely surprised.

A light snow was falling. Tiny flakes alighted on Kabanov's hat and cloak, becoming invisible against the thick, white fur. Around him, Lieutenants Maro and Kuritsin, Father Olov, Enginseer Politnov, Commissar Karif and his adjutant stood awaiting orders and surveying the activity in the square. Sergeant Breshek's squad searched the bodies methodically. Kabanov didn't envy them their grim work.

A voice crackled over the vox. 'This is Captain Sebastev. The relay station is secure. I repeat, we have the relay station.'

Kabanov lifted a finger to his vox-bead, hit the transmit stud and said, 'Colonel Kabanov here, captain. Message received. We're on our way.'

'Very good, sir,' replied Sebastev. 'We await your arrival. Sebastev out.'

Kabanov turned to the others. 'Gentlemen,' he said, 'let's not keep the captain waiting.'

Sebastev stood under the buzzing lights of the relay station's basement, bolt pistol drawn. The gun's muzzle was trained on a man dressed in black, a rebel officer, who sat on the floor, back pressed to the cold, stone wall.

To Sebastev's left, banks of security monitors hissed and crackled, leaking acrid, blue smoke into the air. The rebels charged with protecting the relay station had been supervised from this room. They'd all been killed when Sebastev and his men had stormed the building. Only one man remained alive. Sebastev didn't plan to leave him that way for much longer, but he wouldn't execute the man before Colonel Kabanov gave his permission. There'd be an interrogation first.

Trooper Aronov stood behind Sebastev, also looking down at this killer of Vostroyan Firstborn. The other troopers had been posted to defensive positions around the building, but Sebastev knew from voxed reports that the fighting on this side of the river was essentially over.

Trooper Rodoyev had needed to be physically wrestled from the room after rushing forward with his knife drawn, yelling that he would flay the prisoner alive. He was outside now, posted to the east entrance. Sebastev was torn between Fifth Company's current lack of manpower and his need to see Rodoyev disciplined. The man was setting a bad example for the other troopers and he couldn't go unpunished. Sebastev decided he'd consult with Commissar Karif on the matter when they both had time. Other matters took precedence.

The body of Trooper Vamkin lay in a corner of the basement, another man lost in the effort to secure this place. As Vamkin had entered the room, the rebel officer had surprised him, stabbing him once in the stomach with a wickedly serrated blade. The knife had been coated with a deadly neurotoxin. Vamkin's lungs had stopped working almost immediately. He'd died of suffocation long before he could bleed to death.

Trooper Petrovich, a scout from Second Platoon, had been following right behind Vamkin. Petrovich, who'd lost an ear in a knife fight a few years back, was well known for his cool head. He'd shot the enemy officer in the thigh, crippling him and sending him to the floor, but sparing him to face the colonel's wrath.

For his part, the rebel seemed strangely unconcerned that he'd been taken alive. He sat nursing his wounded leg, occasionally raising his eyes to meet Sebastev's gaze. There was something in his look that disturbed Sebastev greatly, but it was impossible to define. Sebastev felt deeply uncomfortable around the man. He wished Colonel Kabanov would hurry up.

The captive was dressed surprisingly similar to an Imperial commissar. He wore a long, black coat with gold brocade and buttons. His face was clean-shaven. The greatest visible difference was in his headwear. While commissars across the Imperium proudly donned the peaked, black cap of their station, these rebel officers wore tall, pointed hats that swept backwards like the dorsal fin of some sea mammal or shark.

How will Commissar Karif react when he sees this man, Sebastev wondered? I've heard a lot about them but, to my knowledge, this is the first time a so-called officer-patriot of the Danikkin Special Patriotic Service has been taken alive. They usually take suicide capsules prior to capture. Why didn't this one do so when we took the building?

The men and women of the Special Patriotic Service were hated and feared by their own people. Here was an agent of the secession whose task it was to purge Imperial loyalists from the populace, and to ensure absolute dedication to Lord-General Vanandrasse among the forces of the Danikkin Independence Army. They were reputed to be masters of torture and intimidation.

Not only do they look like commissars, thought Sebastev, but they share much of the same remit.

To some extent, however, the limits of their authority differed. The Danikkin officer-patriots had power over both civilian and military conduct. The history of their organisation, going back only a few decades according to Imperial intelligence reports, was bloody and brutal.

Booted footsteps sounded on the ferrocrete floor. 'Cover him, Aronov,' said Sebastev. Aronov raised his lasgun. Sebastev holstered his bolt pistol, turned, and saluted Colonel Kabanov. Kuritsin, Maro, Politnov and Commissar Karif filed into the room.

'Solid work in taking this place, captain,' said Colonel Kabanov. 'I had no doubts whatsoever that you'd manage it. Now tell me, who do we have here?'

'I'd like to make the introductions, sir' replied Sebastev, 'but the bastard hasn't told me his name yet.'

'I see,' said Kabanov. He faced the patriot-officer and said, 'Your attire says you're an officer. Act like one. Tell me your name and rank. My own name is–'

'Colonel Kabanov of the Vostroyan Sixty-Eighth Infantry Regiment,' interrupted the rebel with a grin, 'formerly stationed at Korris, now occupying Nhalich East with the barest remnant of your force.' Lifting his hand slowly, he adjusted his fin-shaped hat. 'I know who you are, colonel. I know your reputation. Had I realised you were not among the dead of yesterday's battle, you might have found breaching our defences a lot harder than you did. Still, you won't hold the town for long with so few men, and no help will come. Your Imperium has forsaken you just as it did the people of Danik's World.'

'By Terra,' spat Sebastev, 'you don't have to listen to this, sir. Just say the word–'

Kabanov held up a hand. 'In due course, captain, in due course. The man was just about to tell me his name.'

'Very well,' said the rebel. 'I am Brammon Gusseff, a patriot-captain attached to the Danikkin Eleventh Mobile Infantry Division.'

'Patriot-captain, my eye,' hissed Commissar Karif from Kabanov's right. 'You are a faithless traitor to the Imperium of Mankind.'

Gusseff actually laughed at that. 'The similarities between us offend you, commissar. That is most amusing. What is your name? You're no Vostroyan.'

'There are no similarities between us, traitor.'

Sebastev looked over at Karif and saw his face twisted with hate.

'So you say,' replied Gusseff before returning his attention to Colonel Kabanov. 'It seems, colonel, that there's no shortage of Imperial slaves in this room who'd bloody their hands on your behalf. Perhaps they should fight amongst themselves for the privilege. That would provide some fine entertainment. Of course, if you do kill me, you'll never open the case the machine-man is so interested in.'

Gusseff inclined his head towards the far corner, where Enginseer Politnov was occupied with something. The enginseer had spotted the case while the others were talking and was about the business of trying to open it. Despite his mastery of all things mechanical, he was having some difficulty.

'What do you have there, enginseer?' asked Colonel Kabanov.

Politnov turned his hooded head and said, 'The case contains something of significant weight. There is a mechanism to avoid forced entry. If I attempt to open it without the relevant codes, the mechanism will destroy the contents. I believe there is a high probability that this case contains something of strategic importance.'

'Can't you bypass the mechanism somehow?' asked Colonel Kabanov.

'Not with the equipment at hand, colonel. A number of the devices I require can be accessed at the Mechanicus facility in Seddisvarr.'

'What makes you think we give a damn what it contains?' growled Commissar Karif, stepping forward, ready to draw his chainsword. Colonel Kabanov put a hand on his shoulder and halted him.

'Case or no case,' said Gusseff, 'I'm the first officer-patriot your idiotic forces have ever taken alive, and I expect to stay that way. Contact your superiors in Seddisvarr and inform them of my capture. You'll find establishing contact somewhat easier than before.'

Lieutenant Kuritsin stepped forward. 'Do you mean to say that you've disabled the jamming device? Where is it?'

'Jamming device?' asked Gusseff sardonically. 'I really couldn't say. Just call your superiors. I might be the only hope you have of getting back behind your own lines.'

'Enginseer,' said Colonel Kabanov, 'do you judge that case adequate to hold a possible jamming device?'

'I do, colonel. It would need to be attached to a large vox-array in order to be effective, but such a device could be built to fit this case.'

'Is the device in the case, patriot-captain? Don't play games.'

'I'll say no more on that, colonel. Contact Seddisvarr, unless you want your men to die here when the next DIA armour columns come rolling into town, as they soon will.'

'Fine,' said Colonel Kabanov. 'Enough of this. Where is the main communications console? I want to speak to Twelfth Army Command at once.'

'The console is on the uppermost floor, sir,' said Sebastev. 'I can take you there.'

'Very good, captain' said Kabanov. 'No one is to kill this prisoner without my express consent. Any soldier who attempts to do so will be executed by Commissar Karif for disobeying a direct order.' Kabanov fixed his gaze on Patriot-Captain Gusseff and added, 'We'll find out soon enough, faithless wretch, whether you live or die.'

* * *

Lieutenant Kuritsin sat down at the console on Colonel Kabanov's orders and began adjusting dials as he called into the vox-mic, 'Six-eight-five to Command HQ. This is six-eight-five calling Command HQ. Are you receiving?'

There was nothing but the hiss of static and whining tones that rose and fell but never gave way to speech. Kuritsin adjusted his dials and tried again, but with the same results. He turned to Kabanov and said, 'I don't know what to think, sir. It could be the weather, I suppose. Even with an array like this, sir, the atmosphere of the planet could still be playing hell with long-range signals. Things aren't too bad at our end, but I can't vouch for the weather over Theqis.'

Just as he finished his sentence, a tinny voice sounded through the console speakers. '...Command... eight-five...'

Kuritsin hurriedly adjusted the dials, desperate not to lose the signal before he could lock onto it. Soon, the voice at the other end was coming through loud and clear. Kabanov let a look of great relief show on his face.

'This is Command HQ. We are receiving you, six-eight-five. Name and rank.'

'Command HQ, this is Lieutenant Oleg Kuritsin, speaking on behalf of Colonel Maksim Kabanov, commanding officer of the Firstborn Sixty-Eighth Infantry Regiment. The colonel is present and wishes to communicate directly with General Vlastan.'

'Very good, Lieutenant Kuritsin. My encryption glyph is lit. Please confirm that your own is also lit.'

Kabanov watched Kuritsin scan the console for the glyph that said comms encryption was active, securing the content of their transmission from enemy comprehension. There, on the left of the console, the glyph shone with a green light.

'Glyph is lit, command. I can confirm encryption is active.'

'Understood, lieutenant. I've got a standing order to patch any communications from regiments in your sector straight through to General Vlastan's personal staff. Await further instructions.'

After a moment of relative silence, a different voice spoke. 'This is Lieutenant Balkariev of the general's communications staff. The general is on his way. In the meantime, please report your status.'

Kuritsin looked up at Colonel Kabanov, who nodded for him to proceed. 'Fifth Company is currently occupying Nhalich East. Forces of the Danikkin Independence Army are entrenched in Nhalich West. The bridge between the two halves of the city has been destroyed by the enemy. We are unable to proceed across the river at this location. Our forces are down to...' Kuritsin pulled a piece of parchment from his greatcoat pocket and read, 'Down to one-hundred and eleven men, eighteen of those seriously wounded. The rebel presence on this side of the river has been eliminated. Civilians are present in the town, currently being kept under guard. We have also taken a prisoner who claims to be a member of the Danikkin Special Patriotic Service. He claims to have something of strategic importance to both sides.'

'Have you... One moment, lieutenant. General Vlastan has arrived and wishes to speak directly with Colonel Kabanov.'

Lieutenant Kuritsin stood and offered Kabanov his seat. Kabanov sat down and immediately felt his body settle into the chair. He hadn't realised just how fatigued he was. Now, with his legs able to rest for the first time in hours, he dreaded having to haul himself out of it. His muscles ached and he longed for sleep. He forced himself not to let it show in front of the others.

'This is Kabanov.'

A wet, wheezy voice sounded from the console speakers. Even through the distortion of long-range vox, General Vogor Vlastan sounded a lot like he looked: a physical ruin of a man kept alive artificially.

'Maksim, Maksim,' he said, calling Kabanov by his first name, greeting him as an old friend. 'Praise the Emperor you're still alive. Damn this world and its bloody storms. We heard the DIA were moving up from Ohslir, but I knew the White Boar would see them off.'

'I regret to report, general, that we didn't exactly see them off. The 701st and most of the Sixty-Eighth were lost in a major DIA offensive. The rebels managed to occupy Nhalich, blowing the bridge in the process and isolating the east and west banks. Our losses were... grievous, sir.'

'But you're alive, Maksim. The White Boar lives on. You weathered the ambush and beat them back. There'll be medals for this.'

'Please, general, you misunderstand me. The rebel ambush was a complete success. They wiped out every single Vostroyan company under my command but one. I only survived by the grace of the Emperor and because I arrived after the event with our rearguard company, Fifth Company, sir.'

The vox-speakers went silent for a moment. The only sound was the background hum and crackle of dead air. Then Vlastan spoke again. 'At least you're alive, Maksim.' The blustery tone had gone from the man's voice, 'And you're holding Nhalich. That's something.'

Damn you for an old fool, thought Kabanov. We couldn't hold this place now if we tried. Half a company against Throne knows how many more orks or rebels? Don't be insane.

'There's more, sir,' Kabanov continued. 'We've taken a captive, sir.'

'You surprise me, Maksim,' said Vlastan. 'The Twelfth Army doesn't take prisoners in this campaign. You know that. We're stretched too thin already without worrying about detainees.'

'We believe he's a member of the Special Patriotic Service, sir. He was apprehended in the relay station, coordinating the rebel defence of the building. He seems to think his life is of some significant worth to the Twelfth Army.'

Vlastan seemed to hesitate for a moment before saying, 'A name, Maksim. Has he furnished you with a name?'

'He calls himself Patriot-Captain Brammon Gusseff, sir, attached to the Eleventh Danikkin Mobile Infantry Division, if I heard him correctly. His accent is very thick.'

Again the vox-speakers went silent. Kabanov had the distinct impression that General Vlastan was engaged in urgent discussions with others at his end. After almost a full minute, the speakers crackled to life again.

'Stay by your comms unit, Maksim. Just stay exactly where you are and await further communication.'

'Understood, sir.' Kabanov turned from the microphone. 'Damned strange, all of this. It doesn't feel right to me at all. Have any of you something to say?'

Atypically, it was Lieutenant Maro who spoke up first. 'He recognised the traitor's name, sir. I'm sure of it. He sounded unusually anxious. Throne knows why.'

Commissar Karif nodded and said, 'I must agree with Lieutenant Maro, colonel.'

'Very well,' said Kabanov, 'but I'm not sure what that suggests. We're talking about a man directly responsible for the death of Vostroyan Firstborn. I don't want to believe Twelfth Army Command is willing to deal with this devil.'

'The man did seem extremely confident that his life would be spared,' said Lieutenant Kuritsin. 'Could he have pre-arranged his own defection on the promise of handing over the alleged Danikkin jamming device?'

Sebastev shook his head. 'He's not defecting. Why would anyone switching sides kill Vostroyan Firstborn? Something is wrong in all of this. I've got a very bad feeling about the man. Part of me thinks killing him would be a kindness.'

A sharp burst of static preceded Vlastan's return to the airwaves. 'Are you there, Maksim?'

'I am, sir,' replied Kabanov.

'Good. Listen carefully, old friend. I have new orders for you. They must be followed to the letter.'

Old friend he calls me, thought Kabanov, but would I have saved his life all those years ago if I'd known times like these would follow?

Kabanov ordered his adjutant to record the general's words. Maro dug a battered old data-slate from a side pocket and began writing on the screen as General Vlastan said, 'You are to take what's left of your force, excepting anyone that can be expected to slow you down, and head north immediately to the town of Grazzen. When I say immediately, Maksim, you can be sure I mean exactly that. According to the most recent transmissions, our forces at Grazzen are under heavy attack from the greenskin horde. The orks have launched a major offensive there. If they reach either of Grazzen's bridges, our Thirty-Fifth Armoured Regiment have been ordered to destroy them. I'll send additional forces to Grazzen as soon as we've finished talking. That should help to keep the corridor open a little longer, but you must hurry. If you don't reach Grazzen in time, Maksim, you and everyone with you will be stranded in Varanes. You will be lost to us. No further support will be available.'

Kabanov shook his head in disgust. What kind of support have you offered up until now. he thought?

'Grazzen is over three hundred kilometres from our current position, general, and we'll be lucky if the orks haven't already taken the mountain pass. Just how long do you think we have?'

'It's impossible to say, Maksim. You've got as long as the Thirty-Fifth can hold out against the odds. This is your only way home. You say the bridge at Nhalich is gone. I say Grazzen is your last chance. The DIA will roll more armour up from the south now that you've ousted their people from the relay station. Nhalich West will already have put a call out for support on the east bank. Fifth Company should leave at once.'

'Very good, sir. Unless there's anything–'

'One second, Maksim. I'm not finished. It is vitally important that the prisoner, Brammon Gusseff, remains completely unharmed, likewise, the case that accompanies him. You are to spare nothing in ensuring that both prisoner and case reach Command HQ here in Seddisvarr. This objective is your highest priority and supersedes all other considerations. The life of every last man under your command is secondary to the achievement of this task. I repeat: the prisoner and case are to be delivered intact to Command HQ on Seddisvarr. Is that clear?'

'Sir...'

'These are my orders, Maksim. If there were any other way...' There was a pause before Vlastan said, 'You know I've always been grateful for–'

The general's voice was cut off as the entire relay station shook. The walls and ceiling cracked and rained dirt down on the heads of the men in the communications room.

'Artillery,' shouted Sebastev. 'They're hitting us from the far side of the river. Get the khek out of here now! All of you!'

Kabanov felt Sebastev's powerful grip on his upper arm as the captain hauled him out of his seat and pulled him after the others, just in time. Another artillery shell smashed into the relay station, bringing massive chunks of the shattered roof crashing down on top of the communications console. Kabanov saw enough in the moment he was yanked through the door to know he'd have been crushed where he sat were it not for Sebastev's reflexes.

The captain still had a grip on Kabanov's arm as they raced down the stairway followed closely by a thick cloud of choking, grey dust. Lieutenant Kuritsin was descending at the head of the group, shouting to the rest of the soldiers in the building as he went. 'Everyone outside now! Assemble on the east side of the building.'

Sebastev and Kabanov hit the bottom of the stairs and raced out into the open air as another artillery round thundered into the building, shaking the ground under their feet. The thick ferrocrete structure collapsed in on itself, transforming into a vast pile of rubble with a rumble and a great cough of dust and smoke.

'Not Basilisks,' shouted Kabanov over the noise of more shelling.

'No, sir,' replied Sebastev as they ran. 'One of their own machines. An Earthshaker would have snuffed us all out with the first shot.'

'I need to know, captain,' said Kabanov, 'did we get the prisoner out in time?'

Sebastev grunted. 'Look up ahead, sir.'

There, among the Firstborn assembled on the street, Patriot-Captain Brammon Gusseff of the Danikkin Special Patriotic Service stood eyeballing Trooper Aronov. The big scout had his knife pressed to the prisoner's neck. Kabanov could see the trooper was itching to use it, too.

'No one must hurt him,' said Kabanov as he slowed his pace. 'Orders are orders, captain, no matter how damned irregular they are.'

'I know that, sir,' said Sebastev, the distaste plain in his voice. 'The prisoner won't be harmed. I'll see to it myself.'

Kabanov was quiet as they walked. His body was screaming at him to rest, but there wasn't time for that. Once Fifth Company was under way, he'd lie down and close his eyes for a while. A mug of hot ohx' wouldn't be a bad idea either.

Just before he and Sebastev were within earshot of the other men, he turned to the captain and said, 'Thank you for pulling me out of there, Grigorius. Damn this body of mine. I'm trying to hold out as long as I can, but it's getting harder. Fifth Company must make it through. For the honour of the regiment, you understand.'

Sebastev didn't meet the colonel's eye. 'For the honour of the regiment, sir,' he said. 'But the White Boar is the only man who can see us back to Seddisvarr. You've got the Emperor's work still to do, I tell you. I'll assist you in any way I can.'

As they rejoined the others, Kabanov said, 'Very well. You can start by getting us out of Nhalich.'

CHAPTER TEN

Behind Sebastev, the sound of the Danikkin long guns could still be heard raining heavy shells down on the east side of town. The shelling was sporadic. The rebels weren't trying to level the place; their own forces were already on their way up from the south-east with the intention of taking it back. Fifth Company didn't plan to be there when they arrived. More Vostroyan wounded had already been loaded into one of the Pathcutters and were being administered to once again by Sergeant Svemir. The able-bodied men, barely a hundred of them now, were busy loading weapons and gear into another of the heavy transports. With so few men left to ride in them, two of the Pathcutters would be left behind, scuttled so the advancing Danikkin couldn't make use of them.

Lieutenant Kuritsin stepped up beside Sebastev. 'I've got some bad news, sir.'

'What is it, Rits?'

'One of our spotters reports Danikkin armour approaching the town, coming up the southern highway, strength unknown. At their current speed, they'll be here within the hour.'

Sebastev was about to respond when a call came in over his vox-bead. 'Tarkarov to Captain Sebastev. One of my men watching the east reports movement, sir. It looks like orks, a lot of them. They're still some distance away, but they appear to be covering ground quickly.'

'Orks and rebels at the same time,' said Sebastev. 'Someone really doesn't like us. Tell our men to speed things up. Anything not loaded within the next ten minutes gets left behind.'

'Sir,' said Kuritsin. 'Colonel Kabanov ordered a squad to salvage provisions from the town. Our own stocks are running dangerously low. Sergeant Breshek took a few men from Fourth Platoon and went to take care of it. They're on their way back with supplies, but with time running out, perhaps we should send extra men to assist them.'

'Fine, send the extra men. The longer we wait, the more chance we'll get entangled with either or both of the oncoming foes. In fact, our chances of getting away clean aren't looking good.'

Tarkarov's voice came back over the vox. 'Could we perhaps organise some kind of diversion, sir?'

'I don't think we can afford to leave without one. We don't want our flanks harried all the way to the mountains. We mustn't get sucked into another fight. Our chances of crossing at Grazzen erode by the minute. I'll consult Colonel Kabanov.'

As Sebastev walked towards the colonel's Chimera, vox-reports came in from his platoon leaders. The essentials had been loaded up. The men were, for the most part, ready to move out on the colonel's command. Sebastev ordered them to stand by.

Sebastev knocked on the sealed hatch of Colonel Kabanov's Chimera to announce himself. The hatch was opened by Lieutenant Maro, who ushered Sebastev in quickly and closed the hatch behind him. Father Olov, Enginseer Politnov, Commissar Karif, and the prisoner, Gusseff, sat in the back of the Chimera, still clothed in full outdoor kit. Gusseff's hands and feet were bound tight and his mouth had been taped.

Sebastev spared him only the briefest glance before he faced Colonel Kabanov and said, 'Sir, we're almost ready to move out, but it doesn't look like we're going to get away clean. Danikkin armour is rolling up from the south and orks are coming in from the east. Even if they don't see us, without some kind of distraction they'll pick up our tracks all too quickly.'

Colonel Kabanov indicated a seat and Sebastev took it. No one, it seemed, was particularly eager to sit next to the traitor. The seats beside and opposite him remained empty, despite the otherwise cramped conditions. 'This is grave news, captain. A distraction would need more time to organise than we can spare.'

'We could stand and fight,' rumbled Father Olov.

'As much as I believe that a glorious death should be the final wish of every man, father,' said Commissar Karif, 'I'm also reminded that General Vlastan gave very specific orders. There's little glory in a death that leaves important tasks unfinished.'

'The commissar is right,' said Kabanov. 'Besides, I've no intention of seeing this company meet its end in Nhalich. Twelfth Army Command wants this traitor, and they're going to get him. We must be away at once. Captain, are the men loaded and ready to move out?'

'We await the last few, sir. They're bringing essential provisions. We're running very low, as I'm sure you know.'

'How long before the men return to us, captain?'

Sebastev voxed the question over to Lieutenant Kuritsin, who was still outside, overseeing the final preparations to move out. When the answer came back, Sebastev relayed it to Colonel Kabanov. 'They've just returned, sir. The provisions are being loaded up.'

'Good,' said the colonel, 'but that still leaves us the problem of a diversion. I blame myself, of course for the oversight. We should have rigged the power plants here like we did at Korris. There just hasn't been time. I don't suppose we could...'

'I think it's too late for that, sir,' said Sebastev, 'unless you're willing to sacrifice the few troopers we have left with any demolitions experience. And they'd need one of the Chimeras to get them to the target area in time. Enginseer Politnov would have to accompany them, too.'

The enginseer swung his cowled head in Sebastev's direction. His metallic voice sounded from somewhere in his chest. 'I have no qualms about remaining to lead such an operation. My life, such as it is, belongs to the Omnissiah.'

Sebastev nodded, but Colonel Kabanov held up a hand. 'No, enginseer,' he said, 'I appreciate your willingness, but we've suffered enough losses. Fifth Company can't afford to leave anyone behind.'

'My own analysis of the situation, colonel,' replied Enginseer Politnov, 'tells me that you will lose some men, or you will lose all. Certain losses will be necessary if Fifth Company is to evade pursuit. I have a proposition that I think will help to minimise those losses.'

In the close air of the Chimera, Sebastev found himself very aware of the mysterious clicks and hisses that emanated from the enginseer's body. Politnov always wore the same voluminous red robes. Oil-stained and torn in places, they were utterly inadequate for life in the deep winter, even more so than Father Olov's robes, but the enginseer seemed impervious to the lethal cold. He had little left in common with mortal men. Over hundreds of years, most of his organs and extremities had been replaced or upgraded. Perhaps he had more in common with the Chimeras and the Pathcutters that he worked constantly to maintain.

'Two of our Pathcutter transports are surplus to current requirements,' said Politnov. 'I believe it was the captain's intention to scuttle them prior to the arrival of the advancing rebels. Confirm, please.'

'It still is my intention,' replied Sebastev.

'Aside from my own distaste at the destruction of any machine, captain, I feel you would be in error to do so. My servitors and I are quite capable of driving both of the machines south-east. At a point between both ork and rebel parties, we will generate the sounds and visual signs of an engagement. This will almost certainly draw the attention of the orks. Those among you who have read Anzion's works will already be aware that orks cannot resist a battle. They crave the opportunity to grow in size and strength. It is like a drug to them. I know from your strategy at Korris, Colonel Kabanov, that you understand this well.'

Colonel Kabanov looked displeased but, when he spoke, his tone was one of resignation. 'You intend to draw the orks onto the rebels, enginseer. It's an audacious plan. I'd even call it foolhardy.'

The enginseer was quiet for a moment, but a slight motion of his shoulders suggested to Sebastev that the old machine-man was chuckling to himself. 'It has a reasonable probability of success, colonel. Far greater than an uncovered retreat, I assure you.'

'You and your servants are non-combatants,' said Kabanov, 'I can't order you to do this.'

'It would be a great and noble sacrifice,' said Commissar Karif, 'but who will appease the machine-spirits of our vehicles if you do this thing?'

'The machines will take you as far as you need to go, commissar. This planet has made them fickle, it's true. Offer due obeisance and they will get you to Grazzen. As for my life and the lives of my staff, they belong to the Omnissiah, as they always have. I have lived a very long time. In recent years, I have slowed. Processing takes more time. My functions include more frequent errors. My biological systems are finally collapsing centuries beyond their natural lifespan.'

Sebastev saw a meaningful look pass between the enginseer and Colonel Kabanov as the enginseer continued. 'These are matters I have kept to myself, though Tech-priest Gavaril detected the truth easily enough. I have watched and waited for the moment that my life might be spent for greatest gain. I suspected it would come during these dark times. I was correct. For the honour of the Machine-God, I am ready to face my death.'

Each of the men in the vehicle, with the exception of the gagged rebel prisoner, stared at the old enginseer with silent respect. His offer to stay epitomised the kind of honour and nobility to which every Vostroyan officer aspired.

I always regarded this man as little more than a functionary, thought Sebastev with no small sense of shame. When did I forget that he is a man of Vostroya? Here, he proves himself the equal of our very best, in spirit if not in combat prowess.

'Enginseer,' said Colonel Kabanov, 'you may take everything you need and go about your plan. May the Emperor as Omnissiah ensure your success for all our sakes. Your sacrifice will be remembered in the annals of this regiment.'

The enginseer bowed his hooded head. 'Then, if you'll excuse me, I will attend to the matter with all haste. The Omnissiah's blessings upon you, gentlemen.'

Enginseer Politnov didn't wait for permission to leave. He simply rose from his seat in the Chimera, opened the hatch and clambered out into the cold afternoon. On impulse, Sebastev rose and followed him outside. The enginseer was walking away in the direction of the Pathcutters, his red robes whipping around him in the bitter wind.

'Enginseer,' called Sebastev.

Politnov stopped and turned to face him. 'Captain?'

Sebastev said nothing. Instead, he raised his hands to his chest, made the sign of the aquila, and bowed deeply.

Politnov's laugh was audible this time: a dry, toneless sound like metal scraping on metal. He turned away and continued trudging through the snow. 'Get back inside the Chimera, captain,' he voxed, disinclined to shout over the noise of the winds. 'Flesh is so weak against this cold. Yes, flesh is weak, but the machine... The machine is indomitable.'

Kabanov's Chimera gave a throaty growl as it pulled into position behind the lead Pathcutter. Fifth Company's vehicles moved away from Nhalich in single file, three Chimeras and two heavy transports in a loose column, making the most of the broad channel the Pathcutter's plough carved in the drifts. The setting sun fought its way through thick clouds, casting a bloody red glow over the western horizon and throwing long shadows out across the open snow.

Enginseer Politnov was beyond vox-bead range, but Lieutenant Kuritsin caught a final communication from him on the Chimera's vox-caster. Politnov reported success in drawing the orks south-west from their original path. As he signed off, he was pulling them straight towards the Danikkin armour column in the south.

Kabanov offered a silent prayer of thanks, commending the enginseer's soul to the care of Saint Nadalya so that she might speed its journey to the Emperor's side. Politnov had offered his life to aid them without a second thought, sure that the time was right for him to step up and make a difference. Kabanov could identify closely with that, particularly now, as Fifth Company sped towards its probable doom.

There seemed little hope that the Thirty-Fifth Regiment would hold Grazzen long enough for Fifth Company to cross with the prisoner. It was far more likely they would arrive to find the place overrun with orks, and the bridge destroyed from the Vostroyan side. A few seconds too late might as well be a year too late for all the difference it would make.

Such grim thoughts were cut off by a sudden pain in his lungs. Kabanov scrabbled for one of his handkerchiefs and coughed into it wetly.

The others looked over at him, concern apparent on their faces, but said nothing. Kabanov threw back a weary smile as he stuffed the handkerchief into his pocket, keen to hide the red splotch that he knew would be there.

Kabanov's age wasn't considerable when compared to many high-ranking Imperial officers, but, unlike the others, General Vlastan included, he'd never opted to undergo expensive and often excruciating rejuvenat treatments. He had money enough to pay for them – House Kabanov had more than its fair share of investments on Vostroya and its neighbouring worlds – but he'd always trusted that the Emperor would take him when it was time.

That time isn't far off, thought Kabanov. Will it be on my terms, I wonder? Or will I be denied my last grand gesture?

Winds picked up, driving across from the east, buffeting the sides of the Chimera. Kabanov's body ached for sleep. 'Excuse me, gentlemen,' he said, 'but we've a hard fight ahead of us – our hardest yet, I've no doubt. It's been too long since any of us had adequate rest. So long as we take turns to keep an eye on the prisoner, I suggest we try to get some sleep. The mountain pass is some hours away.'

Captain Sebastev nodded his agreement, looking immensely tired himself. 'We've been running on ohx' for too long. Get some rest, colonel. That goes for the rest of you, too.' He was referring to Father Olov and Lieutenants Kuritsin and Maro. Commissar Karif, barely able to restrain himself in the presence of the captured traitor, had opted once again to ride with the troopers in one of the Pathcutters. 'I'll keep an eye on this rebel bastard for now.'

It was clear to Kabanov that Sebastev needed sleep as much as any of them, but the stubborn captain wouldn't be argued with. Someone else could relieve him later, he supposed.

'If anyone needs extra blankets,' said Kabanov, 'Lieutenant Maro will provide them.'

Father Olov shook his head, lifted a flask of rahzvod to his lips and took a deep draft. Before anyone else had even settled down, he was snoring like a cudbear.

As the others closed their tired eyes, Kabanov nodded to Sebastev and said, 'Wake Maro in a few hours, captain. He'll take over and give you a chance to rest. That's an order, by the way.'

'Yes, sir,' said Sebastev. 'I'll do that.'

Commissar Karif couldn't stand to be near the so-called officer-patriot, Brammon Gusseff. Breathing the same air as a man who had turned from the Emperor's light filled him with righteous fury. He wanted nothing more than to shove his chainsword into the man's belly and watch his life pour out.

At the same time, Karif had to acknowledge that the prisoner was worth far more alive than dead. If the interrogations were handled correctly, what secrets might the rebel give up? The codes to the case that accompanied him? Details of rebel deployment? Perhaps more besides.

Aware that his self-control was being sorely tested, Karif had excused himself from Colonel Kabanov's Chimera and opted to ride in the Pathcutter at the back of the column. Since he'd only been among Fifth Company for a matter of days, he expected to find a few faces that were new to him. But with Fifth Company reduced to less than a hundred men crammed into just a few vehicles, he soon found himself sitting among familiar figures. Directly opposite him, just as he had been on the journey west from Korris, sat Sergeant Sidor Basch of Second Platoon.

'Glad to see you're still with us, commissar,' said the veteran sergeant.

'Likewise,' said Karif. 'Did you take many losses during the assault?'

Basch shook his head. 'Two from my squad. They'll be missed. Considering the odds, though, I'd say we didn't do half bad.' The sergeant paused as if choosing his next words carefully. 'Commissar... if I offended you last time we spoke... I intended the comparison with Commissar Ixxius only as a compliment, I assure you.'

Karif raised a hand. 'I meant no particular disrespect to the late commissar. I merely dislike being the subject of comparisons, sergeant. I'm my own man with my own merits and, no doubt, my own flaws. I'll be measured by those alone if I'm to be measured at all. But let's have no more talk of it.'

'As you say, commissar.' Changing the subject, Basch asked, 'How did you enjoy that pict-slate?'

At first, Karif was at loss. He couldn't recall any pict-slate. He'd

been with Fifth Company for only six days, but so much had
been compressed into that time, he felt he'd been among them
for weeks. Then it came to him; he'd confiscated a porn-slate
discovered by two troopers searching the bodies in Reivemot
Square in order to avoid fighting among the men.

'Naturally I destroyed it, sergeant,' he said. 'A man of the Imperial Creed wouldn't sully his eyes looking at filth like that. He'd
have to flagellate himself.'

'We've got a different word for it on Vostroya, commissar, but
I'm sure the meaning is the same.' The sergeant enjoyed a laugh,
his infectious mirth spreading to the men seated on either side
of him.

Karif had lied, of course. He had examined the images displayed on the cracked screen of the device. He'd been stunned
that such unflattering and clumsy pictography could represent
a source of entertainment to anyone. The subjects were unat-
tractive to begin with.

The Emperor alone knows how you Vostroyans can find delight
in such sturdy, thick-fingered women, he thought. Then again,
they say Vostroya is a cold place. Perhaps the value of such
women is in the heat they generate. And they look like hard workers. I suppose that counts for something.

Stavin, sitting by Karif's side as usual, was being engaged in
conversation by a kind-faced soldier with a long, brown moustache and a patch of burnt skin below his left eye. The burn was
probably the result of a near miss back at Nhalich. Las-bolts could
still singe flesh if they passed close enough without hitting.

'I saw you fighting back there,' said the soldier to Stavin. 'You
got guts for a shiny. What's your name, then?'

'Stavin. What's yours?'

'I'm Kovo, Fourth Platoon. My squad came in from the north-
east and joined up with your lot at the crossroads, remember? I
saw you drop the two traitors manning that bolter.'

'Oh,' said Stavin simply.

'Aye, good kills. Some of the others said you're from Hive Tzurka. That right?'

Stavin nodded.

'Me, too, the Merchant's Quarter. Can't say I miss it much. Anyway, don't worry about the others ragging on you. All the shinies get it. Just so you know, we saw how you toasted those rebels. You're bloodied now, proper Fifth Company. You won't get any grief from us.'

'How long have you been with the regiment, Kovo?' interjected Karif.

Stavin jumped as if he'd been stung, and only just realised that the commissar was listening to their exchange.

Kovo gave a shallow bow before answering. 'I've been with the Sixty-Eighth for over eight years, commissar. I'm proud to serve under the White Boar. Never thought we'd be hit this hard. Curse Old Hungry for the fat bas–'

Suddenly reminded that he was talking to a political officer, Kovo's cheeks flushed, but he held Karif's gaze.

Karif let his smile put the trooper at ease. 'I haven't met the man myself, but I've heard he could do with a few laps around the compound, so to speak.'

A few of the soldiers listening offered polite laughs, but Sergeant Basch leaned forward, elbows on his knees, and said, 'It's a common misconception, commissar, that the name Old Hungry refers to the general's physical appearance. It doesn't. Captain Sebastev never intended for the name to be taken like that. He calls the man Old Hungry on account of all the Vostroyan lives his career has needed to sustain itself. Look under "attritionist" in a lexicanum and you'll see a picture of General Vogor Vlastan. I won't deny he's a wretched figure of a man, mind you, but that's hardly his fault. We were fighting dark eldar pirates on Kalgrathis twenty-five years ago when an assassin managed to slip poison into his food. Together, the Medicae and the Mechanicus managed to save his life. Whether they should have bothered is open to debate, I reckon.'

A trooper with a face criss-crossed by white scar tissue spoke up from Karif's left side. 'If it weren't for Vlastan's political connections with the Administratum and the bigwigs out of Cypra Mundi, he'd never have made general in a million years.'

Someone on the right, hidden from Karif's eyes by the press of bodies, decided to add a few comments of their own. 'Man's a bloody fool. We should have swept on the hive-cities as soon as we made planetfall.'

'Hestor's balls!' another called out. 'Who knew the orks were here, too? If you ask me, it's hardly the general's fault. The Twelfth Army was undermanned from the start. Look to the Lord-Marshal if you want to blame someone.'

More voices chipped in. 'Khek off! It was Old Hungry ordered us to hold Korris when the rest pulled out. Nhalich might have been a different story for the rest of our regiment and the 701st if the White Boar had been there to lead them.'

'You really think he could have saved them?' asked someone.

'Nothing saved Vamkin,' said a man with First Platoon insignia.

'Or Blemski,' added someone else, 'or Makarov.'

Other voices joined in, adding to the cacophony, half of the men battling to be heard, the other half shaking their heads in silent anger at the loss of their brother Firstborn.

Vostroyan truculence, thought Karif. Is this to happen every time I sit amongst them? Their battlefield discipline is impeccable, but the moment the enemy is overcome, they turn to arguing with each other. Well, I've got my own way of dealing with such things.

He took his laspistol from the holster at his hip and aimed the barrel at the floor of the passenger compartment. A sharp crack rang out, killing the raised voices in mid-sentence. The odour of ionised air and metal reached out to every nose in the cramped space. Wisps of smoke rose from a circular scorch mark in the floor.

Karif spoke quietly, knowing it would force the men to concentrate just to hear him. 'Before I joined this company,' he said, 'I heard many great things about Vostroyan discipline. I heard of victories other Guard regiments could scarcely imagine. I heard of a fighting force dedicated to the Emperor's service in every way.'

He turned his head and saw every eye on him. Those farthest from him, near the hatch at the back, craned forward to watch him as he spoke.

'I was honoured to be placed among you. As we fought in Nhal-ich, I was honoured to recite words from the *Treatis Elatii* to spur you on. But twice I've sat with you in the back of these transports, and twice your discussions have degenerated into disordered shouting. I wonder if I should feel quite as honoured as I did before.'

Karif looked to his left and met Sergeant Basch's hard eyes as he continued. 'You are the last hundred men of the Sixty-Eighth Infantry Regiment, and on your shoulders rest the future of the regiment and the honour of both Captain Sebastev and Colonel Kabanov. You owe the very best you can give to these men dedicated to leading you through this struggle. You owe them unquestioning loyalty, just as every man here owes it to the Emperor. Recent arrival I may be, but I have pledged to see this thing through. Fifth Company has fought hard and will need to do so again before this is finished. One last fight to secure our passage to safety. One last fight to fulfil your duties and preserve the honour of the regiment.

'What say you? Will you join me in asking the spirits of our fallen comrades to aid us, to galvanise our hearts for the coming fight? On your damned knees, every last one of you.'

All the troopers in the transport shuffled their backsides off the benches and knelt on the hard, steel floor facing Karif. Some were slower than others, but a glare from Sergeant Basch enlisted even the most reluctant.

Standing before them, Karif made the aquila on his chest and watched the men before him copy the gesture. 'In the name of the Holy Emperor, Majesty Most High, saints we beseech you.'

'Ave Imperator,' came the response.

'For the glory of the Imperium and the tireless efforts of all who sustain it, we beseech you.'

'Ave Imperator.'

'He who gave his life, He who suffers the eternal agonies of undeath that we might live, to Him we pray. Let the souls of our brothers be commended to His side, to offer their essence in death as they did in life.'

'None die in vain that die in His name,' intoned the soldiers as one.

Karif smiled inwardly.

They're a bloody-minded rabble when left to their own devices, he said to himself, but see how pious they are when the moment calls for it. I had thought there would be trouble, a struggle between their loyalty to the Cult Mechanicus and their faith in the Imperial Creed. But no. Over the millennium, they've found a balance between both. It's remarkable.

'Let us commend the souls of the fallen faithful to His side by naming them.'

Between them, the men present made sure that not one fallen soldier from Fifth Company was forgotten in their prayers.

In the early hours of the morning, in the darkness, the driving snows and the howling winds, Fifth Company's vehicles began their steep climb up into the Varanesian Peaks.

The massive Pathcutter at the front of the column hugged the mountainsides, following the pass that connected the Valles Carcavia in the north with the lowlands in the south. The pass was buried under metres of snow, but it was well mapped and had been marked out with beacons placed at regular intervals. The beacons repeatedly transmitted short bursts of noise that could be followed using a standard cockpit auspex. Even so, between the black of night and the relentless snowfall, visibility was extremely poor, and there was no margin for error.

After hours of treacherous climbing, the road finally levelled out. Fifth Company had reached the apex of its journey through the pass. Soon they'd be heading downhill into the valley and straight towards Grazzen.

Trooper Gavlin Rhaiko, the driver of the lead vehicle, gave a sigh of relief when he noticed that the sky over the mountains was beginning to grow lighter. For the first time in long, stressful hours, he could see beyond the plex bubble of his cockpit. He still needed the auspex to guide him through the falling snow, but every few moments, he raised his head from the green monitor screen to peer outside. It was while doing so that he noticed irregular, flickering lights on the road up ahead.

A firefight!

His finger was halfway to the vox-bead in his ear when a bright red rocket flashed straight towards him, smashed through the plex bubble and detonated, killing him instantly.

Sebastev winced as shouting erupted from his vox-bead, sending a jolt of pain into his left ear. 'Get your khekking transports off the road, warp-damn it. You're wide open out there.'

The voice over the vox had the sharp tone of a Vostroyan officer, but Sebastev didn't recognise it. The man wasn't one of his.

'This is Captain Sebastev, Firstborn Sixty-Eighth Regiment, Fifth Company. Identify yourself at once.'

'Captain, get your men out of those bloody transports and off the road now! You're gift shots, the lot of you.'

Sebastev turned to look at Colonel Kabanov. The colonel had jumped awake at the sound of the explosion up ahead. 'I repeat,' he voxed to the stranger, 'identify yourself at once.'

'This is Captain Yegor Chelnikov, Thirty-Fifth Regiment, Second Company. I have orders from Twelfth Army Command to rendezvous with your company and accompany you into Grazzen.'

The sound of gunfire rattled from the snow covered road ahead, loud even through the hull of the Chimera. 'You must get your men out of those transports, Captain Sebastev. It sounds insane, I know, but the orks are fielding a type of guided missile. You... you won't believe it until you see it.'

Colonel Kabanov gave Sebastev a nod and the captain turned to Lieutenant Kuritsin. 'Rits,' he said, 'get our lads out of the transports and into cover. This is a combat zone. There are orks ahead on the road.'

'Aye, sir,' said Kuritsin and voxed the order across to the others.

'I think, captain,' said Kabanov as he stood, 'that we'd better lead by example.'

Maro was already helping the colonel don his fur hat and cloak. Everyone else in the Chimera began readying themselves to disembark as fast as they could. Sebastev looked down at their Danikkin prisoner. 'What about this idiot?' he asked.

'Cut the bonds at his ankles,' said Colonel Kabanov. 'Maro, keep your laspistol at the prisoner's back. There's nowhere for him to go. If he tries to run, the orks will get him. If they don't, the deep winter will.'

Brammon Gusseff, still gagged and with his hands tightly bound, stood at a gesture from Lieutenant Maro. A few moments later, Lieutenant Kuritsin cracked the rear hatch open and they dashed out into the snow, one after the other.

Sebastev raced to the side of the Chimera the moment his boots hit the snow, eager to assess the situation up ahead. The lead vehicle poured roiling black smoke into the sky. Vostroyan Firstborn poured down the ramp in the damaged Pathcutter's belly, shaken by the impact, but unharmed thanks to the shielding between the cockpit and the troop compartment.

Sebastev could see Commissar Karif at the rear of the column, ushering other Firstborn down the ramp of their last operational Pathcutter. The troopers moved in pairs, immediately taking up covering positions to allow the rest of their squads to deploy safely.

Gunfire sounded close by. Ork shells began to zip past. The

lead transport rattled with the impact of fat metal slugs from ork stubbers. On either side of the road, rising up the snow covered slopes, thick forests of pine seemed to offer some shadowy cover.

'Get our fighters into the trees, captain,' ordered Colonel Kabanov. 'I want to push up as fast as possible. Perhaps we can flank the orks while their attention is centred on our vehicles.'

'To the trees, Firstborn,' yelled Sebastev into his vox. 'Flanking manoeuvres on both sides of the road.' Then, to Captain Chelnikov, he voxed, 'Captain, we're moving up under cover of the trees. What's your status?'

'I've got two squads with me. We're pinned down between the treeline on the east slope and a depression by the side of the road.' Sebastev could hear the rapid crack of Vostroyan lasguns in the cold evening air as the squads from the Thirty-Fifth fought for their lives.

He was about to respond to Chelnikov when another explosion shook the lead Pathcutter. The giant vehicle erupted into a roaring ball of flames. Sebastev fought the urge to rub his eyes. It was difficult to believe what he'd seen just before the rocket hit.

For just a fraction of a second, he'd glimpsed a little green figure sitting near the nose of the rocket before it smashed into its target. The creature's face was twisted and insane with glee, baring needle-like teeth in mad laughter as it raced towards death.

They're using gretchin to guide their rockets, thought Sebastev.

Colonel Kabanov was leading men into the trees on the left of the road, huffing clouds of breath into the air as his boots kicked through the deep drifts. Men from Second and Fourth Platoons took up defensive positions around him.

Kuritsin was by Sebastev's side, unwilling to move off without his captain. Another rocket screamed past the smoking transport, heading towards their unprotected position. Both men instinctively ducked, but Sebastev had a much better view this time. His eyes met those of the mad gretchin pilot. The diminutive ork cackled and yanked hard on its guidance levers, but it was too late to adjust the rocket's trajectory enough to hit the vulnerable Vostroyans. Sebastev thought he could hear the frustrated scream of the mad pilot as the rocket blazed a smoky trail over their heads and disappeared into the screen of falling snow.

'Damn us for fools, Rits,' he barked, angered by the close call. 'Let's get our backsides into the cover of those trees, right now!'

They dashed off, using the tracks gouged in the snow by the other men to add speed to their steps. Just as they reached the treeline, chilling screams erupted from both sides of the pass.

'Those are human screams,' gasped Kuritsin.

'What the hell is going on?' voxed Sebastev desperately. 'Someone report at once.'

'It's the woods, sir,' voxed a breathless soldier from the trees up ahead. Cries of agony, shouted orders and the crack of lasguns sounded from between the black trunks.

'What about the damned woods?' snapped Sebastev.

'They're infested, sir,' replied the trooper, 'with squigs!'

CHAPTER ELEVEN

DAY 688

VARANESIAN PASS – 08:42HRS, -26°C

Karif yelled into the cold air as he swept his growling chainsword left and right, chewing through the multitude of brightly coloured spherical bodies that leapt towards him. Thick orkoid blood soaked the carpet of pine needles that littered the ground beneath the trees. For every ten squigs he carved up like pieces of fruit, twenty more poured forward to snap at him with jaws rimmed by long yellow fangs.

There was a powerful smell of ork spores, like rotting flesh, from the mass of squig corpses that were piling up. It had begun to crowd out the scent of the pine. Knowing the woods meant close combat, the Firstborn had fixed bayonets to the ends of their lasgun barrels and were sweeping the deadly monomolecular-edged blades through the tide of strange foes.

The vicious little beasts were knee high and hopped forward on short, powerful limbs. The jabbering noises they made assaulted the senses. There were too many of them to count.

Karif, Stavin and a trooper called Rubrikov had pressed their backs together, emulating the small knots of troopers nearby, eager not to leave their flanks naked to the savage swarm.

Sergeant Basch of Second Platoon wasn't far from Karif's position, just a little ahead and to the left, partially hidden from view by the trees. 'Keep fighting, you lot,' he yelled. 'We're thinning them out. Press forward!'

It was true, Karif realised. The squigs were still attacking in force, but the space between each round body was widening. More of the blood-sodden ground was showing through with each passing moment.

An orange ball of fungal flesh with a face from a child's nightmare leapt into the air in front of Karif and opened its cavernous mouth, eager to sink its rows of razor sharp teeth into his face. It was a close thing, but the commissar's swordsmanship had been tested by many foes both deadlier and more cunning. He swept his whirring blade upwards with both hands firm on the hilt, shearing straight through the orange body. Two symmetrical pieces flopped to the ground and lay there, quivering. A spray of stinking blood spattered Karif's clothes.

Before he had a chance to curse, searing pain raced up his leg.

He called out in agony and Stavin twisted around to face him, ramming the point of his bayonet into the slimy, pink sphere that had fixed itself to the commissar's lower leg.

'Son-of-a-grox,' roared Karif. Even dead, the squig's jaws were shut tight. There was no time to prise the corpse's teeth from his screaming calf muscle. More of the hopping fiends surged towards them.

Immediately behind Karif, so close it almost deafened him, an agonised scream sounded from Trooper Rubrikov's lips. Karif and Stavin both spun away at the same time, turning to face the howling man who'd been covering their backs.

Rubrikov's face was hidden from view by a fat yellow squig. Blood streamed from the troopers head where the beast's fangs had punched through flesh and into bone. Blinded by the creature, Rubrikov couldn't see to defend himself from the other squigs that crowded him, leaping up to bite great mouthfuls of warm flesh from those parts of him that were unarmoured.

A bright green squig closed its mouth over Rubrikov's flailing left hand, severing it completely. The trooper's horrifically shortened arm spouted a river of steaming blood as he stumbled to the ground, thrashing hopelessly at the swarming orks.

Karif did the only thing he could for the man. He pulled his laspistol from its holster and fired a single powerful shot into the body of the squig that was clamped to the soldier's face. The bolt burned straight through the squig's body and ended the trooper's suffering instantly.

Karif and Stavin quickly slaughtered the rest of the squigs that had fixed themselves to the dead man's body. 'Keep on!' shouted Sergeant Basch from up ahead. 'The squigs are almost beaten, but the herders are just up ahead.'

'Ulitsin is dead,' shouted a trooper at the rear.

'Vanady, too' shouted another.

From the corner of his eye, Karif caught Stavin staring at him and turned to face the boy. 'What would you have had me do? It was an act of kindness, by Terra. Could you have saved him from his agony?'

Stavin shook his head in silence.

'Then cover my back, damn you. We move up as the sergeant suggested.'

Karif turned from his adjutant and started moving through the trees, pacing himself with the Firstborn around him. The light of day was getting stronger, but the clouds were heavy and black, and the shadows beneath the snow covered branches of the trees were thick. Still, the Vostroyans knew better than to give their positions away with lamps. The sounds of battle could still be heard from beyond the treeline.

Captain Sebastev's voice broke through the static in Karif's ear, calling to Second Platoon. 'Sergeant Basch, where are you? Have you flanked those damned rocket launchers yet?'

'We're working on it, sir,' replied Basch. 'Had some trouble with squigs.'

'Understood, sergeant. Same on this side of the road. But you have to get moving. Captain Chelnikov's men are in trouble.

They're pinned down. You need to draw ork fire away from them so they can get to the trees.'

Karif could see open snow between the dark trunks up ahead. Sergeant Basch was the first to the treeline and gestured for his men to take cover at the base of the thickest trunks. Karif and Stavin hurried forward to join the sergeant.

Out in the open, in the middle of the road, a Vostroyan Chimera lay overturned. Black smoke billowed into the air from its rear hatch and firing ports. A large ork, its silhouette a confused mass of cables and squared edges, tore at the bared underside of the vehicle with some kind of massive augmetic claw. Vostroyan las-beams blazed out at it from a shallow bank at the side of the road. Karif thought that must be where Chelnikov's men were trapped.

'Who's firing on that ork mech?' barked Captain Sebastev over the vox. 'You're wasting your damned time. Lasfire won't penetrate armour that thick. I want a heavy bolter on him, now. Where the hell is Kashr?'

'Here, sir,' growled a deep voice on Karif's right. 'I'm with Sergeant Basch in the trees to the east of you.'

Karif looked over at Trooper Avram Kashr. He was a huge Vostroyan, so large that he looked ready to burst out of his bronze-coloured cuirass. The fabric of his greatcoat was stretched tight over arms swollen with muscle. As the big trooper hefted his heavy bolter in readiness to fire on the augmetic ork, Karif could see just how he'd built such a massive physique. The oversized gun was usually fielded by a two-man team. Kashr wielded it alone.

'I have the shot, sir,' voxed Kashr.

'Take it,' voxed Captain Sebastev.

'Cover your ears, Stavin,' said Karif.

As Kashr opened fire, the thunderous noise of the heavy bolter shook snow from the laden branches overhead. The gun's muzzle flame lit the woods in every direction.

Karif watched intently from cover. He saw the big augmetic ork shudder as bolt after bolt struck its armour plates. Blue sparks flashed into life with each impact, vanishing just as quickly. Then the stream of bolts found a weak point – the armour was thinnest on the monster's sides. The ork began roaring and howling as explosive rounds punched through metal and deep into the green flesh beneath, detonating within and causing massive internal damage.

Kashr stopped firing. The ork looked down at its tattered torso in apparent disbelief for a moment before tumbling forwards from the top of the ruined Chimera onto the snow below.

'Well done, that man,' voxed Captain Chelnikov. 'You just took out the leader of this damned mob. That should make the others easier to deal with.'

'I still need Second Platoon to move up and flank those ork launchers,' voxed Captain Sebastev. 'Are you listening, Basch?'

'I'm on it, captain,' replied the sergeant. 'Second Platoon, forward at once!'

Karif and Stavin rose and raced forward with the soldiers of Second Platoon, making for the incline at the side of the snow-covered road. Up ahead, several bizarre ork machines – shoddy-looking red trucks that were difficult to classify until one noticed the launchers mounted on top – fired occasional rockets towards the cover that protected Captain Chelnikov's men.

'We're behind their launchers now, captain,' voxed Basch.

Commissar Karif could see gretchin crews manning the vehicles, working in teams to lift more heavy rockets into the launch slings. Among them, small mad figures leapt and chattered excitedly, apparently eager to climb onto the backs of the rockets and launch themselves to an explosive death.

Do not attempt to understand the mind of the alien, he thought to himself, quoting a section he recalled from the *Tactica Imperialis. Let your curiosity perish in the blazing light of your unquestioning faith.*

He turned to Sergeant Basch and said, 'How do you plan to take them out, sergeant?'

'Explosives, commissar,' said Basch. Something in the man's voice suggested to Karif that he was grinning beneath his scarf. 'I think it's time we blew these mindless bags of filth into the next life, don't you?' He turned to his men. 'How many of you dogs are carrying demo charges?'

Five responded in the affirmative and moved up beside their sergeant.

'Five charges, four ork launchers. That's good. Krotzkin, you stay back here as a reserve. You others, set your timers to five seconds. The moment you slap your charges on the back of those heaps out there, I want you to sprint back to the cover of this incline at full speed. Is that understood? Don't stop to engage the enemy. The rest of us will lay down a covering barrage. Your job is to plant the charges and run like khek.'

'Aye, sir,' answered the four men charged with the attack.

With the attention of the orks held by a continuous stream of fire from the Firstborn on the other side of the pass, Second Platoon readied for their attack on the launchers.

'Now!' barked Sergeant Basch. Four Firstborn raced off over the crest of the rise at a full sprint. Each man had been assigned a specific launcher to target. Karif watched without blinking as each of the Vostroyans slapped their charges against the sides of the launchers, hit the arming switches and bolted straight back to cover. The gretchin crews, alerted by the clang of metal on metal, turned and opened fire with their crude pistols as the men ran back to the cover of the slope.

'Open fire,' yelled Basch. His troopers loosed a blazing volley of las-bolts that cut half of the wicked-faced greenskins down. One gretchin managed to shoot the last of the returning troopers in the leg and the man went down screaming just a few metres in front of Karif.

Karif didn't hesitate. He leapt out from cover and grabbed the wounded man by the collar of his greatcoat, hauling him back towards the others. The gretchin turned their pistols on him. Shells struck the ground around him, sending up white puffs of snow. The trooper Karif was trying to help cried out as a number of shots found their mark. He saw the man's eyes roll up into his head. There was no point helping him now.

He turned to leap back behind the cover of the slope, but at that moment, the demolition charges went off with a deafening boom. For a second, the world disappeared in an almighty white flash. He threw himself face down onto the snow as the heat from the exploding launchers flashed past him.

A moment later, hands grasped his coat and pulled him back into cover. It was Stavin. 'Are you all right, sir?'

Karif shook himself. 'I'm fine. Thank you, Stavin.'

Captain Sebastev was shouting orders to his Firstborn over the vox. 'Move in, now. Basch's squad, flank them from the rear. Use the smoke from those burning wrecks to cover your advance. I want all other squads ready to close in.'

Karif scrambled to his feet and took position with Stavin among the men of Sergeant Basch's squad. He drew his chainsword from its scabbard.

'The Emperor protects,' he told his adjutant.

Stavin gripped his lasgun tight. 'The Emperor protects, sir,' he replied.

'Firstborn, charge!' shouted Sergeant Basch.

The orks faltered at first, surprised by the assault on their rear, but that didn't last long. They turned at once to engage the Vostroyans who charged through the smoke of the burning vehicles.

As soon as the orks turned to engage Basch's men, Captain Chelnikov of the Thirty-Fifth Regiment's Second Platoon ordered his men up and into a full charge at the ork flanks. Colonel Kabanov ordered the rest of Fifth Company forward at the same moment, sure that their best hope of a swift victory lay in surrounding the orks on all sides and throwing everything at them. There was no time for anything else. Every second wasted brought Fifth Company closer to being stranded behind enemy lines.

If the Vostroyans had thought their earlier elimination of the augmetic ork leader would hamstring the orks in some way, they quickly found out just how wrong they were. The fighting was close-quarters and intense. At such close range, the orks didn't need accuracy to score with their oversized pistols and stubbers. Vostroyan men were blasted backwards as they tried to move in, their chests smashed open by the impact of the massive ork slugs.

All too quickly, the Vostroyan attempt to surround the orks degenerated into a chaotic melee as the orks surged forward to meet their attackers. The orks threw empty pistols aside to engage the Firstborn with cleavers, axes and clubs. The Vostroyans fought back, slipping under the ork blades to stab at them with bayonets. The Vostroyan officers carved their way through the orks with glowing power sabres. Each Firstborn had been trained well in the *ossbohk-vyar*, and their skills at hand-to-hand combat were outstanding, but the sheer power of the orks couldn't be denied. Where the crude ork weapons connected with flesh, men fell dead to the ground, their bodies broken open, spilling hot blood over the snow.

Commissar Karif's voice sounded over the vox, pouring words of inspiration into the ear of every man as he fought, inuring them to fear and panic with words from the *Treatis Elatii*. Even so, despite the Vostroyan prowess with blades, the orks were impossibly strong. The Vostroyan body count was rising at an unacceptable rate.

It was Father Olov, gripped by a berserker rage, who turned the tide of battle. He ran forward with the men of Lieutenant Vassilo's First Platoon the moment Colonel Kabanov ordered the charge. The priest swung his mighty eviscerator chainsword in broad circles above his head and it quickly became necessary for Vassilo's troopers to move away from him, leaving him to stand somewhat isolated against the orks that charged towards him. Olov laughed and his eyes took on a thousand-metre stare as he walked forward to meet his enemies. When he reached the press of ork bodies, he attacked with a savagery that rivalled that of the greenskins.

Again and again the purring eviscerator chewed its way through ork flesh and bone, sending massive bodies to the ground in so many pieces. Occasionally, the teeth of the blade bit into plates of ork armour and Olov had to physically wrestle the sword free, but his powerful body was more than up to the task. He forced his way forward, carving a wide channel through the greenskin mass.

The orks fought back with everything they had, but Olov's kills tipped the balance heavily against them. The greenskin numbers dropped rapidly. The Firstborn saw this and rallied behind Olov, surging forward in his wake, hewing orks apart with their bayonets.

'Keep the pressure up,' voxed Colonel Kabanov. 'We're breaking them.'

Sebastev stayed close to Colonel Kabanov throughout the fighting, eager to protect him should he tire and falter, but it never happened. The colonel charged forward with the rest of the men, determined to fight by their side and urge them to a swift victory. Perhaps it was adrenaline, or perhaps it was zeal, but the colonel fought with a skill and speed that surprised Sebastev. In the heat of combat, he seemed not to have aged at all.

When the battle was won, however, Colonel Kabanov's age and condition settled back onto him with a vengeance. His breath rasped in his lungs and he was forced to excuse himself, moving back to the trees where Lieutenant Maro waited with his laspistol pressed to the head of the Danikkin prisoner.

Kabanov ordered Sebastev to take temporary command of the situation. It was imperative that everyone return to the vehicles as quickly as possible. Fifth Company had to be under way.

On the road, the last of the orks fell, hacked apart by three troopers from First Platoon, one of whom Sebastev recognised as Aronov.

Good to see you're still with us, scout, thought Sebastev.

'Captain?' said a voice at Sebastev's shoulder.

He turned and greeted Captain Chelnikov. The man was younger than Sebastev by a good few years. He was taller, too, but his body was lean and his cheeks were sallow. He looked as tired as Sebastev felt.

Of course he's tired, thought Sebastev. What must Grazzen be like right now?

Commissar Karif strode across the snow towards them, wiping the links of his chainsword on a rag and sheathing it in the ornate scabbard at his waist. The commissar's adjutant followed a few steps behind.

'The last ork is down,' said the commissar, 'and the men are trying to calm Father Olov. By the Throne, what a fighter!'

'Aye, commissar,' said Sebastev. 'Olov's mother should have borne him first. This, by the way, is Captain Chelnikov. He was sent to guide us into Grazzen.'

Commissar Karif acknowledged the man with a smile and a short bow. 'Then we'd best be on our way as soon as possible. What's the situation in Grazzen?'

The polite smile fell from Chelnikov's face as he said, 'Not good, commissar. When we left a few hours ago, the entire length of our defences was under heavy siege. I'm not talking about the usual rabble, either. This is the most organised attack I've ever seen from greenskins. They're clearly following a pre-established strategy.'

'What do you mean?' asked Sebastev.

'Well, captain, they began by launching a systematic series of probing assaults along our defensive line, fielding just enough of their force to make us reveal the extent of our strength at each defensive position. Subsequently, they launched concentrated attacks on the outposts farthest from our supply depots. Since then, they've pushed through our defensive line and converged on the city centre from several breaches. This side of the river is a warzone. Optimistic estimates have total ork domination of Grazzen's east bank in less than two hours from now.'

'And the pessimistic estimate?'

'A pessimist would tell you it's already too late, captain.'

'Which are you?' asked Commissar Karif.

Chelnikov shrugged. 'So long as the Emperor sits on the Golden Throne of Terra and cares about the men who serve Him, I'd say there's always hope. Wouldn't you? But the Thirty-Fifth is hanging on by a thread.' He turned to Sebastev and added, 'The sooner you get that prisoner of yours across the bridge, the sooner my men can destroy the damned thing. Let's be on our way at once, captain. What's the status of your vehicles?'

'We lost one of our heavy transports, but we've another and three Chimeras intact.'

'It'll be cramped,' said Chelnikov. 'Some of my men will have to squeeze into your Pathcutter, but it's not far from here to Grazzen. We need to leave now.'

'As you say.'

Sebastev raised a finger to his vox-bead and transmitted orders to his platoon leaders. 'Get everyone back into the vehicles at once. I want the wounded on the Pathcutter. Bring their weapons. Leave nothing here that we might use when we hit the ork lines at Grazzen.'

As the affirmations of his officers came back to him, Sebastev turned in the direction of the trees. Colonel Kabanov stood with his back to a black trunk, coughing into a handkerchief. Lieutenant Maro stood close by, still covering the rebel prisoner, but looking at his colonel with obvious concern.

Just a little longer, colonel, thought Sebastev. Hang on until we reach Seddisvarr, damn it. The medicae will fix you up.

CHAPTER TWELVE

As Fifth Company descended the north side of the Varanesian Peaks, Sebastev could feel powerful winds hammering against the side of Colonel Kabanov's Chimera. The mountains that rose up on either side of the Valles Carcavia channelled strong weather-fronts from the east, punishing the length of the valley with heavy snow, battering the city of Grazzen with storms.

Colonel Kabanov sat under two blankets, coughing wetly into another handkerchief. Lieutenant Maro seemed to have brought an endless supply of them from Korris.

Captain Chelnikov fumbled in his greatcoat pockets for something. After a moment, he smiled with relief and pulled out a sheaf of papers. 'Here they are: tactical maps of Grazzen. The situation may have radically changed in the few hours since I left, but these should give you some idea of where things stand.'

The men in the Chimera leaned forward in their seats, eyes on the maps that Chelnikov spread out on the floor of the vehicle.

Much like Nhalich, Grazzen was split in two, straddling the broad, black waters of the Solenne. Unlike Nhalich, however, Grazzen was a major city that had once been home to over two million Danikkin people. Two great bridges spanned the river, linking the eastern nation of Varanes with Theqis in the west.

Sebastev was looking at the southernmost of the two bridges, thinking it would be their quickest way through, when Chelnikov said, 'I'm afraid the south bridge was destroyed early this morning. The orks pushed up from the south-east edge of the city. Major Ushenko ordered the bridge blown before the orks gained access to the west bank.'

'Leaving only the north bridge intact,' said Colonel Kabanov as he wiped his mouth and returned the handkerchief to his pocket. 'From your map, captain, it looks like we've quite a distance to go once we hit the edge of the city.'

Chelnikov nodded. 'True, sir, but once we're back behind our own defensive lines your vehicles can ride the highway straight up the riverbank to the bridge. It hasn't been mined yet. We still need the highway to move our armour.'

'How much armour?' asked Sebastev.

'The Thirty-Fifth has twelve tank platoons guarding all the main roads towards the bridge. General Vlastan sent out five further tank platoons to support us. They arrived last night. I wish I could believe the general would have offered that support in any case, but I'd say that decision had everything to do with ensuring the delivery of your package, captain.' As he said this, Chelnikov nodded towards the bound form of Patriot-Captain Gusseff. Once again, the man had been tied tightly in his seat.

'I don't know what's so important about that bastard, sir,' said Chelnikov, 'but Twelfth Army Command is going to great lengths to get him. It's not like General Vlastan to send armour detachments out from his precious defensive regiments at Seddisvarr. I can't tell you what it did for morale when our men saw all those Leman Russ tanks and Basilisk artillery platforms rolling over the bridge from the west.'

Sebastev glanced at Brammon Gusseff. The rebel sat staring into space as if in a trance. The more time Sebastev spent around the man, the more unsettled he became. From time to time, Gusseff's body would shake with muscular spasms that he seemed unable to control. It wasn't due to the cold, because the shakes were often localised to a single limb. Then there were the man's eyes, one moment, sharp and calculating, the next, filled with panic, flashing from left to right like those of a trapped animal.

'I don't know what's special about him either,' said Sebastev, 'but I'll tell you this: the man is damaged goods. There's something wrong with him, aside from being a traitor to the Imperium, I mean. He's suffering from some kind of mental problem.'

'He'll suffer a lot more than that when the interrogators start working on him,' spat Commissar Karif. The commissar had opted to ride in the colonel's Chimera on the way into Grazzen. Every available space was needed in the remaining Pathcutter now that Chelnikov's men had joined them.

'I suggest we focus on how we're going to get through the ork lines, gentlemen,' said Colonel Kabanov. 'The prisoner's worth is a matter for others to assess. All we need to know is that we've been tasked with his delivery. Captain Chelnikov, since you're familiar with the city, perhaps you've got some ideas?'

'Well, sir,' said Chelnikov, 'no matter where we try to push through, it isn't going to be easy. Major Ushenko has fought orks on a dozen worlds, sir. Before Danik's World he had a reputation as something of a specialist, as I'm sure you know.'

'I know it well,' replied Colonel Kabanov with a smile. 'I was lucky enough to fight alongside him during the skirmishes on Qietto and Merrand. Throne, that was a long time ago.'

'Major Ushenko says he hasn't seen greenskin leadership like this before, sir,' continued Chelnikov. 'We don't know who this ork warlord is, but he's unusually well organised and consistent.'

Chelnikov pointed to the eastern half of the city and said, 'When I left to rendezvous with your company, the orks had already encircled our forces, pressing us back towards the river, forcing us to give up most of the territory beyond the industrial belt. As you can see, this highway cuts through the city between the industrial and residential sectors; that's where we were holding when I left. The highway has proved an excellent killing ground. It's too broad for the orks to cross without getting chewed up by our heavy bolter nests, and their vehicles can't cover the open ground without taking fire from our tanks, Sentinels and lascannon batteries. The result is an impasse all along this road. I'm hoping it's still holding, but we're heavily outnumbered and, as I left, I heard that the orks were consolidating their forces for a big push. Major Ushenko believes the ork warlord will place himself at the head of a major charge. If that's true, it could provide a rare chance to eliminate him. Of course, Fifth Company has other matters to contend with. I apologise for digressing, colonel.'

Colonel Kabanov shook his head. 'Not at all, captain. I wish Major Ushenko good hunting. But, from what you've said, we'll have to push straight through the ork lines and cross the highway on our journey to the north bridge. Correct?'

'Correct, sir. It'll leave our backs open to the orks, and it will put us directly in the firing zone of both sides, but Major Ushenko has planned a little welcoming party for us.'

'Just what kind of party are we talking about, captain?' asked Sebastev.

'We should follow this road here from the south-west edge of the city, heading north-east towards the bridge. There are ork infantry squads entrenched in buildings on either side of the road, facing north-east across the highway, engaged in a firefight with platoons from my company. What the orks don't know is that we have Basilisk artillery in the city parks here, here and here.'

Chelnikov pointed to open areas on the map not far from the Vostroyan defensive frontline. 'On receiving my signal, our Basilisks will begin shelling this part of the city. It should wipe out most of the ork infantry assembled in the area. If it doesn't kill them, it'll force them to keep their heads down, at the very least.'

Kabanov nodded for the young captain to go on.

'A moment later, the guns will stop firing. That will be our cue to race for the open highway. I emphasise the word race, gentlemen. We need to cross the killing ground at top speed. My comrades on the far side can only afford to hold their fire for a very short time. We can't give the orks a chance to cross and engage at close quarters. As for our crossing, I'm hoping the weather will cloak us from plain sight.'

'Once again,' said Colonel Kabanov, 'this damned winter is both a blessing and a curse.'

Chelnikov nodded. 'Once we're safely behind our own lines, my men and I will rejoin our company. You'll be assigned a guide to take you to the north bridge and get you across to Theqis as quickly as possible.'

Colonel Kabanov scrambled for his handkerchief again and began spluttering into it. Sebastev spoke on his behalf. 'Thank you, Captain Chelnikov. So long as the artillery barrage clears our path, it sounds like we've every chance of getting through.'

'By the Emperor's grace,' said Commissar Karif. 'Let us hope the balance of the fighting hasn't shifted in the time you've been away, captain.'

Chelnikov turned to face the commissar. 'I fear the same thing, but I can assure you that our orders from Seddisvarr left no doubt concerning the general's commitment to receiving your prisoner. My company has been ordered to lay down their lives, if necessary, to ensure that this man reaches Twelfth Army Command. You should have heard Major Ushenko's reaction to that. We've got men from the underhives in our company who'd never heard language like that.'

'I can understand the major's feeling well, captain,' said Sebastev. 'Not one of my troopers is stupid enough to believe the corridor back to Theqis would have been kept open for us if we hadn't secured the prisoner in Nhalich. The Emperor smiled on us that day.'

Colonel Kabanov had regained control of his breathing and asked his adjutant for a flask of hot ohx'. The smell of the salty drink filled the compartment as he drank. 'Throne, that's better,' he said. 'Would any of you like some?'

Sebastev felt he could use a mouthful, but before he could say so, Sergeant Samarov began shouting from the driver's seat of the Chimera.

'I have a visual on Grazzen,' he yelled over the noise of the engine. 'We're getting close, colonel. The city is... the city is burning, sir.'

And so it was. As Fifth Company's vehicles rolled onto level ground at the bottom of the Varanesian foothills, reports started coming in from each of the drivers. The city of Grazzen was lit from end to end with raging yellow flames. The thick snowfall and the violence of the howling winds did nothing to put the fires out. The latter actually seemed to be fanning them and pushing them westward.

Kabanov's command Chimera pulled up at the front of the column. The rear hatch dropped and Sebastev clambered out, quickly followed by the others, all dressed for the freezing cold.

'What the hell...?' gasped Lieutenant Kuritsin at Sebastev's side.

'Emperor, no!' said Captain Chelnikov. 'Are we too late?'

'Very clever,' said Commissar Karif, 'incredibly so for a mere ork, don't you think?'

'I'm not sure I follow, commissar,' said Lieutenant Kuritsin.

Commissar Karif stood with his hands in his greatcoat pockets. 'It seems the ork leader needed a little something extra to motivate his troops. We all know that orks are rarely as stupid as their reputation suggests. The ork infantry would've been reluctant to cross the highway without any cover. From what Captain Chelnikov has told us, the heavy bolters of the Thirty-Fifth were waiting to chew them up. Their losses would have been very heavy. So how does one force a reluctant army to charge an entrenched enemy? Excluding the employment of commissars, of course,' he said, smiling.

Colonel Kabanov nodded. 'Light fires behind them.'

Everyone gazed at the burning city. The flames lit the low bellies of the clouds with an angry orange glow.

'Big fires,' said Sebastev.

'Very effective,' said Commissar Karif with a nod. 'Not only does it push the troops forward en masse, but it cuts off any notion of retreat at the same time. I'd call that a very strong motivator indeed. I'd consider employing it myself under extreme circumstances.'

'The Thirty-Fifth must be getting hit hard out there,' said Chelnikov through gritted teeth.

'Perhaps, captain,' said Colonel Kabanov, 'but at the same time, the fires have pushed the orks into the open. The highway you spoke of will be waist-deep in their dead, I'll wager. There's still everything to fight for.'

'What about us?' asked Lieutenant Kuritsin. 'What does this do to our plans?'

'We keep heading for the highway,' said Colonel Kabanov. 'If we can get through those fires safely in our transports, we can keep heading for our own lines along the same north-west road. We may have to fight through the ork lines without Basilisk support, but we'll be coming from the rear. The element of surprise is still with us.'

Sebastev couldn't share the White Boar's optimism.

The Thirty-Fifth will be retreating towards the north bridge even as we stand here, he thought. Prisoner or not, Major Ushenko will have orders to blow that bridge before the orks can gain a foothold in Theqis.

'Back to the Chimera,' ordered Colonel Kabanov. 'Time's running out.'

CHAPTER THIRTEEN

The Vostroyan occupation of Grazzen had at least kept the roads fairly clear of snow. The major arteries of the city were well-used. Fifth Company made good speed through the outskirts. Sebastev watched through a firing port in the side of the Chimera as isolated habs surrounded by open land gradually gave way to clustered buildings. Before long, the streets were crowded with tall tenements in the Danikkin style, their walls crumbling from two thousand years of climatic punishment.

Up ahead, getting closer with each passing second, a solid wall of flame roared and crackled as it danced in the gusting wind. In the light from the fire, Sebastev saw ork corpses littering every blood-slicked street and alleyway. The buildings on either side bore the scars of artillery bombardment and lascannon fire. The Chimera began to buck as it sped over bodies lying on the open road.

'Sergeant,' called Kabanov to his driver, 'give us all you've got. We've got to break through those flames at speed. I know they're well shielded, but I don't want our promethium tanks blowing up when we're right in the middle of that inferno.'

'Maximum speed, colonel,' replied the driver. 'I'll get us through it, sir.' The Chimera gunned forward, diving into the blazing heat and light.

Even through the heavy shielding of the Chimera's hull, with his cloak and hat removed and his greatcoat unfastened, Sebastev felt like he was being baked alive in an oven.

Sebastev doubted Sergeant Samarov could see where he was going. The flames were blindingly bright. He prayed they wouldn't get snagged or smash into a building before they'd cleared the far side of the blaze.

The other drivers reported that they too were racing across the burning ground. Just then, alarms sounded from the front of the vehicle. 'By Holy Terra,' shouted Samarov. 'It's as you feared, colonel. Much more of this and the tanks will blow.'

One of the Chimera's treads began to rattle, and Sebastev felt the vehicle pull to the left. There was a sudden decrease in speed. 'We've lost the left track,' shouted the driver. 'We're khekked!'

There was a deafening boom from below. Sebastev had time to yell, 'Brace yourselves!' before the Chimera flipped over and slammed to the ground on its back, the right track still running fast, clawing at thin air as if desperate to keep running.

'Throne above!' shouted Commissar Karif. 'Tell me we made it out of the flames.'

'The temperature is dropping in here,' said Lieutenant Maro. 'We must have just cleared them.'

Inside the rear of the Chimera, everyone hung upside down from their seats, saved from serious injury, perhaps even death, by their restraints. Sebastev looked over at Colonel Kabanov and saw blood running from the man's mouth and nose. He immediately hit his belt release, crashing to the ceiling, which had now become the floor, and said, 'Are you hurt, colonel? Answer me. Are you all right?'

Colonel Kabanov opened one eye, and then the other. He coughed, and a fine spray of blood misted the air. 'Damned stupid question, Sebastev,' he rasped. 'I'm hanging upside down. Of course I'm not all right.'

Sebastev moved forward to help the colonel. 'Maro, help me get him down.'

Lieutenant Maro hit his own belt release and dropped gracelessly to the floor, groaning as his head struck the metal. But he was up just as fast and moved to aid Sebastev in getting the colonel down. 'You work the belt release,' said Sebastev. 'I'll lift him down.'

Behind them, Commissar Karif, Lieutenant Kuritsin and Captain Chelnikov dropped to the floor with varying sounds of complaint. Maro worked the colonel's seatbelt off and Sebastev gently lifted the man down.

By the Emperor, thought Sebastev, he's so light. All his muscle, all his vitality... This world has stripped it from him. If the Twelfth Army ever pulls out of this campaign, I'll take some consolation in the knowledge that the Imperial Navy will bomb the damned planet to dust.

Kabanov began shouting as soon as his feet hit the floor. 'Hell blast and damn! I'm not some infant to be put over your shoulder, Sebastev. Unhand me, man. The indignity of it, by the Throne!'

Sebastev stepped back, his eyes fastened to the blood that streaked the colonel's face and clothes. 'You're bleeding, sir.'

'There's nothing wrong with me,' barked Colonel Kabanov, challenging the others with his intense stare. 'I'm the White Boar and I'm still in command of this regiment. You'll damned well do as I say, all of you.'

'Orders, sir,' said Lieutenant Maro. 'What are your orders?'

'Get the bloody prisoner down for a start,' snapped Kabanov, pointing a shaky finger at Gusseff. The man hung from the upturned seat into which he was still firmly strapped. Gusseff didn't even look at them. He simply sat upside down, his legs dangling in front of his chest, his expression as blank as a servitor.

'I'll get him down,' said Lieutenant Kuritsin. He stepped over with his knife drawn and cut the prisoner's ropes. Sebastev would have let the rebel drop to the ground, but that wasn't Kuritsin's way.

Do you pity him, Rits, wondered Sebastev? After what he did

at Nhalich? Broken-minded or not, this man turned from the Emperor's light. How can anyone pity him?

Kuritsin looked up at Sebastev, almost as if he'd heard the captain's thoughts. 'If we're beyond the flames, sir, we'd better get moving. For all we know, the orks might have noticed us already.'

Colonel Kabanov spoke. 'Get your kit on, all of you. I want that hatch open at once. Sergeant Samarov, join us outside please.'

There was no answer from the colonel's driver. 'Sergeant, did you hear me?'

Sebastev moved forward towards the driver's compartment. What he saw made his shoulders drop. Sergeant Samarov's blackened body hung upside down. Small tongues of flame still fed on his flesh and clothes. The plex window of the forward view-port had cracked and broken in the heat of the crossing. Even while he was burning alive, the Vostroyan driver had pressed on, guiding their Chimera through to the other side. Sebastev had never heard the man scream once. He had died like a true Firstborn, and he had saved them.

'Samarov is gone. If we make it though this, I want him put forward for the Honorifica Imperialis.'

Colonel Kabanov's jaw clenched as he struggled with his sadness. Samarov had served as his driver for twelve years. Rather than voice his sorrow, he faced Sebastev and said, 'Open the rear hatch please, captain. Maro, help me to clean this blood off my face, would you? The troopers mustn't see me like this.'

'Yes, sir,' said Maro.

Sebastev stepped to the hatch and struck the rune that should have released it. Nothing happened. The rune wasn't even glowing. The Chimera had lost all electrical power. He'd have to work the hatch free manually. He put all his strength into the effort, throwing his weight against the manual release lever. The metal lever groaned and started to bend, but the locking bolts didn't move. The hatch was stuck tight.

'What's wrong, captain?' asked Commissar Karif. He lent his

strength to the effort, but the lever simply bent a little more. 'I hope to Terra the damn thing isn't welded shut on us. Does anyone know exactly where on this door the locking bolts are?'

Lieutenant Maro stepped forward. 'There are two, commissar,' he said, 'here and here. Both are well shielded and made of titanium. If you're thinking of blowing your way out, I would remind you that any type of blast will almost certainly kill most, if not all of us.'

'I was hardly suggesting that, lieutenant,' said the commissar sourly. 'I'm not entirely sure that my chainsword could manage the task, but couldn't a power sabre slice through the bolts? Would anyone care to try, or are we to sit in this metal coffin until the orks cut us out?'

Sebastev immediately drew his power sabre and hit the activation rune on its hilt. The blade hummed to life, glowing and crackling with dangerous energy.

'Move back, gentlemen,' he said as he pressed the point of the blade to the seam where the hatch met the frame of the Chimera and pushed forward. The machine-spirit of the power sabre protested, changing its hum to an angry buzz as it slowly carved a path through the thick metal. Smoke drifted up and sparks showered the toes of Sebastev's boots.

'May the machine-spirit of this great vehicle forgive us,' said Lieutenant Kuritsin.

After a few moments, Sebastev lurched forward suddenly. His blade had punched straight through to the outside of the vehicle, severing the first of the bolts. The sword gave a last loud crack as the charge cell in its hilt died.

'That's one of the bolts cut,' he said. 'I'll have to swap cells before I tackle the other.'

'Here,' said Lieutenant Maro, 'let me take care of the last one.' He stepped forward with his own blade drawn, hit the activation rune, and began carving his way through.

Sebastev moved back and switched the cell in his sword. Maro gave a triumphant laugh a few moments later as his blade sliced through to the far side of the hatch. The last bolt was severed. 'Let's get out of here,' he said. He pushed the hatch open and climbed out.

As Sebastev followed, he saw that the remnants of Fifth Company had taken up defensive positions around the colonel's ruined Chimera. The crump of artillery echoed down the street. The fighting sounded heavy in the north of the city. Sergeant Basch and Lieutenant Tarkarov stepped forward to greet him. Father Olov, standing with men from Second Platoon, smiled over at him with obvious relief and bowed his head in thanks to the Emperor.

'Good to see you're all right, captain,' said Tarkarov. 'We considered using one of the melta-guns as a last resort, but it might have cooked you all. How is the colonel?'

Sebastev turned to see Colonel Kabanov clamber out from the hatch. Maro had made sure there was no trace of blood on the colonel's face, but his clothes still bore telltale stains.

'The colonel is... fine,' said Sebastev. 'He's eager to get us over that bridge. What's our status?'

Commissar Karif moved past them, calling for his adjutant. Trooper Stavin had been riding in the last Pathcutter with most of the other troopers. Now he dashed forward to stand before his commissar, relief plain on his face.

Lieutenant Tarkarov dropped his gaze as he said, 'One of the Chimeras didn't make it through, sir.' His voice was heavy with sorrow, close to breaking as he added, 'It's Fifth Platoon, sir.'

Lieutenant Kuritsin's voice sounded from over Sebastev's shoulder. 'Captain,' he said, 'Lieutenant Severin is asking to speak with your, sir. He... he doesn't have long. Vox-channel delta.'

Sebastev keyed the appropriate channel and said, 'This is Captain Sebastev. What the hell is going on, Severin?'

Severin's voice, when it came, was strangled as if he fought back screams of agony. 'Caught on wreckage, sir,' he voxed, 'tracks mangled. We're really cooking in here.'

'Emperor above,' roared Sebastev at the lieutenants standing close by. 'We've got to get those men out of there!'

'We're in deep, sir,' voxed Severin, 'pulling pins now. Grenades will be quicker. Make it easier on the... just wanted to tell you, sir...'

'Severin!' shouted Sebastev over the vox.

'And Colonel Kabanov... honour to serve...'

'Severin! Throne damn it, man!'

There was no answer. A muffled boom sounded from somewhere within the wall of flames. The vox at Severin's end went dead. Sebastev roared into the air.

That's no way for heroes to die, he raged to himself. Grey Lady, grant me dire vengeance on the orks. By the Golden Throne, I'll visit such a slaughter on them...

All around, the men of Fifth Company shifted uncomfortably. They'd heard Sebastev's half of the voxed exchange. With the absence of Severin's Chimera, it wasn't hard to work out what had happened. There were troopers among them who belonged to Severin's platoon. They'd come across the flames in the Pathcutter transport with most of the others. As the full weight of the situation struck them, they looked ready to drop. Sebastev knew how they felt.

That was when Colonel Kabanov stepped up to his side and laid a hand on his shoulder. 'Focus, captain,' he said quietly. 'Remember what I told you: the time for mourning comes after the battle. We have to get across that bridge. Time's running out on us. Don't let the sacrifices of brave men go to waste.'

The colonel stepped forward and addressed the men. 'Stand strong, Fifth Company. We've got a hard fight ahead of us. I want you organised into squads at once and ready to move out on my command. We've got a mission to complete for the honour of the regiment.'

As the men jumped to it, the colonel returned to Sebastev's side and ushered Captain Chelnikov forward. 'How far from here, captain?' he asked.

'Half an hour if we double time it, sir,' replied Chelnikov, 'much more if we meet resistance. And trust me, sir, we will meet resistance.'

'The way I'm feeling,' growled Sebastev, 'I hope we do. I'll soak my hands in ork blood before we're done, Throne help me.'

Colonel Kabanov shook his head. 'We all feel the same, captain, but it's a feeling you'll just have to get a damned grip on. Our sole objective is to deliver Gusseff. This regiment's revenge will not interfere. My word is law on the subject. Make sure you understand it well.'

Sebastev held the colonel's blistering gaze as he nodded.

'Good,' said Colonel Kabanov. 'Are all our men assembled? This is it?'

'This is it, sir,' said Lieutenant Kuritsin. 'We've got sixty-three men, excluding the wounded on the top deck of the Pathcutter and the survivors of Captain Chelnikov's squad.'

'Sixty-three,' replied the colonel. 'By Terra, let's not lose any more.' Though the bloodstains were bright on his golden armour and the collar of his greatcoat, he seemed to have regained control of his breathing. His coughing had stopped for the moment. 'And the vehicles, lieutenant? The Chimeras?'

Kuritsin shook his head. 'The heat caused irreparable damage to their treads. Ours is the only one that suffered a fuel tank incident, but the others are practically fused to the road. The Pathcutter is still operational, but it suffered heavy damage. It can manage little more than a crawl. Its width restricts it to travelling the open highway. We'll be much faster on foot, but that doesn't help our wounded.'

'By the saints, that's grim,' sighed the colonel. 'We need all the speed we can get. I want all able-bodied men moving forward on foot. We can't slow ourselves down. The Pathcutter will just have to lag behind. If we reach the bridge and get the traitor across, perhaps there'll be time to hold the crossing open for our wounded. It doesn't give them much hope, I know, but I'd say it's the best we can do for them. Captain Chelnikov, follow Lieutenant Tarkarov over to First Platoon and guide them out, please. The others will follow.'

'At once, sir,' said Chelnikov.

As the other officers moved off, the colonel shot out a hand and stopped Sebastev. 'Listen to me, Grigorius,' he said in a low voice. 'Keep it together. Do you understand me? I know you're eager to punish the orks, but the mission comes first. You need to understand that. You'll be in full command soon.'

'I'll do what's needed, colonel,' said Sebastev. 'Let's just get you to Seddisvarr, so the medicae can restore you. If you need me to step in for a while, that's fine, but it'll be temporary, I assure you.'

Kabanov shook his head. 'You never change, do you, Grigorius? I guess that's why Dubrin chose you: stubborn to a bloody fault.'

Before Sebastev could respond, the colonel moved off, calling for his adjutant to get the rebel prisoner up off his knees and marching alongside the others.

CHAPTER FOURTEEN

DAY 688

EAST GRAZZEN – 15:02HRS, -21°C

The surviving men of Fifth Company crouched in the lee of a crumbling hab-stack, checking their weapons, and fixing bayonets to their lasgun barrels in preparation for the imminent order to push forward. An icy wind whipped along the street, tugging at their tall hats and the tails of their red greatcoats. Captain Sebastev peered out from behind a pile of rubble that had once been the building's south-east corner and scanned the road ahead.

He'd never seen so many orks in his life. The streets were absolutely teeming with them, an impossible press of massive green bodies waving every conceivable type of blade or blunt weapon in the air. Tattered banners bearing the Venomhead clan crest whipped in the icy winds. Many of the largest orks wore trophies from their victory at Barahn: grisly necklaces made of human skulls that seemed impossibly small compared with the heads of the monsters that wore them. Some of the largest orks boasted bulky augmetic limbs that ended in spinning blades or gleaming pincers. The roaring and jabbering of the terrible horde threatened to drown out all but the loudest sounds of Vostroyan artillery and gunfire.

Captain Chelnikov had led Fifth Company up through the streets, heading north-east towards the bridge with all due haste, but the closer they got to their goal, the harder it became to move without drawing unwanted attention. So far, they'd been lucky. Ork aggression was utterly focused on the enemy directly in front of them. The men and machines of the Thirty-Fifth Regiment bore the brunt of the ork attack with bravery and resilience, but they wouldn't last much longer. They were being pressed back further and further with little hope of slowing the orks' forward momentum.

If Fifth Company hoped to gain the bridge before the orks forced its destruction, they'd have to break through the enemy lines from the rear and move ahead of the greenskin advance, and they'd have to do it soon.

As his men crouched in positions of hard cover, Colonel Kabanov moved forward to consult with Sebastev. 'This is it, captain. We have their backs. If we can break through the line up ahead, we've got a solid shot at making the bridge in time to cross.'

'I can't advocate a simple charge, colonel,' said Sebastev. 'The moment they notice us, all the orks in the vicinity will turn to engage. They always fixate on the nearest target.'

'There must be thousands of them,' said Lieutenant Kuritsin. 'If I can raise a nearby Basilisk on the vox, perhaps I can arrange some kind of artillery support. That would go a long way to clearing our path. Captain Chelnikov might be able to help with that.'

'It's worth a try, lieutenant,' said Colonel Kabanov. 'Grab Chelnikov and get to work. He's with Lieutenant Tarkarov's men. As for you, Sebastev, I want you to recommend a man to take responsibility for the prisoner. It may be that none of us get through the ork lines alive, but if even the slightest gap opens up, I want our prisoner rushed through it and carried over that bridge. If you've got a fast man that you trust, make him known to me now. Lieutenant Maro will continue to look after the traitor's case.'

Sebastev didn't have to think on it for long. There, by the far corner of the building, talking quietly with Sergeant Basch, was the man he had in mind.

'That would be Aronov, sir,' Sebastev said with a nod towards the big scout. 'He's particularly capable.'

The colonel voxed a summons over to Aronov, and the scout jogged over to their position. After a smart salute, he crouched beside his superior officers. 'What can I do for you, sirs?'

'The captain here has rather good things to say about you, trooper,' said the colonel. 'He seems to think you might be the man for certain special duties.'

Aronov grinned. 'The captain's a famous liar, sir.'

Colonel Kabanov grinned back. 'Is he, indeed? Well, he'd better not be lying this time, because I'm about to give you a very important job. This is absolutely top priority, trooper. I need you to guard the Danikkin prisoner. If you see an opening in the ork lines during the fighting, I want you to take the prisoner and run for the bridge. This man,' the colonel indicated Gusseff with a thumb, 'must make it to the west side of Grazzen. We're talking about duty and honour here, trooper, not just that of Fifth Company's, but of the entire regiment. Are we clear?'

Aronov nodded. 'Like good rahzvod, sir. How much trouble is he likely to be? Is he suicidal? Will he try to run during the fighting?'

It was Sebastev who answered. 'He's been strangely compliant since leaving Nhalich. I don't think he wants to die. So, no, I don't expect him to give you trouble. You can knock him out and carry him if you think it necessary, but no broken bones and no permanent damage.'

'You take all the fun out of life, sir.'

'I know I do, trooper,' replied Sebastev, 'it's in my job description. Now grab the prisoner and get ready. We'll be push–'

Vox-chatter cut Sebastev off mid-sentence. It was Commissar Karif. 'By the Throne! We've been spotted. Ork warbikes coming in from the east at high speed. Get to cover, damn it. I need heavy weapons over here, now! Colonel Kabanov, Squad Grodolkin is under heavy fire. The orks on the street ahead are turning, sir. They've noticed us.'

The commissar had attached himself to Squad Grodolkin and taken up position guarding the company's east flank. The sound of ork stubbers came from that direction.

'Don't get cut off from the rest of the company, commissar,' voxed Colonel Kabanov urgently. 'Move this way. We have to hold together.'

'It's too late, sir,' voxed Commissar Karif. 'My squad is pinned down. The orks are spilling down the streets on either side. Wait! I think I see a way out, sir. I'm going to try something.'

'What are you going to do?' voxed Sebastev. 'Commissar?'

There was no answer.

'Warp damn and blast,' spat Colonel Kabanov, 'we've lost him.'

'Squad Grodolkin, respond,' voxed Sebastev. 'Anyone from Squad Grodolkin, respond at once.'

Again, there was no answer.

'Khek! It'll be a matter of seconds before those orks come round that corner, colonel. We fight or die.' Sebastev pulled his bolt pistol from its holster and drew his power sabre from its sheath. 'Rits,' he shouted, 'where's the damned artillery barrage?'

Kuritsin looked over. Captain Chelnikov was busy talking into the lieutenant's back-mounted vox-caster. 'All the Thirty-Fifth's vox-channels are choked with traffic, sir. We're having trouble getting through to anyone. Captain Chelnikov is trying the command channel, but the weather is cutting our range.'

Orks appeared on the road that ran east, just a score of them at first, boots pounding the black rockcrete as they raced towards Fifth Company with their cleavers held high. Then, behind them, hundreds more spilled out onto the road from the adjoining streets.

'Engage the enemy!' bellowed Colonel Kabanov, standing to unsheathe his own power sabre. In his right hand, his hellpistol cracked and an ork at the front of the charge tumbled to the ground, headless. 'Try to press north. Don't be drawn away from our objective. We must gain the bridge at all costs!'

'For the White Boar!' added Sebastev. His men lifted their weapons into the air and roared. Then Fifth Company broke from cover, rushing north up the street to meet the massed orks. The enemy on their east flank came straight on, and soon Fifth Company was surrounded, fighting desperately for their lives in a sea of massive green bodies.

To Sebastev, this looked like it might be the end of them.

But it's not over yet, he told himself. If we fall here, we'll sell our lives dear, by Terra. Maybe, just maybe, we can open a path for Aronov and the bastard rebel.

As the orks charged down the street, Karif looked around desperately for the best position of hard cover he could find. Instead, he spotted a dark crevasse in the road, a tear in the rockcrete surface that had probably been caused by a Vostroyan Earthshaker round during the Thirty-Fifth Regiment's attempted defence of the town. The impact on the street had punched a hole straight through to the sewers beneath. Inky blackness had never looked so appealing to Karif.

'Sergeant Grodolkin,' he shouted. 'We're going down that hole at once. Choose three men to cover the descent of the others.'

So Grodolkin had chosen, quickly and calmly, and three men had stayed above, fighting to their last breaths so that the rest of their squad could escape into the sewers.

The orks hadn't followed. In part, Karif was relieved, but he was also concerned. It suggested to him that they'd spotted Colonel Kabanov and the rest of the company and had opted to engage them instead. He offered a quick prayer for the safety of those men as he led Squad Grodolkin along the tunnel, trusting his instincts, secure in the knowledge that his training on Terrax had prepared him for almost anything.

He tried his vox-bead again, but communication with the other squads had been lost the moment he'd leapt into the hole.

Sergeant Grodolkin walked beside him in silence, radiating

intense anger over the deaths of good men. The sergeant was big and broad shouldered, and had lost an eye at some point in his past. It was difficult for Karif to imagine that this dangerous man was as respected for his beautiful paintings of the Emperor's saints as for his combat prowess and solid, squad leadership abilities.

'Those men died bravely,' said Karif. 'We'll honour them at the proper time.'

Grodolkin didn't respond.

The tunnels were dark, and still stank of sewage despite long years of disuse. Trooper Stavin walked on Karif's left, carrying a promethium lamp in one hand and his lasgun in the other. The orange glow of the lamp threw dancing shadows on the curved black walls of the tunnel.

The heavy boots of Grodolkin's squad, just six men left, caused echoes that raced ahead of them into the darkness. Karif cursed the noise, and hissed at them to step lightly. As they pressed forward, however, the sounds of battle overhead became louder and covered the noise of their passage. Tanks and artillery platforms could be heard booming and rumbling through the metres of rockcrete between the tunnel's ceiling and the streets above.

'I hope the others are all right,' whispered a trooper behind Grodolkin.

'I'm more worried about us,' replied another in hushed tones. 'They've got the White Boar with them. He'll get them through. But I've never liked tunnels.'

Sergeant Grodolkin grunted and turned. 'Shut the khek up, you two, or the commissar will execute you on the spot for poor discipline.'

Karif turned and scowled. 'Listen to your sergeant. I'll cut the head off any man that gives us away to the foe. Is that clear?'

'Rahzvod,' said one.

'What?'

'Rahzvod, sir,' he repeated. 'It's clear.'

The sound of metal clanking on stone echoed down the tunnel towards them. By reflex, every man dropped into a crouch with his lasgun raised. Nothing happened. After a moment, Karif ushered them cautiously forward. Soon, they could hear scratching and chittering sounds from up ahead.

'Douse that khekking lamp, trooper,' said Grodolkin.

Stavin hesitated only long enough for Karif to say, 'Do it, Stavin.'

When the lamp was shuttered, it became clear that there was another light source ahead. At a bend in the tunnel just a hundred metres away, the stone walls glowed softly with a pulsing light that suggested a naked flame.

Karif didn't dare speak out loud. Instead, he signalled the others to prepare for an engagement.

Remember your Anzion, Daridh, he told himself. Remember what you read in the man's books. Orks can't see in the dark any more than we can. The noise up ahead doesn't sound like your average orks. They're not sneaky or subtle, but it may be ork stealthers like those we encountered in Korris. What in the warp are they doing up there?

The Vostroyan squad numbered nine men, including Stavin, Sergeant Grodolkin and himself. Karif decided their best chance to minimise casualties lay in a full and sudden frontal assault, catching the enemy right in the middle of whatever business they were about.

Using hand-signed battle language, he communicated to Grodolkin and his men that he believed the sounds to be coming from ork saboteurs. With more gestures, he readied the men to rush forward as one, firing on the foe as soon as they were within sight.

The Vostroyans nodded their understanding and moved into assault formation under the direction of Sergeant Grodolkin. Stavin stayed beside his commissar. He put away his lamp and gripped his lasgun tight in both hands. His bayonet was fixed securely under the weapon's long barrel.

Karif's heart quickened and adrenaline coursed through him, lending extra power and speed to his limbs. His laspistol and chainsword felt reassuringly weighty in his hands.

Who knows how many there are, he thought? Or what we're walking into? The men are ready. There's no point speculating. We attack!

He gave the signal to charge. Squad Grodolkin surged forward along the bend in the tunnel, holding formation as they ran. Before them, a great mob of gretchin, scores of them, spun at the sudden noise, freezing for a moment in absolute surprise.

Squad Grodolkin opened fire immediately. Lasguns cracked with uncommon sharpness in the enclosed confines of the sewers. Beams slashed out, cutting green bodies into smoking pieces. The echoes in the tunnel made it seem as if thousands of Vostroyans were attacking at once.

As the screams of dying xenos filled the air, the gretchin snapped out of their shock and launched into a retaliatory action. But it was too late. Scores of them fell howling as las-bolts carved deep black wounds in their flesh. It was a massacre. The gretchin had been so intent on their task that they were utterly unprepared to defend themselves.

In the light of the gretchin torches, Karif realised with a start just what their task had been.

'Stop firing!' he yelled at the top of his voice. 'Hold your fire, Throne damn it!'

Stavin must have seen it too, because he joined the commissar, his high voice cutting through the noise as he yelled: 'Hold your fire!'

The surviving gretchin, of which there were just over twenty, began firing back. They hefted their heavy pistols with two hands and loosed shots off towards Grodolkin's men. But the Vostroyans saw the reason for the commissar's order. They saw for themselves how close they'd come to disaster. There, fixed to the ceiling overhead, was a mass of ork explosives. Long fuses dangled all the way to the floor, waiting to be fixed to the timing device that lay in the middle of a ring of fresh, green corpses.

A single stray shot, thought Karif, and we'd be dead already.

'Bayonets,' yelled Sergeant Grodolkin. 'Engage at close quarters.'

The gretchin fired again and again as the Vostroyans rushed forward, but the weight of their pistols made it difficult for them to aim properly. Even so, given the volume of fire they loosed at the charging men, it was inevitable that some shots would find their marks. The Vostroyans' cherished carapace armour saved their lives, absorbing most of the impacts from those shots, even at close range.

Only two of Grodolkin's men went down in the hail of bullets. Karif was right behind one of them when it happened. The luckless man was thrown backwards, lifted clear off his feet with his head demolished. Before the responsible gretchin could reload, both Karif and Stavin raced forward, closing the distance at a sprint. Stavin pierced the creature's belly with a thrust of his bayonet, but the gretchin lashed out with its long arms at the same time. Fingernails like talons cut deep red gashes in the adjutant's left cheek.

As Stavin reeled from the blow, Karif swept his chainsword up and lopped off one of the creature's arms. He immediately followed with a savage kick to its bleeding belly. The kick was a blur, launched with a speed and technique developed over long years of daily training on Terrax. The gretchin was blasted backwards, howling pitifully until its skull cracked against the tunnel wall behind it.

As it slumped unconscious to the tunnel floor, Karif turned to his adjutant. The young trooper was shaking with anger and adrenaline. 'Finish it off, Stavin. No mercy for the Emperor's foes. Kill it.'

Stavin stepped forward wordlessly and ran his bayonet through the unconscious creature again and again, driven by rage and shock, fear and pain.

That's the stuff, Stavin, thought Karif. *Mercy has no place in a soldier's arsenal. I told you back in Nhalich, remember? The graveyards are full of merciful men.*

High-pitched alien screams filled the tunnel as Grodolkin's troopers exterminated the last of the gretchin. The stunted green-skins were no match for Vostroyan Firstborn in hand-to-hand combat.

'Damn, but that was a close thing, commissar,' said Sergeant Grodolkin, stepping up to Karif's side. The big sergeant noticed that Stavin was still ramming his blade into the lifeless xenos corpse. 'That's enough, trooper. It's dead. Save your energy for the next one you meet.'

Stavin stepped back, his chest rising and falling with deep breaths.

'If a single las-bolt had struck the explosives, sergeant,' said Karif with a gesture at the bomb clusters on the ceiling, 'we'd have met a very noisy and, in my opinion, early death.'

'Why here?' wondered Grodolkin.

'I suspect we're very near our destination, sergeant. We must try to find an exit hatch nearby. There must be a ladder leading to a manhole cover. I can hear the rushing waters of the Solenne, so the bridge can't be far. The gretchin were trying to bring down the road.'

Grodolkin nodded. 'Meaning we might just be behind Vostroyan lines?'

'More likely, we're right under them.'

As if to confirm this, the tunnel shook with a mighty boom. Karif said, 'The orks must be closing on the bridge even as we speak, sergeant. We've got to get a move on.'

Another blast shook the tunnel. One of Grodolkin's troopers shouted for his sergeant's attention. Karif and Stavin followed Grodolkin over to the trooper and discovered that the man had found a series of steel rungs set into the stone wall. At the top of the ladder there was a manhole cover, their way out of the sewers.

'Outstanding,' said Karif. 'Sergeant, order your men to carefully dismantle the gretchin explosives. We don't want any accidents after all we've achieved down here.'

'Aye, commissar,' said Grodolkin. He turned and began barking orders to his men.

'As for me,' said Karif, 'I could do with a bit of fresh air.'

CHAPTER FIFTEEN

The sky above was dark and heavy as Fifth Company charged straight towards the greenskin horde. The churning black clouds matched the moment well. Sebastev bore little real hope that they'd make it through. Mere men, even soldiers as brave and skilful as the men of this company, couldn't hope to survive for long in close combat against enemies as powerful and savage as the Venomhead orks.

Colonel Kabanov had ordered the men into a fighting wedge with heavy weapons spread evenly along the line. Sebastev placed himself near his colonel with Lieutenant Kuritsin at his side. Father Olov was nearby, as was Lieutenant Maro. The other officers placed themselves by the surviving men of their own platoons. Leading the thirty-nine troopers that remained, the officers of Fifth Company charged up the street with weapons blazing, eager to fell as many of the enemy as they could before the two sides crashed together.

The orks ran, too, roaring and laughing as they hefted their blades into the air. They loved nothing more than a bloody battle at close quarters. This was a fight on their terms. For Fifth Company, there were simply no alternatives. If the Emperor was with them, there would be an opening somewhere. Some of them had to make it through. Trooper Aronov ran just a few metres off to Sebastev's right. The rebel prisoner was slung across the big scout's shoulder, hanging limp. Aronov had immediately knocked him unconscious rather than wrestle him forward during the fight. The prisoner was a terrible burden on Aronov. His fighting would be seriously hampered. Still, Sebastev was sure he'd made the right choice. If anyone could get Brammon Gusseff across the ork line, it would be the big scout.

'Vostroya!' shouted Colonel Kabanov as he charged, firing at the closest orks with his powerful antique hellpistol. Adrenaline and desperation had overcome his ill health, at least for the moment. His every blazing shot sent another smoking ork corpse down under the feet of its fellows, but there were just too many. Ten kills, twenty, thirty, it seemed to make little real difference to the wall of green bodies.

'For Vostroya!' yelled the men, pouring fire ahead of them as the distance closed. The buildings on either side of the street lit up with the intensity of the Vostroyan las-fire. The air echoed with cracks, and became thick with the smell of scorched ork flesh. Troopers Mitko and Pankratov, both of whom wielded plasma guns, loosed devastating rounds that were almost too bright to look at. The orks were packed so close that every blast of superheated plasma obliterated dozens of them.

Troopers Kovo, Grishna and Tzunikov sent burning streams of promethium out towards the enemy, scorching scores of them to death and forcing the others back. But the press of bodies was so tight that the greenskins had nowhere to go. In those first few seconds of the battle, the toll taken by the flamers was gratifyingly heavy.

Fifth Company had already lost most of their heavy bolters on the journey. Only a single man armed with such a weapon remained among them. Trooper Kashr strafed the orks with deadly explosive shells, killing scores of them as he ran forward. The weapon's rate of fire was incredible but, all too quickly, his ammunition was spent. He dropped the heavy gun to the ground and pulled his sidearm from its holster, drawing his knife at the same time.

A part of Sebastev's mind processed all of these details, assessing where best to place his own shots, and where the ork line was thinning, if at all. His bolt pistol barked again and again, and thick ork skulls detonated with sprays of blood, brain matter and bone fragments. But it was Sebastev's power sabre, gripped tightly in his right hand, that he knew would do the most damage.

As orks and men crashed together with bone crunching force, Sebastev launched himself into a sweeping series of strokes from the twenty-third form of the *ossbohk-vyar*. The Vostroyan combat art had taught him to target his enemy's extremities first, removing their offensive capabilities at the first opportunity. The orks that came towards him swinging their crude weapons quickly lost their hands. They fought on, attempting to kick out at him, or batter him with the bleeding stumps of their wrists. That was the nature of orks. They seldom fell from anything but a lethal strike to the brain or to certain vital organs, but by stripping them of their weapons, he rendered them far less of an immediate threat. Disarmed in this way, the orks in question could be dispatched far more easily, though they were still frustratingly tough.

As Colonel Kabanov's fighting wedge bit deep into the ork line, the colonel called out for his men to change formation, to form a tight circle with their backs to the centre.

With the orks closing around them, the Vostroyans arranged themselves into a bristling wall of bayonets and power sabres. They fired las-bolt after las-bolt into the faces of the orks that pressed forward, but they were truly surrounded, and in the most desperate fight of their lives.

The manhole cover was frozen shut. It may as well have been welded shut given the incredible hold the ice had on it. Even the powerful figure of Sergeant Grodolkin couldn't push it off, though he slammed his armoured shoulder against it again and again. After a moment, Commissar Karif called the man back down to the bottom of the ladder.

'Is there a flamer in your squad, sergeant?'

'There was, commissar,' said Grodolkin with obvious remorse, 'but he stayed behind to cover our escape.'

'Well, I suppose there are a few other options available to us. The one that immediately springs to mind would be lasguns.'

'Lasguns, commissar?'

'They won't damage the manhole cover itself, but if we fire enough las-bolts at its underside, I think they should provide more than enough heat to melt the ice that's fixing it in place, don't you?'

'Easy enough to find out,' said Grodolkin. He called three of his men forward and ordered them to stand at the bottom of the ladder, firing vertically at the disk of black metal above their heads. After a moment, Karif called for them to stop.

'That ought to do it,' he said as he gripped the first of the rungs and hauled himself up towards the exit. At the top of the ladder, he reached out a gloved hand and checked the temperature of the cover's underside. It was still warm, but no longer scalding hot. He braced his shoulder against it and pushed.

As the cover lifted, the pale light of the winter afternoon washed over him. The cold wind rushed past him and down into the tunnel. With his head above ground again, his left ear immediately filled with a stream of vox-chatter. There were reports of Leman Russ tanks being crippled by ork anti-vehicle squads. Platoons across the city were desperately trying to fall back towards the bridge, but the orks had already cut them off in many places. Some of the vox-traffic consisted of little more than screams that cut off sharply.

Karif pushed one more time and heaved the heavy manhole cover from his back. As he pulled himself out of the hole, he listened hard for any mention of Fifth Company. To his incredible relief, he managed to catch the voice of Colonel Kabanov ordering his men to fight hard for the glory of Vostroya and the Imperium.

They're still alive, he thought. There's still time to help them.

'Quickly,' he called down to Grodolkin's squad. 'Follow me up.'

Something very sharp and cold slid into position by his jugular. Karif suppressed his reflex to turn.

'Who the khek are you?' asked a harsh voice from behind him. The owner of the voice kept the edge of his blade pressed tight to Karif's neck.

'I am Commissar Daridh Ahl Karif of the Emperor's own Commissariat. I'm attached to the Vostroyan Sixty-Eighth Infantry Regiment's Fifth Company. And, while I applaud you for both your vigilance and your suspicious nature, if you don't get that bloody bayonet away from my neck, I'll use it in your execution. Is that understood, trooper?'

The blade withdrew from his neck immediately.

'That's better,' said Karif as he stood and turned. 'Now move back while my men exit the tunnel. And get someone in charge over here now. I'll need to speak to him at once.'

Good men fell screaming behind Kabanov and the sound filled him with rage, adding speed and power to the strokes of his sword. His hellpistol was empty and there was no time to reload. For every ork that went down, another stepped forward swinging wildly with club or blade. Instead, Kabanov focused on his sword craft, letting his power sabre become an extension of his body and his will. The ground at his feet was slick with freezing blood, slippery with greenskin viscera. The footing was bad, but Kabanov had spent his whole life training for fights such as this. As old as he was, he still retained some of the balance and agility that had made him a regimental combat champion so many years ago. The orks weren't quite as graceful. One slipped on the entrails of its fellows and dropped to one knee. Kabanov lunged forward in a flash and plunged the point of his power sabre into the creature's brain.

'Lieutenant Kuritsin,' he shouted. 'Where in the warp is my damned armour support?'

Kuritsin was close enough to hear. 'Sorry, sir. The vox-channels are absolutely choked. I can't get through.'

Colonel Kabanov knew they were choked. He could hear the panicked transmissions of the Thirty-Fifth Regiment's armour platoons in his own ear. His vox-bead insisted on telling him just how grim things were for Vostroyan soldiers all across this doomed half of the city. As he listened, he recognized the voice of Sergeant Svemir.

'This is Svemir to Fifth Company command,' voxed the medic. 'Can you hear me?'

'I hear you, Svemir,' replied Kabanov. 'What's your status? Where is the Pathcutter now?'

'We've been crippled, sir. We're stuck out on the highway. The orks are cutting their way in. I just wanted to say good luck, sir. I'm giving our wounded something to send them on. I'm sure you understand, sir. I couldn't let the orks kill helpless men. For my part, I intend to go down fighting.'

There was little Kabanov could say to that except, 'You're a brave man, sergeant. The Grey Lady waits to take you to the Emperor's side. Have no doubt about that.'

'Thank you, sir,' voxed the medic. 'They've broken through now.'

At the sergeant's end, the vox went dead. Kabanov felt his stomach twist with anger at the foul xenos. He wouldn't allow this to be the end. 'We have to press north,' he shouted. 'We have to cut through them. Maro, I want you to move into the centre of our circle and start throwing grenades ahead of us. We must thin the ork ranks there if we want to push through.'

Lieutenant Maro did so without question. From the centre of the circle, he began lobbing hand grenades into the packed orks. The resulting explosions showered Fifth Company with hot blood and sent broken green bodies tumbling through the air. The momentary gaps these explosions created lessened the pressure on the circle's north side and allowed Fifth Company to push towards their goal a little at a time. But it was far from enough.

There were fresh screams from the southern and eastern sides of the circle. Fifth Company was losing more men all the time. Pain flared in Kabanov's leg as a cleaver whistled past, tearing a red slash above his knee.

'Fight on, Firstborn!' he roared. 'The sons of Vostroya will never fall!'

But he knew, even as he said it, that he was tiring fast. The fire in his lungs was returning. He started wheezing again. Adrenaline and natural endorphins couldn't hold the pain of his illness at bay any longer.

Just a little more, he thought. Emperor help me. Just give me a little more time.

More screaming sounded behind him and the Vostroyan circle grew smaller and smaller.

'You're in charge?' asked Karif, eyeing the tall, slim officer that stood before him, resplendent in Vostroyan finery that remained unsullied by battle.

'Of this particular platoon, commissar, yes I am. Lieutenant Vemko Orodrov, commanding officer of the Vostroyan Firstborn 41st Armoured Regiment's Second Tank Platoon, at your service.'

'Excellent, lieutenant,' replied Karif, 'It's your services that I require. You arrived here yesterday from Seddisvarr with very specific orders from General Vlastan, is that not so?'

'It is. We're to hold the bridge open for as long as possible so that your Fifth Company might cross with an important prisoner. I see you and your men, commissar, but I don't see any prisoner. I'm afraid there is little time left before the ork horde forces us to fall back. We'll have to withdraw in the next few minutes if we're to be clear before the bridge is blown. The orks mustn't set one foot on Theqis under any circumstances. The general was very clear about that. You may cross with us, commissar, but you won't find a warm welcome in Seddisvarr with your mission unfulfilled. The general will be displeased.'

'Displeased with you, lieutenant, if you don't do everything in your power to aid me now, particularly with the prisoner in question so close at hand.'

'He's close by?'

'Very,' said the commissar. 'Colonel Kabanov and the rest of the company are attempting to force their way through the ork lines as we speak, but I'm sure you've seen how many orks they're up against.'

'They're trying to cut a path through on foot?' asked the lieutenant incredulously. 'It's impossible, commissar. They're dead men for sure.'

'They will be, unless you assign me three tanks and their crews to help open a corridor for them.'

The lieutenant shook his head emphatically. 'I– I can't, commissar. The ork armour is rolling right towards us. We need every machine we've got just to withdraw safely. No, you... you're asking the impossible.'

Before the lieutenant could blink, Karif whipped his chainsword from its scabbard and up to the officer's neck, thumbing the power rune in mid-motion. The weapon purred threateningly into the young officer's left ear.

Karif smiled. 'Impossible is not a word they teach at the Schola Excubitos, lieutenant.'

Sebastev couldn't risk a glance behind him, but he heard Lieutenant Maro cry out and knew that something was wrong. A trooper yelled, 'The White Boar is wounded!'

As those words filled the air, there was a roar of anger from the surviving men. The fighting intensified as if every single ork they faced was personally responsible. More orks fell, and yet more pressed forward. The Vostroyans were few, and each moment was met by the screams of another man as he was cleaved apart by laughing alien brutes.

A monstrous black ork pushed its way through the front ranks and roared at Sebastev, spraying thick mucus into the air. It tossed its head and gnashed its massive yellow tusks together, lifting its axe to launch a horizontal stroke that missed by a hair. The blade of the axe lodged deep in the body of another ork on the right. Before the monster had time to pull his weapon free, Sebastev leapt forward, placed his boot on the bent knee of the ork's lead leg, and stepped up to plunge his blade down through the top of the ork's head.

As the giant body collapsed, Sebastev jumped backwards, returning to his position in the circle. 'Lieutenant Tarkarov is down!' shouted someone.

Hestor's balls, thought Sebastev, not Tarkarov!

'Captain Chelnikov is dead!' shouted another.

'Captain Sebastev,' yelled Lieutenant Maro, 'you have to take command. The White Boar is wounded. The prisoner must get through.'

Khek the prisoner, thought Sebastev, but he knew Maro was right.

'Aronov?' yelled Sebastev. 'Aronov, are you alive?'

A laspistol appeared at Sebastev's shoulder and burned the face from the ork right in front of him. 'I am, sir,' growled the big scout in his ear. 'I won't be for much longer if this keeps up. We can't thin the bastards out, sir. Let me drop the traitor and fight unhindered alongside the rest of you.'

It was a fair request. Aronov wanted to die giving his very best. He clearly believed they couldn't prevail. Sebastev could only agree. Perhaps it had been hopeless from the start. There were just too many orks and every single man who'd fallen so far had sold his life dear. He was proud of them, proud to be their captain.

This is how a Guardsman is meant to die, he thought. There's no dishonour in this, not in fighting with all you've got until your very last breath.

'Fair enough, trooper,' said Sebastev. 'Drop the pris–'

The air was ripped by a mighty explosion. Just a hundred metres or so to Sebastev's left a great cloud of dirt and green bodies erupted into the air. It was deafening. Moments later another cloud burst upwards, throwing hunks of ork meat down onto the Vostroyans. It was much closer this time. The ground shook.

'Armour!' shouted Lieutenant Kuritsin. 'Leman Russ tanks on the north side.'

A cheer went up from the remaining Vostroyans as the sound of heavy bolter fire filled the air. The vicious buzz of lascannons followed before the ground shook again at the impact of another shell from the tank's demolisher cannon.

The orks started to turn their heads.

Sebastev was too short to see over them, but from the frequency of the cannon-fire he counted three separate tanks firing on the ork horde.

'I don't have all day,' voxed a familiar voice.

'Commissar,' voxed Sebastev, 'we thought...'

'I don't care what you thought, captain. We've got the orks blindsided and we're thinning their ranks for you, but if you and your men don't get a bloody move on, it'll be for nothing. The orks have got armour moving in from the east at speed. You've got minutes until the north bridge is sent to the riverbed.'

More explosions rocked the street. 'Maro,' shouted Sebastev, 'get the colonel up and get ready to move. Aronov, don't you dare drop that prisoner. We're getting out of here, now.'

Sebastev stopped shouting long enough to sever the hands of an ork wielding two iron clubs. Then he drove the point of his blade through the beast's throat. A flick of his wrist sent the ork's head rolling to the surface of the street.

'Fifth Company,' he yelled. 'Move, now. For the White Boar and the Sixty-Eighth, go!'

The circle broke and the men surged forward behind Sebastev. He heard Kuritsin urging them on. Father Olov charged ahead, cleaving a broad path through the orks now that there was more room to swing his huge eviscerator.

'Get behind me,' bellowed the old priest. 'I will cut a way through.'

The eviscerator chainsword growled as it chewed through thick ork bodies. Dozens fell in front of the redoubtable priest. Troopers rushed in behind him to protect his back.

Sebastev hacked and slashed as he moved, aware of Aronov beside him, the prisoner still slung over his shoulder. Maro, too, was close by. He carried the White Boar while troopers surrounded him, stabbing out at the greenskins with their bayonets.

Sebastev realised that Maro was struggling to carry both the colonel and the traitor's case. With his free hand, he wrestled the case from the adjutant. 'I'll take care of this thing. You just focus on getting the colonel to safety, Maro.'

The lieutenant nodded.

The ground exploded so close to Sebastev that he was almost knocked from his feet. 'Watch your fire, commissar,' he voxed angrily. 'You'll kill us before the orks do.'

As he uttered these words, more troopers fell howling at the rear of the charge, their bodies smashed apart by savage blows from the greenskins that harried them.

Sebastev kept his sword moving as he pushed through. Everything was a high-speed blur of ugly alien faces and gleaming weapons. More explosions sounded close by and shook the rockcrete underfoot. He could feel the heat from lascannon beams where they strafed the ork line. Heavy bolters chugged as they cut down scores of unprotected greenskins with enfilading fire.

Then, with an explosion that was too close for comfort and a yell of triumph from Father Olov, Fifth Company broke into the open. They'd made it through to the other side of the ork line. Sebastev could see the Leman Russ tanks just ahead. Commissar Karif could be seen at the hatch of the leading tank, manning a pintle-mounted heavy bolter and yelling orders to the crews inside.

'Run to the tanks,' yelled Sebastev. 'Give it all you've got!'

His men raced forward as the Leman Russ continued to pour fire on the orks, dissuading them from pursuit. Orks weren't easily dissuaded, however. They charged forward, unmindful of the horrendous casualties they were taking.

Despite the weight of the prisoner, Sebastev saw Aronov racing ahead. The moment he reached the first Leman Russ, he threw the man up onto the back of the tank, turned, and began firing at the orks with his laspistol. 'Someone, give me a proper bloody weapon,' he shouted.

Other men reached the tanks: Sergeants Basch and Rahkman, Lieutenant Vassilo, Troopers Kovo, Kashr, Akmir: more, but still too few. The moment Sebastev reached the commissar's tank, he threw the traitor's case up beside the man, reloaded his bolt pistol, and turned to stand with Aronov, firing shot after shot back towards the orks, concentrating on those that threatened Lieutenant Maro as he carried Colonel Kabanov forward.

'Don't be fools,' shouted Commissar Karif. 'Get up onto the tanks and hold on. We've got to make the bridge before they blow the damned thing.'

Sebastev stopped firing long enough to help Maro and Kuritsin lift Colonel Kabanov up onto the vehicle. When the colonel was safely onboard, everyone else scrambled up onto the back.

'Go, commissar,' called Sebastev over the drumming of the heavy bolters. 'We're all on board.'

Each of the huge tanks was covered in Fifth Company survivors, clinging on for their lives as the tank drivers kicked their machines into high gear. Colonel Kabanov lay between Maro and Sebastev on the back of Commissar Karif's machine. As the tank moved off, he gripped Sebastev's sleeve and said, 'Grenades, captain.'

Blood was leaking from his mouth and nose. His skin had turned a ghostly white.

'Good idea, sir,' said Sebastev. He pulled two grenades from his bandolier.

The colonel struggled to sit up. 'No, Sebastev. Give them to me, both of them.'

Sebastev was confused, but he did as he was ordered.

Colonel Kabanov faced Lieutenant Maro. 'You'll explain it to him?' he asked.

Maro nodded sincerely, and Sebastev saw tears in the man's eyes.

'Good,' said Colonel Kabanov. 'Then it's time the White Boar looked after himself for a change.'

With that, he slid off the back of the Leman Russ.

Sebastev immediately reached out to grab for him, but Maro restrained him. 'You know it already, captain. This is what he wants. Would you have him wither and die in some hospital bed? I don't think so.'

Sebastev wanted to deny it. He wanted to order the Leman Russ to a stop and go back for the man who'd been his hero since the day he'd joined the Sixty-Eighth Regiment, but he knew Maro was right. Legends like the White Boar were meant to die in battle. When his own time came, he wished no less for himself.

As he watched Colonel Kabanov walk back to meet the orks, Sebastev saluted.

'To me, you filthy devils!' shouted the old man as he staggered towards the foe. He pulled the pins on his grenades. 'One last gift from the Emperor of Mankind!'

Sebastev forced himself to watch. He owed the colonel that much and more. He couldn't be sure of the exact number, but it looked like the White Boar took a good many of the green khekkers with him as he died.

The tanks rumbled around a corner and the scene shifted from view.

'Almost there,' said Commissar Karif from behind Sebastev. 'The bridge is just up ahead.'

Captain Grigorius Sebastev and the scant remains of his Fifth Company crossed Grazzen's north bridge at 16.02 hours on the

688th day of the Danikkin Campaign. The north bridge was destroyed precisely two minutes later, sending a significant number of pursuing Venomhead orks and their vehicles to the bottom of the Solenne.

Patriot-Captain Brammon Gusseff, known to personnel with the appropriate clearance as *Asset 6*, was delivered to Twelfth Army Command HQ in Seddisvarr in the early hours of the following day.

Captain Grigorius Sebastev was placed under arrest at that time.

A TRIAL ENDS

Thirteen days.

For thirteen days, Sebastev had listened with furrowed brow and gritted teeth as men who'd never set foot on the Eastern Front berated him, belittled the valorous efforts of his men, and placed the responsibility for each and every death firmly at his booted feet.

The trial reached its conclusion. There was General Vogor Vlastan, Old Hungry himself, strapped into his life preserving mechanical chair behind the judges' bench. He would pass sentence personally. Sebastev figured the general must have been anticipating this moment for quite some time. The spectators were anticipating it, too. The grand hall had gone deathly quiet.

The council of judges ended their whispered conversation and turned back to face Sebastev in the dock. Servo-skulls, yellowed with age and bristling with sensors and recording devices, descended from above, drifting through the air on suspensor engines that hummed softly. They registered every word spoken in the hall, by officials and spectators alike. The records would be carefully checked later to help identify dissenting voices and potential troublemakers.

'Stand,' ordered a wizened old major on General Vlastan's immediate left. 'Stand, Captain Sebastev. The general wishes to pronounce.'

Sebastev got heavily to his feet, mentally fatigued by so many days of endless talk, of recounting over and over again the events that had transpired since leaving Korris. He saw, there on the far right, in the shadows below the hanging balcony, the figure of Commissar Karif, dressed, as always, in black. He'd attended the court martial every single day since the beginning, and had given evidence of his own on eight of those days, though Sebastev had been ordered out of the court on those occasions, and knew not what the commissar had reported.

Just as it had on every previous day, the hanging balcony that jutted out over the seats of the spectators contained the same two bizarre, inscrutable occupants.

Sebastev's blood chilled inexplicably every time he looked in their direction. He could feel the eyes of the hunched old woman on him, burning into him as if she sought to scorch away his flesh and view the naked soul beneath. The incredible alabaster giant, whose blood-red eyes missed nothing, sat next to her.

And no one can tell me who the khek they are, he thought.

The general coughed and began burbling through a vox-amp attached to his chair. 'We've heard, honoured attendants, from a broad range of witnesses, analysts and assessors over the course of this trial.' The general's small, black eyes panned across the assembly. 'We've heard how the accused conducted himself throughout the period in question, the ways in which he influenced Vostroyan men of both higher and lower rank. And we've heard in great detail how the events that transpired after the loss of the Twelfth Army's dominion over Korris have affected the status of this war.'

Sebastev's stomach rumbled quietly, reminding him that he hadn't eaten since daybreak. His appetite was starting to come back, but his complaining stomach would have to wait.

'This honourable council,' continued the general, 'has listened carefully to all that has been put before it. We have consulted with learned bodies and scoured the histories of our proud military past for precedents.'

Sebastev caught Old Hungry casting his glance to the two strange figures on the balcony, just as he had done throughout the trial. It was further confirmation of something Sebastev suspected: General Vlastan was terrified of the strange pair.

Just who are they, he wondered, and why are they here for this?

The general continued, but Sebastev was sure he detected a loss of confidence in the man's amplified voice. 'We have reached our conclusions and shall now make our pronouncement. In the name of the Emperor of Mankind, and the honoured tradition of the Vostroyan Firstborn who serve in his name, I now address Captain Grigorius Sebastev of the Sixty-Eighth Infantry Regiment's Fifth Company.'

As was the form, Sebastev saluted the Twelfth Army leader.

'Captain Sebastev,' said the general. 'It has long been held by many worthy officers in the Twelfth Army that your field commission to the rank of captain was a grievous and reproachable error on the part of Major Alexos Dubrin. Indeed, some of your senior officers consider your appointment to the rank of captain little more than a favour from one friend to another. Naturally there is no room for such things in the ranks of the Firstborn, but the late Major Dubrin is beyond our judgement now. You, however, are not.'

Sebastev scowled and gripped the wooden railing of the dock. His knuckles whitened. He'd known all along that the man would make the most of this final, grand opportunity to offend and aggravate him.

'Of course, the matter of your promotion is not on trial. We must turn, instead, to matters of acceptable conduct and proper performance. A man in command has responsibilities to many, both above him in rank and below, but especially to those above. That, I'm afraid, captain, is the root of your worst transgressions.

'Throughout your career, you have consistently been shown to suffer from the regrettable delusion that it is your job to safeguard the lives of each and every one of the men under your command. Let me address that delusion by telling you directly, captain, that it is not so, nor has it ever been. The responsibility of any officer is both clear and singular: it is the execution of those orders given to you by your superior officers no matter the cost in blood, pain, lives or anything else you wouldn't care to spend or endure.

'This regular prioritising of your men's lives above all else constitutes a definitive failure on your part to live up to the duties, honours and expectations placed on you by men of vastly superior lineage, intellect and judgement.'

A sharp sound echoed through the great hall. Sebastev flicked his eyes to the source. The alabaster giant sat glaring at General Vlastan, but it was the old woman next to him who'd interrupted the general's speech. She had struck the floor of the balcony with the metal-shod heel of her walking stick.

A long moment of silence stretched out, during which Sebastev watched the general wither under the old woman's gaze before finally turning back to face Sebastev. The general's usual arrogance and confidence had bled right out of him.

'As I was saying,' he said, shifting uncomfortably, 'it is the opinion of some members of this military council that you, Captain Grigorius Sebastev, have consistently placed the lives of individual Guardsmen above the best interests of the Twelfth Army.'

The general was interrupted again by the sharp rapping of metal on wood. Sebastev followed General Vlastan's eyes as they again darted over to the tiny old woman.

'By the Throne,' snapped Vlastan, immediately regretting it. With obvious effort, he reverted to a more placatory tone. 'Please, honoured madam, I have not forgotten your decree. If you'll just allow me to finish what I was saying without further... interruptions.'

In response, the old woman folded her tiny, childlike hands and nodded from beneath the hood of her cloak. Sebastev couldn't shake the impression that she was laughing, though no sound or motion gave evidence of this.

'Some members of this council believe that, for the role you played in the death of Colonel Maksim Kabanov, a greatly respected man among the ranks of the Firstborn, you should be precluded from any commission for the rest of your life. Others felt that the mere stripping of your rank was overly lenient. Extended incarceration and expulsion from the ranks of the Firstborn were considered as alternative punishments.'

This time, Sebastev had the impression that General Vlastan was deliberately trying to avoid glancing at the figures on the balcony.

'However,' continued the general, 'the reality of our war against secession and treachery on Danik's World has changed dramatically in the short time since Barahn and Ohslir fell. The Twelfth Army finds itself facing unprecedented pressure on two fronts, and this war has attracted the attention of certain Imperial bodies that wield a level of authority even greater than that of Twelfth Army Command. As such, this court is forced to acknowledge your part in the successful delivery of a valuable prisoner, the recovery of a device crucial to the continuation of the war effort, and the survival of a regiment whose long and unbroken history is filled with honour.'

General Vlastan's brows knitted together in frustration as he continued. 'There is also the matter of Commissar Karif's testimony to consider. The statements made by the commissar go a long way to suggesting that your purported bravery, piety and prowess in combat were responsible for the deaths of a great many orks and rebels. With these things in mind, and at the insistence of certain high ranking individuals outside the Vostroyan military structure, this court decrees that you will retain the rank of captain.

'Henceforth you are charged with conducting yourself in a manner more fitting to your responsibilities. And to those responsibilities, this court now adds the command of all remnants of the Sixty-Eighth Infantry Regiment, until such time as an officer of adequate rank and potential can be found to replace you. Once this replacement has been selected, you will immediately revert to your former position as Fifth Company commander.'

Voices filled the air of the court as the spectators reacted to the council's pronouncement. People began chattering, eager to share their opinions with those seated next to them. Sebastev looked for Commissar Karif, stunned that the man had spoken out on his behalf, but the commissar had already left his seat. He was nowhere to be seen.

Sebastev looked up at the balcony, but the strange duo had likewise vanished in the last few seconds.

General Vlastan cleared his throat and raised his voice over the hubbub. 'Captain Sebastev, pay attention.'

Sebastev met the general's glare.

'Your men are billeted in the city's south-east quarter, district eleven. My staff will provide a map and arrange transportation for you. Twenty-eight men are listed as the last survivors of the Sixty-Eighth Infantry Regiment, captain. It's not many, but I'm afraid there won't be time to reinforce you before your next deployment.'

For the first time in over an hour, Sebastev parted his lips to speak. 'Deployment?'

The panel of officers who'd acted as Sebastev's judges rose at a gesture from the general and left the bench. General Vlastan's chair gave a loud, mechanical hiss as its piston legs unfolded. The walking chair shook as it rose to its full height, causing General Vlastan's abundant flesh to wobble.

The general's lips stretched into a lop-sided grin. 'I've always thought you disconcertingly short for an officer, Sebastev. A leader should be tall so that men are forced to look up to him, you know.'

Sebastev didn't bother to respond to that. Instead, he met Vlastan's gaze and held it.

The general's grin dropped. 'Yes, redeployed. The Sixty-Eighth

Regiment, such as it is, has been temporarily placed in the service of a higher authority. You'll find out the rest for yourself soon enough. You're no longer of any concern to me, at least for the moment.'

The general grasped the controls of his chair, turned it, and skittered out of the hall, leaving Sebastev speechless. A staff officer led him down from the dock and out through a side door as the rest of the court emptied.

Seconded to a higher authority, he thought? What in the twisted hells of the warp is going on?

Sebastev had a partial answer soon enough.

Commissar Karif awaited him outside the court, accompanied, as always, by his adjutant. As Sebastev walked towards them, he couldn't fail to notice the wide smile on the young trooper's face.

'It's wonderful to see you, sir,' said Stavin with a salute. 'I'm so glad everything... Congratulations on the verdict.'

Sebastev saluted back and said, 'Thank you, trooper. At ease.' He met Karif's gaze. 'As for you, commissar, I don't know what kind of grox-balls you told them in there...'

Karif stiffened.

Sebastev fought back a grin, and added, 'But thank you. Your presence in that hall over the last thirteen days is appreciated, I assure you.' He reached out and gripped Karif's hand, shaking it firmly.

'I'm sure I'll think of some way you can pay me back, captain,' said Karif with a smile and a nod. 'Let's walk together. There are many things we have to talk about.' Trooper Stavin fell into step a few paces behind them as they began their stroll.

'You're not wrong, commissar,' said Sebastev. 'I can't work it all out. We've been seconded? To whom?'

From behind a thick marble pillar on the left, a voice rumbled. 'Seconded to us, captain, and I promise you, you'll soon wish it weren't so.'

Sebastev gasped as the alabaster giant from the balcony stepped across their path. The huge man wore a simple black tunic, cinched at the waist with golden rope. The contrast between his robe and his deathly white skin was striking. His blood-red eyes, so strange and unnatural, fixed on Sebastev's own, measuring him, freezing him where he stood.

Karif and Stavin halted at Sebastev's side, but their reaction was muted. They hardly seemed surprised at all. Karif looked at Sebastev and shook his head. 'My first reaction was exactly the same, you know, captain.' He raised a hand, palm up, and gestured towards the giant man. 'May I present Brother-Sergeant Ischus Corvinnus, of the Death Spectres Space Marines.'

'By the Throne!' muttered Sebastev.

The brother-sergeant lifted his massive hands to his chest in the sign of the aquila, offered a shallow bow, and boomed, 'Good beginnings, Captain Sebastev. There will be time to become acquainted later perhaps. Your new commander is waiting to brief you on urgent matters even as we speak. Let us not dally here.'

Sebastev was still speechless. An Astartes, he thought. Here!

'Come on, captain,' said Commissar Karif, 'we should get moving.'

Sebastev felt Karif nudge him, and wrestled with his sense of awe.

'Follow me,' said the Space Marine as he turned and led the way. 'Milady's patience is famous only for its tiny measure.'

As Sebastev, Karif and Stavin struggled to keep up with the giant Astartes warrior, Sebastev felt his mind racing, trying to understand just how much the war had changed. The Death Spectres Space Marines were here, and something had forced General Vlastan to release Sebastev into the service of another authority: this 'lady', of whom the Space Marine spoke with obvious respect.

Surely it's the old crone from the balcony, thought Sebastev. If the Astartes are here...

'Well?' asked Karif. 'Aren't you going to answer?'

Sebastev shook himself. 'Sorry, commissar. I didn't catch the question.'

'I asked you how you felt about returning to active duty so soon. That farce of a trial... I'm sure you're eager to get back to what you're good at.'

Sebastev thought of the men he'd lost, the friends he'd watched die. He levelled his gaze at the commissar. 'If you're thinking I want revenge for the men we lost, commissar, you're damned right.'

The Space Marine turned his head just a fraction as he listened to Sebastev's words.

Commissar Karif smiled and nodded sagely. 'That's the spirit, captain. I would expect no less from a fighter like you. After all, what would men like us do without a good old-fashioned war?'

A TRANSCRIPT

Source: Partial Audio Feed from Pict-Recording 22a/1F31

Originator: Inquisitor Zharadelle Inphius Faulks (OM/613-7980.1 SC.3)

Date of Recording (Imperial): 5.232.767.M41

Location: Twelfth Army Command HQ, Seddisvarr, Danik's World, Gamma Kholdas, Kholdas Cluster, Segmentum Ultima

Faulks: 'Try again. What is your name?'

Asset 6: 'I told you, damn it all. What do you want me to say? I'm Patriot-Captain Brammon Gusseff of the Special Patriotic Service, attached to the–'

<screams>

Faulks: 'Brammon Gusseff is a construct, nothing more. He's a role you've played perfectly for the last four years, but it's over now. Stop resisting. You're just making this more difficult. Oh, to the warp with this. I want the witch brought in. The drugs aren't enough.

Asset 6: Witch? Please, I- I don't understand. What do you want? I've given you the codes for the case. You have the jamming device. I was promised immunity.'

<door opens, closes>

Jardine: 'You summoned me, milady?'

Faulks: 'Get to work on him. The last program is rooted too deep. If you can't draw him out, he'll have to be retired. This one is a highly prized and decorated asset, so do your best. Understood?'

771

Jardine: 'Yes, milady.'

<door opens, closes>

Asset 6: 'Who in the warp are you? Please, get me out of here. The old crone is insane. I- I don't know what she's talking about.'

<chants>

<screams>

[2 hours 11 minutes of audio censored under security directive 15.331C.]

Faulks: 'Take a drink. You're shaking quite badly.'

Asset 6: 'So would you be, warp damn it. The things I do for the Imperium...'

Faulks: 'Quite. And we're very grateful, lieutenant. It's good to have you back. For a while there it looked like that last graft was going to be permanent.'

Asset 6: 'At which point, you'd have killed me, inquisitor.'

Faulks: 'But I wouldn't have relished the task. Now please, for the records this time, name and rank.'

Asset 6: 'My name is Lieutenant Pyter Gamalov, Vostroyan First-born, Office of Special Operations, Twelfth Army Division.'

Faulks: 'Excellent, lieutenant. Now I need to know just how much of Gusseff's memories you have access to. How close were you able to get to Vanandrasse? What's wrong, lieutenant? You're shaking. Why the tears?'

Asset 6: 'You're going to make me remember everything, aren't you? Every act he perpetrated while I was with him.'

Faulks: 'As always, lieutenant. It's how you serve the Emperor.'

Asset 6: 'But this one, milady. Oh, Throne above, no. This Gusseff... I... he did such terrible things!'

THE CITADEL

Steve Parker

General Vlastan's chair beeped in alarm, unfurled a tiny articulated servo, plunged a needle into his neck and, with a sharp hiss, injected another grey-brown dose of nutrimilk.

Vlastan girded himself against the dizzying rush of the powerful medication. His pulse raced. Sweat beaded on his brow. His hands shook, and blood-flecked spittle gathered at the corners of his mouth. Soon enough, though, his body had stabilised again. He was well used to the effects of the cocktail after so many years.

The frequency of the injections, however, had been increasing. He knew his condition was worsening, and the thought exacerbated his current mood.

He sat alone in his office, gazing sullenly at the formless white void outside his window. The snow-choked streets of Seddisvarr, site of Twelfth Army's Command HQ, were shrouded in freezing white mist. His room, on the other hand, was warm, ably heated by twin thermacoils. No wind rattled the thick glass. The only sounds now were the wet wheezing of his lungs and the whirring gyro-stabilisers of his multi-legged, mechanical chair. Both sounds had long ago ceased to intrude on his thoughts.

Despite the insulated silence of the room, he knew the streets below would be busy with troops. Seddisvarr had been abuzz since the recent fall of Grazzen. If he really strained his hearing, he might make out the faint rumble of Vostroyan tanks and armoured transports rolling along the city's broader avenues.

With his precious Danik's World campaign largely going to hell since the orks had overrun Barahn, there was a particular comfort in the presence of so much heavy armour nearby. The Vostroyan tanks were powerful, reliable and enduring.

It was, he realised, exactly how he would have described Maksim, and the realisation gave his solitude an unwelcome and bitter edge.

'Damn it all,' he swore softly to the empty room, 'isn't it time yet?'

Soon, there would be a knock at the door and his adjutant would enter to help him dress his ruined body for the afternoon service.

He wished the whole matter were over already. His grief confused and disgusted him. He'd long thought himself beyond such things. Indulging one's emotions was the province of far lesser men.

Still, he told himself, I should have expected to feel something. Today, after all, I commemorate the death of the last man I ever called friend.

51 years earlier,
Mount Megidde (South-east Face, 504m),
The Sambar Basin, Valis II

'Get some suppressing fire on that stubber-nest,' growled Sergeant Sergiev. 'Mirkov, Brebnik, flank left and grenade those bastards, or we'll be stuck here all day!'

In the sky above the mountain, seeming almost close enough to touch, thick black clouds roiled and boomed. Torrents of water raced down every crack and crevice as if fleeing in terror from the dark, hulking shape of the enemy fortress at the top. Sergiev thanked the Omnissiah, tech-aspect of the God-Emperor of Man, for the warmth and protection of his hat and greatcoat.

Both utilised special fibres developed to counter the lethal chill of his home world.

Corporal Brebnik leaned from the cover of a broad rock and threw a smoke grenade. When the billowing cloud was large enough to conceal them, he and Mirkov moved out, working their way left while the enemy fired blind.

Sergiev growled and hunkered down a little further as the raking fire of the heavy-stubber chewed rock chips from the boulder that shielded him.

'By the Emperor's holy balls!' he hissed.

Despite repeated requests over the vox-net, Regimental HQ would not allow him to lead the shattered assault force back down to level ground. 'Push on,' they had commanded. 'The citadel must fall at any cost!'

But what could they possibly hope to achieve now? The taking of Mount Megidde had effectively ground to a halt. The mountain's south-eastern ascent was littered with the cooling bodies of Vostroyan dead, and Sergiev, a mere sergeant, had found himself the ranking man by default.

He had lost his commanding officer, Lieutenant Lymarov, three hours earlier to a mutant flamer-team. Pairs of these sadistic freaks descended from the citadel to scour the slopes and ridges for luckless victims.

A nightmare image returned to him of the lieutenant screaming and flailing as bright flames devoured him. Desperate to escape his agony, Lymarov had thrown himself from the closest precipice, plummeting like a meteor to the sharp rocks below.

At the time, Sergiev had felt a guilty, nauseating relief. He'd been about to shoot the lieutenant himself, as much to end the man's terrible screams as to put him out of his misery. Lymarov's leap had relieved him of that burden.

The lieutenant had been a good man. It was no way for him to die, and the memory twisted Sergiev's stomach and filled him with righteous anger. Perhaps falling back *would* be a mistake. Any ground lost now would cost more lives later. And there was vengeance yet to be had. The bastard muties had to be punished, not just for the lieutenant's death, but for all of it: all their corruption and treachery, the wanton torture and human sacrifice they practiced, the atrocities he'd seen in the cities to the south, everything that had forced Sector Command to deploy Imperial troops here en masse.

After overthrowing the planetary government, the Valisian mutants had launched a pogrom against their pureblooded kin. Millions were slaughtered in the name of the Ruinous Powers. They had cast their lot in with the vile enemies of the Golden Throne, and marked themselves for destruction – a filthy stain on the glorious Imperium of Man.

Duty and honour, Sergiev! he told himself. *We'll move up, secure more ground, fix more ropes, and lay a path for those that follow. If we die, we die. The next assault will get that much closer to the summit. Sooner or later, whether it takes a thousand of us or a hundred thousand, we'll smash that damned citadel and burn those twisted freaks out.*

'Check your ammo counters, lads,' he voxed to the men behind him. They were all that remained on the south-eastern slope – nineteen men cobbled together from the remains of four whole platoons. He wondered how many still fought on the mountain's west face. Regimental HQ had stonewalled him when he'd asked for an update. 'Get ready to move forward as soon as that stubber-nest is down. Cover-to-cover. Confirm your targets. We'll make the best of this mess, by Terra!'

'What about the wounded, sir?' voxed one of the troopers. Sergiev realised he had been tuning out the groans of pain all around him.

'They rest,' he replied. 'RHQ will send medics up once we've secured the next ridge.'

It was a poor lie, but a necessary one. Most of the wounded were beyond help. They'd bled out past the point of saving. It just didn't help anyone to say so.

He slammed a fresh powercell into his lasgun, primed it,

watched the counter illuminate and, with a prayer on his lips for the Grey Lady's favour, readied himself to lead his patchwork squad further up the mountain.

They'd have to move fast, despite the steep gradient, the endless downpour, the hunger and exhaustion. There were snipers and stubber-nests dotted all the way up the slopes, dominating the cliff-tops and ridges, firing down from the overhangs. There was little choice but to face them. The muties had laid dense minefields on the easier alternative ascents.

There was a bright flash up ahead followed by a muffled boom. 'Stubber's out!' someone voxed. It sounded like Mirkov.

'Good work, trooper!' Sergiev answered. 'We move up till we hit the next one.' He stepped out from behind his rock, raised his lasgun over his head and shouted, 'Follow me, lads. We'll teach the khekking freaks a thing or two!'

'Belay that!' barked a crisp voice from the rear. 'Stay exactly where you are. You will not break cover until I order it. Not until my order.'

Sergiev, his body responding by reflex to the tone of command, stepped back into cover before he knew what he was doing. Confusion, however, quickly gave way to a great wash of relief. There was no mistaking the sharp consonants in the voice of a Vostroyan aristocrat.

An officer? That meant... reinforcements!

He saw them now, a full platoon, clambering up the narrow trail to the rear behind a broad-shouldered young man in officer's dress. Forty men! Forty of them in their tall hats, long red greatcoats and bulky carapace armour.

But Sergiev's joy was short lived. As the officer made a beeline towards him, the sergeant's heart sank.

They've sent a boy, he thought. A bloody *shiny*. He must be seventeen if he's a day!

Sergiev was thirty-two.

The officer drew nearer, marching now in smart, measured

steps. Despite the boy's solid-looking physique, his features were soft, unscarred and unweathered, and his upper lip was hardly dressed at all, save with the very scantest sign of manhood.

Still, moustached or otherwise, the boy wore lieutenant's stripes, and Sergiev knew his place. On Vostroya – a world of dangerously proud men – the high-born were the proudest of all, and it was a foolish trooper who dared openly disrespect them. So, when the boy halted two yards in front of him, Sergiev stood ramrod straight, puffed out his chest and whipped his hand to his brow in salute. He received a short, sharp salute in return.

'Name and rank, soldier,' said the boy.

'Kitko Sergiev, sir. Sergeant, 112th Magdan Lasgunners, Eighth Company, Second Platoon.'

The boy nodded. 'Good to know you, sergeant. Are you in charge here?'

Was that a test? Sergiev wondered. 'Not anymore, sir.'

The boy smiled then dropped unceremoniously into a crouch behind the cover of Sergiev's rock. Looking up with a cocked eyebrow, he gestured for Sergiev to do likewise, and the sergeant dropped down beside him.

'My name,' said the boy, 'is Second Lieutenant Maksim Kabanov, commanding the 116th Sohlsvodd Infantry, Tenth Company, Sixth Platoon.' He glanced in the direction of his men as he spoke. They had taken up positions of cover alongside Sergiev's lot and were dispensing hot ohx' from their flasks. Their medic was already about the business of treating Sergiev's wounded.

'My honour and pleasure, sir,' said Sergiev.

Lieutenant Kabanov turned his eyes back to the sergeant. 'To answer your unspoken question, I'll be eighteen by next Emperor's Day. Yes, my men and I are as green as grass, and every last one of us is a good decade younger than you, I imagine, sergeant. But we've come to do the Emperor's work nevertheless. My troopers are well trained and will quickly prove themselves.'

'They're Firstborn, sir,' replied Sergiev. It was the only proper answer he could give.

Kabanov grinned. 'Yes, they are. Just like you. So, if you'll fight alongside us, if you'll take my orders and give me the benefit of your experience, I'm sure we can make General Krupkov a happy man.'

Sergiev stared hard into the lieutenant's fierce blue eyes. Young nobles fresh from the military academies were notoriously eager for swift advancement, and usually paid for the privilege with other men's lives. Why should this boy, this Kabanov, be any different? Was it Vostroyan zeal that lit his face, or a raging thirst for personal glory? The two were difficult to tell apart.

'You harbour doubts, sergeant,' said Lieutenant Kabanov, 'and so you should. I'll prove myself through action, in any case. But I'm not here to win you over. I'm here to cripple that citadel's aerial defences. If you think you might be up for that, let's push on!'

Despite reservations, Sergiev found himself grinning. The young man's audacity was certainly infectious. If he lived long enough to back it up...

Kabanov stood and raised his voice. 'Listen up, Firstborn. The freaks think they've got Third Army beat. Right now, they're pissing on a picture of the Emperor and calling Vostroyan mothers pigs. I'm not having it. What about you?'

'Sir! No, sir!' the men yelled back at him, angered by the images his words evoked.

'Good. That's what I thought you'd say. So let's get our backsides up this bloody mountain and kill some mutants!'

While the troops roared approval, Sergiev leaned across and said, 'The wounded, sir?'

Kabanov half-turned towards him. 'My medic will do what he can, then follow us up. I'll have my vox-man call in an evacuation request. It's the best I can do for them right now.'

Sergiev nodded and dared to hope that this unbloodied pup might not get them all killed.

* * *

Third Army Headquarters, Cadenna,
Sambar Basin, Valis II

Vlastan and Kabanov sat stiff and unspeaking in the austere outer room while a torrent of screamed abuse emanated from inside the captain's office. The captain's adjutant, sitting silently at his desk, feigned preoccupation with loose papers, but it was clear to Kabanov that he was listening intently. His expression was miserable.

Someone isn't popular, thought Kabanov, but is it the captain or his visitor? It doesn't bode well for Vogor and I in either case.

Abruptly, the shouting stopped and the heavy wooden doors to the captain's room crashed open, ejecting a tall, thin man in a long red greatcoat.

Ignoring the adjutant, he stormed towards the exit, boots clacking sharply on the marble floor.

Vlastan, seated on Kabanov's left, whispered urgently, 'By Terra, Maksim! That's General Krupkov.'

The general's hearing must have been exceptional because, at the barest whisper of his name, he halted and spun to face the two young lieutenants. His hard, angular face was still flushed from shouting.

As one, Vlastan and Kabanov bolted to their feet and threw up razor-sharp salutes.

Kabanov felt his gut lurch. He was sure that, with two new targets in his sights, the furious general would resume his tirade, for no other reason, perhaps, than he was madly angry and not at all ready to calm down.

But, as General Krupkov eyed them, taking in their crisp, clean uniforms and the look of fearful admiration in their eyes, his rage seemed to dissipate. When he spoke, his voice was level. 'You're new,' he said. 'I suppose you came in with the last lot.'

Kabanov, as was his habit, let Vlastan answer for both of them. His charismatic friend was older by almost a year, taller by a good fifteen centimetres, and typically eager to do the talking for both – something that Kabanov had been thankful for many times during their friendship.

'We landed two days ago, sir,' said Vlastan, 'and arrived at the front just this morning. Second Lieutenants Vogor Vlastan and Maksim Kabanov, at your service. And the Emperor's, of course, sir.'

The general pursed his lips, lifted a hand to stroke his splendid grey moustache and said, 'Vlastan and Kabanov. So, those worthy names are among us once again.' With a sidelong glance towards Captain Tyrkin's office, he added, 'New blood is just what's needed around here. The north-eastern front is the most critical theatre of operations in this war today. Absolutely critical, mark you! There's plenty of opportunity here for fine young officers to earn a reputation.'

'Yes, sir!' said the young lieutenants in unison.

Eschewing further comment, General Krupkov, high commander of the Vostroyan Third Army and the much-lauded Hero of Hell's Ridge, spun on his boot-heel and marched off, leaving Vlastan and Kabanov standing stiffly to attention in a room suddenly silent.

Silent, that is, until a weary and impatient voice shouted, 'Georgiev! Where in blazes are those two wet-arses I'm supposed to brief?'

Roughly ten minutes later, Vlastan and Kabanov stood together with Captain Tyrkin and his adjutant, Georgiev, on soft, muddy ground, facing north-east in the pouring rain. The air was thick with dampness and the smell of wet earth. The line of the horizon lit intermittently with the flicker of distant explosions.

Tyrkin, shielded from the rain by his adjutant's umbrella, pointed to a vast, shadowy shape and said, 'There she is, gentlemen. Mount Megidde, all nine hundred and seventy-three metres of her. And on her summit sits the notorious enemy stronghold – Megiddzar.'

Vlastan and Kabanov squinted against the rain. The mountain sat black and forbidding against a low, thundery sky but, as Kabanov looked, he realised that the storm accounted for only a small percentage of the flashing and booming near the mountain's peak. 'Heavy artillery, sir?' he asked.

The captain nodded. 'From that altitude, their long guns can punish our forces on the valley floor with absolute impunity. Until three days ago, when the Emperor Himself blessed us with these rains, nothing we put across the River Aimes was safe. Even now, we can get infantry across in trickles, but any attempt to move armour onto the far bank brings down a punishing barrage. Our own artillery can't even get close.'

'Air support, sir?' asked Vlastan. 'A bombing run, or paratroopers?'

Under the umbrella, Tyrkin turned to face the tall, darkly handsome youth. 'Neither is feasible, lieutenant, until we do something about their damned anti-air batteries. Anything we fly in gets torn apart at range. Say what you will about these warp-blasted mutants, but they've got the Sambar Basin held vice-tight. If we don't break through the Murgoth Line within the next five days, the offensive at Therabourg will have to be cancelled. Who knows how much longer the war will last if that happens?' His face creased in a deep scowl. 'General Krupkov needs someone inside that citadel to knock out their damned anti-air batteries, and he needs it done yesterday.'

Vlastan's mind, Kabanov knew, would already be weighing the honours he might win. He made no secret of his vast ambition. Military greatness, he'd often boasted, ran in his bloodline. Vostroyan military records seemed to bear that out.

Kabanov's father, on the other hand, had never advanced beyond the rank of major, but was somewhat famous in his own right. His mastery of the *ossbohk-vyar* – the brutal Vostroyan close-quarters combat art – had earned him regimental honours year after year, and Kabanov was keen to follow in his footsteps, though he was far less inclined to talk about it.

Glory or not, he didn't like the look of Mount Megidde. Its slopes seemed filled with threat, steep and jagged like the serrations on a cruel blade. It stood alone, tall and grim, utterly dominating the broad, open farmland that surrounded it. The troopers, he'd heard, had nicknamed it Black Tooth because it chewed up every man who tried to ascend it.

This whole region had been one of the most productive agrizones on the planet. Now, between the constant shelling and the torrential rain, it was a blood-soaked quagmire, and all too many of the bodies that covered it were Vostroya's sons.

Vlastan seemed oblivious to that. 'If the general wants this mountain, sir,' he said, 'rest assured that we're the men to take it. Both Lieutenant Kabanov and I intend to make our mark early on.'

Tyrkin's smile was more polite than genuine, for he knew how many lives Mount Megidde had reaped since Third Army's advance had faltered here, but he said, 'That's the spirit, lieutenant. Your fathers would be proud, you know. I had the honour of serving alongside both of them before they passed over to the Emperor's side.'

'You did, sir?' prompted Vlastan eagerly.

'Indeed, and they were great man, both. Your father, Vlastan, was a real force among the officer class – a strong traditionalist and much missed.' To Kabanov, he added, 'And your father inspired us all with his prowess in the regimental tournaments. If you've any of his martial skill, I shall enjoy seeing you compete.'

Kabanov bowed gratefully at the compliment. Vlastan, he noticed, had turned to face the mountain again. Tyrkin, though, wasn't quite finished.

'Since neither man lived to see you take your first battlefield commissions, I feel some responsibility in passing on the wisdom they would surely have imparted themselves. The vast majority of new officers, you see, are apt to make the same mistakes. They may feel ready to face foul greenskins, insidious eldar or unspeakable mutant scum, but few are prepared for an enemy that strikes at the heart. Few are ready to wrestle their own conscience.'

Vlastan and Kabanov listened while the rain drummed steadily on their hats and shoulders. One at a time, the captain fixed them with his gaze. 'This may sound distasteful to you, given any youthful idealism you may cling to, but you must remain objective in putting the proper value on the lives of your men. We officers are noble-born and must bear the requisite burden of our class. We live to command, elevated to it by birthright. The troopers, however, were born to die serving the Divine Will. Understand that from the beginning. Your fathers would have impressed this upon you most strongly.'

From the corner of his eye, Kabanov saw Vlastan nodding in wholehearted agreement, but his own reaction was markedly different.

His father's letters and journals betrayed Tyrkin's lie. Major Urien Kabanov had been a humanist and squandered no man's life, guided firmly by the core precepts of the *ossbohk-vyar*. Back on Vostroya, Kabanov's mother had fondly corroborated this.

Tyrkin, Kabanov realised, was watching him closely, waiting for some cue that said the lesson had been absorbed, so he nodded grimly despite his inward thoughts.

It was enough to satisfy the older man. He mumbled to his adjutant and, together, they turned back towards the shelter of their Chimera armoured transport. Over his shoulder, he called out, 'Come, gentlemen. I'll drop you at the barracks. It's time you briefed your men on the specifics of the assault.'

Mount Megidde (West Face, 696m)

'Keep pushing, you worthless dogs,' roared Vlastan. 'By the blasted warp, what's gotten into you. This is the Emperor's work, for Throne's sake!'

His sergeants immediately took their cue and began shouting the men onwards, pressing them up the mountain metre-by-metre, though stubber-fire stitched the rocky ground all around them.

He'd lost four men already taking this ridge – the first men to crest it. Taking the brunt of the enemy's defensive fire, they'd jinked and shuddered for a moment in the withering barrage, then tumbled backwards, falling past him and out over the cliff towards the jagged lower slopes.

An infuriating loss.

Screams of agony sounded from left and right now as the enemy's bullets found other unfortunates. Mud-splashed suits of carapace armour protected vital organs, but some of the whining slugs bit deep into unprotected arms and thighs, ripping open the arteries there.

The wounded went down howling, blood pumping out over the cold ground. Their plaintive cries for aid further angered Vlastan. That they were all boys of his own age mattered not a bit.

Selfish fools, he cursed. We're in the middle of a firefight! Should I ask the blasted mutants to take a caffeine break while we patch you up?

He and his Fourth Platoon had been charged with storming the mountain's western face – one of the hardest ascents and, for that very reason, the least mined and defended. He wondered bitterly if Kabanov's ascent was any easier. RHQ believed the mountain's natural defences had made the mutants complacent on the western and south-eastern sides.

As more enemy fire peppered the rocks around the ascending Vostroyans, it certainly didn't seem so to Vlastan. Every metre he won was bought with blood.

Once at base of the citadel walls, Vlastan was to throw his force against the defenders, drawing their reserves to the western battlements so that Kabanov and his platoon could penetrate the south-eastern defences with minimal resistance.

He was far from satisfied with the plan.

It's a load of rot, he cursed. A man of House Vlastan charged with leading a diversionary force? Nothing less than a damned insult!

A pale, stooped figure with overlong arms and huge, bulbous eyes lunged from cover up ahead and levelled a stubber at the advancing line. Before the mutant could pull the trigger, however, Vlastan's laspistol found him. There was a sharp crack and the acrid smell of ozone. The mutant's body toppled forward, trailing steam from the large, cauterised hole that had appeared in his face.

'Nice shot, sir!' voxed Vlastan's comms officer, Corporal Korgin.

Seeing the kill, other mutants vented their rage from higher ground, leaning out from shielding rock to send deadly volleys down the mountainside.

'Blast them, Firstborn!' yelled Vlastan into his vox-bead's microphone. 'Squads Borgoff and Gurelov, flank left. Sergeant Niriev, I want suppressing fire front-right! Move up, move up, damn you! Any man who falls behind will be shot!'

Swept up in the noise and madness of the fight, the men didn't hesitate to follow Vlastan's every word. More fell screaming to the concentrated fire of the enemy, but the Vostroyan advance was inexorable. The mutants on the slopes were a rabble, relying on sheer numbers to see them through. They lacked the lifelong training of the disciplined Firstborn. With confidence overfed by earlier success, they were unprepared for such a continuous, determined assault on ground they had presumed secure.

Pausing momentarily behind good, solid cover, Vlastan slid a new cell into the grip of his pistol and looked up the slope towards the summit.

There, up beyond the next ridge, he saw the colossal black walls of Megiddzar. They seemed so mighty he could almost believe they were propping up the storm-heavy sky. Misshapen figures moved to and fro on the parapets and, from the right, he heard the rippling boom of the enemy's heavy artillery, unmistakably near. The mountain trembled under his feet.

I'm sorry, Maksim, he thought. I know you're counting on me for your diversion, but I can't pass up this chance to make my mark. You'll have other chances, my friend, but this day is mine.

Troopers surged past him, yelling and roaring as they ran. One was struck hard in the face by a stubber-round and knocked from his feet. He died instantly, lasgun clattering to the ground.

Vlastan felt a sudden, wet warmth and looked down to see his clothing and armour splashed with fresh gore. He felt a moment's panic before he realised it was blood from the young trooper, not his own.

His relief soon turned to anger. 'Slaughter those mutant freaks!' he bellowed, careful to stay in cover for the moment. 'Show them no mercy, Firstborn! Charge!'

Mount Megidde (South-east Face, 802m)

Kabanov's men were having no easier time of it on the south-eastern ascent. The steep cliffs, sharp rocks and tangled lines of razor wire were bad enough, but every time the young lieutenant sent men forward to cut a way through, there were screams of agony as yet another died or was horribly wounded.

We've come too far, thought Kabanov, to be waylaid by their blasted snipers and stubber-nests. The citadel must be less than a hundred metres further up.

But a creeping nausea was slowly taking hold of him. Each loss twisted his guts tighter and tighter. He felt each death, each howl of agony, keenly. These men were following his lead, depending on him. The orders they obeyed were his.

And they were hardly men at all, he reminded himself. Most of the dead were from his own platoon – teenagers just as he was.

Father, he thought, did you suffer such doubts? How can I prevent their slaughter and still do my duty? It seems... impossible.

Had Tyrkin been right after all? Was he being an idealistic fool? Had he read too much into his father's writings?

If he thought his subconscious mind might answer the question for him, he was disappointed.

The only answer was the rattle of gunfire from further up the mountain, followed by the earth-shattering boom of the citadel's long guns.

Behind him, about two kilometres to the south, on the flatlands of the Sambar Basin, great fountains of earth and flame burst majestically into the air. The enemy was shelling the town of Sambariand.

At least here, thought Kabanov, momentarily glad to be on the mountainside, we can strike back at our foes. The Guardsmen dying down there have no such chance.

The thought lent him further purpose. Megiddzar simply had to fall today.

A stubber-round ricocheted close to his head and he pushed himself flat against the cold, wet surface. 'Holy Throne!' he spat.

Sergeant Sergiev rose from cover, returned fire, then hunkered back down.

'Mind yourself there, sir. Those bastards will be keen to bag any man with stripes.'

Through the vox-bead in his ear, Kabanov heard his comms officer hailing him on the platoon's command channel. 'Message from RHQ, sir.'

'Let's have it, Pitkin.'

'One word, sir: Orpheon.'

'Orpheon,' Kabanov repeated. 'Excellent, corporal. Keep me updated.'

'Yes, sir.'

'Orpheon?' asked Sergiev. 'As in the Flaming Saint?'

'It's the go-word, sergeant. Our comrades on the western face have initiated their diversion. We'll give the Valisians some time to be drawn away. And then the real work starts.'

* * *

Mount Megidde (West Face, 962m)

Vlastan looked to left and right, making sure his men hadn't revealed themselves. They kept down, tight behind jutting spurs of rock on the final ridge. The citadel's defenders certainly knew that attackers had come, but Vlastan had been careful not to show his full numbers as he'd neared the citadel's curtain wall. Moments ago, he'd sent false confirmation of his attack to RHQ. His vox-man, Korgin, had protested. 'I thought you said, sir, that we were to create a diversion?'

'No plan remains intact on the battlefield, Korgin. Don't you even know that much? Diversionary forces have a nasty habit of getting obliterated. Is that what you want, soldier?'

Korgin gulped and the blood drained from his face. 'But Sixth Platoon, sir... Lieutenant Kabanov and his men–'

'Have no better chances of taking out those anti-air batteries than we do. No, simultaneous attacks on two sides will double the likelihood of operational success.'

Korgin didn't look satisfied, but he caught the dangerous look in Vlastan's eyes and said, 'Understood, sir.'

'Excellent,' said Vlastan. 'Trust me, Korgin. There will be decorations for this. Now, get my sergeants over here. It's time they received new orders.'

Mount Megidde (South-east Face, 951m)

'Khekking hell!' growled Sergiev as he threw himself prone and rolled into the lee of the nearest boulder. Stubber-fire blazed out in torrents from atop the rain-slicked citadel wall. He called over to Kabanov. 'Are you sure about that transmission, sir? This doesn't seem like much of a reduced defence to me.'

The citadel towered over them, ancient, dark and utterly menacing. A utilitarian structure, its only artistry was in its solid construction. It was not a fortress built to inflate some warlord's ego. It had been built for a single purpose only – to resist assault. But its architects had lived in the days when even basic las-technology had seemed lost forever. No matter how thick its rough-hewn walls of black stone were, they could not resist the modern Imperial Guard for long.

Still, Kabanov's expression was grim. The wall was one matter, the godless mutants were quite another.

He was sure he'd held his men back long enough for the enemy's defensive focus to shift west. Had Third Army intel got it wrong? Was the enemy garrison far larger than expected?

Either way, he thought, we're committed now. We breach that wall and take out their anti-air, no matter what.

'Squads Tolgin and Zunelov,' he voxed, 'move into position. Mortar teams, deploy behind those outcrops on the left and right. When I give the word, I want coordinated fire section-by-section. Herd the defenders towards the centre. They'll get a nasty surprise when the whole damned thing collapses under them. Lasgunners, help keep the bastards occupied while the sappers work.'

A series of short acknowledgments broke the static.

'Sapper-team, move under cover of smoke only. I don't want you taking unnecessary risks. Is that clear? If we lose you now, we might as well pack-up and go home.'

'And everyone would hate that, sir,' quipped Sergeant Ivanenko.

On hearing his voice, Kabanov could picture the man's wry grin. The nineteen year old Ivanenko was a gambler, a notorious risk-taker. That made him a natural choice for a sapper-team leader, but it also made him unpredictable.

'I mean it, Ivanenko,' voxed Kabanov. 'Your sappers are no good to me dead. Just open me a nice big hole in that wall.'

'We'll get it done, sir. You'll see.'

Squads Tolgin and Zunelov were in position now and raking the battlements with las-fire. Kabanov saw the bodies of careless defenders fall from the heights like stricken birds. There was a sickening crunch every time one of them struck the rocks.

'Mortars ready,' crackled the vox.

'Sappers in position, awaiting your go, lieutenant,' voxed Ivanenko.

'Mortars are cleared to fire,' said Kabanov. 'I repeat, mortars are cleared to fire.'

There was a familiar, almost musical *whoomping* sound from left and right as the mortar tubes spat explosive loads up onto the parapets.

Kabanov watched with satisfaction as the old stone defences exploded outwards in a rain of shattered blocks and dust. Pale bodies were thrown outwards too, smashing open on the mountainside like sacks of raw meat.

'Let's have that smoke, sergeants,' voxed Kabanov. Squads Tolgin and Zunelov immediately began lobbing their smoke grenades into the mossy depression between their cover positions.

'Sappers, move up!'

'Yes, sir!' answered Ivanenko.

Kabanov watched the sergeant and his men race forward from their cover into the protective shroud. They wouldn't have much time to wire the charges. He ordered his lasgunners to standby with another round of smoke grenades.

The mortars were traversing their fire inwards, bunching the surviving defenders into an increasingly small space atop the wall and keeping them too busy to pour significant fire on the smoke-shrouded sappers below.

Soon enough, however, they noticed the smoke below. Worse still, the rain and wind was stripping it away faster than Kabanov had expected. One of the mutants shouted something and others leaned over the top of the wall to fire straight down.

There were howls from within the smoke as some of the sappers were hit.

'Ivanenko,' voxed Kabanov. 'Report!'

'Two of my lads down, sir. Where the khek is our covering fire?'

'Mortar-teams, keep the pressure up,' Kabanov barked. 'We've men dying out there.'

The mortars could only fire so fast, however. The protective smoke dissipated further, laying the sappers naked to fire from directly overhead.

'More smoke, now!' roared Kabanov over the vox. Another sapper cried out, struck hard in the thigh. He went down. Kabanov saw one of the man's comrades turn to aid him. Ivanenko shouted furiously, and the sapper reluctantly turned back to the matter of the explosives.

Squads Tolgin and Zunelov lobbed the last of their smoke, and the remains of the sapper team enjoyed cover once again. Kabanov prayed they'd have enough time to finish up. There was little he could do for them once the smoke cleared for the last time.

The wall was vast and wide, and the mortar-teams were overwhelmed with targets. Kabanov's lasgunners did all they could, but the crenulated parapet offered the mutants outstanding defensive cover. Having watched their fellows fall screaming to the rocks, few of the mutants were careless enough to present viable targets now.

Instead, they poked out only briefly and, when they did so, they fired directly downwards again. Kabanov saw that the last of the smoke had cleared.

'Ivanenko,' he voxed. 'Status!'

From a team of eight, only three sappers remained, working frantically at the base of the wall. 'More time, damn it. I've lost too many. I need more time!'

Even as Ivanenko said this, another of his men crumpled soundlessly, shot through the top of his hat.

Kabanov felt sick, almost dizzy. 'Ivanenko,' he voxed. 'Get to cover, damn you. We'll work something else out.'

The last of the Ivanenko's men screamed and spun, his face a bloodied mess, and only Ivanenko himself was left.

'Did you hear me sergeant?' shouted Kabanov.

'No time, sir!' replied the sapper-team leader. He stood alone at the base of the wall, hands working frantically. Above him, a score of mutant guns zeroed in. His time had run out. There was only one option left.

'Good luck, you men,' he voxed. 'Keep your heads down, won't you?' With that, he stepped back from the wall, raised his lasgun and fired into the central mass of the high-explosives.

'Ivanenko!'

Kabanov was thrown onto his back by the blast. Utterly deafened, the breath ripped from his lungs, he felt as if the universe itself might be ending.

Stone blocks rolled down the slopes in a great, dust-trailing torrent, and only good hard cover prevented more Firstborn from being killed.

The dust, thought Kabanov as he coughed and spluttered. Don't let the dust settle.

Sergiev was standing over him, hauling him up by the edges of his breastplate. 'He did it, lieutenant!' he gasped. 'The damned citadel is wide open!'

In Kabanov's mind, he saw Ivanenko's face staring back at him with a sardonic smile. There was grief, like a lead weight in his belly, but he knew he had to put it aside, at least for now.

'Firstborn,' he voxed determinedly. 'You know what to do!'

With a booming battle cry, the men of Sixth Platoon surged forward towards the breach.

Megiddzar (West Wall)

Vlastan snarled as another of his men fell screaming from the face of the western wall. 'Keep climbing, you dogs,' he yelled over the vox. 'Mortars, keep them covered, damn you!'

Only moments ago, he had seen groups of defenders running southwards along the parapet. It was exactly what he'd been waiting for. Sure that Kabanov's efforts in the south-east had secured the mutants' attention, he had ordered his men to scale the walls using the grapnels they carried. RHQ had issued the grapnels for the mountain ascent, not for the citadel walls, but to Vlastan, that mattered little. It only mattered that his plan was working.

Even with the distraction of Kabanov's assault on the far side, however, Vlastan's men still had to climb under enemy fire.

His mortar-teams launched shell after shell onto the parapet with worthy accuracy and, slowly, the Vostroyans charged with being the first up the ropes made progress towards the top.

There was a rattle of gunfire and one fell screaming to his death, followed all too quickly by another. Hard contact with the ground cut their screams off sharply.

'Heavy covering fire, ground-teams,' demanded Vlastan. 'They're almost at the top. Damn your eyes, give them cover!'

Three of his troopers were within centimetres of the parapet now. Then, as Vlastan watched with growing excitement, the first crested the wall. There was a shout and the glare of raking las-fire. The mutant defenders turned to return fire on the Vostroyan intruder, but Vlastan's mortars spat at same moment, and the mutants were blown from their roosts in a shower of rock and ruined bodies.

The second climber hauled himself over the wall, ably covered by the las-fire of the first. Then the third scrambled over. At the bottom of the ropes, others began their climb.

'That's it, Firstborn,' voxed Vlastan excitedly. 'Keep moving!'

With ropes secured and an increasing section of the wall being taken and held, more and more of Vlastan's men were able to clamber up and over. Soon, it was the turn of Vlastan, his vox-man, Korgin, and the mortar teams.

Vlastan – young, fit and long-limbed – climbed the rope with impressive speed. Korgin was slower, but managed despite the weight of his back-mounted vox-caster. The mortar-teams followed, tying their heavy firing-tubes to the ends of two lines, and hauling them up after themselves once they'd reached the top.

The rest of Vlastan's platoon had deployed in textbook defensive patterns, pressing back the waves of mutants that raced towards them from other sections of the wall.

We made it, thought Vlastan. I knew it could be done. Diversion, my eye! Just wait till Maksim hears about this.

The citadel's interior lay before him, its low, square buildings whipped by sheets of driving rain.

He scanned the flat rooftops for a moment, noting those that vented smoke. One building boasted a long-range communications antenna. Still, these things were of secondary importance. There, on a series of broad platforms built atop the southernmost section of the wall, Vlastan's eyes found what they were looking for – the enemy's devastating long-range artillery pieces. And there, flanking them on either side, were the deadly anti-air batteries – the ultimate target of this entire operation.

I take those down, thought Vlastan, and I'll have my first damned medal at the age of eighteen.

'Push south along the wall,' he ordered his men. 'Our victory is close at hand. Press those damned freaks back!'

Megiddzar (South-east Quarter)

Having penetrated the citadel's south-eastern extent via Ivanenko's breach, Kabanov's men soon found themselves fighting desperately through the dark, cobbled streets that criss-crossed the interior. Wind gusted between the buildings, stinging their faces with battering rain, but the Firstborn were hardy, had trained since childhood in far worse conditions than these, and didn't stop to notice. They were far too busy strafing the insane enemies that poured through the streets towards them.

The Chaos-crazed mutants displayed an almost suicidal eagerness to engage. They were utterly insane and, despite superior numbers, seemed unable to exploit the tenuous position of the attacking Vostroyans. It occurred to Kabanov that these freaks had never been drilled for this. Valis II had never raised Imperial

Guard regiments and had maintained only a small PDF force before the coup.

More likely than not, these sickly, long-armed aberrations were the mutated offspring of simple farmers who had laboured far too long in the corrupting radiation of the system's twin suns.

'We should press west, sir,' offered Sergiev. He had remained close to Kabanov's side throughout, almost as if he'd charged himself with personally protecting the young, inexperienced lieutenant. 'The anti-air defences will be clustered close to the main artillery.'

'Agreed, sergeant. All squads, cut us a path west. We can't afford to get pinned down here. I don't want to be here any longer than necessary.'

Of course, it wasn't as easy as that. Even as his platoon poured blazing las-fire on another wave of charging foes, Kabanov wondered just how many of the defenders Vlastan had actually drawn away. There seemed to be an awful damned lot of them where there shouldn't have been.

Megiddzar (South-west Wall)

Vlastan fired shot after shot into the enemy ranks as they charged desperately along the wall towards his men, ready to die to save their precious artillery from the Vostroyan assault.

The parapet was becoming littered with smoking, twitching mutant corpses. Without the advantage of high ground, the enemy was taking tremendous losses now, and Vlastan was losing very few of his own. The tide had turned. His men, he knew, had the treacherous twists completely outclassed. He stepped over another pale body, noting with distaste the ugly Chaotic sigils branded on its cooling, naked flesh.

The sickening fools, he thought, grinning as his pistol carved a smoking black crater in the body of another on the wall ahead. They race towards us as if they're invincible, and we slaughter them like grox before a feast.

His men were gaining ground quickly. The proximity of their objective had re-energised them. The artillery platforms were only metres away, and many of the mutant gunnery crews now broke from their duties to engage. As his men slaughtered them, Vlastan ordered his sergeants to organise two-man demolition teams. They were to knock out the anti-aircraft batteries at once.

The massive, devastating artillery pieces could wait. His first priority was to make the skies safe for a subsequent aerial assault.

Unlike Lieutenant Kabanov's platoon, Vlastan's men hadn't been issued with satchel charges. They were meant to provide a mere diversion, after all. They would have to make do with grenades. Still, Vlastan thought, five or six detonated in the firing mechanisms of each quad-barrelled anti-aircraft gun will render them just as useless.

'Korgin,' he shouted. His vox-man trotted over, pistol in hand, firing at anything that moved.

'Sir?'

'You and I will have the personal honour of destroying that battery there.'

Vlastan nodded towards the battery on the farthest platform.

'I'm with you, sir.'

Vlastan turned to the nearest troopers and barked, 'Give us good, solid cover all the way, you lot.' Then he and Korgin broke into a crouching run while stubber-shells whizzed and whined over their heads.

Loping mutants raced to intercept them, but both men fired their pistols with deadly accuracy, and the troopers behind them laid down good cover as they'd been told to. A dozen mutants fell by the time Vlastan reached his objective.

Over the din of gunfire and incomprehensible battle-cries, Vlastan shouted, 'Hurry now! Give me your grenades.'

Korgin stepped over a scarred, smoking body and handed his commander a bandolier with four 'fraggers' fixed to it.

Vlastan snatched it from the young trooper's hands. As he did so, he saw movement on the floor of the platform. 'Watch out!'

The warning came too late. One of the downed mutants was only wounded. He sprang up, whipped his long arms out towards Korgin, and caught him by the belt and breastplate. Then, holding the young trooper in an iron grip, the mutant plunged them both over the parapet wall.

Korgin's chilling scream stopped abruptly on hard contact with the rocks below.

Vlastan cursed angrily as he fixed Korgin's bandolier to the anti-aircraft gun, pulled one grenade pin after another, and ran like hell towards the protection of his men.

Twice he staggered as enemy rounds struck his carapace armour with frightening force, but he ran on in adrenaline-fuelled desperation. He'd gone about thirty metres when the grenades went off with a deafening crack. Sharp metal fragments whipped through the air, wounding a dozen nearby mutants. Vlastan threw himself to the ground.

He looked back towards the gun and saw only a twisted metal ruin shrouded in black smoke.

Pushing himself up quickly, he continued his stooping run, skidding to a stop when he reached the relative security of his troops.

'Sergeant Gurelov bit one, sir,' reported Sergeant Niriev immediately. 'But all anti-air batteries have been destroyed. Permission to pull out?'

Vlastan shook his head. 'Permission denied, sergeant.' He turned his eyes to the citadel's interior once again. Among the buildings in the streets below, he found what he was looking for. The comms antenna he'd noticed earlier was much closer now.

'Sir?' queried Niriev.

'We just lost our vox-caster, sergeant,' said Vlastan stiffly. 'But, if I'm not mistaken, that building by the fountain down there is a communications bunker. RHQ must be informed of our success immediately. Move out, gentlemen!'

Megiddzar (Southern Quarter)

Corporal Pitkin threw himself into cover behind the thick stone wall of the hab that shielded Kabanov and gushed, 'Just had that damnedest transmission from RHQ, sir. I can't get my head around it.'

Stubber-shells spanged off the stonework all around them.

'Well, don't keep it a secret, corporal,' said Kabanov.

'Well, it seems, sir... it seems that Lieutenant Vlastan and his men have successfully managed to destroy all of the citadel's anti-air defences.'

'They what?' exploded Kabanov.

'My reaction exactly, sir, but RHQ are adamant about it.'

'The enemy must have compromised our communications network, Pitkin,' said Kabanov, but he already suspected the message was genuine. It had Vogor's ambition written all over it.

'I double-checked, sir. The broadcast codes were spot on, verified by the Officio Communicatus and everything. It's definitely legitimate.'

'What the hell happened?' asked Sergeant Sergiev. 'Wasn't he supposed to lead a diversion?'

'That would explain the massive opposition we've faced so far. Damn him. What does RHQ advise?'

The diminutive Pitkin blew a breath out between his teeth. 'We've been ordered to pull out, sir. A naval assault wing is inbound from Fortune Bay. Marauder bombers, sir. Sixteen minutes out. They're going to level the place. And if we're still here...'

'And Lieutenant Vlastan's platoon?'

Pitkin looked deeply uncomfortable now. He wouldn't meet Kabanov stare. 'They're pinned down in a comms tower west of here. Completely surrounded, sir. RHQ says they won't make it out.'

Vlastan, you bloody fool, thought Kabanov. *Damn your ego to the warp, look what you've done to yourself! Am I supposed to just walk away?*

'Pitkin, contact RHQ. Tell them we're close to Lieutenant Vlastan's position and believe we have a solid shot at opening a corridor of escape.'

'Sir?'

'Sixteen minutes, you said, until those Marauders level the citadel. That leaves no time for argument, corporal. Do it. If RHQ objects, I want you to fake a vox-caster malfunction.'

Pitkin reddened and seemed about to argue, but Sergiev preempted him. 'Listen to your lieutenant, corporal,' he said. He gestured at the rest of the platoon. They hugged the corners of the ancient stone habs, poking out to fire back at a gradually thinning enemy force. 'If these men walk away from their brothers now, it'll weigh heavy on them for the rest of their lives.'

Something in Sergiev's voice told Kabanov the man was speaking from bitter experience. 'We're talking about other Firstborn here, corporal.'

Sergiev didn't need to say any more. Pitkin had heard enough. He set his jaw and nodded. 'Firstborn, sergeant. You're absolutely right, sir. I hope you don't think me a coward.'

'There are no cowards among the Firstborn, Pitkin,' said Kabanov with a grin. 'Least of all in my platoon.'

In his mind, however, he was praying feverishly to the Emperor and the Grey Lady, patron saint of Vostroyan, for the protection of his men. He'd already suffered more than enough losses for one day.

Megiddzar (Communications Bunker)

'All sides, sir,' reported Sergeant Niriev. 'If there's a way out of this, I can't bloody well see it.'

Vlastan stood with Sergeants Niriev and Borgoff in a small room dominated by a communications console and several low-grade cogitator units. The concrete walls were covered in bizarre, blood-painted glyphs that hurt to look at, and the floor was strewn with bodies – mutants in strange, ribbed uniforms of black metal and leather.

These freaks – Vlastan guessed they represented some kind of officer class – had been caught off-guard when his men had stormed the building.

He cursed under his breath. 'Then you're not looking hard enough, Sergeant Niriev. If you think I conquered Megiddzar only to be flattened when the place gets bombed, you're out of your mind.'

The sergeant looked angry, but he said, 'The men will fight on, of course, sir, but the enemy has us locked in tight. We lost a lot taking this place. I understand that you had to get a message out, sir, but unless we get external help, we won't survive this.'

Damn and blast, thought Vlastan. To have come so far, to have achieved so much, only to be trapped here at the very end. I won't have it. A posthumous decoration doesn't appeal to me at all.

'Have the men hold firm, sergeant. Tell them that the honour and reputation of all Vostroya is at stake here.'

Sergeant Borgoff cleared his throat and said, 'Sir, we've barely ten minutes left until the bombers arrive and we're running low on powercells for the lasguns. We should lock ourselves in and meet our deaths honourably in prayer to the Emperor as Omnissiah.'

'Bloody fool! I have no intention of meeting my death here. This is a comms tower. I'll petition RHQ to delay the bombard-ment. I'll request assistance from Sixth Platoon if I have to. We will not fall!'

'Be serious, sir! Sixth Platoon must be halfway down the moun-tain by now.'

Vlastan almost cuffed the young sergeant for his tone, but he struggled to rein in his temper. No, he thought. Kabanov *will* come. He would no more leave me here than he would renounce his beloved *ossbohk-vyar*. I'm sure of it.

Unsettled by the faraway look in their commander's eyes, the sergeants backed away, returning to their men to fight, and most probably die, alongside them.

Kabanov and his platoon found Vlastan's position all too easily. The sounds of stubber-fire and las-fire, and the smell of ozone, led them there like shift-workers to a fresh pot of ohx'. They could see a veritable army of mutants firing at shuttered windows and gun-ports in the thick walls of a two-storey comms bunker. The mutants were using stacks of supply crates and water barrels as cover, but their backs were wide open.

'All sergeants,' voxed Kabanov quietly, 'have your men take up assault positions now.'

'Aye, sir,' came the response.

'There won't be time to set up mortars,' voxed Sergiev. He stood only a metre from Kabanov, but spoke low over the vox rather than give their presence away.

'We still have grenades and satchel charges. It might be enough to drive a wedge in their forces.'

Kabanov wasn't wrong. On his command, Sixth Platoon hit the mutants from the rear with everything they had. Fragmentation grenades wreaked terrible damage on the unwitting freaks. The satchel charges blew their cover positions to pieces, killing dozens in a hail of flying debris. The mutants turned to defend themselves far too late, with predictably grisly results.

Inside, Vlastan's men didn't hesitate to exploit the change in the situation. They saved their cheers and shouts of joy for later. Instead, with the mutants forced to fight on two fronts, they launched a concentrated attack on those whose backs were now turned towards them. Searing volleys of las-fire blazed out from the comms bunker.

Kabanov watched scores of the enemy fall with a dark feeling of enjoyment. 'Vogor,' he voxed, 'if you can hear me, get your men out of there now. We've opened a corridor for you, but we can't hold it forever, man!'

Vlastan's voice returned to him through the static. 'I was just about to call you, Maksim. I knew you'd come. Late to the party, perhaps, but here all the same. Hold that corridor steady, we're coming out!'

A heavy steel door was kicked violently open and the survivors of Vlastan's Fourth Platoon surged out to take positions of cover alongside Kabanov's men. Lasgun powercells were quickly shared and, together, the united Vostroyans loosed a staggering amount of fire at the howling, raging mutants.

Vlastan was the last to exit the comms tower. When he came out, he kept his head low, his laspistol high, and ran in a zig-zag towards Kabanov's position. Stubber-rounds whipped at the soaked cobbles and crates all around him.

'Warp damn and blast it all!' he spat. 'Let's get a move on, Maksim. Those bombers will be here in a heartbeat!'

Kabanov scowled, keyed the open channel on his vox-bead and said, 'All squads pull out at once. Make for the breach. Don't stop to engage. I want every last man sprinting for his life. This whole damned mountaintop will be dust and flame in about four minutes!'

Sergiev rose to send lethal las-bolts into the bodies of two closing mutants, then turned to Kabanov. 'Better lead by example, sir.'

Kabanov nodded. 'That goes for all of us. Let's move!'

Four minutes. Not nearly enough time to get clear. But, if they could just make beyond the citadel walls and into the cover of solid rock...

With a final burst of las-fire, Kabanov, Vlastan and Sergiev broke from cover and began pounding the cobbles in the direction of the breach. Enemy stubber-fire smacked into the stone walls on either side as they ran.

The surviving Firstborn followed close behind, though a number were cut down by the mutants as they tried to break from cover. Others, too, were struck in the back or legs as they raced through the wet streets.

Kabanov could hear their cries of agony and frustration, but he dared not look back. He had already detected the throaty growl of Marauder engines on their deadly approach vector.

As he, Vlastan and Sergiev turned a corner, they ran into tall, emaciated mutant who had looted a lasgun from the corpse of a fallen Firstborn.

Kabanov, running at the head of the group raised his pistol just a fraction too late. The hideous mutant, his face a gaping mess of fleshy strips and strange, bony ridges, pulled the trigger and emptied the weapon's remaining charges at them.

Kabanov's pistol barked a moment later, burning a deep tunnel into the brain of the disgusting freak. Strained curses from behind him made him turn.

Sergiev was down. He rolled on the wet ground in agony. One of his knees had been reduced to a cauterised stump. The severed lower leg lay where it had fallen, smoke rising in wisps from charred tissue.

'Sergiev!' gasped Kabanov as he turned and crouched by the older man. 'Damn it, Vogor. Help me get him up.'

'There's no time, Maksim,' hissed Vlastan. 'He's too badly wounded. We've got to get out of here.'

Kabanov replied without turning. 'I said help me, you son of a bitch!'

Vlastan cocked his head and listened to the sound of the bombers closing fast. 'You're a fool, Maksim. We have to go now! Where the hell is that damned hole you made in the wall?'

Booted feet sounded on the cobbles and the surviving Firstborn charged round the corner. When they saw Kabanov crouching by Sergiev, they skidded to a halt.

'I need two fast men!' Kabanov barked.

Sergeant Zunelov reacted immediately. 'Vlenin and Borsky, front and centre!'

The troopers in question quickly had Sergiev supported between them. The men resumed their sprint and, in moments, the massive, ragged gap in the citadel wall loomed before them.

The bombers were much louder now, almost deafening. Kabanov knew they must be almost directly overhead. His legs began to throb as a dull pain worked its way through the damping effects of adrenaline, but he kept on.

Seeing their prey leap over the rubble and out onto the bare mountainside, the pursuing mutants roared and screamed. Shots whizzed through the air all around the Vostroyans as they ran, slid or tumbled down the uppermost slope.

'Get to cover,' shouted Kabanov over the vox. 'Get into cover right now!' The roaring of the Marauder engines was joined by the whistling of bombs as they fell in their hundreds.

'Down, all of you!'

The mountain erupted like a volcano. Fire exploded in great pillars that thrust upwards from inside the walls. Then, with the massive outward pressure of the blast-wave, the walls themselves blew out.

After long millennia on the very crest of the mountain, the ancient citadel of Megiddzar, offering protection to local people since before the Age of Strife, was utterly obliterated.

Flaming rubble rained down from the sky.

Mount Megidde (South-east Face, 961m)

Kabanov shut his eyes tight and hugged his rocky cover until long after the cascade of stones had stopped. Then, slowly, he arose, shook off the debris that covered him, and began leading his men down the mountainside. He did not look back.

As he passed Vlastan, he didn't feel like speaking. Vlastan's mood, however, was jubilant. 'Stop and look for a moment,

Maksim. Revel in our glory. We did it, man, you and I. We'll be decorated for this. Decorated. Mark my words!'

As his friend spoke, Kabanov caught sight of Vlenin and Borsky carefully helping the one-legged Sergeant Sergiev down the difficult terrain.

Good troopers, thought Kabanov. All of them. And so many lost.

Vlastan hadn't stopped. He stood, still crowing about honours and medals and all the worthless tin that men died for, and suddenly Kabanov had had enough.

Before he could stop himself, he'd raced over and gripped Vlastan tightly by the throat. His face twisted into a vicious snarl. 'You make me khekking sick, Vogor, you know that? Don't ever, *ever* compromise the lives of my men again!'

Vlastan was taken aback for only the briefest moment. Aristocratic indignation quickly took over. With a disgusted snort, he tried to knock Kabanov's hand away, but he'd forgotten just who he was dealing with.

Kabanov moved in a blur – none who saw it could later demonstrate the technique – and before Vlastan knew what was happening, he was on his back with the wind knocked painfully from his lungs.

Kabanov stood over him, eyes aflame, poised to deliver a killing blow.

To a man, the Firstborn stopped and watched in statuesque silence.

Vlastan waited, heart racing, muscles tense, staring into his friend's wild eyes. It was in those eyes that he saw a terrible rage being slowly, gradually mastered, and he knew the blow would never come. 'Striking a fellow officer is a capital offence, Maksim,' he said softly.

'That's not why I hesitate,' hissed Kabanov through clenched teeth. He rose, turned and continued his long march down the mountainside while the exhausted men behind him followed in heavy silence.

* * *

51 years later,
Seddisvarr Cathedral, Danik's World

The God-Emperor towered over the congregation, dominating the cavernous interior of the cathedral, making even the largest of men feel almost microscopic by comparison.

It was a mere statue, of course, but it radiated an undeniable power over all present. The points of its stylised halo reached the frescoed dome some fifty metres above a white marble altar draped, today, in the rich red silks of a Vostroyan remembrance service.

While Bishop Zarazov, Twelfth Army's senior ecclesiarch, droned on in his gravelly bass tone about honourable servitude and the afterlife, Vlastan gazed at the Emperor's golden face in numb silence, waiting to be called forward onto the dais.

Hundreds of wooden pews had been removed from the cathedral hall so that every off-duty trooper in Seddisvarr could attend the service, whether they wished to or not. Almost two thousand men stood packed together, standing in silent respect for fallen comrades. Their breath misted in the freezing air of a space far too large to heat.

'And now,' said Bishop Zarazov, 'if General Vlastan will approach the altar...'

Vlastan tore his eyes from the Emperor's golden face and willed his mechanical chair into motion, his brainwaves translated into spidery movements by the augmetic interface at the base of his skull. As the chair jerked its way forward, each metal claw struck the marble steps with a ringing sound that echoed loudly from the grey stone walls.

Vlastan was angrily conscious of the clatter. It felt disrespectful to make such a terrible din here, and it seemed to take forever to reach the lectern at the altar's side. In fact, it was only seconds before he faced it, his eyes on the red book that rested there.

Beside the book, which lay open, sat a gold inkpot and a single white quill. Vlastan leaned forward slowly, dipped the quill's nib in the ink and, with all the steadiness his ravaged body could muster, began to write in the book.

As he carefully scribed each letter, he felt the eyes of all those present upon him. One pair of eyes in particular burned hotter than most.

Grigorius Sebastev, that damnable upstart captain, stood with the remains of his shattered Fifth Company, his eyes stabbing at Vlastan from the front row. The old woman, the inquisitor to which Sebastev and his men had recently been assigned, had sent one of her Astartes giants too – a man whose unnatural proportions resembled no other in the cathedral so much as the great statue of the Emperor Himself.

A special honour for you, Maksim, thought Vlastan, to have a legendary Space Marine present at your remembrance. But then, you were something of a legend yourself.

He finished inscribing the last of the letters and rested the quill in the inkpot. Then, for a quiet moment, he sat unmoving, staring at what he'd written.

Colonel Maksim Kabanov, 68th Infantry Regiment (699—767. M41), KIA.

His eyes kept returning to the first of the words.

Here it ends, Maksim, he thought. A four-star general writes a colonel's name in the Book of Remembrance, and fifty years of soldiering are over. I wonder if you ever resented it, that I made general and you did not. You must've known why. Old Tyrkin laid it out so plainly, that first day.

One of Vlastan's useless legs shuddered in a brief spasm, and he looked down at his ruined, artificially-sustained body.

I never hated you, Maksim. You saved my life twice, though our friendship was long dead that second time. I sometimes think you should have let me die. That's weak, I know. And, besides, that was never your style. The great White Boar left no man behind, eh? Only, here I am, and you are gone, and I find no victory in that.

He turned from the book and, as the clattering legs of his chair carried him back down the altar steps, found himself inexplicably angry, though whether at himself or at his old friend, he couldn't say. In his head, he imagined Maksim's voice. It said:

History will not be kind to you, Vogor.

Then, it was gone.

From his pulpit, Bishop Zarazov waited until the echoes of the chair's footfalls had faded, then lifted his hands and said, 'Sanctioned hymn number two-six-six.'

The cold air filled with the mournful sound of the *Cantus Militaris Deorum.*